CONDENSED BOOKS

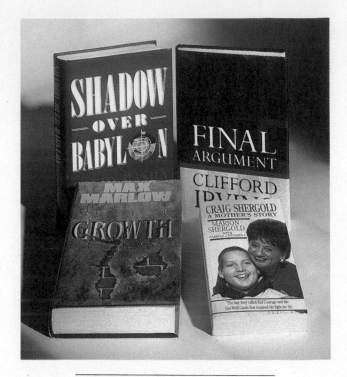

THE READER'S DIGEST ASSOCIATION LIMITED
Berkeley Square House, London W1X 6AB

THE READER'S DIGEST ASSOCIATION
SOUTH AFRICA (PTY) LTD
Reader's Digest House, 130 Strand Street, Cape Town

Page make-up by MS Filmsetting, Frome, Somerset
Separations by Magnacraft, London
Printed by BPC Magazines (East Kilbride) Ltd,
A MEMBER OF THE BRITISH PRINTING
COMPANY LTD
Bound by BPC Hazell Books Ltd, Aylesbury

CONDENSED BOOKS

SHADOW OVER BABYLON
David Mason

PUBLISHED BY BLOOMSBURY

CRAIG SHERGOLD
A Mother's Story
Marion Shergold with Pamela Cockerill

PUBLISHED BY BANTAM

FINAL ARGUMENT
Clifford Irving

PUBLISHED BY HAMISH HAMILTON

GROWTH
Max Marlow

PUBLISHED BY SEVERN HOUSE

CONTENTS

SHADOW OVER BABYLON

David Mason

Former special services officer Ed
Howard has faced some pretty strange
requests since setting up XF Securities,
but none as remarkable as the task
outlined by English business executive
Sir Peter Dartington. It is a top-secret
operation that, if successfully carried
out, could mean that Howard and his
men will be able to retire for good.
Quite simply, Dartington wishes to
commission the assassination of
President Saddam Hussein of Iraq.

A gripping thriller about the
meticulous planning and execution of
an extraordinary operation, with an
amazing twist in the tail.

CRAIG SHERGOLD

Marion Shergold
with Pamela Cockerill

Marion Shergold knew that her nine-
year-old son, Craig, was ill. He had
been complaining about pains in his
ears. But the news that he had a brain
tumour came as a terrible shock. As
doctors at London's Great Ormond
Street Hospital struggled to save her
son's life, Marion battled to keep up
Craig's spirits with a worldwide appeal
for get-well cards. Millions of people
around the globe followed Craig's story
and sent cards to the brave young
English boy who wanted to get his
name in the *Guinness Book of Records*.
Now Craig's mother tells the full story.

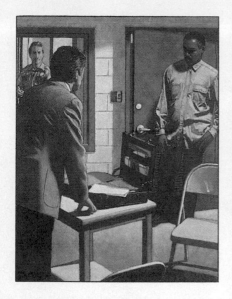

FINAL ARGUMENT

Clifford Irving

Twelve years ago Ted Jaffe left the rough-and-tumble world of the Florida state attorney's office for a slice of the good life. Now a partner in a plush law firm, he is shocked to learn that the only man he ever put on death row may be innocent—convicted because witnesses lied at the original trial. Luckily, the sentence of death has not yet been carried out. As Ted Jaffe races to get a new trial, he knows that this time his own future, as well as his client's, will depend on the outcome.

Full of suspense and surprises, this is an edge-of-the-seat legal drama by a favourite Condensed Books author.

page 297

GROWTH

Max Marlow

Designed and built by George Playle, one of Britain's most prominent architects, the Ashmore Tower should have been one of the safest buildings in London. So when it collapses, causing serious loss of life, everyone is shocked. Playle's daughter Georgina—herself a successful architect—cannot believe her father is to blame. As similar disasters in other countries come to light, she suspects that they may be connected. If so, many of the world's largest buildings may be in imminent danger.

This is an exciting novel of one woman's race against time, as she seeks desperately to avert catastrophe.

page 413

SHADOW OVER
Babylon

David Mason

Illustrated by John Beswick

Danny MacDonald might conceivably be the best shot in Britain, but it would take a great deal to persuade him to line up his sights on another human being. His quarry has always been the deer of his native Scottish hills. But there is one very special mission that just might lure Danny away from his job as a Highland stalker to become a professional sniper in a band of mercenaries.

Thus begins a thrilling novel about a top-secret attack on Saddam Hussein. It is the work of a talented new author, a one-time soldier who writes from close personal knowledge and experience of clandestine operations.

Chapter ①

The stalker studied the ground thoughtfully through his binoculars, then stowed them away inside his jacket. 'We'll have to take this next bit very, very slowly, now,' he whispered to his companion. 'Those three hinds on the left aren't making it easy for us. We'll be in full view of them for the next forty yards, until we reach that wee burn yonder.'

The 'rifle', a former British Army colonel, nodded in acknowledgment. He had absolute faith in the stalker's judgment: if Danny said that was the only way forward, then it was the only way. For the past hour they had picked their way slowly past scattered groups of red-deer hinds and calves; it seemed to him miraculous that they had not been winded by the deer. Even the minutest breath of wind carrying the smell of man to the super-sensitive nose of just one of the hinds would have done it: she would have cleared off, taking with her every other beast for hundreds of yards around.

Even if this stalk came to nothing, reflected the colonel, it had been his most exciting for a very long time. He raised his head cautiously and scanned forward across the bare patch of boggy grass they must now cross. There was no cover at all, and they would be in full view of the hinds, scarcely a hundred and fifty yards away.

The two men crawled slowly and with infinite care, flat on their stomachs. The hillside was sodden from the persistent October drizzle of the previous week; both men were soaked to the skin. It took them twenty minutes to cover the fifty yards to the shallow depression of the burn, and the colonel was breathing hard with concentration.

The water in the burn gurgled noisily, but the stalker still spoke in a whisper. 'The stag will be about two hundred yards away now. We'll go up the burn about sixty yards to that wee knoll on the right; we may be able to get a shot at him from there.'

Again the colonel nodded, and followed as the stalker led the way along the burn. When they reached the small knoll the stalker motioned to the colonel to wait and crawled forward a few yards, disappearing almost immediately in the grass and heather. The colonel had been stalking for over thirty years, but the thrill and tension of it had never diminished for him. He was by nature a hunter; he loved his annual week's deerstalking in the Scottish Highlands.

The stalker returned as soundlessly and invisibly as he had departed. 'He's still where he was, lying down. I think we can get a reasonable shot at him from the side of this knoll.'

'Where is he?' asked the colonel. 'What sort of range?'

'He's about a hundred and forty yards away,' replied the stalker.

'What sort of beast is he?'

'He's a very old stag, could be in his last year. He'd weigh about twelve stone, maybe twelve and a half. A good beast to get off the hill. He's been with the hinds, and he's taking a rest just now. He's very black from the peat hags, and he looks pretty well tired out.'

The colonel was glad. He had never had any desire to shoot a trophy head, or a stag in his prime. He knew the slow death that awaited a stag whose last teeth had finally loosened and gone. Far better to end it with a bullet.

The stalker took the Rigby out of its canvas sleeve. Very quietly, he worked the bolt, easing a .275 cartridge into the chamber, and then applied the safety catch. A hundred and forty yards was as close as they were going to be able to get. It was a reasonable distance for a competent shot, and the colonel was pretty good. He motioned to the colonel to follow and they crawled up the last few yards onto the side of the knoll.

The landscape ahead gradually came into the colonel's view. Straight in front of him were the hinds and calves. Beyond, he could see the old stag, lying down. The stalker eased the rifle across to him, and he began to settle into a comfortable firing position.

Suddenly, the nearest hind flicked her head round, facing directly towards him. The colonel froze. She's looking straight at us, he thought. She's bound to see us now.

The hind had seen a tiny flicker of movement out of the corner of her eye, and she stared intently at its source. Nothing was moving now, but something, something very small, had changed. She was uneasy, and her uneasiness communicated itself to her calf, which moved closer to her. The calf appeared confused, looking one way and then another. After another minute or so, its mother looked away again. She resumed feeding, but remained wary.

The colonel let out a slow sigh as the hind finally lowered her head to graze. He brought the telescopic sight to bear on the stag and eased the safety catch off. The stag's body was obliquely facing him. The colonel aligned the cross hairs low down on the front of the stag's chest. The light was improving and, as he took his last breath in before the shot, a shaft of sunlight broke through, throwing the stag's body into sharper relief. *Perfect*, thought the colonel and his finger tightened on the trigger.

The hind had caught a flash of light from the telescopic sight. Thoroughly alarmed, she barked loudly and bolted away.

The colonel's mind registered the hind's bark and he saw the stag turn his head sharply towards him. He squeezed the trigger.

The old stag had only just started to struggle to his feet when an enormous blow hit him on the right side of his body, about a foot behind his foreleg; it nearly knocked him back down. He wrenched himself up on his feet and took off in headlong flight.

'He's hit, Colonel.' The stalker was looking through his binoculars as the beasts raced away. 'Yes, he's hit, right enough, but I can't tell for certain where. If it's a heart/lung shot, he'll go down in a hundred yards or less, but you'd better give me the rifle just in case.'

'The old beggar moved, Danny!' The colonel was suddenly voluble after the tension and silence of the stalk. 'He bloody moved, just as I fired! Half a second more, that's all I needed!'

The stag ran. His legs seemed a little unsteady, but his survival instinct propelled him on.

The hinds had already fled, covering the rough ground at speed; the stag followed them. After a hundred yards the herd streamed over a brow down into a corrie, and was lost from view. Danny jumped to his feet. 'Come on, Colonel, we mustn't lose him.' He raced off.

Danny was still well short of the edge of the corrie when he threw himself to the ground and started to bring the rifle to his shoulder. He worked the bolt, feeding another round into the chamber. Some hinds had now come into view, way off in the distance, climbing fast up the far side of the corrie. The colonel reached his side. 'Why have we stopped?' he panted.

'You see those hinds, Colonel? They're the same ones. Either your stag will be dead in the corrie below, or he'll take much the same path

11

out as the hinds. If you don't mind, I think I had better take the shot.'
The colonel lay down beside Danny, and glanced sideways at him.
What did he mean, he'd better take the shot? From *here*? It was a
ridiculously long range.

The stalker's face was calm. After a few seconds his eyes narrowed
in concentration. The colonel followed his look. The stag had
appeared as Danny had predicted, climbing directly away from them
on the same track the hinds had taken.

Danny locked the rifle into his shoulder, his eye to the scope.

The stag had stumbled a couple of times descending into the corrie,
but now he was climbing it was easier to keep his footing. The strange
feeling in his body gave him the extra edge of fear he needed. He
wanted to lie down and rest, but instinct drove him on.

Danny squeezed the trigger. The bullet streaked across the void of
the corrie at nearly two thousand miles an hour. Five hundred yards
and just under three-quarters of a second later, it struck.

The old stag never heard the shot. Instead, he felt a second crashing
blow on the back of his neck, and then—oblivion.

The colonel could hardly take it in. The stag had collapsed, stone
dead. 'Bloody hell,' he breathed, 'I've never seen anything like that in
my life! The beast was *miles* away! And he was still running! That was
the most fantastic shot I've ever seen!'

Danny was calmly getting to his feet. He unloaded the Rigby and
put the rifle back in its sleeve. 'Och, I don't know about that,
Colonel,' he said easily. 'Maybe it was just a bit of luck. Come on, sir,
let's go and deal with your stag.'

The colonel followed Danny, still marvelling in disbelief. He had
been watching the expression on the face of the stalker as he fired.
Luck had had nothing whatever to do with it.

'MR ASHER, IT IS VERY KIND of you to have come. I really am most
grateful to you for sparing me so much of your valuable time.' The
Minister hoped he was not overdoing it. He had a tendency to be
perhaps a little too effusive when greeting someone he disliked.
Fortunately, he had sufficient personal charm to carry it off; few
people had proved entirely immune. His charm had been just one of
the factors that had contributed to his successful career in politics.

He surveyed Asher's face with distaste, his friendly smile giving no
hint of his feelings. He realised that he should not have worried.
Roger Asher was used to flattery.

'My pleasure entirely, Minister,' boomed Asher. The Minister
politely gestured towards a large, comfortable chair. Asher eased
himself down into the leather upholstery, which wheezed under his

gargantuan frame. He was unfit and grossly overweight.

'A glass of lemonade? It is homemade. I find it a refreshing drink.'

'That would be most kind.'

The Minister poured the lemonade. He sat down in an easy chair opposite Asher and watched as the big man greedily gulped the drink down. The Minister wondered. Had bad manners somehow assisted Asher in amassing his enormous wealth, or had the wealth, once acquired, merely rendered good manners unnecessary? Asher appeared to pay only lip service to the finer points of social behaviour. He had an ego to match his physical size. Still, there was no doubt that hobnobbing with powerful men, and being consulted by ministers, were pursuits Asher revelled in.

'A comfortable flight, I hope?' The Minister was solicitous. Asher had just flown in from New York in his private Gulfstream IV jet.

'Perfectly satisfactory, thank you, Minister,' replied Asher, 'although I can't say I really enjoy flying. I never cared for it much.'

The pleasantries over, the Minister studied his fingernails briefly and spoke. 'The government has a rather awkward problem.' He paused, as if wondering how to continue. He knew what he was going to say, but wanted to convey an impression of slight embarrassment. He was skilled at dealing with people. He did not delude himself that this man was a blundering oaf. Asher had been enormously successful; he was shrewd, cunning and manipulative.

Well, two can play at that game, thought the Minister. He himself had had to show great skill to maintain his position during the radical changes of the 1980s. His privileged background had not exactly marked him out for advancement in the way that it might have done in the old days. An old family, Eton, Oxford ... that sort of upbringing and education was nowadays considered anachronistic. The Minister had played down these things, and had survived unscathed. Now, with a new leader, a more moderate approach was being signalled. The election due in the spring of 1992 would, he hoped, set the seal on this new approach.

He continued. 'There is a matter that has caused the government some difficulty. We are now anxious to see this resolved, and we considered that you might be able to offer us some suggestions as to what measures we might take.' The Minister glanced up at the big man's face, and could see that he had his attention. 'It is a matter of some delicacy,' he said finally, trying to look even more embarrassed.

'Minister, I am honoured that you think I might be of assistance,' began Asher. 'Naturally, I would be willing to help.'

Asher was not being honoured, thought the Minister; he was being flattered. He just could not tell the difference. He would, however, have picked up on the phrase 'a matter of some delicacy'. Asher would be well aware that the expression invariably meant that the matter was one of extreme *in*delicacy. So far so good, thought the Minister.

'We have come to the reluctant conclusion that this matter now calls for fairly uncompromising action.' Still no sign of perturbation on Asher's face. This was going to be easier than he had thought. 'The problem is an individual one,' he said, and paused again to let the remark sink in.

He was startled by Asher's blunt reply. 'There must be many individuals who could be deemed to be a problem to the government. I assume that this is not a matter of merely minor inconvenience?'

'I can see that it will be unnecessary to skirt around the subject any further. I have always greatly admired your perceptiveness.' Good Lord, he thought, the man is actually nodding in agreement! 'Perhaps it would be best for me to come directly to the point.'

FIFTEEN MINUTES LATER, the Minister shook Asher's hand warmly and thanked him profusely for the assistance he had promised to give. The meeting could not have gone better. Asher had agreed to handle everything. The government would not be involved. There would be—what was that dreadful expression?—Yes, a 'cut-out'.

As the big man left, the Minister closed the door of his office and for a moment leaned back against it, his mind almost reeling at the thought of how childishly easy it had all been.

SIR PETER DARTINGTON had been intrigued by the invitation and, he had to admit it, rather excited. Respectable businessmen like him were not supposed to get excited, he reminded himself. Dartington set great store by his respectability; he had earned the label the hard way.

Yes, he thought, his had been a life of hard work. He never tired of telling people of his humble origins, and of the metamorphosis of his father's company, Dartington & Son (Builders) Ltd, into Darcon International plc. He knew the tale was impressive, and he had no doubt that it had inspired many people to believe that by hard work and determination anyone could succeed as he had done.

An inspiration to others—how many times had he heard himself being introduced in speeches in those terms? And Dartington was a good, natural speaker; he had never for a moment considered attempting to disguise his broad provincial accent. He was a well-liked figure, well liked by all. He received more invitations to attend society and business functions than he could possibly have accepted.

But this invitation had been irresistible. 'Mr Roger Asher hopes that you might care to join him for the weekend on the *Princess Scheherazade*, off Cannes.' Asher's personal assistant had gone on to explain that should Sir Peter find this proposal convenient—the woman sounded confident that he would—Mr Asher's private jet would be placed at his disposal for the journey to Cannes and back, and a car would take him from the airport to the marina.

So now here he was on this great big flashy yacht, lying on a sun-lounger, with flunkeys waiting on him hand and foot. It had come as another surprise that he and Asher were the only two on board—apart, that was, from the crew: eleven of them, just to look after two passengers!—but that had been nothing compared with the surprise he had felt when Asher had dismissed the steward after dinner the night before and got down to business. And what an extraordinary proposition! His head was still spinning. Pete, my boy, thought Dartington to himself, you'll have to watch yourself here.

'Morning, Peter.' Dartington turned his head to see Asher emerging from the saloon wearing a dressing gown. The big man lumbered out onto the deck and collapsed into a large chair. 'Another drink? Andrew!' he bawled back in the direction of the saloon door. 'Drinks for Sir Peter and myself.'

'Good morning, Roger,' replied Dartington. He decided not to point out that it was well past midday.

Andrew appeared with a large beaker of orange juice for Asher, who took it without a word and gulped it down, and a fresh gin and tonic for Dartington. Dartington thanked the lad. Andrew smiled at him and withdrew.

'Had any further thoughts about what we discussed last night?' Asher wiped a dribble of orange juice from his jowls.

Dartington got up from the lounger and moved to a chair under the shade of the awning, pondering his reply. 'I'm sure you'll understand, Roger, that I feel a bit out of my depth. I mean . . . I've never had anything to do with this sort of thing before.'

'Neither have I, my dear chap,' said Asher cheerfully. 'But the main thing is that it is in the national interest.'

'I accept your assurance on that, Roger. In fact there can be no doubt about it. But why don't they get the SAS or someone to deal with it?'

'I don't think I would be revealing any secrets if I were to tell you that they have in fact looked into that. The problem is threefold. In the first place, a very long lead time would be required to get them into a position where they could pull it off. Something in excess of a year, I believe. Secondly, the chance of failure and subsequent embarrassing exposure would be absolutely unacceptable to the government. Asher paused to take another swig of orange juice. 'Thirdly, and probably most significantly, there is a sort of unwritten rule that governments never get personal. They can be as beastly as they like to a whole country, and frequently are, but they can never be seen to be going for individuals.'

Dartington had risen to his feet and was pacing the deck, a frown on his face. 'So you are telling me, Roger, that when they want some dirty work done, they come to someone like you or me?'

'I have no idea,' replied Asher nonchalantly, 'as I have not been approached before. But I assume that this is what happens, yes.'

'And why me, in particular?' *Why you?* he wanted to ask.

'That's easy. They didn't approach you. They approached me. They don't yet know that I am sounding you out. I approached you, first because I know you are a patriot who has shown that his country is important to him, and second because your company is well established in the region concerned, and could therefore provide a base for the operation. The third reason is a little more complicated, but I think I owe it to you to explain what it is.'

Asher stopped for a moment's reflection before going on. 'The British Government is very careful to remain within the law. However, now and then the government finds itself under pressure to act in a way that is contrary to this principle. Such a case has arisen here.' Asher paused again to drain his glass. 'As you know, we are negotiating a treaty to be signed at Maastricht. My personal opinion is that the government is right to refuse at this stage to commit itself to more federalism. Those of us with a true vision of Europe are prepared to wait until we can carry the people of our country with us.

'But I'm digressing. The fact is, some of our other partners are more insistent on fast progress towards federalist principles. One country in particular is most insistent.'

The French, thought Dartington. It has to be the French.

'France's trade,' continued Asher, 'has taken a few knocks over the last year, owing to the international situation. They have shown themselves to be prepared to sign trade agreements with any country, of any political stance, no matter what. You will no doubt recall the glee with which they sold Exocet missiles to the Argentinians during the Falklands War.

'Unfortunately for them, they now find themselves under constraint. One or two lucrative contracts have been frozen. The French desperately want this situation to be reversed. There is one obstacle to this—just one. Do you see what I am driving at?'

Dartington was beginning to see. 'But how does the British Government come into this?'

16

'It's simple,' said Asher. 'The French apparently do not have sufficient expertise to remove this obstacle themselves. So the British Government has promised to do it for them. In return for this, they will agree to our terms for signing the Maastricht Treaty. And the British Government is covering its position by going private with this operation, rather than using the SAS.

'Anyway, that is the background. I imagine,' Asher went on, holding Dartington's eyes steadily with his own, 'that you can understand why I came to you. I know you are pro-Europe, and at the same time a patriot. The two are not, as some would have us believe, incompatible. I hope I have given you reason enough to agree to take this on. There is an additional reason, but before I tell you what it is, I shall need your assent to the project.'

'Forgive me, Roger, but it's all a bit much to take in at once.' Dartington was well aware that this was a pretty hard sell he was being given. 'Can I think about it for a while?'

'Good idea,' answered Asher. 'Very sensible. Let's go in and have some lunch.'

They ate lunch largely in silence. Asher knocked back glass after glass of pink champagne, and rarely paused between huge mouthfuls of food for long enough to speak, while Dartington, in contrast, merely picked at his food, remaining pensive. Asher's speech about European unity had cut no ice at all with Dartington. On the business level he saw the necessity of remaining at the heart of Europe. All his business speeches had stressed this, and no doubt that was where Asher had picked up on his 'pro-Europeanism'. On a personal level, however, he would have preferred to keep Britain at arm's length from the increasing interference of Brussels.

But he had to admit that the project Asher had put to him had appeal. What a thing to be able to tell his grandchildren! It was exciting! He wasn't getting any younger, and every man should have something to look back on.

The two men finished lunch just before three o'clock, and wandered outside again. Andrew served coffee from a silver pot. The weather was balmy and relaxing, and Dartington realised that he felt on top of the world. What a life, he thought. Sixty years old, and something like this suddenly comes your way. *Why not?*

'OK, Roger, I'm interested. I've a good mind to do it. I think I know where to start.'

'Splendid!' boomed Asher. 'Splendid! A very sensible and patriotic decision, if I may say so.' He paused, and his voice took on a portentous tone. 'I can now confidently assure you that the government will not be ungrateful.'

'I don't understand. I thought you said that the government doesn't know I am being approached.'

'That is correct. And officially, they will continue to know nothing about your involvement. However, I am authorised to conclude an agreement on behalf of the government.'

'What do you mean?'

'Times are hard,' said Asher, 'for all of us. It is no secret that the construction business has suffered badly over the last year or so.'

'What are you driving at, Roger?'

'Darcon is, if I am correct, currently preparing tenders for eleven major contracts worldwide. By major,' he added, 'I mean tenders for contracts exceeding fifty million US dollars in value each.'

Dartington's mouth was hanging open as Asher ploughed on, unstoppable now.

'Any one of these contracts, should Darcon be successful in its tender, would enable your company to keep its head above water for a while. If *two* contracts were to be awarded to you, Darcon's future would be rosy. But competition is fierce.' Asher drained his coffee cup loudly. 'I shall be blunt. Should this project be a success, the government will ensure that two of your tenders are accepted. You may win a third contract on merit alone. But you have a guarantee from me that you will get at least two.'

Asher stood up; he clapped Dartington reassuringly on the shoulder and went inside, leaving Dartington sitting where he was in utter astonishment.

ED HOWARD WAS FORTY-FIVE years old. He was tall, thin and dark-eyed, and had thirteen years of active military experience behind him; from 1966 to 1979 he had been a commissioned officer in the Royal Marines and the Special Boat Service.

He had married in 1976; his wife, Claire, soon began to put pressure on him to leave the Forces and find a job offering better pay and more regular hours. When he was offered a job in the City, he resigned his commission and accepted the offer.

Howard had known he would miss Forces life, but he had had no idea how much of a wrench leaving would be. He felt uncomfortable in London. He stuck it in the City for the next three years and then decided to set up his own business, advising companies and individuals on security problems.

Claire was horrified when he told her he was jacking the job in, and when he told her what he was going to do instead she ranted at him for two weeks. Finally he got bored with it and told her she would do better to find herself a doormat, not a husband—someone who could put up with her tantrums. In the subsequent proceedings for divorce, Howard's savings went on legal fees, a hefty financial settlement for Claire and a small flat in Wandsworth; precious little was left over to put into his new business.

An old friend from the American Special Forces, Mike Ziegler, helped with the finances. They went into business together and recruited a team of acquaintances, mostly former Special Forces, to join them. XF Securities was born. Mike Ziegler and his team of four handled the American and Far Eastern market from Los Angeles, while Howard and half a dozen others looked after the larger market of Europe, Africa and the Middle East from London.

They had an early success when there was a kidnap attempt on a wealthy Italian client; it was the kidnappers' bad luck that one of Howard's men was with the client at the time. The three Sardinian kidnappers were disarmed and spent several weeks prior to their trial in hospital, under police guard. The lawyer at the trial made much of what he said was the excessive degree of violence to which his unfortunate clients had been subjected by Howard's operative, the sinister-looking Mr Harris. The judge, however, said that in his opinion Mr Harris had performed a valuable public service.

The trial received considerable publicity; as a result work flooded in for XF Securities. There was a temporary setback when Howard himself, along with one of his men, spent six months in jail in Ankara, Turkey. They had been arrested and convicted of paying off a ransom demand on a kidnap victim, but the victim had been released unharmed. The kidnapped man's company had been duly grateful; the Turkish authorities, however, had not been so understanding. Howard and his colleague had been prosecuted. The victim's company had appreciated the fact that Howard had not implicated them, and had since retained XF Securities for all its security work.

The company concerned had been Dartington & Son (Builders) Ltd, later Darcon International plc. Howard now sat facing its chairman across the desk, in the study of the chairman's house in Kent.

'Peter, are you serious about this?' Ed Howard already knew the answer. He could see the determined look in Peter Dartington's eye. He wondered briefly whether Dartington had gone mad.

'I'm deadly serious, Ed. I would like you to examine the problem and let me know what you think. If you come to the conclusion that it's a non-starter, then we will both have to forget this conversation; but if you think it might be possible, I want to know how it might be done and who might be prepared to do it. Could you let me have a report, say in a couple of weeks' time?'

Howard stroked his chin thoughtfully. 'I won't get far in just two weeks, Peter. But I'll have a look at it for you, do some background research, yes.'

'Good. Now there are various constraints you will have to build in, I'm afraid. First, this must remain between you and me. No one in Darcon must know about it. If you need to talk to any of your own people, they must not *in any circumstances* learn of my involvement.' Dartington paused to light a cigarette. 'Second, and equally important, you must not approach anyone who might report back to the authorities. I'm afraid that must rule out any contact with friends in the police or the security forces. Silly, in the circumstances, but there it is.'

'Peter, I have a couple of questions. First, I take it that if I can come up with a feasible plan, you will actually want me to set it up and run it. Is that correct?'

'Correct.'

'Right. That was just for the record, so that I know. Now my second point. This is a very high-risk project. Certainly more high-risk than anything I have done before. We're talking major business here, so I hope you don't mind. What is the budget?'

Dartington drew on his cigarette and fixed Howard with a level gaze before answering. 'Ed, this is big, I know. If you can pull it off, I am prepared to pay you five million pounds.'

'Peter, I'm afraid that just isn't going to be enough.' Howard paused and studied Dartington's face. Had there been a flicker of surprise? 'Look at it this way. I will need to put together a team of highly specialised people for this. Together, such a team could pull off a series of major robberies, with a potential total reward of ten million or more to split between them. And they wouldn't face the risk of being killed in the process. OK, anyone I chose would be legit, so they wouldn't go for something like that. But what you are asking them to do isn't exactly legit.'

Without lowering his eyes, Dartington tapped cigarette ash into a small silver ashtray on the desk in front of him.

'For a start,' Howard went on, 'I must ask fifty thousand for preparing the report. If you accept it and commission the job, we're probably talking about a further half a mill in retainers. Then there will be expenses.' He paused again; Dartington's face was impassive. 'Expenses alone may amount to a million quid. On top of all that, there is the question of remuneration. I'd say you're looking at at least a tenner, all up. I honestly don't think anyone competent would touch it for less.'

Dartington looked hard and finally spoke. 'I quite see your point,

Ed. Go ahead with the report. I'll see where I can get to with the finance. You'll understand'—he smiled reassuringly at Howard—'ten million pounds is a lot to come up with. But I'll see what I can do.'

Howard stood up. 'I'll get back to you in a fortnight. I'll bring the report with me for you to read. Then I'll destroy it. Is there anything else?'

There wasn't. Dartington showed Howard out to his car and waved him off as he drove down the gravel drive.

Howard's thoughts were only half on his driving as the Saab cruised up the M2 motorway back to London. His mind was turning over the implications of the meeting with Dartington. He forced himself to concentrate on the things Dartington *hadn't* said. Leave aside the project, he thought to himself; concentrate on the possible reasons for Dartington's wanting it done. Dartington had sounded unsure of his ground when finances were discussed; he hadn't seemed agitated, just unsure. And why would Dartington want to undertake this project by himself? Howard knew the extent of Darcon's current operations. None of them was being threatened to a sufficient extent to warrant the sort of action Dartington was contemplating.

Howard arrived home and let himself into his flat. He poured himself a whisky, and sat down in his armchair. Who's behind you, Peter? he thought. Government?

He went to his desk, switched on his computer, and waited as it whirred into life. When it prompted him for his password, he tapped this in, and opened a new file under the 'memo' template. This was one file, he thought, that he would not save to the computer's hard disk. He would keep it only on a three-and-a-half-inch floppy while he worked on it, and it would stay in his safe or on his person at all times. The computer prompted him with the line 'To:—¶', and he typed simply 'PD'. Below this, it already showed 'From:—EH¶'. The prompt moved to 'Subject:—¶'. Howard typed in the single subject line: 'The assassination of President Saddam Hussein of Iraq¶'.

Chapter ②

Over the next ten days, Howard spent his time in what a casual observer might have considered to be a state of unproductive idleness. Initially, he emerged from his flat only to make forays to bookshops, returning with piles of books on the Middle East, the 1991 Gulf War, and Saddam Hussein; he paid for all of them in cash rather than by credit card. He spent hours poring over the books, annotating passages with a green highlighter pen.

A friend in the BBC, who had covered the Gulf War from Tel Aviv, obtained videotapes from the BBC archives of all the reports of the invasion of Kuwait and the Gulf War. Howard studied each reference to Saddam with care, taking in every detail of his appearance and surroundings.

He spent hours in the British Newspaper Library in Colindale Avenue, poring over back numbers of newspapers and periodicals, occasionally taking photocopies; and he visited Edward Stanford Ltd in Long Acre, where he bought copies of all the maps he could find of Iraq and the Middle East.

By the end of a week the beginnings of a plan were formulating in his mind, but he knew he didn't have enough. For one thing, there was not quite enough detail on the maps he had been able to get. For another he was no expert on the Middle East; he would have to talk to Johnny Bourne and get his reactions. The third problem seemed insuperable, and he doubted whether Johnny would be able to help.

He would start with the maps; it was probably the simplest problem, although it would involve a potential security risk. He picked up the telephone and rang the home number of a friend in 21 SAS who had been on the staff at Northwood during the Gulf War.

'Derek? Ed Howard. Can you do me a favour?' Howard spun a plausible yarn about a client getting involved in postwar reconstruction projects in Kuwait and Saudi Arabia. 'The problem is there seem to be no detailed maps of the region apart from the 1:500,000 Tactical Pilotage and 1:1,000,000 Operational Navigation Charts I've got from Stanford's. They're not quite detailed enough for what I need. I was wondering whether the MOD might have any satellite-generated ones made for the Gulf War?'

'Well . . .' Derek sounded a little doubtful. 'There were some things like that floating around, but they were pretty highly classified, and only produced for specific targets and areas. They might not be classified any more, now that the war is over, but they would still be pretty up to date, apart from various structural modifications made to the landscape, courtesy of the RAF and USAF. Bridges and buildings blown up, you know.'

Getting warmer, thought Howard. 'They sound more like the business. Any way I can get hold of a set of them?'

'I've still got mine, somewhere . . .'

Bingo, thought Howard. Careful, now. 'Any chance I could borrow what you've got for a day or two, just to compare them with mine?' His voice sounded light and casual.

'Don't see why not. Come round for a drink and I'll let you have the whole set.'

An hour later, Howard was back in his flat with Derek's set of maps; a quick look had confirmed that they were exactly what he needed. He would get them Xeroxed first thing on Wednesday and return them. One problem down, two to go.

'WELL, HOW DO I LOOK?'

'Hmm? Fine, just fine.' Johnny Bourne was sitting at his desk in his shirtsleeves, facing the window, going over a report he had to finish drafting before the morning.

'Hey, at least look at me, you rat!'

'Oh, sorry, Juliet, I was concentrating.' Johnny swivelled the chair round and looked at his flatmate. 'Hey, not bad!'

He hardly recognised her. Gone were the shapeless jeans and sloppy, paint-stained pullover, the tied-back hair and the unmade-up face that he had grown used to since she had moved in three weeks earlier and started doing up her room. When she hadn't been deep in her books, she'd usually been covered in paint and wallpaper glue.

She had struck him as a straightforward, down-to-earth character when she had answered the ad for the room and they had quickly come to an agreement for her to move in. She had actually proved to be a very good flatmate, thought Johnny. She replaced things she'd finished off—coffee, sugar, stuff like that; she'd helped keep the place tidy, and her boyfriend Mark had been no bother—he'd only called round for her a couple of times, and he'd never stayed for more than a few minutes. Yes, she'd turned out to be an excellent flatmate. But he hadn't really *noticed* her before.

Now she looked terrific, thought Johnny. The simple, classical black shift dress, modestly showing off the curves of the slim figure which hadn't registered with him before, the dark hair tumbling down over her shoulders, framing her face, the touch of make-up accentuating her dark eyes. Yes, she looked wonderful. 'Big night out, huh? Where's he taking you?'

'Oh, just out to dinner. He's supposed to be calling round for me in about twenty minutes.' She had caught the expression of surprise on Johnny Bourne's face as he turned round. A little smile began at the corner of her mouth. She turned away before he could notice it. 'Can I get you a drink, Johnny?'

'Hmm? Oh, yes—thanks, that's kind of you. Whisky, please, with a couple of ice cubes if they're there. Hey, Juliet. Sorry I was flippant. You look really nice.' She glanced at him over her shoulder as she poured his drink, smiling at his compliment. He returned to his work, tapping his pencil on his chin as he read.

Juliet brought the drink over to his desk. She set the glass down and stood next to his chair. 'What's all this stuff you're working on?' She leaned forward, peering at the papers.

'Oh, just a security report for one of our German clients.' He looked up at her, smiling. 'It's rather dull, really.'

'*Really* dull?' She returned the smile and rested her hand on his shoulder as he took a shot of the whisky. He set the glass down, tilted the chair back and slipped his right arm round her waist, looking up at her. Careful, Johnny boy, he thought. Remember your golden rule. Never fool around with flatmates. It always ends in disaster.

'Yes, Juliet, you wouldn't be at *all* interested.' He gazed up into her eyes, grinning mischievously.

Juliet's long fingernails moved, and played delicately on the back of Johnny's neck, beneath his thick brown hair. Her fingers were ice-cold from the whisky glass. The effect of her touch was electric; a tingling feeling seemed to break out down his back, and he shivered involuntarily. He allowed his hand to slip down the outside of her leg, caressing her through the soft material of the dress. She swayed towards him, her hip gently resting against his shoulder.

'Mmm. Juliet, you know something? You feel really nice.'

'You're a kind man, Johnny Bourne. And *you* feel nice, too.' Her hand continued moving on his neck. His heart was pounding now, and he knew his eyes were betraying him.

'You've forgotten your drink, Johnny.' Her voice was low and husky. As he looked up again into her eyes he could see they had turned a smoky black, and her pupils were almost completely dilated.

Slowly, he stood up, shaking feverishly, and their bodies pressed urgently against each other, abandoned to the irresistible force of their desire. He picked her up lightly. She clung tightly to him, nuzzling his chest and neck, as he carried her through into the bedroom, kicking the door shut behind him.

'GOOD LORD, JULIE!' Johnny's voice was soft, almost reverent. 'What happened back there?' He lay on his back amid the chaos that twenty minutes before had been a tidily made bed. He held the girl to him, her scent still intoxicating. Their breathing had now eased; they lay relaxed, entwined across the bed.

She looked up into his eyes and smiled. 'Well, I rather think we both happened. To each other.' She reached for his face.

They kissed, slowly, grateful for each other. Johnny didn't think he had ever known anything so powerful as the feeling that had overcome him. *How on earth have I never noticed her before—have I been blind?* This woman had just completely blown his mind away; he had been powerless to resist. 'Julie, my darling, you are dynamite. I didn't know what had hit me. I still don't.' His voice softened. 'You're so lovely, so beautiful . . .' He pulled her closer, and held her tight.

Juliet bit her lip and suppressed a shiver at his display of tenderness. 'So it was all my fault, huh? You old goat, you. So much for your rule about flatmates.'

Johnny grinned and kissed her again. Her heart pounded as he whispered into her ear. 'Julie, I really mean it. You are . . . a wonderful, lovely girl.' His eyes burned into hers, then softened again. 'I never imagined . . . I mean, you will stay, won't you?'

Her eyes softened and she smiled down at him, her face radiant. Then, seeing his expression of anxiety, she said, 'Of course I'll stay, you big gorgeous ape. But on one condition.' She raised herself on one elbow and wagged her finger in his face with mock seriousness. 'You only break that rule of yours with *me*, understand?'

'Deal,' said Johnny happily, kissing her, tasting again the gentle sweetness of her mouth.

The telephone rang, and Juliet stirred.

Johnny grimaced in irritation. 'Let the damn thing ring. The machine will get it.' He couldn't remember if he'd set the answering machine. Who could it be, anyway? . . .'Hey, Julie!' He sat up, a blur of movement, and was on his feet.

Juliet, astonished, found herself flung on her back on the bed. *Goodness*, she thought, *he moves so fast. Like a cat . . .*

'Mark! What about Mark! He'll be here any minute now!'

'Relax, lover.' With a peal of laughter she pulled him back down onto the bed. 'Mark's not coming.' She giggled. 'It's OK. I called him at work this afternoon and put him off.'

'You did what?' Understanding dawned on his face. 'Do you mean you set this up . . . you little smoky-eyed minx!' He lay down again, resting on one elbow, his eyes travelling slowly down her slim figure. Then his mouth came down on hers and he pulled her close again, kissing her eyes. 'How long have you been planning this, you wicked, perfect girl?'

She clasped him more tightly. *Ever since the start, you stunning man*, she wanted to say. *But I had to find out what you were really like before I made yet another of my mistakes, so I wore baggy old clothes so you wouldn't notice me just for my looks . . . And you were so nice, so considerate, so kind and good to me . . . still the little boy in there—the little boy, slightly embarrassed as you told me about your rule with flatmates . . . That was when.* But she knew she would never tell him, because if she did, he might change . . . 'Would you settle for sudden mad impulse?'

'No, I wouldn't.'

She giggled again and curled up gently against him. After a few seconds, her hand moved up round his neck. 'Johnny?'

'Still here, smoky eyes,' he murmured.

'Do you have any more rules we could break?'

'Just the one, I'm afraid.' He caressed her shoulders and back, his fingers running lightly down her spine. 'Shall we break it again?'

'SO WHY DO THEY GO along with it? Why do they put up with Saddam, let him inflict all these disasters on them, one after another?'

'Oh hell, Ed, that's a huge question—we could discuss it for hours.' Johnny paused to draw on his cigarette, and continued. 'The simple answer, that he rules by terror, is too simplistic, and although it's obviously true, the oversimplification also partly explains why the West has made so many blunders in the region over the years.'

Howard let Johnny talk, absorbing his knowledge. He was a fluent talker and he obviously knew his subject. If XF Securities had anyone who knew the Arab world it was Johnny Bourne. The tape was running so that he didn't have to take notes.

' . . . so let's just look at the question of truth for a minute. It is a key issue, because attitudes to it are so misunderstood. Westerners have exploited these people and lied to them for years—ever since we first came into contact with them, actually. They think of us as robbers, liars, out to destroy their culture.

'So when a strong man like Saddam rises up amongst them, and tells them how there will be glorious victories over the exploiters, that the Arab culture will triumph, they believe him—believe him because they *want* to believe him.

'To an Arab, everything is subordinate to Islam and honour—even truth, because to them honour *is* truth. It's just a damned shame that it so often seems to be the rogues, the monsters with no morals, who rise to the top of the heap . . .'

That's the way of the world, lad, thought Howard. You've still got a lot to learn, Johnny. But he sat and listened as Johnny ranged over the complexities of the Arab world, getting a sense of the respect this idealistic young man felt for these people.

Later they got down to specifics: military capabilities, hierarchies, administrative details. They broke off for a snack at one o'clock; Howard had bought some sandwiches at the corner shop and they washed them down with a can of beer each. The two men sat, relaxed, in the comfortable armchairs in Howard's flat. Johnny suddenly looked tired, Howard thought. Tired, but . . .

Howard looked at him closely. The younger man was wolfing his sandwiches down as though he hadn't eaten for a week. I'll be damned, he thought after a few seconds, a smile starting at the corner of his mouth. 'Johnny?'

'Uhuh?'

'What's her name?' The smile was a grin now.

'What? How . . . ?' The younger man started, staring at him.

Young Johnny was actually *blushing*! 'Come on, Johnny. Give. Who is she?' Howard groaned inwardly. This was all he needed.

Johnny was indeed tired; but his elation was obvious. It all spilled out in a rush, while Howard listened in astonishment. 'Oh Ed, she's wonderful! I've never been so knocked out by anyone before . . .' He gushed on for a few minutes, then faltered to a stop, smiling sheepishly as he looked at the amused expression on Howard's face. 'Come on now, Ed. Don't look at me like that. I'm serious.'

I can see that, thought Howard. 'When did you meet her?'

'Well, last night, really . . .'

'Last night?!'

'Well, what I mean is, I never really noticed her before then. She's my new flatmate.'

'Oh Johnny!' Howard burst into laughter. 'After all you give out about your rules with flatmates.'

'Ed!!' Johnny's eyes momentarily blazed with anger.

Back off, Ed, Howard thought to himself. Don't be so rude to the boy. 'Johnny, I'm sorry. I really didn't mean it that way. You must admit, there is a funny side to it—you and your golden rule. But I'm sorry. So—this is the real thing at last, eh?' He smiled, the tension gone.

Johnny subsided again, and his eyes dropped to the floor. He spoke in a soft, low voice. 'Yes. It is. I can hardly believe it, but yes. I asked her to marry me and she said yes.'

Oh, hell!! Howard slumped back in his chair. *I don't believe this. Not now, when I need him for this.*

With a huge effort, Howard composed himself. 'Johnny, hey, look, I'm delighted for you. Congratulations!' Think, now, he told himself. Think positive. 'Tell me about her. What does she do?'

'Well, it's funny you should ask.' Johnny was off again, happily, his eyes alight as he talked about Juliet. 'She's studying for a career promotion. Her exams are coming up. She's going to be a detective inspector! CID—you know. Imagine that! Me married to a police-woman! Hey, Ed . . . are you OK?'

Ed Howard had collapsed backwards into his chair with a groan.

HALF AN HOUR LATER Johnny was still sitting opposite Howard, his brow knotted in thought. He now understood Ed's initial reaction—inexplicable as it had seemed at the time—to his news.

Howard had decided to tell Johnny about the project; he could see no alternative. He knew he could trust Johnny to keep quiet about it, even with the girl, and he knew Johnny would give the project—if it got the green light—his usual two hundred per cent. Nevertheless, he had felt it necessary to point out the higher-than-normal degree of risk that Johnny's new liaison posed to the security of the operation.

'What you'll have to think about, Johnny, if you can bear with me for a moment, are two separate factors here: one from your point of view, and one from hers. First, right now you are emotionally very vulnerable. You have just opened up to your girlfriend, and you're going to want to share all your thoughts with her. That's entirely natural, and I wouldn't expect anything else. All I'm saying is, you'll have to find some way of squaring with your conscience any guilty feelings you may have about deception on your part. I hope I'm not offending you—I'm just being logical here.'

Johnny had nodded, his face thoughtful.

Good lad, thought Howard; he was not going emotional on him. 'Fine. Sorry I had to mention it, but I knew you'd understand. Now, the second thing. She has obviously gone for you like a ton of bricks. I'm very happy for you both—good for you. But most women in this state want to know absolutely everything about the new man in their life. What you do, all that. It's only natural. Do you see?'

Again Johnny nodded.

'She is obviously very bright. To have got where she has with CID at such a young age, she must be bloody smart.' Howard paused to drain the last mouthful from his beer can. 'And if there's something there that doesn't fit, she's going to spot it, take it from me.'

'Add all this up, and what have we got? We've got a big potential problem, that's what. I'm sorry for spelling this out so baldly—I wish I could have put it better.'

Johnny remained silent for a while, thinking about Howard's analysis of his situation. 'No, Ed, you're right. I can't deny it. I'm not much good at deceiving friends. But one thing I *am* quite good at is compartmentalising my life. I can forget my work when I go home and I can leave personal considerations behind when I'm working. As a back-up position, I think I'll start reviewing one of our client operations in Saudi Arabia, Darcon maybe.'

Howard's face remained completely expressionless. He had not mentioned Sir Peter Dartington or Darcon; Johnny did not know the identity of the person who had commissioned the report.

Johnny went on talking, unaware of the significance of what he had said. 'We're going to need to tap into one or two of the Saudi concerns anyway, if this thing gets off the ground. That way, if she asks me what I'm doing, I'll be able to say I'm working on a confidential project to do with Saudi Arabia, and it will be true. I don't want to have to lie if I can help it. But I think I can live with not telling her the whole truth.'

The two men began to go over Howard's plan with a fine-tooth comb, covering every aspect. Johnny whistled in admiration at one or two of Howard's ideas, and occasionally interjected points of his own, animated again, concentrating with his usual intensity. They covered transport, routes, equipment, documentation, administrative details, fall-back protection, security and deception plans.

By 5.30pm, having put a full day's brainstorming into the project, Howard decided to call a halt. They had covered almost everything, and Howard had virtually all he needed for his report to Dartington. He let Johnny out, then moved the chair he had been sitting on out of the way and pulled back the carpet. He opened up the floor-safe and took out the floppy disk to continue working on the report.

TWO MILES AWAY and four hours later, Johnny Bourne and Juliet Shelley lay relaxed and contented in each other's arms in the darkness of the bedroom.

'Johnny?' A sleepy murmur from his side. 'You're under arrest.'

'Huh? What for?'

'Assaulting a police officer. Me,' she added.

'It was entrapment, honest. Oh, all right, I plead guilty. What's the sentence, officer?'

'Life.'

'With you?'

'Yes.' She reached up and kissed him. 'Johnny, are we really going to a jeweller's tomorrow?' She wriggled happily, nuzzling his neck.

'Yep.'

'Which one?'

'You'll have to wait and see, nosy. If you must know, it's run by an old friend of mine from my army days.'

'You haven't told me much about your time in the army. I want to hear all about it.' She yawned dreamily, drifting off to sleep. 'I want to know all about you. Everything. Every tiny detail. Every single tiny little thing . . .' She fell silent, breathing softly and regularly, asleep in his arms.

'I love you, smoky eyes,' whispered Johnny.

HOWARD SAT IN SILENCE as Dartington read through the thirty-page report. For the first twenty minutes there had been no comment from Dartington, other than a muttered 'You've done your homework, haven't you?' after the first few pages. Howard had half expected Dartington to skip through the background sections covering the history of Iraq, its geography, climate and people, but, on second thoughts, it was perhaps not surprising that Dartington was reading the report carefully; it had, after all, cost him £50,000.

Finally, Dartington set the report down on the desk in front of him. 'Yes,' he said, giving Howard a beady look, 'you've certainly done your homework. I've got a few questions, as you probably expected. I didn't much like that last paragraph, but we'll come on to that later.'

Since Howard said nothing, only nodded, Dartington carried on. 'First of all, are you sure about all the previous attempts on his life? Is it as many as that?'

'No. There have almost certainly been *more* than the six I've mentioned in the report. The only difficulty is in establishing who was behind each attempt. Some were almost certainly initiatives of individual Iraqis. Others were initiated outside Iraq; the Israeli Mossad being the most likely protagonist. The CIA is another possibility. Whatever the case with these attempts, no actual Israeli or American citizens were directly involved—they simply provided funds, encouragement, organisation, equipment, that sort of thing. The actual dirty work in each case was done—or rather, wasn't done—by Iraqi citizens who hated Saddam.'

'How did you get to hear about these plots?'

'Oh'—Howard gestured vaguely—'I keep my ear to the ground. Do you remember that report a couple of months back in the papers about a purge in the higher echelons of the Iraqi Army?'

'Yes. Was it true?'

'Pretty accurate. Large numbers of senior officers were rounded up, tortured and shot. Saddam supervised it, and shot a number of them himself. The ones who didn't die under torture, that is. Amongst them were the plotters of one of the assassination attempts.'

'So how are you going to do it? You haven't gone into detail about that at all.'

'That is deliberate, I'm afraid. It'll be safer that you don't know. No offence intended, but if someone gets at you, I have to be able to protect my own back.'

'I'm afraid nevertheless that I must ask you for some idea of how you are going to do it.'

The question confirmed Howard's view that Dartington was not the prime mover behind the operation. He answered carefully. 'We would be a small team. We would adopt a hit-and-run approach, spending minimal time within Iraq, and using bluff and deception rather than pure stealth and concealment, although everything will be

30

geared to getting in and out without anyone realising who we are. I'm sorry, Peter, but I mustn't tell you any more than that.'

Dartington nodded resignedly. He changed tack. 'What about this other stuff in here, the bit about Saddam having all these doubles? Won't that make life more difficult for you?'

'Quite true; it could. He has twelve doubles who are used to impersonate him. He sends them out and about so that he is seen by his people, while he stays safe in his bunker in Baghdad. Some of them bear only a passing resemblance to him, others have had plastic surgery and are more convincing. One of them is supposed to be particularly good—apparently he even has the voice right. But although Saddam always carries a pistol, the doubles are not allowed to carry their own weapons.'

Dartington was shaking his head in amazement. 'So how the hell are you going to get at Saddam?'

'That's the big problem, Peter,' Howard said gently. 'I won't be able to, without good intelligence. I can't simply take an army into Baghdad and attack one of the myriad bunkers on the off chance that Saddam is lurking inside. I have to know when and where I'll have a chance of getting near him. Without information, we might as well forget the whole thing here and now.'

'Is that what you mean by "talking to my principal"?'

'Let's not beat about the bush any more, Peter. I know you're not behind this. You're a rich man, but not so rich that you can spring for ten million quid without batting an eyelid. None of Darcon's operations is threatened by Saddam—at least, nowhere near enough to justify the cost. That means someone else is paying the bills. And that someone else must be straight, otherwise you wouldn't have anything to do with it. The only candidate I can think of that fits the bill is the government, but that's just my guess and I don't particularly want to know—all I'm saying is, I have to talk to the guy in charge. I don't have to meet him—we can talk by phone. I'll just have that one question to ask him, and I'm afraid I have to insist that you don't know what he tells me. I need a date and a place to get Saddam, and your principal may be able to provide that information.'

There was a long silence as the two men stared into each other's eyes. Finally, Dartington shrugged. 'I thought you would guess sooner or later. You're right, there is someone else behind this; for obvious reasons I can't tell you who. I will have to talk to him.'

'OK,' said Howard. 'This is how we'll play it. In order to safeguard security for both of us, he will ring me on a portable telephone. Not mine; yours—that one you use for outgoing calls only, so I won't get any calls intended for you. Ask him to ring me on any Monday morning between eight and nine. I will answer, calling myself Mr Hatcher; your principal should identify himself as Mr Jethro.'

'All right,' agreed Dartington, 'I'll set it up.'

'Good,' said Howard. 'There is one other thing, which I hope you won't mind. I'll have to burgle this house at some stage.'

'What? What on earth for?' Dartington looked startled.

'Mainly to protect you. I'm going to have to use the Darcon set-up in Saudi Arabia as a cover for certain things. For that I will need information. Someone will realise in due course that Darcon has been used, so there will need to be an explanation as to how the information was obtained. The burglary will be it. I'll be in touch with you again by phone to give you a date. On that date, it would be better if you were away from here. Perhaps you could take Lady Dartington up to London for the night to the theatre or something.'

Dartington agreed. Howard told him which files would need to be left in the desk, and the two men rose; Dartington handed Howard his cell-phone and the report, and Howard left for London.

EARLY ON OCTOBER 28, Howard drove out of London and by eight o'clock was stuck, as he had intended, in the Monday-morning rush hour on the M25. Even in the unlikely event of someone's attempting to monitor the call he was expecting, there would have been no possibility of the signal being pinpointed to his car.

At 8.10 the cell-phone warbled its ringing tone and Howard answered. 'Mr Hatcher here. Who is speaking, please?'

'This is Mr Jethro. I understand that you wish to speak to me.'

Howard was momentarily startled by the disembodied, metallic sound that came over the telephone. Then he realised that 'Mr Jethro' was using an electronic device to disguise his voice. 'Thank you for calling, Mr Jethro. As you know, I have been asked to do some business on your behalf. Unfortunately, the person I will need to contact is extremely difficult to track down. Would you be able to give me details of a suitable appointment I might keep with him?'

'I will need some time to find out the information you require, Mr Hatcher. I'll have to ring you back. Perhaps next week at the same time. Failing that, the week after.'

'Thank you very much. I look forward to hearing from you.'

'Goodbye, Mr Hatcher.'

The phone went dead. Despite the disguised voice, Jethro had come across as powerful. Howard wondered who he was. Either Jethro was a very careful man, or his voice was well known. Howard shrugged. He took the next slip road off the M25 and headed into London. He had an appointment with a friend at the Travellers' Club.

AT 12.45 THE TAXI drew up outside the Travellers' Club and Howard got out. The hall porter informed him that his guest was waiting for him in the bar.

Howard walked through. 'Henry! Glad you could make it.' The two men shook hands and Howard ordered drinks.

Major Henry Stoner was in his early fifties, and had been Howard's company commander when Howard had joined 42 Commando, Royal Marines. Stoner was now retired and was the London Branch Secretary of the National Rifle Association. A good organiser, he spent much of his time down at the ranges at Bisley, helping to organise rifle meetings, as well as coaching the southeastern regional team.

The two men chatted about old times over lunch, but then the conversation turned to rifle-shooting and Bisley.

'It's getting rather more technical nowadays, Ed,' said Stoner. 'I must get you down for a day, so that you can see what goes on. It's amazing what developments there have been.'

'Don't you find that a bit of a shame? I mean, isn't it something of a pity, compared with the old days, when it was all down to skill?'

'Not a bit of it. It's still a question of whether you've actually got it or not.'

'So how does a good rifle shot come to your attention? Do you go round all the regiments looking for their best marksmen?'

'Surprisingly enough, no. The good Service shots will turn up at Bisley sooner or later as part of their regimental shooting teams. One can spot the really promising ones quickly enough. But, nowadays, it's more often civilians who are the most exciting discoveries. With a bit of coaching they are soon as good as the best of the Service boys.'

'So among other things, you're a sort of talent scout, are you?'

'Well, I enjoy spotting talent and bringing it on. Every now and then I hear of someone who sounds exciting, and try to persuade him to come and give it a go. Sadly, it doesn't always work.'

'How do you mean?'

'Well, for example, a friend of mine recently told me about a young chap called MacDonald, a professional deerstalker. All stalkers are competent shots, but this fellow sounded quite remarkable. I wrote to him, asking him to come down for a trial, but he wasn't interested. I'd love to get my hands on him and see what he could do.'

'Tell me about him,' said Howard.

THE MINISTER PUT DOWN the receiver and remained sitting for a few minutes, thinking carefully. He was uneasy that Asher had telephoned him at home, but he supposed it couldn't be helped. On the face of it their conversation had sounded pretty innocent, even if someone had been monitoring it. But he couldn't risk it again. Asher had served his purpose in this matter; now that the Minister had a telephone number for 'Mr Hatcher', he would deal direct with him. Meanwhile, there was much to do . . .

ON THE AFTERNOON of October 30, two days after his telephone call to the Minister, Asher received a letter delivered by hand. The motorcycle courier had refused to hand it to one of his secretaries, adamant that he must deliver it in person.

'Tell Mr Asher that it concerns Mr Jethro.' The courier's voice was indistinct inside the crash helmet.

'Very well, but I can tell you that it will not make any difference,' the secretary replied, contriving to look both disdainful and alarmed. Privately, she was dreading a bawling-out from Asher.

She proved to be wrong. Asher immediately asked her to show the courier in; still wearing his crash helmet, he handed Asher the envelope without a word and left. Asher tore it open and waved her out of the room. Ten minutes later, he buzzed her on the intercom and told her to arrange for the Gulfstream to be ready to leave for Gibraltar early the following morning.

FOUR DAYS LATER, and 2,000 miles to the south, Asher put down his telephone. *Another* change of plan, but the way things were going, he had little option. And the potential rewards . . .

But it was annoying. He was due back in London the following night, Monday, November 4, to make a speech, and he'd wasted a day and a half kicking his heels in Madeira. Oh well, it couldn't be helped. He would ask his son to make the speech in his absence. He pressed the intercom button to the bridge. 'Gus, I'm not going home yet after all.' He glanced out of the window. The sea outside was almost flat calm; it was a gentle, hazy day. 'Tenerife,' ordered Asher. 'Make for Tenerife.'

At four that afternoon, the *Princess Scheherazade* sailed south from Madeira. Asher, alone on board apart from the eleven crew members, worked on in his office below deck.

ON TUESDAY, NOVEMBER 5, Dartington was a worried man. The lead item in the news that morning was about Asher's death at sea. It had shaken him to the core. After reading what had happened to Asher, he had rung in to his office saying that he was feeling unwell, and then sat around for most of the day wondering what to do.

Shortly before seven that evening, a motorcycle roared up the drive to his house. Dartington's wife answered the door; the helmeted rider handed her an envelope and roared off again.

Lady Dartington walked through to her husband's study. 'This has just arrived for you, darling.'

'Oh? Thanks, dear.' He studied the plain white envelope, which bore just his typed name and address.

Dartington's wife left the room and he slit open the envelope. There were just four lines of plain, anonymous typing.

Sir Peter: You will be understandably concerned at the events of the last twenty-four hours. This is to reassure you that the agreement made with you will be honoured, and that you have nothing to worry about. The project should proceed as agreed.

Chapter ③

On the morning of Monday, November 4, Howard had been in the Saab on the M25 awaiting a telephone call, but none had come. The following Monday, the 11th, the phone rang at 8.32am.

'Mr Hatcher here. Who is speaking, please?'

'Mr Hatcher, I am speaking for Mr Jethro. I am his assistant.' This time there was no electronic disguise; the speaker had an English public-school accent, and sounded calm and self-assured. 'I hope you do not mind my contacting you on Mr Jethro's behalf?'

'No, that's fine,' said Howard. 'I assume that Mr Jethro has told you that I need some information about the overseas contract I am hoping to conclude on his behalf?'

'He has. The request for information was reasonable—this particular client is not easy to get hold of. He will, however, be attending a large meeting in his home town next April on the twenty-eighth.'

Howard thought fast. He would have to examine the map of Iraq carefully, but from what he could recall the place shouldn't be too difficult to reach. 'His home town, April twenty-eighth. Thank you. Is there anything else you think I ought to know?'

'There may be representatives from other firms at the meeting. You should not regard them as important. That is all I can tell you.'

'Thank you; I think that should be enough to go on. Can I suggest that you or Mr Jethro call me again, as before, in case I have any further queries? If there is no reply, you may assume that all is proceeding to plan.'

'One of us will telephone again in a fortnight's time, and fortnightly thereafter. Thank you for your assistance.'

The line went dead. Howard tossed the phone onto the passenger seat and turned his mind to the matter of Jethro's 'assistant'. That guy was no mere assistant, thought Howard. He was government; little doubt about it. He had implied that there might be a foreign diplomatic presence at the 'meeting', and by saying that the diplomats were not to be regarded as important he had dropped a heavy hint that it would not matter if they ended up being caught up in the affair—or even killed. Phew, thought Howard. Serious stuff.

One thing mildly puzzled him—the date. Anniversary of the Revolution? No, that was February 8. Ba'ath Party Day? No again—that wasn't until July 17. He was still wondering about the date when he reached the M40 slip road. He abandoned his speculations for the time being and headed back into London along Western Avenue.

ON THURSDAY, NOVEMBER 14, Howard waited at Heathrow for the arrival of British Airways flight 282 from Los Angeles. The arrivals board reported a punctual landing at 12.25pm; forty minutes later a tall, rangy figure appeared with a rucksack and a briefcase.

'Mike! Good to see you!'

'How you doin', Ed?' Mike Ziegler shook Howard's hand warmly, and the two men made their way towards the exit.

They collected the Saab from the car park and headed towards central London.

'You've got me on fire with curiosity about this one, Ed.' Howard had given little away over the telephone; he had simply told Ziegler that there was 'an interesting new project'. When Ziegler had asked *how* interesting, Howard had just remained silent. He had known Ziegler would not be able to resist anything *that* interesting.

Howard cast his mind back to when he and Ziegler had first met, more than twenty years earlier. He had been sent over from the Special Boat Service on a liaison posting to the US Navy, and Mike Ziegler had become a firm friend.

'This is a big one, Mike.' Howard decided to string it out a little further. The old adrenalin highs were starting again; it was all beginning to slot together. 'I'll let you guess what it is. Who is the most unpopular man in the world?'

'Easy. Patrolman Morton Kleinberg of the LA Police Department. He gave me a speedin' ticket the other day. Why, we got to knock him off?'

'Wrong guy.'

Ziegler shot Howard a sharp glance. The older man was concentrating on the road, but Ziegler noticed that his eyes were glittering with a fire he hadn't seen there for years. *Oh, boy* . . . 'Old Saddam? We gonna pay him a visit? That it?'

'Got it in one.'

During the remainder of the journey into London, Howard filled Ziegler in on the background to the project. He found that Ziegler had a similar concern about the security of the operation, and was relieved to hear that Howard's report to the man he called 'the cut-out' had not contained details of the assassination plan.

'What about the two guys on the phone?' Ziegler asked.

'Difficult to say. Jethro is definitely somebody big. He has to be, if he has this particular cut-out in his pocket. The other guy, his so-called assistant, I really can't place. English, very cool—could be a senior civil servant. One way or another, this smells of government involvement. I'm sure the cut-out wouldn't have agreed to have anything to do with it otherwise.'

'Yeah, I guess you're right. OK, what about the game plan? How are we goin' to do it?'

'I'll go over that when we meet up with the rest of the boys. They're waiting for us at my flat.'

'I'VE PICKED EACH ONE of you because you are the best I know at what you do.' Howard glanced round the room. Seven pairs of eyes were watching him. 'So far, only Johnny and Mike know what this is about, and they're in. The rest of you have been told simply that it's big, that we're talking about retirement money—and I mean *luxury* retirement money—for all of us, and that we have only about a fifty-per-cent chance of pulling it off. We have an even worse chance of getting away with it afterwards. And we're not just talking about imprisonment here. This is action. Do any of you want out?'

'You mentioned prison, boss. How illegal is this?' Bob Usher, a hard-looking man in his late thirties, spoke up. Usher had developed a distaste for prison life during his six months in jail with Howard in Ankara. The diet in the prison had been atrocious, and the deficiency of vitamins had been responsible for his losing nearly all his hair. Before joining XF Securities, Usher had been a sergeant in the 22nd Special Air Service Regiment.

'I'm afraid we will have to break one or two little rules here in the UK. Where we're going, it will be terminally illegal, if we're caught. But we'll be doing everyone a favour.'

'Oh gawd,' grimaced Usher, 'here we go again.'

'Thanks, Bob,' said Howard with a grin. 'I'll try to get you remission for good behaviour.'

'As far as I'm concerned, if you, Mike and Johnny reckon it's OK, you can count me in, boss.' The new speaker, Mel Harris, was a restless-looking man; he sat on the edge of an upright chair, leaning forward with his elbows on his knees. His eyes were piercingly blue; no one could fail to notice the intensity of his stare. Harris wore dark glasses when he did not want to be noticed. Like Bob Usher, he was an ex-sergeant from 22 SAS. It was he whom the three Sardinian would-be kidnappers had underestimated so badly.

'Thanks, Mel. Tony, how about you?'

'Count me in too, boss,' said Tony Ackford, 'I could do with a holiday from the missus.' Howard grinned. Ackford was a large-boned ex-Marine, as big as a small giant. He had served fifteen years with the Special Boat Service, and had always turned down promotion. His tiny Irish wife was legendary for her temper; Ackford, despite his physical strength and ability in combat, was no match for her.

'Fine, Tony, but what's she going to do to you when you get back, huh?'

'I'll bring her a bunch of flowers, boss. They got flowers, where we're going?'

'I doubt it.' Howard turned to the last two men. 'Andy, Chris, how about you?' Andy Denard and Chris Palmer were the only two who were not on the XF Securities payroll. Howard's telephone call to Denard had been if anything even more cryptic than those to the others, since Denard was a citizen of Zimbabwe. It had been Denard's own suggestion to bring Palmer along, because his 'qualifications' would prove indispensable—Palmer was an aircraft mechanic. Howard already sensed that the two ex-Rhodesian Special Forces men had been accepted by the others. Their dry humour, and their no-nonsense, modest style, seemed to have gone down well. Denard was small and wiry, while Palmer was built like a rugby prop forward.

Denard spoke up. 'What will the flying involve, Ed? Do I get to play with an F-16 or something nice like that? I'm bored flying tourists around, you know.'

'Sorry, Andy, nothing as fancy as that.'

'I might have known. Oh, well, I might as well come along anyway. Bloody taxi-driver, that's all I get to be nowadays.'

'All you're good for, nowadays, you bum,' growled Palmer. 'Don't worry, boys, I'll keep the little squirt in line.'

Howard looked round the room with satisfaction. All of them had agreed in principle to join the team, as he had been almost certain they would.

'OK, lads, here it is.' Howard gave it to them rapidly, in a few clipped sentences. There were two or three whistles of surprise, and some approving looks on the faces around him. Mel Harris's eyes lit up in fierce delight; he slapped a fist into the palm of his other hand.

'This operation,' Howard continued, 'is not going to resemble anything we might have done in the military. This is a smash-and-grab job, not a sneak in and out. But I think it can work.

'Anyway, first things first.' He produced seven fat manila envelopes and tossed one to each man. 'There's twenty gorillas in each of these envelopes. I want you each to spend up to half that on getting yourselves some good wheels. Nothing too flashy. Anonymous, reliable secondhand motors. Pay cash, and fill out the registration details yourselves—in false names. Tell the seller you're buying the car for a girlfriend. The cars must not be connected with you. Leave them parked away from home when you aren't using them.

'Johnny's the only exception—he needs a more up-market car for what he'll be doing. The rest of the money is for incidental expenses. No flashing it about. I want receipts. Now, here are some more envelopes.' Howard handed them round; each man's envelope had his name on it. 'Open them up.'

Inside each one were instructions, a tasklist and more money. The amount in each case depended on the likely expenses.

'Mel, you'll see that you and I have a small job to do next week—a break-in down in the country. Then you and Andy are going to make a trip to the States. Your job is to find a cowboy pilot who looks sufficiently like Andy to pass muster. He must be a competent flier with a valid commercial pilot's licence. Andy can check out his flying ability, but I want you to assess how easy it will be to keep him in line. We don't want a drunk or a hothead. Put the cowboy on a retainer of ten thousand dollars, with a further ninety thousand when the job's done. Tell him as little as possible, and don't let him know your names. OK?'

Mel Harris nodded, his eyes still bright with anticipation.

'Good,' said Howard. He turned to Ziegler. 'Mike, you're headed back to the States too, but on a separate job. There are some high-tech items we need.' Next he turned to Palmer. 'Chris, the first thing you've got to do is start growing a beard.'

The stocky Zimbabwean's blond eyebrows lifted slightly; then he nodded in assent.

Howard continued. 'You have to find and lease or buy a plane. Eight seats or more, good tough workhorse machine—something like an Islander or a Twin Otter, suitable for rough landing strips—and reasonable spares back-up. Johnny will handle the finance as it'll be the most expensive item and we won't be able to use cash.

'I still have a major job to do myself. We need one more man, with a specialist skill that none of us has, or not to the standard we are going to need.' Drawing on his cigarette, Howard watched the others trying to figure out the expertise not represented in the room. At last he said, 'We need a top-class sniper. The best there is.'

There were slow nods of understanding from all the seven except one. Tony Ackford had been slowly reading through his shopping list, his brow knotting into a deeper frown with each successive item. Finally, the big man spluttered into indignant life. 'Boss, what the hell is all this rubbish that Bob and I have to get? I can just about understand how the tape recorder and Arabic tuition tapes might come in handy—I mean, I can imagine it might be useful to be able to say "Stand completely still you lowlife or I'll blow your poxy head off" in Arabic, but what's the use of a sixteen-foot rubber dinghy, wet suits, paddles and an outboard motor in the middle of the desert? And this—*four tons* of tinned margarine? Chemical toilet and camping kit? A forty-foot-long commercial freezer container? What sort of a caper are we going on—a camping expedition to Baghdad, where we deep-fry a camel in margarine and bring the effing thing home deep-frozen, towing it behind a dinghy?'

The others were rocking with laughter, and eventually Ackford's face broke into a grin too. Howard waited until the laughter had subsided; then he began to explain.

SOMETHING WAS NAGGING at Howard as he sat poring over his maps of Scotland. He had bought a complete set of 1:50,000 Landranger Ordnance Survey maps, and was methodically working through them. He had two clues—a place name and a surname.

He studied the area. Wild-looking country, he thought; steep, magnificent, desolate. The village was marked, and there was a PH sign which made him reach for his motorist's handbook. Yes, the public house was listed: an inn. Rooms were available. Probably fairly basic, but it would do. He felt a brief sense of achievement at having tracked it down—without needing to ask Stoner too many questions. But a fat lot of good it would do him, unless he could find out a bit more—something that would give him a handle on this fellow.

MacDonald. Not an unusual name, in its various forms—as hundreds of fast-food outlets reminded him practically wherever he went, but a very common name up there. Yet he had noticed a particular reference to it somewhere, and there might be a connection. Why had it registered? Where had he seen it? He could not remember. He would have to start again from scratch.

He set off again for the British Newspaper Library and by 11.30 he was deep into the stack of newspapers he had requested. At 4.36pm he located the reference he had noticed. He was fairly certain it would be enough to persuade MacDonald to cooperate.

MEL HARRIS REVERSED his recently acquired Golf GTi into the farm gateway and switched off the lights. He and Howard sat for ten minutes in silence while their night vision adjusted. Eventually, Howard nodded and they got out. Howard pointed out the big house on the other side of the field; at three in the morning, only the porch security light was still on. The two men put on overalls and gloves, and unloaded a bulky black bag and a metal tube from the boot.

Harris's voice was a whisper. 'I feel a proper Jumblatt with these kid's trainers on, boss.'

'Don't let it bother you, Mel,' murmured Howard. 'Think of the admiring glances you'll get down the nick after we get picked up for this little caper. Come on, let's go.'

Harris and Howard walked briskly across the field and climbed the wall into the kitchen garden at the back of the house. Making no sound, they skirted round the flowerbeds until they came to the window of the study at the front. Howard examined the window and gave the thumbs-up: the latch was open.

While Howard noiselessly pushed the sash window up, Harris unpacked the telescopic fishing rod from its tube. He taped a small wire frame to the tip of the rod and stuck pieces of putty on the arms of the wire that ran at right angles to the rod. He peeled the backing off a double-sided adhesive strip, the other side of which was already fixed to a six-inch-square piece of card, and then pushed the reverse side of the card against the putty of the frame. The frame and putty now held the card in place at the end of the rod.

Careful not to put his hand through the window, Howard silently indicated the location of the infrared alarm sensor. Harris eased the rod through the window, card first.

The sensor was in the corner of the room, on the same wall as the window. It covered the whole room; it would sense a change in position of any heat source, such as a human body, within the four walls. It could not detect the window being opened—since it was on the same wall the sensor's gaze swept right past it. Because the card gave off a neutral infrared signature, its presence did not register. The sticky strip on the front of the card made contact with the sensor's surface and stuck tight. Harris gently pulled the fishing rod, which disengaged itself from the loose grip of the putty. The card was now stuck fast to the sensor, covering its small window and leaving it completely blind. They climbed soundlessly into the room.

They stood listening for a while, but there was no noise from inside the house. Howard snapped on his small pen-torch and went to the desk. Checking the drawers, he took a small crowbar out of the bag and quietly and slowly began levering open the only two that were locked. Then he switched on the photocopier at the side of the desk. Leafing through the three files he had taken from the desk, Howard extracted thirty-eight pages; he laid the first of these on the flat glass platen of the copier, closed the top cover, and pressed the 'copy' button.

The noise from the photocopier was almost inaudible. When all thirty-eight pages had been copied, Howard gave a nod, and Harris switched off the machine. The copies of the documents, along with some Darcon headed paper and company envelopes, were placed in a document folder in the bottom of the black bag.

Howard deftly rifled through the desk; a pocket dictating machine, a camera and some loose cash joined the folder in the black bag. Harris disconnected Dartington's fax machine and video recorder. Both went into the bag. Two silver candleholders, the only small objects of obvious value in the room, were placed by the windowsill. The two men then spent three minutes creating the impression that someone had been searching hastily for valuables.

When Howard was satisfied, he strewed the contents of the files about the floor. The room now looked a shambles. Switching his torch off, he climbed out of the window, taking the silver candleholders in his gloved hands and lowering the bag to the ground. Harris replaced the fishing rod in its tube and handed it out to Howard. Then he walked across to the alarm sensor and removed the card, checking that all the tape came away with it. He folded and slipped the card into his inside pocket.

The alarm sensor immediately registered the presence of an intruder. Down the hall, the control box sent its instruction to the autodialling unit in the cupboard nearby; the unit began dialling the number of the alarm company's central monitoring station.

By the time the unit finished dialling, Harris had climbed out of the window and dropped lightly to the ground. Reaching up, he drew the window down, then used one end of the fishing-rod tube to smash a pane of glass near the latch lock. He pushed the window up again and left it open.

Taking one handle each of the bag, which was now heavy with all the booty, Howard and Harris retraced their steps to the kitchen garden and the wall beyond. At the wall, Howard dropped the candleholders in the mud before climbing over.

A POLICE PATROL CAR arrived at the house thirty seconds after the GTi had pulled unnoticed out of the farm gateway. All the evidence, from the imprints of the training shoes in the flowerbeds to the nature of the stolen goods, would lead them to conclude that 'youngsters' had been responsible—a view that would be reinforced by the discovery later that morning of the items of silver amateurishly dropped near the kitchen-garden wall.

Harris headed back towards London. He drew in briefly at a lay-by to allow Howard to dump two almost brand-new pairs of training shoes, two pairs of dark blue overalls, and a perfectly good camera, dictating machine and video recorder into a rubbish skip.

THE YOUNG ESTATE AGENT could hardly credit his luck. One minute he had been sitting in his office twiddling his thumbs and gloomily pondering over his future, and the next, this round-faced fellow had walked in off the street and said he wanted to lease some of the deadest property on the firm's books. Unbelievable!

The Loundis Road industrial units had been completed in 1988: ten of them, in a row. Eminently lettable—in theory, at least. Easy access to the M4 at junction 16; good, versatile units, all things considered. The problem had been the recession.

All ten units were still empty—Loundis Road was deserted. There had been no interest at all. Until today, that was. The round-faced guy had just walked in a couple of days ago, said he liked the units, and asked if he could rent—wait for it—not one, not two, but *three* of them. Just like that. Talk about a kick-start! The round-faced Mr Bryce had been delightful to deal with. He had read through the draft tenancy agreement and agreed all the terms on the spot; he had been ready with bank references (which had checked out *very* nicely); the two of them had driven out in Bryce's car to look the units over; they had shaken hands on the deal and driven back.

Nice motor, Mr Bryce had. Very nice. BMW 325i, leather seats, CD sound system, went like a rocket. No cash-flow problems for Mr Bryce, that was obvious. The lease had been completed in a record two days, and the bank draft had been cleared. Six months' rent in advance, too. Oh yes, thought the estate agent as he waved Mr Bryce off, it would be drinks all round in the office today.

THE BMW DROVE AWAY from the estate agent's office, heading out of Swindon towards the M4. Johnny Bourne opened his mouth and extracted two pink rubber cheek-pads, stowing them away in a plastic bag in the glove compartment next to a small bottle of 'plastic skin'. The pads made him look as though he had just been for a painful visit to the dentist, he thought; but to anyone who didn't know what he normally looked like, they just gave him a more rounded face. He rubbed his fingertips against the upholstery of the BMW; the coating of plastic skin on each finger began to peel off.

Bourne had had a busy week. The flight to Liechtenstein, the formation of a company there and the transfer of a million pounds into a new bank account, then back to England and the formation of three more UK-based companies: one in the food wholesale business, one in freight and the third in general trading. Firms of solicitors and accountants in three separate towns had handled the paperwork and VAT registration. Then there had been further transfers of funds into newly opened accounts at three different British banks. There would soon begin a series of transactions between the companies which would satisfy the banks that they were trading healthily. None of the transactions would survive a proper audit, but they wouldn't have to.

In the meantime, Bourne would have to keep remembering the plastic skin and the cheek-pads. If Juliet saw him like that ... the consequences didn't bear thinking about. He smiled as he thought of her, and found himself pushing his foot down on the car's accelerator.

ON FRIDAY, NOVEMBER 29, Howard arrived at Edinburgh on the midday shuttle from Heathrow. Collecting his luggage, he went to the Avis desk and completed the car-hire formalities for the Ford Escort he had booked. He drove out of the airport and headed north towards Spean Bridge and Fort William.

It was a cold day, with squalls of wind gusting across the road, at times strong enough to rock the car. By 3.45 in the afternoon, the light was failing; it would be dark well before he arrived.

Five miles past Spean Bridge he turned off onto the single-track road to the small village of Carvaig. Howard drove slowly and carefully. The eyes of black-faced sheep by the roadside were lit up by his headlamps as he passed; a couple of times he had to stop and toot his horn to clear them off the road itself.

Finally, just after five o'clock, he saw a small scattering of lights ahead in the distance, and ten minutes later he arrived at Carvaig itself. The inn was prominent among the twenty or so cottages. He parked the car, collected his bags and rang the doorbell.

A young auburn-haired girl of about eighteen appeared, wearing jeans and a thick pullover. She had a pretty face and a soft, lilting west-coast accent. 'Good evening—can I help?'

'My name is Hatcher, Edwin Hatcher. I rang and booked a room for a couple of nights. I hope that's still all right?'

'Oh, yes, of course, Mr Hatcher—I'm sorry. Come away in! I

should have known it must be you!' The girl smiled at him and offered to help with his bags.

She busied about, chattering and making him feel welcome. Then she showed him into the small sitting room and went off to make him a cup of tea. A woman appeared, smiling and wiping her hands on her apron as she came up to shake his hand. She was a small, trim figure, perhaps forty years old.

'Mr Hatcher—welcome to Carvaig! I'm Morag Cameron—Sheila's mother.' Hers had been the voice on the telephone when Howard had rung to book the room. A nice voice, soft and gentle, sounding slightly surprised at the idea of someone coming up to such a remote place in November for a weekend break.

Morag Cameron showed Howard up to his room, which was small but comfortable and spotlessly clean. Howard opened the window and caught the unique, wild smell of the air and memories began flooding back to him. He breathed in contentedly and began to unpack.

Half an hour later, after a hot bath in wonderfully soft, peaty water, he went down to the bar. He settled into a chair with a book, to all appearances a tourist relaxing after a day's motoring.

Sheila came in and asked him if he would like a drink. She was visibly pleased when he chose an expensive malt whisky.

For a while, Howard was the only customer in the bar, and he and the girl chatted amiably. Many years ago, he told her, he had come up here with his father; he had been a youngster of twelve at the time. His father had been invited for three days' stalking on the Glen Carvaig estate. He had always meant to revisit the place, he said, but had only now finally got round to it. 'So it's really just a little bit of nostalgia, if you like.'

His story was partly true, but the true parts had happened somewhere else. He had memorised enough details from the map to be able to mention some of the hills in Glen Carvaig if she asked.

He changed the subject. 'I was wondering if it would be possible to take a walk up the glen—perhaps tomorrow morning. I could take a sandwich or something with me. Is there anyone I should see to ask permission?'

'Oh, I'm sure that would be fine, Mr Hatcher. The stalking is finished for the season now, and they've not started on the hinds yet. I'm sure that as long as you stay on the road up the glen you'll be fine. And I can make you a piece for your pocket, if you tell me what you would like—we've some good beef, or there's ham or cheese.'

'The beef sounds fine. That would be very kind. How would I get there? Would I drive to the lodge? It's a couple of miles or so on up the road, isn't it?' It was. He had that portion of the map clearly in his mind's eye.

'Aye, you could take your car up there. It's a nice walk—about ten miles up the river from the lodge to the head of the glen.'

'Shouldn't I see someone before just setting off on my own? The stalker, perhaps?'

'Well, you may see Duncan up there at the lodge, if he's not away up the glen himself. Duncan Macrae. He's the stalker.'

Howard was momentarily nonplussed. Duncan Macrae? That was the wrong name. He thought quickly. 'Glen Carvaig's a big forest for just one stalker, isn't it? I thought there were two beats.'

'Aye, there are, right enough. But Duncan is the head stalker. Danny only works there part-time, during the stalking season.'

'Danny?'

It all came spilling out; she couldn't have hidden her feelings if she had tried. She was obviously in love with Danny MacDonald. The two families had been friends for years; then had come the tragedy, when Sheila was only nine years old. Her parents and Danny's were driving back home late one rainy night when an oncoming van suddenly rounded a corner at speed on the single-track road. Danny's mother was driving the car. She swerved to avoid a collision and the car went off the road, careered down a steep bank and burst into flames. Sheila's mother was thrown clear; Sheila's father and both Danny's parents were killed. Morag Cameron was found two hours later, nearly dead from exposure and shock, by a passing motorist. The van and its driver had never been traced.

Danny had been eighteen at the time of his parents' death, and Fergus, his brother, sixteen. Both had worked part-time during the holidays as gillies for their father, who had been head stalker at Glen Carvaig, and so when Duncan Macrae had been appointed to the post, he was wise enough to recommend that Danny, a natural at it, should be given the second beat.

Fergus had gone to Aberdeen to work in the North Sea oil business. He had travelled abroad and married; he had hardly ever come home. Then there had been the second terrible tragedy, and he would be coming home no more . . .

Howard could see Sheila was upset, and he quickly switched the conversation back to Danny. As the girl talked about him, a picture of the young Scot began to build up in Howard's mind. Determined, self-reliant, tough, fit and strong—all good points. A hot temper— not so good.

'So what does he do outside the season?'

'Och, he runs his uncle's sports shop in Fort William. Well, now,

46

Mr Hatcher'—she straightened up and assumed an air of brisk
efficiency—'I'd best see to your supper before the others all come in.
We've some very nice trout, which I can recommend.'

ON NOVEMBER 29, Harris and Denard had been in Texas for exactly
a week. They had covered nearly a thousand miles around the
southern part of the state in their hired Chrysler.

They had visited dozens of airfields. Some surprised them by their
size and sophistication; others proved almost deserted. Harris had six
flying lessons from six different instructors, Denard chartered three
half-hour flights in light aircraft, and they both went up on two
tourist flights. On chatting afterwards to the pilots, however, they
drew a blank each time. Three of the pilots seemed hungry enough for
work, but the rest were apparently contented and settled in their jobs.
Even the three more promising ones would not fit the bill: two were
over six foot tall, and the third was about sixty years old.

'It's true, what they say about this state,' groaned Denard, as they
drove off having drawn yet another blank. 'I haven't seen anyone my
size since we've been here.'

'We've got plenty of time,' Harris reassured him. 'There must be
somebody smaller around here somewhere who wants to earn an easy
hundred thousand bucks.'

On the afternoon of Friday 29, they arrived at Los Morelos
airfield, thirty miles northwest of Austin. Large hoardings at the
entrance to the airfield listed the facilities on offer from a number of
operators: charters, flying lessons, scenic flights over the Colorado
River, freight services, air taxi. It looked promising.

The airfield control centre was empty except for a dispatcher
behind the counter and a man sprawled in an armchair, drinking
coffee from a styrofoam cup.

Harris approached the counter. 'We saw the notice advertising
flights over the Colorado. Do we have to book, or is there a plane
available to take us up for a flight right now?'

The dispatcher was polite and helpful. 'You'd want Dan Woods or
his partner Gene Barcus. River Flying Services is their outfit. They're
both up right now with a party each, due back in twenty minutes.'

Harris looked at his watch and shrugged, thinking of the extra time
they would have to spend waiting. Denard caught his eye and was
about to speak when a drawling voice from behind them broke in.

'You could sure do worse than try Ray Sullivan.' They turned and
looked at the man in the armchair, who got slowly to his feet. 'He's
got an office out back. Ain't far. I got to go over there anyhow.'

Harris and Denard looked at each other, then Harris said, 'OK.'

The man led them out of the control centre, leaving the dispatcher frowning with disapproval.

'What kind of work does this guy Sullivan do?' asked Denard, as they walked across the apron.

'Oh, he'll do any darn thing you might want. One-man outfit, glad of the work. Good pilot. Does all his own maintenance, too.'

Harris and Denard exchanged another glance, following behind their guide. They reached an old Nissen hut, and the man opened a small side door. There was a small desk in one corner, with a telephone and a mass of papers. There was no one in sight.

Their guide turned and held out his hand. 'Well, howdy, folks! Nice of you to drop in. Ray Sullivan here, at your service.'

He grinned. 'Sorry about the charade, but I could use the work.'

Harris looked at Denard again, a slow smile starting on his face.

NINETY MINUTES LATER, they climbed down from a twin-engined Cessna and had a quick conversation as Sullivan finished securing the plane for the night.

'I think he'll do,' said Harris. 'Plenty of experience. He seems pretty unflappable and steady, and he's admitted he could use some extra dosh. Let's talk to him.'

'Mel, he's still a couple of inches taller than me. There's some facial resemblance, I admit. But I'm fair-haired and he's got dark hair and a moustache.'

'If he agrees, I'll buy you some hair dye,' said Harris. 'And you can start growing a tache. OK?'

Later that evening a delighted Ray Sullivan, now unexpectedly richer by $10,000 in cash, waved the Chrysler away. He would carry on at Los Morelos for a while; then he would wind down his business and move away from the area. He would be given a date in late March to fly to London, England. A month after that, his job done, he would be able to go anywhere he liked in the world.

HOWARD DRESSED in walking clothes and took an unhurried breakfast. Collecting the 'piece' that Sheila Cameron had made for him, he left in the car for Glen Carvaig Lodge. He spent the morning walking up to the head of the glen and back.

He then drove back through Carvaig and down onto the main road. He arrived in Fort William just before two o'clock, parked in the station car park, and went for a walk through the town.

The Yellow Pages book in the inn had listed three sports shops in Fort William; he had made a note of the addresses. He crossed over the road, past the Alexandra Hotel and into the High Street. The window of the first shop on his list had a display of running shoes, track suits and windsurfers. Inside he could see a young man attending to customers. The young man was barely twenty and had hair flopping down over his forehead and eyes.

The second shop was two hundred yards further along the High Street, its window packed with boots, wet-weather clothing, climbing gear, clasp knives and camping equipment.

Howard moved on to the third shop, which proved to be small and principally for the fisherman. He opened the door and went in. A rather dour man in his late fifties showed Howard a selection of trout flies in response to his enquiry. Howard bought two flies and left.

He collected his car and drove back to the second shop, parking fifty yards away. He settled down to wait. At about 4.30 a large Volvo estate car drew up outside the shop; the driver got out and went inside. Five minutes later he re-emerged, followed by a man in his late twenties carrying two boxes of shotgun ammunition. The man loaded the boxes into the customer's car and went back inside. At five o'clock the man left the shop, locking up as he went. He walked a few yards down the street to a side road, where he got into a blue Toyota pick-up and drove away.

Howard followed the Toyota out towards Spean Bridge, keeping fairly close behind. Four miles outside Fort William, the Toyota signalled a right turn and pulled into a half-concealed gateway. As Howard drove on past, the name of the cottage was briefly caught in the Toyota's lights. Howard carried on for a further half-mile, then did a U-turn and headed back to Fort William, where he stopped at a telephone kiosk. There were 183 entries in the Highlands and Islands phone book under 'MacDonald, D'; Howard found the one with the address given as Glenside Cottage. He picked up the receiver and dialled the number.

HOWARD SWUNG THE DOOR of the phone booth shut and drove the Escort back out of Fort William towards Spean Bridge. Ten minutes later he pulled into the gateway of MacDonald's cottage, got out of the car and walked up the short gravel path to the front door.

The fair-haired man who answered the door looked as fit as Howard would have expected a professional deerstalker to be. His level gaze met Howard's, and the two men studied each other; Howard was struck by the paleness of the blue-grey eyes—you almost felt you could look right through them.

'Mr MacDonald? I'm Peter Hanbury. I rang you. It's good of you to see me.'

'Danny MacDonald. My pleasure. Come in, Mr Hanbury.' They

shook hands, and MacDonald led the way into the small sitting room. 'Take a seat. Can I get you a cup of tea?'

'That would be very kind.' Howard glanced cursorily round the room as MacDonald disappeared into the kitchen. The sitting room was simply furnished. Along one wall, under the window, was a large workbench covered with tools and assorted pieces of machinery. No woman's influence here, thought Howard. Not yet, anyway. Apart from the bench, there were two chairs, a table, a television and an old mains radio. The only personal touch was a pair of framed photographs on the chimneypiece. One showed a man and woman in their thirties, with two young boys of about six and eight; the other was of the same two boys in their teens, smiling happily at the camera.

MacDonald reappeared in the doorway with two mugs of tea. Howard took the proffered mug and they sat down.

'Well, Mr MacDonald,' he began, 'as I told you on the telephone, I do occasional pieces for an American magazine which is widely read by gun enthusiasts in the States. I heard through the grapevine about a remarkable shot you pulled off last year, and I thought it would make a story. I'd be prepared to offer you fifty pounds for telling me about it.'

MacDonald remained impassive while Howard talked; then, when he had finished, he nodded. 'Well, I don't see any great harm in that. What exactly is it that you want to know?'

'I've spoken to the colonel, and he's told me about the stalk itself.' Howard was lying. He had never met the colonel and did not know him—he had only spoken to Stoner. 'So perhaps you could just tell me how you pulled off the shot. He was genuinely impressed.'

'The colonel is a fine gentleman,' said MacDonald, 'and quite a competent shot himself. He just had a wee bit of bad luck. The stag moved just as he committed himself to the shot; the shot went behind, going into the gut. The beast took off with the hinds and we didn't have another chance until he was about five hundred yards away.'

'But why did you take a shot at that range?' Howard was leaning forward in his seat, looking intently at MacDonald.

'A fair enough question, Mr Hanbury,' replied MacDonald, 'but I was reasonably confident about the shot. And it could have been an hour or more before we came up to him again; I don't like to see a beast suffer unnecessarily.

'The shot was a lot easier than it sounds. There were several things that helped. First of all, there was next to no wind. In the second place, it's not difficult to estimate the speed of a beast. The stag was climbing at a vertical rate of about four feet per second, allowing for the steepness of the slope. At five hundred yards the time of flight of the bullet will be a little less than three-quarters of a second, so I had to aim about three feet in front of where I wanted the bullet to hit.'

Howard was nodding, so MacDonald went on. 'Then there was the range itself. At a distance of five hundred yards an error of fifty yards in one's estimation can make a difference of a foot in the elevation of the bullet. However, this beast was running directly away from us and uphill, presenting the length of his spine almost vertically. A shot anywhere in the spine from the top of the neck to about the eighth thoracic vertebra is a killing shot. D'you see what I'm getting at? The target area was narrow, but nearly three feet high. Of course I had to take into account that a .275 will drop fifty inches below the point of aim at five hundred yards. It was a good shot, yes, but not really a risky one. At least,' he added, 'that was the theory. In practice, it wasn't like that at all.'

Howard was puzzled. 'How do you mean?'

'Theory is all very well,' said MacDonald, 'but you can hardly sit down on a hillside with a calculator and start working things out. It's almost entirely a matter of instinct.' MacDonald paused for a moment, studying Howard. 'Anyway, I think that covers the shot itself, unless there's anything you aren't clear about?'

Howard was elated. The stalker had demonstrated his competence and knowledge beyond question. 'No, Mr MacDonald, you have explained it all very clearly. I followed all that perfectly.'

'I rather thought you would, Mr Hanbury.' MacDonald's eyes narrowed, and now he too leaned forward in his chair, watching Howard's face closely. 'So perhaps you can tell me why you're really here. You're no more a journalist than I am. You didn't take any notes when I was talking. You followed me out here this evening, then you went back to telephone me before returning here. Someone fitting your description is booked into the inn at Carvaig, and has been asking questions about me. I think, Mr Hanbury—or is it Mr Hatcher—that you had better explain yourself.'

Howard had been trying hard to remain expressionless while MacDonald spoke; now he could contain himself no longer. His face broke into a broad grin.

Chapter ④

After giving MacDonald his real name, Howard apologised for the subterfuge and said that he had an interesting proposition. Before he explained the proposition, said Howard, he wanted to establish whether or not it was a feasible one.

MacDonald was puzzled, but he had lost some of his initial wariness. 'So let's get this straight, now, Mr Howard. You are asking me whether it is theoretically possible to hit a target six inches in diameter at a range of twelve hundred yards. Is that it?'

'That's right.'

'Fine. Well, the answer is that in theory it *is* possible. A top-quality long-range sniper's rifle is capable of grouping better than a half a minute of angle. That means an error of less than half an inch diameter at a hundred yards. At twelve hundred yards the possible error will be twelve times as large, so a group of shots should fall within a circle less than six inches in diameter. But that assumes no error at all on the part of the man firing the rifle. And there are all sorts of other things to take into consideration too.'

'Such as?'

'Well, the standard 7.62mm NATO bullet loses velocity and goes below the speed of sound at about nine hundred yards. After that it becomes very unstable. So you'd need a very powerful cartridge—one that's still supersonic at twelve hundred yards. But there are other factors to take into account—humidity, air temperature and barometric pressure. We can pretty well ignore variations in humidity. Air temperature is much more significant. A single degree centigrade difference in temperature will make a difference of about one inch in twelve hundred yards. So, for example between dawn and midday, when you might have a temperature variation of perhaps ten degrees or more, the difference will be ten inches—putting the margin of error outside the six-inch target.'

'As much as that? I had no idea.'

'I'm afraid so. But unfortunately,' continued MacDonald, 'that's only the start of it. Let's go on to barometric pressure. This is affected by weather and altitude. The higher the altitude, the thinner the air is; so there is less air resistance and the bullet doesn't slow down so quickly. D'you follow me?'

'Yes, I think so.' Howard was impressed.

'Fine. So if the rifle had been sighted in on a cold day, say at ten degrees centigrade, on a firing range in the south of England three hundred feet above sea level, you could not expect it to perform the same way up here in the hills on a warm day. At an altitude of fifteen hundred feet, and in an air temperature of twenty Centigrade, the bullet would go somewhere between two and three feet high of your six-inch target at twelve hundred yards. You can begin to see how easy it would be to miss the six-inch target, can't you?'

'Yes, I can.' Howard was beginning to feel slightly worried.

'That's not all,' said MacDonald. 'A bullet with right-handed spin will veer off to the right. Luckily, the effect is a predictable constant for a given range, so you can adjust your sights to compensate. There are two other factors—both far more important. Range and wind. You get just one of these even *slightly* wrong, and you've had it. Let me give you an example, still using our super high-velocity ammo. Taking our distance of twelve hundred yards, let's assume you make an error of one hundred yards, that is, you think it's thirteen hundred yards. Let's also say that your average error in estimating the wind speed is five miles per hour—not a big error at all, over a long distance like that. D'you realise by how far you will miss your six-inch target?'

'Tell me,' said Howard, gloomily.

'About six feet above the target and four feet off to the side.'

'Oh, Lord,' groaned Howard. 'I had no idea it was quite that bad.'

'It's not an insurmountable problem, of course,' said MacDonald, 'and for target shooters it's easier, because they know the distance between them and the target to the nearest yard. Also, there are usually flags flying all the way down the side of the range, so they can see what the wind is doing.'

'Well,' said Howard, 'let me be more specific. Let's say we know the altitude, we can read the barometric pressure, take the temperature and the humidity and allow for those . . .'

'Just a second,' cut in MacDonald. 'It takes time to work it out. You'd probably need about twenty minutes.'

'Five minutes maximum.'

'Not a chance, unless you'd worked out a whole lot of different possibilities beforehand. That would take literally days. But anyway, you haven't mentioned range and wind.'

'Maybe we could put one or two little flags out. As for range, I don't know. Let's say we get it right to within fifty yards.'

'That would be imprecise. I don't know . . . What about sighters?'

'What do you mean?'

'How many sighting shots can the shooter take?'

'He can't take any at all.'

'Mr Howard,' said MacDonald, shaking his head and smiling dismissively, 'I can tell you straight away that in those circumstances the best shot in the world wouldn't stand a chance of hitting it with his first shot. He would be doing very well to hit a target six *foot* square with his first shot, let alone six *inches* square. It just isn't on.'

'Is there no way we could get round the problem of estimating the distance?'

'Well, you could if you had an accurate range-finder. You look like a military man. Does the army have anything like that? Laser range-finders? I seem to remember hearing something about them.'

Howard considered the matter. He dared not ask his SBS contacts. 'I wouldn't be able to get one for this particular job.'

'Hold on, I've had an idea. You could use an optical range-finder. They're large, but quite accurate over that sort of distance. My uncle has an old naval instrument from the war.'

'Good,' said Howard, relieved. 'Now, what about wind, if we can't use flags?'

'You'd definitely need something to gauge the wind speed. The best thing would be proper meteorological anemometers. You know, those things with three little cups on them which turn round in the wind. You can get small handheld ones.'

'Excellent!' exclaimed Howard. 'A friend of mine is an electronics expert. I'm sure he'd be able to get hold of a type of anemometer that he could fix up so that two or three of them could radio back the wind speed. We couldn't have them manned—they'd have to be on a remote read-out.'

'What d'you mean, you couldn't have them manned? Why not?'

'Mr MacDonald, before I answer that, I just want to know one thing. Given the range-finder, the anemometers and tables for temperature et cetera, could *you* hit such a target with your first shot?'

MacDonald thought for a moment, then gave Howard a sideways look before answering carefully. 'Yes, Mr Howard, I think I would have a good chance. I couldn't guarantee it; nobody could. But it might be possible.' MacDonald looked directly at Howard and leaned forward. 'I assume there is a point to all this. I've been patient, Mr Howard. Now you can level with me, please. What is this all about, and what is this six-inch target you want me to hit?'

Howard held MacDonald's eyes with his own and replied softly, 'The target is a man, Mr MacDonald.'

'What?' MacDonald was up on his feet in an instant, his eyes wide with incredulity. Gradually he turned a furious red, then began jabbing his finger at Howard. 'Give me just one good reason, right now, you madman, why I shouldn't go straight to the police!'

Howard's voice remained soft and steady. 'The target is Saddam Hussein.'

The blood drained from MacDonald's face, and he sat down. Howard watched carefully as conflicting emotions seemed to hit MacDonald all at once. Howard discerned more about the stalker's character in those seconds than he had in the whole of the previous hour's conversation. MacDonald's blue-grey eyes seemed to change colour to a fierce bright blue. The stare was as fixed and hard as any Howard could remember. The voice, when it came, was little more than a whisper. 'Tell me you're not joking. *Tell me!*'

'I'm deadly serious, Mr MacDonald. This is no joke. You know it isn't and there are three good reasons why I don't think you'll go to the police.' Howard's eyes deliberately flickered to one side—to the photographs on the chimneypiece.

MacDonald saw the movement of his glance; his hands tightened on the arms of the chair. His voice had risen to a quiet hiss as he spoke through tightly clenched teeth. 'Oh, you bastard. You complete *bastard*. You knew, didn't you? Yes. I'll do it. *I'll do it!*'

THE NEXT MORNING Howard drove back to Edinburgh, deep in thought. He checked in the hire car and caught the shuttle to London. It was Sunday, December 1. With the successful recruitment of Danny MacDonald, the last major piece of the plan was now in place.

On Monday morning he drove down to Swindon, where he found Bob Usher checking off goods delivered to Unit 8 on the industrial estate. Bourne was sitting at a desk in the side office, dealing with paperwork. The unit had taken on the appearance of a warehouse, with packing cases and pallets stacked in neat lines. A fork-lift truck was parked in the corner, plugged in for recharging.

Howard walked over to the office and went in. 'Morning, Johnny. How's it going?'

'Pretty good. We're well ahead of schedule. Mel and Andy arrived back from Texas yesterday—looks like they've already found themselves a suitable pilot.' Bourne told him about Ray Sullivan. 'He's coming over on March twenty-eighth. Apparently he's raring to go.'

'Must be the thought of that ninety thousand dollars. It's funny to think I might never have to meet him. Any news from Mike?'

'No. He's been in the States a week now. Those night-vision goggles are probably tricky to get hold of. I expect he'll ring if he has problems with any of it. How did you get on in Scotland? You look pretty cheerful.'

'No problem at all. Danny MacDonald is good—really knows his stuff. He's better than I dared hope.' Howard recounted the details of their meeting, relishing the part when MacDonald had challenged him for his real name. 'He's pretty alert. Bearing in mind that he has no reason to be watching his back, he did well to put two and two together.'

Bourne nodded approvingly. 'I look forward to meeting the guy. By the way, when Andy and Mel rang in, I told them to join up with Chris—he's still looking for an aircraft.'

Howard nodded. Chris Palmer had warned him that finding a

suitable plane might take some time. 'Right; I'm off to talk to the others. Where's Tony? I've got a job for him.'

'Next door in Unit Nine. He's already got his machine tools set up. He's busy on those AK silencers.'

'Anything in Unit Ten yet?'

'No. The container's coming later this week; we'll put it in there. We'll have to work on it in situ, on its trailer.'

'Fine. OK, back to your statutory company duties, lad!' Howard left him in the office and went next door to find Tony Ackford bent over a workbench, wearing protective goggles. A five-inch cylinder of steel was spinning between the chocks of a lathe, the bit cutting into one end to form a neck.

Ackford looked up as Howard's shadow fell over the bench; he switched the machine off. 'Morning, boss. Good trip north?'

'Yes, thanks, Tony. Our boy has agreed. He's given me a list of requirements. How are you getting on?'

'Fine. I've done one silencer already.' Ackford showed Howard the finished article. 'Here, I've got a deactivated AK 47 to show you how it fits. I bought it at one of those places that sell replica guns.' Ackford screwed the finished silencer in place.

Howard inspected it. 'It looks fine, Tony. Do all AKs have this same threading on the end of the barrel?'

'Yes. AK 47, AKM, AKMS, the lot. Even the Chinese versions do. The AK 74 doesn't, of course—it has its own special muzzle brake.' The AK was the most widely produced and most copied assault rifle in the world. The original design of the Avtomat Kalashnikova 47, named after the Soviet citizen who had designed it in 1947, had remained largely unchanged since then. The AKMS was a version with a folding stock, issued to Soviet airborne forces and tank crews. Most of the Warsaw Pact countries had produced their own versions of the same design. The AK 74 was a newer version; it fired the smaller 5.45mm calibre, in place of the old AK 47's 7.62mm.

'How long will it take to finish all eight silencers?'

'Another few hours should do it, boss. It's a simple job with this machinery.' Ackford indicated the other tools—stamps, cutters, presses, drills, and tap and die machinery.

'Good. I've got the details of the sniper rifle we need. Does this mean anything to you?' Howard passed him a piece of paper.

Ackford studied it. 'Accuracy International, eh? Couldn't have chosen better. What are we going to get—the L96?' Accuracy International Ltd had designed the L96 sniper rifle to replace the British Army's ageing L42.

'Actually, no. There's now a second-generation version of the L96 called the AW. We're getting the specialist version of that—the Super Magnum. It's based on a necked-down Rigby .416 case. It's a great big cartridge, firing a two-hundred-and-fifty-grain bullet at a muzzle velocity of three thousand feet per second.'

'Phew. That'll give him a sore shoulder. You want me to put the order in? Accuracy International are extremely security-conscious. They won't sell to just anyone. I'll have to use the firm's RFD licence to get it as a request from a friendly government.' XF Securities was, among other things, a Registered Firearms Dealer. Clients occasionally requested specialist weaponry for security purposes, and the RFD licence officially enabled Howard's company to supply it.

'Fine. Use Colombia. Ziggy can fix that when he comes back—he's doing some work for the authorities out there, with the British Government's blessing. You know, the drugs problem. The new Colombian government is trying to stamp out the cartels. Can you see any problem with the other gear he's asked for?'

Ackford scanned down the list. 'No problem with that. In fact, Accuracy will fix it all up and sight it in for the ammo. OK, boss, I'll get on with it.'

Howard slapped him on the back and returned next door, pleased at how things seemed to be progressing.

ON THURSDAY, Palmer telephoned Bourne from Dublin to announce success in locating a suitable aircraft. The normally impassive Rhodesian sounded delighted with his find: the plane, a twin-engined Pilatus Britten-Norman Islander BN2B-20, was in excellent condition and had recently been given a major overhaul. Tip tanks had been fitted, giving it a maximum range of 1,075 nautical miles.

The Islander had almost all the other fittings required, including an autopilot; the only modifications Palmer would need to make would be to strip out the rear seats and install a GPS satellite-navigation system. The two rear doors were wide enough for cargo-loading, and the low-pressure tyres were suitable for soft-field operation.

'She's just about perfect for what we want, Johnny,' said Palmer, concluding his run-down of the Islander's specifications. 'I think we ought to move fast, and snap her up.'

Bourne congratulated Palmer on his find. 'Excellent work, Chris,' he said. 'I'll come straight out tonight and close the deal.'

THE BIG ARTICULATED LORRY pulled into Loundis Road and drove slowly up towards the end. The driver climbed out of his cab and rang the bell on the side door of Unit 10. A round-faced man wearing jeans emerged and introduced himself as Mr Bryce; he and the driver had a brief conversation, then the driver returned to the wheel.

Ten minutes later, the trailer had been reversed into the empty industrial unit and Mr Bryce was completing the paperwork, signing for the trailer and its cargo. As the lorry-driver drove away, Mr Bryce lowered the large roller door. He removed the cheek-pads, and became Johnny Bourne once again, then went to fetch the others.

Usher, Harris and Howard walked slowly and in silence round the large yellow-painted container sitting on the trailer. Externally, it was forty foot long, eight foot wide and eight foot high. Ackford went to the rear end; pulling up a set of steps, he reached up and undid the two heavy loading doors. As he swung them back, he muttered a curse. 'They've had the thing switched on. It's freezing. We'll have to wait until it warms up before I can start working on it.'

'They probably thought we'd be loading it up straight away, Tony,' said Howard. 'We've got all the time we need, and more. In between working on this, most of us can go back to our normal work with XF, to keep up appearances. There's nothing much more to do for the next three months. It'll be Christmas soon and everyone can take the usual time off. Have you got everything you need?'

'Everything's here, boss. There shouldn't be any problem.' Ackford climbed down and went to the other end to examine the protruding refrigeration unit. He frowned. 'There's not much space here, as I thought.' He pulled out a tape measure. 'The freezer unit takes up nearly the whole end. There's only twenty inches either side of it. The largest opening I'll be able to cut will be about eighteen inches wide. Is that going to be enough? What's the biggest item to go in?'

Howard thought about it. 'The domestic refrigerator, I'd say. Everything else ought to fit. You'd better see what the actual opening is when you've stripped it down and cut it.'

'I'll start on it tomorrow. By the way, boss,' Ackford added, 'I'd just as soon work on over Christmas and New Year. The wife'll be off on her annual pilgrimage to her family in Dublin and I can't stand the thought of going there again. Also, I won't be interrupted. Can you give me a chit or something I can show her to prove I'll be working?'

'OK, Tony.' Howard smiled. 'I'll fix something. But get the noisy work done before the holiday, will you? I don't want too much attention drawn to this place.'

CHRISTMAS CAME AND WENT; Ackford worked on. He was enjoying himself; he liked the peace and solitude. By Tuesday, December 31 he had completed his work; he went across to Unit 8 to fetch Bourne, who had dropped in briefly to collect the mail.

Ackford grinned. 'Come inside, boss.'

The two men climbed into the container through the rear loading doors, and Ackford led the way down to the front end.

'OK,' he said. 'The freezer unit is on the outside of this end wall. It works by drawing in air, cooling it and pumping it round the inside, through these ducts. Now, you see this panel here?' He indicated the right-hand panel; like the one on the left, which looked identical, it was held in place by screws. Ackford took out a screwdriver. 'All the screws are dummies except for these three . . .' He selected the three screws, turned them each through ninety degrees, and then pulled. The entire panel hinged away, folding flat against the side wall.

'Now,' he continued, 'you can see the doorway I've cut in the outside steel shell of the container. If you unfasten these four clamps the door opens outwards, forming an opening eighteen inches wide and seven foot high. I'm not going to demonstrate that now, as I've just finished filling and painting the outside.'

Bourne was nodding his head as Ackford explained.

'The joins where I cut the door are sealed with filler, so to help open it, I've welded on two jacking points. A couple of car jacks will push it open, no problem. So, that's that hatch.' He swung the panel shut and locked it into place. 'Right, let's go back outside again.'

They climbed out and went to inspect the freezer unit. Ackford connected the unit to a power supply. Shouting above the noise of the fan, he indicated the unit's motor housing. 'Can you spot anything in there?'

'No, it all looks the same as before.'

Ackford unplugged the lead. 'Well, it looks the same, but it ain't. First of all, this isn't a normal seagoing refrigerated container—what they call a "reefer". This is the sort that goes on lorries. It's got what's called a "nose mount"—the unit sticks out. A proper reefer has the whole end taken up by the freezer unit itself—there wouldn't have been any space for a door. This unit has two power sources—a diesel motor here for when it's standing alone, and an electric one. The electric one can be hooked up to the reefer point on a ship. Can you see anything funny about this unit?'

Bourne looked closely and shook his head.

'What do you suppose these two gismos are?' Ackford indicated two small items nestling amid the freezer unit's machinery, connected to separate pipes, tubes and wires.

'Oh, of course. Now I know what I'm looking for, I've got it. That's where you've put them. And where's the thermometer?'

'Here, on the outside. I'm rather pleased with this part. All I did was take the thermostat to bits and reassemble it with the wrong setting. When it's set on minus twenty centigrade, it will maintain normal room temperature instead of deep-freeze. I've also fixed the thermometer read-out to give the wrong reading—it will say that the interior is cold when it isn't.'

'Ack, it's brilliant. It's a fantastic job. You'd never know, to look at it.' Bourne peered closely at the outside of the steel container. He ran his finger over it to feel for any raised metal.

'Aw, watch out, boss, the paint's still wet . . .' Ackford grinned as Bourne's hand came away with a smear of yellow paint on it. 'Look what you've gone and done. Ruined me paintwork.'

'Sorry, Tony.' He wiped his hand on his jeans. 'I haven't wrecked it, have I?'

'Nah. The filler's hard, that's what matters. It'll only take a couple of minutes to retouch it.'

'Well, Ed's going to be delighted. It's a marvellous job. I suggest you take a few days off now. I'll see you on Monday.'

Ackford nodded. 'Yeah, I suppose I ought to go and drop in on me mum and dad for New Year. The wife's still away in Ireland.'

That evening the various team members—with the exception of Mike Ziegler, who was still in the USA—celebrated the New Year in their own ways, scattered around the country. Tony Ackford took his parents out to their local pub for a quiet drink; Mel Harris and his wife went to a party in Worcester; Bob Usher, further north in Manchester, was with his girlfriend; Johnny Bourne, in his London flat, opened a bottle of champagne and toasted the future with the newly promoted Detective Inspector Juliet Shelley; and Andy Denard dragged Chris Palmer off to Trafalgar Square.

Ed Howard spent the midnight hour alone, in his flat in Wandsworth. A glass of whisky in his hand, he sat thinking, his dark eyes expressionless and his mind far away. As the last chime of Big Ben sounded over the radio, he wondered briefly how 1992 would turn out. A thin smile crossed his mouth, and he raised his glass. Here's to your fifty-fifth birthday, Saddam, he thought to himself. We'll be there. We're going to come and spoil your party.

ON THE MORNING of Monday, January 6, Bourne collected the mail from each of the three industrial units and went into the inner office of Unit 8. The last letter in the pile caught his eye; it was postmarked Portsmouth. It was from Accuracy International, informing 'Mr Arndale' that his order for two rifles was ready for collection.

By four in the afternoon, Bourne had been to Portsmouth and returned with two long, slim cases and a smaller, heavy box. Inside Unit 8, he and Ackford opened them up.

Ackford's eyes widened as he saw the two big rifles. 'Oh, boy. Now that is what I call workmanship.' He picked up one of the two heavy rifles and worked the bolt action. 'Just feel that.'

'Quite something,' Bourne agreed. 'But don't get too attached to them. Remember what you've got to do to one of them.'

'It'll be vandalism, boss. I'm not sure I can do it.'

'The best way is to get on with it right now. Let's see, what are the serial numbers?' Bourne quickly checked the numbers engraved on the barrels of the two weapons. 'OK; this makes your job easier. Not only are they consecutive numbers, but they end in "eight" and "nine". That settles it. Here's "nine". Go and wreck it right now. Drill out that breech block, and weld up the firing pin. Make it a neat job—it's still got to look good from the outside.'

Ackford departed with the rifle, looking mournful. A few minutes later, Bourne heard the whine of a high-powered drill.

By Wednesday morning, the job was finished. Ackford handed the useless rifle to Bourne, who set off in the BMW to the Birmingham Proof House. Returning that afternoon, he gave the rifle back to Ackford. 'OK, Tony, I've got the Deactivation Certificate. Now change that "nine" to an "eight". I'll get on with the Export Licence papers.'

Bourne sat down in the office and began filling out the Department of Trade and Industry Export Licence application form, entering the details of the rifle and those of the Colombian governmental firearms dealer with whom XF Securities did regular business.

The application would take four weeks to process; a licence would be granted for the export of the rifle whose serial number ended in '8'. The deactivated rifle, '9', with its serial number carefully altered to '8' by Ackford's engraving, would be air-freighted to Colombia. Customs at Heathrow would not check that it actually worked. Why should they? Who would go to the bother of filling out a DTI Export Licence application for a rifle that didn't work and therefore needed no licence? The arrival of the rifle would puzzle the Colombian dealer, who would immediately notice that it was inoperable. Bourne would telephone him to confirm the error and advise him to scrap it.

As far as the British authorities were concerned, rifle '8'—the one that worked—had been exported; meanwhile rifle '9' had officially ceased to exist as a firearm—there was a certificate to prove it.

The switch would not come to light.

MacDonald arrived in London on Tuesday, January 14 on the overnight sleeper train from Fort William. Howard collected him from King's Cross Station and drove him out to Swindon, where the rest of the team, less Ziegler, were assembled, curious to meet the stalker. Howard introduced them to him, one by one.

The last man he came to was Ackford. 'Tony is our armourer. He's ready to fit the rifle to your measurements whenever you are.'

Ackford and MacDonald disappeared next door into Unit 9, locked in conversation about weapons in general and the big Super Magnum rifle in particular.

Howard waited until they had gone then turned to the others. 'Well, Tony seems to be getting on well with him already,' he said. 'What do the rest of you think of him?'

'He seems OK,' began Harris. 'He looks steady and alert, and if you say he can shoot, well . . .'

'But he's never seen action, boss?' Usher wanted to know. 'How do you reckon his nerve will stand up to it? And is he fit?'

'He's got good nerves, from what I've seen,' Howard reassured him. 'I've got a feeling he'll do just fine, even though it'll be his first taste of real action. Now; I've got some more news. Mike is on his way back. Says he's got everything we wanted, including the new satellite-navigation gear. When he gets here, I'm going to send him off up to Scotland with Danny. The rifle will need sighting in and zeroing. Danny has a place in mind on the Glen Carvaig estate, way up in the hills, where they'll be able to do it without being bothered. It'll give Mike a chance to suss him out, and see whether he's as fit as he seems.'

There were nods of assent and approval all round, and the team went back to work on the fitting-out of the freezer container.

MIKE ZIEGLER and Danny MacDonald set off at six in the morning a week later from Danny's cottage where they had spent the night. In the back of the car were a rucksack and an H-frame carrier with a rifle case strapped to it; each load weighed nearly seventy pounds.

They left the Sierra at Glen Carvaig Lodge. It was 6.30, long before dawn, and the January air was cold, crisp and still. They hefted the two weighty loads onto their shoulders and set off along the track.

The stalker led off at a good fast walk and gradually increased his pace. They reached the head of the glen, after ten miles of steady climbing, in an hour and forty-five minutes. They had climbed 600 feet, and now there was a light dusting of snow on the track.

'It gets steeper now. About five miles to go. The ground is a little rough in places—you'll need to mind your ankles.'

'No problem, Mac.' The American was not even breathing hard.

Off the track now, the going was much slower; the snow covering became thicker as they climbed. When they finally came to the place they had been aiming for, high in the hills, it was nearly ten o'clock.

The fifteen-mile walk had taken them just three and a half hours.

With the advent of dawn, Ziegler could now see the ground they had covered. In front of them was a freshwater loch, its smooth, inky-black surface stretching out before them. He drank in the scenery. 'Why have I never come here before? This place is just beautiful, Mac. Fantastic.'

MacDonald glanced at him and smiled. 'Aye, I love it up here in the hills myself.'

The two men started to unpack some of the equipment, including a range-finder, which MacDonald had borrowed from his uncle. Ziegler set up the range-finder on its tripod on a grassy knoll by the side of the loch. Then he collected the components of a target frame. Taking a walkie-talkie radio, he set off along the shore of the loch at an easy jog, leaving MacDonald at the firing point. Ten minutes later, he came to a promontory about twelve hundred yards from the firing point. He assembled the target: a wooden frame four foot square, covered with yellow-painted canvas. In the centre was a black circle six inches in diameter. He called MacDonald on the radio and held the frame still for the range-finder.

A minute later, MacDonald's voice came over the radio in reply. 'I measure that at twelve thirty-five. Come back this way thirty-five paces and I'll take another sight.'

In a matter of minutes the posts of the target frame had been hammered into the ground, exactly twelve hundred yards from the firing point. Ziegler took cover behind a boulder ten yards away and reported that he was ready. Thirty seconds later, there was a whiplash crack as the bullet passed him. A second later there was a distant thump as the sound of the muzzle blast of the rifle caught up.

MacDonald took his time between the shots; he had used an electric blanket to prevent the rifle from becoming cold, and now he did not want the barrel to heat up too much from firing.

As the report of the last shot died away, Ziegler walked back towards the target. The four shots were in a five-inch group; the centre of the group was just below the black, five inches from the centre of the six-inch circle, and four inches to the left. 'This is unbelievable shooting, man,' he reported over the radio.

'Thanks. I'm going to do some final adjustments, then take three more shots. With luck, that'll be enough.'

Ziegler covered the four bullet-holes with stickers and retired behind the rock. When MacDonald had fired three more shots, the American went over to the frame. His jaw dropped as he saw the result. He spoke into the radio. 'Mac, I just don't believe what I'm seein' here. You've shot a three-inch group, smack in the middle of the black. This is incredible! I guess we're through here, right?'

'Yes, that'll do! It's gone very well indeed.' MacDonald's elation was evident in his voice. 'This is a fine rifle. I think you could say we're in business!'

By the time Ziegler rejoined him, MacDonald had finished packing up the rucksack and the rifle was again secure in its case, strapped to the H-frame carrier. The two men chatted easily on the descent, elated with the success of the day's work, exulting in the splendour of the harsh winter scenery and the occasional glimpses of deer in the distance. Their friendship was sealed.

The next morning Ziegler loaded up the Sierra with the rifle and other equipment for the journey back south.

Chapter ⑤

The chill March rain lashed down; the thunderstorm was one of unusual ferocity. The suddenness of the downpour had caught the two running figures by surprise, but they were laughing, splashing through the water pouring down the track.

Then the girl slipped and fell. She cried out, and the man stopped and turned round. He went back to her. She was sitting on a rock clutching her left knee; the wet denim of her jeans was torn and there was a streak of blood mingling with the rainwater. She tried to stand, but winced, giving another little cry. The man caught her before she fell a second time; he picked her up in his arms. She felt very small and light. 'Come on,' he said, 'I'll carry you. Let's get inside that stable before we both drown.'

'Oh, thank you, Danny,' cried Sheila Cameron, biting her lip; the pain from her knee was sharp.

Danny MacDonald glanced down at her as he strode along the sodden track, carrying her against his chest. Her hair was soaked, plastered to her face and neck, and she looked as young and vulnerable as ever he remembered. He reached the stable, undid the hasp and pushed the door open. Inside, out of the rain, he set her down on a stack of straw bales. 'That's some storm,' he said. 'Now, let's have a look at your knee.'

'Mum will kill me for this,' moaned Sheila as he took out his knife and carefully enlarged the hole in the knee of her jeans to examine the cut. Her teeth were chattering from the cold.

Danny looked up at her face. She really *was* cold, he thought. 'Here,' he said, taking off his tweed jacket. 'It's wet, but it'll still be warm.' She let him wrap it round her shoulders.

'What about you, Danny?' she asked. 'You've only got a shirt now, and it's soaked through . . .'

'Och, I'll be fine,' he said. He glanced out of the door. The rain was coming down in torrents. 'We'd better stay here a while, until it eases off.' He looked at the girl again; she was shivering uncontrollably. He frowned. 'I'll light a fire,' he said. 'That'll help to dry you out a bit.'

The small stable was a long-disused cottage. On one end wall was an old fire-grate; Danny pulled a handful of straw from one of the bales, then started breaking up a discarded piece of furniture. The straw flared as he lit it; soon the old dry wood began to crackle.

'This should do us fine. Come on,' he said, picking Sheila up again, 'let's be moving you nearer to the heat.'

He kicked a couple of straw bales over to within a few feet of the fire-grate, and set her down on one. She was still trembling with cold, her arms wrapped tightly round her body under his jacket. He sat down beside her on the straw bale and put his arm affectionately round her shoulders. Heated by the fire, their wet clothes began to give off steam. The thick smell of the stable and the damp tweed filled their nostrils.

The girl snuggled up to him; he was used to feeling protective towards her. Her head leaned on his shoulder, then lifted again. 'Danny, your shirt's all wet and horrible. Take it off and dry it.'

He looked at her for a moment, then stood up and took off his shirt, wringing it out and hanging it on a low wooden rafter near the fire. 'You ought to do the same,' he said eventually. 'It'll do you no good sitting there in soaking wet clothes. Don't worry—I won't look. I'll turn the other way. Here—let me help you with your boots first.' He unlaced her boots, pulled them off, then peeled off her socks. He held her cold feet in his hands and rubbed the circulation back into them. Then he stood up and turned away. 'I won't look,' he said again.

Sheila began to undress in front of the fire. Danny heard her exclamation of pain as she forced the wet jeans down over the injured knee. She sat back down on the straw bale. 'Ouch! This straw is prickly!' She giggled. 'All right, Danny, you can turn round now.'

She sounded more cheerful now, thought Danny. He turned to see her slight figure huddled in his thick tweed jacket, her bare legs stretched out towards the fire. His jacket reached almost to her knees. 'When did you last have this old jacket cleaned, Danny? It smells like something died in it!'

Danny grinned, glancing down at her. 'What did you expect, girl? I can't afford to have the thing dry-cleaned after every day out on the hills, can I? It's got sweat, blood, peat hag . . .'

'Oh!' said Sheila, pulling a face. 'Don't be so disgusting!' Then she smiled. 'Come and sit down here and keep me warm!'

He sat down, leaning over again to look at her knee. 'Doesn't look too bad,' he pronounced. 'Can you move it?'

She straightened the knee, wincing, but nodding. 'It'll be OK. It's just a bruise and a cut. It may be sore for a while but I'll be fine when I warm up.' She looked directly at him. 'Would you put your arm round me, Danny? I'm still cold.'

He did so, still staring ahead into the fire. Her head dropped to his bare shoulder. Danny said nothing; he felt suddenly awkward. She was no longer a little child.

'Do you have many girlfriends, Danny?'

He was startled by the question. 'Och, Sheila. What would you be wanting to ask something like that for?'

'Well, we might as well talk about something. We always used to talk, when we were children. Anyway, do you?'

'Well, if you must know, the answer is yes, I have had one or two girlfriends. None serious at the moment, though.'

She wriggled a bit closer to him. 'There's only ever been one man for me,' she said in a low voice, barely audible above the crackling fire. Her cheek slipped down off his shoulder and rested softly on his bare chest. 'But I don't think he's ever realised it.'

The shock of realisation hit Danny MacDonald, and he felt as though a fire had suddenly been lit inside his head. His arm tightened involuntarily round her as he became aware of how blind he had been. He had always thought of her simply as little Sheila; she had been like a sister to him, the little child he was so fond of . . . How blind he had been . . .

Slowly, he turned to look at her, comprehension on his face, his eyes fixing at last on hers and reading confirmation in her expression. Without a word, he cupped her face in his hands. He had kissed her out of affection before, when she had been a child, but the familiar face now so close to his was that of a young woman. Closing her eyes, she pushed her mouth upwards towards his, and then her arms went round his neck and their mouths met as they kissed again. She was suddenly the loveliest, most irresistible thing he had ever seen.

Sheila Cameron sank gently onto the rough straw next to Danny MacDonald. They stretched out together, desperate for each other, everything else forgotten. Outside, the rain still poured down, drumming heavily on the corrugated-iron roof of the stable; inside, steam rose from the damp clothing draped along the rafters. The fire roared eagerly in the grate, casting a flickering red glow on the two young lovers.

ON MONDAY, MARCH 23, six large commercial skips were delivered to Unit 8. Ackford had been busy with an oxyacetylene cutter, reducing his machine tools to unrecognisable pieces of metal; the other team members had systematically smashed every other item of equipment left over. The whole lot went onto the skips; in twenty-four hours Units 8 and 9 were stripped completely bare. In Unit 10 the large freezer container still sat on its trailer. A smaller, twenty-foot freezer container had joined it, its refrigeration unit working. In a corner was a small pile of equipment to be loaded onto the aircraft.

At midday on Tuesday 24th, the delivery lorries returned to remove the skips; they drove away to the county-council tip, where the skips' contents joined thousands of tons of other anonymous rubbish.

The following morning, Wednesday, the equipment for the aircraft was loaded into Howard's, Palmer's and Usher's cars, which then set off in convoy for Southampton Airport. At the airport, Palmer and Denard supervised the loading of the Islander. Leaving the plane, they returned to Swindon, and Howard then went back to London.

On the morning of Thursday the 26th, Bourne drove Howard and MacDonald back out to Swindon where, inside Unit 10, they waited for Harris. He arrived at ten o'clock, driving a large Volvo HGV tractor unit. The final items were carefully loaded into the container; last to be loaded were pallets of food, transferred by fork-lift from the smaller container, which had been keeping them frozen. The doors of the big container were closed and locked; Harris reversed the Volvo carefully into the trailer coupling and connected the power, hydraulic and air lines. The fan of the big container's refrigeration unit hummed noisily. Harris collected the paperwork from Bourne and drove the lorry away.

Bourne switched off the refrigeration unit on the smaller container, which was now empty, and went into the office to arrange for its collection. He made two further calls, one to arrange for the fork-lift to be collected, and the second to a firm of contract cleaners.

As Harris drove the container out onto the M4 heading east, there began a series of incidents which would have made any police crime-prevention officer despair. In Bristol, a Vauxhall Astra was parked in a street not far from Temple Meads Station; the driver got out and walked away, leaving the door unlocked, the driver's window four inches open and the keys in the ignition. The same happened with a Rover 820 in Oxford, a Peugeot 205 and a Ford Escort XR3 in London, a Sierra in Leytonstone and a Toyota in Wembley.

With the strange exception of the Peugeot 205, which sat undisturbed for two days, all the cars were stolen within a matter of hours of being abandoned. No thefts were ever reported.

Harris arrived at Felixstowe's Trinity Terminal at three in the afternoon. Reporting to the shipping agents, he completed the paperwork, made a last check on the diesel-driven generator and watched while the container was lifted off the trailer by crane and deposited in one of the 14,000 slots in the huge parking area, its fan still humming. Harris departed for London; stopping at a lay-by, he unhitched the empty trailer, removed its number plate and left it there. On his arrival back in London, he returned the Volvo tractor unit to its owners. The trailer would stay in the lay-by for several weeks before the police noticed that it had been abandoned.

The shipping agents in Felixstowe submitted the usual Form C88 to HM Customs; an officer scanned the list of contents, mentally totting up the stated weights of the cargo of frozen food to check that they tallied with the container's given gross weight of twenty-six tonnes. They did. The officer stamped the form and authorised the Customs seal; the container was then transferred to the mile-long quay where the Cyprus-registered MV *Manatee* was berthed. At two o'clock in the afternoon the container was swung across over the ship and set down in a slot at deck level. A deck hand secured the container to four anchoring points on the deck and connected a hookup cable to the refrigeration unit.

Within two hours, most of the remaining containers for MV *Manatee*'s voyage to East Africa had been loaded on board; there were eight hundred of them, stacked in twenty rows across the ship, each row five high and eight wide. The MV *Manatee* was due to sail the following morning, Friday, March 27.

If the Customs officer had decided to inspect the contents of the container, he would not at first glance have noticed anything unusual. On opening the rear doors he would have seen four cargo pallets of frozen vegetables, stacked two pallets high and two across. There was no more than an inch of spare space, either in width or in height. The pallets appeared to be standard wooden ones, but in fact they had been cut precisely to size so that they would fit tightly and make it almost impossible for anyone to see what lay beyond.

Behind the four pallets of vegetables, the officer would have found pallets of tinned margarine, also frozen. There was normally no reason for margarine to be frozen, but it acted as an efficient cold pack, insulating the vegetables from what lay nearer the closed end of the container.

Behind those closely stacked pallets of food, thick insulation boards formed a bulkhead barrier across the container, preventing the frozen cargo from chilling the remaining thirty feet of the container behind it. The floor of this remaining section was covered by a one-foot-deep layer of concrete blocks, to make up weight. This concrete floor, along with the walls and ceiling, was covered by thick rubberised carpeting, as an effective means of sound insulation.

The thirty-foot space was fairly cramped; along one wall were stacked bundles of equipment and stores. The Customs officer would have found the contents of these bundles very interesting indeed; they contained all the contraband items for the operation, such as the rifle, ammunition, AK silencers, satellite-navigation gear and night-vision goggles. Along the other wall were a refrigerator, a fire extinguisher, a vacuum cleaner, a camping stove, cooking pots, a chemical toilet, a table and two folding canvas chairs. At the far end, spread out on the floor near the ventilation ducts, were two mattresses.

As the container bumped gently down onto the deck of the ship and the fan unit came back to life, Ed Howard stirred, unzipped his sleeping-bag and climbed out. Two small thermostatically controlled air conditioners were running. They were the items that Ackford had fitted into the freezer unit's housing and which Bourne had not spotted until they were pointed out to him. They would continue to circulate air at a constant twenty degrees centigrade.

'Twenty-four hours like this, I'm afraid,' muttered Howard. 'Tomorrow night we can start chucking the extra food overboard and make a bit more space.' He looked across to his companion. 'Danny?' Well, I'll be damned, he thought admiringly. He's a cool one.

Inside his sleeping-bag on the other mattress, Danny MacDonald was fast asleep.

THE NOISE, A SLIGHT CLANG, was lost among the creaks and groans of the ship as MV *Manatee* made her way southwards through the night in the swell of the Bay of Biscay. Almost invisible in the dark, a thin line of paint on a forty-foot refrigerator container cracked. A section of the container wall near one corner swung slightly ajar, leaving a one-inch aperture. The hatch Ackford had cut was open.

Howard carefully pushed the hatch open another two inches and applied his eye to the gap. There was no one to be seen to the right, the side visible through the small opening. He could see that there was a space between the container and the ship's superstructure in front of him. Other containers stacked on either side formed a solid wall, leaving a passage from one side of the ship to the other.

Satisfied, he turned to MacDonald.

'Couldn't be better,' he said in a low voice. 'There's plenty of room to open the hatch, and we're on the lowest level, on the container deck. I'll just go and check out the other end, the cargo-loading doors. It'll be a bonus if we can get at them. I'll be back in five minutes.'

Outside, he pushed the hatch door almost closed and took stock. The container was two from the end in the row; three more were stacked on top of each one, forming a solid steel wall thirty-two foot high. At each end of the passageway formed by the containers and the ship's superstructure there was a small companionway down to the main deck, ten feet below; Howard descended and made his way aft. There was no sign of life. Looking up, he saw that there was a gap about six foot wide separating the row of containers from the row behind it. It would be enough for them to be able to open the main doors. He returned to the hatch and let himself back in.

'OK, Danny; they've made life really easy for us. We'll be able to get at the doors. Not only that, but we won't be disturbed there. There's no direct access to that part of the container deck. We've got a lot to do before it gets light. I want to finish chucking all the surplus stuff overboard, so that we can seal up this hatch and repaint it. We'll only need the main doors after that. Let's go.'

They stepped out of the hatch, pushing it closed. Howard began pressing quick-setting filler into the cracks with a palette knife, while MacDonald opened a small tin of yellow paint. When Howard brushed paint over the cracks, the hatch was once more invisible.

Descending the companionway to the main deck, the two men moved noiselessly aft; Howard shinned up a heavy steel girder to the container deck at the cargo-door end of the container. MacDonald, watching him climb up, saw Howard scale the girder with ease and disappear over the edge onto the container deck. Howard fastened a thin climbing rope to one of the containers and lowered it to MacDonald, who climbed up after him. They pulled the rope up and untied it. There was no safety rail along the side of the container deck. The edge hung directly over the sea.

Using a pair of pliers, Howard cut the wire of the Customs seal on the container and pocketed it. Then he swung open the doors.

The packs of frozen vegetables had thawed considerably but they were still very cold; wearing heavy insulated gloves they began lifting the packs off the pallets. One by one, the ten-kilogram packs of food were dropped fifty feet into the sea below. The splash in each case was inaudible, lost in the wake of the ship. They took nearly seven hours to jettison the surplus vegetables and margarine. By five o'clock in the morning the last pack had gone, as had the pallets. The blank wall of the insulation boards faced them. The boards too were dismantled and thrown over the side of the ship.

'OK, Danny. That'll do for tonight. We'll start shifting the breeze blocks tomorrow. Let's go in and have a brew.' Pulling the heavy doors shut behind them, they went back inside.

It took them two more nights to jettison all the concrete blocks. Finally, they were left with just their camping equipment and the waterproof stow-bags of contraband items. The space inside the container seemed less confined and claustrophobic with the extra foot of headroom; Howard reckoned that the boxed-in feeling, which he himself had hated, had subsided largely because they now had two means of escape—one at each end of the container. In three days, they had seen no sign of the crew; they knew there would have been a twice-daily check to ensure that the units were functioning correctly, but they had neither seen nor heard any sign of this.

By the fourth night at sea, Howard and MacDonald had settled into a routine of sleeping by day and being awake by night. Howard spent the fourth and fifth nights outside the container, deep in the shadows of the main deck observing the movements of the crew. He was encouraged to see that night activity was minimal, and that patrols by crew members were infrequent and at fixed times.

With no more manual work to do for another ten days or so, Howard brought out the language tapes and began boning up on his limited knowledge of Arabic. He concentrated on a handful of standard opening phrases, trying to get the pronunciation right. He hoped he would not need to speak the language at all.

His thoughts wandered from the Arabic lesson. 'How are you getting on with your tables, Danny?' he asked. MacDonald had occupied himself with his book of tables and trajectories, working with a pocket calculator and making copious notes.

He looked up at Howard. 'Nearly finished, I think. I've worked out pretty well every variation we might come across.'

'Well, I've got a little present for you from Bob Usher. I don't know whether it'll be any good, but I'd like you to try it.'

MacDonald looked puzzled as Howard unpacked one of the stow-bags and handed him a flat, gunmetal-grey package measuring twelve inches by ten. Howard pressed two catches, and a lid flipped up, exposing a small screen. He pressed the power button on the right, the screen came to life and the machine emitted a tiny hum.

Howard explained the rudiments of the machine to MacDonald. 'It's a lap-top computer, a Grid 386NX. The MOD has bought a lot of them. Bob saw you wrestling with those tables and thought there must be a better way. See what you think.'

'A computer? Are you joking?' MacDonald gave Howard a disbelieving look. 'You realise April Fool's Day was yesterday?'

'No joke, Danny. But I don't know how useful it'll be. The ballistics program may not be as accurate as it's supposed to be. Give it a try, anyway.'

MacDonald's surprise turned to fascination as he followed the simple instructions Usher had provided. Starting at the standard 'C:>' prompt, he typed 'EXTBAL6.EXE', then pressed the return key. After a short pause, the LCD screen flashed up the logo of the computer program: 'EXTERIOR BALLISTICS OF SMALL ARMS', followed by a series of rows and columns of figures, giving full details of a specific load of ammunition, together with a complete set of weather conditions. The details had already been set for the .338 Lapua Magnum sniper ammunition, along with a series of standard readings for temperature, altitude, humidity, range, barometric pressure and windage. He studied them eagerly. 'Now just type "SUM",' Usher's instructions told him. MacDonald did so. Immediately the screen cleared again and 'PLEASE WAIT' appeared. Two seconds later, several long columns of figures appeared.

'Will you just look at that,' breathed MacDonald. He compared the readings for elevation and windage that the computer had worked out in just two seconds with those in his notebook. They tallied exactly. He looked at Howard, an accusatory look on his face.

Howard held up his hands apologetically. 'Danny, I know you're wondering why we didn't give you that machine before, and save you all your hard work. But I reckoned it would be best if you got all your tables down before using the computer. You might not have entirely trusted it otherwise.'

MacDonald pursed his lips, then shrugged. 'You're right, I probably wouldn't. I don't mind telling you, I'm astonished. It's amazing—so quick. I think we'll take both with us—the computer and my notebook. Then if this thing breaks down at least I'll still have my notes.'

'That's just what I wanted to hear,' said Howard. 'I've got another little toy to show you. It's a satellite-navigation unit. With this thing,' he added, holding up a small device about eight inches long, 'we can find out where we are, to the nearest hundred yards.'

ON THE MORNING of April 7, Harris and Denard waved Ray Sullivan off from Southampton Airport. Harris was well pleased. The American pilot had behaved himself during his stay in London and had appeared anxious to do a good job. He had checked the flight plan and had even suggested a couple of sensible modifications.

'I think our boy will do nicely,' mused Harris, as they watched the Islander climb away and head out over the sea on the first leg of its journey to Saudi Arabia. 'Nursemaiding a cowboy out in Saudi could prove to be quite a headache, but I don't think this one'll give any trouble. Hell, he doesn't even drink much—just the occasional beer.

More than I can say for you, Andy, you mad little devil.'

'I never drink when I fly,' retorted Denard. 'Come on, let's get back to London. The first beer's on me. It'll be our last for a while,' he added, mournfully.

That evening, Bourne, Denard, Palmer and Harris took a British Airways flight, BA133, to Jiddah. Ziegler, Ackford and Usher followed the next morning, taking BA125 to Riyadh. All seven entered Saudi Arabia under their own names and travelling on their own passports. In his capacity as security consultant to Pan-Arabian Petroleum, Bourne had had no trouble in concocting adequate PAP contracts of employment for the team members.

Entry into Saudi Arabia is tightly controlled. Two categories of visitor are permitted: pilgrims to the holy cities of Mecca and Medina and businessmen, workers and their families. There are no tourists. A visa application has to be supported by proof of employment by a sponsoring firm. All seven men from Howard's team had stated that they were employees of PAP which, aside from its 750 Saudi employees, had forty-five Britons, twelve Americans and eight Pakistanis working in Saudi Arabia.

Initially, a person taking up employment in Saudi Arabia is granted a visitor's visa, valid for one month. If he intends to stay longer, he must apply to convert his visitor's visa into a business visa. An *iqaama* (work permit) is then granted. The *iqaama*, a small six-page booklet with a brown cover, must be carried at all times by the bearer, who will normally surrender his passport—stamped to show that the *iqaama* has been issued—to his employer.

On arrival in Jiddah in the early hours of April 8, Harris and Denard took a taxi straight to the Sheraton Hotel, where they checked into the adjoining rooms reserved in their names. At reception, they handed in their passports. No comment was made about Denard's new moustache or about his hair, which was darker than in his passport photograph.

Denard went straight up to his room; he would stay there for three days, not showing his face and using room service for all his meals. The room-service deliveries would be made to Harris's room, and signed for by Harris, before being taken through the connecting door.

Bourne and Palmer checked into a different hotel, the Marriott. After breakfast that morning Bourne telephoned Tony Hughes, the senior Darcon director in Saudi. Hughes had been expecting to hear from 'Mr Bryce' and sent a driver round to their hotel to pick him and 'Mr Potter' up. When they arrived at his office, Hughes examined the proffered Darcon identification Bourne had prepared, giving their occupations as geologist and surveyor. The fax messages Hughes had been sent on Dartington's machine had had a convincing tone of confidentiality and importance, and he was now satisfied.

Hughes was a small, energetic man and he didn't seem to feel in the least slighted that Dartington was apparently organising new projects on his territory behind his back; Bourne soon realised from the way Hughes spoke about Dartington that Hughes had an unqualified admiration for his boss.

'Everything's ready for you, Jim,' said Hughes, addressing Bourne. 'You've got the run of the old construction camp up at Badanah. It's been empty for four months now, ever since we finished that resurfacing job on the road there. I've had the four vehicles you wanted driven up there, and there's a couple of our mechanics going over them right now to check that they're in good order. The other staff are three security guards, a storeman and a cook. All Saudis except for the cook, a Pakistani. Do you need anyone else?'

'No, thanks,' answered Bourne. The first thing he would do would be to give the Saudi staff three weeks' paid local leave. 'We're pretty self-contained, Tony. We'll be out of camp most of the time, as soon as the others join us. You've been extremely kind.'

Bourne and Palmer took their leave and returned to the hotel, where they were joined later by Ziegler, Ackford and Usher, who had arrived on a flight from Riyadh.

The following day, April 9, Bourne, Palmer, Ackford and Usher flew to 'Ar'ar, in the far north of the country. The Darcon construction camp was ten miles along the main Trans-Arabian Pipeline (TAP) road past the nearby town of Badanah. They arrived there at 11.30, in the heat of the day, and began settling in. The Saudi staff were delighted at being given three weeks' leave and disappeared with alacrity.

Ziegler, who had accompanied the others to the airport, went to the Avis car-rental desk and hired the largest vehicle available. It was a big Dodge Ram Charger covered pick-up, with a double cab and plenty of room in the rear compartment. He drove north out of the city, and after just over an hour's driving he joined the coast road, continuing north towards Yanbu' al Bahr. He arrived there at midday.

About 500 miles to the northwest of Yanbu, the MV *Manatee* was approaching Port Said, at the northern end of the Suez Canal.

HARRIS WAS WAITING when Sullivan touched down at King Abdul Aziz International on the morning of the 11th. The Texan, travelling on his own passport and with supporting Darcon documentation prepared by Bourne, passed through immigration control without trouble. His friendly, relaxed manner went down well with the Saudi officials. His cheerful if linguistically incorrect 'Well, howdy and salaam to you, old buddy!' made the immigration officer smile. The paperwork for the Islander was completed without a hitch.

Harris drove him back to the Sheraton and began the well-rehearsed tale he had prepared for the pilot's benefit. 'Look, Ray, there's been a change of plan. The boss is out of town for a while. Unexpected, like. It could be as long as three or four weeks. We're to stay on standby. We're booked into the Sheraton. We've got to stay there and not move until we hear from him. That OK with you?'

'Sounds fine by me,' said Sullivan. 'I'll do just whatever you say.'

'Fine.' Harris continued the fabrication. 'I'll need your passport and other papers for hotel reception. Pilot's licence, the lot. You wouldn't believe the bureaucracy here. The hotel will hold it all till we check out. I'll deal with it—I speak the lingo.'

'OK. Here's my folder—everything's in there.' He grinned at Harris. 'I guess that old folder'll look a little better at the end of this job, with an extra ninety thousand bucks in it, huh? In the meantime, I ain't asking *no* questions at *all*.'

'Thanks,' said Harris. 'I've got your room key here—sixth floor. Just go straight on up when we get there and I'll sort the rest out. Charge anything you like to the room bill—it's all paid for.'

They arrived at the hotel a few minutes later. Sullivan went up to the sixth floor and settled in; the room had been vacated that morning by Denard, who was now waiting next door in Harris's room, his bag packed and ready. Harris gave Sullivan ten minutes to get to his room, then rang Denard from reception, telling him to come on down.

Denard walked straight to Harris's car. Five minutes later, Harris joined him and handed over Sullivan's folder before driving him out to the airport. Denard, using Sullivan's identity, filed a flight plan for Al Wajh, a small town on the Red Sea coast 200 miles to the north of Yanbu; Harris did not wait around to see him take off.

ON THE NIGHT of April 11, Howard and MacDonald stripped the container almost bare. Howard had been consulting the tiny satellite-navigation receiver. He had calculated that they would be roughly where he wanted to be the following night, the 12th.

The two men emerged at six o'clock on the evening of the 12th, dressed in black neoprene wet suits. Working quickly, they began to empty the container, stacking the items they would need on the narrow section of the container deck by the rear doors. Everything else, including the domestic fridge, went over the side into the sea.

Howard used the vacuum cleaner to sweep every last trace of their occupation from the interior. Closing the two cargo doors he turned to MacDonald, who was bending over the camping stove outside on the deck. A small covered pot on the stove contained four ounces of lead. When it had melted, MacDonald carefully poured it into a plaster-of-Paris mould Howard had made from the original Customs seal. Howard passed the original sealing wire through the locking latch on the container door and into the mould so that it would pass through the solidifying lead. The two men jettisoned the vacuum cleaner and the final surplus items over the side of the ship. Howard glanced at his watch; it was 19.56 local time.

Fifteen minutes later, they had lowered all their equipment down to the main deck. Acutely aware now that this was when they stood most risk of being discovered, they worked hurriedly to move the large rubber stow-bags and other items to the stern of the ship, where they began unpacking the bulkiest of the bags. Inside was the sixteen-foot inflatable Gemini craft. MacDonald began inflating the air compartments using a diver's air-bottle, while Howard returned to the container. The mould was cool to the touch; he broke the plaster away and washed the new lead seal with water. He gave it a brief inspection under his torch; it would do. He flung the bits of plaster overboard, then returned to help finish inflating the Gemini.

Once all the cargo was securely lashed down inside, Howard and MacDonald lowered the craft, using two of the ship's heavy steel stanchions, until its transom touched the sea. The water under the *Manatee*'s stern boiled and frothed from the ship's propeller; Howard had a moment's anxiety that the Gemini would capsize, but the rubber craft settled satisfactorily and was towed along steadily fifty yards astern.

Howard adjusted MacDonald's life jacket and clipped a ring on the Scot's harness onto one of the two towropes. MacDonald climbed over the side. Howard used a third rope to brake his descent along the towrope, and watched as MacDonald slowly lowered himself down along the towline towards the Gemini.

When MacDonald was safely aboard, Howard partially inflated his own life jacket and cut loose the towropes attached to the Gemini, which floated away. He cut away the remaining rope ends from the stanchions, threw them overboard, then jumped over the side himself and began swimming towards the green glow of a beta-light in the bow of the Gemini. MacDonald helped him aboard.

It was 22.00 local time. If the calm weather held, they should cover the seventy miles to the Saudi coast by about three in the morning.

MacDonald was no stranger to small dinghies. At that moment, however, as the forty-horsepower outboard engine caught on the third pull of the starter rope, and they started out on their passage halfway across the Red Sea, he felt as alone and vulnerable as he had ever felt in his life. He thought of home, and of young Sheila . . . so far away . . . a different world, another existence. He looked around him—there was nothing. Nothing except the lights of the MV *Manatee*, gradually disappearing into the night.

Chapter ⑥

They made better time than Howard had expected. By 03.00 he reckoned they must be within ten miles of the Saudi coast. He stopped to get an exact fix from the Global Positioning System (GPS); the reading gave 36° 54′ E, 25° 31′ N. Holding a beta-light to the chart, he immediately saw that the wind had driven them further north than he had expected; they were right off Shaybara Island, only a few miles from the coast. In daylight, the island would be clearly visible.

Hurriedly, he beckoned to MacDonald to fit the sound-muffler box to the outboard engine. A few minutes later MacDonald saw a light approaching from the south. Howard headed north, away from the light, but it continued to draw nearer until it was perhaps two miles distant. A searchlight stabbed on and probed the dark. A patrolling Saudi naval vessel, thought Howard grimly; time to hide.

They slowed to a crawl, edging towards the shore. The light of the other vessel was still approaching. A rocky promontory showed up ahead; Howard gently steered the Gemini up to it, the engine burbling almost inaudibly. MacDonald grabbed a spur of the rock and held on to it, while Howard unrolled a bulky camouflage net and draped it over themselves and the whole craft.

They were just in time. The searchlight caught the now shapeless lump of the Gemini full in its beam. They held their breath; the beam passed on. Underneath the thickly camouflaged net, everything in the Gemini was matt black. The vessel kept going past until eventually its light was lost from view. Howard stowed the net and signalled to MacDonald to let go of the rock.

A mile further on they reached the eastern end of Shaybara Island; Howard turned north through a narrow channel and began to thread his way through the little archipelago near the main coastline.

At 03.55 they made landfall. Howard did not beach the Gemini straight away; the shore was too flat and bare. A mile up the coast they came to a small inlet with steep rocky sides. It was perfect,

Howard decided—little more than a crevice in the coastline.

Howard jumped out, leaving MacDonald to secure the dinghy to a rock. Climbing the small rockface, he was rewarded by a rumbling sound in the distance; minutes later the lights of a truck passed by, half a mile away. Good, thought Howard; the coastal road was close by. He returned to the boat, and the two men began unloading it.

Stripping off their wet suits, they towelled themselves dry and put on black trousers, T-shirts, windcheaters and balaclavas, and desert boots. Then Howard set off for the road, where he put three small marker flags by the roadside, 400 yards apart. He returned to the inlet.

At 04.40 a second set of lights approached. The vehicle lights passed his first marker. A car horn sounded three long blasts and one short. At the central marker it sounded again, three short and one long; then it stopped, switching off its lights.

It was Ziegler and the Dodge Ram Charger. He had been camping out for three days, and had been driving back and forth along the road each evening after dusk and each morning before dawn. Glad as they were to see him, Howard and MacDonald were even gladder that he had brought a large Thermos of hot coffee. By 05.15, the three men had the equipment loaded and were on the road north.

It was 06.45 when they arrived at Al Wajh. Denard was waiting for them; by 07.30 he had clearance for the flight. Ziegler drove the Dodge up to the aircraft for loading, then returned it to the airport car park where he locked it up, pocketed the keys and left it, walking back to the plane. At 08.00 precisely, the Islander took off and headed northeast on a course for 'Ar'ar.

'NO LUCK WITH WEAPONRY yet, I'm afraid, Ed,' reported Bourne as he watched Howard and MacDonald attack large plates of food. The three men were sitting at a table in the Badanah camp cookhouse; it was midday. 'But everything else seems OK. Bob and I have found some spare medical equipment, and Tony and Chris have knocked up some other things that look convincing enough. I think our two fake ambulances will pass inspection.'

'What are the vehicles themselves like?' asked Howard through a mouthful of hot curry and chapattis. He and MacDonald were ravenous after the journey; the smiling Pakistani cook had prepared a huge lunch for them.

'Couldn't be better. Identical and almost brand new. Only a couple of thousand miles on the clocks, except for one which has done ten thousand. We should have all the mechanical work finished in a couple of days, then we'll do the repainting.'

'Good. I'll come and have a look in a minute. Mmm, this is good. Living in a tin box and eating tinned food for a fortnight has not been my idea of fun.' He cleaned his plate with a piece of chapatti, reflecting. 'I think we'd better forget the idea of getting weapons here. We'll have to nick some when we get into Iraq. Right,' he concluded happily, 'I'm full. Let's go and have a look at things.'

They walked over to the camp workshop. Tony Ackford was working underneath a Toyota Land Cruiser on a ramp, assisted by Bob Usher. Nearby were two identical vehicles, and the wheelless shell of a fourth, stripped for spare parts.

'How's it going, Tony?' Howard walked over to examine his handiwork.

'Fine, boss. No probs at all. Let me show you an idea I'm working on. We can bypass the silencer, so it'll sound like the exhaust's clapped-out. We'll be able to turn it on and off whenever we want.'

Howard nodded his head. 'Good idea—I like it.'

JULIET SHELLEY HAD IMMERSED herself in her work to take her mind off Johnny's absence. It was her second-last working day at her old job. She would have Saturday and Sunday to herself, then on Monday, the 13th, she would report to her new post at New Scotland Yard. She put on her coat to go. Just one more day, and then on to a new challenge. A new life . . .

As the bus ground slowly along through the heavy evening traffic, she thought about her future with Johnny. He had only been away for eight days, and she missed him dreadfully. How much longer was it? Another three weeks . . . she would never let him go away and leave her again. Never!

The bus reached her stop and she got off. Instead of walking straight to the flat, she went round the corner to the shops. The cleaners were still open, thank goodness.

As she searched for the ticket, she realised to her annoyance that she had mislaid it. 'I'm sorry, but I seem to have lost the ticket. The name's Shelley. I brought a black skirt in this morning.'

'Address, love?' Juliet gave it, and the assistant went off to look.

He returned a few minutes later and handed the package over. 'That'll be two pounds sixty-five, love. Do you want to take this other piece as well? That would be another two-forty.'

'What other piece?'

The assistant handed over a wire hanger, with a pair of blue jeans. 'Same address on the ticket, love.'

Juliet looked at the ticket; it had the name 'Bourne' on it. Johnny's jeans. 'Yes, I'll take them. They're my fiancé's.' She paid and left.

As she walked home, Juliet swung her bag lightly in time with her step. Silly man, she thought. It was ridiculous, sending jeans to the cleaners; far too expensive. She smiled to herself.

She let herself into the flat and took off her coat. In the bedroom, she removed the flimsy plastic covers from the skirt and jeans and opened the wardrobe door to hang them up. She noticed a yellow mark on the seat of the jeans and frowned. Stupid man! Didn't he know that if you had a stain, you had to tell the cleaners what it was?

She carried the jeans through to the kitchen and rummaged in the cupboard under the sink for the Stain Devil tubes.

She began to scrub at the mark. Five minutes later she held the jeans up and inspected them. The stain had vanished.

HOWARD AND THE OTHERS had time on their hands. They were not due to leave Badanah until April 25. Meanwhile Denard took Howard and Ziegler up in the plane on the 17th. Denard had filed for a local survey flight to the west, along the Trans-Arabian Pipeline road; sixty miles out from 'Ar'ar they passed over Al Jalamid airstrip; there was little sign of life. The TAP road itself was busy; it was the main highway from Jordan to the Gulf States, and large lorries thundered along it.

The landscape beneath them was almost entirely featureless: mile upon mile of rocky, boulder-strewn nothingness. Fifteen miles beyond Al Jalamid, Denard indicated a dark slash in the desert a couple of miles north. 'Al Mira strip,' he said through the throat mike to Howard.

Howard peered out of the right-hand window as Denard circled over the airstrip; it looked deserted.

'Your track is only a few miles away now, if your map is right,' Denard continued. 'This may be the best place to land if we need to. The road would be better, but it's too busy—someone would see us.'

Satisfied that the Al Mira strip would do, Denard climbed to 11,000 feet and flew on west. Almost immediately, he pointed out a dirt track leading off from the TAP road to the north. 'I think that must be it. What do you reckon?'

Howard spent several minutes studying the map and comparing it with the almost featureless panorama below him. The terrain was crossed by many tracks visible from the air; only a few of them were marked on his map. 'OK, Andy, I'm pretty sure that was the right track. Take her down and we'll confirm it and leave a marker. How far north do you think you can get away with?'

'At radar altitude, maybe five or ten miles. That's as far as I'll be able to explain away as accidental. The authorities here are quite strict. Understandable, I suppose, after the events of last year.'

'Fair enough. Keep us at a height no one will think is suspicious, and follow the track as far as you think won't cause any comment.'

After Howard was satisfied that the track was heading in the direction indicated on the map, Denard brought the plane round, heading back towards the TAP road. Howard turned to Ziegler in the rear of the plane, signalling to him to get ready. Ziegler took three one-litre plastic cans out of a bag and eased open the rear cargo door.

'OK, Andy,' Howard said, 'we're ready to mark when you are. Give Mike a countdown—"one" for four hundred yards short, "two" for the junction itself, and "three" for four hundred yards past it.'

'Will do.' Denard circled for a minute. Then he put the Islander into a steep dive. He levelled out at a hundred feet, then went down to ten feet, skimming along the road. Ten seconds later, he gave Ziegler the signal to drop the first can out of the door. Eight seconds later came the second signal and after another eight seconds the third.

He hauled back on the control column and the aircraft climbed steeply. Howard began to feel queasy at the aerobatics. When they got back up to 2,000 feet, he looked down.

Spaced out along the road there were three splashes of bright white paint where the cans had burst on impact with the tarmac. They would be unmistakable, even in the dark. The middle splash was right next to the junction of the track leading north into Iraq.

'OK, Andy, that's fine,' said Howard. 'Time to go home.'

IT TOOK A MORNING to prepare the two vehicles for painting. The third Land Cruiser was a sandy beige and they decided to leave it as it was. It was to be used by Denard and Palmer. Bourne, Usher, Howard and MacDonald worked with adhesive tape and paper to mask off all the glass, chrome and other unpainted surfaces of the first two Land Cruisers, while Ackford set up the paint-gun and practised on the hulk of the cannibalised vehicle.

At last everything was ready. The others left, closing the workshop doors behind them to prevent dust or sand particles from blowing about. Ackford fitted his goggles and face mask and began to spray. Forty minutes later he emerged, closing the doors quickly behind him.

They left the two Land Cruisers to dry for twenty-four hours, then opened up the workshop to inspect Ackford's handiwork. The white paint looked immaculate.

'Oh, *beautiful* work, Tony,' said Usher with exaggerated praise. 'Just gorgeous. You've missed your vocation, mate.'

'You've just voted yourself into a job,' retorted Ackford with a grin. 'You can do the next coat, when we've finished all the modifications.'

'I thought you'd never ask.'

Ackford supervised the careful denting of several panels on the vehicles, and removed one rear bumper. When the team had finished, Usher applied the next coat of paint. The following day, when they opened the workshop doors, the two vehicles were matt green.

Once all the masking tape and paper had been removed, they inspected the Land Cruisers carefully. Declaring himself satisfied, Howard produced a handwritten list from his pocket. 'Right,' he said. 'Let's make the final modifications.'

As they walked round the Land Cruisers consulting the list, sharp blows were administered to the glasses of two taillights, smashing them. Bourne opened a large packet of red stickers with Arabic lettering and red crescent shapes and applied them to the bonnets, front passenger doors and tailgates. With the flashing roof-lamps, the Land Cruisers now looked like paramilitary ambulances that had seen a lot of service and been poorly maintained.

'OK, boys,' said Ackford, handing out large paintbrushes, 'that'll do. It's top-coat time. Get painting.'

Ziegler examined the large can of liquid in front of him. 'What in hell's this, Tony? It looks awful.'

'It is, mate,' said Ackford cheerfully. 'It's a nice mixture of old engine oil and grease. Now, get it on there. Not too thick, and keep it off the glasswork—we want to be able to see out, don't we?'

Twenty minutes later the Land Cruisers were covered with a thin smear of dirty oil.

'Bloody hell,' muttered Howard, impressed. 'These Land Cruisers look ancient. Even *I'm* convinced they won't last ten miles. And under all that muck they're brand new.'

It was the afternoon of Thursday, April 23. The next night, if all went to plan, they would cross the border into Iraq.

IT WAS DUSK AS THEY LEFT Badanah. Howard reflected that, for some reason, setting out on an operation was always the part that made him most nervous. It was ridiculous, he thought. All that it involved was driving seventy-odd miles along the TAP road until they saw the paint splashes, then turning off onto the track. What could be simpler? But the risk of discovery was there. A chance police patrol, a breakdown . . . It just needed one bit of bad luck, and months of work would disappear down the drain. Howard hated contemplating failure. He scowled at the thought and tried to shake himself free of it. Unnecessarily, he consulted the GPS receiver one more time.

Bourne, in the driver's seat beside Howard, noticed the tension in his passenger and said nothing. He felt a keen excitement, a sense of anticipation—something he had not felt for a long time. He thought of Juliet, and his heart gave a momentary lurch. He tried to picture her face; the vision was only a hazy one. It surprised him. It was barely a fortnight since he had said goodbye to her. Their wedding was set for Saturday, May 23—only a month from now. But there had been something in those smoky eyes as she had said goodbye. Johnny frowned at the memory. He had been scrupulously careful. His two lives, as Bryce and Bourne, had been kept completely separate. There was no connection that she could have made; she knew nothing of Bryce, of the BMW, of his other work. He shook his thoughts clear and glanced at the Land Cruiser's trip milometer.

'I've got sixty miles on the clock since Badanah, Ed. How are we doing?'

'Al Jalamid should be coming up any minute. The turning's about fifteen miles past that.'

In the back of the Land Cruiser, lying on the ambulance stretcher, Danny MacDonald too kept his thoughts to himself.

Occasionally he turned his head to peer out ahead into the dark. To his surprise, he realised that he was having the time of his life. He liked these men. They were tough, fit, self-reliant, unflappable—as he was. They were good men to be with. A good team.

Danny considered each of his companions in turn. Big, level-headed Tony Ackford—confident, easy-going and friendly and, although the last one he would have expected to be good with his hands, amazingly precise and patient. Bob Usher, that small, tough, shiny-headed bullet of a man, usually reserved and quiet, but with flashes of bubbling humour. Danny had been puzzled by the others' occasional references to Bob as 'TV star'. Eventually he had asked what they meant, and had been startled to hear that Bob had been one of the first two men to enter the Iranian Embassy in London, during the SAS operation to rescue embassy personnel in 1979. Those pictures had been replayed on TV dozens of times since, and Danny had often wondered about the men involved—what they were like. Now he could count one of them as a friend.

He hadn't really fathomed Mel Harris at all—a restless, mercurial character, never still for long, his bright little eyes always darting about. Danny suspected he had the shortest fuse of any of them.

Andy Denard and Chris Palmer were a team apart, in a way. Andy was clearly the joker, but Danny knew from what Howard had told him that he was a brave and skilled pilot. And then there was Chris—stolid, utterly dependable, as calm and professional as Tony.

Johnny Bourne was another, thought Danny, who was difficult to read. Howard had told Danny a little about Bourne's army record during their sea voyage. As a young platoon commander in the Falklands, Johnny had stumbled with his platoon into an unmarked Argentinian minefield at night, shortly before the battle for Mount Longdon. It was sheer bad luck. His platoon sergeant trod on a mine, losing a foot. Another soldier panicked and ran, treading on a second mine. His foot was also blown off, and a third soldier nearby, who had correctly stood his ground, was badly injured by mine fragments. The medic, courageously trying to make his way forward to assist the wounded, trod on a third mine and lost his foot too. In the space of two minutes, Johnny found himself with four horribly injured soldiers on his hands. He calmly picked up the wounded sergeant and led the platoon back out of the minefield, each man following exactly in his footsteps. Just as they reached the safety of a rocky outcrop, flares went up, and half a dozen Argentinian machine-gun nests opened up on them from the hill in front. Johnny Bourne returned alone into the minefield under heavy fire, three times, to bring the other wounded men out.

Danny could certainly understand why Mike Ziegler had been chosen. Mike was one of the most impressive men he had ever met—a powerhouse of energy, an athletic, cool, humorous, brilliant soldier. And a charming, likable man.

Ed Howard himself, mused Danny, was a complete enigma. One could never tell what he was thinking. What was one to make of those dark, expressionless eyes, and the calculating, manipulative mind that must lie behind them? Howard was something of an organisational genius, and probably the best soldier of all of them.

Danny gave up speculating. He knew that his companions were the sort of men he would choose to be with him in time of trouble. He reflected once more on the job he was to do, and the hot anger rose in his throat again. Soon, now. He lay back and tried to relax.

Ackford, behind the wheel in the vehicle behind, came alert. Passing a large smear of white paint in the middle of the road, he said, 'I think we've arrived. Got them NVGs ready?'

'Yeah,' Ziegler replied.

The two ambulances pulled off the road by the second paint splash. Bourne continued along the track until he was well clear of the road, before stopping. Howard passed Bourne a flying helmet; it had two protruding optical devices attached to the front, like mechanical eyes. Bourne put the helmet on and switched on the optics. Howard, and in the second vehicle Ackford and Ziegler, did likewise.

The night-vision goggles gathered in the tiny amount of available light and magnified it fifty thousand times; night was turned into day, in astonishing detail.

'Let's try it with the infrared lamps,' said Bourne to Howard. He flicked a switch on the dashboard. Ackford had fitted each Land Cruiser with an extra set of driving lamps; these were completely covered by filters which blocked out visible light. Only the invisible infrared wavelengths penetrated the filter. The NVGs were sensitive to infrared as well as visible light, and the transformation was dramatic. Good as the visibility had been before, now it was like a bright summer's day, except for the fact that the picture was green.

To the naked eye, the vehicles were invisible; for the occupants, however, who could see perfectly with their goggles, it was a simple matter to pick out the track and travel northwards at a reasonable speed. Ahead, fifty miles away, was the Iraqi border.

'LIGHT THERE—up ahead.' Bourne's voice had tensed.

'Got it,' said Howard. 'Slow right down. Creep up closer.' He took another reading from the GPS. It gave 39° 40′ E, 32° 04′ N. The light was about three kilometres ahead. That put it over the Iraqi border.

For ten miles now they had been travelling more slowly and carefully. This section of the track was abominable; seasonal flash floods had carried parts of it away. The two vehicles crept towards the light, their engines running almost silently. At a distance of one kilometre, Howard motioned to Bourne to halt. They got out and peered at the light, trying to discern exactly what it was.

Howard felt a tap on his shoulder. Ziegler had joined them from the second vehicle. 'Movement,' he whispered in Howard's ear. 'A man, I'm pretty sure. The light's movin' in the breeze. My guess is a pressure lamp, hangin' outside. There's a building on the left, set back a little from the track. A border post, probably.'

'I agree,' whispered Howard. 'This is a chance to get some weapons. Three of us should do it. We'll move up four or five hundred yards closer, in the ambulances. Then Johnny, you stay there with the vehicles. I'll cause a diversion. Mike, you take Tony and Bob and see what ordnance you can sneak out of their armoury. How long do you reckon? One hour be enough?'

'Let's make it twenty-two hundred hours exactly for the diversion,' said Ziegler. 'I'll get clear by then.'

'Fine. Johnny, at about twenty-one forty-five hours, move up very slowly as close as you dare. Come through without lights when you see the diversion. Anything else, anyone?'

'Ed?' hissed Ziegler. 'Mind if I take Danny with me instead?'

Howard shot him a glance, then smiled. 'An excellent idea. He's used to sneaking up on things unobserved, isn't he?'

'Just what I was thinkin',' replied Ziegler. He went over to Howard's vehicle and whispered, 'Mac, the boss has picked you and me to sneak up on that border post and do a bit of thievin'.'

MacDonald felt absurdly flattered to have been chosen.

HOWARD'S TASK PROVED EASY. Approaching the border post with his NVGs on, he clearly saw the main building. Outside, a solitary sentry sat hunched on a bench, wrapped in a heavy overcoat against the chill of the night air, his head buried in his chest. There was another, smaller building behind the main one, and a third—a long, low structure—next to that. The size of the buildings suggested a platoon-strength position.

A hundred yards or so further off, he saw what he was looking for: a low, walled emplacement without a roof. Slowly, he crawled up to a gap in the wall and looked inside. It was a fuel dump containing 45-gallon drums of petrol and kerosene. Bingo, he thought. A ready-made diversion.

ZIEGLER MOVED LIKE A WRAITH through the dark. Following him, Danny felt utterly confident. He had quickly absorbed the basic hand signals and night-movement techniques Ziegler had taught him on night training outside the Badanah camp. The two men approached the rear of the main building. Ziegler motioned MacDonald to the ground and covered the last few yards alone, working his way round the side. Removing his goggles, he peered through the window. Inside was a desk, with a chair behind it. A man with the shoulder flashes of an Iraqi lieutenant was asleep in the chair, several days' growth of stubble on his face and his beret askew, covering his eyes. A wooden partition with a door separated the guard commander's office from the rear section of the building, which Ziegler guessed was a storeroom. He returned to MacDonald. The loud chorus of snores emanating from the second building told them that it was the main bunkhouse. The third building housed a communal mess-room; inside there were six men, the current guard detail.

'OK, Danny,' whispered Ziegler in the dark. 'My guess is that there will be some spare arms in the front buildin'. Let's go take a look.'

The rear door to the store was unlocked. Two dozen AKMS rifles hung in a long rack on the wall inside; nearby on the floor was a stack of green-painted metal canisters about fourteen inches long, looking exactly like oversized sardine tins. In another rack were the long, funnel-ended tubes of six RPG-7 antitank rocket-launchers, with several wooden crates of projectiles underneath them, and in a third were four light machine guns. Three more wooden crates proved to contain fragmentation hand grenades.

Working quietly, Ziegler handed six AKMS rifles and six of the heavy sardine-tin canisters out to MacDonald. He ignored the machine-gun rack and selected one of the RPG-7s and a crate of projectiles. Finally, he bent to pick up one of the crates of hand grenades.

A floorboard squeaked loudly and Ziegler froze. Almost immediately he realised that the sound had come from behind the partition, not from under his own feet. The lieutenant had shifted in his chair. There was no further sound and, after two precautionary minutes of immobility, Ziegler walked silently outside with the crate of grenades. Infinitely slowly, he closed the door behind him.

Not long afterwards, Ziegler and MacDonald had filled one ruck-sack with canisters; into the other went the projectiles and the grenades, the crate of projectiles sticking out of the top. Taping the AKMS rifles together so that they would not rattle against one another, Ziegler hefted one of the packs and checked his watch. Twenty minutes to go. One more thing to do—empty a water-bottle into the fuel tank of the truck parked in front of the building. MacDonald, with the other pack, followed him into the darkness.

Nineteen and a half minutes later, several things happened almost at once. First, a small alarm clock in the office sounded. The lieutenant yawned and woke, and the sentry outside jerked into consciousness, glancing guiltily behind him in case he had been caught sleeping at his post. At that moment, there was a dull *whoompf!* from behind the building.

The sentry got to his feet, uncertain. As he did so, the lieutenant emerged from his office and ran round to the side of the building, where the sight of fire and explosions that met his eyes froze him to the spot. He let out a bellow of fear and anger; in the second hut, soldiers were jolted awake. In the darkness and confusion, they cursed and scrambled for their boots and weapons, and began piling out into the night—except it no longer seemed like night-time.

The lieutenant made a futile attempt to goad his men into action, swearing, threatening and screaming at them above the roar of the blaze from the fuel dump.

If he, or any of his soldiers, had turned round to look behind him at precisely 22.05, he might just have seen the dark shapes of two rather dirty ambulance vehicles pass by on the track leading north, not thirty yards away.

But none of them looked. The two vehicles slipped past, unnoticed.

Howard's team was inside Iraq.

Chapter ⑦

John Kearwin glanced up at the console on the left of his desk as the 'alert' light came on. Positive trace from the Defense Support Program (DSP) downlink, thought Kearwin, absently; not strictly speaking his territory yet. North American Aerospace Defense Command (NORAD) would already be dealing with it, and he would know soon enough if it needed further investigation. He tapped in a code on the console's keyboard to run a standard analysis program of the trace, and went back to work on his main screen.

Kearwin was fairly short, with a round face and a slightly squeaky voice, and he wore round metal-framed glasses. He loved his job and he took his work seriously. All his colleagues in the US National Reconnaissance Office in Washington did, he reflected. They were all exceptionally talented and able people, he knew; and he knew that he too was good at what he did. It would have amazed and baffled him, however, to be told that the others all thought of him as something of a whiz kid, even by their standards. In his eyes he was no different to them. If he had a fault, he was perhaps a slightly too serious young man, but because he was so unassuming and modest, he was genuinely liked and respected.

The installation of the DSP satellite real-time console four years previously had been one of Kearwin's own ideas.

'Not our job, John,' his boss Walter Sorensen had said, gravely. 'Real time ain't our job. We just deal with the medium and long-tail stuff. NORAD does the real-time analysis and handles quick-reaction situations. That's what they're for. We get the more interesting job, figuring out later what they didn't have time to do.' For what must have been the fiftieth time, Sorensen had gone off into one of his favourite standard finger-wagging lectures, patiently explaining the role of the National Reconnaissance Office.

But Kearwin had rehearsed his pitch. 'You're absolutely right, Walter, but it's the time lag that bothers me. Remember what happens every time there's a positive? Every time the Soviets launch a satellite or run a test firing? The brass scream for an instant analysis. They figure we're the guys who can give them the detail, so they holler at us for it every time.' Kearwin knew he had Walter Sorensen's attention. It was a sore point with the man known by the young analysts as the Walrus, because of his similarity to that creature. He was a patient man, but he got exasperated with having to explain that his department was not the one to ask for quick-reaction analysis—and not only that, but that he didn't even know there was a positive trace yet—NORAD hadn't yet got to the stage of passing it on down the line.

So now there was a DSP console sitting on the side of Kearwin's work-station, occasionally blinking up positives. The Defense Support Program satellites watched for the intense infrared signatures emitted by missiles, and gave a fix on the launch site. After launch, by the use of readings from several DSPs, a 3-D image was obtained, giving a trajectory and likely target within sixty seconds. The DSPs always monitored the same area, giving a new reading of the whole of their patch every ten seconds. The DSP satellite that Kearwin monitored was geostationary, not moving relative to the earth, monitoring the same area over the Gulf.

The flashing light on the DSP console caught Kearwin's attention again. The analysis was coming through. He looked at it and frowned. *I'll be damned*, he thought, running a quick request for more information on the positive trace. He called over his shoulder to the Walrus. 'Walter, we've got a positive on the DSP. Western Iraq. Looks like a Scud launch. You want to see it?'

Sorensen got up from his desk and wandered over. 'Whaddya mean, a Scud? You crazy? The war's over.' He studied the data, his forehead creasing deeply.

'Yes, but look at the location.' Kearwin was tapping out instructions on the keyboard, and more information appeared on the screen. 'Right on the border, would you believe it?'

'How does the signature fit?' Sorensen asked, peering at the screen and fingering his moustache.

'Fits with Scud parameters on the four-point-three-micrometre band, maybe a little low on the two-point-seven band.' The short-wave infrared sensors on the DSP routinely monitored these two wavelengths; from them it could be established what type of missile had been fired; each propellant gave off its own signature. Once the CIA knew the propellant, you pretty well had the missile.

'Where is it now?'

Kearwin tapped in the instruction on the keyboard. A few seconds later he blinked in surprise. 'It hasn't moved! Maybe an engine test.'

Sorensen grinned. 'Engine test, my foot. You ain't got nothing but an oil-bucket job! Never thought you'd fall for that one.'

Kearwin was annoyed with himself for his mistake. He thought back to the Gulf War, when the tactic had been used to mislead the F-16 Falcons on Scud bombing raids. By the time the F-16s arrived, the Scud launchers were already well clear, usually hidden underneath a bridge; a mock-up launcher would be left in place with containers of burning oil around it for the F-16 attack sensors to lock onto. Many 'successful' bombing raids just destroyed mock-ups. Oil-bucket jobs, thought Kearwin. And now he had fallen for one himself.

But was it? It didn't make sense. Why would the Iraqis want to try the old oil-bucket scam in peacetime, right on the border? Irritated, Kearwin decided to take a closer look. He tapped out an instruction calling up the track of the most recent Keyhole satellite pass over the area. A diagram of the tracks appeared on the screen under an area-map overlay. Perfect, thought Kearwin; a KH-12 had passed over the area only five minutes earlier. The information would already have been received via the relay satellites and the ground-link station, and the signal would now be being computer decoded and relayed on for archiving. It would take a few minutes for the computer to find the coordinates he wanted. He would have a quick look at it to see what it was, and then head on home.

He sat back in his chair, thinking, then leaned forward again. Might as well get a couple of earlier passes for comparison while he was waiting. He tapped in another instruction. The previous pass had been a KH-11 only twenty minutes before, and would do fine. He called it up. The pass before that had been nearly two hours earlier. He called this one up as a second back-up. One minute and thirty-five seconds later, the more recent of the two previous passes appeared on Kearwin's screen.

A godforsaken spot by the look of it, right in the middle of the desert. The only feature was a small cluster of buildings in the centre of the screen, next to a dirt track. A truck was parked by the main building. A little border post.

The sub-console light blinked, telling him that the pass of two hours earlier was now ready. He put it on screen. There was no difference to the naked eye. He ran the code to overlay the two and cancel out the differences.

Kearwin watched as the two pictures overlaid each other exactly and the computer started trying to merge them. The screen slowly changed as the pixels started to cancel each other out. Gradually, the dots disappeared and the screen became emptier; finally, it was almost entirely blank except for two tiny clusters of pixels near the top of the screen and another two nearer the centre. Kearwin magnified the area at the top and saw two vehicles. They were there in the earlier pass, but not in the more recent one.

He knew what he would find in the second set of clusters nearer the centre: two vehicles again, this time in the second picture but not in the first. Kearwin wondered idly why they had moved only four hundred yards or so in an hour and a half.

The console indicator light flashed again; the latest picture, the

KH-12 pass which should show up the heat source the DSP had spotted, was now ready for downloading. Kearwin sent a print command for the two earlier passes he had compared, along with separate blowups of the vehicles in each case. He also ordered a digital read-out of the actual infrared signatures of the vehicles. Then he ran the latest pass. The picture came on screen.

He saw his oil-bucket fire straight away. A nice little blaze, it looked like. The border post's fuel store had gone up. No more to it than that, he thought, disgusted. He ran the close-down sequence on the keyboard, and started tidying up his desk, preparing to leave.

Ten minutes later he was ready to go. He collected the print-outs and walked back to his desk. He would have a look at them the next day, if he had time.

It was then that Kearwin noticed that his screen was still active. By mistake he had run the 'compare' sequence, not the close-down one. Now his screen was showing comparisons between all three pictures.

There was the fire, a big scattering of white pixels inconsistent with the two previous pictures. There were the two tiny sets of clusters near the top and the two near the middle—the two vehicles in their different positions. And there they were again, near the bottom of the screen. Leaving the fire. Why? He checked back on his log, to see the time of the first indication of the fire. That would give it an accuracy to within ten seconds. The time flashed up: exactly 15.00 USA Eastern Time. That meant 22.00 in Iraq. A precise time. Rather too precise for an accident. Deliberate?

Frowning, he studied the read-outs of the vehicles. Both the same: small and boxy. Not trucks. Cars—probably four-wheel drive, judging from the poor state of the dirt track. The spectral analysis showed that they had their headlamps on; one could tell that from the shadows the lights cast. But there was something not quite right about those shadows. They showed up in the infrared band, but not in the visible spectrum. Infrared lamps!

Frowning hard now, Kearwin got up slowly, and walked over to Sorensen's desk. 'Walter, I've something odd here. Maybe Langley can clear it up for us. Could you come and have a look?'

The two walked back to Kearwin's station as he explained what he had got. 'It's this oil-bucket fire. I took a closer look at it.'

The Walrus broke in with a smile. 'You know what I like about you, John? You're competitive. You hate being beaten. You just never give up on something, do you?'

'It just bothered me, Walter. Look.' Kearwin ran through the data. 'Here's the fire, OK? Now, here's a couple of previous passes.' Kearwin brought in the two earlier pictures and ran the cancellation sequence. The three sets of clusters came up on screen.

'A couple of vehicles?'

'Right. A couple of long-wheel-base four-by-fours, is my guess. But look at the times. At twenty-thirteen, they're up here, about five hundred yards away from the post.' Kearwin pointed at the set of clusters near the top of the screen. 'Twelve minutes before the fire, at twenty-one forty-eight, they've moved to within two hundred yards of the post. Then, thirteen minutes after the fire, they're through the border and down here. Now look at these.' Kearwin laid out the spectral-analysis sheets showing the shadows cast by the vehicle headlamps. 'Faint, not conclusive, but I got a ten-dollar bill says those are IR lamps they're using, not white light. What does that tell you?'

'If you're right, it tells me covert,' said Sorensen. 'So, what's your theory?'

'Two vehicles approach the border by night. They drop off some guys back here. These guys sneak up on the border post, while the vehicles wait. Fifteen minutes before the prearranged time, the vehicles mosey carefully on up to near the post. At twenty-two hundred hours on the button, they torch the fuel depot as a diversion. In the confusion, the vehicles drive through, no visible lights, and wait up here, the other side of the border, to pick up the saboteurs.'

'Yeah, it fits, except there would be some light from the fire. Someone would have spotted them.'

'They can't have. The guards must all have been trying to put out the fire. Listen, Walter, I'd like to get Langley to let us know if they've got anything going on there.'

'Now hold on, hotshot,' the Walrus protested, 'don't get carried away here. OK, some guys jumped the border. Wouldn't you wanna do the same in their place? They'll head straight for the Saudi cops, like as not, and demand political asylum. Good luck to 'em.'

'Sorry, Walter, I forgot to explain something. My fault. These pictures are inverted. The top of the screen is south, not north. These guys, whoever they are, are busting *into* Iraq, not out of it.'

HOWARD HAD DECIDED to put as much distance between them and the border post as possible before he made a stop. He wanted to get past Ar Rutbah before midnight if at all possible.

Fortunately the track was easy to follow. The corrugations across it were severe in places, and there were frequent deep potholes and ruts, but Howard reflected that the going was rather better than he had expected.

MacDonald, being bounced around in the back of the Land

Cruiser, had other opinions. He attempted, with little success, to stow the stolen weapons safely out of sight where they wouldn't rattle about. After twenty minutes he gave up, and concentrated on trying to fit the silencers Ackford had made. Bracing himself with his feet against the roof of the vehicle, he managed to screw the three silencers onto the AKMS rifles.

After about thirty miles they reached a main track junction, where they would turn north. They pulled the vehicles off the track into a shallow wadi, allowing MacDonald and Usher to complete the stowage of the weapons. Each man was given an AKMS to conceal beneath his seat.

It took ten minutes' work with a hacksaw to open the heavy metal boxes of AK ammunition. Each man charged six thirty-round magazines. The rest of the ammunition was stowed under the stretchers. Dumping the empty crates and boxes in the wadi, they checked that there was no sign of traffic before setting off.

It wasn't until they were eight miles short of Ar Rutbah that they saw the first sign of life: four sets of lights coming towards them on the road. They removed their night-vision goggles and switched their headlights on; it was time to start acting like a couple of ambulances.

'Looks like military,' muttered Howard.

'What do you reckon we do?' asked Bourne.

'Flash the headlights, toot the horn a couple of times, wave cheerily and bellow something patriotic in Arabic.'

Bourne complied. The occupants of the four vehicles barely acknowledged them as they swept past in the other direction.

'Land-Rovers,' muttered Howard. 'Anyway, it's good news that there doesn't seem to be any alert out for us.'

The lights of Ar Rutbah, such as they were, appeared in the distance. The town gave the impression of being almost deserted. Howard guessed that the only well-lit area, a mile or so off the road to the east, was a military installation with its own generator. Behind him, as they drove through the empty-looking town, he heard a roaring sound as Ackford tried out his exhaust-bypass lever. Howard grinned. No one hearing that racket would guess that this was a group of assassins attempting to pass unnoticed through Iraq.

The first main road they came to was Route 10, the old highway from Baghdad to Jordan. They turned left onto this, then a mile out of town turned right and picked up the road that would lead them past the cryptically named H1 air base towards Kirkuk.

'All being well, we should reach H1 by about zero one forty-five.'

The latter part of the road to H1 was almost dead straight. What little of the scenery they could make out was featureless and empty, a stone and gravel desert with occasional patches of low scrub. Traffic was sparse and they made good time.

Ten miles short of the air base Howard ordered a halt. They pulled well off the road and killed the lights. 'Might as well refill the tanks.'

The fuel tanks took three jerry cans of petrol each. Glad of the extra space this would make, they slung the empties away.

Soon afterwards, the lights of H1 pierced the darkness along the skyline. 'With luck, we should be able to motor straight past it,' said Howard. 'The road's pretty straight, and . . .'

A flashing light appeared in the road about 600 yards in front. More lights snapped on.

'Hit the screamers, Johnny! Flashers, the lot! I'll get in the back with Danny.' Howard dived over the back of his seat, wrenching on a white coat. Danny was already on the stretcher, covering himself with a blanket. 'OK, Danny, time for your pill. Bite hard on it when I say so. Keep your eyes closed and moan loudly.'

Sirens wailing, the ambulances raced up to the roadblock and screeched to a halt. Running figures appeared as Bourne leaped out, gesticulating excitedly. An officer approached, and Bourne tugged him round to the back of the ambulance, jabbering in Arabic.

'*Now*, Danny,' whispered Howard in MacDonald's ear, just as the rear door was opened.

Danny bit hard on the pill and found himself spraying bright red liquid out over his chest. He tried to close his mouth, but the liquid kept bubbling out. He let out a convincing moan.

As the door opened, Howard turned and snarled one of the two speeches he had painstakingly rehearsed under Bourne's tuition. The Arabic came fluently. 'Shut that door, you imbecile!' he shouted furiously. 'Can't you see this man is badly injured? And get your men out of the way, or his death will be on your hands!'

The officer recoiled, shutting the door. Still gabbling away, Bourne hauled the officer to the second ambulance. Screams were coming from inside. Bourne pulled the door open. A wild-eyed Ziegler, in white coat and stethoscope, was attempting to hold a struggling and screaming Usher down onto the stretcher. Protruding from beneath the blanket was Usher's left leg, dripping with blood.

The officer had had enough. Waving furiously at his men, he yelled for the road to be cleared and the ambulances let through.

The vehicles blocking the road were hurriedly removed; Bourne jumped back in behind the wheel and set off with a squeal of tyres. As Bourne passed the soldiers, he was still shouting and wailing out of the window; he kept up the performance until they were out of sight round a bend in the road.

JOHN KEARWIN HAD BEEN BUSY. He and Walter Sorensen had quickly identified the first problem—tasking priorities. Strictly speaking, the US National Reconnaissance Office existed to operate the satellites and interpret the evidence they supplied. Its Director did not have a free hand with tasking. It was the CIA that allocated tasks and decided what the satellites were to look at.

Sorensen had had a word with the NRO Director, Martin Faga; because there wasn't much else going on, Faga gave him seven hours. 'You've got until zero six hundred hours Iraqi time, Walter,' said Faga, whose interest had been aroused. 'That's twenty-three hundred Eastern. If you haven't come up with anything by then, I'm afraid we'll have to revert to normal daytime operations.' Although he hadn't said so, Faga hoped that Sorensen *would* find something, something everyone else had missed. The CIA had known nothing about an incursion into Iraq; it had been a shot in the arm for the NRO to have discovered it first.

'Thank you, Director,' said Sorensen. 'Can I have your authorisation to task the JSTARS aircraft as well as the KH satellites?'

Faga thought about it. 'All right. Yes. I don't suppose the crews will mind.' The Joint Surveillance and Target Attack Radar System (JSTARS) was to ground movement what the Airborne Warning and Control System (AWACS) was to air movement; its radar apparatus could detect vehicle movement 200 miles away and had proved its worth in the Gulf War.

Kearwin's first instruction was to give the JSTARS an area to look at, with an order to locate and track the two vehicles that had left the border post. It proved to be a simple task for the JSTARS and it quickly came up with a positive sighting, forty miles south of Ar Rutbah. Now that he had an approximate speed and track of the vehicles, Kearwin lined up a KH-12 for a 'bounce' pass and at 23.41 it swooped down to an altitude of 150 kilometres. By the time the pass took place, the JSTARS had reported that the two vehicles were approaching the town of Ar Rutbah. Kearwin married up the two times and the location, and at 23.47 the picture appeared on his screen.

Because the 'bounce' had brought the satellite down to nearly half the altitude, the picture of the vehicles was much better than the previous rather indistinct ones, and would be as good as he would get. He zoomed in on the image and ran a computer enhancement sequence to optimise the picture. When he was satisfied, he stored the image in background memory as a template for future matching.

So far it had been pretty straightforward, thought Kearwin. They had made it easy for him. A deserted area, nothing else moving ... but who were they, and where had they come from?

Kearwin decided that for the time being he could do nothing more to affect the tracking exercise. He called over to a colleague and explained the situation. 'Jerry, I want you to keep a close eye on progress here.'

Working alone, Kearwin began to sift through data from previous Keyhole passes. Thousands of miles of recording tape in the archive section stored data from satellite images of every part of the world.

He studied the map overlay, zooming out so that it showed northwestern Saudi Arabia. He marked the screen with the co-ordinates of the border post and the subsequent sighting; they flashed up as blips with the date and time given alongside. OK. He looked at the track network south of the border. There were two ways they could have come, if they had used the main tracks: either from Turayf, near the Jordanian border, or from Wadi Al Mira, which didn't look much of a place. Either way, their rate of travel would put them on one of those tracks for at least an hour before the sighting near the border at 20.13. What coverage was there available for about 19.13?

Within seven minutes, he had his answer. The computer checked through data from two KH-11 passes at 19.17 and 19.35, and showed the two vehicles at 19.35 ten miles north of Al Mira. Fine. Where had they come from before that? He ordered the computer to search through archive material on the TAP road. Sure enough—there they were again, at 19.04, coming along the road from 'Ar'ar.

Ten minutes later, Kearwin had his first big stroke of luck. A KH-11 pass had picked up the two vehicles at the moment they had turned out of a compound outside Badanah, near 'Ar'ar. A previous pass of the compound showed a twin-engined plane that a standard template match confirmed to be a Britten-Norman Islander. He checked one more previous pass, from the day before. The aircraft was missing from the construction camp; but a few miles away, at 'Ar'ar airport, there it was, parked on the apron.

Kearwin leaned back in his chair and rubbed his eyes.

How long had the plane been there? Easy. One check back for each day, say at 18.00 or thereabouts. Not too difficult. He started punching in the instructions on his keyboard.

Half an hour later, the pass for April 12 showed the plane missing. He checked the two previous days, but there was no sign of it: it must have arrived some time on the 13th.

He decided to put someone else onto it and check on real-time progress. It was coming up to 01.45 in Iraq. Where had these guys got to? He walked over to Jerry's work-station.

'JSTARS has lost them in clutter, John, about a minute ago! They report stationary clutter on the road, probably other vehicles. They can't be sure.'

'Tell them to keep watching that spot until something moves again. Maybe they ran into a roadblock or something.'

Kearwin decided to check the AWACS records to trace flight movement. The process took longer than getting data from the Keyhole archive; the older AWACS database demanded exact requests. You couldn't just say, 'Give me all details on flights heading away from 'Ar'ar for April thirteenth.' You had to give the exact heading and aircraft type. With a sigh, he began to type.

He found it after only fifteen minutes. An aircraft matching the Islander's description had been tracked by a routine AWACS flight on the morning of the 13th. It had been flying on a heading for 'Ar'ar. He fed the Islander's course in and the ground track flashed up on his screen on the map overlay. There were two airfields on that approximate heading: Sakakah, only seventy-odd miles from 'Ar'ar, and Al Wajh, way down on the Red Sea coast. He decided to try Al Wajh first. He interrogated the computer for a probable departure time, given the AWACS computation of ground speed: it calculated 08.05. The Keyhole log indicated a KH-12 pass over Al Wajh at 07.43; that would do. He pulled the picture.

Kearwin was lucky. There was no cloud cover; the picture was a good one. The other element of luck was not so much that the plane showed up clearly on the ground at Al Wajh; it was that right alongside it was a vehicle.

Kearwin thrust his fatigue to one side. The vehicle was distinctive, the picture excellent. It was a large pick-up, with a covered rear cargo compartment. He studied the map, and decided to follow a hunch that it had come from the south, along the coast road.

'John?' It was Jerry. 'I think we've got a problem.'

Kearwin looked up anxiously. 'What gives? JSTARS didn't pick them up again after the roadblock?'

'No, it's not that. We got them again, still heading east along the same road. That means they probably intend crossing the Euphrates.'

'So, what's the problem?'

'Come and have a look at the picture we have of the bridge.'

'HADITHAH COMING UP, Johnny. About five miles.' Howard anxiously scanned the road ahead.

'Usual routine?'

'Flashing lights on, but no sirens unless we run into trouble. There's a big bridge there over the river, leading to the road to Bayji.'

It was 02.30 when they reached the town, which was deserted. They had descended from the plateau, down into the valley, and it was noticeably warmer, though still cool. There were orchards and fields surrounding the town. The road ran along the bank of the Euphrates. It felt humid after the dryness of the desert; a pungent smell of animals and humans wafted in through the windows.

'The bridge should be coming up on the right.' Howard consulted the GPS. 'Yes—there it . . . Oh, damn!'

Bourne braked the Land Cruiser to a halt. They sat in silence, staring at the sight alongside them. The huge bridge was a wreck. The central span was completely gone and the main pier on the far side had collapsed sideways. The gap was 200 yards wide.

'Any other bridges, Ed?'

'There were. But the other three are shown here as definitely down.'

'So, what do we do?'

'The next bridge downstream is twenty miles away, right by an army base. And maybe that one was hit too. There's a big dam about five miles upstream but that's bound to be heavily guarded. No, there must be a temporary ferry or something here. Keep going along slowly, and I'll look out for it.'

Howard saw the pontoon ferry just a mile further on. They stopped and examined the pontoon through binoculars. It looked deserted. 'There'll be someone there on duty,' growled Ziegler, hefting his AK. 'I guess I'll just have to go wake him up.'

Ten minutes later, on Ziegler's light signal, the two Land Cruisers slipped gently down the muddy incline to the jetty. Ziegler waved them straight onto the large floating pontoon tethered alongside it. He himself was kneeling down, one knee on the chest of a now wide-awake Iraqi corporal, the silencer of his AKMS jammed between the man's teeth. Howard and the others got out of the Land Cruisers.

'This here's Corporal Abdul,' said Ziegler conversationally. 'He's kindly goin' to act as our tour guide of the Euphrates tonight. Isn't that right, Abdul?' Ziegler grinned down at the Iraqi soldier, who had not understood a word he had said.

Bourne grabbed the corporal and hauled him roughly to his feet, talking in a low, fluent voice full of menace. He kept close to the Iraqi as he moved to the rear of the pontoon and started the diesel engine.

The pontoon began to swing out into the lazy current of the big river, heading for the opposite bank through the black, oily water. Howard and Usher scanned the west bank behind them for any sign that the pontoon's departure had been noticed; they saw nothing.

At the far bank, they slipped alongside the jetty and made fast. Bourne turned to Howard. 'Ed, take the Land Cruisers on up the bank a little way. I'm just going to have a word with the corporal.'

The two vehicles moved forward off the jetty and drove up the incline. A minute or two later, Bourne rejoined him. 'Everything OK?' asked Howard, as they set off eastwards.

'Fine.'

In the back of the vehicle, MacDonald shuddered. Intuition told him that the corporal's body had joined the other flotsam in the water of the Euphrates, floating slowly southwards towards Baghdad.

KEARWIN'S EYES WERE RED with fatigue, but curiosity had now overridden all thoughts of rest. He had traced the pick-up truck back south along the coast road. A pair of successive KH-11 passes, at 04.47 and 05.05 on April 13, had shown the pick-up to have been stationary for a period of at least eighteen minutes at a remote-looking spot about seventy miles south of Al Wajh.

The vehicle must have stopped for some reason. To rendezvous with some other vehicle along the road? No. There had been no other vehicle present. Besides, the pick-up had driven off the road, a few hundred yards down towards . . . the sea!

But there was no sign of a boat. Nothing, except a tiny two-pixel-sized blob right by the shore in the earlier of the two passes. Kearwin thought about it. It was ridiculous. Something just one foot across? One *foot*? Forget it.

But the heat source was there, definitely. A man? No, this object, whatever it was, was too hot—much too hot for it to be a human.

An engine! It had to be an engine!

Hammering out instructions on his keyboard now, Kearwin called up a KH-12 pass from thirty minutes before the two KH-11s. It began to appear; he fixed his eyes on the screen. There was the sea, a uniform grey, warmer than the land. He studied it keenly. Then he saw it. The tiny bright spot. And it was 700 yards out to sea! That meant . . .

Of course, a boat or dinghy might not show up—the temperature difference would be too slight, especially if spray was cooling the boat. But an outboard engine . . .

Yes, it must be the same object. It *was* an engine! *Now* he had something to work with!

Half an hour later, Kearwin threw his head back and let out a piercing whoop of triumph. The work of the NRO ground to a temporary halt as analysts looked up in astonishment.

Walter Sorensen, despite his tiredness, jumped to his feet and hurried over to Kearwin's desk.

'I've got them, Walter! I've got them!' Feverishly Kearwin began to explain, his voice cracking with excitement. As his words came pouring out, other analysts drifted away from their stations and gathered round to hear what all the fuss was about. Walter Sorensen listened with pride as Kearwin talked. This was one of *his* boys. The excited murmuring of the other analysts washed over him as he thought about what Kearwin had achieved.

Covering a period of two weeks and a vast expanse of territory, he had tracked targets that would normally have been reckoned too small to rate any attention. And he had done it with archive material—not even special tasking. *Wow*, was the Director going to like this!

This would make the CIA at Langley sit up and notice. Oh *boy*, would they sit up! He could give them the route, the timings, the vehicles, the camp they had come from, the aircraft—he could give them the lot.

Best of all, he could give them that damn great container ship.

TWENTY MILES CLEAR of the Hadithah crossing, Howard was the first to spot the warehouse, standing in a wire compound. He made a decision. 'Pull up, Johnny.'

They pulled off the road and studied the compound. 'Nothin' movin' at all,' observed Ziegler.

'There are only about two hours of dark left,' said Howard. 'I think we'll take a look, see who's here. We won't find a more deserted spot than this, and I don't want to get too close to Bayji.'

They drove the Land Cruisers quietly up to the gatehouse; Bourne got out and rattled the gate, shouting in Arabic. An old man appeared, only half awake. Bourne chatted amicably to him for a minute or so, and then suddenly produced his AK. The old man paled. He jabbered in terror, hurrying to open the gate.

They drove the vehicles through; Bourne made the old man lock the gate and hand him the key. He pulled him over to the back of the second ambulance and pushed him inside. 'Look after him, Bob. We'll take a look at that warehouse. He's guarding an empty building; an unused food store, would you believe.'

'Right,' said Howard. 'Time for a bit of vehicle maintenance, something to eat, and some rest. We've done well. But first things first.' He pulled out his packet of cigarettes. 'Anyone got a light?'

HARRY CRESSWELL HAD NO IDEA who the ambassador had spoken to, but it must have been someone with clout. The Kenyan Foreign Minister, probably. Whoever it was, it had had the required effect. A chief inspector of the Kenyan police was waiting for the CIA head of station when he arrived in Mombasa, and he was whisked straight down to the docks. The port had been sealed off; there were Kenyan army people everywhere, unsmiling, mean-looking men with loaded rifles. Out in the harbour, the lights of three patrol boats circled as the MV *Manatee* was slowly towed into her berth.

Cresswell was in a foul mood. For one thing, he didn't like being woken up at three in the morning. What was more, he didn't like the sound of this at all.

The Deputy Director (Intelligence) had sounded pretty mad about something. 'Get down there pronto, and check it out!' he had yelled at him down the line.

In the port director's air-conditioned office more than five hours later, Cresswell put down the telephone and sat for a moment, thinking. The DD(I) had sounded in a slightly better humour. Cresswell's initial report following the questioning of the *Manatee*'s captain must have mollified him somewhat. Not that there had been much to report. The news that the ship's port of origin was Felixstowe, England, and that she had not stopped en route, apart from Suez, seemed to have given him something to chew on.

Cresswell looked out of the window again and raised his eyebrows at the sight of the pandemonium on the dockside. He could see Chief Inspector Robert Mwanza in the middle of a throng of African bodies, giving orders, directing the operation.

There was a knock on the door, and a young policeman entered. 'Excuse me, sah. The chief inspector says to come.'

'I'll be right there.' Cresswell left the office and ambled down the stairs. As he opened the door, the clamour of the activity on the quay hit his ears like a volley of gunfire. He walked across to Chief Inspector Mwanza, who was leaning over a table working his way through a pile of documents. 'How's it going, Chief Inspector?'

Mwanza gestured over his shoulder at a big yellow-painted freezer container. 'That one is empty.'

'Is that unusual?'

'The Customs say yes, but not unheard of. Occasionally they go empty if the owners cannot find a cargo for both ways.'

'What does it say on the bill of lading?'

'That is what I am trying to find, Mr Cresswell.' Mwanza continued sifting through the stack of papers.

Cresswell walked over to the container. Four Customs men were standing by the open doors, examining the British Customs seal. Cresswell approached the Customs officials. 'Is the seal OK?'

One of the men looked up and nodded. 'Yes, sah.'

Cresswell poked his head inside the container. Clean as a whistle.

He wandered round it slowly, examining the outside. The fan unit was running noisily; it obviously had an integral power supply.

Wait a minute. What was the thing running for? It was empty, right? Some idiot had switched it on by mistake. 'Anyone know how to turn this thing off?' Blank looks greeted his question. Cresswell shrugged. Fine. Let it run. Why should he care that fuel was being wasted, keeping the thing froz . . .

Just a minute! *It hadn't been cold at all.* The fan was running; it was even dripping with condensation. And the temperature gauge said . . . *minus twenty!*

Cresswell hurried back over to the table. 'Inspector! I think we got something here!'

It would be an hour before an engineer reported the existence of two air-conditioning units mounted inside the refrigeration-unit housing, and explained how the thermostat had been tampered with. At 03.09 USA Eastern Time, the phone began to ring in the DD(I)'s office in Langley, Virginia. The DD(I) flicked on a light, rose sleepily from his couch and picked up the receiver.

When he heard what Cresswell had to report, he instantly forgot his tiredness. 'Thank God for that,' he muttered as he rang off. 'London can take the heat from now on.'

Chapter ⑧

The emergency meeting of the British Joint Intelligence Committee broke up and its members began to disperse. As he headed for the door, the Commissioner of the Metropolitan Police was approached by a trim, grey-haired figure wearing a regimental tie.

'Commissioner, may I make a suggestion?'

The Commissioner looked at the speaker with interest. 'Yes, Mr Goodale? I would welcome your ideas.'

Max Goodale smiled. 'Naturally, anything MI5 can do will be on the basis that the investigation will be entirely under your control. It is simply that we have various resources at our disposal that could be of assistance. I would like to offer them. After all, none of us yet knows what we are dealing with here.'

'Mr Goodale,' said the Commissioner, 'that is a generous offer, and I very much appreciate it.' He smiled back at the Deputy Director of MI5. 'I think it is an excellent idea, and I would like to take you up on it.'

As they walked out to the Commissioner's car they discussed the unusual nature of the task the police had just been assigned.

'I'm going to throw this job at SO11,' said the Commissioner. 'Initially, at any rate, it looks like a job for the Criminal Intelligence Branch, with help of course from other departments—including, as you have kindly offered, your own.'

'Let's hope that together we can come up with something. Can I ask who will be the officer in charge?'

'The Commander of SO11. One of the best, if not *the* best. Jones. Patrick Jones.'

'ALL RIGHT, GENTLEMEN. This is what we're going to do.' Commander Patrick Jones leaned over the table and looked round the faces in the room. His glance settled on a small, stocky man with thinning red hair and close-set eyes. 'Hughie, I want you to get down to this Swindon address on the bill of lading. Liaise with the Thames Valley people when you get there, but make it quite clear that this inquiry is centralised here in London. Give the place a going-over—I want every speck of dust analysed. Find out who has been there, who owns it. If it's rented, get hold of the agent and get all the details. Names, descriptions, the works. Who has made deliveries or collections? Post, refuse collection, milk? Grab anyone who has seen any of the occupants. OK?'

Detective Superintendent Hughie Carter had been making notes; he looked up and nodded. This was going to be a major job, he was beginning to realise. The first thing he would do would be to call his newly appointed assistant and hand over all his other work. It would give him a chance to see how the kid handled things in his absence. A competent enough kid—or so she seemed so far. She had to be competent, he supposed, to have been promoted that quickly. Well, he would soon find out what she was made of.

The Commander was now addressing a tall, blond, scholarly-looking man wearing heavy-framed glasses. 'Paul, I want your team to find out where this outfit had an account. When you find it, get copies of all the bank statements since the account opened, details of all transactions and who the payments were to or from. Go and talk to the people they did business with. Find out who audits their accounts and pull them in. Again, I want names and descriptions of these characters. Clear on that?'

Detective Chief Inspector Paul Hallam of the Fraud Squad nodded. This one sounded interesting. He liked grabbing respectable citizens out of bed on a Sunday morning.

Jones moved on to address a dark-haired man who looked like what he in fact was—an ex-middleweight boxer. 'Jerry, I want you and your boys to find out about this aircraft. Get some of your team to work on the registration mark and find out where they bought it. Has it been re-registered? If so, who to? Get the others backtracking it from Saudi Arabia. It arrived there on April eleventh. Give it three or four days, for the journey, and find out where it left from. Find out who saw it and who the pilot was. Get a name and description.'

'Right.' Detective Inspector Jerry Willson privately doubted whether he would get much joy out of civil airfields on a Sunday, but, like Hallam, he had every intention of making someone else suffer for yet another ruined weekend.

'Now; I would like to introduce Mr Goodale here. Mr Goodale is from the Security Service.' There were a few startled glances. 'I suggest each of you thinks carefully about what MI5 can offer, in terms of either personnel or resources. Mr Goodale and I will be joint coordinators on this.' Jones let the remark sink in. The men in the room studied Goodale with new interest, realising that he must be a high-ranking member of MI5. Jones nodded as he saw the interest. 'You will have a man from security attached to each of your teams. I want the highest degree of cooperation. I hope that is understood. I also,' he concluded, 'want results. And I want them fast.'

OVER THE NEXT FEW HOURS the results began to come in. The container-leasing company confirmed that the container in question had been delivered to Unit 10. Soon, a team of a dozen analysts was at work, searching the building for evidence. At the same time, a startled young estate agent, whose firm had conveniently been identified by the TO LET hoarding at the entrance to Loundis Road, was hauled unceremoniously from a Sunday-morning lie-in with his girlfriend and subjected to a session of questioning by two determined-looking CID officers. The search team widened its area of operation to Units 8 and 9, and the descriptions of 'Mr Bryce' and his BMW were circulated.

The estate agent was very specific about the car. It was a blue four-door saloon, he said; it had a manual gearbox and silver-grey leather seats, and the body was the new version introduced in 1991. Police forces all over the country were given the description and asked to keep a lookout.

It would turn out to be a dead end. Bourne's BMW was in Italy. It was no longer blue, and its new owner would remain blissfully innocent of its chequered history for ever.

Detective Chief Inspector Hallam, too, had initial success. Barclays Bank cooperated by producing the records of the freight company Bourne had set up. These revealed the existence of the two other companies. Hallam immediately set a team of detectives to work on each one, and was soon gleefully ordering solicitors and accountants to be brought in for questioning, and impounding documents for fingerprinting. When the payments from the Liechtenstein bank were uncovered, he reported back to Commander Jones.

Patrick Jones pursed his lips and drummed his fingers on the desk. 'That one will probably have to wait until tomorrow, Paul. We can't go after an overseas organisation just on my say-so. But I'll see what I can arrange.' He put down the telephone and frowned. Liechtenstein, indeed. So far, they had covered their tracks pretty well. The three industrial units were as clean as a whistle, as far as Hughie Carter had been able to tell. No useful evidence of anything: the place had obviously been scrubbed clean. The only evidence they had found was a small spot of yellow paint; it would probably match up with the paint on the container.

Damn it, thought Jones. The fellow must have slipped up *somewhere*. Hughie Carter would find something. *Someone* must have seen something going on. One of the many people making deliveries, most likely. Hughie had already talked to the driver who had delivered the container, but all he had seen was . . . chubby-face. The guy didn't mind being seen. Why? Obvious—disguise. The face? Contact lenses, dyed hair maybe . . . Voice? A normal-looking man, medium height, sometimes in a suit, sometimes in working clothes . . . It was pretty hopeless, unless Hughie came up with another witness.

The telephone rang; it was DI Willson. 'We've traced the plane, Chief. Southampton Airport. It left there on April seventh. And we've traced it back to Ireland, where they got it from.'

'Any description or names?' Jones leaned forward in his chair.

'I was rather hoping you would be able to pull a few strings with the Garda in Dublin, Chief. You know, ask them to talk to the plane's previous owners.'

'Consider it done,' said Jones, warmly. 'What about the pilot?'

'We pulled the records from the airport log. His name's Sullivan. US citizen, commercial pilot's licence. We've got his address, passport number, everything. He flew out alone in the Islander.'

'Good work, Jerry.'

'Thanks, Chief.'

Jones replaced the receiver with a grin. Now *that* was more like it, he thought. Some hard information to work on. Not bad going, for just over half a day's work.

COMMANDER JONES'S PROGRESS report was rapidly passed up the line; Sullivan's details were relayed to CIA Headquarters in Langley, where at 9.25am Eastern Time they landed on the desk of the Deputy

Director (Intelligence). The DD(I) was not best pleased to learn of the involvement of a US citizen in an affair that he thought he had safely passed to London for action. When, a short time later, the FBI came back to him with full details of Sullivan, his spirits rose a little. A no-good, small-time bum who had recently closed down a one-man air-charter business wouldn't have the know-how to organise a major international stunt like this. Sullivan must be a bit-part player. Perhaps even a stooge. It still looked like a British operation.

The DD(I) turned his irritation on James Ansell, the head of the Mid-East desk. 'What does that idiot in Riyadh think he's up to? Why haven't we heard any more from him about this airplane?'

'You mean Kennings?'

'Yes—Kennings. Get him moving on this, will you?'

Ansell fixed the DD(I) with a level gaze and replied, 'Alvin Kennings is a good man. He did well to get the registration mark of the plane in the first place. It's not easy to communicate any sense of urgency at all to the Saudis.' Yes, reflected Ansell, Kennings had done pretty well, so far, correctly guessing where the Islander had entered Saudi Arabia and then concentrating his enquiries on Jiddah.

The DD(I) thought about it. 'Well, keep him at it, would you?'

UNFORTUNATELY for Alvin Kennings, the Islander had disappeared nearly twenty hours earlier. Denard had left Badanah shortly after dark, having filed a flight plan with 'Ar'ar air-traffic control that afternoon. He had given his destination as Tabuk, 300 miles south-west across the Nafud Desert.

Taking off at 19.00, an hour after Howard and the ambulances had left Badanah, he climbed to 10,000 feet and settled onto the course of 204 degrees magnetic he had filed with 'Ar'ar control tower. After half an hour of steady flying, he switched off all his lights, dropped altitude and skimmed north towards the Iraqi border.

The desert was flat and featureless, but flying at little more than 100 feet above the ground in the dark, and without instruments, was a test of nerve and skill. After another half an hour he was streaming with sweat, but he did not dare climb any higher.

Soon after crossing the TAP road, Denard switched on his GPS unit and checked his position on the map: only two miles off-course. Eighteen minutes later, he saw the two parallel lines of lights on the ground. Easing back on the throttle and lowering the flaps, he brought the aircraft in to land on the improvised runway.

Chris Palmer was waiting for him in the third Land Cruiser. They had made a reconnaissance and decided on the landing strip two days earlier, fixing its exact position using the GPS. It was in the middle of nowhere, twenty-five miles short of the Iraqi border.

Denard was exhausted from the concentration of low-level flying. Palmer had a Thermos of sweet tea ready, and Denard drank two cups, sitting in the front seat of the vehicle while the engineer finished anchoring the aircraft down against possible winds.

'Rather my job than yours, Chris,' commented Denard when Palmer joined him in the vehicle. 'I don't envy you that drive.'

'No problem, man,' answered Palmer. 'You behave yourself out here, hey?'

'Oh, sure,' said Denard, sarcastically. 'What could I get up to, anyway?' He handed over Sullivan's folder with the documents inside. 'Drive carefully, and don't go bumping into any camels.'

Denard climbed out of the vehicle and walked over to the tent Palmer had put up; he was looking forward to a long sleep. Tomorrow, he thought, yawning, he would shave off his moustache and wash out the hair dye. There was no need for him to look like Sullivan any more.

Palmer started the engine and set off on the eighteen-hour drive to Jiddah. He hit the TAP road at 22.11, just after Bourne had led the two ambulances past Howard's diversionary fuel-depot fire.

'ALVIN? JONATHAN MITCHELL. This is unofficial, but it might be a good idea if we pooled our resources.'

Kennings knew Mitchell well, and liked him, but he had not yet received the go-ahead from Langley to work with him on this. He feigned surprise. 'I don't think I quite understand you, Jonathan.'

'Oh, come on, Alvin.' The English voice on the other end of the line was serious, not mocking. 'I know where it is. The Islander, I mean. Or at least,' he added, 'I know where it should be.'

'What!' Kennings's response reverberated noisily down the telephone line. 'How did you find out? Where is it?'

From the other end came an equally resounding silence.

Kennings gave in, wearily. 'OK, what's the deal?'

'Simple. You've got transport. HMG doesn't quite run to private jets. You share your wings, and I share my info.'

The deal was a fair one. Kennings capitulated. 'OK. It's a deal. I'll meet you at King Khaled International in twenty minutes. American Airlines ticket counter.'

Forty minutes later, the two senior representatives of the British SIS and the American CIA in Saudi Arabia were seated in a tiny Lear Jet as it taxied for takeoff from Riyadh. Kennings turned to the Englishman. 'OK, Jonathan, tell me how you found out.'

'Simple, really. My embassy people have been ringing round every airfield and airport in the country. We got lucky at a place called Tabuk. It's been overdue there for more than fifteen hours now. They only noticed its absence when I asked if it was due in.'

'So why are we going to 'Ar'ar?' asked Kennings.

'Two reasons. First, that's where it took off from yesterday. Second, that's where it's been based for the last couple of weeks.'

'What!' For the second time in less than an hour, the normally calm Kennings exploded with incredulity. He had been sent on a wild-goose chase when Langley must have known all along exactly where to send him. He shook his mind clear and changed the subject. 'Tell me about this company Darcon, Jonathan. Are they on the level?'

'Why do you want to know?'

'Because the Islander's documentation on entry into Jiddah made out it was their airplane. I phoned a guy called Hughes—he's the senior Darcon man here—but he said he knew nothing about it.'

Mitchell looked thoughtful. 'That puts a new slant on things,' he said, frowning. 'A couple of days ago the Islander received clearance from 'Ar'ar to base itself temporarily at a construction camp called Badanah. My contact in 'Ar'ar told me the pilot and his friends were living there. And the camp happens to be owned by Darcon.'

'Well,' said Kennings, 'I think the first thing we'd better do is have another chat with Mr Hughes. He's got a bit of explaining to do.'

Using the radiotelephone in the Lear, Mitchell called Hughes at his office. Hughes sounded genuinely perplexed and indignant, but insisted that the visitors were all bona fide, with all the correct documentation from London, signed by Sir Peter Dartington himself.

'Mr Hughes,' said Mitchell, 'I'm going to send round one of my people from the embassy to see you right away. I would be grateful if you would cooperate with him in full.'

Hughes promised to do so.

'One more thing, Mr Hughes. You say they asked for the use of four vehicles—you're sure that's correct?'

Hughes said that it was.

'Good. I'd like you to make a report straight away to the Saudi police. Tell them that these vehicles have been stolen and give descriptions of the men you saw.' Mitchell ended the conversation and turned to Kennings. 'Let the police do the legwork, eh?'

The CIA man smiled. 'Nice touch, Jonathan,' he said. 'I like that. I like it a lot.'

THE SAUDI POLICE wasted little time. Descriptions of the two men and the four stolen Land Cruisers provided by a baffled and angry Tony Hughes were flashed to police stations all over the kingdom.

110

Hughes had given descriptions of the two men, but had seen Bourne and Palmer only in disguise. Bourne had worn his 'Bryce' cheek-pads and Palmer a thick beard, which he had shaved off as soon as he arrived in Badanah. They had entered Saudi Arabia under their true identities, undisguised. The visa photos would be of little value and Hughes would later be unable to identify them.

Consequently, when Palmer arrived at the routine checkpoint on the approach to Jiddah, near the end of his long drive south from where he had left Denard and the Islander, he was waved through without a problem. The bored and uninterested police officers on duty at the checkpoint paid little attention to the heavy-set driver of the Land Cruiser, opting instead to concentrate on a pick-up truck behind it containing five Indian migrant workers. By the time the details of the stolen Land Cruisers came through, the policemen at the checkpoint had forgotten all about the Land Cruiser, and Palmer, exhausted after his 900-mile journey, had arrived at the Jiddah Sheraton and was relaxing in the lobby with a long cool drink.

ALVIN KENNINGS and Jonathan Mitchell arrived at Badanah to discover the construction camp empty but for the camp cook. The highly nervous Pakistani, immediately sensing that something was badly amiss, was pathetically anxious to help. On being asked questions to which he did not know the answers, he adopted the procedure of telling his interviewers what he thought they wanted to hear. The result, as Kennings soon realised, was an almost worthless stream of particulars, many of them fabricated and misleading.

Kennings drew Mitchell to one side. 'We're getting nowhere with this guy. About the only useful information he's given is that there were eight of them, all white, and that they all left here last night in the three vehicles and the plane. I think we can rely on what he said about two of the vehicles being painted up to look like ambulances. Those will be the two inside Iraq. The third vehicle has definitely left too, and we have to assume that it's still in Saudi. The fourth must be that hulk in the workshop; I guess they stripped it clean for spares. I suggest we report that we're now looking for eight white men, three vehicles and one airplane. If we give people any more than that it will just add to the confusion.'

'You're right,' said Mitchell. 'I'll go and phone Hughes and get him to report that to the police. Let's hope they pick up that third vehicle.'

Mitchell telephoned Hughes, who quickly relayed the information to the Saudi police. The scope of the search was accordingly widened and orders were issued for all white Darcon employees to be investigated. It was, of course, an entirely understandable assumption on Hughes's and the police's part that the criminals were posing as Darcon employees.

The trouble was, the assumption was wrong.

At 17.55, as Palmer was ordering his second drink in the lobby of the Sheraton, Harris was arranging check-out formalities for himself and Sullivan, who was still upstairs. Two police officers approached the desk and demanded to see the duty manager, who duly appeared from his office. Harris heard the senior of the two officers ask to see the hotel register. He understood enough Arabic to follow some of what the police were saying, but it was only when he heard the word 'Darcon' that alarm bells began ringing. Then he saw one of the policemen hand a photograph across the counter and ask the duty manager if he had seen the man. Casually, Harris moved closer to get a look at the picture.

His heart sank. The photograph, though not a good one, was plainly identifiable as Sullivan. The duty manager shook his head regretfully and handed the picture back to the police officer.

Harris thought quickly. He had taken the precaution of having the other room registered in Denard's name and both men were recorded as employees of Pan-Arabian Petroleum, not Darcon. The manager had not recognised the photograph. It was as well, thought Harris, that he had insisted that the American shave off his moustache.

But they were blown. He finished settling his and Sullivan's hotel bills, collected his own and Denard's passports and walked over to join Palmer. Talking rapidly in a low voice, he outlined his suspicions. 'Chris, we're in trouble. The police are onto Sullivan—I've just seen them flashing his photo in reception.'

'What do we do now?' said Palmer.

'Well, let's look on the bright side. In the first place, your journey wasn't wasted. The boss was right to insist on the precaution. It means we have to let Sullivan go, and I mean *now*. He's served his purpose—it was only his ID papers that were needed, for Andy. Getting the plane out afterwards would have been a bonus, but it'll have to be ditched. The first thing to do is hand over Sullivan's papers and get him to the airport. He'll have to take his chances there. He doesn't know any of our names; the worst he can do if picked up is give descriptions of me and Andy—we're the only two he's met.'

'OK,' said Palmer, 'but what about the Land Cruisers? Maybe they've got the registration numbers.'

'Exactly,' said Harris. 'That means your Land Cruiser could be hot. We have to assume it is. I'll take Sullivan to the airport by taxi and hire a car there—a similar-coloured Land Cruiser. If I can I'll put its plates on your car so that we can continue to use the same vehicle. We might have to abandon it and the hire car would lead back to me—I'm going to have to hire it with my own credit card.'

'But if you're going to swap the number plates round, all that does is make your hire car the hot one. How does that help?'

'Ah,' said Harris. 'I've got an idea for that.' He outlined his plan; then, holding Sullivan's document case, he went upstairs.

Passing the door of his room, Harris ducked into the service pantry and looked round. There was a plumber's tool-bag on the floor; he opened it, selected a hand-drill, a hacksaw and a screwdriver, and put them inside his document case. His eyes lit on the large worktop surface, covered with off-white Formica. Using a kitchen knife, he levered off a large piece of the Formica; this he snapped into two pieces small enough to fit into his document case. Then he went back to his room to collect the Texan, who was ready to go. The two men descended to the lobby with their bags. Avoiding the front desk, Harris quickly guided Sullivan straight out to find a taxi.

On the way to the airport, Harris informed the puzzled Sullivan that the job had been cancelled but that he would be paid anyway, as agreed.

Harris decided he owed the genial Texan something of an explanation. 'Listen, Ray,' he whispered, to avoid being overheard by the taxi-driver, 'it's possible that there may be trouble at the airport. Keep a low profile. The fact is, you've been registered all along at the hotel under a false name. If you do get picked up, the heat may be quite fierce. But all you have to do is insist that you were at the hotel the whole time and don't know what all this is about. There are plenty of witnesses there who will identify you. All I want is for you to give as vague as possible a description of me if you're asked.'

'No problem, Mitch. Listen, it's been good knowing you. I'd love to know what this has all been about, but I guess I'd better not ask.'

Harris smiled again. He had grown genuinely fond of the easy-going Texan. 'It wouldn't be good for your health, Ray. And, by the way, I wouldn't go back to the States either, if I were you. If the cops are looking for you here, they're probably after you there too.'

'Bad as that, huh? But don't worry. I wasn't planning returning there anyhow.' Sullivan chewed his lip reflectively. 'I've always fancied taking a trip to Thailand,' he added, with a roguish wink.

They arrived at the airport and Harris paid off the taxi. Sullivan disappeared in the direction of the ticket counter. Harris went to the Avis desk and rented a cream-coloured Land Cruiser.

Out in the Avis section of the car park, he located the vehicle and started it up. He drove the vehicle the short distance to the public section of the car park, found a space and reversed the Land Cruiser into it, almost up against the bumper of another car. He got out, and taking his document case round to the rear of the vehicle he knelt down. Hidden from view by the other car, he opened the document case, took out the screwdriver and unscrewed the rear licence plate.

Back inside the vehicle, he used the hacksaw to cut one of the pieces of Formica to size and began to make a copy of the plate on the Formica, using a black marker-pen. When he had finished, he compared the two plates. Not bad, he thought; the copy wouldn't stand up to close inspection but it should do for what he wanted.

He attached the copy plate where the real one had been. He drove the Land Cruiser out of the slot and then back in, this time head first, so that he could repeat the procedure for the front plate. Having placed the two genuine plates and the car-hire documents inside his document case, he locked the vehicle and hailed a taxi to take him to the Sheraton.

Palmer had been unobtrusively hanging around the hotel car park where he could observe his vehicle. 'No sign of any interest at all,' he told Harris. While Palmer kept an eye open, Harris replaced the hot plates with the ones from the hire car. Palmer's Land Cruiser now bore the identity of the hire car. The two men went back into the hotel, where they had a quick snack before setting off on the long drive back to rejoin Denard, waiting with the Islander near the border.

Sullivan had by then passed through passport control without incident and was waiting in the departure lounge for the 21.10 flight to Bangkok.

'SO, GENTLEMEN, the known facts have all been verified by on-the-spot investigations carried out by CIA, FBI and British police and intelligence personnel.' Brent Scowcroft, National Security Adviser to President Bush, looked round the table. 'Now let us move on to supposition.' He glanced at the faces round the table. 'I have to say that what I have heard from the National Reconnaissance Office makes it ninety-nine-per-cent certain, as far as I am concerned, that these suppositions are correct. They run as follows:

'Two or more men are concealed inside the sea container for its voyage from England. On the night of April twelfth-thirteenth, during the ship's passage south through the Red Sea, they empty the container and depart from the vessel in a dinghy and make for the Saudi coast. They are collected by an accomplice driving a pick-up vehicle, and are driven to Al Wajh. They board the Islander and fly to 'Ar'ar, then travel up the road to Badanah. Last night, April

114

twenty-fifth, the two ambulances drive north to the Iraqi border, where they cause a diversion, enter Iraq and travel northeast on the Kirkuk road. Before dawn this morning, Iraqi time, they lay up in a large building east of Hadithah, where they still are. The third vehicle and the aircraft have meanwhile departed for destinations unknown.

'Now before we go on to theorise about what these people might be up to, I have asked the Director of the NRO to bring with him to this meeting the senior supervisor of the NRO section responsible for bringing this affair to light. Mr Director, I would be grateful if Mr Sorensen would explain to us how this was done.'

All heads turned to stare at the big man with the large drooping moustache. The Walrus looked uncomfortable and cleared his throat.

Ten minutes later he had finished the detailed explanation and begun to summarise. 'So you see, gentlemen, the initial sighting was made by chance. I have to say that the tracking work, however, was of the highest quality and was largely the work of just one of my analysts.' He tweaked his moustache and turned to the National Security Adviser. 'Perhaps if you have any questions, sir . . . ?'

Brent Scowcroft shook his head and looked round the table. 'Any of you gentlemen have a question for Mr Sorensen?'

The man on Scowcroft's left spoke up. 'If I may, Mr Chairman?'

'Go ahead, John.'

Under Secretary of State John Kelly leaned forward in his chair, made a steeple of his hands and looked at Sorensen. 'In view of what this may be leading to there could be serious implications here for US foreign policy. We at the State Department consider it essential that we get a handle on these people and put a stop to their activities. I believe the President'—he glanced at Scowcroft, who nodded—'is at one with us in this. It would appear that the men inside Iraq are temporarily beyond our reach; while they are there, we simply can't get at them. So there remain just two avenues of investigation open to us. The first is obvious, but may lead to nothing: to interview Sir Peter Dartington and find out what he knows. The second you say is difficult: the locating of the airplane. The pilot may be in contact with the men and might be persuaded to call them off. My question is this: what chance do you have of finding the plane?'

The Walrus tweaked his moustache more vigorously than usual before answering. 'Very little, I'm afraid, sir, unless it takes to the air again, in which case it will be spotted almost immediately by AWACS. If this plane has gone into hiding, it may be that it's waiting until the men in the vehicles have completed their task and are heading for home. The plane may be their means of escape, and I would guess that it will sit tight until it is called for.'

Across the table from him Robert Gates, Director of Central Intelligence, raised a forefinger and spoke. 'The CIA would agree with that assessment.'

'I think,' said Scowcroft, 'that this brings us on to the possible reasons for the activities of these men. Independently, the NRO, the CIA and the State Department have all arrived at the same conclusion. In brief, we believe they are engaged in an attempt to assassinate Saddam Hussein.'

There was a gasp from a frog-faced man at the far end of the table. The Walrus recognised him as Douglas Longmire, Assistant Treasury Secretary. A powerfully built man wearing the uniform of a US air force general muttered, 'About time someone did.'

'That is beside the point, General,' said Scowcroft firmly. 'The question is, how do we handle this? The President would like to hear our recommendations.'

Charles Burnside, Vice-Chairman of the Joint Chiefs of Staff, weighed in forcefully. 'I say we let 'em get on with it. We should've been allowed to finish the job last year, when we had the chance. Good luck to these guys.'

'If I may, Mr Chairman.' Under Secretary of State John Kelly cut in, his voice icy. 'There are issues of foreign policy here that General Burnside perhaps fails to appreciate . . .'

'Policy, schmolicy,' said Burnside. 'Look where your foreign policy has gotten us. No-place, is where.'

'Gentlemen! Gentlemen!' Scowcroft held up his hands in a placatory gesture, and waited until the murmurs round the table had ceased. Then he addressed Kelly. 'John, I think it would help if you explained the situation as the State Department sees it. I have to say'—Scowcroft shot a warning glance at Burnside—'that the President is entirely in agreement with the State Department's assessment. John?'

Kelly began to speak, controlling with an effort his irritation at Burnside's irreverent intervention. 'The issue at stake, put simply, is the future of the Iraqi state. Without strong leadership at the top, there is little doubt that it would fragment—probably very fast. In the north, the Kurds would seek to establish an independent Kurdistan. In the south, the Shi'ite Muslims would also secede. That would leave the minority Sunni Muslims of central Iraq holding what remained. None of these three states could survive as a separate entity. The neighbouring powers would be too strong. I speak here principally of Turkey, Syria and above all Iran.'

Kelly paused for emphasis, then went on. 'For many years now, Iraq and Iran have balanced each other off in the power struggle in

116

the Mid-East. You will recall how convenient—for want of a better word—the war between these two countries was. Quite simply, the fragmentation of Iraq would leave Iran the dominant economic and military power in the Gulf.

'Can any one of you here,' asked Kelly, looking round the table and reserving an especially hard stare for General Burnside, 'honestly say that you would be happy to see Iran become the unchallenged dominant power in the Mid-East in general, and the Gulf in particular, with all that that would mean?'

There was silence in the room. Kelly ran his gaze round the faces at the table; all eyes were upon him. 'So. We must accept that the continued existence of the Iraqi state is essential to stability—albeit an uneasy stability—in the region. Unfortunately, there is only one man who can guarantee, for the time being, to hold it together: Saddam Hussein.

'It therefore follows,' he continued, 'that this attempt on his life—if that's what it is—is fundamentally against the national interests of the United States. What is at stake here is the peace of the region. That is why these men are so dangerous. That is why, if it can be managed, they must be stopped. There is only one question that we should be addressing. How can this be achieved?'

'We could warn Saddam.' All heads swivelled round towards the new speaker. It was Douglas Longmire. He shrugged at the expressions of scorn on some of the faces. 'Why not? All we have to do is tip the wink to the Iraqi Ambassador to the UN. He passes the warning on to Saddam. Simple.'

'Mr Chairman?' Robert Gates, Director of the CIA, spoke up. 'Unfortunately, it is *not* that simple. It is unlikely that any credence would be given by Mr al-Anbari to such a warning, even if it was passed on by a neutral party. Moreover, just imagine the stink that would be caused if it got out that we had actually intervened to save Saddam's life.'

Scowcroft, at the head of the table, cleared his throat and avoided Longmire's frog-eyed glare. 'I think we must rule out any idea of a warning,' he muttered hurriedly. 'Does anyone else have a better solution?'

'All we can do, Mr Chairman, is to hope that the attempt will fail.' The speaker this time was the Director of the FBI. 'These men have been lucky, so far. I am surprised that they have got as far as they have. We investigated the pilot. He is a nobody, a bum. It could, after all, be nothing more than an amateur operation that just happens so far to have enjoyed an undue degree of success.'

'There is one way they could be stopped. One way that would

guarantee it.' All heads turned again towards the source of the gruff voice. It was General Burnside.

'Please explain what you have in mind, General Burnside,' said Scowcroft quietly.

'Right now,' enunciated Burnside, 'the USS *Missouri* is in the northern Gulf. If the NRO can give me the exact coordinates of the building where these guys are holed up, they can be flashed immediately to the *Missouri*. The necessary weapons-programming could be completed within about fifteen minutes. The distance to the target looks about five hundred miles. Time of flight would therefore be an hour, or thereabouts. Within approximately seventy-five minutes from now,' he looked at his watch, 'say at about nineteen forty-five Iraqi time, a couple of cruise missiles could fly in through the window of that building and blow it and everyone inside to pieces.'

For a full half-minute, there was dead silence in the room. The President's National Security Adviser looked at the faces round the table. He saw no dissent. Slowly, he lifted the receiver of the red telephone in front of him. He spoke briefly, then handed the receiver to Burnside, who listened to the voice on the other end of the line.

'Yes, Mr President,' said General Burnside finally. 'I will give the launch order at once.'

Chapter ⑨

'Peter, there's someone from the consulate to see you.'

'Eh?' Sir Peter Dartington's eyebrows rose fractionally, and he pushed his dark glasses up onto his forehead. 'What does he want?' He set down his glass of planter's punch on the table beside the sun-lounger. He sat up and looked at his wife.

'He didn't say, dear. He's waiting in the study.'

Dartington slipped his feet into a pair of flip-flops and pulled on his shirt, grumbling. 'Damn it, how did anyone find out that I was here?'

'I expect your office informed them, dear.'

Frowning at the interruption, Dartington disappeared inside the villa, still grumbling. He found his visitor in the study.

'Sir Peter Dartington?' The man rose to his feet.

Dartington regarded him coolly. 'Yes. What can I do for you?'

'My name's Smith—Detective Sergeant Smith. I am on attachment to the British Consulate in Nassau.' Smith produced a warrant card; Dartington waved it away with irritation. Smith continued. 'I have been asked by my colleagues in London to investigate a security matter, and we believe you may be able to help us.'

'Couldn't it wait until I get back to London?'

'I'm afraid not, sir.' The man opened his briefcase and produced a slim folder of papers. He selected a sheet and handed it to Dartington. 'I wonder if you could verify that this is your signature, please, sir?'

Dartington frowned again. 'Just a minute, I'll need my glasses . . . oh, there they are.' He retrieved his reading glasses from the study desk and put them on. Smith watched his face closely as he peered at the paper. 'Yes, this is my signa . . .' Suddenly, Dartington's expression changed. 'Just a minute, I never sent this! This is a forgery! Where the hell did it come from?'

Smith continued to study the angry bafflement on Dartington's face, until eventually the protests petered out. Was there something else in the businessman's expression?

Halfway through reading the copy of the fax, Dartington had suddenly realised all too well what it signified. His instinctive reaction of indignation had given him a few seconds to marshal his thoughts. He sat down. 'I think you had better explain what all this means, Detective Sergeant Smith.'

Smith was in fact an officer with the British SIS; he had been carefully briefed on the case, although he was not a trained interviewer of people such as Dartington. DCI Hallam, had he been there, might just have spotted the fleeting moment when Dartington had realised the trouble he was in; Smith had missed it. Nevertheless, he guessed that Dartington had something up his sleeve.

'Sir Peter, perhaps you would care to look at the top of the paper. You will see a series of numbers and letters.'

'Yes, yes,' said Dartington.

'They give the identification code and telephone number from which the fax was transmitted. Would you please compare them with the number and code at the top of this second fax?' Smith extracted another document from his folder and handed it over.

Dartington examined it. 'They are the same. The date and time are different, but all the rest is the same.'

'It is indeed. In fact, both messages were sent by a Canon Fax-220. Do you deny having sent these messages?'

'Of course I do. What I mean is, no, I don't. I sent the earlier one—I remember it. But this other one—the later one—is a forgery.'

'Sir Peter, these two faxes were sent by the same machine.'

Dartington frowned. He made a show of comparing the two documents. For a minute, he sat, apparently racking his brains. Then he exclaimed, 'Just a minute!' and sprang up, going over to his desk. He took out his diary and riffled through the pages as he returned to his chair. He looked at the dates on the faxes again, then up at Smith. 'That explains it,' he said, sitting back with a smile.

It was Smith's turn to look perplexed. 'Please enlighten me, Sir Peter.'

'On the night of November nineteenth last year, my house in Kent was burgled. Among the items stolen were some papers and my personal fax machine—this machine. The date of this forged fax message is December second. The transmitting telephone number shown on here doesn't mean a thing—you have to enter it in manually. All this means is that the thief didn't change the settings. I think you have your answer.' He emitted a small sigh of feigned exasperation. 'Now,' he continued, imparting a hard tone to his voice, 'you will kindly tell me at once what all this is about.'

Smith was taken aback. He jotted down the date of the burglary on a piece of paper, and made a mental note to give London hell for not checking their facts. Then he looked up. 'It would appear, Sir Peter, that we owe you an apology, as well as an explanation. Perhaps you will understand the gravity of the situation when I inform you that the people responsible for sending this message appear to belong to an organisation that has made use of the facilities requested in this message to enter Saudi Arabia and conduct what looks like, ah, shall we say, a terrorist operation.'

Dartington sat bolt upright; his alarm was genuine. 'I see,' he said slowly, his face a mask of concern. 'Good Lord. That certainly explains things. Look, I'm sorry if I was short with you. I had no idea. I hope you catch these people. Is there anything I can do to help . . .?'

'Thank you, Sir Peter. It is kind of you to be so understanding. But we cannot be too careful, as you will appreciate.' Smith got to his feet. 'My apologies again for bothering you with this unpleasantness.'

'Not at all, Detective Sergeant.' Dartington walked Smith to the door and bade him good day.

Julian Smith drove slowly away from the villa. He hadn't believed a word Dartington had said. Oh, he had been glib and convincing all right. But it was too bloody neat, that story about the stolen fax machine. He had no doubt that it would check out all right, but it was too neat. Never mind, he thought. He had had time to wire the villa, and the telephone line was already being monitored. The two bugs and the tapped phone line would turn up something.

THE PROW OF THE MAJESTIC warship sliced through the calm waters of the northern Gulf, leaving a boiling phosphorescent glow stretching out far behind her in the dark. The USS *Missouri* was one of the four greatest fighting ships ever to have been built: nothing less than floating, living history. When Japan surrendered at the end of the Second World War, the surrender ceremony had taken place on the *Missouri*'s deck.

On her bridge, nearly a hundred feet above the sea, her captain thought about the order he had received from the Joint Chiefs. He hoped that it was important. Surely it had to be, if they were targeting *four* missiles at it.

The voice of the weapons officer came over the squawk box. 'SLCMs ready, sir.'

'Radio? Do we have confirmation of the order to fire?'

'Affirmative, sir,' replied the communications officer.

'Commence firing.'

The ignition of the rocket-boost motor in the first launch tube hurled the missile out horizontally over the sea, leaving a trail of white vapour. The firing of all four Tomahawk cruise missiles was completed within thirty seconds. The captain gazed out towards the northwest horizon and watched them disappear into the night.

'HOW'S THAT TRAFFIC now, Mike?' Ed Howard looked up as Ziegler joined him.

'Worse than New York in the rush hour during a state visit. Must be an entire division movin' along there. Mile upon mile of it.' Ziegler sat down and poured himself a cup of coffee. 'How are our visitors?'

The old man's two sons had arrived at dawn to relieve him. The three men had shared the job of guarding the empty warehouse.

'They're scared. Johnny's still talking to them.' Howard jerked a thumb in the direction of the little group huddled in the corner.

'*Sha'ib*,' said Johnny Bourne. 'Old man. Soon we will be leaving here. Maybe in one hour . . .'

The old man had gone beyond fear. He was now resigned to the certainty of death.

'*Sidi*, I am unimportant,' he said. 'But my sons here, they'—he indicated the two younger men who sat with their wrists fastened by handcuffs round a steel girder—'they are young. They work hard. They have women and children. I am an old man. Kill me; my days are over. But if you have it in your heart to spare my sons, God will surely smile on you.'

'We have no quarrel with you, old man.' Bourne's voice was cold.

'I know it, *sidi*. You have treated us well. Given us food. But you are planning to kill us. I ask only for the lives of my sons.'

Danny MacDonald sat a little way off, watching and listening to the exchange. He understood a few words—not many, but he could tell what the old man was saying. With a feeling of revulsion, Danny knew that death was what awaited this old man and his sons when the team left . . . Danny could see the hard look on Johnny Bourne's face. He could watch no more.

He got up and went over to join Howard and Ziegler. 'Ed? Can I ask you something?'

'Go ahead.'

'Is it really necessary to kill these three?'

'Sit down, Danny.' Howard's penetrating gaze didn't leave Mac-Donald's face. 'You knew the rules of the game when you signed up. But I'll tell you something.' He leaned forward, his dark eyes still fixed on MacDonald's. 'We're *not* going to kill them.'

'Wha . . . ? Then why is Johnny giving them such a hard time?'

Howard sighed. 'He came to me soon after the two sons arrived this morning to take over guard duty from the old man. He said he wanted to try something.'

'What do you mean?'

'Johnny said that if he had a chance to talk to them, to strike up a relationship of mutual respect, there would be less chance of their hating us and wanting to blow the whistle. A large part of that mutual respect has to be based on their being afraid of us, which is why Johnny has been giving them such a grilling. When he tells them their lives will be spared, they will feel gratitude. It's a well-known psychological trick, Danny. All Johnny's been trying to do is to telescope the process into the space of twelve hours, rather than several days or weeks. That's why he hasn't taken any sleep.'

MacDonald said nothing. What Howard had told him had taken him completely by surprise. He had misjudged Bourne completely.

Howard was still talking. '. . . And there's one other factor we're going to throw in, which should guarantee their silence,' he said. 'We're going to give them some money. Quite a lot of it. Compensation for the harm we have done them, no strings attached. It will be accepted. It will also,' Howard grinned, 'make it even more unlikely that he or his sons will go to the Iraqi authorities. He'll know that if he talks to them, sooner or later they will find the money. And that would be the end of him and *all* his relatives.'

'Oh,' said MacDonald.

'Satisfied now?' asked Howard. 'Good. Right, onto other things. It's nearly seven; I want to be away from here fairly soon, but we have a problem with the road. That big convoy seems to be endless. I'm going to give it till eight. If it hasn't cleared by then, we'll have to go cross-country the rest of the way. Go and give Tony a call, will you? Mike's going to get some chow and a brew going. We'll eat in about fifteen minutes.'

'TONY? PETER HERE. Would you mind telling me exactly what the bloody hell is going on out there?'

'Peter! Am I glad to hear from you!' Tony Hughes's relief at hearing Dartington's voice was unmistakable. 'Where are you?'

'I'm on holiday. I'm calling from the Bahamas. I've just had the police here with a story about some people who have forged some Darcon documents to get the use of some of our facilities in Saudi. What the hell is all this, and who are these people? What have they been doing?'

Hughes outlined what he knew, mentioning the conversations he had had with 'security men from the British and American Embassies'. After giving as much information as he could, he concluded: 'And that's all I know. I'm sorry about all this, but the paperwork all seemed genuine.'

Dartington injected a note of concern into his voice. 'Listen, Tony, I want you to cooperate in full with the embassy, and I also want you to report all this to the Saudi police.'

'Already done, Peter.'

'Good. I'm bloody angry about this,' spluttered Dartington. 'Not with you,' he added hastily. 'It isn't your fault. But I don't like the idea of these people making monkeys out of us and stealing our gear from under our noses. Please do whatever you can to help catch them. Phone me here if you learn any more.' Dartington gave Hughes his number and rang off.

SEVERAL MILES AWAY, Julian Smith sighed and switched off the tape recorder. Damn, he thought. I'd rather hoped he would give himself away. Perhaps he's on the level after all. Or maybe he's just rather smarter than he appears.

'JOHNNY?' ED HOWARD CALLED over to Bourne, who still sat with the hunched figures of the three Arabs in the dim light on the far side of the warehouse. 'Grub's up.'

Bourne turned his head and gave Howard a slow nod. 'Be with you in five, Ed. I'm just going to explain the situation to them now.'

A few seconds later there was an excited babble of voices from the corner. MacDonald looked up from the pot of thick soup he was ladling out into mess tins. Johnny Bourne was unlocking the handcuffs on the two younger men. In the guttering candlelight MacDonald could see the skinny old man rising stiffly to his feet. He was talking solemnly to Bourne; the hands of the two men were clasped firmly together in a gesture of understanding.

Despite the old man's unkempt appearance, it struck MacDonald that he had never before seen such dignity in a human being.

Howard ate quickly from his mess tin, then looked at his watch. It was 19.25. 'Keep a plateful for Bob, boys. I'm just going to join him and see how that convoy's going. Start packing up.'

THE FOUR CRUISE MISSILES, launched from the USS *Missouri*, reached the coastline within ninety seconds of one another. Two were following a course to the east, while the other two were directed slightly to the west.

The eastern pair had headed towards the Iraqi town of Basra. There, Iraqi forces were brought onto the alert and tracer lit up the sky. But by the time the firing had started, the missiles, screaming over the land at 550 miles per hour, were long gone, and heading in the direction of Baghdad.

The other two missiles had followed the waters of the Khawr abd-Allah, entering the narrows of the *khawr* at the border with Kuwait. Twenty miles further on, they had picked out the Shatt al Basra canal, which took them, like their counterparts, past Basra. At the end of the canal they turned almost due west.

By 19.41 the four missiles were seventy miles from their target and converging. The two western missiles slowed; they were ahead of schedule by twelve seconds. All four were due to impact simultaneously at 19.49, exactly eight minutes away.

THE SMALL SIDE-DOOR swung open as Howard reappeared in the warehouse. 'The convoy has definitely gone. Nearly ten minutes since the last vehicle passed. Let's go.'

Howard and Ackford drove the Land Cruisers out towards the gatehouse, using the NVGs and the IR spotlamps in the dark. Usher, muttering about having had his supper interrupted, helped Bourne and the three Arabs to close the big doors; then they all walked over to the gate, where Usher got into the back of the second vehicle and resumed gulping down the contents of his mess tin. By the gate, Bourne started talking in a low, urgent voice to the three Arabs; when he had finished, he shook their hands once again. Disengaging himself with trouble from the protracted expressions of gratitude, he climbed in beside Howard, who had moved over to the front passenger seat. The old man's two sons, at Bourne's urging, began hurrying home along a track; the old man would remain on duty for the night, as if nothing had happened.

Howard turned to Bourne. 'You OK to drive, Johnny?'

'I'm fine.'

'OK, let's roll.'

THE OLD MAN WATCHED the two vehicles leave, then locked the gate. He thanked Allah for his deliverance. These *Amerikaaniyeen* were not at all what he had been led to believe. They were honourable men; they had treated him and his sons with respect. And he was now a rich man; the unimaginable wealth they had pressed upon him, with the properly humble apologies for the inconvenience and worry they had caused, made the future look bright indeed.

He would be careful about the money. It would not be safe for him to conceal it on his person. No, he thought, he would hide it, straight away. He knew the place for it. There was a large rock behind the gatehouse, with a small crevice at its base, hidden by scrub and a flat stone. The rock was inside the security fence, so no one would find the money by accident. Yes, he thought, he would hide it now. He walked over to the rock, and knelt down to move the flat stone.

The action saved the old man's life. There was a loud *whoosh* as something passed overhead in the dark; then night suddenly turned into day and the whole world seemed to disintegrate about him. A small piece of falling debris from the building caught him a glancing blow on the side of his head and he fell unconscious.

Five minutes later he was found by his two anxious sons, who had hurried back to see if he was still alive. On regaining consciousness, their astounded father opened his eyes to the devastation of the warehouse, now a smoking ruin.

The old man would retell, countless times, the story of how he had survived the terrible air raid, but neither he nor his sons would ever reveal to anyone just why he happened to have been sheltering behind the large rock at the exact moment the bombs fell.

'BLIMEY! DID YOU SEE THAT?' Bourne stamped hard on the brake, bringing the Land Cruiser to a halt. The second Land Cruiser pulled up alongside. All six men turned to look at the scene.

A mile behind them, Howard could see through his binoculars that the warehouse had disintegrated.

'What the hell was it?' Bourne asked.

'I heard three or four explosions, very rapid succession,' said Ziegler from the other vehicle.

'So did I,' said Howard. 'But let's get going. I think we'd better put in a bit of mileage between us and this place.'

They drove off again. For a while there was silence in the lead ambulance. Bourne was the first to speak. 'Must have been an air strike, I guess. What do you think?'

'I don't know,' Howard admitted. 'But it's bad news, whatever it was. It was no bloody coincidence, that's for sure.'

'But if they were after us, they wouldn't just have bombed that place. They'd have sent a helicopter force, and they'd have blocked this road into the bargain,' said Bourne. 'Or maybe,' he added, 'they *have* blocked this road. Don't you think we ought to get off it?'

'No. It doesn't change anything. We'd still be more conspicuous off-road.'

'What about that convoy up ahead?'

'The tail end will be at least five or ten miles on up the road by now,' replied Howard. 'They'll probably have heard the explosions, but they won't come back.'

'I hope you're right.'

'If I'm wrong, we've had it anyway,' said Howard grimly. 'But we could still turn this convoy to our advantage. We'll catch it up and tag along behind it until just short of Tharthar airstrip, as planned. If we come to a roadblock, we'll go through it as part of the convoy.'

Bourne nodded and increased speed. Fifteen minutes later, they caught up with the convoy. Bourne maintained station 400 yards behind the last vehicle. At this rate it would take another hour, he thought, before they reached the turnoff.

Beside him, Howard was thinking hard. Something about that air strike, he thought, smelt very wrong. Very wrong indeed.

THE LONG CONVOY'S PROGRESS had been reported and monitored by the JSTARS; initially, Kearwin had been worried that the two vehicles would slip away from the big building and get lost among the hundreds of other vehicles.

Sorensen came in just after 12.30, straight from the NSC meeting, looking flustered. He hurried over to Kearwin's desk. 'John, are we sure those cars are still in there?'

'Sure as can be, Walter.'

'Right. I want you to keep a real close eye on that building for the next twenty minutes. And I want a good shot of it from the first Keyhole pass after thirteen hundred hours. That's twenty hundred in Iraq. OK?'

'Sure thing.' Kearwin began tapping in instructions, setting up a 'bounce' by a KH-11 at 13.05. He glanced up at the Walrus, who was still standing beside him, a preoccupied expression on his face. Kearwin studied him curiously. 'How did the meeting go, Walter?'

'Don't ask, John. Don't ask.' The Walrus shook his head.

Kearwin smiled to himself and turned his eyes back to the screen.

At 12.42, the JSTARS scan showed movement at the building. The Walrus jumped to his feet and came hurrying across to Kearwin's station again. 'Are you sure?'

'Yep. See for yourself. Two vehicles. They've stopped by that hut.'

Five minutes later, they saw the vehicles move off. 'They've made it!' exclaimed the Walrus with a broad grin, as the trace showed the vehicles drawing clear of the warehouse. 'Just in time!'

'Walter?' asked Kearwin, now consumed with curiosity. 'Would you mind telling me what is going on here?'

'Never mind, John-boy,' said the Walrus. 'You just take another look at that building.'

Twenty seconds later, the on-screen picture of the warehouse dissolved in confusion; it seemed to take a long time to clear. When it did, the building had disappeared.

'It . . . it blew up!' said Kearwin, his voice suddenly shaky. 'I don't believe it! It just blew up!'

'Exactly,' said the Walrus. 'Now, if you'll get back to monitoring the Land Cruisers' progress, I've got a phone call to make. I'm gonna enjoy this,' he added. 'Oh, boy!' He stomped off, chuckling.

HARRIS AND PALMER chatted easily for the first ninety minutes out of Jiddah, Palmer gradually relaxing in the passenger seat after the tension of the close shave back at the Sheraton. 'Mel, if you don't mind, I'm going to get some shuteye for a couple of hours, hey? It was a long drive and I only got two hours last night at stops along the way. You OK to carry on?'

'I'm fine; I've had all the rest I need. You go ahead and sleep.'

'Watch out for camels,' said Palmer. 'They wander across the road and they're hard to spot. There's the BBC World Service on the radio on those three buttons there, and Radio Israel on the right-hand one. You'll have to hunt around from time to time to get the best frequency for the World Service. Wake me in a couple of hours or so.'

AT 21.05, just as Ray Sullivan's flight was about to take off for Bangkok, Howard spotted the turning off to the right. The track looked reasonable, and the GPS confirmed their position. As the two ambulances turned off the main road, the taillights of the convoy carried on away from them, disappearing into the darkness.

'That's it,' said Howard. 'Now for the last leg. It should be fairly open to start with, but the nearer we get to the Tigris the more risk there'll be of being seen.'

By 23.00 Howard calculated that they were no more than ten miles from their destination. The vehicles slowed to a crawl. The signs of civilisation were becoming more frequent now and at 23.20, as they breasted a rise, they saw off in the distance the light of a car or truck moving from left to right, heading south towards Baghdad.

127

'That open rocky area should be just up ahead on the left. About another half-mile.' Howard was now using the large-scale satellite-generated map, which showed the ground in detail. By the dim green glow of a beta-light he saw that they were very near the place he had picked out as a lay-up point. Three minutes later, he said, 'Here.'

Bourne slowly turned left off the track and picked his way carefully through the rocks and scrub. The second Land Cruiser followed. After ten minutes, a building appeared on the skyline 400 yards in front of them. Howard got out of the vehicle and was joined by Ziegler. Without speaking, the two men moved off on foot.

Twenty minutes later, they returned. 'It's perfect, Johnny,' Howard reported. 'We can get the Land Cruisers into that enclosure. It's just a wall surround, no roof on it. Completely deserted, and no sign that anyone's been there recently. Let's get moving.'

'THEY'VE DEFINITELY STOPPED, Walter.' Kearwin was categoric. 'They haven't moved for thirty minutes now. I'm sure this is a planned halt. It's half past midnight out there now.'

The Walrus tweaked his moustache thoughtfully and nodded his head. 'They're about a mile short of that main north–south highway. Maybe they'll go on to Baghdad tomorrow.' He pondered the possibilities, then decided there was little point in speculating. 'OK. What's this town here? Just the other side of that highway?'

Kearwin looked on the map. 'It's called Tikrit. That mean anything to you?'

'Nope. I'd better go call on the Director. Maybe he'll come up with a slant on it. Meanwhile, you keep an eye on them.'

'OK,' ANNOUNCED HOWARD in a low voice, 'we'll be off. Johnny, make sure you check before first light for wheelmarks. And get some sleep, you hear? You look just about all in.'

'I'll sleep in the morning, Ed. See you in about thirty-six hours, OK?'

Howard, MacDonald and Ziegler were assisted in lifting their heavy packs onto their backs. MacDonald nearly staggered under the huge weight; 120 pounds if it was an ounce, he thought. With a brief wave behind them, the three men set off, plodding slowly down the incline towards the highway.

Bourne turned to Ackford and Usher. 'OK, boys, we've got a lot to do. Let's start by getting all that muck off the vehicles.'

Elbow grease, assisted by liberal applications of white spirit, cut through the oily mess that had covered the vehicles. The matt-green top coat of paint proved easier to remove than expected.

Once they had finished cleaning and polishing, they emptied the vehicles and cleaned out the interiors. While Usher went off to relieve Bourne on guard, Ackford began to replace broken light fittings and cracked windows, using spare parts taken from the fourth Land Cruiser. The red filters on the revolving roof lights were replaced with blue ones; only the IR filters on the spotlights were left. A pole was attached to a vertical clamp at the rear of each vehicle; then Ackford produced a flat package containing two new sets of number plates, a new set of stickers and two large flags.

'We'll leave the flags till just before we go, Tony,' said Bourne. 'Let's get the stickers on, then put the camouflage nets up and get some of that thorn scrub over the top as well.'

He looked at his watch. It was 04.00.

HOWARD HAD BEEN WORRIED about crossing the highway, but in the event they negotiated it without incident. Waiting in the shadows beneath the roadside bank, they watched and listened. After a little while there was a long gap in the traffic; they climbed onto the road together and walked across quickly, disappearing into the cover of some palm trees on the far side.

Through the night-vision goggles the scene ahead was strikingly different to the emptiness of the rocky outcrop where they had left the vehicles. It was an area of cultivation, of palm trees and orchards and fields and small, scattered groups of houses. The night felt warmer than the previous one; MacDonald guessed that this was because they were at a lower altitude, having descended into the Tigris valley.

After an hour and a half, they were approaching the town; Howard began to skirt round it to the south. Gradually, the ground began to rise in front of them. By 03.00 they had reached the top of a shallow incline, which stretched obliquely away from Tikrit to the south. From the ridge they could see the town spread out beneath them and, beyond it, the lights of the Sahra military air base.

Howard, stopping to check his GPS receiver and the map more frequently now, began to move closer to the town of Tikrit, working his way along the deserted ridge. A large open area came into view. It was just inside the town boundary and surrounded on three sides by buildings; it looked to MacDonald like a very large town square— almost an arena, he thought. On the far side, nearest the town centre, was a structure lit up by spotlights.

Howard had stopped again. 'OK,' he breathed to MacDonald and Ziegler, 'by my reckoning, this is just about it. Mac, get the range-finder set up and give me the exact distance to that spotlit wall.'

Gratefully, the three men unburdened themselves of their heavy loads. MacDonald erected the short tripod and assembled the range-finder. He slowly moved the instrument round on its pivot until the wall came into view. With a start, MacDonald saw that there was a giant portrait painted on the brightly lit wall; he instantly recognised the smiling, benevolent-looking features of Saddam Hussein. Lining the split-image picture up on one edge of the wall, he turned the drum until the line was unbroken, then he read the distance off the scale. 'Twelve hundred and ninety,' he whispered to Howard.

'Good,' said Howard. 'This will do as our main position. Mike, you and Danny find the best spot within twenty yards forward of here, and I'll go back about a hundred yards and pick our secondary.'

Ziegler spent some time prowling around the area immediately in front of them. Eventually he beckoned to MacDonald, who came over to check the line of view down to the area below. He nodded his satisfaction. They went back to retrieve the packs and move them forward to the place they had selected. Then they unpacked a large groundsheet and a spade each and began to dig.

They completed the first hide when it was still dark. Only when Howard was persuaded that it was satisfactory did they move back up the slope to the secondary position; Howard and MacDonald set to work while Ziegler went off to put out the anemometers.

He returned an hour later; he had found places for two out of the three, at distances 450 and 800 yards from the front hide. The first was on an upper branch of a tall, bare thorn tree, and the second, as close as he had dared to approach to the arena, at the top of an electricity pole. 'Sorry, Danny, but there just wasn't anywhere to put the third anemometer.'

'We'll have to make do with the two of them,' MacDonald shrugged.

By the time they had finished digging the second hide and had covered it over and camouflaged it with scrub, the first glimmers of dawn were beginning to appear. Clearing away any visible trace of their presence, they made their way back down the slope to the first hide, nearer the arena.

Ziegler remained outside as Howard and MacDonald crawled in; he scoured the area minutely, brushing over their footprints and removing any sign that anyone had ever been there. Finally, he crawled in himself, pulling the hatch cover into place behind him.

MacDonald admitted to himself that he was tired. It had been hard work, true, but all his life he had been used to hard work. It was something more—tension. He would have been less than human if he had not been a bit frightened of what he had got himself into. He glanced at his two companions. Ziegler was already asleep, still and soundless. Howard lay motionless on his front, gazing out of one of the observation slits towards the arena. He had taken the first watch. His face looked unearthly, covered as it was by streaks of brown and black camouflage cream, his eyes glittering in the pale orange light of daybreak. MacDonald knew he himself must look equally strange.

'Try and get a bit of sleep, Danny,' Howard whispered. 'It's going to be like an oven in here when the sun gets up.'

'I'll try.' MacDonald lay back, looking at the ceiling of the hide. What was it Usher had told him? *Keep smiling.* That was it. Don't take it too seriously—always find the funny side; it's the only way to survive. Bob had been right. Humour was the antidote to fear, even to disaster. Gradually, MacDonald began to relax; twenty minutes later, he was asleep.

BRENT SCOWCROFT DRUMMED his fingers on the table, frowning. 'So the British have come up with nothing on this guy Dartington?'

'Apparently not, Mr Chairman,' said Robert Gates, Director of the CIA. 'He has been interviewed by the British Secret Intelligence Service in the Bahamas. I have the full details if you need them, but suffice it to say that he has a perfectly adequate explanation for what looked like some incriminating documentation. However, the British will continue to monitor his every move.'

'Hmm,' said Scowcroft thoughtfully. 'Well, please keep me informed. He turned to Martin Faga. 'Has the National Reconnaissance Office got any news about where these people have got to?'

Faga laid out the large composite photograph of Tikrit on the table, and the others gathered round. A red blob marked the location of the vehicles. Faga said, 'Tikrit is Saddam's home town. And the day after tomorrow is his birthday. It could be that he will put in a public appearance there to boost his image. At any rate,' he shrugged, 'these men seem to have some idea that he will.'

Gates chipped in again, glancing across at Faga and nodding. 'I would support that view. The Iraqi News Agency announced this evening that there would be birthday celebrations again this year. They did not, however, specifically say that Saddam would be going to Tikrit. These people could be acting on a hunch, but I do not believe they are. It would be extremely interesting to know where they obtained their information.'

'Does it matter?' asked Scowcroft. 'If we know they are there, we could launch another missile strike.'

'I have considered the idea,' replied Faga, 'but in short, I think we may already be too late. We do not have the capability to track individual humans by satellite. A missile strike might destroy the vehicles, but the only probable result of cutting off their escape route would be that they would subsequently be caught. We already know that at least one of them is an American citizen. What if he were caught and paraded in front of the Iraqi television cameras?'

Scowcroft quickly realised the appalling propaganda implications. Aghast, he stared at the DNRO.

General Burnside broke the silence, his voice calm and low. 'Mr Faga is right. The actual assassination team will have left the vehicles already. It's early morning in Iraq right now; they'll have moved into position, ready for tomorrow.'

'That makes sense to me,' said Scowcroft gloomily. 'So what do you gentlemen recommend that I tell the President?'

'I think,' said Faga, 'that the best thing the President can do right now is to hope that this attempt fails for some reason, but that the assassins manage to escape.'

'All the way back to Saudi Arabia,' said Gates, 'where we can get our hands on them.'

'OH, HELLO, SIR; I wasn't expecting you back.' Detective Inspector Juliet Shelley raised her head in surprise as Hughie Carter came into the room. He looked exhausted, rumpled and cross.

'There's not much more I can do there for the time being,' said the detective superintendent with a yawn. 'Bloody wild-goose chase, if you ask me. How are things here?'

'Oh, pretty quiet. No problems at all, really.' She hesitated, choosing her words. 'Sir,' she went on, 'you look tired. Why don't you go home and get some rest? I can handle things here.'

'Can't,' said Carter briefly. 'I've got to stay on call here— immediate notice. But maybe I'll crash out on the couch for a while.'

'I'll get you a cup of coffee, sir,' said Juliet decisively, standing up. 'Would you like anything else with it?'

'Oh, thanks. Maybe a biscuit or something.'

Juliet left the room. Five minutes later, she was back upstairs in Carter's office with a tray. The detective superintendent was sitting on the couch. He looked up in amazement as she pulled over a coffee table and set the tray down in front of him. 'Hell, Juliet, I . . .'

'Come on, sir, get it down you. You look as if you need it.'

Carter cast his eyes down at the plate of bacon, egg, sausage and tomato. Suddenly, he realised that he was hungry. He began to eat, motioning to Juliet to sit down on a chair opposite him. In between mouthfuls, he grumbled gently about how he had been run ragged for the previous twenty-four hours. 'Not a single clue, would you believe? Clean as a whistle they left that place.'

'What's the panic all about, sir?' Juliet asked curiously.

'Terrorist group, so we've been told,' replied Carter indistinctly through sausage and egg. He snorted. 'Hah. What sort of terrorist sets up an op here, then takes off for the Middle East? Should be the other bloody way round, shouldn't it? Anyway, why should we mind if they go and blow up the Saudi royal palace, or whatever it is they're up to? Dose of their own medicine,' he rattled on, waving his knife.

'Saudi Arabia?' asked Juliet, puzzled. She felt a twinge of alarm. Johnny was out there. 'Why there?'

'Search me, girl,' said Carter, swallowing another gulp of coffee. 'Two men turned up there on April eighth, posing as construction workers. One English, one South African. There were others, including some blokes who smuggled themselves there in a sea container.'

Juliet had stopped listening. Her mind raced. That date—April 8. An Englishman, and others. Johnny left on April 7—he would have arrived on the morning of the 8th . . . Her mind went back, searching for inconsistencies, for something wrong. But her sudden rush of suspicion was ridiculous, she told herself. OK, Johnny hadn't talked much about his work, but the idea that he might be involved in *terrorism*? Never in a thousand years! She forced her voice to remain calm. 'You said they left their base here clean—no clues?'

'About as clean as you can get. No dabs, no hairs, no fibres—nothing. Just a couple of spots of paint on the floor.'

'Paint?' Juliet tripped the word off her tongue as lightly as she could manage; her stomach was like lead.

'Yeah. It'll probably match up with the container.'

'How do you mean?' she asked, barely audibly.

'The container they used to smuggle some of their colleagues out to Saudi,' Carter explained, chewing on a piece of bacon. 'Apparently, they cut a doorway in it and then painted over the cracks. Yellow paint—it'll probably match up when we get the samples back.'

Juliet's head swam. Her knuckles went white as she gripped the arms of her chair. With an effort she got to her feet, then stood for a moment, swaying. 'Excuse me, sir,' she said. 'I must just go and finish something off next door.' She turned, holding onto the back of the chair for support, and launched herself towards the door. It seemed miles away, at the end of a dark tunnel.

Yellow paint, she thought numbly. That mark on the jeans Johnny left at the cleaners. That was yellow paint.

MACDONALD AWOKE to hear a slight *twang*. He was about to sit up when he remembered the low roof. He turned his head to one side and saw Ziegler crouched in front of one of the side observation slits, a catapult in his hand. There was a bleat and the noise of something scampering away.

'Damn goats,' muttered the American.

It was airless and stifling in the hide. The only ventilation consisted of the horizontal observation slits. Howard was still awake, lying on his front and gazing down towards the arena. MacDonald looked at his watch. He had slept for five hours; it was nearly midday.

'Danny?' Howard whispered. 'I think we can leave Mike to defend us from the goats for a while.' He grinned and pointed through the front observation slit. 'There's some action down there.'

MacDonald rolled over onto his stomach and looked out of the slit. There were signs of activity. He reached for his binoculars and examined the scene.

All around the big square men were erecting flagpoles and hanging bunting. Huge Iraqi flags now decorated the buildings.

'Take a look at the far side, just in front of Saddam's picture,' said Howard. 'Here—have a look through the spotter scope.'

MacDonald put his eye to the scope. The scene, magnified sixty times, leaped into view. Just in front of the picture wall, sections of a large wooden platform were being unloaded from lorries. A team of soldiers was bolting the sections together; gradually the platform took shape. As MacDonald looked on, white-painted sections of a second, smaller structure were carried onto the platform and positioned in its centre.

MacDonald handed the spotter scope back to Howard, who immediately took in the set-up. 'Bingo,' he said quietly. 'A saluting rostrum. And in just about the right place, too. Let's get an exact range on it now.'

Manoeuvring the large cylindrical range-finder into place at the observation slit was a clumsy business, but after about ten minutes MacDonald had it mounted securely on its low tripod. He lined the split image up on the white edge of the rostrum and turned the dial; gradually, the two halves of the image came together. When he was satisfied, he read off the distance on the scale. 'One thousand, two hundred and forty-two yards.'

MacDonald reached for the little portable computer and switched it on. Practice at Badanah, with further guidance from Usher, had made him proficient with the ballistics programme.

'OK, let's do a little practice run,' said Howard. 'Wind speed,' he read off the little electronic panel beside him, 'one knot, right to left. Barometer, nine hundred and eighty-nine millibars. Humidity, eighty per cent. Air temperature, thirty-one degrees.'

MacDonald read off the scale for 1,242 yards. 'If I left the zero settings I did at twelve hundred yards, the bullet would go twenty-nine inches low and ten inches to the left. So it needs ten clicks up on the elevation drum and three clicks to the right on windage.'

'I think we're in business, Danny,' said Howard with a fierce grin.

Behind them there was another soft *twang* from the catapult. 'Damn goats,' growled Ziegler.

Chapter 10

The black rage had descended on him again.

The worse the rage became, the more it distracted him; and the more it distracted him, the worse it became. It was a brutal spiral downwards into a Stygian fury. At its worst the rage overwhelmed him, made him lash out at anything and anyone in sight.

Still just in control, the big man flickered his eyes venomously over the food set out on the long table in front of him, then towards the figure of the attendant who stood, stiff with fear, at the side of the room. Useless, worthless little creature, he thought. With a violent flail of his arm he swept the food, the plates, the glasses and the bottles away onto the floor. The echo of the breaking china and glass died away as cold, dark eyes settled menacingly on the figure by the wall. 'Your Excellency, shall I clear up the . . .'

'Get out!' The big man crashed a heavy fist down onto the table. He rose to his feet, his face crimson, shaking with wrath. The terrified servant needed no further bidding. With an anguished whimper he scuttled out of the room, closing the heavy door behind him.

Alone now, the big man aimed a ferocious kick at his chair, knocking it flying. His thoughts wandered. Tomorrow . . .

Tomorrow. It would be dark outside now, above in the streets. Tomorrow would be an important day. Action had been forced on him by circumstances, but he would turn it to his advantage, as he always did. Forced on him, he thought savagely. There had been only two alternatives: it had had to be either the Iranians or the Syrians. He hated them both. But he hated the Syrians more.

A nonaggression pact. He had been left with no practical alternative but to propose the initiative. The economy was in desperate trouble. There had to be an agreement with one of them, before they both combined to squeeze him dry. The Iranian lackey would sign tomorrow in Tikrit.

But neither the minion nor his masters in Tehran could be trusted. Well, he had already taken precautions for tomorrow. If there was a plot, it would fail, as all the others had. Did they think he was so stupid? Well, they would find out that he wasn't. Tomorrow . . .

Deep in the labyrinth of bunkers beneath the streets of Baghdad, Saddam Hussein continued to pace, alone in the darkness.

EVENTUALLY, TO EVERYONE'S RELIEF, the temperature in the hide had begun to fall. The cooler night air sucked the heat from the ground, from the roof of the hide. Howard was at last taking some rest in the well of the hide. Ziegler had taken his place, next to MacDonald. Below, in the town, most of the movement had ceased. Lights still burned and small fires were to be seen on the outer fringes, in the scattered encampments of the soldiers who had been working in the arena.

It had been a day of constant alertness, of tension. Danny had sensed that the other two were feeling it too, although it hadn't prevented them from snatching occasional periods of sleep.

Oddly, it had also been a day of almost stupefying boredom. There was nothing to do except watch the scenery—the same scenery, hour after hour—or eat, drink or sleep. MacDonald was a patient man, but the monotony had become almost too much for him. He wondered how his companions, men who thrived on action, could bear it. It was the waiting.

THE THREE MEN in the hide heard the grinding screech of the tanks long before they saw the tanks themselves. By now, down in the arena, thousands of people had gathered. Foot soldiers stood in massed ranks towards the front and sides of the arena, facing the platform and its white rostrum. In the centre of the arena, an area set aside for civilians began to fill up; the citizens of Tikrit had responded to the blaring calls over loudspeakers bidding them to attend the ceremony that was about to take place.

A wide area round the platform had been left clear. The din of the approaching armoured column grew even louder. Into the arena came a small convoy of wheeled scout cars. Howard was puzzled to see a black limousine among the scout cars; it was ushered into place in front of them and stopped. A small pennant was hanging from a miniature flagstaff on the bonnet of the limousine, but it was too tiny for Howard to make out what it was.

A fifty-strong contingent of purposeful-looking soldiers appeared to be controlling operations. 'Presidential bodyguard,' Howard breathed softly. 'It's happening. Danny, get ready.'

MacDonald slipped the big rifle from its padded case and laid it out, its muzzle peeping through the front slit of the hide. From his breast pocket, he took out the wallet of ammunition and laid it down next to the rifle's barrel. He ran through the weather checks with Howard, entering the details swiftly into the computer.

At eight in the morning it was still relatively cool. 'Nineteen centigrade,' whispered Howard. 'Warming up. Set it for twenty, Danny. That's sixty-nine Fahrenheit. Better make it seventy.'

'Wind?'

'Not a breath. Dead calm!'

MacDonald finished entering the settings. The computer gave the trajectory. He began adjusting the clicks on the telescopic sight's elevation drum. Howard was loading film into the long-lensed camera mounted on its squat tripod next to him.

The line of tanks thundered into the arena, fanning out to either side. The spectacle was awesome, even to the three men in the hide twelve hundred yards away. The roaring of the engines seemed to continue for many minutes; then it began to abate.

The men in the hide took in the scene. Tanks and armoured troop carriers encircled the huge crowd. MacDonald could only guess at the number of men—10,000, he reckoned, possibly more. He was beginning to make an estimate of the number of tanks when his ears registered a clattering noise.

'Helicopter approaching!' Howard's voice was tight with tension.

The big helicopter came skimming in over the town. Over the arena it banked round abruptly and started to hover, descending slowly into the open space to the right of the platform. At a hundred feet above the ground the rotors began to raise the dust, and Howard saw the massed foot soldiers and civilians clutch at their headgear, their clothing whipped by the downdraught from the rotor blades. Then the helicopter's engine slowed. Howard saw the door of the limousine open. A small man in black robes and a turban stepped out and walked towards the aircraft, escorted by an aide. 'Looks like one of those Iranian ayatollahs,' muttered Howard. 'What's he doing here? I thought the Iranians and Saddam were mortal enemies.' The Iranian stood outside the rotor circle as the blades slowed.

The noise of the engine winding down reached the three men in the hide. When the rotor blades came to a stop the helicopter door opened and a burly figure in olive-green uniform and a black beret climbed out, followed by three other uniformed men. The guard-detail commander called his waiting men to attention and snapped off a salute. The burly man acknowledged him briefly, then walked past and approached the Iranian. There was a handshake and a swift, passionless embrace between the two men. The Iranian fell in with the retinue, following a few paces behind the big man.

Howard kept his eye tight against the spotter scope, following the big man's progress. He had seen the face in photographs and newsreel clips countless times before; now he gazed at the man with a sense of unreality. 'OK, it's him,' he whispered fiercely to MacDonald. 'Get ready. Wait till he gets up on that rostrum. Ziggy, all clear?'

Ziegler was still covering the rear of the hide against the approach of any intruder. 'Yeah, clear,' he answered tersely. 'Go ahead.'

MacDonald gradually eased himself into his firing position. He drew back the bolt of the rifle and gently fed the large brass case of the cartridge forward with his thumb. It clinked softly as it slid into place in the chamber. 'I'll need absolute quiet and no movement at all, please,' he said to Howard and Ziegler. 'I have to concentrate.'

The burly figure of the Iraqi President mounted the platform and walked towards the rostrum. The assembled crowd fell silent. Slowly he mounted the steps of the rostrum. The Iranian and his aide had taken up a position on the platform to the right of the rostrum with the President's retinue on the left. The figure of Saddam Hussein raised his right arm to acknowledge the salute of the gathered troops below.

Behind the spotter scope, Howard's face suddenly creased with worry. 'There's something wro—'

The crash of the rifle shook the hide as MacDonald fired. He was reloading swiftly. 'I said quiet, damn it!' he shouted angrily at Howard. 'Watch for the strike!'

The big bullet took nearly two seconds to travel across the open ground towards its target. The motor drive on the camera, activated by Howard, began to whirr noisily. Both Howard and MacDonald were watching through their telescopes; suddenly they saw the burly figure on the rostrum lifted violently off his feet, as though by an unseen force. He was spun round and flung backwards, crumpling below the steps of the rostrum, dead.

The men on the platform stood frozen in shock. One of Saddam's aides drew his pistol and held it aloft, as if ready to fire. In the crowd, the first shrieks of alarm broke out.

Crash. The big rifle fired again. Howard and Ziegler were taken completely by surprise. They seemed to hear MacDonald yell 'Allah!' at the top of his lungs.

'What the hell . . .' Howard turned furiously on MacDonald. 'Stop it! What the hell are you doing?'

MacDonald was still watching through his scope, his eyes ablaze. As he watched, the second bullet hit the aide with the pistol, low in the stomach. The man suddenly doubled up and fell to the floor, writhing. MacDonald's eyes were now triumphant.

'Mac, for God's sake!' bellowed Howard. 'Stop now. Just stop!

That wasn't Saddam, I'm telling you! It wasn't him!'

MacDonald turned to him. 'What do you mean? He's dead! I hit him smack in the middle of the chest. Look for yourself, man!'

Down below in the arena, pandemonium had broken out. People in the crowd were shouting and screaming in confusion and panic. The Presidential bodyguard, as confused and panicked as the rest, had begun firing their weapons at random into the crowd. The Iranian diplomat was grabbed by two men from the bodyguard and wrestled to the ground, his arms yanked up viciously behind his back, his face forced down into the dust.

Boom! The ground shook as a tongue of grey-black smoke erupted from the barrel of a T-72 tank at the left-hand side of the arena. The 125mm shell screeched over the heads of the terrified crowd and the unarmed conscript soldiers. The firing from the bodyguard slackened as they looked round in bewilderment.

'OK, let's get out of here,' said Ziegler, calmly. 'I don't fancy stickin' around to watch the goddamn celebrations.'

'No!' snapped Howard, his eye still fixed to the spotter scope. 'Wait. I'm telling you, that was not Saddam! He wasn't wearing a pistol. He always has a pistol. That must have been a double. We have to wait.'

All three of them now turned to watch the scene. At the side of the arena, heavy steel doors crashed open as a hundred men of the Presidential bodyguard emerged from a line of personnel carriers. After assembling into a disciplined body they approached the saluting platform on the double. The officer in charge shouted a harsh order. His men fanned out, their weapons trained on the men of the first guard detail around the platform. The original bodyguard troops slowly put down their weapons and raised their hands.

When the commander was satisfied that everything was as he wished, he barked out another order. Six men accompanied him as he marched briskly away to the T-72 tank and stood stiffly to attention.

The turret hatch on the tank swung slowly up; the man inside began to lever himself out. His face, below a black beret, came into view; it was smouldering with fury and malice.

Saddam Hussein climbed heavily down from the tank and dusted off his uniform shirt with an elaborate gesture. For a few seconds he stood by the vehicles, staring malevolently around him, his eyes blinking. Inch by inch he unfastened his holster and drew his pistol, cocking the action. There was silence. The bodyguard commander and his men wilted beneath the menacing glare of the tyrant. He waved them aside with his pistol and advanced steadily towards the platform in the arena. The bodyguard fell in at his side as he swaggered through the crowd of people still prostrate on the ground.

Saddam took his time. He spun it out, well aware of the terrifying effect of his appearance. The man's presence was colossal and unmistakable. He reached the platform and glanced briefly at his dead lookalike, and then at the wounded aide, who was still alive and moaning in agony. He spat out an order to the guard commander.

Two soldiers unceremoniously dragged the Iranian diplomat towards the Iraqi President. They flung him down at Saddam's feet. Saddam shot the Iranian in the back of the head. The corpse was dragged away.

The commander of the original guard detachment was next. He too was hauled before the President, writhing and babbling in terror and desperation. Again Saddam's pistol fired; the man collapsed dead.

One by one, the men from the first guard detachment were brought forward for execution. Almost imperceptibly, MacDonald stiffened. Sensing that he was about to fire, Howard and Ziegler held themselves absolutely motionless and watched in fascination.

MacDonald gazed through the telescopic sight. Out of the corner of his eye he saw the shimmer of rising air at the bottom of the sight picture drift slightly off to the left. A very slight wind, he thought. Instinctively, he aimed off a foot to the right. The cross wires of the telescopic sight aligned on the right-hand edge of Saddam Hussein's body. MacDonald squeezed the trigger.

The big rifle bucked in MacDonald's shoulder once more, and the bullet streaked towards its target. What made the shot go low was uncertain. A sudden downdraught of air somewhere along its route, an infinitesimal difference in the bullet weight or the powder load, the minutest flinch by MacDonald, or the fact that the rifle barrel was now hot from the first two shots: MacDonald would never know.

Saddam Hussein was standing stock-still on the platform, his right arm outstretched downwards with the pistol ready to fire at the man sprawled at his feet. The bullet smashed against the barrel of Saddam's pistol and ricocheted off the metal slide. The pistol flew out of his hand and the bullet spun sideways on into the lower part of Saddam's pelvic bone. The bone shattered where the bullet hit it, and Saddam let out a piercing howl and sat down heavily.

The weight of his body on the cracked pelvis was instant agony, and he fell back on the platform, drawing his knees up and clutching his hands between his legs. Blood seeped through his fingers and torn uniform trousers onto the wooden platform. Those standing near him drew back in horror, and the man who had been on the point of being shot scrambled frantically away.

For just one second there was dead silence except for Saddam's noises of distress; then all hell broke loose. The condemned men of the first Presidential guard detachment, seeing their chance, broke free of their shocked captors and scrabbled for their weapons. The second detachment recovered in time to shoot down a number of them, but many managed to grab AKs and turn them on their rivals. A full-scale battle between the two factions of the bodyguard broke out around the platform. In less than a minute, more than sixty members of the bodyguard lay dead or wounded.

Among the conscript soldiers watching helplessly was a regiment of the Iraqi artillery. They were the remains of three entire artillery divisions from the 1991 Gulf War, practically wiped out by American B-52 bombing in the days preceding the land assault by the Allies. Any spirit these men had once had was broken; they were listless and brutalised, and in some cases mentally unhinged. They had been reorganised into a single regiment; an injection of new officers from the Iraqi Republican Guard, drafted in after the war to restore morale, had had little effect. The men's loathing of warfare remained, and to a man they had focused their unspoken hatred on the one individual they saw as responsible for their suffering. Saddam had indeed been wise not to allow such soldiers to be armed on occasions such as this.

Along with the thousands of Tikriti civilians, these men had scattered in panic when the firing from the Presidential bodyguard had begun raking through the crowd. Used to the perpetual, numbing barbarity of their existence, they would probably have offered no resistance even if they themselves had been lined up, one by one, for execution. Except that this time, there was one extraordinary difference. The sight of the dictator himself, lying in agony on the platform, seared itself into their minds. They gaped at him in utter disbelief. Then a young corporal started giggling.

Within seconds others had joined in. The laughter became hysterical. Tears of frenzied hilarity and rage swept through the ranks of the conscripts. Somewhere within these men the last spark of spirit was rekindled. Slowly, at first, and then in a sudden rush, they rose up and threw themselves with deadly purpose on the men of the Presidential bodyguard.

The townspeople of Tikrit rose too. Brainwashed, bereaved, impoverished and starved by the policies of the ruler who had risen to brutal power from their own humble town, they too had seen the dictator lying helpless and humiliated on the platform. The Traitor of Tikrit! They converged on him, fury in their hearts.

Howard, MacDonald and Ziegler had been watching the spectacle unfold, unable to wrest their eyes from the tide of chaotic violence.

'What the hell are they doing now?' Howard muttered to himself.

A small group of civilians had commandeered an army Jeep, and were driving it into the centre of the arena. It was soon surrounded by a tumult of yelling people, waving and gesticulating excitedly. After a minute or so, the crowd parted to form a passage for the Jeep, which started forward. For a moment or two, the three men in the hide could see nothing. The roaring chant of the crowd reached their ears. *'Sahhl! Sahhl! Sahhl!'*

The Jeep began circling the arena. Behind it, tied by the feet and being towed by a rope along the ground, was Saddam Hussein.

'Lord!' breathed MacDonald. They watched open-mouthed as the screaming figure was dragged along at speed, flayed and lacerated by the stones on the hard ground.

'Time to go,' said Howard.

The three men hurriedly began packing equipment into the rucksacks. MacDonald stowed the big rifle in its sleeve, and then pocketed the empty cases of the three rounds he had fired. Ziegler crawled out of the hide and kept watch to the rear. Then they headed back to the vehicles. Behind them, the death screams of Saddam Hussein seemed to rise high above the exultant roar of the crowd, and then fade.

IT WAS 01.35 IN WASHINGTON when the first unusual Keyhole picture came through. It indicated sources of unusual heat in the arena, along with some smoke obfuscation.

Kearwin did an analysis of the heat sources. 'Walter, there are six vehicles on fire!' He spoke rapidly, his voice rising. 'Look at this little Jeep here going round and round. Here's the helicopter. The rest is all military tanks, scout cars. It's chaos down there. They must have killed him, or tried to.'

'I agree. That leaves just one question, doesn't it?' The Walrus spoke in a low voice, almost to himself. 'Is Saddam still alive?'

'He's dead, Walter,' Kearwin replied without hesitation. 'The helicopter hasn't moved. If Saddam was alive, he would have got out pretty fast once the trouble started, wouldn't he? Nothing has got out. He's dead. They did it!' Kearwin's voice had risen to an excited shout. There was an outbreak of unrestrained cheering from the others in the room.

The Walrus held up his hands. 'Quiet!' he bellowed. 'You still have a job to do here. I still want those men to be shadowed. I'm relying on you not to lose them. You've done well so far, and I know I can rely on you to keep it up. Now, get to it!'

THE THREE MEN made little attempt to avoid being seen on the way back to the vehicles. Howard had decided that speed was more important than concealment. Dressed in dishevelled and dirty Arab clothing, they carried the rucksacks slung over their shoulders, instead of wearing them conventionally. The AKMSs were concealed beneath their robes, their stocks folded. The only large item was the big AW rifle; MacDonald, without a rucksack, carried this slung across one shoulder with a bundle of sticks, to make it look as though he was carrying firewood.

In the event, they came across few people, and at 09.20 they breasted the rise and approached the walled enclosure. As they drew near, Howard's simple thumbs-up told the others all they needed to know; the three men were greeted with broad grins and pumping handshakes. Usher remained on guard while Bourne directed them to three large bowls full of clean water; stripping off their dirty clothes, they began washing off the accumulated filth of their thirty-hour stay in the Tikrit hide.

'Well, I think someone ought to put up a sign for this country sayin' UNDER NEW MANAGEMENT,' whispered Ziegler with a grin as he soaped himself down. 'Mind you, I don't suppose anyone's figured out yet who's goin' to be takin' the job on. Nasty end, Saddam had.'

'What happened?' asked Bourne eagerly, laying out three sets of clean clothing.

'Well, our Scotchman gets the first guy clean through the ticker. Trouble is, he's not the real Saddam, see? Then Mac gets a bit overenthusiastic,' confided Ziegler, frowning at the memory and darting a glance in MacDonald's direction. 'He plugs this other guy standin' nearby, just mindin' his own business. Anyhow,' he continued, 'all hell breaks loose, with the bodyguard people loosin' off their AKs into the crowd. Then a tank pops off a couple of shells over their heads, to quieten them down a little. Then guess who climbs out of the tank? Old Saddam himself. And I'm tellin' you, this time there's no doubt about it. He takes over the show and starts shootin' a few guys with his personal handgun. That's when Mac really lets him have it.'

'Come on, you two,' said Howard, towelling himself dry and pulling on a clean shirt, 'stop gassing and let's go. Johnny, Ack, get the camouflage nets off those vehicles and put the flags up.'

All six men were ready, dressed in ordinary civilian shirts and trousers, by 09.30. Bourne, Ackford and Usher had already shaved; MacDonald, Ziegler and Howard attacked their two-week-old stubble with electric razors and watched as the camouflage nets were pulled off the two Land Cruisers. With the dirt and the top coat of matt green now gone, the two vehicles looked almost brand-new.

They mounted up, started the engines and headed down the slope and towards the main highway past Tikrit. Now that all need for concealment had passed, they drove at speed. They reached the highway at 09.45 and turned north, towards Bayji.

Seven time zones away in Washington, John Kearwin breathed a sigh of relief as the JSTARS screen picked up the movement.

THE ROAD WAS EERILY EMPTY. Behind the wheel of the lead vehicle, Bourne was visibly tense. After a while, he asked Howard, 'How long do you reckon before they put up some air cover?'

'Impossible to say,' shrugged Howard. 'With any luck, things are so confused right now that they're in a state of complete paralysis.'

'We've done nearly thirty miles from Tikrit already. Should be at Bayji soon . . . Oh, *hell*,' said Bourne as they rounded a bend in the road, 'look at that!'

Two hundred yards in front of them, the road was completely blocked with military vehicles and barriers. Armed soldiers leaped to their feet and levelled their rifles at the two Land Cruisers.

'Republican Guard,' said Bourne. 'Hundreds of them. OK, is it going to be you or me?'

'My turn,' replied Howard, 'but you'd better come along just in case. Danny, you stay in the car.' The vehicles rolled to a stop in front of the barriers. Howard and Bourne slowly climbed out and faced the line of rifles and machine guns pointed at their chests.

MAJOR HASSAN OMAIR looked up, annoyed, as a lieutenant barged rudely into his command tent. '*Shu tureed?*' he snapped. 'And stand to attention, curse you!'

'*Inglizi.* English. They demand to see you—sir,' drawled Lieutenant Saleh Masoud with a sneer.

The major stood up, surprised. Squaring his red beret on his head, he followed his subordinate out into the sun. Two Westerners were leaning nonchalantly against the front car. The major grinned. 'You fool,' he said contemptuously. 'Have you never seen such vehicles before? Have you checked their papers? No? Well'—he waved his arm in disgust—'get back to your post, imbecile. I will do it myself.'

Lieutenant Saleh Masoud scowled and moved off, muttering under his breath.

The major walked over to the Land Cruisers and addressed the older of the two men standing by the first vehicle. '*Sabaah al-khayr,*' he said. 'Good morning.'

The tall man allowed his companion to answer on both their behalves. '*Sabaah an-noor,*' came the second man's fluent rejoinder; he continued with a polite expression of hope that the major was well, then finally introduced himself and his tall colleague.

'I congratulate you on your command of our language, Sayyid Bourne,' said the major in Arabic. 'It will make our conversation much easier. May I examine your credentials and those of your colleagues?'

'Certainly, Major,' replied Bourne, continuing in Arabic. 'We have all the necessary documentation in the other vehicle. Perhaps if you would care . . . ?' He gestured towards the second Land Cruiser; he and the major walked over to it.

Ziegler wound down the window and flashed the major a bright smile. 'Hi,' he said.

The major looked momentarily nonplussed.

'The papers, Mike,' prompted Bourne in English.

'Oh, sure,' said Ziegler, fishing under the dashboard. He produced a folder of documents and handed them through the window.

The major glanced through the papers in the folder, his face expressionless. Behind him, three soldiers had taken up station with their rifles, still suspicious of the foreigners. Underneath his seat, Ziegler's hand closed on his AKMS.

146

'Where have you come from today, Sayyid Bourne?' asked the major in a matter-of-fact tone.

'We have driven up from Baghdad, Major,' answered Bourne.

'What's he sayin', Johnny?' asked Ziegler conversationally.

'Well, Mr Bourne,' the major said pleasantly, suddenly switching to English, 'it is unfortunate for you that not only can I speak your language, but also I can read it. Furthermore, I have had occasion to examine similar papers recently. There was a Mr Kay here a few weeks ago. His papers were in order. Sadly,' he added, 'your documentation is not, shall we say, quite of the calibre of his. These papers do not authorise your presence in this part of the country.' He gave Bourne a look of unconcealed interest. 'Well, Mr Bourne?'

While the major was speaking, Ziegler had seen Howard casually inching closer, blocking the view of the soldiers behind the major. The major's hand began to move to the holster on his belt.

'Don't do it, Major,' growled Ziegler, poking the silencer of his AKMS just above the windowsill of the vehicle. 'This here is a silenced AK. It's the real thing. Don't even twitch a muscle.'

Before the major could react, Howard addressed him from behind, his voice light and affable. 'OK, Major. As my colleague says, don't do anything rash. We are all armed, and we will not hesitate to shoot if we have to. Just keep looking at those papers and listen carefully to me. We'll take things one step at a time. Do you understand?'

'Yes,' said Major Hassan Omair in a shocked whisper.

'Good. First of all, we'll try something very simple. I want you to turn round slowly and tell those three soldiers to get back to their posts. And don't even think of warning them—Mr Bourne here speaks excellent Arabic, as you have heard. One word from him and Mr Ziegler will shoot you down. Are you ready, Major?'

'Yes.'

'Good. Do it.'

The major turned round, his face a blank mask. 'You three,' he croaked at the soldiers in Arabic, 'return to your posts.'

The soldiers obeyed. Howard said, 'That was fine, Major. Now, we're going to walk slowly over to the other vehicle. When you get there, I want you to stand with your back to the front passenger door. Understood?' The major nodded, and they walked the few yards across to the other vehicle. Howard inclined his head to speak through the rear window. 'Danny, keep your AK trained on the back of the major's head. If Johnny says fire, shoot him instantly. Now, Major,' he smiled, straightening up, 'we're going to try something a little more complicated. Let me explain what you're going to do.'

MacDonald carefully trained his AK on the Iraqi officer's back. He listened as Howard continued to give instructions to the major, stopping every now and then to check that he had understood.

The major was still in a state of shock, and nodded his acquiescence. Finally, mustering his thoughts, he said, 'You cannot hope to get away with this.'

Howard's mouth was still smiling, but his eyes were not. 'We have nothing to lose, Major. I'm sure you will understand that from our point of view, death would be infinitely preferable to capture. But if we die, you will die first. There is no necessity for that to happen if you do exactly as I say. Do you understand?'

'I understand.'

'Good. Give the orders.'

Ten minutes later, the small escort convoy had been drawn up. Ackford had reversed a few yards to allow an armoured scout car to slot into place between the two Land Cruisers; two trucks, each with a complement of fifteen red-bereted Republican Guardsmen, were lined up behind. Two officers and two sergeants came over to report to the major, who began his briefing.

'These foreigners,' he said, 'have authority to proceed to the Jordanian border at Trebil. I have decided'—he managed a faint swagger of self-importance—'that in accordance with standing orders, we will accompany them to the border to make sure that they do not deviate from their route. I will travel in front, in their vehicle. The remainder of the escort will follow. Lieutenant Aziz Ali,' he continued, turning to the second officer, 'you will remain here, in charge of this position.' The officer nodded eagerly. 'We shall return tomorrow morning,' concluded the major. 'Now, get those barriers moved aside and we'll be on our way.'

As the convoy moved off behind the leading Land Cruiser, Ziegler breathed a sigh of relief. 'Jeez,' he murmured to Ackford as they followed the scout car through, 'I do believe we've pulled it off.'

MAJOR HASSAN OMAIR sat silent and brooding in the front of the Land Cruiser. He had recovered from his initial shock. He realised, too late, that he should have made some attempt to avoid what had happened, but the tall Englishman, Howard, had given him no time to think. And the other man, Bourne, spoke perfect Arabic—any attempt to warn his soldiers would have resulted in his own death; there was no doubt in his mind that they meant what they said.

Who were these spies, the major wondered, and what were they doing? Where had they got these vehicles from? Perhaps they had stolen them in Baghdad. They seemed genuine . . . The black 'UN' letters on the doors and rear would have been simple to fabricate, but not the blue flags with the white globe-and-laurel motif . . . Yes, these men must have come from Baghdad, as Bourne had said.

Or had they? The road closure extended all the way south, down to Samarra. The major's company had been ordered to the Bayji power station, to close the road to all traffic. Another company had been sent to Samarra to set up a roadblock there. With the road blocked both north and south, how had the spies managed to pass along it? They couldn't have come from Baghdad—they would have been stopped at Samarra. That meant they must have joined the road somewhere north of Samarra—at, say, ad-Dawr, or . . . Tikrit!

The blood drained from the major's face as he realised what that meant. If it was true, it explained the roadblocks. Today's celebrations . . . Saddam must have been at Tikrit—his home town. It was the only explanation. These spies must have made an attempt on the President's life! He shot a keen glance sideways at the Englishman, Bourne. There was a smile on the man's face and his eyes were bright; there was a look about him of confidence, of success.

The major decided that he was not going to let these spies get away with what they were doing. If they had disposed of Saddam, they had done Iraq a favour, in his view. Nevertheless, they must not be allowed to escape. Much as he hated Saddam, the major was an honourable man and a patriot. He had decided what he would do. At Trebil he would have a chance to act, when they had to stop at the border with Jordan.

Half an hour later, the major was taken by surprise when Bourne swung the Land Cruiser off the road and began to pick his way down towards the Euphrates. 'What are you doing?' he asked.

'The bridge at Hadithah is blown, Major. Wrecked. We have to take a ferry.'

Shortly afterwards, they arrived at the ramp, and the major saw that what Bourne had said was true. 'How did you know about the bridge?'

'Air photographs, Major.'

'I see.'

They reached the jetty at the bottom of the ramp. 'Get out of the car slowly, Major, and stand next to the door,' said Howard.

The pontoon ferry was at the far side of the river, and they waited fifteen minutes for it to arrive. It was manned by a daytime crew of five army engineers, commanded by a sergeant. The sergeant took one look at the red-bereted major and was at once attentive, ushering the vehicles politely on board the large craft.

'Don't talk to him, Major,' said Howard. 'Just tell him to get on with it and take us across.'

The sergeant was not about to ask any questions of the stony-faced major who barked the instruction at him. He had had enough trouble two days before, when it had been discovered that one of his corporals had apparently deserted.

The crossing went without a hitch, and by 13.30 they were on the open road leading to Ar Rutbah, retracing the route they had taken three nights before. Progress was slower owing to the lumbering presence of the two trucks at the rear, but Howard was well satisfied. The biggest potential problem, he thought, was the major. The man had clearly regained his wits. He would need to be watched.

'ARE YOU ABSOLUTELY certain of this?' The DNRO studied Kearwin's face closely.

'As certain as I can be, sir. They're masquerading as a United Nations inspection team. Can I show you what I've got so far?'

'Please do.' Faga leaned over the table as Kearwin spread out the series of Keyhole satellite photographs.

'Here they are at a roadblock, sir. You can see that the reflection signatures of the vehicles are different to that of the Iraqi armour. It's not much, but we checked with the CIA agent who went to the Badanah camp, and he confirmed that white gloss paint had been used. We followed them from the roadblock, using the JSTARS. We got a second Keyhole shot. Here it is. The template matches up. It's them, and they have an army escort.'

Martin Faga nodded. 'I think you're right about them pretending to be a UN team. For one thing, I can't think offhand of any other way they could have convinced the Iraqi Army that they have any business even *being* in Iraq. And there's another reason. They're breaking the oldest rule in the military book. You never, *ever* take the same route to exit enemy territory as you took to enter. They wouldn't be doing that unless they were now effectively a different outfit. The UN idea fits.'

'These people have been unorthodox right from the start,' said Kearwin. 'What you say about them breaking that rule convinces me all the more.'

Faga smiled. 'You've done a fine job with this, Kearwin. You too, Walter—and all the others involved. I'll be going to the NSC with this assessment. When they hear about the phoney UN cars, they'll probably have a fit. Anyway, thank you, and keep it up.'

THE TALL, SCRAWNY MAN sat hunched forward at the end of the table. Ugly pockmarks pitted the face below his henna-tinted red hair. His eyes flickered round the faces of his colleagues.

He noticed that they were all glancing round too; all appeared unsure, even frightened. All except the bespectacled former Foreign Minister sitting halfway down on the left; he appeared inscrutable and smiling, as always. They had been stunned when he had broken the news to them just five minutes before. The stench of terror pervaded the room like a stinking fog. But there was no time now for idle speculation as to the state of mind of any of his colleagues. He must strike hard, fast, like a snake. He must give them no chance to think, leave no room for argument.

He was already halfway there. The significance of his taking the Chair had certainly not been lost on them as they filed into the room and saw him sitting there.

As Vice-President, he was the automatic successor. But if one of the others had heard the news first, it would not have been automatic at all; perhaps he, Izzat Ibrahim, would not be sitting in the Chair now. One of them would have grabbed it—probably that diseased hyena the Deputy President.

But Sa'adi Tumah Abbas, formerly Minister of Defence and recently demoted to Presidential Military Adviser, subservient to the last, had come to him for instructions when he had heard. Izzat had known that one day he would. Had he not flattered the man, cultivated him, praised his ability? Had he not led him to believe that the Vice-President's influence counted for something? And had the dolt not believed it all? Yes.

Izzat Ibrahim addressed him direct. 'Brother Sa'adi, we are all grief-stricken to hear your report. Do you have anything to add?'

The Presidential Military Adviser looked around miserably. 'Alas, no, brother Izzat Ibrahim,' he said. 'Details are still very sketchy . . .' He began to repeat some of the information he had already given.

The Deputy President, the hyena Taha Yasin Ramadan, smacked the palm of his hand down on the table, silencing Sa'adi Tumah Abbas with a poisonous glance. 'You mean to say that this is all you can tell us? That our beloved brother the President has been assassinated and that there has been an insurrection? In *Tikrit*, of all places? What is being done about it?'

'And why was I not informed immediately?' The aggressive shout came from Hussein Kamil, Defence Minister and son-in-law of Saddam Hussein.

Sa'adi Tumah Abbas attempted convincing answers to the questions. He failed dismally; he had none. Izzat Ibrahim said nothing; sitting back in satisfaction, he allowed the man to become the focus of everyone else's rancour and dismay.

Eventually there was a lull; Izzat Ibrahim held up his hands.

'Brothers, fellow members of the Revolutionary Command Council, it is with the greatest sadness that I feel we must conclude that the report, however incomplete it appears to be, must be true. We must for the time being suppress our terrible grief, and face the fact that our beloved brother and leader, Saddam Hussein, has been the victim of a treacherous and cowardly assassination plot. There were eye-witnesses to the events in Tikrit early this morning. The commanding officer of the third regiment of the Medina division of the Republican Guard escaped, along with elements of his command staff. The men have all been interrogated and all gave the same story before being executed for cowardice. On my instructions, Tikrit has been sealed off. No information will emerge except via the divisional commander personally, and he will report direct to this council.'

Izzat allowed himself another glance at the Defence Minister, Hussein Kamil, and bared his yellowing teeth at him in a parody of a smile. 'I am sure, brother Hussein Kamil, that you will forgive me on this occasion for exercising my authority as deputy commander in chief of the armed forces without prior reference to you. Swift action was required, and attempts to contact you at midday proved unsuccessful. You had important duties to attend to, at a certain address in . . . Khulafa Street.' Izzat bared his teeth even wider; the hideous grin was now mocking. Hussein Kamil had suddenly turned a deathly pale; his mouth opened, then snapped shut.

There was silence from the others. Hussein Kamil eventually managed a response. 'You were undoubtedly correct to take the action you did, brother Izzat Ibrahim,' he spluttered.

'Thank you,' purred Izzat Ibrahim. His yellow teeth flashed again, then he turned to the others. 'So. The question to which we must now address ourselves is simple. What further action should be taken to avoid a major crisis and further upheaval? The answer is equally simple. There must be a continuity of leadership, leadership of the greatest strength. At this dreadful time, devastated as we all are, I find one shred of comfort: that you, my brothers around this table, are of the unquestioned calibre and heroic resolve to pledge your full support to the leadership that circumstances demand.' There, thought Izzat Ibrahim. He had said it. There could be no possibility that anyone had failed to grasp the implication of his words.

The first sign of dissent, when it came, was from a completely unexpected quarter. 'I imagine that none of us, brother *Vice* President,' sneered the Minister of the Interior, 'would dispute that strong leadership will be required. The question is simply one of identifying those areas of policy where strength—and experience— will need to be demonstrated.'

Izzat was taken aback. Ali Hassan al-Majid was a cousin of Saddam's, and Izzat knew exactly what he meant by his remarks. His record was horribly impressive. It was he who had ordered the gas attacks on the Kurds during 1987 and 1988, and he whom Saddam had appointed Governor of Kuwait following the 1990 invasion. Along with his henchman, Ala'a Hussein Ali, he had presided over the rape and despoliation of Iraq's 'nineteenth province'. If anyone had adequate credentials for suppressing further internal disorder, it was he. So, thought Izzat, he was making his own bid for power, was he? It wouldn't work. The dog had too many enemies—they would gang up against him to ensure that he never rose to absolute power. Izzat decided to let the others chop him down.

The hyena, Taha Yasin Ramadan, was not slow to begin the process. 'Our brother the Interior Minister,' he snarled, 'is correct in one respect: experience in the exercise of power will be required. But we are beset on all sides by enemies who will undoubtedly attempt to take advantage of the disaster that has today befallen Iraq. The leadership of Iraq would ignore the foreign dimension at its peril. Skill, and resolution in dealing harshly with all our enemies—external as well as internal—will be vital.'

'Our brother Taha has spoken well.' Startled, Izzat jerked his head round to look at the new speaker. Halfway down the table, the bland face of the former Foreign Minister—now Deputy Prime Minister— was smiling broadly beneath his heavy spectacles. 'One might almost think that he was proposing my own candidacy for the Presidency.' Tariq Aziz chuckled at his own joke; Izzat's eyes narrowed in suspicion. What was this wily old fox driving at? 'Naturally, if such an honour were to be offered to me, I would decline.' Tariq Aziz's expression became more serious. 'In truth, I believe that the office of President must, for the time being, remain unfilled.'

Izzat Ibrahim was dumbfounded. There were murmurs of bewilderment from around the table; out of the corner of his eye Izzat noticed the hyena, Taha, sit back in his chair with an air of smug satisfaction. The two of them were in league! But what were they up to?

'Not only would any deliberation regarding a replacement for the President be premature at this stage,' continued Tariq Aziz, 'but I would go further. To make such an appointment now would be to court disaster. I hasten to say,' he said with a disarming smile, 'that by this I do not mean that there are no suitable candidates among those present in this room. Far from it. No; the reason that we must not seek a new President is a far more compelling one. It is also blindingly simple.'

Izzat was completely lost. What was this grinning fox driving at?

'Any change, or even any *appearance* of change, would be utterly catastrophic,' declared Tariq Aziz emphatically. 'If it became known that our brother Saddam had been assassinated, it would be a sign that *the Presidency*, not simply the President, was vulnerable—fatally vulnerable. If, alternatively, we were to issue an announcement that he had been replaced—it would be taken as a sign of internal dissent within this council. There are enough enemies, both within Iraq and without, waiting to seize on such news. We must therefore carry on as before. No change must be apparent.' He turned to Yasin Ramadan. 'Taha, my brother,' he asked, 'how many remain of the imposing lookalikes?'

The hyena grinned. 'There are nine,' he answered. 'Of these nine, seven bear only a superficial resemblance to our late brother and leader. The remaining two were selected to undergo special surgery. The first, the lookalike Bakr Abdullah—'

'Is dead.' Izzat Ibrahim's voice was a hiss. 'He was shot this morning, along with the President.'

Shock distorted the hyena's face. 'How do you know this?'

'The same way,' snorted Izzat, 'that I knew about the assassination. The interrogation of the witnesses, of course. You will kindly explain what this reference to the lookalikes is about. What possible use can they serve now? They should be eliminated.'

'On the contrary,' the hyena spat back at him, recovering his equilibrium. 'They are now more vital to the security of Iraq than ever.' He glared at Izzat Ibrahim. 'The news about the lookalike Bakr Abdullah is unfortunate but the crucial thing is that the last one on the list, the lookalike Muhsen Hashim, remains at our disposal. He is the best of them all.'

'So what exactly is it that you propose?' Izzat was now certain that he knew.

'It is simple. There will be no announcement of an assassination, no announcement of a replacement as President. Instead, a film will be made as soon as can be arranged. This film will feature the lookalike Muhsen Hashim. It will be more comprehensive than anything he has featured in before. He is capable of it, I know. Only a few people outside this room, other than the traitors responsible for this morning's outrage, will ever know the truth. The traitors, along with all witnesses and anyone else who might have heard rumours, will be eliminated. This imposing lookalike will take the place of the President.'

Izzat Ibrahim was staggered. 'Are you suggesting that this lookalike should sit on this council? That he should become one of us?'

'Of course not,' retorted the hyena contemptuously. 'He will merely receive his instructions from us. He will do what he is told.'

'Might I ask,' hissed Izzat, 'who it is that you have in mind to give him his instructions?'

'The matter is of no consequence,' snapped the hyena. 'The instructions themselves will of course be important, but the duty of relaying them to the lookalike will be one of little significance. However, as it appears to be something to which you attach such importance,' he snickered, a note of triumph in his voice, 'perhaps I might propose that you take on this task yourself?'

The deadly insult implicit in Taha Yasin Ramadan's words stunned the room into silence. Livid fury suffused Izzat's pockmarked face, and he glared at the hyena with a bitter ferocity. 'The idea is an utterly preposterous one! It could never work!'

'This plan is infinitely less preposterous than any alternative on offer. I have given the matter much careful consideration. This plan will work. It must be *made* to work. If it fails, then we are all, every last one of us'—the hyena, in full control now, slowly swept his malevolent gaze round the room—'doomed.'

Izzat Ibrahim, beaten, stared fixedly at the hyena Taha Yasin Ramadan. The small unblinking eyes radiated pure hatred.

Chapter ⑪

Lieutenant Saleh Masoud was ready to explode with frustration. Despite the fact that the sun was now sinking fast, the armoured car was still baking hot inside; he had not had a chance to stop for a rest, for food, for anything. He imagined the guardsmen in the trucks behind would be about as fed up as he was. His driver certainly was, and had let him know about it at length.

Curse the major, he thought indignantly. It was typical that he would ride in comfort in the foreigners' car while his men were being bumped about in these bone-shaking rattletraps. A curse on the major, and ten thousand curses on these filthy foreigners. The lieutenant made up his mind. Half an hour more was all he was going to give them. If they went on any longer than that without stopping for a rest, *he* was going to stop. He would refuse to go any further.

The lieutenant had by now become so preoccupied with preparing the bitingly effective speech he would make to his commanding officer that he didn't take any notice when Bourne turned off the main highway to Trebil. The convoy had almost reached Ar Rutbah; Bourne abruptly took a turning through the town. He headed south towards the Saudi border, the same way they had come.

UNLIKE HIS SURLY SUBORDINATE, Major Hassan Omair had realised straightaway what had happened. Suddenly they were heading south—out into the middle of nowhere. Quickly, the major thought about what he might do. His plan for having the spies arrested at Trebil had now gone out of the window. He immediately decided that he would give them no hint that he thought anything was amiss. Perhaps that fool Saleh Masoud, in the scout car, would twig what had happened. If so, he would probably do something about it. Maybe even fire off his 14.5mm cannon at them. Good for him if he did.

But what were the spies doing now? The man Howard had picked up a strange flying helmet—it had a device like a pair of binoculars fitted to it. Of course—a light-amplification device! And the man was temporarily distracted . . .

Howard, in the back seat behind Bourne, had been watching the major carefully. As he reached for his NVG helmet in preparation for operating in the dark, it occurred to him that pretty soon the major would guess where they were now headed. They had passed the turnoff to Ar Rutbah South airfield, and the dirt track began only a mile or two further on. He passed MacDonald a second NVG helmet and handed another forward to Bourne.

Bourne was putting on his helmet when two things happened more or less at once. The first, unnoticed by him, was that the scout car behind braked to a halt.

The second thing was that the major, recognising what was perhaps the only chance he might have, made a sudden grab for the steering wheel. Bourne, temporarily preoccupied with his helmet, was wholly unprepared. Howard, however, was not. He hit the major hard on the side of the neck with the edge of his hand; the major slumped unconscious over Bourne's lap. Bourne, recovering quickly, pushed the inert Iraqi roughly back into his seat.

The incident was over in less than four seconds, but in that time the Land Cruiser had drawn about seventy yards clear of the rest of the convoy. Howard and Bourne registered the fact simultaneously; Bourne braked hard.

Ziegler, Ackford and Usher, sandwiched between the scout car and the first of the trucks, realised there was something wrong. 'Not yet,' said Ziegler tersely, 'wait till we find out what this is about.'

Lieutenant Saleh Masoud was already out of the scout car. The lead car, he noticed, had not stopped immediately; presumably it would now reverse back to see what was up. Then he would give the major a piece of his mind.

In the meantime, the lieutenant decided, he would make sure these

Shadow Over Babylon

foreigners got a rough time of it. He walked back to the second Land Cruiser. 'Get out of the car,' he snarled menacingly at Ziegler, jerking his thumb backwards in an unmistakable gesture.

Ziegler raised his AKMS and shot the lieutenant in the throat. He motioned abruptly with his elbow to Ackford and Usher. 'Out now,' he ordered. All three men dived out and rolled away, leaving the dead body of the lieutenant lying by the vehicle.

The sergeant in the cab of the first of the two trucks had heard the soft cough of the silenced AK and had seen the lieutenant collapse dead. He reacted quickly. With a yell of 'Out of the vehicle!' at his men in the back, he jumped out himself, loading his AK 47. He was about to fire when he heard a shout in English. There was a bright flash from somewhere near his feet, and he too fell dead.

The shout he had heard was 'Grenade!' from Ackford. Almost simultaneously he, Usher and Ziegler had hurled hand grenades at the two trucks behind. The first exploded between the front wheels of the lead truck, killing the sergeant and setting the vehicle on fire. The second exploded near the rear of the truck, dispatching three soldiers. The third grenade, aimed by Ziegler at the second truck, misfired.

Ackford and Usher were now raking the two trucks with AK fire. Many of the soldiers inside never managed to get out, but thirteen of the occupants of the second vehicle, undamaged by the grenades, jumped to the ground and began returning fire. Ziegler took careful aim at the four headlights on the two trucks and shot them out, plunging the scene into darkness.

The driver of the scout car had reacted with speed and initiative when the first grenade had exploded. Wrenching himself out of his seat, he grabbed the turret-mounted 14.5mm cannon and fired it without aiming. The cannon had been pointing directly ahead, down the road, and the first three rounds went straight into Howard's Land Cruiser as it reversed towards him. The car slewed off the road and turned over on its side, catching fire.

MacDonald had felt a violent thump on his left arm as a bullet passed through it; the blow was strong enough to make him drop his AK. Immediately after that, the world seemed to turn upside-down, and he crashed down on his head. He was saved by the NVG helmet. He scrambled out of his door, which now opened towards the sky.

While MacDonald was climbing out of the door above, Howard dived over into the back of the vehicle and kicked open the rear door. The RPG-7 antitank rocket-launcher was underneath the back seat; he grabbed it and rolled out onto the ground, lining up the weapon on the scout car. There was a deafening bang from the RPG as the projectile fired; it detonated almost immediately on its target,

157

punching through the thin armour plate. The front of the armoured car disintegrated and the interior began to burn.

Johnny Bourne had been hit in the lower leg. Another bullet had hit a rear wheel and shattered it; it was this that had caused the vehicle to swerve out of control and turn over onto the driver's side. As it did so, the body of the unconscious major once again fell across Bourne, pinning him down. The vehicle was starting to burn.

MacDonald felt utterly helpless. He couldn't fire his AK for fear of hitting Ziegler, Ackford and Usher, who were engaged in an ear-splitting firefight with the remaining Iraqi guardsmen. Flattening himself to the ground, he turned his head to see Howard racing off to one flank.

It suddenly struck MacDonald that Bourne was nowhere to be seen. Behind him, the Land Cruiser was starting to burn; in a flash, he realised Bourne must still be inside. He ran to it and dived into the back. He found Bourne pinned down, and using his one good hand he pulled the major's weight off his wounded leg.

'Thanks, Danny,' shouted Bourne hoarsely above the din outside, as by their combined efforts they managed to get the unconscious Iraqi off him altogether. Bourne dragged himself out of the rear of the vehicle, following MacDonald. Outside, they crawled away from the wrecked car, which was now burning fiercely.

'What shall we do, Johnny?' shouted Danny.

'Not much we can do at this stage,' shouted Bourne, grimacing. 'My leg's wrecked, anyway. Best stay here and see what happens.'

Howard had seen that Usher and Ackford were on the right flank. He headed out to the left, where he knew Ziegler would be. Gradually, the crossfire laid down by the four men began to take its toll. The Iraqis, blind in the dark, confused, tired and caught completely off their guard, were no match for their adversaries. Only eight out of thirty-five were now left alive.

There was a loud bang as the burning Land Cruiser exploded. Major Hassan Omair died without regaining consciousness. The bright flash of the explosion illuminated the scene enough for the Iraqi sergeant from the second truck to see movement from one of the enemy. He let off a long burst from his AK 47. The figure he had fired at jerked convulsively and then lay still. *Got him*, thought the sergeant. Then came a series of shockingly forceful thumps to his own body. Before he could grasp what had happened, the Iraqi sergeant drew his last breath, a look of surprise on his face.

The gunfire died away; the last Iraqi soldier was dead.

'Mike?' called Howard.

'Here. AOK.'

'Johnny?'

'Here,' called Bourne, his voice sounding strained. 'Hit in lower right leg. Bones not broken.'

'Good. Danny?'

'Here. Hit in left forearm.'

'Tony?'

'Here. My helmet got hit, but I think the contents are still OK.'

'Bob?'

There was a long silence. Ackford said, 'He's over here, boss.'

'OK. I think we're clear. Mike, take over. Find out if any of those vehicles are serviceable.' Howard walked over to Tony, who was kneeling by Usher's body. Usher had taken three bullets in the head and chest. He had died instantly.

'Lousy luck, boss,' said Ackford. 'We nearly made it.'

'THIS EFFING TRUCK'S a pig of a thing to drive,' shouted Ackford above the din of the engine.

'So would anything be, with a flat front tyre,' answered Howard. He smiled weakly to mask his uneasiness. The second Land Cruiser had refused to start. It had taken several hits; the distributor and the battery were smashed. Thank heaven the second truck worked, he thought, despite the shot-out tyre.

Howard hadn't wanted to hang around at the scene of the fight a moment longer than necessary. It didn't matter that the truck's lights didn't work—they wouldn't have used them anyway. Ackford was wearing his night-vision goggles, and could see perfectly well.

'Just keep going as far as you can, Tony,' said Howard. 'I want to get as much distance between us and those wrecks as possible.'

'I'm doing my best, boss.'

There was a tap on the cab and Howard turned round to see Ziegler poking his head through the canvas cover behind. 'Andy's on his way, Ed. Airborne now. You got coordinates for us to give him?'

'Not yet, Mike. We'll keep going for a few more miles and look for a suitable place for him to land.'

'OK.'

'How are Johnny and Danny?'

'Danny's OK. A big hole, but straight through the muscle. Not bleedin' too bad. I'm not so sure about Johnny, though. I've put a pressure dressing on it, but he's been losin' quite a bit of blood.'

'You'll all just have to hang on for a while. We daren't stop yet.'

'OK.' Ziegler's head disappeared back behind the canvas flap.

Howard had an afterthought. He leaned his head out of the cab window again. 'Mike?'

Ziegler's head reappeared. 'Yeah?'

'Any dead Iraqis on board?'

'Yeah. Two who never made it out of the truck. I was about to start chuckin' them out of the back.'

'Don't. We'll need them. I'm pretty sure we're blown in Saudi,' said Howard. 'We're probably going to have to ditch the plane on arrival and think of some other way.'

'Hell,' said Ziegler. 'What makes you think that?'

'The air strike on that warehouse,' said Howard. 'I'm quite sure it wasn't Iraqi.'

THE IRAQI AIR FORCE colonel commanding the Ar Rutbah South air base looked up in surprise at the sudden loud knocking on his door. 'Come in,' he called.

The door flew open and an agitated army captain appeared. 'Sir, there has been a mutiny!'

'What? Explain yourself!'

The captain explained. He had been driving back to Ar Rutbah, he said, when he had seen something burning, about two miles away from the turning to the base. He had gone to investigate. He had seen the vehicles and the soldiers' bodies. All dead, he said.

The colonel was perplexed and angry. 'What was anyone doing down there?' he asked.

'I don't know, sir,' said the captain. 'But the Republican Guard never inform us of their movements in advance.'

The colonel knew. It was a sore point with him. But . . . *Wait a minute!* 'Captain, did you say Republican Guard?'

'Yes, sir. About twenty or thirty of them. All dead.'

'Order a full alert at once, Captain!'

'Yes, sir!'

The colonel hurried to his car and sped across the airfield to the control tower. All round the air base, security lights were coming on as the sirens began to blare. He had decided what to do. 'Get H3 air base on the radio! I want to speak to Colonel Suba Ali! Urgently!'

'Yes, sir!' replied the operations officer with a salute.

Yes, thought the colonel. H3 air base was the answer. There was nothing here at Ar Rutbah South except transport planes. They had a squadron of helicopter gunships at the H3 base, only forty miles away to the west. The Mi-24 Hind was a fearsome machine—as Afghan Mujahideen guerrillas had discovered to their cost—heavily armed and armoured, almost impossible to shoot down, and equipped with sophisticated radar and optical target-acquisition devices. The situation called for nothing less.

ANDY DENARD WAS FLYING as low as he dared, heading for the last reported position of the team. Harris, beside him in the copilot's seat, took the coordinates again ten minutes later, and Denard altered course slightly to compensate for the truck's new position.

'How did they sound, Mel?' he asked tersely, his eyes not moving from the scene ahead.

'Hard to say, with Johnny talking Arabic and me trying to remember mine. I don't know. Tense, certainly. But so am I, the way you're flying this thing.'

'Don't worry, man. We'll soon be there. Ten minutes more.'

'I'll have aged ten years by then!'

Denard laughed. Harris, glancing at the pilot's face, saw that just for once his eyes weren't laughing too.

THE MI-24 HIND had almost arrived at the site of the reported incident. The Iraqi pilot was confused. What was all this rumpus about the Republican Guard? What were they doing down here, getting themselves slaughtered? The pilot didn't like the sound of it. Mutinies were nothing but trouble.

The navigator-gunner broke his train of thought. 'Coming up to target now. One kilometre.'

The pilot saw it straightaway. Four burning vehicles, as reported. Two of them almost completely burnt out already. The pilot circled the scene. Bodies were strewn around; it *had* been a massacre. He spoke into his microphone. 'Anything on the FLIR?'

The observer studied the forward-looking imaging radar display and answered, 'One aircraft approaching from the south. Twenty-two miles distant. But the infrared imaging shows an unusual track pattern leading that way. A vehicle has left here recently. It looks as though it's got a damaged wheel.'

'We will investigate,' said the pilot. 'There are no air bases down there, and there are no scheduled movements in that sector. And that vehicle may contain the dissidents responsible for this massacre.'

The Hind banked round and began to pick up speed, heading almost due south down the track.

MACDONALD'S ARM was beginning to ache like hell. Beside him, Bourne lay on the ground, his leg raised as Ziegler finished binding up the wound. His face was taut with pain. A Saudi hospital, followed by a long stretch in prison, MacDonald thought numbly; that was all either of them could look forward to. They had so nearly made it.

'I think I can hear the plane, boss,' called Ackford.

'Right,' said Howard. 'Lights now!'

'THE AIRCRAFT HAS JUST LANDED,' reported the forward observer in the Hind. 'It's a twin-engined light aircraft. The vehicle is stationary, two kilometres distant.'

The pilot spoke to the navigator–gunner. 'Engage the vehicle. Fire one AT-3. Then prepare to engage the aircraft with the 12.7mm nose-gun. We're going to have some fun.'

The navigator–gunner armed one of the four antitank missiles on the starboard wing, and locked onto the target. He waited until he was one kilometre from the target and then fired.

MACDONALD NEVER HEARD the missile coming. Forty yards behind him, the truck dissolved in a sheet of flame. The force of the explosion knocked him flat. As he sat up again, slightly stunned, something thundered overhead. He flipped on his night-vision goggles.

'Helicopter!' screamed Bourne, grabbing his AK. 'A Hind! Danny! Get the sniper rifle and put some armour-piercing rounds into it! That's the only thing that might stop it!'

'No good!' yelled MacDonald in reply. 'It was destroyed in the fire in the Land Cruiser!'

Harris had just jumped down from the Islander when he saw the truck a hundred yards away disintegrate with a flash. By the light of the burning vehicle he saw Ackford and Ziegler firing their rifles at something airborne. He ran to join them. 'What is it?' he bawled.

'Hind, I think,' shouted Ackford.

Harris suddenly saw it through his night-vision goggles. It was wheeling round and coming in again. It was going for the Islander. 'Any weapon for me?' he shrieked.

'Back there, by Johnny and Mac,' bellowed Ackford.

Harris sped off towards the others.

Denard hadn't waited. Ramming the twin throttles forward, he had begun taxiing the Islander. His goggles had given him a brief glimpse of the Hind, and he knew he would be no better off in the air. The twin engines howled as Denard raced the plane along the strip, juggling the throttles and the rudder to throw it into violent pirouetting movements. It was all he could do. He had to rely on the others to destroy the helicopter.

The pilot of the Hind had seen the aircraft's pathetic attempts to escape. He smiled: this was going to be more entertaining than he had thought. Bullets were whacking into the side of the helicopter. He ignored them, and brought the Hind into a static hover, to get a shot at the aircraft with the 12.7mm nose-mounted gun. It would be good target practice. Then he would finish off those idiots firing rifles at him. The 12.7mm nose-gun began to chatter beneath his feet.

Harris reached Howard, who was in the process of loading the RPG-7. 'Let me take it,' he yelled, 'I'm good with an RPG! You load for me.' Howard nodded and thrust the antitank weapon at him. Harris shouldered the RPG and brought it to bear on the Hind, which was hovering 200 yards away. He fired.

The Hind's copilot saw a sudden flash of light over near the remains of the truck, and momentarily caught sight of something streaking past him in the dark. 'Missile!' he screamed.

The pilot had not seen it; he was concentrating on the aircraft, which was proving a difficult target. 'What missile?' he asked.

'It just missed us! I'm sure of it!'

The pilot frowned. That put a different complexion on things. He would have to deal with it—urgently. He pushed the control forward and applied throttle, to take the Hind out of the hover. As he did so, a second RPG-7 projectile impacted on the thick, armoured-glass cockpit window beside him. A stream of white-hot metal plasma was blasted through the window into the cockpit, where it exploded with a dazzling flash, killing all the crew instantly. The Hind fell from the sky like a dead bird, smashed into the ground and burst into flames.

Harris and Howard stared in silence at the burning wreckage of the helicopter. Then Howard spoke. 'That was a bloody good shot, Mel,' he muttered. They both watched as the Islander began taxiing back towards them. Howard stood up slowly. 'Come on. Let's get going. I think I've had about as much trouble tonight as I can take.'

'EIGHT MINUTES, ED. I'm going to start climbing now.'

Howard looked across to Denard. The pilot's face was very pale and tense, and there was a sheen of sweat on his forehead. Howard frowned momentarily, then swivelled round to shout the instruction to the others in the rear. He turned back to Denard. 'Come on, Andy. Set the autopilot and come back to get fixed up with a chute.'

'No point, Ed.'

'Huh? What do you mean, no point?'

'I'm hit.' Denard coughed.

Howard was stricken. Denard's face was now a mask of pain. 'Why didn't you say? Where? How bad?'

'Gut, somewhere. Losing blood. Can't feel my legs any more. Haven't you noticed? I've been flying without rudder control since we took off.' Denard made a weak attempt at a smile. 'I've had it, Ed.'

'I can fix you up, Andy! Don't give up now!'

'No!' Denard coughed again; some blood ran down his chin. Almost whispering, he forced the words out with great effort. 'Autopilot's had it, too. Tried it ten miles back. That bloody chopper got me and it, both. You and the others bale out. I'll give you the signal.'

'Andy, *please* come! We can land instead! I'll get you to a hospital. I can't just leave you here!'

'No, Ed,' whispered Denard. Howard strained forward to hear him. 'Never liked the idea of prison. I wouldn't make it, anyway. You go. Here's all my ID. Give my regards to Chris.'

Numb with sadness, Howard stumbled into the rear of the plane and began preparing himself for the jump. Going through the motions like an automaton, he finished strapping on the parachute. He had hoped they would not need to jump, but the fact that they were compromised now made it imperative. Harris's story of his and Palmer's near-miss at Jiddah had confirmed it to him.

He looked up; the others were ready. He could see from their faces that none of them had yet realised what had happened to Denard. Ziegler opened the large cargo door and the night air rushed in.

Howard watched Denard for the signal; when it came, he whacked MacDonald on the shoulder. The Scot, eyes tight shut, jumped out of the door. Behind him, Howard and Ziegler were helping Bourne out of the plane. The others quickly followed.

As Howard floated down to the ground under his parachute, the rumbling engine noise of the departing Islander gradually faded into the night.

KEARWIN WAS PUZZLED. Forcing himself to look up from the Keyhole satellite image of the burning truck and helicopter, he turned his attention to the AWACS plot of the Islander's flight. Where was it going to land? He shrugged. It didn't matter. Wherever it landed, there would be the vehicle; JSTARS could follow that, until the decision was made to intercept it. Kearwin wondered why the Islander was making no apparent effort to conceal itself this time. It was the first stupid mistake these guys had made.

Kearwin's instinct suddenly told him he had read it wrong. These people just didn't *make* mistakes. The plane must be a blind. But they *had* to have left Iraq in the plane! Yet it hadn't landed to let them out. That meant . . .

'Jerry!' he shouted. 'Get JSTARS to monitor offroad vehicle movement along the track of that airplane. Start near the TAP road itself. They've jumped!'

Two minutes later, they had got it. It had been a very close thing. The JSTARS had picked up a vehicle leaving Al Mira airstrip. Five minutes more and it would have been just another car on the busy road. The JSTARS picture fitted the template for a Land Cruiser. The third vehicle had surfaced at last.

THE SEVEN MEN in the third Land Cruiser were subdued and silent. Howard's news about Denard had hit them hard. Harris and Ackford were squashed into the front passenger seat; beside them Palmer drove, grim-faced, as smoothly and steadily along the tarmac road as he could.

MacDonald sat in the luggage compartment in the rear with Ziegler, who was dressing the wound in the stalker's forearm. MacDonald felt quite comfortable; the injection the American had given him had already taken the edge off the pain, and he sensed himself becoming strangely detached and light-headed.

'What on earth was in that injection, Mike?' he asked dreamily.

'Morphine,' grinned Ziegler. 'You'll be flyin' for a while. Make the most of it, though. I'm not givin' you any more after this. Don't want to make a junkie of you.'

Bourne was lying across the rear seat, his damaged leg on Howard's lap. He had been nearly unconscious when they found him after the parachute drop, and Howard had lost no time in applying a tourniquet above the knee and putting in a plasma-expander drip.

His blood pressure had stabilised, but he was very pale. He had passed out soon after being hefted into the Land Cruiser, and Howard was now taking advantage of his semiconscious state to attend to his leg. Working quickly, he cleaned it and packed the wound. It was nasty. Howard pulled a long face. Somehow, Bourne was going to have to recover enough to be able to make it through the exit channel at the airport without appearing too ill to travel. He knew Bourne was tough, but things didn't look too promising.

ANDY DENARD DIED seventeen minutes after crossing the TAP road. The Islander kept on flying by itself, steadily losing height. Ten minutes later, it encountered a downdraught which made the nose pitch forward. The movement was enough to dislodge Denard's lifeless body. His corpse slumped against the control column, pushing it forward and sending the aircraft into a steep dive. Unobserved, except on the AWACS monitor, the Islander smashed into the ground in a remote desert region northwest of Sakakah and caught fire.

The US Air Force AWACS passed the information on the crash direct to the Saudi Arabian air-traffic-control authorities, and Saudi investigators found the remains of three bodies: those of Denard and the two Iraqi soldiers from the truck. The next day they discovered a fourth—Usher's. All four were burnt beyond recognition.

The Saudi police autopsies would be inconclusive, but the evidence of the bullet wounds and the aircraft's course would point overwhelmingly to the likelihood that the four men had been shot while attempting to flee from Iraq. The police would assume that the pilot was the one they had been seeking—Ray Sullivan.

JAMES ANSELL, head of the CIA's Mid-East desk, sat in silence as the Deputy Director (Intelligence) read through the transcripts of the news report. 'These are verbatim?' the DD(I) asked.

'Pretty much, sir, yes.'

'This Iranian news-agency report is very specific,' said the DD(I). 'And it fits with what we know about this assassination team and their movements. I mean, it says here that Saddam was shot yesterday at eight in the morning, Iraqi time. And one of their own people was killed too, a diplomat. Why would the Iranians specifically say he was shot, and give a time, unless it's true?' The DD(I) paused, trying to piece it all together in his mind. 'Apart from the fact that it fits exactly with the movements of the hit squad, can we confirm any of this?'

Ansell nodded. 'It fits with rumour that the Iranian Ambassador to

Iraq has disappeared. He had an appointment at the Swedish Embassy in Baghdad last night, and he didn't show up. I think we have to take it seriously.'

'But then there's this other report,' snorted the DD(I). 'The Iraqi Government denies it all. A ridiculous rumour, they say. There have been pictures broadcast of Saddam presiding over a meeting of the Revolutionary Command Council. They deny the whole thing as complete nonsense.'

'That's exactly the sort of thing one expects from the Iraqi news agency,' said Ansell. 'I can't think of a single word of truth they've broadcast in the last ten years. If Saddam *has* been assassinated, they're hardly likely to tell anyone about it until his successor is announced. There would be massive civil unrest, possibly an uprising.'

'Hmm,' grunted the DD(I). 'Well, I must say I'm inclined to agree with you. The clincher is that it all fits exactly with the NRO reports on the movements of the hit squad.'

'That's what convinced me, too,' said Ansell. 'But for that, I don't think I'd have attached quite so much credibility to it.'

The DD(I) stared out of the window. 'Well, thanks for this, James. I'd better get it to the DCI. I guess he'll want to tell the President.'

'MR PRESIDENT, I have Prime Minister Major on the line.'

'Thanks.' The President picked up the telephone. 'John? George here. I'm sorry if I woke you up.'

'That's all right, Mr President,' replied John Major sleepily. He had retired late, just half an hour before, only to be woken by the telephone. 'What can I do for you?'

'John, you ought to know that the Iranian news agency has reported that Saddam Hussein was shot yesterday morning. My people here are inclined to believe the report.'

'Oh,' said Major, suddenly awake. 'How sure are they?'

'They can't be certain,' answered the President, 'but it all fits with our satellite-monitoring operation. The question now is what are we going to do about it? On the diplomatic side, I think we have to prepare for the fragmentation of Iraq. On the practical side, I think we must decide what we do about the assassins. I would welcome your thoughts.'

John Major mustered his thoughts and voiced them. 'Diplomatically, things will clearly be awkward. If Saddam is dead, I suppose it rather depends on who takes over. If it's another strong man, fragmentation might be avoided.'

'That's possible,' drawled the President, 'but we don't think there is anyone else strong enough. Baghdad is denying the whole thing. If there had been a strong man ready to take over, he would probably already have made his move. If Iraq does break up, we'll end up with three rump states—the Kurds in the north, the Sunni Muslims in the centre, and the marsh Arabs in the south. We don't think any of these three states would last long either.'

'Shi'ites,' corrected Major. 'We must remember to refer to the marsh Arabs as Shi'ites. If we call them "marsh Arabs" it makes them sound more innocuous. If people started thinking of them as harmless victims, public opinion might force us to do something about protecting them from Saddam.'

'OK, Shi'ites, if you like,' grunted Bush, irritated at being lectured by the Prime Minister. 'But that just reinforces my point. The Iranians are Shi'ites too, and they'll use that as an excuse to intervene. This is the main threat, as we see it—Iranian intervention. The implications of that are scary.'

'Things in Iran aren't as bad as they were,' countered Major. 'Mr Rafsanjani has consolidated his power in recent elections, and he is a moderate. I feel that the Iranian situation is a lot more promising now than it was under Khomeini.'

'We'll just have to disagree on that,' declared Bush. 'Those ayatollahs still have a lot of influence. I want to discuss a joint approach to Iran. I think we must present a united front. I think we must offer Rafsanjani our support. If we stay on better terms with Iran, we might be able to persuade them that moderation pays.'

'That sounds like a very sensible approach, Mr President,' agreed Major. 'Very sensible indeed. Perhaps my Foreign Secretary and your Secretary of State could come up with recommendations.'

'Fine,' said Bush. 'Now, we must also decide what to do about these assassins. The CIA should have caught up with them soon. The question is, what do we do with them?' Major's answer to that might be revealing, he thought.

'I suggest we let the Saudi police handle the matter,' replied the Prime Minister simply.

'You do realise that we have tapes of radio conversations they had, and two of the voices had English accents?'

There was a note of testiness in the Prime Minister's voice. 'There may well be British subjects involved, Mr President, but I can assure you that they are not employees of Her Majesty's Government. I wouldn't want you to think that they might be.'

'Of course I didn't mean to imply that, John,' said the President, his voice placatory. 'For my part, I give you a categoric assurance that the United States is not behind this attempt on Saddam.'

At the other end of the line, John Major sat silent for a moment. So, he thought, that is what this telephone call is about. The President does suspect that the British Government is involved, and he wants a confirmation or a denial. He thought hard for a few seconds, then spoke. 'And I give you a similar categoric assurance, Mr President. These men are not acting for the British Government in any capacity, and I don't think we should interfere,' said Major firmly. 'No, I think it would definitely be better if they were arrested and tried out there. Perhaps if the sentences they receive under Saudi law are particularly harsh, we might appeal for them to be reduced.'

'Well, I for one would like to know who was behind this job,' said Bush with feeling. 'The situation out there is quite bad enough without people taking it on themselves to knock off heads of state, however nasty they are.'

The Prime Minister considered his response. 'It would certainly be interesting to know who was behind it,' he began slowly, 'of course it would.' He cleared his throat briskly. 'But what's done is done. I think we can do no more than let justice take its course.'

'Well, I'll let you get back to bed now. It's been interesting talking to you.'

'Good night then, Mr President,' said the Prime Minister with relief, not entirely sure that their conversation had settled anything.

George Bush put down the telephone. He too was a little perplexed by the way the dialogue had gone, particularly the last part. Maybe the CIA was right about this, after all: that the Brits were the ones behind this whole operation. OK, he thought; if the British Prime Minister was happy to let his own agents rot in a Saudi jail, so be it.

Chapter (12)

Howard had been sitting awake thinking; he hadn't slept at all. There were quite a few pieces to the puzzle that simply didn't fit. His suspicions about the air strike on the warehouse had hardened into certainty; there was no doubt that they had been compromised. He turned to Ziegler. 'Mike? How much do you know about the capabilities of aerial surveillance?'

'What—air photos, that kind of stuff?'

'Perhaps. Look, we've assumed that Saudi radar picked up the aircraft. What if something more sophisticated picked it up?'

'You mean AWACS? Yeah, it's possible. The Saudis have got AWACS.'

'I wasn't thinking of the Saudis, Mike.'

The implications of Howard's remark slowly sank in. 'Oh no!' said Ziegler. 'You mean, our side?'

'Yes, I'm afraid I do. I can't see any other explanation for it. I think we've been shadowed since quite early on. And for some reason, they aren't acting friendly at all. The warehouse was evidence enough of that. The question is, if they're using AWACS, what can it do? Could they have been tracking us all along? Might they be tracking us right now? My feeling is that they have—and they are. I don't see any other way they could have known we were in that warehouse.'

'I don't know the latest technology. But there was some capability they used in the Gulf War to spot Iraqi tanks movin' about.'

Howard had made up his mind. 'OK. We'll assume they've got us on some sort of a monitor right now. Here's what we're going to do.'

'THEY'RE JUST PASSING through Al Wajh, Walter,' called out Kearwin. 'They haven't stopped there. Where are the CIA boys now?'

'Never mind about them,' said the Walrus. 'All you gotta do is keep your eyes glued to that Land Cruiser on the screen. It's after dawn there now, and there'll soon be other traffic on the road.'

'That shouldn't be a problem. They're so close now. JSTARS is practically overhead. It couldn't miss that Land Cruiser, even in traffic.'

Kearwin watched the Land Cruiser continuing south along the coast road towards Yanbu and Jiddah. He wondered what they were going to do. Were they going to stop where they had landed the dinghy, and take to the sea again? Or were they going to carry straight on to Jiddah?

Twenty miles out of Al Wajh, the Land Cruiser stopped briefly; then it was off again. No more than ten seconds, thought Kearwin. Probably changing over drivers. It was another fifty miles to the place where they had landed the dinghy. That would be the next point of interest—would they stop there? He leaned back and waited.

Forty-five minutes later, Kearwin sat up with a start. The Land Cruiser *had* stopped at the landing point. It had turned off the road, down towards the sea. They *were* going to take to the boat again!

Five minutes later, the information was flashed to the American Embassy in Riyadh; from there it was relayed to CIA agent Alvin Kennings, who was on the road north of Yanbu. Kennings looked at the map and cursed. He was an hour away from where the Land Cruiser had stopped; they could be away in the boat before he got there. But it didn't really make any difference. There was a US frigate standing about twenty miles offshore. On board were two Sikorsky Seahawk helicopters. No dinghy was going to get past *them*.

UNKNOWN TO KENNINGS, the rear door of the Land Cruiser had opened just before Al Wajh, a little more than an hour earlier. Ziegler, clad in several extra layers of clothing from baggage in the rear, and wearing the last of the NVG helmets, had rolled out onto the road. The Land Cruiser did not stop; Ziegler hit the ground hard but apart from a headache and a few bruises he was unhurt. He waved at the departing Land Cruiser and set off at an easy jog towards the northwest. Al Wajh airport was six kilometres away; he reckoned that it would take him no more than twenty-five minutes.

Twenty miles beyond Al Wajh, as Kearwin noticed on the JSTARS screen, the Land Cruiser stopped briefly. The drivers did indeed change, as Kearwin conjectured: Harris took over. What Kearwin could not have known was that everyone else got out of the vehicle in the few seconds it was stationary. Howard and Ackford lifted Bourne out and laid him on the ground beside the road, while Palmer helped MacDonald to get the luggage out.

When the Land Cruiser was empty, Harris drove off. The stop had lasted for less than ten seconds.

They carried Bourne and the baggage well off the road and took shelter out of sight behind a bush. Howard returned to the road and put out two small marker flags. They sat down to wait.

Ziegler had arrived at Al Wajh airport at 06.45, at about the same time the others had left the Land Cruiser. He went straight to the car park and got into the hired Dodge Ram Charger he had used to collect Howard and MacDonald from the dinghy. He started it up and drove away, following the route the Land Cruiser had taken just under half an hour before. At 07.18 he spotted the first of the two marker flags and slowed, stopping when he reached the second. Howard and the others emerged from cover, climbed into the Dodge and drove off, still following the route south towards Jiddah.

When Harris reached the spot on the coast road Howard had described to him, he drove down towards the shore, then stopped and got out. He removed the vehicle licence plates with a screwdriver and set off at a fast jog down the road. He wanted to be well away by the time the Ram Charger caught up with him.

Half an hour later, Harris was nearly five miles clear of the abandoned Land Cruiser, on a quiet stretch of road. He heard the pick-up's car horn toot the signal; he looked round and prepared to jump on board. It was 07.51.

Exactly thirty-five minutes afterwards, at 08.26, the Ram Charger passed a large Chevrolet saloon going in the opposite direction. Neither car took any notice of the other among the traffic. At 08.52, the Chevrolet arrived at the reported location of the Land Cruiser and stopped; Alvin Kennings and two burly Marines from the US Embassy climbed out.

'There's no one here,' said one of the Marines unnecessarily.

Kennings ignored him. He was scanning the sea with his binoculars for any sign of a boat. He saw a helicopter circling in the distance, way out to sea. 'The Seahawks will pick them up,' he muttered to himself. He continued watching.

He would have to wait until 10.32 before he received the message that neither the radar systems on the frigate nor its Seahawk helicopters had seen any sign of a boat.

Alvin Kennings immediately realised that the team must have changed vehicles, but neither he nor John Kearwin, several thousand miles away in Washington, would ever know how.

'IT WOULD THEREFORE APPEAR, gentlemen, that these men have slipped through the net cast by the CIA.' The Director of MI6, Britain's Secret Intelligence Service, concluded his summary and looked up from his notes. There were a few raised eyebrows, but little other reaction from the members of the Joint Intelligence Committee.

'Thank you, Sir Arthur,' said the Intelligence Coordinator. 'Gentlemen, before we discuss any further action that might be taken to identify the individuals concerned and deal with them, I think it would be useful to examine the possible repercussions of their actions in Iraq.' The Intelligence Coordinator paused for a moment and studied the faces around the table. 'First of all, we should perhaps try to establish exactly what has transpired. The evidence, as you have heard from Sir Arthur, is compelling: in short, it is the view of the American intelligence community that yesterday morning President Saddam Hussein was assassinated by a sniper's bullet. The broadcast by the Iranian news service—not something to which great credibility would normally be attached—gave a specific time and place. These particulars happen to coincide exactly with observations made by American, ah, surveillance satellites. The official Iraqi news network has put out several broadcasts denying the Iranian report, and Saddam Hussein himself has been shown on television . . .'

Max Goodale, Deputy Director of MI5, the Security Service, allowed his mind to detach itself from the proceedings. So it had been a sniper, had it? That was the first he'd heard of it. Interesting. He cast his mind back over the almost total lack of evidence the police had been able to obtain, and the dubious connection, still unproven, with Sir Peter Dartington. He decided there were a few more things he needed to find out; he refocused his attention. The Intelligence Coordinator was winding up.

'So, gentlemen, that is the proposed policy of Her Majesty's Government. Unless there are any comments, I would now like to discuss what action we might take against the assassins.'

Goodale broke in. 'Mr Chairman, I think it would be useful to have an idea of the type of people we are dealing with. I think the view of the Director of Special Forces would be most useful.'

The Intelligence Coordinator nodded his assent. 'Yes, Mr Goodale, that might be useful.' He turned to a man sitting at the far end of the table. 'Brigadier? Perhaps you would enlighten us?'

The Director of Special Forces was a former commanding officer of the 22nd Special Air Service Regiment. He spoke economically and to the point. 'On the evidence of what they seem to have achieved, these are men of high calibre, probably ex-Special Forces. These particular men are unconventional but effective, and highly resourceful. On a purely professional basis, I have to confess some admiration for their ability. But there is one thing that puzzles me about this affair.'

'Yes, Brigadier?' prompted the Intelligence Coordinator.

'It is the question of where they got their information. If we had been asked to do this job ourselves, we could probably have done it, but I must stress that we would have got nowhere without precise information, well in advance, as to Saddam's whereabouts. It would be most interesting to know where they got this information from.'

The Intelligence Coordinator was anxious to bring the discussion back to the point. 'Thank you, Brigadier. I am sure that is a question that will exercise us all until the matter is resolved. Perhaps we could now address the issue of what is to be done about these men, when they are found . . .'

Goodale was thinking hard again. He considered the type of individual who would be capable of doing what these men had done. He had come across such people when he had been younger. In fact, he had once thought of volunteering for the SAS himself, but had instead found himself recruited into the shadowy world of army intelligence . . .

The Joint Intelligence Committee broke up half an hour later, and Goodale left the building to return to his office. As he sat back in his car, something was nagging at his mind. It was only a small thing, something just to make him wonder if by chance . . .

'George,' he said suddenly to his driver, 'change of plan. Could you take me out towards Edgware, please.'

THREE HOURS LATER, Goodale was back in his office, a gleam in his eye. He picked up the telephone and rang an old friend. They talked for a few minutes and Goodale asked one question. He got the answer he expected. He made two further calls; one was answered by a machine; at the other number there was no reply. Just as he had expected. Well, well, thought Goodale. He went down to the basement and picked out six files, returning with them to his office. When he had finished reading, he leaned back in his chair and let his eyes go out of focus.

There was a knock on the door and his secretary came in. She looked ill at ease. 'Sir? Could you spare me a moment? It's something, er, personal, about a friend of mine.'

'Certainly, Janey. Come in and sit down.'

The young woman was relieved. Her boss was clearly in a good mood. She blurted out her story in a rush. 'Sir, one of my oldest friends is in trouble. She has this boyfriend, you see, and I said I thought you might know what to do. I mean, she doesn't know who you are, but she knows I work in Security. It's all right—she's a police detective inspector. It's her boyfriend. Well, her fiancé, actually. She thinks he's mixed up in something. She'd like to talk to you.'

Max Goodale smiled. 'This fiancé of hers, Janey,' he said, glancing at one of the files on the desk in front of him. 'His name wouldn't by any chance be Bourne, would it?'

'THE CHECKPOINT OUTSIDE Jiddah is only about twenty miles away now, boss,' Harris called out to Howard from the rear section.

'OK, Mel. What's the usual form there?'

'It shouldn't be a problem. If you smile at the guys and make an effort to speak a bit of the lingo, they normally just let you through.'

'Do they check the paperwork?'

'Yes. Passports, vehicle documents— you know. No problem.'

'Unfortunately, there *is* a problem. Two of the passports—mine and Danny's—don't have Saudi visas in them.' Howard thought for a moment. 'I'll tell you what,' he said. 'We'll hand them all the passports in a bunch, but we won't give them mine or Danny's—we'll give them Andy's and Bob's instead. There's a danger that they might match the faces, but I think it's a lesser risk.'

'OK, boss.'

Howard turned to Bourne, who was lying along the rear seat of the big double cab, his leg still up across Howard's lap. He shook his shoulder gently. 'Johnny? Time to wake up. How are you feeling?'

Bourne opened his eyes. He had drifted in and out of a restless sleep, occasionally wakened by the pain from his leg. 'Weak,' he croaked. 'But the pain has eased. It's not so bad as it was.'

'Good,' said Howard. The painkillers were obviously doing their job. 'Listen, Johnny. We're coming up to a police checkpoint. You're going to have to sit up and look reasonably normal when we pass through it. D'you think you can manage that?'

'Sure,' said Bourne. He raised himself on one elbow. 'Help me up, will you?'

Howard eased Bourne up into a sitting position. He saw Bourne set his jaw in determination, but ten seconds after sitting him up he noticed the pale face grimace; the blood flow to his leg had brought the pain back with a vengeance. There was a sheen of sweat on Bourne's face, and Howard was worried that he would pass out.

Ziegler gave the bored-looking Saudi policeman a radiant smile, and mustered his best Arabic. '*As-salaam aleikum*,' he greeted him. '*Kayf haalak?*' He handed out the passports and the Ram Charger's hire documents, along with his driving licence.

The policeman seemed to take an age to check through the papers, and made a show of leaning down and looking into the vehicle to study each face. Then he disappeared round the back of the vehicle to look into the rear, where Ackford and Harris were sitting with MacDonald. Oh God, thought Howard, he's checking the faces.

Suddenly, the policeman was back. He handed the passports and documents back through the window to Ziegler and waved him on through. As the vehicle started forward, Bourne gave a groan. 'Ed,' he muttered weakly, 'I don't know how much more of that I can take. You'd better leave me behind. I'll never make it onto a plane.'

Howard made up his mind. 'I'm going to give you another shot of morphine, Johnny. All you have to do is remember not to talk too much. We'll get you a wheelchair at the airport.'

'What about the passports, boss?' called Harris. 'How are you going to deal with that? Bamboozling a traffic cop is one thing, but trying to hoodwink an immigration officer is quite another. Neither you nor Mac looks anything like Andy or Bob.'

'I'm going to change the photos. You, Mike and Tony drop the rest of us at the airport; then I want you to go shopping.' Howard gave Harris a list of purchases.

Harris nodded in understanding. 'Do you think it'll work, boss?'

'No. Not a chance,' said Howard drily, grinning. 'But do you have a better idea?'

When they arrived at the airport, Howard and MacDonald hurried off to find an automatic passport-photograph booth, while Ziegler and Palmer went in search of a wheelchair. Harris drove the pick-up a short distance to a temporary parking space and waited in the cab with Bourne and Ackford. Ten minutes later, he saw Palmer and Ziegler returning with a borrowed wheelchair.

'Luxury model, Johnny,' beamed Ziegler. 'It's got a leg-rest, so you'll be able to keep your foot up—don't forget, it's a sprained ankle you've got.' They lifted Bourne into the wheelchair and Palmer trundled him off towards the terminal. Ziegler climbed into the front of the cab beside Harris and Ackford. 'OK, guys; let's go shoppin'.'

Half an hour later, the team reassembled in the departure hall of the airport. Howard had bought tickets for them all on the first available flights out; he and MacDonald would travel on a separate flight from the others. Harris had replaced the original licence plates on the hired Land Cruiser and checked it in. Ziegler handed Howard a small bag containing the things he had bought and went off to check in the hired Ram Charger.

Howard had a brief word with each of the others; then he disappeared to the rest room and locked himself in a cubicle. He took out a scalpel blade and carefully slit around the edge of the photograph in Usher's passport, cutting through the thin transparent plastic film that sealed it to the page. He began to prise the photograph off with the blade. The glue was stubborn, and he managed to get only the edges away. It was enough; the replacement photograph would cover what was left. With a stationery-embossing tool and a set of simple patterned dyes, he began to copy the embossed Passport Office stamp onto a photograph of himself, taken in the booth. It was a slow process, but after twenty minutes he was reasonably satisfied. Laying his photograph over the removed one of Usher, he lined up the embossed lines and stuck it down lightly with glue. Then he took a thin sheet of transparent adhesive film, cut it roughly to size and laid it over the passport page. Using the scalpel blade, he trimmed it to exactly the same size as the original. Howard inspected the finished result. His own face stared out from Usher's passport; he just hoped the Saudi immigration officer would not notice the disparity in the stated height—he was nearly four inches taller than Usher. He began to repeat the process for Denard's passport, using MacDonald's photograph.

Howard emerged at 12.45; he found MacDonald sitting alone. 'The others all get off OK, Danny?' he asked.

'Aye,' answered MacDonald, a strange look on his face. He looked at Howard. 'It seemed wrong, somehow, saying goodbye to them here. They're a hell of a good bunch,' he added with sudden feeling. 'I'll miss them.'

'We had to split up at some stage, Danny,' said Howard gently. 'If we all arrived back home at once, we might attract attention. Especially with two injured. We're the biggest risk, as we're the ones with false passports. So we go last, to give the others a chance.'

'What about the other end? Will these fool British immigration?'

'They won't have to,' said Howard. 'When we get to Rome, we'll go through Italian immigration on our own passports. EEC passports, they won't be stamped. I'll say goodbye to you in Rome— you'll have to get a ticket for the next flight back to the UK. There'll be nothing in your passport to show that you ever left Europe. Come on, let's go.'

As they walked towards the immigration counter at the entrance to the departure lounge, MacDonald felt that every eye in the huge airport building was on him. He sneaked a glance at Howard.

'Keep it natural, Danny,' murmured Howard casually.

In a half-daze, MacDonald handed over Denard's passport. He tried to appear nonchalant, but as the immigration officer flicked through the pages of the passport his heart was pounding.

Then there was a thump as the stamp came down on the page; the officer handed the passport back to him. 'Thank you, Mr Denard,' he rattled off in English. 'I hope you have enjoyed your stay in Saudi Arabia.'

'Aye,' said MacDonald with a sudden smile. 'I've had the time of my life.'

THE CAR TURNED OFF the Spean Bridge road into the cottage gateway and stopped; the Deputy Director of MI5 got out and walked up the path. He knocked twice and waited, glancing idly at a workbench standing under a lean-to shelter at the side of the cottage.

The door opened. Danny MacDonald stood in the doorway, one arm in a sling. His face registered surprise and then pleasure. 'Well, hello, sir! This is a pleasant surprise! Will you come in?'

'Thank you, Danny,' said Max Goodale. He followed MacDonald through into the sitting room. It was a warm, welcoming room; a pretty young woman with auburn hair was busy hanging a pair of curtains on a rail. She got down from the stool as Goodale entered.

'Sir, I'd like you to meet my fiancée, Sheila.' MacDonald introduced them; Sheila blushed and smiled.

'Delighted to meet you, my dear,' said Goodale, also smiling.

'Can I offer you a cup of tea?' asked Sheila.

'That would be very kind,' said Goodale. 'Then I'm afraid I must have a private talk with Danny. I do hope you don't mind?'

Sheila looked puzzled, but a nod from Danny reassured her. She went into the kitchen and the two men sat down. Goodale and MacDonald exchanged small talk until Sheila reappeared carrying a tray with tea and shortbread biscuits. Goodale thanked her and she returned to the kitchen, leaving the men alone.

For a few seconds there was silence, then Goodale spoke. 'Nasty wound, that, Danny,' he said quietly. 'Has a doctor seen it?'

MacDonald looked uncertain of himself. 'Just a cut, sir, that's all it is.' He forced a smile.

'From what I've heard, it's a bloody great big half-inch-diameter hole, not a cut,' retorted Goodale, his eyes suddenly steely.

The blood drained from MacDonald's face. 'Who . . . who on earth told you that, sir?'

'I saw a friend of yours yesterday,' replied Goodale, his eyes never leaving MacDonald's face. 'A fellow called Johnny Bourne. But he didn't give me your name. I already knew. And that nice suntan you have,' he added caustically, 'does rather confirm it.'

MacDonald was shattered. His voice, when it came, was a whisper. 'How did you find out? What gave us away?'

'A combination of things. Bad luck and sheer coincidence, mostly. But more of that in a minute. First, I'll tell you a story. Perhaps you'll correct me if I get any of the details wrong.'

MacDonald nodded dumbly.

'I never knew how your brother Fergus died,' began Goodale, looking keenly at the photograph above the chimneypiece, 'but last Wednesday I remembered something I had read in the newspapers and hadn't connected with you at the time. So I went to a library to look up some back numbers. Fergus was married to a Bahraini girl, wasn't he?' MacDonald did not contradict him, so he carried on. 'He went to live out in Kuwait, to work for an oil company. When the Iraqis invaded, he and his family were taken prisoner. He was tortured, and his wife and young daughter were beaten and repeatedly raped by Iraqi soldiers, then dragged away. Their mutilated bodies were found two days later. Your brother was held as part of Saddam Hussein's "human shield" hostage programme, and eventually released. He died about three months later, a broken man. Have I got it right?'

'Yes, sir,' said MacDonald hoarsely, the pain of the memory showing in his voice. Then he blurted out, 'It was only because of what happened to him that I agreed to do this thing!'

'I know, Danny.' Goodale's tone was gentle. 'Ed Howard knew about Fergus too, didn't he? That was how he recruited you?'

'Yes,' answered MacDonald. 'He said he knew of three reasons why he thought I would do the job, and I realised immediately what he meant. Fergus, his wife and his daughter. How did you find out about Ed?'

'An acquaintance of mine called Henry Stoner remembered being asked about you by Howard. You've heard of Stoner. He wrote to you to try to get you to join his rifle-shooting team.'

'Yes.'

'When I rang Howard's number, I got a prerecorded message saying that he was away. I rang you here, too, and there was no reply. It all seemed to fit. Now, Danny'—Goodale again looked Mac-Donald straight in the eye—'I want you to answer my questions. First, what exactly happened that day in Tikrit?'

The story took Danny MacDonald nearly an hour to relate; he described the events vividly and in unstinting detail. Goodale hardly interrupted. It all poured out of Danny with passion; his eyes lit as he told of the death of Saddam Hussein, then darkened as he recounted with sadness the deaths of two friends.

When he had finished, Goodale fixed his gaze on MacDonald. 'Who was the other man you shot, Danny? The one standing on the platform behind Saddam's double?'

'His name was Ala'a Hussein Ali,' said MacDonald slowly. 'When the Iraqis invaded Kuwait, he was a colonel in their secret police, the Mukhabarat. Saddam made him nominal Prime Minister of Kuwait. He personally supervised the torture of my brother—Fergus told me, before he died. I recognised him on the platform.' MacDonald's voice had become tight and hard. 'Ed never asked me why I'd shot the man, but I think he knew. The other man with us in the hide thought I'd gone mad. He thought I'd yelled "Allah", as if I was some sort of religious maniac. It was the name Ala'a that I was shouting.'

Goodale was silent for a while before speaking. 'I have one more question, Danny. I want you to think very hard before answering it.' He paused and leaned forward, his eyes stern. 'Do you know who was behind this operation? The man who recruited Howard?'

The reply was instant. 'No. Ed never told me. He never told any of us. The general consensus was that the British Government was behind it.'

Goodale appeared satisfied. 'Right, Danny. I believe you. You've given me the answers I wanted.' There was a look of puzzlement on MacDonald's face; Goodale continued. 'I shall now tell you what is going to happen, and why. Before I do, I must ask you to give your solemn word that you will never again speak about what you have done, to *anyone*. Nor will you ever discuss our conversation today. Is that understood?'

MacDonald nodded. 'You have my word, sir,' he said simply.

Goodale inclined his head in acknowledgment. 'Good. Now; it would be possible to prosecute you, Howard, Bourne and the others. Between you, you have committed a large number of serious offences in this country. Am I making myself clear?'

'Yes, sir,' replied MacDonald miserably.

'However,' Goodale went on, 'any defence lawyer would use the background to the story, and the details of your deeds abroad, to maximum potential. There would be the most almighty rumpus. Quite apart from the possibly catastrophic diplomatic repercussions *vis-à-vis* a number of other countries—Saudi Arabia being the most obvious—it's quite clear to me that your prosecution would be pointless. Do you see what I'm driving at?'

'Not really, sir,' mumbled MacDonald, now thoroughly perplexed.

'It's quite simple, Danny. If the full story got out, which it would be bound to do, you and your colleagues would, in the eyes of public opinion, become national heroes overnight. I cannot see any jury in the land giving more than two minutes' thought to the matter. You would get off scot-free, if you'll excuse the expression.'

'Oh,' said MacDonald blankly.

'So,' Goodale pressed on, 'I intend to spare the British taxpayer the expense of an unnecessary trial, the outcome of which would be not only a foregone conclusion but also a miscarriage of legal justice— which might encourage other hotheads to think that they could get away with a similar exercise elsewhere. The Director of Public Prosecutions has confirmed to me that a prosecution would not be in the public interest.

'So,' concluded Goodale, 'it seems that you and your colleagues escape the axe. This time. But don't ever, *ever*, even *think* of doing anything like this again.'

MacDonald was dumbfounded. Goodale was going to let him off. He cleared his throat. 'Thank you very much, sir,' he managed to say, his voice shaking with gratitude and relief.

Goodale smiled and relaxed. 'Johnny Bourne sends you his regards, by the way. His leg won't be quite what it was, but he will walk again. And I can assure you that when he does, he'll walk the straight and narrow. His first journey'—Goodale gave a little chuckle—'will be down a church aisle in two or three weeks' time. Have you met his fiancée? No,' he went on without waiting for a reply, 'I don't suppose you would have. She's a detective inspector with the Metropolitan Police. A quite remarkable girl.'

'How did you find out about Johnny?' asked MacDonald.

'It was a simple matter of deduction, once I had Howard's name,' replied Goodale. 'Bourne was an obvious choice for Howard to make from among the people in his security company. I'd like to meet Howard himself one day, but he is proving, shall we say . . . elusive. I expect Ziegler is another, and possibly Harris . . . I don't know yet. The American pilot, Sullivan, is a bit of a riddle. And the South African . . . but I am retiring next month—for good, this time,' he said with a grin, 'and it will give me something to do, trying to piece it all together. But never mind. Let's forget it, shall we?'

MacDonald felt as if an enormous weight had been lifted from his shoulders. 'I don't know what to say, sir. I'm very grateful . . .'

'Nonsense, Danny, nonsense,' beamed Goodale. 'Now,' he said, standing up, 'I must be off. My congratulations on your engagement—your Sheila seems a delightful girl. And I much look forward to seeing you again at Glen Carvaig this October, for our annual outing on the hill. But,' he added pointedly, 'no more long-range shots, understood?'

MacDonald grinned. 'You have my word on that too, Colonel.'

SIR PETER DARTINGTON sat alone in his office in London, pondering the extraordinary events of the day. Tuesday, May 5, 1992; he wouldn't forget it in a hurry.

First thing that morning, he had gone downstairs to the study in his house in the country. On top of the pile of post was a plain manila envelope addressed to him from Italy. He opened it and then sat down heavily when he saw the sequence of photographs. The pictures clearly showed the shooting of Saddam Hussein. *Ye gods*, he breathed, Ed Howard has done it. He's done it! Hurriedly, he locked the photographs in the safe and left for London.

On his arrival at the office, the second extraordinary event of the day unfolded. Everyone was smiling, shaking his hand, congratulating him. Bewildered, he asked what all the fuss was about. Dorothy Webster broke the news to him. Darcon had been awarded three major contracts it had bid for. Not one, not two, but *three*! He felt triumphant, ecstatic.

He thought about the two contracts he had been promised as payment for setting up the assassination. Yes, two of these three must have been awarded in that connection. One was obvious—the motorway-widening in the north of England—but Dartington could not think how the government could have swung either of the others. But it didn't matter. He opened several bottles of champagne to celebrate with his delighted staff.

That was when the third thing happened. Dorothy Webster announced a visitor, who was apparently very insistent on seeing Dartington in private. 'It's a Mr Goodale, Sir Peter. He has shown me a card. He's from the police.'

Dartington had soon found out exactly who Goodale was. He wasn't a policeman at all. The man had come straight to the point; Dartington had been badly rattled.

Now he sat in his chair, reflecting on what the MI5 man had said to him—Goodale, the sprightly little man with those intense blue eyes which missed nothing. For a moment, when Goodale had told him that he knew about the deal, Dartington had been too shaken to concentrate. Then, as he was leaving, Goodale had made some other remark. 'Just give a bit of thought to those other two contracts, would you? Who do you imagine would have been able to swing those for you?' What could he possibly have meant by that?

It made no sense at all. None whatsoever, brooded Dartington, unless . . . No. That was ridiculous. Dartington's mind quickly ran over the implications. The unease he felt turned to horror as he realised that it was a perfect explanation for the puzzle; it tallied with all the facts. But it wasn't possible! It couldn't be!

The truth of it, suddenly so obvious, hit Dartington in a blinding flash. He grasped the enormity of what he had done. He buried his face in his hands.

THE MINISTER WAS ON CLOUD NINE. The meeting with the Prime Minister had gone better than he had dared hope. He had been congratulated for the success of his plot to assassinate Saddam Hussein, and was now assured of promotion.

Asher had had to be disposed of, of course. A pity, thought the Minister; the man had been useful over the years. A repulsive pig of a man, unprincipled, gluttonous and degenerate—but useful. Scandals had been looming; Asher had been involved in all sorts of financial chicanery. If he had been exposed . . . No, he had had to be dealt with. The Minister had taken charge of it. The 'accident at sea' had been his own idea, and it could not have worked out better; his men had made no mistakes, left no clues. The Prime Minister had expressed his pleasure about this too, and had not hesitated to sign the final approval for the two construction contracts to go to Darcon. Yes; the Minister had every reason to feel elated.

The Mercedes pulled into the drive of the Minister's luxurious house in the suburbs of the city. His driver opened the door, and the heat hit the Minister as he stepped out of the car's air-conditioned coolness. It was unusually hot, even for the time of year. The noonday call of the *muezzin* sounded in the distance. As Minister for Protocol in the Iranian Government, he knew that it would not do to miss the call to prayers. He decided to say a special prayer for the soul of his country's martyred ambassador.

ON WEDNESDAY, MAY 6, 1992, the Iraqi television service broadcast a short piece as the lead item in its early-evening news programme. The President was briefly shown inspecting a guard of honour; in the background, a large formation of armour could be seen, the soldiers standing to attention beside their vehicles. He was accompanied by Izzat Ibrahim, the cadaverous Vice-President of Iraq, and a number of aides in military uniform. One was carrying a newspaper which he held up to the camera as he walked past. It was clearly dated May 5.

The American CNN, the British BBC and a handful of other broadcasting organisations around the world picked up the item and broadcast it, for the simple reason that it afforded the first confirmed new glimpse of Saddam Hussein that there had been for many weeks.

Some of the more observant viewers formed the distinct impression that the Iraqi President seemed rather more unsure of himself, perhaps less in control, than they remembered from previous footage. There was nothing in particular they could put their finger on, but . . . it was almost as if, somehow, they weren't watching the same man.

Just a handful of viewers, however, were paying very close attention indeed. They noticed one other detail, ostensibly a minor one, which made them sit bolt upright in their chairs and reach for their telephones. There was something missing. The pistol holster on the President's belt was empty. The man was unarmed.

DAVID MASON

David Mason has had a distinguished military career and is a trained sniper. Commissioned into the Welsh Guards in 1970, he was seconded to the Sultan of Oman's army from 1974 to 1976. In 1975 he was awarded the Sultan's Bravery Medal for his part in two actions. In the first he rescued wounded men while under heavy fire, and in the second he extracted more casualties from a mined track on a sheer cliff-face by night.

After his army days, David Mason concentrated on his work as an Oxfordshire landowner, but his family kept suggesting that he ought to write a book capitalising on his military experience.

The subject for such a book took time to germinate. The process started when Mason's nine-year-old daughter learned that there was going to be a war in the Middle East. It worried her and she asked her father: 'Aren't lots of people going to be killed?'

When he agreed that this was probably true, his daughter had another question for him: 'Why doesn't somebody just kill Saddam? Then all these other people wouldn't have to die.' Mason thought that it was a pretty good question, and he started to ask himself how he would go about eliminating Saddam Hussein if he were given the job—as an unofficial operation, of course.

'It's a lot easier to do something like that if you have official backing,' he told us. 'James Bond, for example, could always rely on the British Embassy to supply him with kit and cover stories. Operating on your own is a lot harder.' Nevertheless, he prepared a plan for the operation, and convinced himself that it could actually work. This plan was the basis of his book.

The result, *Shadow Over Babylon*, has been an extraordinary success story for a first novel: snapped up by an eager publisher and now being translated into eighteen languages.

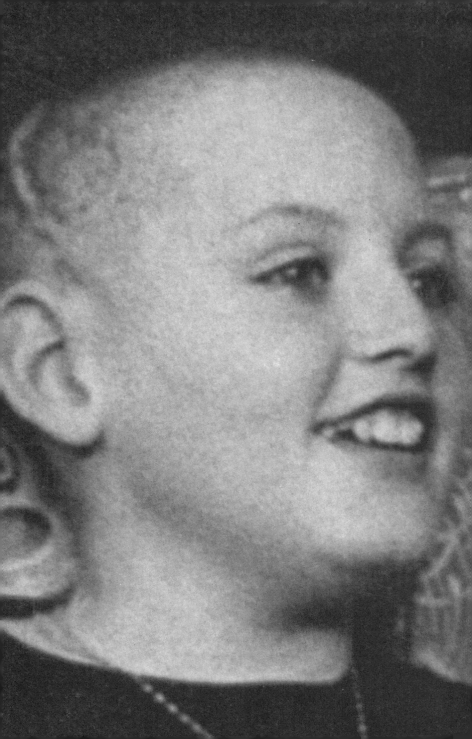

Craig Shergold
A Mother's Story

by Marion Shergold
with Pamela Cockerill

Craig Shergold was as active and lively as any nine-year-old boy—a fanatical supporter of Chelsea Football Club. Then, two minutes into the flight back from a holiday in Benidorm in 1988, Craig started to complain about his ears hurting. The pain came and went over the next few weeks. Antibiotics did not seem to help, and eventually Craig's condition worried his mother so much that she took him to hospital. On their second visit it was realised that Craig was very seriously ill indeed . . .

Introduction

It all began as a bit of a joke really. Not that you're in the mood for jokes when you've just been told your child might be dying, but Richard Hayward was good at getting people to smile. He always had a twinkle in his eye and the whole ward used to brighten up when he came in to see his patients. That morning Mr Hayward stopped with his students, as he always did, at the foot of Craig's bed.

'How are you feeling today, Craig? How's the earache?'

'Well . . .' Craig screwed up his face. 'I reckon it's not quite as bad as it was yesterday,' he said slowly. Something had happened to his voice in the few days since he'd been rushed to Great Ormond Street Hospital. He was drawling his words and leaving long gaps between them. It was as if some other child was in Craig's body. I think Mr Hayward knew how I felt because he looked over at me and smiled. 'All right, Mother?'

I nodded. I couldn't trust myself to speak. Part of me was still hoping I'd wake up and find the whole thing had been a bad dream.

Mr Hayward checked the side of Craig's head where his brain shunt had been put in three days before. They'd shaved half his hair off and the dark red scar stood out like a half-moon against his white scalp.

'That looks fine to me, Craig. All being well we should be able to do the next operation on Monday as we planned.' Then, as he turned to go, Mr Hayward noticed the walls around Craig's bed. 'My goodness, someone's been busy.'

Up until yesterday there'd only been about thirty get-well cards on

189

Craig's wall—the ones that had come in the first day we got there. Since then, as more and more of our friends and family had heard the news, lots more cards had arrived. But I was afraid we might make the other kids in the ward jealous if we made a big show of them. Not all of them had dozens of uncles and aunties like Craig. So I'd just piled the cards on Craig's bedside locker.

But the day before Mr Hayward had spotted that great wobbly pile of cards and he'd given me a real ticking off. 'What are they doing there? Get them up where he can see them.' He'd spread his arms. 'I want this child to have as much spiritual upliftment as possible.'

After he'd gone the nurses had helped me string all the cards round the walls. There were hundreds of them, cards from the family and neighbours, homemade cards from every child in Craig's school, cards from my friends at work and from Ernie's mates at the London Electricity Board. There was hardly an inch of wall space showing around Craig's bed from floor to ceiling. And I had to admit that it had cheered Craig up. He'd taken more of an interest in these cards than in anything since he'd been in hospital.

Now Mr Hayward put on a great act for Craig's benefit, turning slowly round and round as he stared at the walls, dropping his jaw and making his eyes go wide. 'I just don't believe it,' he said at last. 'I have never in my life seen so many get-well cards for one little boy.'

Craig chuckled and a little bit of the old sparkle came back into his eyes. 'It's good, innit?' he said.

'It certainly is. You must have more friends than anyone I know.' Mr Hayward turned to the students behind him. 'I think he should go in the *Guinness Book of Records*, don't you?'

They laughed politely. 'Yeh! Go for it, Craig!' one of the nurses called across the ward as Mr Hayward moved on to the next bed.

He hadn't meant it seriously. I knew that. It was my friend Alison who took him at his word. She'd been sitting next to me while Mr Hayward was doing his rounds and for the rest of the morning she seemed lost in thought. I didn't pay her too much attention as I was too worried about Craig. His face had swollen up and his skin was turning a terrible yellow colour. Every so often he'd moan and his body would give a great jerk as if he'd had an electric shock. I sat on my chair beside the bed, rocking backwards and forwards in despair.

'Marion—why don't we try for it?' Alison said suddenly.

I stared at her. 'What are you talking about?'

'The *Guinness Book of Records*.'

'Alison, Mr Hayward was only kidding. He didn't mean it for real.'

'I know that. I still think we should do it.'

I couldn't believe she was serious. Craig was dying. I didn't care a fig about the *Guinness Book of Records*. I shook my head. 'What's the point, Alison?'

'It would give Craig something else to think about instead of just being ill,' she said. 'That's the point. And you too. It would help take your mind off all this.'

I hesitated. I knew there was some sense in what she was saying. 'What would we have to do?'

'We'd launch an appeal asking people to send him get-well cards,' Alison said. 'I could ring all our customers at work for a start. Write to a few local companies. Maybe the *Sutton Guardian* would run a story about it. What do you think?'

'I'm not sure. How many cards do you think we'd have to get?'

'Oh, I don't know . . . A thousand? Two thousand?'

I thought. A couple of thousand cards didn't seem an impossible target. Craig must have received over two hundred already.

'If we don't do it the cards will stop coming soon,' Alison urged. 'You can't have many friends who haven't sent one yet. And you know how Craig loves getting his cards.'

It was true. He wanted to open every one himself. It was the only time he really seemed to wake up.

'Oh all right then, Alison,' I said. 'I suppose it can't do any harm. Let's go for it . . .'

IF SOME OLD GYPSY had read my tea leaves that day in Great Ormond Street Hospital and told me that over the next four years Craig would receive more than 100 million get-well cards from caring people all over the world, I wonder if I'd have believed her.

And if that same gypsy had told me that our small council house would overflow with sackfuls of get-well cards; that every week for nearly four years I would have to rope in dozens of friends and neighbours to help me open Craig's mountain of mail, would I have believed that? And if I had believed it, would I have gone ahead?

I like to think I would. I pray I would. Because one thing is certain. If I hadn't said yes to Alison's idea that afternoon, my son Craig Shergold would not be alive today.

One

There'd been no reason to think on the night that Craig was born that he wasn't going to grow up to be a healthy little boy.

He came into the world at 10.30pm on June 24, 1979— Midsummer's Night—in St Helier Hospital, South London, just down the road from Carshalton where Ernie and I lived. It was a perfectly straightforward, normal birth.

I know every baby is a miracle to its own mum and dad but Craig was extra special for us because we'd had to wait twelve whole years for him. Steven, our first baby, had been born in 1967 when I was nineteen, and we'd always planned to give him a little brother or sister. But it hadn't happened. Then, in November 1978, when we'd just about given up hope, I'd found I was pregnant again. We were over the moon. We'd thrown such a party to celebrate, the singing and dancing had gone on all night and most of the next day.

And now, at last, our new baby was safely here and our family was complete. After Ernie left for home the nurse tucked me up in bed in a side ward with Craig snug in a cot beside me. 'Now sleep, Mrs Shergold,' she ordered, and she switched out the light. Sleep? She'd be lucky! The minute the door closed I flicked the light back on and dived into the cot. I unwrapped the blankets and carefully checked every inch of him. He was perfect.

He had a mop of the most wonderful dark hair. As I ran my fingers through it and saw the big fat neck underneath I started to giggle. That was Ernie's neck—there was no mistaking it. Still, at least he hadn't got my nose, poor child. In fact he was such a pretty baby, with his long dark eyelashes and rosebud mouth, that he almost looked like a girl. I wrapped him carefully back up and cradled him in my arms. In my whole life I'd never felt such happiness. I remember I said a little prayer. 'Dear God. Please, please, don't let anything happen to him. I love him so much already.'

We decided to call our new baby Craig. 'It means strong and enduring, like a rock,' I told Ernie.

The day before I was due to take Craig home from hospital my best friend Carol came in to see him. She was cuddling Craig, when out of the blue I said to her, 'Do you know, Carol, if anything happened to him I think I'd die.'

She gave me a funny look. 'Nothing's going to happen to him, Marion. What on earth made you say that?'

'It's hard to explain,' I said. 'It's just that I'm so happy now and sometimes when I look at him I get this awful feeling that something is going to come along to spoil it. I don't know why. I wasn't like this with Steven.'

Carol put her arm round me. 'Don't be so daft. Craig's going to be fine,' she said. 'You've got the baby blues, that's all.'

I told myself she was right and whenever the terrible flashes of doubt rose up I did my best to push them away. Gradually the feeling came less and less often. But it never quite went away.

EVEN BEFORE I HAD KIDS of my own I'd always believed that family life was the most important thing in the world. I grew up in a big tenement building in the Boro'—the local name for the Borough of Southwark just south of the Thames. We only had two rooms, one for eating and one for sleeping, and twelve families had to share the toilet on our landing. I had a really happy childhood. My mum came from a very big family and our living room was always full of people. My brother Kevin and I grew up surrounded by singing and laughter and love, and I wanted that for my own kids. I've never had time for those who think you spoil kids by showing them too much affection.

So, though Ernie and I were often short of money, and there weren't many toys while Craig was growing up, I made sure that there were always plenty of cuddles. I don't know if that was why, but Craig grew into a very contented baby. He was always smiling and laughing, and boy, did he love an audience! He was a real performer.

He was musical too. Almost from the day he could talk he could sing. My mum had a lovely voice and she and Dad taught him the same old cockney songs that they'd taught me and Kevin—by the time Craig was three or four years old he knew them all off by heart.

When he was five Craig announced that he wanted to be an actor when he grew up. I took him seriously. Performing is in the blood on my side of the family. My mum's father was a musician and played the trumpet in some famous band before I was born. When we were growing up in the Boro', Dad boosted his wages from the brewery by playing the piano and singing down the pub every Saturday night. Sometimes my mum would sing as well and if Kevin and I behaved ourselves we were allowed to sit in a corner and listen. My sister Kate was born after we moved from the Boro' and, although she never saw those pub concerts, nevertheless she grew up to be a professional singer.

Sadly the family voice missed me out, but I did inherit the Blydes' love of an audience. Ernie tells people that the restaurant is my stage, and I think you have to be a bit of an actress when you work as a waitress. You put on different faces for different occasions—jokey for a football-club dance, polite for a black-tie dinner. I could put on different voices too. I'd talk as if I'd been to finishing school if I was serving at a Buckingham Palace garden party, but in the clubhouse serving breakfast to the Chelsea team after training you'd never know I'd left the Boro'. Being a waitress was one long performance, and I loved it!

I need people around me. People and parties have always been like food and drink to me. I'm different from Ernie who's quiet by nature and a bit of a loner. Also Ernie is easy-going and doesn't get worked up as easily as me. We do have plenty in common, but I think it's our differences which have helped Ernie and me through the rough times. Our temperaments seem to balance each other out.

IN THOSE FIRST FEW YEARS of his life I often thought I'd chosen the wrong name for Craig. 'Strong as a rock' sometimes seemed like a bad joke. Steven had never suffered from a single childhood illness, but Craig caught everything. He'd only just got over chickenpox and measles when he caught whooping cough (he hadn't been vaccinated because one of Ernie's nephews had epilepsy). He whooped and whooped until he foamed at the mouth, and by the end of every day he had a blinding headache from coughing so much. At least I used to think then it was from the coughing. Sometimes now I wonder.

It was in March 1984 that Craig gave us the biggest fright. One morning when I went to wake him up he wouldn't get out of bed. 'Come on, lazybones,' I told him. 'You'll be late for nursery.'

His face was white. 'Mum,' he said, 'I can't walk.'

Ernie and I carried him downstairs and put him on the settee and I called the doctor. 'It's just a virus,' he said when he'd examined Craig. 'It's made him feel weak, that's all. It'll pass.'

But it got worse. The next day Craig was admitted to hospital and he stayed there for five days. At first he just slept and slept. Then slowly he started to be more alert and once he was able to stand up and hobble around they let him come home again. They did all sorts of tests on him but they never found anything wrong. 'Don't worry about it, Mrs Shergold. There's no reason anything like it should happen again,' the consultant assured me. But I did worry.

Craig took to school like a duck to water. Like most kids he could be a holy terror, but he could usually talk his way out of trouble and I couldn't stay cross with him for long. Steven didn't often lose his temper with him either, though Craig used to push him to the limit. He always wanted to play with Steven and his friends but, being twelve years older, they didn't always want him hanging around. 'Upstairs! Hop it!' Steven would say when his mates came in. But Craig would pull a pathetic face and go, 'Ohhhh, Ugly!' (Ugly was his pet-name for Steven) and Steven would end up letting him stay.

Craig got hooked on football when I started working at the Chelsea Football Club at Stamford Bridge. The job involved serving breakfast to the players after training and dinners to the directors on match days. Ernie and his whole family had always been mad keen Chelsea fans, and with me working there as well, there was only one team that Craig could possibly support. Even his pop idol, Kylie Minogue, had to take second place to Chelsea.

THAT YEAR WAS A BAD TIME for me. My mum found a lump on her breast and the doctors told her it was cancer. When they'd finished giving her chemotherapy at the Royal Marsden Hospital I nursed her at home until she died in July 1988. Everyone had loved my old mum. She was a real old-type cockney who called a spade a spade. It had been a struggle for her to make ends meet but I never heard her complain. Her family was always more important to her than money. Craig was the apple of her eye.

After she died I started to have bad dreams. One terrible night in September I dreamed that Craig was dead and lying in a white coffin across my feet on the bed. When I woke up the sweat was rolling off me and Ernie was shaking me. 'What's the matter, Mal? What is it?'

'I've got to see Craig.' I was trembling like a leaf. 'I've got to see if he's all right . . .'

For days afterwards the image of Craig in his coffin haunted me. I saw it everywhere I looked. I knew I had to pull myself together. I was run down. What I needed was a holiday.

We booked a week in Benidorm in November. A whole crowd of friends and family cottoned on to the idea and there were thirty-six of us! Steven and Ernie took a week off work—Ernie was a driver for the London Electricity Board now—and we got permission to take Craig off school. We even persuaded my dad to come along.

We had a terrific time. The nightlife was great. We played my party-music tapes every night in the bar and stayed up till the early hours dancing and singing. Craig joined in everything we did. He was a party person like me, and it was always Ernie and Steve who'd be yawning before him.

On the last day of the holiday six of us decided to go on a coach trip to a place called Guadalest—high in the hills above Benidorm. Craig didn't want to come and we left him in the hotel with Steven, his girlfriend Sharon and their friends.

The view from the top of the old stone steps at Guadalest was wonderful. 'Isn't that absolutely magnificent, Ern?' I pointed down to the brilliant blue lake below us. The holiday had done its job. I felt ready to face life again. '*Adios amigos*,' I shouted.

At the top of the steps there was an old cemetery with a high stone wall around it. On the wall I noticed a plaque with some lettering. The inscription was in Spanish and English. I read it aloud to Ernie.

'*Wanderer stop awhile and think of the marvellous works of God and of your short passage on earth.*'

It was as if a bubble had burst. That plaque brought it all back to me: how much I missed my mum. The inscription touched something deep inside me and I wanted to remember it. I shivered. Suddenly all I

Craig at three years old—my pride and joy.

The Mutual Admiration Society: Craig and my wonderful mum, Kate.

The start of 'the cards'. Under doctor's orders, we strung them up all over the ward.

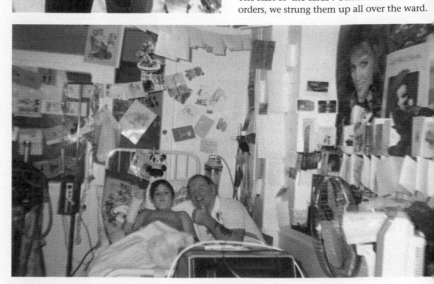

wanted was to get back to the hotel and to Craig.

'Come on,' I said. 'Let's go.' And Ernie tucked his arm through mine and we walked back to the bus.

IT STARTED IN THE PLANE on the way home from Benidorm.

'Oh Mum, my ears hurt,' Craig complained a couple of minutes after we took off. He started to moan and hold his head. The stewardess found some inhaling capsules in the first-aid box, and I broke them on to a handkerchief and held them to Craig's nose. After a while he stopped crying and dozed off. As we were coming in to land the stewardess brought me some paper cups to hold over his ears and it seemed to help.

The next morning Craig came in, his face all screwed up with pain. 'Oh, Mum, my ear does hurt,' he said.

'All right, darling, you can stay off school today,' I said, still half asleep. 'Come on, climb into bed and have a cuddle.' Craig didn't need asking twice. He was always ready for a cuddle.

When the pain hadn't gone away by the afternoon I took him to the local surgery. The doctor thought the flying had probably upset the pressure inside Craig's ears. 'It should settle down in a day or two. Give him a couple of paracetamol if it gets any worse,' he said.

By the third day the pain had eased off and Craig was nagging me to let him go back to school. In the end I gave in, although he was screwing up his eyes and blinking a lot, and I thought he needed sleep. But he was desperate to tell his mates all about Benidorm.

Over the next few days Craig started to look very pale. 'Stay off school, darling,' I urged him. 'There's only a couple of weeks to go before you break up—you won't miss much.' But he was set on going.

'We've got the play. And I'm King Herod. I must go, Mum.'

For a week the earache came, went and came again until after another sleepless night I took Craig back to see the doctor. After he checked Craig's ears he said, 'Would you go and sit in the waiting room, Craig. I'd like a little word with your mother.'

'There's no infection at all in Craig's ears,' he told me when we were on our own. 'I'm not saying the pain isn't real but I'm wondering if it could have been brought on by a delayed reaction to his grandmother's death. He was very close to your mum, wasn't he?'

I was a bit taken aback. But he was right—Craig *had* been terribly close to his nan. He'd idolised her.

'Can you give him anything for it?' I asked.

He shrugged. 'It should get better with time. Give him painkillers if it gets too bad, and try not to worry about it.'

I decided to take his advice. I had something else to worry about now anyway—Steven had just informed us that Sharon was having a baby and that they were going to get married. Compared with that bombshell Craig's earache seemed a minor problem.

By the afternoon of the school nativity play life had settled down again. I was beginning to get used to the idea of being a grandmother, and Craig's earache seemed to be getting better. I went along to the school to see his acting debut. He swaggered on stage wearing his shiny tinfoil crown and gold epaulettes, strode around looking important, and said his lines loud and clear. The next day school broke up and we started to get ready for Christmas.

I'm always very silly at Christmas. It's like Selfridges in our house—you can't get another decoration up on the walls and I always make a sack for everyone, even for Ernie. This year Steven had been invited to Sharon's for the day and, after he left, Craig brought his sack downstairs to open his presents in front of the telly. But after he'd opened them he just said, 'Thanks, Mum,' in a little voice and curled up in the armchair to watch the telly.

I sat down and began to fold up the crumpled paper from his presents, watching him out of the corner of my eye. Craig was still blinking a lot, I noticed, and screwing up his eyes as he stared at the screen. Maybe he was just tired. 'Perhaps we ought to be stricter about his bedtime,' I said to Ernie that night.

Over the next few days I made sure that Craig caught up on his sleep so that he'd be able to enjoy New Year's Eve. We always had a big 'do' to see the New Year in. The day before the party, I woke up with earache myself. The pain was so bad I could hardly speak. I dragged myself to the doctor who shone a light in my ears. 'Well there's no mystery about *your* trouble anyway,' he said. 'You've got a really bad infection in both ears. I'll give you some antibiotics.'

By New Year's Eve I was in agony. 'Come on, Mal, let's call the party off,' Ernie said. 'Everybody'll understand.' But I couldn't face letting people down. I doped myself up with painkillers and spent the day making sausage rolls. At eight o'clock the house started filling up. There was my old dad, wearing a brave face for his first new year without my mum, Steven and Sharon, Ernie's brother Fred and his wife Joyce, Craig's godparents John and Sandra, my sister Kate and her husband Jimmy, and dozens of aunts, uncles and friends.

Craig really seemed to be back to his old self and was doing his bit to help. I stayed in the kitchen carving turkey, pouring drinks and nursing my ear, but I kept catching glimpses of him in the other room offering plates of prawns and cockles around.

Steven came into the kitchen at about ten o'clock. 'Where's Craig, Mum?' he asked. 'I haven't seen him for a bit.'

We found him in his bedroom—curled up tight under his duvet with just the top of his head showing.

'Craig?' I said. 'Aren't you coming down to see the New Year in?' Craig peered out at me. 'No. I'll say Happy New Year tomorrow. I'm very tired.' And his head disappeared again under the duvet.

I closed his door and walked downstairs. The way this ear business seemed to be draining all his energy was beginning to bother me. Then, at midnight, when all the poppers were going off and everyone was singing 'Auld Lang Syne', a pair of feet appeared at the top of the stairs. 'Can I have a popper, Mum?' a little voice asked.

Ernie nudged me. 'Look—there's not much wrong with him now.' For some reason I burst into tears and he put his arm round me. 'Come on, cheer up. It's been a bad year. It's nineteen eighty-nine now—things have got to start getting better.'

But over the next few days, although Craig did seem more like his old self, my earache got steadily worse. Then, two weeks into the new year I woke up to find Craig holding his hand over his ear and sobbing. What I'd been dreading had happened. I'd given Craig my ear infection. By the time we got to the surgery Craig was huddled into a ball, rocking backwards and forwards with the pain. 'Yes, he has an infection,' the doctor confirmed, 'but it's not too bad. I think we've caught it early.' He scribbled on his prescription pad. 'I'll give him some antibiotics. It should start to improve in a day or two.'

After two days Craig was getting worse rather than better. 'I can feel water in my ears, Mum,' he kept saying. Yet again I picked up the telephone to make an appointment with our GP.

'It's not very inflamed,' the doctor said, shining a light in Craig's ear. 'I can't understand why he's in so much pain.' He gave Craig a puzzled look. 'Have you been sick?'

Craig shook his head. 'No. But I feel a bit sick.'

The doctor picked up his pen. 'I'll write a prescription for something to help that. This should take the nausea away.'

'Doctor, he says there's water in his ear,' I remembered.

'It can sometimes feel like that if there's an infection. It should clear up by the time he finishes the antibiotics.'

Our pharmacist was a little Chinese man who could only speak broken English but was always very friendly. I gave him the prescription and saw him frown at Craig before he disappeared. A couple of minutes later he hurried back holding Craig's medicine, but instead of handing it over the counter he came out into the shop and stared into Craig's eyes. Then he looked up at me and his face was worried. 'I no like!' he said.

I felt scared. 'What do you mean, you don't like?'

He shook his head and waved his hands about excitedly. 'Me no happy with your son. Hospital! Hospital!'

Suddenly I was filled with energy. 'Right,' I said. 'Thank you very much.' I bundled Craig back into the car. 'We're going to hospital, Craig,' I said. 'We'll see if *they* can find out what's wrong with you.'

I decided to take him to Queen Mary's, the big children's hospital in Carshalton about a mile away. The casualty department was like a madhouse, with queues of children waiting for attention. It was two hours before we were seen. Craig had gone drowsy again and was lying across my knee by the time a nurse bustled up. 'Now, what's the problem here?' she asked. I told her about the earache and she nodded and stuck a thermometer in his mouth.

Craig's temperature was normal. But the nurse said she would ask a doctor to have a look at him 'just in case' and led us into a cubicle. It was a lady doctor, who looked as tired as I felt. She listened as I told her the whole story and then shone a torch in Craig's ears and tapped his cheekbones. He winced.

'He seems to have blocked sinuses,' she said. 'I think we'll change his antibiotic to a stronger one.' She wrote out a prescription and handed it to me. 'You can collect that from the dispensary here. And I'd like you to get some inhaling crystals for him—you can buy those from any chemist. I'll ask the ENT department to make an appointment for him to see the ear specialist next week. They'll send you a card to let you know what day.'

She seemed very sure of her diagnosis and I left the hospital feeling much calmer. Sinuses weren't too serious.

Ten minutes later I was back at the chemist. I'd given a lift to Theresa, my Irish next-door neighbour, and I left Craig in the car with her. He was dozing and there didn't seem any point in waking him up.

I smiled at the little Chinese pharmacist. 'I've been to the hospital,' I told him. 'They said to get some inhaling crystals.'

'For Craig? No! No!' He did fetch a packet down off the shelf but he wasn't happy about it. I paid for the crystals and he followed me out and peered through the car window. Craig half woke up and stared back at him. 'No like! No like!' the pharmacist said to me again. Then he walked back into the shop, shaking his head.

I felt frightened as I drove home. I knew Chinese people understood things that couldn't be explained by Western doctors, like acupuncture and herbal treatments. What if he had seen something in Craig that English doctors couldn't see?

Ernie pooh-poohed the idea. 'Craig'll be all right. You're just scaring yourself for nothing. Give the new medicine a chance.'

The next morning, when I tiptoed into his bedroom, Craig was sleeping peacefully and his breathing sounded easier. Ernie left for work and I was clearing up his breakfast things when Craig came downstairs, rubbing his eyes. 'Hello, Mum,' he smiled.

'Hello, darling,' I said. 'How are you this morning?'

'I'm unbelievably tired,' he said slowly. Then he gave me a cheeky grin. 'I am hungry though.'

I felt like giving three cheers. Craig hadn't been interested in food for days. He decided that what he really fancied was a bowl of Shreddies in hot milk. I was humming as I warmed up the milk.

Craig sat down at the table. I put the Shreddies in front of him and watched him wolf it down. Typical, I thought. After all my worrying. All he'd needed was a change of antibiotic. I sat there as Craig polished off the bowl of cereal. 'Delicious,' he grinned and pushed his chair back from the table and walked over to the settee.

And then, without any warning at all, he vomited. Only when I say vomited the word doesn't really describe it. What happened was more like an explosion. Craig's breakfast shot out of his mouth across the room and hit the wall so hard it splattered in all directions.

For a moment I stood rooted to the spot. Then I screamed, 'Theresa! Theresa!' I kept yelling my neighbour's name like a mad thing until she rushed in from next door.

'What's the matter, Marion? What's happened?'

I pointed at the walls. 'Craig's been sick.'

Theresa let out her breath. 'Oh Bejasus,' she said. 'Is that all? I thought someone was being murdered. Sure he'll be fine now all the muck's come up. It's just what he needed.'

'He's not *fine*!' I was beside myself. 'You don't know what it was like. Just look at him.'

Craig lay on the sofa, his eyes open, staring into the distance.

'Theresa, please.' I grabbed her shoulder. 'Just watch him while I phone the hospital. I'm afraid to leave him.' Theresa stared at me, but she stood obediently in the living room while I ran to the phone.

I found the number of Queen Mary's Hospital but my fingers were shaking so much I could hardly dial. I asked to be connected to the ear, nose and throat department, and the phone seemed to ring for an age before it was picked up.

'Can I help you?' a bored voice asked.

I tried to stay calm. 'This is Marion Shergold speaking. My son Craig has an appointment some time next week, but he has just been very, very sick. I want to change the appointment to today.'

'I'm sorry, Mrs Shergold, but all the appointments are taken today. Your son has an appointment on Thursday.'

Something told me I was fighting for more than a place in the queue now. 'Listen, lady,' I spat, 'my little boy is not a whinger. I'm telling you he is ill. This sickness was like a *bomb!*'

There was a heavy sigh at the other end. 'Well, I can't promise you anything, Mrs Shergold, but I'll see what I can do. Leave me your telephone number and I'll ring you back.'

Five minutes later the phone rang again. 'I have an appointment for you at three o'clock. I'm afraid that's the best I can do.'

I looked at my watch. Five past nine. How on earth was I going to fill in the next six hours? I ran downstairs. Theresa went back next door and I sat down next to Craig on the settee. He looked up at me. 'Oh, Mummy,' he said, 'I'm so tired.'

Craig didn't often call me Mummy—since he'd been at school it had been Mum. Now it was as though he'd gone back to babyhood. 'Would you like to go on Mummy's bed, Craig?' I asked and he nodded. I cleaned him up as best I could and then half carried him upstairs to our bedroom. I sat by the bed until he fell asleep. Then I covered him up and came downstairs.

It took me nearly an hour to clear up all the mess and disinfect the carpet and walls. Every ten minutes I ran upstairs but Craig was in a very deep sleep, his breathing slow and regular. 'While they're sleeping, they're getting better,' my old mum used to say when kids were ill. I just hoped she was right.

QUEEN MARY'S IS A BIG HOSPITAL made up of lots of single-storey red-brick units separated by neat lawns. I parked the car next to the ENT unit and steered Craig inside. I told a receptionist Craig's name and we sat down in the waiting room. 'There's no one else here, Craig,' I whispered. 'We should be first in.' But before long the tiny room was packed, not just with patients but their brothers and sisters too. There was a box of toys in the corner and some of the kids started having a go at toy drums and xylophones—the din was terrible. Craig was flinching at every sound.

Then one by one the kids who'd arrived after us were called in to see the doctor. I could feel my blood rising. By a quarter to four Craig was looking green. 'Oh Mum, the noise,' he moaned. Every time a child banged on a drum he recoiled as though someone had hit him.

And then, suddenly, his face changed and I moved like lightning. I'd brought a carrier bag with me in case he was sick again but the bag just filled up and overflowed in seconds and Craig continued to throw up all over the floor—it was like a hosepipe gushing out.

No room ever cleared so fast. All the parents just swept their kids out and within seconds we were on our own. Craig stopped vomiting at last and began to cry. A nurse in a blue uniform—I guessed she must be a sister—appeared and bent over Craig. 'All right, sweet-heart,' she comforted him. 'It's all right. Don't cry.'

'I couldn't help it,' Craig sobbed. 'I didn't mean to. I'm ever so sorry.' He was really upset about making such a mess.

'Don't worry.' The sister was looking into his eyes as she spoke and I saw her expression alter. Reaching into her breast pocket she pulled out a small torch and flicked it on. She shone the torch into Craig's eyes. First one, then the other. It was the first time since Craig had been ill that anyone apart from that Chinese pharmacist had looked into his eyes. She stood up and put the torch away. I felt her hand touch my shoulder and when I looked up her face was full of pity.

'Mother,' she said gently, 'your son is very, very ill.'

I stared at her in horror, then I burst into tears. 'I knew he was ill,' I sobbed. 'I kept saying he was ill. Why wouldn't anyone believe me?'

Two

Suddenly Craig was the centre of attention. An Indian lady doctor wearing a sari hurried up and led us into a consulting room. 'Sit down here, Craig.' She pointed to a chair and picked up a headset.

I thought the sister was going to explode. 'You're surely not going to do a hearing test now?' she said, and they started to argue. The sister wanted Craig to go straight down to see the paediatrician, but the ear doctor disagreed. They both seemed to be in a state of panic. Then the consulting-room door swung open and a man in a white coat, who turned out to be the senior registrar, came in. Someone had rung him to say there was an emergency. He took charge of the situation, and before I knew what was happening Craig had been bundled into a wheelchair and the sister was pushing him out of the ENT unit.

The sister pushed the wheelchair straight across the grass outside with the registrar and me running alongside to keep up. The sister carried on through the casualty ward, following a red line on the floor which led into a glass-sided cubicle with a bed in it. Carefully she lifted Craig out of the wheelchair onto the bed.

'Please sit down, Mrs Shergold.' The registrar waved me towards a chair. 'Now, Craig, I'd like you to do a few tests for me. Do you think you can manage to do that?'

Craig nodded. The doctor held up his fingers and asked Craig to count them. He made him touch his nose with his forefinger. He got him to walk along lines on the floor. Craig wasn't very good at any of the tests—he got the numbers wrong, he kept missing his nose and he wobbled like a drunk when he walked the line. By the time the registrar finished Craig was exhausted. We helped him up onto the narrow bed. He turned his head to look at me and I saw his face was beaded with sweat. 'Mum,' he said, 'there's water in my ears.'

'He keeps saying that,' I said. 'Everyone seems to think he's imagining it but he *keeps* saying it.'

The registrar nodded. He was busy writing something at a desk. 'We're going to admit Craig into hospital, Mrs Shergold,' he said.

I'd been expecting it ever since the sister had looked in his eyes, but hearing him say it out loud still came as a shock. All I could think was, I have to ring Ernie. 'Mummy'll be back in a minute, darling,' I told Craig. I stumbled out of the cubicle and wandered down the corridor until I found a payphone. I took out my purse. There was a twenty-pound note inside. I was in a total panic. I put the receiver down and ran back to Craig.

A new nurse was waiting with him. She told me he was to be admitted to Ward B1 which was in a different part of the hospital. This time he was put on a stretcher and lifted into one of the hospital's small blue ambulances for the 200-yard journey.

Less than ten minutes after being put into a hospital gown and tucked up in bed, Craig had fallen asleep. I sat on the bottom of his bed, hugging myself for comfort. I thought of the thousands of times I'd sat on Craig's bed watching him sleep like this, hurting inside with loving him so much. But I'd never ever hurt the way I was hurting now. I sat there in a sort of trance watching him. Then at eight o'clock the ward door swung open and Ernie hurried in followed by Mitchell, my brother Kevin's son. I was so relieved to see them. Somehow I expected poor Ernie to make everything all right.

He put his arms round me. 'Oh, love, I've been looking everywhere for you. Why didn't you leave me a note?' Then his eyes moved to the bed and I felt him go rigid. 'Oh, Mal . . .'

I started to gabble. 'I had to get him here, Ernie. He's very ill. They've said he's ever so poorly.'

Craig must have heard Ernie's voice and his eyelids fluttered open. 'Hello, Dad,' he said and he gave Ernie a lovely big smile.

'Hello, son,' Ernie said in a choked voice. 'What's all this then? You're going to be all right, aren't you?'

'Yeh,' Craig said, as breezy as anything. 'Course!'

'Craig looks better than you do, Marion,' said Mitchell, trying to lighten the atmosphere. But Ernie was shaking now. I was too.

'Go on, Mitchell, you go home,' Ernie said. 'Thanks for the lift.'

We sat beside Craig's bed and I started to tell Ernie everything that had happened. Suddenly the ward doors opened and the registrar walked up to Craig's bed. 'I've arranged for Craig to go to St Helier Hospital for a brain scan,' he said quietly. 'The ambulance should be here in a few minutes.'

Twenty minutes later we found ourselves sitting in the ambulance beside Craig for the short journey to St Helier. Craig was wide awake again, and I felt calmer. At least things were moving along now.

But when the two young female radiographers met us at the scanner room I knew there was something very wrong. These women were wearing white coats but underneath they were dressed up to the nines. I nudged Ernie. 'They've come in specially,' I said. 'They've come in just for our Craig.'

'No.' Ernie shook his head. 'Course they haven't. They'll be working an evening shift.'

'Were you on your way out tonight, then? Have we messed up your evening?' I asked.

One of the girls shrugged and said, 'Yes, we have come in specially but please don't worry about it. He'll be all right.'

They wheeled Craig into the scanner room and the door closed behind them. And suddenly it came to me what must be wrong with Craig. The papers had been full of it recently—there was an epidemic among school kids up North.

'You know what I think, Ernie?' I said slowly. 'I think he's got meningitis.'

Ernie glared at me. 'Shut up, Marion,' he said. 'Don't you start all that! Just don't you start thinking like that!' Then suddenly his face cracked and he ran out of the room.

Poor Ernie was still in shock from finding Craig in hospital. After all, I'd had a whole day to get used to the idea of how ill he was. But Ernie hadn't had any idea. It wasn't surprising he couldn't handle it.

He came back, his eyes all red and swollen. 'I'm sorry, love.' He sat beside me and took hold of my hand and I put my arm round him.

The doors opened at last and the radiographers wheeled Craig out. He was asleep again. I went up to the trolley and held his hand.

'Has he got meningitis?' I knew the radiographers weren't supposed to tell you what they'd seen—the leaflets in the waiting room told you not to ask them—but I couldn't help myself.

One of the girls smiled brightly. 'No, no he hasn't got meningitis,' she said. 'Don't worry. I'm sure he'll be all right.'

'Oh!' I wanted to kiss her. 'Thank heavens for that!'

A nurse took us downstairs to the foyer to wait for the ambulance to take us back to Queen Mary's.

When it did come, Ernie and I sat opposite each other, both

watching Craig as he made little whimpering noises in his sleep.

'Maybe it's just a virus,' Ernie said suddenly. 'Like he had that time when he was four.'

'Yes.' I nodded. 'He was better in a few days then, wasn't he?' But I knew deep down neither of us believed it.

Outside the ambulance the rain was bucketing down. I could hear the windscreen wipers going and I suddenly remembered a scene from an old black and white film I'd seen years ago, where the hero and heroine were escaping into Mexico in a rainstorm. 'Listen to the windscreen wipers,' the hero had said to his girl. 'Do you hear what they're saying? "Together. Together. Together." '

I listened to the ambulance's windscreen wipers, and I prayed, 'Oh, dear God, please let us always be together. Please don't take our little boy away from us. Please, please, dear God, get him well . . .'

It was past midnight when we got back to the ward at Queen Mary's. Ernie and I sat by Craig's bed watching him, not speaking, our arms round each other. Some time later I heard a noise, and when I looked up I saw the senior registrar talking to the ward sister.

The sister came over and caught my eye. 'Mrs Shergold? Will you and your husband come into the office for a moment. Would you like a cup of tea?'

I jumped to my feet. 'No. I don't want a cup of tea. When you give people a cup of tea you're telling them bad news.'

She reached out to take my arm. 'Look, my dear, come into the office so we don't wake Craig up.'

That worked. 'All right.' I took Ernie's hand and we followed the sister into her office. The registrar was standing in the corner.

'Please sit down,' the sister said.

I shook my head. 'What is it then?' I asked.

The registrar cleared his throat. 'Mr and Mrs Shergold, I'm very sorry to have to tell you this, but I'm afraid that the scan has revealed that Craig has a brain tumour.'

For a long, long moment I felt numb. 'Is he going to die?' I heard myself asking.

The registrar looked at me and his eyes were sad and very tired. 'I'm afraid it's a possibility,' he said.

THE WORLD HAS GONE BLACK. Far away I can hear a voice screaming 'No! No! No!' and I know it's my voice. Not my little boy. Brain tumours happen to other people. It can't happen to us. It just can't . . . I'm trembling all over and I can feel Ernie's arm tight around me trying to calm me down. Then, all at once, I start to feel angry. The doctor's a fool, I think. They've been getting it wrong for the last six weeks.

They've got it wrong again, that's all. How dare he say such a thing about my lovely son? How dare he?

I push Ernie away and run back into the ward and bend over Craig's bed. He's still asleep. He looks so perfect. How can he possibly have a brain tumour? I stand by the bed taking deep breaths, then I go back into the office. 'You're wrong,' I say. 'He's in a lovely sleep.' I glare at them, and then suddenly I double over in sobs because deep inside me I know that my happy, jokey, lovely little boy is going to die.

'WON'T YOU SIT DOWN, Mrs Shergold?' Somehow the sister and a nurse got me onto a chair and Ernie stood behind me and gripped my shoulders. I could feel his sobs shaking through me. The registrar sat down facing us and clasped his hands together. 'I'm afraid there's no way I can make this any easier for you,' he said. 'What the scan has revealed is a very large tumour in Craig's mid-brain. It's about the size of an orange and it doesn't resemble any of the brain tumours I've come across before. There's no one in this hospital who's qualified to interpret the scans in any more depth. What Craig needs now is specialist neurological care and I've arranged to have him transferred to Great Ormond Street Hospital.' He stood up. 'Sister will tell you about the practical arrangements. I really am very sorry.' He closed the door quietly behind him.

I turned to the sister. 'I haven't even got any fags,' I wailed and I gave a hysterical giggle—crying and laughing all at the same time. The sister put her arm round me. She half carried me down the corridor, with Ernie behind, and led us into a room with a bed and a sofa. Then she brought out a packet of cigarettes and lit one for me, and went to get some tea, while Ernie sat down next to me and cuddled me. I'd never needed Ernie's arms round me like I did then.

The sister came back with the tea and sat opposite us. She waited until I'd finished my tea, then said gently, 'We've just had a call to confirm that they're waiting for Craig at Great Ormond Street. Why don't you go home and pack a few things? You'll probably have to stay with him so you'll need sponge bags and a change of clothes for yourselves as well as for Craig. If you get back here by six o'clock you'll be able to travel over with him in the ambulance.'

It was a quarter to two. Outside in the hospital car park the rain was still sheeting down. In the distance I could see the illuminated cross of the hospital chapel. 'Ernie.' I pointed. 'Can we just go in there for a minute?'

We crept inside and I fell to my knees in front of the altar. Ernie has never been a religious man, but he knelt beside me and for five minutes we both prayed as we'd never prayed before. Then Ernie touched my shoulder. 'We'd better go, Mal. Steve'll be waiting.'

By the time we climbed into the car we were both soaked to the skin. The rain was coming down so fast the wipers just couldn't cope with it. Between that and Ernie's tears I don't know how we got home safely that night.

As we turned the corner into Selby Road, I saw Theresa's porch door standing open with the light streaming out onto the garden. Even before we'd opened the gate Steve was at the door. 'Mum, Mum, is he all right?' He looked terrified.

'Come inside, Steve,' said Ernie quietly and pushed him gently back into Theresa's hallway. The door into her front room was open and I could see my brother Kevin and his wife Carole sitting on the settee. They looked just like the last time I'd seen them. Our whole world had turned upside-down. Why did everything still seem so normal?

'Mum. Please tell me what's up. What's wrong?'

I tried desperately to pull myself together. After all, Steve was my son too. I took a deep breath. 'Steve, I'm afraid it's very bad. Craig has got a brain tumour.'

Steve's face twisted in pain. I tried to throw my arms round him but he wouldn't let me. 'No, Mum! No!' he yelled. 'He can't have! Not my brother!' Tears streamed down his cheeks. 'God has got the wrong house. We've never hurt anyone. Why does it have to be us? What have we done wrong? He's taken my nan,' he cried. 'No more!' and he ran out into the night.

'Ern, get him back,' I screamed.

'No. I'll go.' Kevin pushed past me. 'You two get inside.'

Everyone in the house was crying now. Suddenly I heard Kevin calling and I rushed outside. Steve was standing with Kevin in our front garden. I put my arm round Steve and tried to get him in out of the rain. 'I'm sorry, Mum,' he sobbed, 'but I can't take it. I love Craig. He's the best kid in the world.'

He let me cuddle him. 'Come on, Steve, let's go indoors,' I said.

Kevin and Carole decided to drive to my sister Kate's house to tell her the news and they set off, promising to be back by five. We said good night to Theresa and went inside.

'Come on, mate,' I said to Steve. 'You'd better get some sleep. It's nearly three o'clock.'

Steve shook his head. 'No, don't make me go upstairs, Mum. I couldn't sleep on that bunk-bed knowing Craig wasn't there.'

'All right then, lie on the settee,' I said. He fell onto it with a little groan. I knew he was hurting just the same as Ernie and me.

We went upstairs and lay on our bed and held each other close. Ernie tried to reassure me, but I kept seeing that image of Craig in a coffin surrounded by white lace. 'That nightmare's coming true,' I told Ernie. 'Maybe I dreamed the future.'

'No.' He sat up. 'Don't even think it.'

A tumour, they'd said. I remembered Mum lying terrified on the bed, waiting for the results of her breast biopsy, and the doctor's voice as he announced, 'Mrs Blyde, you have a malignant tumour.' And I remembered his astonished look as she cried in relief, 'Oh, God bless you, Doctor! Thank you!' because she hadn't known he meant cancer . . . Did they mean cancer this time too?

Neither of us could keep still. All we wanted to do was to get back to the hospital. At five, Kevin and Carole returned and I made us all a cup of tea before we left. Ernie and Steve sat with me in the back of Kevin's car as he drove to the hospital.

Craig looked like a china doll, his eyelashes dark against his white cheeks. The nurse sitting with him put her hand on my shoulder. 'I've not left him for a second,' she said. 'He hasn't woken up at all.'

I sat on Craig's bed aching to hug him, but afraid to disturb him. Then at last a voice said, 'The ambulance is here. You can wake Craig up now,' and I touched his cheek with my hand.

'Hello, Craig,' I whispered. 'Mum's here.' His eyelashes fluttered and he opened his eyes. I kissed him and he smiled.

'I know,' he said quietly. 'I love you, Mum.' His voice sounded strange and slurred. 'I'm sorry I'm ill.'

Before we'd set off from home I'd promised myself I wouldn't cry in front of Craig, but now I couldn't stop the sobs. His hands came up and cradled my head. 'Don't cry, Mum,' he said. 'I'll be all right.' He looked across at Steve and gave him a sleepy smile. 'Hello, Ugly,' he said. 'Have you been crying over me too?'

By the time they got Craig into the ambulance he was drifting in and out of sleep. Steve and Carole climbed up the ambulance steps after me while Ernie travelled in the car with Kevin.

Now and then Craig's eyes flickered open. 'I've got water in my ears, Mum,' he kept saying. I rocked backwards and forwards. I'd never felt so frightened in my life.

Finally the ambulance stopped and the driver switched off the engine. 'Here we are then.' The driver's mate opened the door and I looked up and saw a dingy building with crumbling concrete balconies. The Great Ormond Street Hospital for Sick Children. Everyone had heard of it—GOSH was one of the best hospitals in the country—but it didn't look too inspiring to me that morning.

We followed Craig's stretcher through the main doors of the hospital into the busy entrance lobby. Craig had dozed off again. Two nurses came up and said they'd been waiting for us. 'Craig is being admitted to the Punch and Judy Ward,' one smiled. They led us to a small lift and Ernie and I piled in after Craig's stretcher.

We got out on the first floor and were met by the ward sister. 'Sorry.' She held up her hand to the others. 'Mum and Dad only.'

I was taken aback when I saw the ward. All the hospital wards I'd ever seen had been orderly with neat rows of beds on either side. But the Punch and Judy Ward was packed with beds laid higgledy-piggledy in all directions so that we had to walk through a sort of maze to reach Craig's bed in the far corner.

Gently the ambulancemen and the pretty nurse who'd travelled with us transferred Craig to the bed and pulled the metal sides up to stop him falling out. Then, with a cheerful 'All the best, Craig', they left to return to Queen Mary's.

There were strange noises coming from further down the ward. I looked over and saw a young boy sitting in a chair. One side of his head was shaved bare showing a long operation scar on his scalp. He was dribbling and he didn't seem able to hold his head up properly. In the cot opposite Craig's bed a baby was crying. He had a row of metal clips right round the front of his head—I shuddered and turned back to Craig.

He was complaining again to Ernie that there was water in his ears. 'Mum, help me,' he said. 'They feel like they're going to break.' I called one of the nurses, who fetched some swabs and probed his ears gently. When she pulled the swabs out they were damp.

She hurried off. Very quickly a doctor arrived at his bedside, took more swabs and sent them off for testing. I felt really upset. Why hadn't anyone listened to him till now?

All morning the tests continued. Three times he was put on a trolley and wheeled away for X-rays, brain scans and sight tests. By the end of the morning he was exhausted and fell into a deep sleep.

Because there was only one chair beside the bed, Ernie, Steve and I took it in turns to sit with Craig. Every time I went out to the visitors' room someone else had turned up. My dad, not able to say a word, shaking his head. My sister, Kate, her face white. My best friend Carol. Ernie's brother, Fred. By midday more than twenty people were waiting their turn to spend a couple of minutes at Craig's bedside. I was touched by all the support and love.

Kevin and Carole were still waiting patiently. When they were finally allowed into the ward, Carole handed Craig a big poster of Kylie Minogue. Craig's face lit up. Kylie was his idol—he had all her records and he watched *Neighbours* on TV every day. Then Kevin handed Craig an envelope. Craig had trouble opening it, but in the end he managed. It was his very first get-well card. It had a clown's face on the front and when you pulled the tab at the bottom the clown poked his tongue out and on his tongue it said 'Get Well'. Craig beamed. I stuck the card up on the wall behind the bed. 'That's the first of many—you wait and see,' I said.

At two o'clock a nurse came over and asked Ernie and me to go to an office up the corridor. She promised to stay at Craig's bedside until we got back. As we went out into the corridor I noticed a board on the wall with pictures of the staff. At the top were photographs of the Great Ormond Street neurosurgeons. One was handsome and distinguished looking, with kind eyes and dark hair turning silver at the temples. As I read the name underneath the photo a strange calm came over me. Mr Richard Hayward. 'That man is going to save Craig's life,' I told Ernie. I'd never felt so sure of anything.

'Come on now, don't start,' said Ernie. 'We won't have any choice.'

We knocked on the door and stepped into a bright modern office. Sitting behind the desk sat the man in the picture.

'Well that's my first prayer answered,' I said.

Richard Hayward smiled, he had a twinkle in his eye. 'Oh? What's that?' he asked.

'I saw your picture,' I said. 'I want you to do my Craig's operation.'

He asked us to sit down and the twinkle in his eye disappeared. 'You must have realised by now that Craig is very ill,' he said gently. 'The scans have shown us that he has a very large tumour in the region of the mid-brain.'

'Is it cancer, Doctor?' I had to know.

'We don't know yet. It has an unusual appearance. It's far too dangerous to try to do a biopsy, so we won't know if it's malignant until we try to remove it. What we're most concerned about at the moment is that the tumour is causing fluid to build up in Craig's brain. That's the reason he's experiencing such severe earache.'

'Is that why he's got water in his ears?' I asked.

'That's right.' Mr Hayward nodded. 'We've started treating the problem with drugs and we plan to put a small plastic device called a shunt into Craig's brain to drain away the fluid. Once the pressure's relieved we'll be in a better position to try and remove the tumour.'

'He will be all right though, won't he?' I interrupted.

Mr Hayward stood up and came round to our side of the desk. 'Mr and Mrs Shergold, I'm not going to mislead you. Craig is a very sick little boy. You can thank God that you got him here today. If you hadn't he might well have been dead by tomorrow.'

Craig had been literally dying and yet nobody had realised it. How was it possible in this day and age?

'Now that he's here he has a chance, but his condition is still very,

very serious,' Mr Hayward went on. He looked from Ernie to me. 'Craig could die before we're able to operate. Or he could die on the operating table. Even if he comes through the operation, removing the tumour could cause permanent damage. It's in an area of the brain which controls a lot of important functions. There's a possibility that the surgery could leave him blind or paralysed . . .'

I held up my hand. 'Don't tell me any more.' I took hold of Mr Hayward's hands and pressed my hands around them, willing every bit of power in my body into his hands. 'You can do it, Mr Hayward.'

He probably thought I was a nutty old cockney mum but he didn't try to take his hands away and I was grateful. He smiled. 'I'm glad you've so much faith, Mother,' he said. 'But please—not too much.'

I shook my head. 'God will bless your hands,' I told him. 'Craig is not going to die. You are going to get him well.'

While we were in Mr Hayward's office Ernie and I had managed to stay quite composed. But the minute we left we broke down. It was a few minutes before we were able to face walking back into the ward. To our relief we found Craig had been given some painkillers which had sent him to sleep.

Ernie went back to see our family while I sat beside Craig's bed, holding his hand. There was a shelf above Craig's bed and someone had left a big furry green elephant on it. Elephants were my mother's lucky mascots. I felt a strong sense that she was here with us. A couple of weeks before she died Mum had called us all in to see her. 'I'll always be with you,' she'd promised then. 'I'll be watching over all of you. I'll never leave you.' I stared at the elephant. 'Mum,' I prayed, 'if you're there, please ask God to get him well.'

Craig stirred and opened his eyes. I guessed the noise in the ward had woken him. Some of the kids were watching television. A little girl had a cassette player going full blast. And there were builders hammering in the closed-off ward next door.

'Mum?' Craig was looking at me and his eyes were huge. 'Mum?' he said again. He stared at the other kids on the ward, frowning at their bald heads and operation scars. In a minute I knew he was going to ask me what he was doing here. I knew I had to be honest with him.

'Craig,' I said softly, 'you do know you're very ill, don't you?'

He stopped me. 'I know, Mum. I've got a brain tumour.'

My jaw dropped. 'How do you know that, Craig?' I asked.

'I guessed,' he smiled. 'Lucy in *Neighbours* has a brain tumour.'

'Oh, Craig.' For the first time that day I was laughing. Thank heaven for *Neighbours*.

Craig's eyes were fixed on my face. 'Lucy's getting better, Mum.'

'I know she is, Craig. And so are you.' I squeezed his hand tightly.

Three

Ernie and I spent Saturday night dozing on two reclining chairs in the visitors' room, and I woke up feeling stiff and numb. Ernie had already been into the ward to check on Craig.

'They've put him on a drip,' he reported. 'The sister said it's only because he's dehydrated from being sick and they want to get some fluid into him. She said he's had a peaceful night.' I fished in my handbag for my compact. I looked about a hundred years old—my eyes were red and my hair was standing on end. I rubbed some foundation on and dragged a comb through my hair. It wouldn't help Craig to have his mum looking like something out of a horror film.

Craig squinted up at me as I arrived at his bedside. The ward lights seemed to hurt his eyes. For most of the morning I sat with him while he drifted in and out of sleep. The painkillers weren't working as well as they had yesterday, and the noise of the ward was bothering him more—even the sound of my voice when I spoke to Ernie made him flinch. The nurses gave me cold compresses to hold against his head but they didn't seem to help much.

A new doctor came to check him and to my relief he increased Craig's painkillers. Halfway through the afternoon, while Craig was sleeping, a pretty dark-haired nurse came up holding something in her hand. 'Hello, I'm Sally,' she said. 'I've come to show you what a shunt looks like so you'll understand a bit more about the operation tomorrow.' She handed me a plastic thing attached to a long piece of fine tubing. 'The tube will run down a vein inside Craig's neck so all the excess fluid in his brain drains into his blood system,' Sally explained. 'As soon as the pressure inside his head gets less his earache should improve.'

Far from reassuring me, seeing the shunt frightened me even more. It looked such a big thing to put inside a little boy's head. Sally patted my arm. 'Try not to worry about it. It really is quite a routine operation. Most of the kids in this ward have got a shunt. I'm sure he'll be all right.' Suddenly she put both her arms round me and gave me a big hug. 'Why don't you go and have a cup of tea?' she said. 'You both look as though you need a break.'

I knew she was right. Ernie's face was grey with worry and I'd felt sick ever since I woke up. We decided to go out for a bit of fresh air. As we passed through the reception area I noticed a sign saying CHAPEL, pointing up a ramp laid over some worn stone steps.

I'd been brought up to go to church. I'd stopped going since I'd grown up, but I still said my prayers every night and now it felt as though this chapel was calling me. I walked up the ramp, pulling poor Ernie after me. We found ourselves in a very old part of the building, older even than the wards in Craig's wing. Ahead of us was a door, and as I pushed it open I stopped, astonished. It was beautiful. Most of the hospital needed a lick of paint but not this chapel. The lighted candles reflected off gilt paint and polished brass. There was an arch over the altar and on the wall above it was a large painting showing Jesus with two children, one on his lap and one by his side. Above his head in gold lettering were the words, 'Suffer the little children to come unto me.'

I started to cry, then I prayed, then I cried again.

On the way out we passed a table with a visitors' book and a pen on it. I stopped and read the last message in the book. Straight away I recognised Steve's handwriting. 'Please don't let Craig die,' he'd scribbled. Above that, my niece Sue had written, 'Please God, let my cousin Craig live.' Almost everyone who'd visited Craig in hospital yesterday had written a few words.

I picked up the pen and started a fresh line. 'Dear God,' I wrote, 'I love Craig so much. I couldn't live without him. Please don't make him suffer. Please don't take him from me. Take me instead.'

CRAIG WAS JUST WAKING UP when we got back to the ward. A great crowd of visitors was waiting to see us and they were allowed in, one at a time. Some of Ernie's brothers and sisters had travelled from Hemel Hempstead and Nottingham just for those two minutes at his bedside. Steve had spent the night at Sharon's mum's house and Sharon had come in with him to see Craig this morning. 'You know Sharon is having a baby, Craig?' Steve said. Craig nodded slowly. 'Well we know it's going to be a girl and we've decided to call her Kylie because she's your favourite.' Craig put his thumbs up and mouthed, 'Thanks, Sharon. I love you.'

We'd discovered a canteen where you could get a cup of tea and a bite to eat and Ernie and I took turns to go there with our visitors. I was gasping for a cigarette as well so after I finished my tea I went out through the main hospital door and sat on the bench in the drizzle to have a smoke. I was on to my second cigarette when a young woman came up. 'Have you got a kid in the hospital?' she asked. I nodded.

'Come with me. I know where you can have a cig in the dry.'

She took me up in the lift to the fifth floor of the hospital. 'Here.' She opened a door. 'We call this the fag room, though I don't suppose *Blue Peter* would like it!'

She explained that the *Blue Peter* TV programme had paid for the room so the parents of sick children could have a break from sitting in the ward all day. Its proper name was the family room. But you could see why it was called the fag room. Three women and a man sat in comfortable armchairs drinking coffee and smoking. The room was bright and warm and it felt welcoming, not like the dingy visitors' room downstairs where Ernie and I had spent the night.

I sat down and started chatting. 'You don't want to worry about the state of the place,' one girl said. 'They're too short of money to keep up appearances. It's the staff that count. The surgeons here are the best there are, believe me.'

Other mothers chipped in to back her up. Most of them were old hands, and they told me how to get a parking permit and where to shop and how to fit in with the hospital routine. Some of them had been sleeping in the hospital for days and looked as rough as I did. Meeting them did me good. Afterwards I didn't feel so much on my own, and knowing I had a bolt hole was a big comfort.

On Sunday evening the lights had been dimmed and most of the children were asleep when a nurse came over and whispered, 'There's a telephone call for you, Mrs Shergold. You can take it in the family room.'

It was my old boss Joan Spears. Years ago I'd organised parties and charity functions for her and she'd remained a very dear friend. The sympathy in her voice was too much for me and I broke down. Her voice was firm as she listened to my sobs. 'Marion, please, I want you to listen to something,' and she began to read me the tale of the suffering man who looks behind him and when he sees only one set of footprints in the sand thinks God has deserted him. But in fact God has been carrying him through his time of trouble. When she'd finished Joan said quietly, 'Marion, God will carry you too. Never forget that . . .'

I walked slowly back to the ward. I'd always believed that friendship and love were the most important things in life. After Joan's call I was more certain of it than ever.

At six the next morning after a quick wash and brush-up in the visitors' room we headed back to the ward. Craig looked dreadful. His body was bloated and his skin had turned an ugly yellow colour. We sat with him until eleven, when the ward door opened and a porter pushed a trolley in. Craig hardly seemed to be conscious as the porter and a nurse lifted him onto it.

They hadn't told us how long the operation might take. An hour went by. I went to the chapel, wanting to be on my own. I threw my whole heart into my prayers this time. It felt as if an electric current was running through my body as I begged God to spare Craig's life. Then, feeling calmer, I went back upstairs.

It was half past three when the waiting-room door opened and Sister Lindy the day sister came in. She was smiling. 'Craig's all right,' she said. 'You can come back into the ward to see him now.'

He was asleep, his head propped high on pillows to help the shunt drain the fluid from his brain. One side of his head was shaved bare and there was a crescent-shaped incision where the shunt had gone in. His face and body were still swollen but I could see a definite improvement. His sleep was more restful—he even seemed to be a slightly better colour. While Ernie sat and held Craig's hand I slipped back once more to the chapel. This time the message I wrote in the visitors' book was short. 'Thank you, God.'

Craig slept for the rest of the afternoon while Ernie and I sat beside him chatting quietly. There was a pile of envelopes on his locker—cards from relatives, friends and neighbours. There were seventy-four, most of them with a long handwritten message for Craig. I decided I'd read them all out to him. It would do him good to know so many people were thinking of him. There was a parcel at the bottom of the pile and I opened it carefully. It contained an almost full bottle of aftershave, a card and a letter on crumpled paper torn out of an exercise book. It was from Craig's best friend Lee.

To Craig.

Hope you get better soon, because we have been haveing a good time at school and we have been haveing good football matches. Me and Jay's dad have billt a tree-house down the park and I havent got any one to argue with on the way to school. I no them hospital beds are uncuftuble becos I have been in won myself. I hope you get better soon from Lee.

P.S. Your probably the goodest boy in the world even when your mum cant see you . . . This aftershave might make you smell a bit better Ha! Ha!

I stuck the letter on the side of Craig's locker so it would be the first thing he saw when he woke up.

Early in the evening Mr Hayward's registrar came into the ward and made straight for Craig's bed. 'So far so good,' he said cheerfully. 'Craig's operation went well. We're pleased with him.'

I jumped up. 'Oh, thank you, Doctor.'

'I should go and eat something if I were you. We don't want you two cracking up on us. Craig still has a long way to go . . .'

Craig was still sleeping peacefully so we went to the canteen and ordered fish and chips. At the last moment I pushed my plate away. 'It's the hospital smell,' I said to Ernie. 'I can't face it.' Ernie could though, and he put away first his plate and then mine. It was good to see the old Ernie back, and I had a lump in my throat as I watched him. I loved Ernie so much. He'd always been a wonderful father and husband. I squeezed his hand. 'Nothing's going to part us whatever happens, is it, Ern? 'Cos I do need you, you know.'

He gave me a little choked smile. 'We need each other, Mal. United we stand, divided we fall. Right?' It had always been our song.

Next morning I thought Craig looked better.

'Look at all my cards, Mum,' he said as soon as he woke up.

While Ernie slipped out for a wash I read Craig his messages, first the letter from Lee, then all the cards I'd stuck up the day before.

The porters arrived to take him down for more scans and I went too. When we arrived back there was another huge bundle of cards on his locker.

'Do you want me to open them for you?' I asked.

'No. I want to do it myself.' His voice was still slow.

It took Craig nearly two hours but he did it. Some cards were from people we hadn't seen for ages. I'd never been so grateful for being a waitress: through my work I'd met hundreds of people and now the bush telegraph was working.

Ernie held up a card with an elephant on. 'This one's from Betty. She must have known your mum thought elephants were lucky.'

My eyes wandered round the ward, and I realised that none of the other kids had as many get-well cards as Craig did. 'Craig,' I said gently, 'I don't think I'll put today's cards on the wall. I think it might look a bit greedy to the other kids, is that all right?'

'I don't mind.' Craig's head slipped back on his pillows and he closed his eyes. But the smile stayed on his face.

That Tuesday was a wonderful day. Ernie and I knew the real test, the big op, was still to come, but for now we just enjoyed the fact that he'd got over this first hurdle so well.

Our visitors shared our relief. Steve was working as a building labourer just down the road and he popped in during his lunch-hour to bring Craig some fruit. Craig's bed looked like a Covent Garden stall, and there were dozens of packets of chocolates. Craig couldn't eat them—he was still on a drip—but we shared most of the goodies out among the kids on the ward.

On Wednesday morning my dear friend Jan, who had looked after Craig whenever I was working, came in carrying two huge carrier bags full of cards. 'From the kids at Craig's school!' she said. 'They've made them all themselves.' Then she put a parcel on Craig's bed. 'The Parents' and Teachers' Committee gave me five pounds for you, Craig, so I bought a Kylie Minogue tape at the shop.'

'Oh great,' said Craig. 'I'll play it when my earache's gone.'

I looked at Ernie. Craig hadn't told us his earache had come back. Early in the afternoon when Craig was asleep Mr Hayward came into the ward. His face was concerned. 'I've just seen the latest scan,' he said. 'It shows that the tumour is growing very fast which means we must operate as soon as possible. It will take too long to get an operating theatre ready here, so, if you agree, we'd like to do the operation in the National Hospital on Monday.'

I felt my heart jump. I reached out for Mr Hayward's hands and this time he held them out to me. I held them tightly, willing all my strength into them. It was as he was leaving that Mr Hayward noticed the cards on Craig's locker and gave me strict instructions to put them up at once. The nurses thought it was a great idea and we spent the afternoon stringing them across the walls.

A play therapist, Janet, was on the ward that day. When she saw all Craig's cards she decided to get every kid on the ward to make him a get-well card as well. I was so relieved that the other kids weren't jealous. Instead Janet was turning it into a project everyone could take part in. The aim now was to completely cover the walls of the ward with Craig's get-well cards.

But the kids' excitement was lost on Craig. The noise was really getting to him. Some workmen in the road outside were using pneumatic drills. And if that wasn't enough, Caroline, the little girl in the cot opposite, was bawling 'Don't worry, be happy' over and over. 'Please, Mum. Stop her,' Craig whispered. 'She's driving me mad.' I felt my blood rising. They knew Craig had earache. What had they been thinking of to put him in this noisy ward? I asked a nurse to give him some painkillers and eventually he dozed off.

Craig stayed asleep or unconscious—I couldn't always be sure which—for the rest of that day. He was running a temperature now and the nurses brought a fan to cool him down, but soon he became delirious. Doctors came and did more tests. I was so frightened. I wanted to rescue Craig from this madhouse of radios and televisions and workmen's drills. If only I could get him home. Maybe the nightmare would stop then.

He only regained consciousness once more that day and when he did he looked straight at me and whispered something. I bent my head closer to hear.

'I'm glad it's me who's ill and not you.'

There was a lump in my throat. 'Why, Craig?'

He stared up at me with great big eyes. 'I love you too much, Mum. You couldn't have stood the pain.'

All my resolutions flew out of the window and I hugged him to me and sobbed.

Craig Shergold

IT WAS NEARLY THREE O'CLOCK in the morning before the nurses managed to persuade us to leave Craig's bedside. We were back in the ward by six. The duty nurse walked over to us as we sat down by Craig's bed. 'He's had a restless night, I'm afraid,' she said.

My blood boiled. 'Why didn't you fetch us then?'

She shrugged. 'I tried to,' she said. 'I couldn't find you.'

'I don't believe her,' I told Ernie as she walked off down the ward. 'She doesn't care about Craig. I don't think any of the nurses really care. It's just a job to them.' I knew I was over-reacting, but yesterday I'd heard one of the agency nurses complain that there was no swimming pool or tennis court in the hospital. She said she only put up with it because the money was good. I'd been brooding about it.

'Come on, Mal,' Ernie patted my arm. 'They're not all like that. Don't get yourself upset.' But I was furious at not being called. I needed someone to blame and the nurses were easy targets. I forgot about the ones who'd cuddled me and comforted me. I forgot about Sally patiently explaining the shunt. Now I saw the nurses as enemies: they wouldn't let you stay in the ward all night, but you couldn't trust them to fetch you if your child needed you. I scowled at the nurse until she went off duty, seething every time she smiled.

Craig was listless and far away that morning but at least he was awake and his temperature had gone down. The post came early—another couple of dozen cards for Craig. He was in no state to open them so I did it for him and stuck them on the walls.

Alison, a new friend I'd met three months ago in Benidorm, turned up at eleven. She hugged me without saying anything and sat down while Ernie went out to take a break. Alison's first husband had died of a brain tumour and it was hard for us to find the right things to say. I was quite relieved when Mr Hayward came into the ward. I was even more relieved when he commented on Craig's cards and made a joke about getting into the *Guinness Book of Records*.

I might have guessed Alison would jump at the idea. She was a born organiser and this sort of thing was right up her street. She was also personal assistant to one of the directors of Gilbey's Gin so she had lots of business contacts. By the time she was ready to go she had a plan of action all drawn up.

'I'll circulate the idea to all the firms we deal with,' she promised. 'I'll get them to ask all their employees to send a card. We should get hundreds that way—maybe even thousands.'

After Alison left I had more important things to worry about than record-breaking. Craig was getting steadily worse. I sat by his bed talking to him, trying to keep him alert. I didn't feel any longer that sleep was healing: if Craig was asleep I felt his tumour could take

219

control. I felt certain that to fight it he had to stay alert.

All afternoon I sat by his bed talking to him, telling him how much we loved him, reading him stories. Whenever he shut his eyes, I'd bend close and say sternly, 'Listen to Mummy.' I told him stories of when I was a kid playing on the bombsites and chasing rats round the back of the local factory. I told him about my rich Uncle George and the day that Kevin and I let the handbrake off his posh car so it rolled into a cobblestone pillar and brought all the family running out of the pub yelling blue murder. Craig loved the idea of me getting into the same sort of scrapes as him.

I opened some of his presents. There were about a dozen furry toys now. I arranged them so they were all sitting up, paying attention, and when I looked again Craig was asleep. I went out to the visitors' room, asked Ernie to take over the vigil and set off towards the chapel. In the past week it had become my second home.

Today two figures were sitting in one of the pews. I felt cross. This was 'my' chapel. I wanted a good chat with God. How could I do it with other people here? While I waited for them to go I wandered over to look at the messages in the visitors' book. Tonight there was a fresh one. *'Please God help little Craig Shergold to get well and please help his mum and dad. From a nurse who cares.'*

Tears rolled down my cheeks. How could I have told Ernie that nurses were heartless? The couple in the far pew stood up and left, smiling at me as they passed. I knelt down in the candlelight and prayed to God to forgive me.

WHEN I GOT BACK to the ward Craig was awake. He grinned. 'Hello, Mum. I've been to the toilet! I feel a lot better.' Then he frowned. 'You haven't been crying, have you?'

'No,' I fibbed. 'It's just the rain on my face.'

Ernie told me they'd given Craig an enema. I was relieved. Craig hadn't had his bowels open since he'd been taken ill. But an hour later he was seized with an attack of diarrhoea and vomiting and soon afterwards the hot and cold sweats started again. The nurses were wonderful. They were changing his sheets every half-hour but they never complained. I felt completely useless. Every time Craig retched I was retching in sympathy: I just couldn't stomach it. Thank heaven for Ernie who ran backwards and forwards to the sluice with the soiled sheets without turning a hair.

By the time it was over and Craig lay once more in a deep sleep I was completely drained. We went out and told everyone waiting patiently outside that visiting wouldn't be possible this evening. A few of Ernie's workmates had come in, tipped off by John, who also worked at the LEB. John told us he'd applied for compassionate leave for Ernie, something which hadn't crossed our minds in the confusion of the last few days. I was so grateful we had such wonderful friends.

After they'd gone we started to get ready for 'bed'. Tonight especially, with him being so ill, it felt as if we were deserting Craig. 'Ernie,' I said, 'ask the nurses if we can sleep on a chair by his bed just this once.' Up until now the nurses had always made us leave the ward during the night shift, but to my surprise they agreed to Ernie staying. Perhaps they thought his efforts in the sluice room deserved a reward.

That night I tossed and turned on my reclining chair. I missed being able to reach out and touch Ernie for comfort and I couldn't stop worrying. I dreaded what Friday might bring.

Ernie woke me at six and we went back to the ward.

Mr Hayward was already by Craig's bed. He examined him, studied his charts, then looked at me. 'Could I see you and your husband outside for a moment?' he asked.

In the corridor Mr Hayward turned to face us. 'I'm afraid the poor little chap's in a bad way,' he said. 'Unless he recovers very quickly we're not going to be able to operate on Monday. It will be a long operation and the condition he's in now he just wouldn't survive it.'

I felt numb. I couldn't face going back to the ward with Ernie and letting Craig see me upset. I walked downstairs and out of the hospital. Outside I wandered round the courtyard. I sat down on the wooden bench, and stared up at his window, shivering with cold. Then the tears started rolling and I hung my head.

After a while I sensed someone come and sit down beside me and I looked up. A little boy, about ten years old, was looking at me with wide eyes.

'Have you got a child here who's very ill?' he asked.

I choked as I tried to answer him. 'He is very ill,' I said shakily.

At that the little boy leaned over and his lips brushed my cheek. 'He won't die,' he said. 'The doctors here will save him. They saved me.'

I threw my arms round him and hugged him. I hardly noticed his mother sitting down on my other side, putting her arm round my shoulders. When my tears slowed down she told me that her son had received a lung transplant at Great Ormond Street. A few months ago he'd been dying like Craig. Now he was almost ready to leave hospital. 'Keep your faith,' she said. 'Your son will get well.'

I felt full of hope again. I thought of Joan's words, 'God will carry you,' and realised with astonishment that they were true. Every time I'd felt I just couldn't carry this burden any longer, something had given me the strength to keep going. The sense of peace when I'd first seen Mr Hayward's photograph, the nurse's message in the visitors' book, and now this wonderful little boy.

THE OPERATION WAS POSTPONED for a week. But now I knew God was looking after us, and I think Ernie was beginning to share my faith. Once or twice he slipped quietly out to the chapel on his own.

As if in answer to our prayers Craig started to eat—only a mouthful of porridge and a sip of tea—but it was his first solid food for a week. Things were looking up.

A few days later Craig's temperature was back to normal, his response to the coordination tests seemed better, and, best of all, his sense of fun had come back. One day Alison brought her husband Norman to visit and they gave Craig a huge pair of slippers shaped like bear paws with long nails. Craig loved them, and we lifted the sheets and put them on his feet. He gave me a wicked look then suddenly yelled out, 'Nurse! Look what the medicine's done to my feet. My toenails are growing.' One of the nurses came rushing over, then saw the slippers and collapsed in giggles.

Steve had great news that week. He came in late one evening, looking very excited, and gently woke Craig up. 'Guess what, Craig? They've accepted me into the fire brigade.' Craig gave him a huge smile. 'I'm proud of you, Ugly. I knew you could do it.' He closed his eyes. 'Now let me sleep. I'm happy.' Steve grinned at us and crept out. Seeing the love between my two sons gave me a warm glow.

The next day when Steve came in again he and Craig sent Ernie and me to the canteen saying they had something private to talk about. When we came back Craig grinned. 'You'd better listen to Radio GOSH at five to four, Mum,' he said. 'It's a surprise.'

We had to go into the ward kitchen to listen to the radio because there was so much noise in the ward. At five to four Craig's voice came out of the radio loud and clear. 'Mum, I love you, and you too, Dad. I'm sorry I'm ill, but I'll get better I promise. I'm going to be at my brother's wedding. This song is for you. It's "I Just Called to Say I Love You".'

As we listened to Stevie Wonder singing that lovely song there wasn't a dry eye in the kitchen. Afterwards, back in the ward, Craig tutted at my tear-stained face. 'Cor, I knew you'd cry, Mum. But I do love you and I will get well. Me and Ugly arranged that while you and Dad were having tea. Clever, weren't we?'

Alison had been busy spreading the word about Craig's cards and that week we saw the first results of her hard work. Every day Craig got cards from people we'd never heard of. The nurses had been telling everyone that Craig wanted to break the world record and soon all the kids were involved: the cards had become a project for the Punch and Judy Ward as much as for Craig. Every day when the post arrived there'd be screams of delight and the new cards would be passed round for everyone to have a look at before they were put up.

Now that Craig had got the taste for food again, we couldn't stop him eating. I thought it was a sign that the pressure in his brain was going down but the ward sister said it was a side effect of the steroids. The reason they were giving Craig steroids was to shrink the tissues around the tumour before they removed it. The sister said it was the steroids that were making him so bloated. 'Once he comes off them he'll start to look better,' she promised.

I wondered what it would take to make us look better. Ernie and I hadn't been home since we arrived at the hospital. Neither of us was eating proper meals—we were getting by on chocolate biscuits and cups of tea. I worried about Ernie. I felt as if I'd got new strength now, but Ernie was exhausted and kept falling asleep.

Then one day Sister Lindy said, 'There's a vacancy in Rainbow House. How would you like to stay there for a couple of weeks?' Rainbow House was a guesthouse for the parents of very sick children, just round the corner. We went to see it. The contrast with our seedy visitors' room was dramatic. It was beautifully fitted out with luxury carpets and curtains and there were proper bedrooms with twin beds. The thought of sleeping in a proper bed again and taking a shower was wonderful.

ON THE MORNING of Monday, February 6, I woke up with one thought running round my head—I had to buy Craig an elephant for luck. I was sure it was my mum sending me a message.

Craig was quite drowsy when we got to the ward and didn't want to talk much. I sat by his bedside with Ernie until the Wishing Well Appeal shop at the hospital entrance opened, then I ran downstairs. 'My little boy's having an operation today and I've just got to have an elephant,' I told the woman behind the counter.

'I haven't got any elephants,' she said. 'Would an owl do?'

I felt devastated. I'd been so sure there'd be an elephant here waiting for me. Then I remembered that Craig's godmother Sandra collected owls—maybe that was the lucky sign I was looking for. I fumbled in my purse but the shop assistant held up her hand. 'No. Give him this from me.' She pointed to the sign above the shop and smiled. 'Tell him I am wishing him *well*.'

Gratefully I took the owl from her and set off back for the ward. Craig was lying on a trolley in the ward talking to Ernie and clutching the teddy bear that his cousin Kerry had given him. I put the owl on his trolley. It was better than nothing, but I was still upset I hadn't managed to get Craig an elephant. I felt it was a bad omen.

I was explaining to Craig how the Wishing Well lady had given him the owl when a group of mums came across from the other side of the ward to wish Craig luck. 'We wanted Craig to have this,' one of them said and she handed me a grey furry elephant. I was speechless. Who had told them? Almost before I could say thank you the porters started to wheel Craig out of the ward. As we reached the door Janet the playleader called, 'Marion—don't forget Craig's present.' She was holding out the green elephant that had been on the shelf above Craig's bed ever since we'd arrived here.

'That's not Craig's,' I told her. 'It belongs to the hospital.'

Janet shook her head. 'No. This was Craig's admission present. All the kids get a toy when they come in. Didn't anyone tell you?'

I was over the moon. Who could doubt now that my mum was watching over us? I took Ernie's hand and we followed the trolley carrying Craig and his big pile of furry toys into the lift.

I'd thought we'd be travelling by ambulance but I was wrong. 'We're going to walk to the National,' the porter told me as we came out of the lift. 'It'll give him a smoother journey.' He explained that all the hospitals in this area—Great Ormond Street, the National Hospital for Nervous Diseases, and University College Hospital—were connected by tunnels built during the war.

The nurses arrived and put blankets over the trolley to keep him warm and we all walked through some wide rubber doors into the tunnel. It felt very cold and a bit eerie. Our footsteps and the sound of the trolley wheels echoed around us. The walls were whitewashed brick with little dim lights set into them, and every so often we passed metal staircases vanishing up into the darkness. At last the floor started to slope upwards and we emerged into daylight to find ourselves facing the main entrance of the National Hospital.

Compared with Great Ormond Street it looked very modern. The porter pushed Craig through the entrance and into a swish stream-lined lift. We came out on the operating floor and there was Richard Hayward waiting for us. 'Hello, Mother. Hello, Dad.' He held out his hands to me. I took hold of them and looked into his eyes. 'You're going to do it,' I told him. 'God will bless your hands.'

'I hope so,' he nodded.

The theatre team came out to meet us, dressed in their greens, and my stomach turned over. Craig stared up at me, looking worried.

'You're going to be with me, Mum, aren't you?' he said in a frightened voice.

I knew I wouldn't be allowed in the theatre. I thought quickly. 'I'm not going to leave you, darling. I'll be right outside this door,' I promised.

'Come on, Craig.' A big fat guy came up to the trolley. 'Let's label the teddies, shall we?' He put a name tag on the two elephants, the teddy and the owl, and then, last of all, he put one on Craig's wrist.

When Craig was growing up he and I had always sung songs together and now it seemed the natural thing to do. I sang Craig's radio request gently to him, 'I just called to say I love you. I just called to say how much I care . . .' Struggling for each word, Craig sang the next two lines back to me, 'I just called to say I love you. And I mean it from the bottom of my heart . . .'

'We're ready for him, Mrs Shergold,' one of the nurses called. Ernie and I stood back and the trolley started to move slowly away from us into the theatre. Craig's eyes, wide and scared, stayed fixed on me.

'Don't forget, Craig,' I called, 'I love you so much . . . And I'm here.' And then the doors closed behind him and he was gone.

Ernie and I put our arms round each other and sat down on the stairs near the lift. After a few minutes a sister came up to us. 'You must go out now,' she said. 'Go and have a drink.'

'I don't want a drink,' I said. 'I promised Craig I'd stay here.'

'I'm sorry but really you can't.' She looked at her watch. 'It's twelve o'clock now. He'll be in the theatre for several hours. Why don't you go back to Rainbow House and I'll make sure they ring you there as soon as he's out of theatre. Then you can be with him when he comes round. He won't know that you haven't been here, and you'll be better off getting some rest.'

I knew what she said made sense though it still felt as if I was betraying Craig's trust. 'I'll be sitting by the phone,' I promised. When we got to Rainbow House I left Ernie with our visitors in the sitting room, took a chair to the phone in the kitchen and sat waiting, rocking to and fro.

A support party of family and friends had turned up to sit with us—all of them took it in turns to sit with me in the kitchen.

It was ten when the phone rang. I snatched the receiver off the hook. It was Sister Lindy. 'Craig's just come out of theatre,' she said. 'He's very cold and we're wrapping him in silver foil to warm him up but you should be able to see him at about half past ten. He's on a ventilator and various machines so don't panic when you see him.'

I put the phone down. Ernie looked at me anxiously. Behind him another dozen faces waited for news. 'He's out,' I said.

Twenty minutes later Ernie and I led the way up the steps to the Punch and Judy Ward. Craig had been brought to the small intensive-care unit next to the sister's office. We walked in nervously with Steve, leaving the others in the corridor.

They'd warned me not to be scared by all the machinery but I didn't even see it—all I could see was Craig. He was wrapped in a shiny case of silver foil and a thick white bandage covered his head. His lips were swollen and held open by the mouthpiece of a ventilator which was pumping air in and out of his chest. His eyes were closed, the long dark eyelashes brushing his cheeks. It was as if I'd stepped back in time. He looked like my baby.

I leaned over and started to sing softly, my face close to his. 'I just called to say I love you . . .' I sang the whole song through. He didn't move. The only sound was the pumping of the ventilator. I took a deep breath and started to sing the song again. Every time I reached the end I kissed his face and started again. And suddenly, as my lips touched his cheek, I felt his eyelids flutter. I drew back and his arm lifted shakily towards me. His lips moved around the plastic tube. 'I . . . love . . . you,' he whispered.

Behind me I heard a soft sighing and when I looked round I saw that everybody in the room was crying. I was crying too. I kissed Ernie. I kissed Steve. I kissed the nurses. Through the glass I saw Richard Hayward standing outside in the passage with his registrar. I went out and he held his hands out to me. I took hold of them. 'I told you God would bless you, didn't I?' I said.

He smiled and nodded. 'You did.' He looked exhausted. He'd been operating for ten hours. 'You must be absolutely knackered,' I said. 'God bless. Thank you from the bottom of my heart.'

He smiled. 'I'll talk to you in the morning,' he said. 'Don't forget there's a long way to go. These first twenty-four hours are critical. We're not out of the woods yet.'

Four

The next day Craig was given morphine for the pain and slept for the whole morning. It was nearly lunchtime when Mr Hayward called us into the sister's office. Ernie and I sat down opposite him, and he told us that he wanted to explain what he had done during the operation.

'We managed to cut out almost three-quarters of the tumour,' he said. 'As you know it was growing right at the centre of Craig's brain, very close to the brain stem. That's the area which controls breathing, heart rate and blood pressure. It meant we had to tread very carefully and we were forced to leave some of the tumour behind. If we'd cut any deeper we might have lost him.'

I felt uneasy. 'Won't it grow back?' I asked.

'Not necessarily,' Mr Hayward said. 'I hope not. The pathology lab will do an analysis on the part of the tumour we've removed and let us know whether it's malignant or not.'

Ernie caught hold of my hand. 'How long will that take?'

'About a week.'

A whole week more of hoping and praying . . .'Don't you have any idea just from looking at it?' I asked.

'From its appearance we're fairly certain that it's a teratoma,' Mr Hayward said carefully. 'It's the first time I've ever seen this kind of tumour in the brain. Usually we find it growing in the abdomen. It's a congenital tumour, which means it's there at birth, but it usually doesn't start causing trouble until puberty. Then it can grow very rapidly. When these tumours develop in the ovaries or testicles they can get very big indeed.'

My stomach was turning over. 'How big?'

'Up to fifteen pounds in weight. But, of course, it wouldn't reach that size in the brain. It's a very unusual tumour—it's actually a living thing. It has hair, it has nails, sometimes it even has teeth.'

I stared at him in horror. What was he telling me? That some sort of monster was living in Craig's brain?

'I'm sorry,' Mr Hayward said. 'I can't tell you any more at the moment. All we can do until the pathology report comes back is to wait and hope.'

For most of the afternoon Craig slept peacefully. His nurse stayed the whole time at his bedside watching over him. He was still on the respirator and was lying on his back, propped up on pillows. From time to time he opened his eyes but he didn't try to speak. I just lived for the moment, enjoying the fact that he was alive.

As the day drew to a close I let myself start to get hopeful. 'We must be over the worst now,' I told Ernie. 'Why don't you go back in to work tomorrow for a couple of hours?'

I was tempting fate. The next morning, while Ernie was away, the pain started. Every sound was torture for Craig. I even had to stop opening his cards—just the sound of the envelopes tearing made him moan. Worst of all, he hated the sound of my voice. I've always had a loud voice, and now Craig begged me not to speak. Even when I tried to whisper he shushed me.

By Wednesday he didn't need the respirator any longer, and he was moved out of intensive care into a cubicle. But he didn't show any other improvement. In fact he was getting worse. Ernie didn't dare go in to work again. By Wednesday evening the pain was so bad they had to increase the dose of morphine and at last, at ten o'clock, Craig fell asleep. I refused point-blank to leave him and the nurses found a Z-bed for me to sleep on which we crammed in the cubicle.

Every morning a porter lifted Craig onto a trolley and wheeled him away for scans and tests but we never found out what the results were. I asked to see Mr Hayward but I was told he was away. It may have been unfair, but I felt we were being deliberately kept in the dark, and on Thursday morning when Craig started moaning worse than ever, I flipped and demanded to see a doctor. One of the nurses disappeared and came back with a young doctor.

'Thank you for seeing me,' I began. 'I just want to know what's wrong with Craig. Why is he in so much pain?'

The doctor studied the floor and said in a bored voice, 'He's got blood clots.'

His attitude was the final straw. '*Look* at me when you talk to me,' I exploded. 'I'm only a mum,' I went on. 'I'm only a waitress. I don't understand. What do you *mean* he's got blood clots?'

He hesitated, then shrugged. 'Well, you can have a look at the scans if you want.' He went into the sister's office and came back a few moments later carrying a scan which he held up to the light. 'Look,' he pointed. 'Each of those dark areas is a blood clot.'

I stared at the scan. Craig's whole brain was a mass of blood clots. 'What's going to happen? What are you going to *do*?'

He wouldn't meet my eyes. 'We're hoping they'll self-disperse,' he said. He sounded so indifferent I could have hit him.

I stumbled back into the cubicle and started to tell Ernie about the blood clots. I was still trembling with shock when the door opened and Bobby Campbell, the manager of the Chelsea football team, walked in. What timing! He'd brought a football and a team photograph, signed by all the players. I knew Bobby Campbell quite well. The last time we'd met I'd been serving him dinner at a Christmas function at Stamford Bridge. He was a big strong man, but now he took one look at Craig and his face just crumpled. 'Oh Marion,' he said. 'I'm so sorry. I'd no idea he was so ill.' I nodded. I could hardly speak. 'What's wrong? I'd heard he was getting better.'

I explained to him about the blood clots and he looked more and more upset. I sensed he was about to break down. Then he pushed a note into my hand. 'Read this. We're all praying for you.'

After he left I opened Bobby's note. 'Listen to Capital Radio at five to six tonight,' it said. 'Keep your chin up.' At ten to six a nurse found the station for us on my little radio and turned the volume down till it was quiet enough for Craig. They played a couple of requests then we heard the DJ's voice say, 'Hi, out there. This is a very special message for a great Chelsea supporter—Craig Shergold, who is nine years old.' Craig's eyes had been shut, but when he heard that they opened wide. 'He's in Great Ormond Street Hospital with a tumour on the brain,' the DJ continued, 'so hi there, Craig. Are you listening? This is from all your friends, the players at the Chelsea Football Club. We know you're very sick at the moment but we also know that you're going to get well.' Then the Chelsea team song rang out and Craig beamed from ear to ear. When the record finished the DJ said, 'When your bus is late tonight and you're moaning away, remember this little boy, count your blessings and say a prayer for him.'

Bobby Campbell must have told the team about the record attempt because the next day a get-well card was delivered with personal messages from every single player. 'Get well soon, Craig.' 'Hurry up and get back down the Bridge. We all love you and miss you.' The way Craig reacted you'd have thought the card was a cheque for a million pounds.

But on Friday evening the pain got worse. By Saturday it was so bad that at times it took three of us—Ernie, me and a nurse—to hold Craig down on the bed. It was terrible to see him suffering. All day I stayed by his bedside, rubbing his hands to try to get them warm—his hands and feet had been icy cold ever since the operation—and talking to him nonstop. 'Come on, Craig. You can do it. Fight it. Come on, you can win.'

At last, late on Saturday evening, Craig fell into a little sleep. Until then he'd been so restless with the pain that you couldn't say he'd slept at all—but now he slept quietly on his side for a whole hour. Then at nine o'clock he stirred. His eyes fluttered open and he stared at me with a puzzled look on his face. 'Hello, Mum,' he said. 'Have I got any visitors?' The pain had completely gone.

The next day, as I sat by his bed watching him lying peacefully at last, Craig turned his head towards me. 'Mum,' he said slowly, 'I've had a very funny experience.'

'Have you, darling? What's that?' I asked.

'You was there, Mum. Nanny was there.' He stopped.

'Yes?'

'And someone else was there. I don't know who this other person was though.' He frowned. 'It's as if I was two person—' he hesitated, 'two personalities,' he said at last, struggling with the word.

'Yes?'

He moved his hands around, anxious for me to understand. 'It was so clear,' he said. 'I was lying on the bed, but I could see myself lying on the bed. And Nanny was there . . . But you kept calling me, Mum. You kept calling me. You wouldn't let me go.'

The rest of Sunday was wonderful. Visitors crowded in with presents and cards. The pain had gone now but Craig was still having trouble seeing clearly. Late in the afternoon the door opened and I did a double take as I realised who it was—George Best, Ernie's football idol. Ernie was sitting on Craig's bed and nearly fell on the floor.

Georgie grinned. 'Hello,' he said. 'My good friend Bobby Campbell asked me to come in and see you.'

Craig squinted up at him. 'Who *are* you?' he asked.

I thought Ernie would die of embarrassment but I just cracked up. 'I bet that's the first time anyone's said that to you, isn't it?' I said.

He grinned. 'I think it's been a while.'

Ernie was so excited. 'Craig,' he gulped, 'this man was the best.'

Georgie stayed a long time with Craig, talking football—teams, players, famous goals—men's talk. 'Chelsea don't need any other supporters with you around, Craig, do they!' he teased.

After Georgie's visit Craig really bucked up. He was still weak and he couldn't sit up on his own, but he looked miles better and he started to read his cards and to chat to his visitors. He even started to eat again. Ernie went to work every day that week—the LEB were letting him work short days on compassionate grounds.

On February 13, the day before Valentine's Day, Janet the playleader was helping everyone make Valentine cards in the playroom. Craig had fallen asleep and I'd left Ernie with him and gone to the playroom to give the kids a hand with cutting and gluing. Suddenly a voice said, 'Mrs Shergold?' I looked up. Sister Lindy was peering round the playroom door. 'Would you fetch your husband and come in to the office please?'

I stood up slowly, my stomach turning over. I knew what her summons meant—the results had come back from the path lab. This was it. The day we'd all been dreading.

It was Richard Hayward's registrar who stood behind Sister Lindy's desk as Ernie and I walked into her office. 'Please sit down,' he said. I could feel myself trembling and I gripped the arms of the chair. Oh God, I prayed, let it be benign. But I knew. His face gave him away.

'I'm very sorry to have to tell you this,' he cleared his throat then continued, 'I'm afraid it is cancer, and it's very aggressive. We need to start treatment straight away, initially radiotherapy—then chemotherapy. But we can't do the treatment here, I'm afraid,' the registrar continued. 'There are two options. One is the Royal Marsden which has the advantage of being quite near your home.'

'Oh no! Not again!' I felt the tears rolling down my face.

'Mrs Shergold,' he said kindly, 'we do know that your mother was in the Royal Marsden last year so it's quite understandable if you don't want Craig to have his treatment there. If you prefer he could receive it at the University College Hospital.'

Both Ernie and I were in tears now. My mind was in such a muddle. I remembered visiting Mum in the Marsden, finding her distorted with pain after the last short sharp shock of chemotherapy. I remembered her consultant telling her, 'Katie, we're going to give you some more chemo,' and the way she'd smiled at him. 'Darling,' she said, 'you save that for the youngsters. I've had my life. You save that chemo for the little kids.'

Was it possible she'd known what was going to happen to Craig when she said that? Don't be daft, Marion, I told myself.

'We'll leave you both for a little while,' Sister Lindy said. 'I'll get you a drink of tea.' She disappeared and we sat in her little office lost for words. I dabbed at my eyes with my soaking-wet hanky but the more I dabbed the faster the tears came. By the time Sister Lindy came back with a pot of tea I was in a terrible state.

'Do you want to go back to his room?' she asked me gently after I'd drunk a cup.

'I can't go to him,' I said. 'I can't go to him like this.' I could hear the rain beating a tattoo on the office window. 'Every time something happens it's raining,' I sobbed.

'Take her to the pub,' Sister Lindy said to Ernie. 'Craig's asleep. You two go out and have a drink.'

I let Ernie lead me down the stairs and out into the street, but I wouldn't go into the pub. We wandered aimlessly along Theobalds Road, the rain mixing with our tears. 'Let's look for a card shop,' I said suddenly. 'I'm going to buy him the biggest Valentine card there is.' We found a shop in Leather Lane market. The card I wanted was about two feet high. Covered in hearts and flowers. I knew Craig would think it was dead soppy but he was going to get it anyway.

'Right,' Ernie said as we came out of the shop. 'Now I *am* going to get you a drink. You look terrible.' But I had to get back to Craig. It was still bucketing down, and we looked like drowned rats by the time we got back to his little room.

As we went through the door dripping water all over the polished floor, I saw he was wide awake. I sneezed, pretending I had a cold. 'We've just been to the shops,' I said. 'Oh, achoo—I can't stop my eyes watering.'

He peered at me puzzled. It was the only time I'd been glad of his blurred vision.

'Well you'd better hurry up and dry them,' he said excitedly, 'cos two of the Chelsea footballers are coming up to see me!' Sure enough, a few moments later, Gordon Durie and Clive Wilson walked in and for the rest of the afternoon all Craig's thoughts centred on football. The two players sat with him telling him all the Chelsea news, promising he could be team mascot, and joking about how terrible the breakfasts were now his mum had stopped working there. Craig was on cloud nine. Thanks to those boys he had no idea his mum and dad had just been breaking their hearts over him out in the rain.

After the players left, Craig fell asleep and Ernie and I sat watching him quietly. Ernie put his arm round me.

'Come on, Mal,' he said. 'We can't give in. Look how Craig enjoyed himself with those lads. He hasn't given in, has he? He's fighting every inch of the way. They've taken most of that tumour away, and if we let him have the chemotherapy we'll get rid of the rest of it. He's come this far—we've got to keep going now.'

It wasn't the first time I'd thanked God for Ernie. He might be quiet and shy, but when I needed him he was there, solid as a rock. I hugged him, knowing he was right. Think positive, I told myself. Craig had cheated death once—why shouldn't he do it again?

WE DECIDED TO LET Craig have his treatment at the Royal Marsden Hospital after all. It made sense because the Royal Marsden was only a twenty-minute journey from our home.

Mr Hayward arranged that Craig would be transferred on Friday, February 17, but there was an ambulance strike and we had to use our own car. A nurse helped me make a little nest of pillows and blankets on the back seat and Ernie and I lifted him gently in, trying anxiously not to touch his head. Two days before, they'd taken his clips out and the scar ran all the way from the top of his head to the nape of his neck. I sat in the back seat with Craig, plucking up courage to explain about the biopsy results.

'Craig,' I said, 'the hospital where we're going is special. There are lots of children there who are very ill and they'll ask you what's wrong. They'll probably tell you they have cancer and—'

He interrupted me. 'Oh blimey, Mum, I hope it's not catching. I've got enough to put up with, with this brain tumour.'

My eyes filled up. 'Oh, Craig,' I said, 'you are funny. Tumours are called cancer as well. But I don't want you to worry—they have some very good treatments there.'

He seemed to accept it and fell asleep, but he wasn't at all well. His forehead felt very hot and he was moaning as he slept. Being driven over bumpy South London streets in our little Fiat wasn't helping him at all, and by the time we turned into the driveway of the Royal Marsden he was in a dreadful state.

A specialist had been waiting all afternoon for Craig to arrive, but as soon as she saw him Diana Tait shook her head. He was far too ill for treatment, she said, he needed to recuperate first.

'I think the best plan is to send him back to Queen Mary's for a week,' she told us. Ten minutes later Craig was put into one of the Marsden's own ambulances and transferred back down the road to the hospital where his tumour had first been diagnosed.

So far the day had been one long nightmare, but the moment we arrived at Queen Mary's everything changed. The staff came out to welcome us and the nurse who had taken Craig to Great Ormond Street planted a big kiss on Craig's cheek and then hugged me. 'We've been ringing up every week to check how he was doing,' she said. 'We'll look after him.' He was put in a cubicle at a quiet end of Ward B2 and after an hour or so he started to look a lot better.

We stayed in Queen Mary's for ten days. At first I felt frustrated by the delay but in fact a breathing space was what we'd all needed. It did Ernie and me good, while Craig just blossomed. The very first morning he woke up bright as a button and asked if he could give himself a bath. The surprises weren't over. As I helped him out of the bath he said, 'Mum, do you think I could go to Janet's wedding?' I couldn't believe my ears. Janet was the daughter of our next-door neighbour, Theresa. We'd been invited to her wedding months ago, but when Craig got ill I'd put it out of my head.

After a conference the staff gave their blessing and found him a wheelchair. While Ernie dashed home to fetch my best green trouser suit, I dressed Craig in his Chelsea Football Club tracksuit.

We only stayed an hour at Janet's wedding reception but it was a very special hour. Craig even got up from his wheelchair and swayed a few shaky steps with me in the disco while Steve watched us, his eyes shining. I was so proud. What guts my little boy had.

On Monday Ernie had the day off work and I left him minding Craig while I nipped home to pick up my bank book. I was nearly broke by now. Money just seemed to disappear in hospital, what with phone calls, stamps, cups of coffee and so on. Last week my best friend Carol's mum, Thelma, had sent in £50 to tide us over—she'd organised a raffle for us at the OAPs' Bingo Club—but that had nearly gone. I was going to have to break into my savings.

It felt strange turning the key in the lock again—I hadn't been through our front door for a whole month. The door wouldn't open all the way, and as soon as I got into the hall I saw the reason: there was a great pile of envelopes on the floor.

I'd just put the kettle on when the doorbell rang. It was our postman John. He grinned at me. 'What's going on in this house? It's worse than the Christmas deliveries!' He handed me a big brown package addressed to Master Craig Shergold and covered with Australian stamps.

'I think I know what this might be, John,' I told him. With butterflies in my tummy I went into the kitchen and held the package over the kettle so I could peel the sealed end open. I didn't want Craig to get excited for nothing if I was wrong.

But I wasn't wrong. Oh bless you, Alison, I thought. Sealing the flap back down, I grabbed my portable cassette player, jumped in the car and tore back to the hospital. This was going to be the best medicine Craig had been given so far.

I ran into the ward and put the package on Craig's bed. 'A present for you, darling,' I said, trying to look casual as he opened it. Out tumbled a photograph, a record and a tape. 'Oh yeh!' he yelled. 'Yeh!'

One at a time he picked them up, his eyes popping. The photograph was a head-and-shoulders portrait of his idol Kylie Minogue with a handwritten message. *To Craig, Get Well. All my love, Kylie.*

'Put it up where I can see it, Mum,' Craig said. He picked up the record. 'Her latest single!' he exclaimed. '"Especially For You." That's the one she made with Jason Donovan, and it ain't even been released yet!' I thought he was going to fall out of bed he was so excited. Then he saw the cassette. 'I dunno what's on this though.'

I passed him my cassette player. 'Here, you'd better find out.'

We listened as Kylie's voice said, 'Hi, Craig—Sorry to hear you're not well. Hang on in there. You'll be better before you know it. Keep smiling and I hope to see you sometime. All my love, Kylie Minogue.'

Craig went potty. He didn't come down to earth all day. The news spread round the ward and all the kids and their visitors came over to his bed to have a look and a listen. Andy Coulston, a reporter from the *Sun* newspaper, rang up—I never discovered how he found out about it—and he wrote a story about Craig.

'Watch it, Craig—you'll be famous if you carry on like this,' I teased him.

There were lots of other cards that week. Since we'd left GOSH Alison had been giving people our home address so Ernie or I collected the post each day from Selby Road—usually there were at least thirty cards—and brought them in. Every day I sorted through the new cards with Craig and picked a few out. Usually it was the funny ones I put up—I was so anxious to keep Craig laughing.

I didn't count the cards. Breaking the world record was still only a hazy idea in the back of my mind. When my mum had been dying I'd read lots of articles about cancer which said how important positive thinking was. What could be better than the cards for getting him to think positive?

But they weren't the only weapon I used. That week I thought up one idea after another to keep Craig's spirits up. I quoted Steve's kung fu at him. 'I am the master. I am going to win! Come on,' I ordered, 'say it after me. I am going to WIN!'

Craig laughed at me. But he did say it, to please me.

His clothes were another area where I took control. He was allowed pyjamas now instead of the awful white hospital gowns but I felt wearing pyjamas all day would make him feel like an invalid so I brought in colourful clothes—bright pink Bermuda shorts and emerald green T-shirts. It made him look a lot better.

Before we left Great Ormond Street Mr Hayward had given Ernie and me a pep talk. He'd been keen on positive thinking too. 'Every kid needs a dream,' he told us. 'Do you have a dream you could share with him?'

I'd told him that Ernie and I had always joked about taking Craig to Disneyworld when Ernie was fifty.

'Do it,' Mr Hayward urged. 'Give him something to look forward to. Hold up a light at the end of the tunnel for him.'

At first I'd dismissed the idea. A trip to Disney would cost thousands and we were worrying where the next mortgage payment was coming from. But now I decided to go for it, and my friend Carol egged me on. 'We'll get people in Carshalton to fund-raise,' she said. 'Tell him you'll take him there for Christmas.'

Our time in Queen Mary's went quickly and with every day that passed Craig seemed to get stronger. He was sitting up in bed now rather than slumping and he could walk a few steps unsupported.

At last, on February 25, the doctors judged that Craig was well enough to be transferred to the Royal Marsden. Craig was admitted to the Princess Chula Ward, the children's cancer ward. Compared with the cramped Punch and Judy Ward it seemed huge, but Craig was in a cosy side ward with just four beds.

Craig's consultant at the Marsden, Diana Tait, called us in to see her on the first day. She was young and very attractive and Craig fell instantly in love with her.

'Hello, Craig,' she smiled. 'Would you like to know a little bit about what's going to happen while you're here with us?'

Craig nodded, open-mouthed.

'Well,' Diana Tait said, 'today you'll be going down to the theatre for what we call a lumbar puncture. That'll help us learn something about the way your body is fighting the tumour. Then in a couple of days' time we'll start your chemotherapy.' The doctors at Great Ormond Street had told us Craig would have radiotherapy first. I didn't ask why she'd changed the plan though. I doubted I'd

It was my good friend, Alison Ingram (left), who took up Mr Hayward's suggestion of trying for the Guinness world record.

Our nightmare begins (below). Craig's first major operation had to be postponed because he was too weak to undergo surgery.

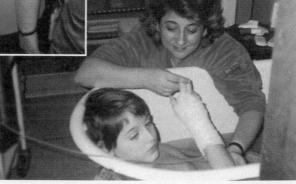

One of Craig's visitors was the great footballer of the sixties, George Best.

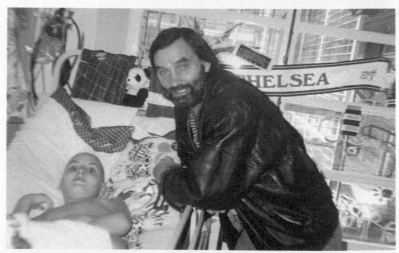

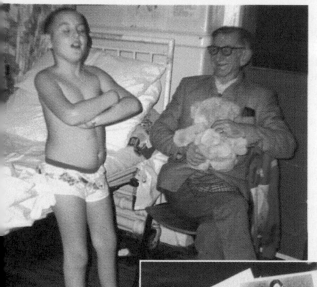

'I am going to WIN!' —
Craig demonstrating
his kung fu techniques
for my dad (left).

Craig with just a
tiny selection of the
autographed celeb-
rity photographs
that arrived.

understand. Half the time now the technical terms being used were going straight over my head.

Diana Tait told us a little bit about chemotherapy and how the drugs would weaken the cells in the tumour. She warned him that he might feel sick and his mouth might get sore. 'You'll probably lose your hair too I'm afraid.' She smiled. 'What's left of it.' (Craig still only had a downy covering on his scalp.)

'Oh, well,' Craig grinned, patting his head. 'It'll save me having a haircut.'

There was another thing about chemotherapy I learned, and it came as a terrible shock. Craig and Ernie had gone for the lumbar puncture and the registrar was describing the chemicals they'd be giving Craig, when he said casually, 'You do realise that Craig will never be able to have children after his treatment, don't you?'

I felt as though I'd been kicked in the ribs. I hadn't realised any such thing. I fled outside and drove to Carol's house and when she answered the door I collapsed in tears. Carol sat me down and made me a mug of tea. 'Now stop crying and tell me what's the matter.'

'He'll never be able to have kids, Carol,' I sobbed. 'Oh, it's not fair.'

Carol banged her fist on the table. 'Marion, stop crying. Don't you realise what this means?'

I sat up startled. 'No. What?'

'If they're saying he can't have kids then they're talking *long-term*!'

'Oh!' I gasped. 'Oh yes. So they are!'

If they were talking long-term they must think Craig was going to live! I drove back to the hospital with my heart singing.

They'd warned me that Craig would have a terrible headache after the lumbar puncture and might be sick, but when I got to the ward I saw Craig was sitting up in bed surrounded by visitors. He was eating a big sticky doughnut, and there was a huge smile on his face. 'Hello, Mum,' he said. 'Look what Joyce brought me. My favourites!'

THE FOLLOWING DAY Craig had to have something called a Hickman line inserted. Dr Tait explained that this was a fine piece of tubing which was inserted into a vein and left there. They would be able to feed the chemotherapy drugs and others straight into Craig's body without having to give him a fresh injection each time.

Two days later Craig started his chemotherapy. A bag of chemical was hung on a stand and connected to his Hickman line and then it was a matter of waiting. Each bag took hours to go in, but Craig's reaction didn't take so long. First came the vomiting then the diarrhoea, but Craig didn't once complain. He knew he had to have it and that was that.

The fact that the other kids on the ward were also receiving chemotherapy kept him and us from feeling too sorry for ourselves. There were three other children in Craig's room: two girls, Emma and Samantha, who were being treated for leukaemia, and Kelvin, who had a tumour on his leg. Craig was soon good friends with all of them, but it was Emma that he took under his wing. She was nine, the same age as Craig, and very frightened of the treatment—she used to scream in terror whenever they came to give her a blood transfusion. I think Craig felt he had to set her a good example by being brave and he never let her see that his chemotherapy bothered him—straight after he'd been sick he'd crack a joke about it to Emma.

There was a wonderful atmosphere on the ward. All the parents supported one another, and someone would always look after kids who didn't have visitors and make sure they didn't feel left out. Ernie was good like that—he'd spend hours playing cards with Kelvin, whose parents ran a pub and couldn't always come in during opening hours. I was amazed at how these kids could still laugh. In the next room to ours there were kids who were too poorly to get out of bed and sometimes I'd go in and play the fool with them, doing head over heels and cartwheels. 'Bet your mum can't do this,' I'd say and they'd have hysterics. 'Oh, do it again! Do it again, Marion!' they'd scream. Sometimes Craig would hobble in, put his hands on hips and say, 'What's *she* been doing now?'

Ernie slept in the hospital most nights, though that hadn't been the way we'd planned it. I'd decided that there was no way I was going to leave Craig on his own at night—not after I'd read the booklet we'd been handed when he was admitted. It was a depressing publication called *Childhood Cancers*—I hadn't let Ernie read it. One of the things it said was that children with brain tumours can die suddenly in their sleep. After reading that I'd asked for one of the hospital Z-beds and set it up on the floor next to Craig's bed.

But Craig soon got fed up. 'Cor blimey, does Daddy have to put up with this?' he asked on the third night. 'Do you keep asking *him* if he's all right and if he's warm enough and keeping him awake?'

I tried to stop myself fussing but I couldn't, it was just my nature.

'Go home, Mum,' he said two evenings later. 'Please. I don't need you to sleep with me.' He grinned. 'I'm a big boy now.'

I didn't want to but I knew I wasn't helping him by keeping him awake. After that Ernie slept on the Z-bed instead while I went home. But I always wrote a little note to him each night and left it on his pillow so that he would have a love-letter to wake up to.

They were running a test called myelography on the fluid they'd taken from Craig's spine during his lumbar punctures. Craig seemed so much better that when Diana Tait told me the results were ready and called me into her office I felt quite optimistic.

Ernie wasn't there. He'd fallen off a lorry while delivering a fridge and was up in St Helier Hospital having his foot X-rayed.

'Our family's keeping the hospitals round here in business!' I joked to Diana Tait, but she didn't smile.

'Marion,' she said, 'sit down.'

My heart stood still. 'Why? What's wrong?'

She gave a sigh. 'I'm afraid I've got bad news. The myelography shows that the cancer has travelled to Craig's spine. There's one definite tumour and three probable tumours in the lumbar region.'

I was stunned—it had never occurred to me that there might be more tumours. I gaped at her. 'Where have they come from?'

'The spinal cord and the brain are well connected—it's very easy for cancer cells to travel between them. They're what we call droplets—they're not very big, and we're going to try and treat them, but I have to be honest with you—it doesn't look good.'

I wouldn't believe it. 'It can't have travelled. He's getting better. He's better than he's ever been. Go and look at him.'

Diana Tait shook her head. 'Marion, I'm sorry, but the tests tell a different story.'

'He's *not* going to die,' I yelled. I stood up and pushed my chair away. 'You can think what you like, he is *not* going to die!'

I stormed out of the office. I thought about going to the chapel to pray but went to have a cigarette instead.

Samantha's mother was having a cup of coffee in the Juno Room. She was a big black lady who'd had a lot of troubles—she'd lost her husband very young and now her daughter had leukaemia. She took one look at my face and said, 'Do you want to talk?' I told her what had happened and she took my hand. 'Don't ever lose your faith, Marion,' she said. 'There are two powers in life. There is the power of evil and the power of good. You've got to pray to God *every* day to take the power of evil out of your life.'

I wasn't convinced. 'How can God let children get cancer?' I asked her. 'And what about earthquakes and hurricanes and famines—how can God let them happen?'

She smiled. 'They happen *because* there are two powers and unless we all pray to God then the power of evil can take over. The more people that pray, the more God will answer their prayers. It says so in the Bible.'

Samantha's mum put me back on the right road. I hadn't realised it until now, but my faith had been really shaken by the suffering Craig had been going through. After that day I started to pray again. Not in the Marsden chapel, where somehow I never felt at home, but wherever I happened to be. And it did help, just as she'd said.

I didn't tell Craig about the new tumours. 'As long as he's laughing he won't give in to the cancer,' I told Ernie. 'It's up to us.'

The other kids helped Craig keep cheerful. Most of them had great attitudes to their illness. There was always more laughter in that ward than tears.

In addition to all the targets I had set for Craig he had set one of his own—he wanted to be a pageboy at Steve's and Sharon's wedding. I didn't encourage the idea. He had gone to Janet's wedding, but that was before the chemotherapy started. He hadn't been weakened by all this vomiting and diarrhoea. But Craig had made his mind up, and the doctors didn't argue. Kevin's sister-in-law measured him up for a pageboy suit and six weeks after his brain operation Craig walked down the aisle behind Sharon. He had trouble keeping his balance and as soon as Sharon took her place at the altar, he walked over to Ernie and me in the front pew and collapsed back into his wheelchair, but he did it. I was so proud of him. There wasn't a dry eye in the church, and after the ceremony the vicar came over and put his hands on Craig's little bald head and blessed him.

After the wedding I was sure I could see an improvement in Craig. He was walking better, his headaches were getting further apart, his eyesight was improving. He could recognise people much more quickly now, he could read his cards for himself, and he could watch television and videos with the other kids on his ward.

Each of Craig's chemotherapy treatments was given over about ten days. Then he'd be given a couple of weeks to recover before the next treatment. On the day Craig was due to start his third course of chemotherapy I was at home getting ready to leave for the hospital when the phone rang. It was Andy Coulston from the *Sun*. 'Kylie Minogue is appearing in the Children's Variety Performance tonight,' he said. 'How would Craig like to go?' I didn't have to ask Craig to know the answer to that one! The hospital agreed to put off his chemotherapy and also agreed that Emma could go with us—Andy had said he could take a friend and Craig was determined it should be Emma. They'd become inseparable.

We travelled with Emma and her mum up to the Dominion Theatre by taxi and were put at the front. All Craig's favourite stars were there. Jon Pertwee, the pop group Brother Beyond, Philip Schofield, Sue Pollard, Jason Donovan and of course Kylie . . .

After Jason and Kylie had stopped the show with the duet, 'Especially For You', Jason stepped forward. 'We've got two very special kids here tonight,' he said, and he came right down off the stage, introduced Craig and Emma to the audience and gave them a big cuddle. Kylie came down and chatted to them too.

It was after midnight when we finally got back to the hospital. Emma put her little head on her mum's lap and closed her eyes. Even in her sleep she was still smiling. Craig leaned against my shoulder and snuggled up. 'How do you feel, Craig?' I asked.

'Great,' he murmured.

'Who is the master?'

He grinned up at me. 'I am the master,' he said.

Five

Craig's mouth ulcers were causing real problems—they'd spread outside his mouth and up to his nose. The nurses gave me a little sponge on a stick which I had to dip into a jar of brown liquid and dab all round his mouth. One day early in April we were going through this routine when a voice behind me said, 'Hello, Craig,' and I turned round to see Diana Tait.

Dr Tait grinned at Craig, then turned to me. 'Marion, I'd like to see you for a minute.' My heart sank, as I followed her out of the ward, but out in the corridor Dr Tait smiled. 'Marion, I don't see why you can't take Craig home for a day or two.'

I stared at her. 'When?'

'Today if you like,' she said. 'Take him home overnight. It'll do him good. Being with other sick children all day isn't helping him to get well. What he needs now is a bit of home life.'

I could have kissed her. Craig had been getting really low recently. All his mates had gone or were going. Kelvin had finished treatment and gone home and Emma seemed to be a lot better and was also due to be discharged soon.

I dashed to telephone Ernie—and screamed the news down the phone at him. Craig was so excited. He couldn't wait to see how I'd papered the living room with his cards. Twenty minutes later Ernie arrived and Craig and I got into the back of the car. It was a lovely warm day. All the cherry blossom was out in Carshalton Beeches and Craig and I started singing 'I'll be with You in Apple Blossom Time', full of the joys of spring.

The last time Craig had seen Selby Road there'd been snowdrops peeping out in the front gardens. Today, when we pulled up outside our home, there were pink buds on the roses in front of the house. As we made our way up the garden path he stopped, his hand on my arm, and looked around him. 'It's good to be home, Mum.' He sounded like a soldier coming back from the wars. My eyes filled up and I put my key in the lock. It wouldn't turn. Ernie took it from me, but he had no more luck. While he was trying I glanced through the window and saw that the brass box where I kept my video tapes and magazines was in the middle of the room. I wondered why Ernie had left it there.

'It's no good,' Ernie said. 'The latch must be down inside. I'll have to climb over and get in the back door.' He heaved himself onto the fence and down the other side and then I heard him shout, 'Oh no!'

'What's the matter, Ern?' I called.

'We've been burgled,' he yelled. 'They've cleaned us out.'

I waited, clutching Craig's hand until Ernie opened the front door. Then nervously we walked inside and looked around. The cards were still all over the walls as I'd left them, but the whole place had been ransacked. The telly had gone, the video . . .

I sat Craig down on the settee and left him with Ernie while I ran upstairs to our bedroom. Our bed was upside-down on the floor and my dressing table was smashed to pieces.

In a daze I wandered into Craig's room. He'd had his own little fourteen-inch telly in there and a computer. I wasn't surprised to find them missing. What I hadn't expected was to see the Chelsea wallpaper hanging off the walls in shreds, or the muddy footprints all over Craig's Chelsea bedspread. I stared in horror, feeling absolutely numb. Craig mustn't see this, I thought.

Downstairs Ernie was sitting on the settee with his arm round Craig. 'I've rung the police, Mal,' Ernie said. 'They're sending someone round. They said we're not to touch anything.'

I sat on the other side of Craig cuddling him until the police arrived. Ernie showed them into the front room and the two great big coppers looked round, their faces deadpan.

'Well, they've done a proper job here, haven't they?' The one who'd spoken turned towards me and his face changed as he saw Craig's bald head and the big scar down the back of his head. He went upstairs to see the bedrooms and when he came down again he looked as though he'd seen a ghost. He stared at the layers of get-well cards on the wall. 'Are these all his?'

I nodded.

He looked at his mate and shook his head. 'I've met some villains in my time,' he said, 'but I don't think any one of them would have done this. The hardest criminal would have come in here and said, no—this is the wrong house.'

They never did find out who did it, but whoever they were, they couldn't have guessed the publicity the break-in would bring. The

Sutton Guardian ran a story on the burglary and dozens of sympathetic letters arrived. The evening after the robbery there was a knock at the door and I opened it to find two of our neighbours, Chris and Carol Pilbeam, holding a television set. Chris was the manager of Sutton Athletic Football Club and he told me the club had organised a whip-round to buy a TV for Craig. Soon afterwards a local builder, Len Carpenter, came round with a video.

Both events were written up in the local paper and in the course of one article the reporter mentioned Craig's Disney fund. The idea caught people's imagination. Within days Peter Pink, the owner of Pink's gym in Carshalton, had organised a body-building display which raised more money towards the Disney trip and as an extra thrill Peter arranged for Mr Universe, Lance Dreher, to present the cheque to Craig. Thelma, Carol's mum, had already been running small raffles to help get Craig to Disney. Now she decided to take advantage of all the publicity to organise some serious fund-raising. Over the next few weeks a pub in South Croydon raised £1,000, a Battersea postman volunteered to run in the London Marathon to raise money for Craig's trip, and the firemen from Croydon fire station also started collecting for him. Ironically, thanks to our burglars, this trip to Disneyworld was beginning to look a real possibility.

When the national press found out they took an even bigger interest in the story. While Craig was home the *Sun* newspaper sent a pretty young girl reporter called Ruki Sayid to talk to him. It didn't occur to me to tell Ruki about the card record. To my mind the main point of the get-well cards was to keep Craig's spirits up, and I thought thirty or forty cards a day was quite enough to cope with. It took Craig a couple of hours to open them each morning and finding room for them was getting to be a problem. Once or twice I'd thought of asking Alison to find out how many more we needed to beat the world record, but somehow it slipped my mind.

Craig continued to come home for a few days at a time between treatments, and getting away from the hospital atmosphere did seem to make him a lot brighter. We still hadn't told him about the spinal tumours. He understood that he was fighting cancer—and Ernie and I felt that was enough for him to cope with.

In June, Craig completed his final chemotherapy treatment and the following week he had more tests to assess how well the treatment had worked. While we waited for the results we took Craig home again. The doctors wanted to give him a couple of weeks to recover before they started radiotherapy. He'd lost a lot of weight and was very weak now—he'd been having some very heavy nosebleeds and he needed transfusions of special blood cells called platelets, which helped with clotting, to try and control them.

Before he was allowed home I'd been warned not to take Craig into shops or public places where he might pick up an infection. The doctors were especially concerned about chickenpox, which they said was very dangerous to children receiving chemotherapy. I wrote a big notice in red felt-tip pen and put it on the front door.

PLEASE DO NOT ENTER THIS HOUSE IF YOU OR YOUR CHILD HAVE CHICKENPOX OR ANY INFECTIOUS DISEASES. CRAIG HAS NO IMMUNE SYSTEM AND I'M SURE YOU'LL AGREE HE HAS BEEN THROUGH QUITE ENOUGH!!!

Craig enjoyed that break at home. His best friend Lee came daily—he was a gem—and Maxine, who'd sent Craig a card nearly every day since he'd been ill, also visited regularly. On June 24, he was ten years old and we had a little birthday party for him. Afterwards we took a birthday cake into the Princess Chula Ward to share with the children still there. To Craig's joy we discovered Emma in the isolation room. She'd been brought back for a bone marrow transplant, and the two of them sat for an hour chatting and nibbling birthday cake.

On June 29, Sharon's and Steve's baby girl was born and they kept their promise to Craig by calling her Kylie. Craig was able to visit them in hospital which gave him a big lift. The same week I drove him up to the Marsden because Diana Tait wanted him to have a CT scan, which produces detailed, accurate pictures of the deep parts inside a patient's body, before starting radiotherapy. While we waited for her to assess the scans, Ernie and I took Craig back to Great Ormond Street to see Mr Hayward. He was delighted with the progress Craig had made since February. He could stand on one leg now and count to nearly fifty. We came away feeling very optimistic.

We were unprepared for the bombshell waiting for us. The following Tuesday we had a routine appointment with Diana Tait and Craig was very bright and breezy as he did his tests. After ten minutes Dr Tait said, 'Craig, I want you to go with the nurse to be measured. Your mum and dad can stay here.' The nurse took Craig away, and she waved us towards two chairs. 'Marion, Ernie, sit down a minute.' We obeyed. 'I'm sorry,' she said. 'The chemotherapy hasn't been very successful. There's some change in the spine, but it doesn't seem to have touched the brain tumour at all.' She sighed. 'We could give Craig radiotherapy but it would have to be very deep radiotherapy and the chances are the end result would be the same.'

I went crazy. After all he'd been through. All the pain. All the vomiting. And for what? 'Is he dying?' I asked.

She shrugged helplessly. 'He could be. Look, if you want to try radiotherapy we can. Why don't you go away and think about it.'

Poor Ernie looked shell-shocked and I was completely distraught as we came out of the office. Jane and Shirley, two of the nurses, came over and offered their support. 'Come on, now,' Jane said. 'You haven't given up before. Don't do it now.'

Ernie went to find Craig while Jane walked with me up to the Juno Room. I just couldn't take it. I fell sobbing onto a chair.

'Oh, Marion, please stop,' Jane said.

'I can't,' I gasped. 'I can't.' Hours seemed to pass. Jane brought me a cup of tea and poor old Ernie came up the stairs about three times before I felt ready to face Diana Tait again. There was no argument. Ernie and I were agreed on what had to be done.

'We want you to do the radiotherapy,' I told her.

She spread her hands. 'All right. If that's what you want. But I'm not promising anything—you must remember that.'

Craig could receive radiotherapy as a day-patient which meant that I would take him to and from the Marsden by car each day. The treatment would be given every day for nine weeks.

The radiotherapy took place in a windowless room in the hospital basement. Before it started Craig had a mould taken of his head so that a Perspex mask could be made to immobilise his head during radiation. Marks could be made on the mask to allow the radiotherapists to target the tumour. Ernie and I weren't allowed in during treatment, but we could stay with him while he was prepared. By the time they'd finished getting him ready he looked like something out of a horror film—his head was encased in Perspex except for a hole for his nostrils, but Craig didn't seem bothered by it.

We'd been warned that Craig would be as sick after the radiotherapy as he'd been after the chemo. But at least the diarrhoea and the nosebleeds stopped. He was put back on steroids and his weight started to creep back up. Every morning I had to load the wheelchair, half carry Craig out to the car, strap him in and drive through the rush-hour traffic to the Royal Marsden. The radiotherapy itself only took a few minutes but there was always a long queue for treatment and it was usually after midday when we got home. It was exhausting for me so it must have been even more so for Craig. After eight weeks of treatment he looked listless and bloated and his speech had got very slow. His coordination was bad too. The only good sign was that his eyesight didn't seem too bad now.

I was sure the radiotherapy treatment was causing most of his symptoms. It was due to finish at the beginning of September and I expected a magic improvement then, but although he stopped being sick, he was still lethargic and depressed. Looking at him, I had a terrible suspicion that he had given up. The thought terrified me.

The news that Craig had been chosen to present a bouquet of flowers to Princess Diana couldn't have come at a better time. The Princess was opening a Malcolm Sargent holiday home for the families of children with cancer at Jaywick Sands near Clacton. After the ceremony Craig would stay for a week's seaside holiday.

But he was too ill. The morning of the opening he didn't get out of bed when I called him. I rang up Maureen O'Sullivan, the Marsden-based organiser for the Malcolm Sargent Fund, to call the whole thing off.

Maureen consoled me. 'Never mind, Marion,' she said. 'There's a royal film première in aid of the fund at the Odeon, Leicester Square, in ten days' time. I'm sure he'll be feeling better by then. I'll see if I can get Craig an invitation to that so he can meet Princess Diana then instead. Prince Charles will be there too.' A few days later she rang to tell me Craig and two little girls from the Marsden would meet the royal couple at the première of *When the Whales Came*.

Maureen was right, Craig did start to look better that week. It looked as if we'd make it this time.

The performance was due to start at seven thirty. I don't think Craig was as excited as me—he would rather have seen *Batman*—and he certainly wasn't as excited as the two little girls. They were over the moon at the idea of meeting Princess Di. Their hair was just starting to grow again in little wisps after their chemotherapy and they did look lovely, wearing long dresses bought specially for the occasion.

At seven o'clock we were all told to get into line and the little girls took their places next to Craig in his wheelchair. By seven twenty it was clear the royals were late. Officials rushed around speaking into walkie-talkies, then without any explanation we were taken down some stairs into a room. Suddenly there was a buzz of excitement outside and we all surged to the door to see what was going on. But although we saw the flashbulbs going off we didn't catch a glimpse of the royal couple, who were ushered straight into the cinema.

I couldn't believe it. Both the little girls were sobbing their hearts out. I sat through the film absolutely seething. Not for Craig—Kylie Minogue had meant more to him than Princess Di—but for those little girls, still sick from chemotherapy, in their pretty long dresses.

Next day, when I took Craig in for his check-up at the Marsden, I was still seeing red. The two little girls had come in for their weekly check-ups too, and their mothers came over. We were grumbling away to each other about the fiasco of the night before when Brian

Sadler, the Appeals Director for the Royal Marsden, walked into the treatment room and headed towards us.

I knew Brian quite well and anyway I was in the mood to stir up trouble. 'What do you want, Brian? Have you come about last night?' I asked. 'I think it's disgusting. The papers ought to know.'

He shook his head. 'I've heard about that. But it's not worth getting upset about.' He smiled. 'What's all this about the *Guinness Book of Records*?'

All the wind was taken out of my sails. I could feel the blood rising in my cheeks. 'How did you know about that?' I asked.

'I've had a phone call from ICI in Cheshire asking about Craig. They said someone called Alison Ingram had written asking them to send get-well cards to Craig because he was trying for a world record—is it true?'

I had to admit it was.

'How many have you got now?'

I shrugged. 'I don't know. Maybe about three thousand.'

Brian Sadler stared at me thoughtfully. 'How would you feel about going for it properly?' he said. 'Making it an official world-record attempt. With the Marsden behind you.' Before I had time to say anything he added, 'You'll never break the record if you do it on the quiet, you know. The world record is over one million cards.'

My jaw dropped. 'We'll never do that.'

'Oh, I'm sure you could. You just need to publicise it better. The Marsden could let the papers know, the TV people, all the radio stations, we could turn it into something really big. The publicity wouldn't just help Craig—it would help the Marsden. We have a big fund-raising appeal going, and anything that brings the Marsden's name to people's attention helps. But it's entirely up to you. I don't want to force your hand.'

I thought about it and suddenly found myself grinning at Brian Sadler. 'Right. You'd better tell us what to do,' I said.

THE STORY BROKE in the *Daily Mirror* on Monday, September 25. There was a big picture and an article telling of Craig's wish to get into the *Guinness Book of Records*. Two days later the *Sun* launched an appeal. Thanks to the Marsden publicity people Craig's address was given out on ITV's *Good Morning Britain* programme, and on *This Morning*. Radio presenters also plugged the appeal.

The public response was dramatic. Craig was due to be discharged the day after the *Mirror* story was published, and at eight thirty that morning I was making the house nice for his return when there was a knock on the door. I opened it to find John, our postman, holding a great pile of cards between his hands and his chin. At midday Ernie had just brought Craig back from the hospital when there was another hammering on the door. This time John was on a moped and I could hardly lift the bag he handed me.

'I think you'd better come in, John,' I said.

John stared at me flabbergasted as I told him about the appeal. 'Well, good luck, mate, I hope you make it,' he said to Craig. 'I'd better get myself a bigger bike.'

At teatime a post office van pulled up outside and we watched the driver carry four bulging mailsacks up the path to the front door. He and Ernie struggled to carry them in. Craig was lying on the settee and he laughed so much I thought he was going to make himself sick. 'Oh, *Mum*, I don't believe it,' he said. 'I just don't *believe* it.'

Then the phone rang. It was Pauline, the receptionist for Princess Chula Ward. 'Marion, you should see behind my desk! The mail-sacks are blocking up the foyer. They're everywhere. Do you think Ernie could come up and get them?' Ernie set off in the car and while he was away there was another knock on the door. This time it was a tall, pleasant-looking man with glasses and a moustache who introduced himself as Charlie King, the delivery-office manager at Wallington Post Office. I asked him in.

Craig was looking really very ill, and Charlie seemed quite upset when he saw him. He sat down opposite Craig. 'I read the story in the *Sun*,' he explained. 'I just wanted to ask you if you're sure you want to go ahead with this? It's going to be a lot of work.'

'Of course I'm sure,' I said. 'It's going to make him better. Don't you worry about us. We'll manage.'

He smiled. 'I'm not trying to stop you. I only wanted to say that if you do go ahead the Post Office will be right behind you. We'll give you all the help we can. We can even make the Princess Chula Ward one of the Post Office's nominated charities this year. That way, when problems arise, you can always call on me to help.'

'What sort of problems?'

'Well, one of the difficulties is going to be actually counting the cards.' He leaned forward. 'Where are you going to do it? Who's going to help you? You can't count a million cards yourself.'

I shrugged. 'I've got loads of friends, a lovely family,' I said. 'They'll help—I'll get the vicar to loan us the church hall.'

Charlie nodded. 'Good idea, but you'll have to organise the counting very strictly. For an official record you can't have any mistakes. It'll have to be done like a vote count at an election.'

I hadn't really thought about the practical side of this appeal before. Suddenly other difficulties started to occur to me. 'What'll we do with the cards after we've counted them, Charlie?'

Charlie looked around him and laughed. 'Well you can't put any more up on the walls, can you? Maybe we can find some paper recyclers to take them.'

'It doesn't seem right to destroy them,' I said.

'No. But paper recyclers pay money and the money could go to help other people with cancer,' said Charlie. 'No one would mind that. We could raise money from the stamps. There are firms that'll pay for used stamps—they package them up and sell them to stamp collectors.' He looked at his watch. 'I must go.' He stood up and touched Craig gently on the shoulder. 'Bye, Craig.' You could see his heart going out to him. 'Don't worry. I'll help you.'

At the door he turned. 'This could go on for a long long time, you know, Marion. I hope you won't regret it.'

'I won't.' I felt so certain about that. This was going to help Craig more than anything so far. We were going ahead.

Brian Sadler rang the next day to tell us the telephones at the Marsden were jammed and the cards were causing 'a bit of an administrative problem'. On Friday, when we went into the Marsden for Craig's weekly check-up, I saw what he meant. There were cards everywhere, in the entrance hall, in the corridors . . . I carried a sack into the Juno Room to open while I was waiting for Craig. The other mothers in there helped me count them, and after half an hour there were cards all over the floor.

A week before, Craig had been getting thirty or forty a day; now it was more like ten thousand. Brian had discovered that the card record was held by a little boy from Leicestershire called Mario Morby who had 1,000,265 postcards. If I'd known that before I might have abandoned the whole idea but now, seeing all these sacks of mail flooding in, I knew it wasn't an impossible dream.

Every night that week Dad, Carol, Thelma and Fred came round to help but even though we stayed up till three in the morning, we only managed to open a few thousand each day. By the end of the week we'd counted 22,500 cards, but there was a growing mountain of unopened sacks in the garage. We had to have more help.

I went to see Bill, the vicar of All Saints, Hackbridge, who agreed to lend us his hall. The minute I got home I started to telephone people asking them if they'd be willing to spend three hours opening cards. Local radio stations mentioned the card-opening night, and the papers were very keen to know how we were coping. Ruki rang to say the *Sun* wanted Craig to come into the office and be their 'editor for a day', and on Sunday, a big limo took Craig to Wapping where he had a wonderful time, meeting all the staff and touring the newsroom. He even sat in the editor's chair and both Kelvin McKenzie, the editor, and Peter Cox, the assistant editor, were wonderful with him.

The card-opening session was due to start at seven. Fred and Ernie went early, ferrying sacks to the hall in Fred's big van. By the time I arrived with Craig in his wheelchair the church hall was overflowing with people. Charlie had brought his whole team of posties from Wallington and with Ernie's help they had arranged long trestle tables around the hall. When he saw me he came over beaming. 'We've sorted out the stamps,' he said. 'The Leukaemia Research Fund are going to take them.'

Well over a hundred people had turned up—aged from eight to eighty. The counting continued steadily for three and a half hours. Charlie had organised it like a military operation. The posties brought in the sacks of envelopes and tipped them onto the tables. The openers had to slit open the envelopes and check every card to see if it had a special message or money inside. Then they collected the cards into bundles of two hundred. The bundles were carried to the end of the hall where John, our own postman, counted them and entered the running total in the official tally book. Other people were given the job of tearing the stamps off the envelopes and putting them in boxes in the middle of the table to go to the Leukaemia Research Fund. The envelopes were put into special wastepaper sacks under the tables.

I was anxious for people to enjoy themselves and I'd brought my party tapes so we could have a sing-song while we counted. It worked, and the atmosphere was great. Charlie had put up a blackboard at one end of the hall and every half-hour or so he wrote up the total so far. By half past eight it had reached 21,000, nearly as many as we'd managed to count in the whole of the past week.

I'd hoped we might get a few cards from famous people and I wasn't disappointed. Early in the evening my friend Jean suddenly waved her arm in the air. 'This one's from Des O'Connor!' she yelled. There was a cheer and I rushed over and brought it back to show Craig. Soon afterwards we found cards from Seve Ballasteros, Tessa Sanderson, Linford Christie and Henry Cooper.

Finally, at ten thirty, Charlie called it a day. Since seven o'clock we'd opened 43,000 cards. On top of what we'd already opened that made a grand total of 69,000. Everybody went crazy, cheering and laughing. 'When are we going to do it again, Mal?' someone called.

Clearing up would take at least another hour but Charlie insisted we took Craig home. 'He's tired. Get him to bed. I'll sort things out.' He promised to drop the opened cards off in my garage the following day—I still felt they were too precious to recycle.

AN ITV FILM of the card opening and interviews with Charlie and Craig were broadcast the following morning. That afternoon a man turned up at our house from Securicor. He said his boss had seen an appeal by Charlie about the waste paper and wanted to help. It seemed that one of Securicor's subsidiary activities was recycling paper. They would pick up the waste envelopes direct from the Post Office and pay the Royal Marsden for every ton they recycled.

It was evening before I got a chance to sit down and take out the letters I'd saved from the night before. I started to read them to Craig but I was soon in tears. Craig raised his eyes to heaven at my 'soppiness' but I couldn't help it, the letters were so moving. Every pupil in a Belfast school had sent a letter and a card. A little boy of five, also called Craig, said he'd spent all his pocket money on his card. There was even a poem and a long letter from a prisoner in Shepton Mallet Prison in Somerset: *Go for it son, get in the 'Guinness Book of Records'. We might be in prison but we have got hearts as well and we are human.*

'I've got to answer some of these letters,' I said to Ernie.

'Love, you haven't got time,' Ernie protested. 'And we can't afford the postage. There must be a hundred letters there.'

Charlie came to the rescue. He told me to draft a standard letter of thanks. 'We'll get someone at the office to duplicate it and the Post Office will supply you with two thousand pre-paid envelopes,' he said. Charlie was proving to be an absolute gem. 'Don't be silly,' he said when I tried to thank him. 'The Post Office is doing good business out of this. The least we can do is to put a bit back.'

Dear Charlie put more than a bit back. The day after the first opening session he talked a firm in Harlow into lending us two letter-opening machines. The same day he contacted Sutton United Football Club, where he was a member, and asked them if they'd let us use their ballroom for card sessions. I was very relieved when they said yes, as Hackbridge church hall really wasn't big enough. Charlie booked the ballroom for Thursday evenings and Sunday mornings. 'There's about two hundred thousand cards in the sorting office waiting to be counted,' he said. 'We're going to need at least two sessions a week to keep on top of them.'

I had enough on my plate dealing with the press. The phone hardly stopped ringing with people wanting to interview Craig. I never said yes without asking him because I didn't want to overtire him, but when he was asked to appear on *Good Morning Britain* with Mike Morris and Richard Keys there was no chance of him saying no. To be on television as a celebrity guest was a dream come true.

The interview went really well, then after the programme we went to the Marsden for Craig's weekly check-up. Craig was being weighed when the registrar came in and gave me a beaming smile. 'Good news, Mrs Shergold,' he said. 'The latest scans show that the tumours in Craig's spine have completely cleared.'

I was so ecstatic I screamed. I took the registrar's hand. 'It's the cards,' I said. 'It's all those people praying for Craig. Do you know what this is? It's a miracle.'

I didn't ask about the brain tumour. I didn't want to risk spoiling my happiness. I had more energy than I'd had for months. I wanted to thank every single person who'd written to Craig, so I took up Charlie's suggestion and drafted a thank-you letter. He came back the next day with 2,000 copies, each with a gap at the bottom for me to add a personal message. Before long it was taking up nearly all my time: when I wasn't opening cards, I was writing letters.

We held the first meeting at Sutton United Football Club at ten thirty on the morning of Sunday, October 8. Charlie had booked a morning session because of all the children who wanted to help: the Carshalton Brownie and Cub leaders had rung to say their packs wanted to be involved and so did most of Craig's school.

The posties had arranged tables all around the room with bundles of cards already opened by machine, and I did my bit too by putting boxes out labelled 'money' (for the Marsden), 'famous' (for celebrity cards), 'funny' (for anything people thought might make Craig laugh), 'holy' (for things like prayers, mass cards and religious medals) and 'presents'.

The session was another great success: by two thirty we'd opened another 59,000 cards. Everyone seemed to have had a really good time and Charlie announced that we'd meet again on Thursday.

This time the 'famous' box contained cards from George Cole and Dennis Waterman. And we had found one from the Duchess of York! She'd enclosed one of her Budgie books and a handwritten note. It thrilled Craig. One which thrilled him even more came from Captain Al Haynes, an American airline pilot who had saved his passengers from drowning when his plane crashed into a river in Iowa. Captain Haynes sent him the pilot's wings he'd been wearing in the crash. 'I hope these bring you as much luck as they brought me,' he wrote.

Then on Wednesday Craig picked an envelope from a sack I'd brought home, opened it and yelled, 'Oh no! I don't believe it!' My heart jumped. I took the typewritten letter from him and read it:

Dear Craig,
    I have just heard that you have been in hospital and wanted
to write at once to wish you well. Nobody ever likes being in

hospital but you are obviously keeping busy and I hope this get-well message helps you achieve your ambition.

With warmest good wishes to you, your family and all those looking after you at the Royal Marsden Hospital. With love and all very best wishes . . .

Margaret Thatcher

I put it on the hearth in pride of place. Craig was on top of the world for the rest of the morning, and so was I. When the phone rang I skipped to answer it.

'Marion? It's Brian Sadler. Have you heard from Donald McFarlane?'

'No. Who is Donald McFarlane?' I asked.

'He's the editor of the *Guinness Book of Records*. He announced this morning that Craig won't be allowed an entry in the *Guinness Book* even if he does break the record.'

'What?' I sat down suddenly on the stairs.

'He made a statement to the press this morning,' Brian went on. 'I'd better read out what he said, shall I? "Long experience of similar situations tells us that such appeals have the potential to get out of control. In the long term they cause more distress than positive value." I don't know what to say, Marion. What do you think?'

What I thought was unprintable. I was absolutely beside myself.

Craig had heard my side of the phone call so I had to tell him. His face fell. 'Ain't they mean, Mum?'

'Never mind, darling, don't give up hope,' I told him. 'I'm not going to lie down and take this.'

The phone started straight away. All the papers wanted to know my reaction, and when I told them I was going to fight Donald McFarlane's decision most people said they were behind me. Ruki telephoned from the *Sun* newsroom. 'Are you going to carry on, Marion?'

'Of course I'm going to carry on,' I said. 'It'd be silly not to. Anyway if I stopped I'd be letting people down.'

'Good for you,' said Ruki. 'Don't forget we're on your side.'

Ruki's story in the *Sun* was headlined: GUINNESS MEANIES. But it did no good. Donald McFarlane had made up his mind. No matter how many cards Craig received he could not win a place in the *Guinness Book of Records*, and that was that.

The hall was booked for the next session. Ernie and I had to decide what to do. It wasn't difficult. These cards were helping Craig to fight his cancer and that mattered far more to me than the record. I telephoned Charlie. 'Tell everyone that the meeting at Sutton United Club on Sunday is *on*,' I said. 'We're going to carry on counting.'

Six

As I walked into the Sutton United Club ballroom on Sunday morning people looked over expectantly. I took a deep breath and raised my fist in the air.

'Guinness! Up Yours!' I yelled. 'We're going to go for it!'

The hall just exploded.

That morning, we found hundreds of letters saying, Don't give in. Every single national newspaper had sent a card to support us. 'That Donald McFarlane should be here today!' Charlie said.

We counted 60,000 cards that day. The following Thursday, two hundred and fifty people turned up, and we counted 70,000. But even that wasn't enough—Charlie reckoned 200,000 cards were arriving each week now—and for the rest of October we decided to hold three card sessions weekly and to appeal for more volunteers.

The ballroom had an extra advantage over the church hall—apart from its size—it had a bar. Counting cards was still what mattered, but now people could have a drink while they worked.

Our family and friends never flagged. Steve and Sharon came whenever they could, though Sharon's mum was very ill and Steve was studying for his fireman's exams so they couldn't always make it. But some people, like my dad, and Tony and Jean, my old friends from work, never missed a night.

The list of celebrities who'd written to Craig grew longer and longer. By the end of the month the celebrity box contained cards from the Rolling Stones, Sean Connery, Eric Clapton, Neil Kinnock, Ronald Reagan, Richard Gere, Tom Jones (I grabbed that one!) and Arnold Schwarzenegger. Craig was thrilled by all the big names but when an interviewer asked him who his favourite card was from he didn't have to think twice. 'Buster Merryfield . . .' he said.

She looked puzzled. 'Who?'

Craig gave her a despairing look. 'You know—Uncle Albert off *Only Fools and Horses.*'

The sacks of opened cards had overflowed out of my garage and were piling up in the garden. Everyone was urging me to recycle them but I still hated the thought. Then I had an idea. Handicapped kids had been sending us cards made by cutting up old Christmas and birthday cards. I thought maybe schools for the handicapped could use Craig's cards for occupational therapy. It turned out they could. And Charlie and his mate Tony in the Post Office were soon sending sacks of cards to handicapped schools all over the country.

We weren't just getting run-of-the-mill get-well cards any more.

One card, the size of a football pitch, arrived in separate rolled-up sections. There were miniature ones too. Someone had sent Craig a card the size of a postage stamp, with a message you could only read with a magnifying glass. One man in Germany had sent a piece of the Berlin Wall with 'get-well' carved into it, and someone from Easter Island sent a message written on a coconut shell.

The cards were coming from all over the world. Everyone's geography was getting better. 'Where the heck is Swaziland?' someone would say. If nobody knew, someone would look it up on the map Charlie had stuck up behind the card-opening machine.

After each card night I'd collect the 'special' boxes. Cheques were continuing to pour in and the hospital had opened a fund in Craig's name to receive all the money.

I would take the other boxes home to sort out later. The contents of the 'present' box took up most room. Craig's bedroom was filled with furry animals now, so he decided to give the rest to the kids on Princess Chula Ward. There were also sweets, books, video tapes and literally hundreds of cassette tapes.

The 'holy' box usually took me even longer to sort out. I'd started a holy box to collect all the mass cards that were arriving, telling Craig that candles were being lit and masses said for him in Catholic churches all over England. But I hadn't expected to get so many things from other religions. We had holy ash from a mountain in India, little plaster Buddhas, a chant that he was supposed to repeat six times a day.

Sometimes I'd find miracle cures in the 'holy' box—lotions and potions with messages urging me to feed them to Craig or rub them on his head. Someone in Russia had sent Craig a mushroom in yellow liquid with black lumps floating in it, which he was supposed to drink. Then there was the bottle of red syrup from Hungary with a letter saying, 'This will cure your son'. It didn't say what we were meant to do with it. I took all the folk medicines up to the Marsden thinking that maybe they could use them for research.

The box of letters took me longest to sort through. Some of them had me in tears, especially the ones from people who'd lost a relative to cancer, wanting advice on how to cope. I knew I wasn't qualified to help, but I'd sit up in bed scribbling away while Ernie snored beside me. There were the notes from children all around the world, saying they were praying for Craig. I wrote to as many of them as I could.

I didn't ask Craig to help me answer his letters. His hand still trembled so much he had trouble holding a pen and I felt writing would use up too much of his precious energy. But I'd get him to sign his name on my letters or sometimes on a photo of himself.

By the first week in November we'd opened 700,000 cards and Charlie estimated that the sacks waiting at the sorting office contained at least another half a million. Despite warnings I didn't feel as if I was going to have a nervous breakdown—we were all having so much fun and it was doing Craig so much good that both Ernie and I were on a real high. How could we feel ill when we were surrounded by all this love and affection? How could we possibly feel alone with all these people sharing our concern for Craig?

There was one thing worrying me though. Our household bills were being delayed because everything with our address on it was being put into Craig's sacks, and some would be stored for weeks before we got round to opening them. We were so late paying the electricity bill we were nearly cut off and in November our telephone was disconnected. After that I started giving people my friend Jan's address if they wanted something to come direct to me.

On Bonfire Night, Carshalton Athletic Football Club held a charity match for the Princess Chula Ward with Craig as special guest. He loved every minute. The following week Securicor made the first payment for our waste paper and I took Craig to present the cheque to the Marsden. But Brian Sadler stopped us at the entrance to the ward and took me aside. 'I'm sorry, Marion, you can't go in,' he said. 'Jamie has just died.' The day crashed around my ears. Jamie had been in the ward when Craig was admitted. Now I could hear his parents' grief echoing up the corridor. We made the presentation in the foyer and then I whipped Craig away.

The count was rapidly approaching one million now, and Charlie worked out that we should finally break the world record on Thursday, November 16. We set about organising a gala celebration. By seven, Sutton United's ballroom was jam-packed with people. Television crews from TV-am, Sky TV, France and New Zealand had turned up, and with the cameras filming every move we counted madly for two hours. Craig was on top form, entertaining the crowd by singing along with a Kylie Minogue record. Then at five to nine Charlie called for a bit of hush.

'I forecast we would hit this record tonight by eight thirty,' he said. 'Well not only have we hit it, we have *smashed* it, by a quarter of a million! Our total of counted cards so far is one million, two hundred and fifty thousand, two hundred and sixty-five cards.'

There was a wild cheer and everyone started clapping.

Charlie handed Craig a card in a frame. 'This is for all the hard work you've caused me and my postmen, mate. And good luck with the next million.' Everyone roared, but Charlie shook his head. 'No, I mean it,' he said. 'This is not the end. I need your support because we need to count again. And again. And again. We're going to get to two and a half million. We'll show the *Guinness Book of Records*.' The whistles and cheers nearly took the roof off.

The celebrations went on until nearly midnight. I sang until I was hoarse. All the good old happy songs. 'We'll Meet Again', 'You'll Never Walk Alone', and, of course, 'I Just Called to Say I Love You'.

Next day was out-patients' day at the Marsden and I had to dig Craig out of bed and drive him up to the hospital. After the usual eyes, ears and balance tests we arrived home in the afternoon. Craig was tired out after the excitement of the night before and went up to bed for a nap. I was downstairs when the phone rang.

'This is Norris McWhirter's secretary,' a woman's voice said. 'I'm ringing to tell you that Mr McWhirter has agreed to recognise Craig's record. He will receive an entry in the next *Guinness Book of Records*.'

The scream I let out must have deafened her. She waited a moment then said, 'Norris plans to come to your house this weekend to present Craig with his certificate.'

After I'd put the phone down I rushed upstairs. 'Craig, Craig, they're going to put you in the book! Norris McWhirter's coming to see you!'

Craig gave me a sleepy little smile. 'Magic,' he said.

In fact, Craig missed being presented with his certificate. On Saturday he had been invited to see a matinée performance of the show *Starlight Express* and at one o'clock a car arrived to take Ernie, Craig and me up to the West End. We had a wonderful time. The show was great and there was a special surprise. After the performance the cast lined up to meet Craig and presented him with nine thousand *Starlight Express* get-well cards. It turned out that for the past two weeks they'd been getting everyone in the audience to sign a card for Craig!

We arrived home at seven, tired but happy. Soon afterwards there was a knock on the door. I answered it to find a neighbour from a few doors down standing on the step, looking all excited. 'Here,' he said. 'Some geezer knocked on my door and he left this . . .' And he handed me a large piece of card.

This is to certify that Craig Shergold of Selby Road, Carshalton, Surrey, England, became the first person ever to receive more than one million get-well cards.

I took the certificate back into the front room and waved it at Craig. He took it from me and, screwing up his eyes, read the words slowly out loud. 'Wow! I'm in the *Guinness Book of Records*!' He gave me a great beaming smile.

IN JUST TWO SHORT MONTHS Craig had become a celebrity. Something about him had caught people's imagination. He was asked to appear on television, to open fêtes, to start sponsored events. Then, on November 23, the Nolan Sisters, Bobby Davro and Hearts of Gold did a benefit concert for Craig's Disney fund at the Working Men's Club in Willesden. At the end of the concert they got Craig up on stage and he danced with the stars while everyone sang 'You'll Never Walk Alone'. The audience never stopped putting their hands in their pockets. By the end of the evening we knew that we would be going to Disney. The only question was when.

We knew we couldn't think of going away for more than a few days at a time yet because Craig still needed weekly check-ups at the Marsden. He was having MR scans every couple of weeks too. The MR scanner worked by using magnetism and radio waves rather than X-rays like the CT scanners. Ernie and I took him for an MR scan a fortnight after breaking the record. After Craig came out of the scanner we went to look for Emma who was back in the Princess Chula Ward for more treatment because her bone marrow transplant had been unsuccessful. We'd seen her the week before and I'd been shaken by how ill she looked. Emma was such a pretty girl, but she'd lost all her lovely hair and her skin had turned a terrible angry red. She'd spent our whole visit planning to do things with Craig—she'd been so thrilled by his cards and all the people he'd met. 'Do you think you could ask Lenny Henry to come and visit me, Marion?' she begged. I promised I'd try but in my heart I knew it would take more than a comedian to make Emma feel better.

Today, when we asked after her, we were told she was off the ward having treatment. 'Never mind,' I said to Craig, 'we'll go and see her next week.' But the following Friday, as we arrived in out-patients, one of the mothers took me aside. 'Emma's died,' she whispered.

I felt as if my legs had been knocked from under me. It shouldn't have been such a shock, after the way she'd looked last time. But it was. I just couldn't believe Emma was gone for ever. She'd been so bright, so full of life. Every time a kid died, a knife went through me. But with Emma it was the worst yet. She'd been Craig's first real friend in hospital.

Somehow I managed to carry on as normal for the next hour. I drove Craig home and left him with Ernie. Then I drove the car up to Mitcham Common, parked in a quiet spot, and howled like a wild animal. I felt absolutely terrified. Who was going to be next? But even in my grief I knew I couldn't let Craig find out. For his sake I had to keep going as if nothing had happened.

Luckily there was plenty to keep my mind occupied. Once the

record was announced I'd expected the cards to die down, but they were still flooding in. Charlie had predicted two and a half million by Christmas. It was three million. Everyone was working overtime to try to keep up. I would never be able to thank the counters enough but I organised a Christmas party as a token of our gratitude.

I was starting to get worried about Craig's schooling. He'd missed nearly a year. It was obvious he couldn't go back to school while he was still in a wheelchair and spending most of each day in bed, but he needed something. After a bit of a fight the education authority agreed to pay for a tutor. Mrs Dinnage started just before Christmas and taught him on Mondays, Tuesdays and Wednesdays from half past ten to twelve. Craig loved it, and I was amazed by what Mrs Dinnage managed to achieve without a proper classroom.

For a week or two before Christmas, though, schooling would have to take second place to travel. A couple of weeks earlier Craig had given an interview to French TV thanking all the French people for their cards and wishing them 'un joyeux Noël'. Now the same TV crew wanted to interview Craig again, and to our delight the French airline Air Inter had offered to pay for us to spend five days in Paris.

None of us had ever been to Paris before and we loved it. We stayed in a small hotel near the Arc de Triomphe, with shutters on the windows and a wrought-iron balcony.

That weekend Craig went into the bathroom to clean his teeth and let out a yell. 'Hey Mum, look, my hair is growing.'

I dashed in and sure enough there was a faint dark fuzz all over his scalp. I was thrilled—the doctors had told us his hair might never grow again—and Craig was tickled pink, I could tell.

The TV interview went well. An interpreter translated the questions through our earphones and Craig thanked the French people for all their cards and kindness and said how beautiful France was. The next day we returned home to Carshalton for a quiet family Christmas.

The new year provided another thrill for Craig—an invitation to meet Princess Diana when she visited the Marsden on January 29, 1990. Craig finally got to shake hands with the Princess and was rewarded with a beaming smile. 'Well done, Craig,' she said.

Since October our life had revolved around television, radio and magazine interviews. But at least the media let you know they were coming. Other people dropped in unannounced. It never crossed my mind that we were taking a risk asking strangers into our house. People often told us we should have our heads read, but after all that had happened to us since Craig had been taken ill, why shouldn't we have faith in human nature?

I often regret not keeping a visitors' book during that time. We had so many interesting people in our house, including all the Chelsea football team and countless TV personalities. I'd been afraid that all this attention might make Craig big-headed, but he still talked to everyone in the same way. 'Hello, mate, how are you?' he'd ask, whether it was a pop star or a neighbour from the estate who'd dropped in to see the latest cards.

Mrs Dinnage was finding teaching more difficult. Every time she started on a lesson the doorbell would ring and she'd have to break off. Eventually we decided to buy an old caravan and use it as a schoolroom. Now, if people turned up during lesson time I just told them Craig couldn't be disturbed. He was doing quite well in his schoolwork and Mrs Dinnage was pleased with him. I still wished he could go back to school though. Lee was very good about coming in to see him, but most of his other mates had dropped off.

By February the card count had risen to six million and I rang Guinness and asked them if they'd change Craig's entry in the *Book of Records*. They agreed but said we had to submit a figure by the middle of May to catch the printing deadline for the 1991 edition.

IN ALL THE EXCITEMENT of the cards we'd never forgotten our other aim of getting Craig to Disneyworld, but it was March before Diana Tait finally decided he was well enough.

We left Heathrow Airport on March 15. In the end we didn't spend much time in Disneyworld itself. Although he enjoyed the Magic Kingdom, the crowds and heat were too much for Craig and after a couple of hours he flopped. The one thing he really wanted to see was the Disney parade, and we managed to find a good place for that. Because Craig was in a wheelchair all the characters came over to him and patted him on the head or shook his hand.

I suddenly realised that the Fairy Godmother was heading towards us. She stopped and touched his head gently with her wand. 'Hello, little boy,' she said. 'Now, what do you wish for?'

Craig looked up at me. 'I've only got one wish, ain't I, Mum? I just want to get better. I want to live.'

I started to cry, I couldn't help it, and the Fairy Godmother stepped back. 'I hope it comes true,' she said softly.

That was the last day we went to Disney. Craig was just too tired afterwards. I realised that I'd been kidding myself in thinking he was almost well again.

Next day we decided to take it easy and stay by the hotel pool. Craig hadn't been swimming since our holiday in Benidorm sixteen months before, and it was wonderful to see him doing breast stroke across the pool. Something shocked me though—how thin he looked next to the other kids in their swimsuits. I hadn't realised how much weight he'd lost.

Although we didn't go back to Disney we did take Craig to lots of other places. We went to Gatorland, we fed the dolphins and watched water-ski displays at Sea World.

I was still uneasy when we came back. It was nearly eight months since his radiotherapy had finished yet he could still hardly walk. And his speech, if anything, had got slower than it had been last September. I was very aware that conventional medicine had nothing left to offer Craig and I began to look around for other help.

I've always been a believer in spiritual things. I know there's more to life than what we can see and hear and touch. When I was a little girl of eleven I started having premonitions—I used to call them my 'witchy' feelings. Once, daydreaming in class, I pictured the trestle table which carried our morning bottles of milk collapsing on top of a girl called Margaret. A week later it happened, just as I'd imagined it.

That sort of thing happened a few times over the next twenty years. The time I remember best was when Steve was a toddler and I was taking him and some other kids to a funfair at Mitcham. I was in the kitchen when I actually heard a voice saying, 'You're going to have a car smash tonight. Don't go out.' But the kids were all screaming to go and I told myself not to be stupid and we went. We'd only got as far as the traffic lights at Mitcham when a drunken driver jumped the lights and hit us . . . The car was a write-off, though, luckily, none of the kids was seriously hurt.

Because of my experiences I found the idea of faith healing quite reasonable. So when I read an article about a psychic surgeon two days after we arrived home from Florida, my interest was caught at once. This man was supposed to be able to do operations without instruments because power was being sent to him from the spirit world. Two reporters said he had diagnosed their illnesses correctly.

I might not have taken it any further but the next day a stranger knocked on the door. The man, whose name was Tony Sales, said he'd been reading about Craig just before he saw the piece about this psychic surgeon. 'I had the feeling it might be the answer for Craig,' he said. 'Would you let me pay for him to see this man?'

I didn't take much persuading. I said he could go ahead and make an appointment. On Good Friday, April 13 (why didn't that date make me think twice?) Tony Sales picked Craig and me up and drove us eighty miles to the psychic surgeon's house in a beautiful village. Two women dressed in white coats appeared and one of them showed us into a waiting room filled with lovely antique furniture.

Craig was quite ill. The long journey had upset him and there was a terrible smell of liniment everywhere which was making him feel sick. I asked for a drink for him and one of the ladies in white coats sighed and fetched him a thimbleful of water in a tiny glass.

Suddenly a door opened and a great big man came in, all smiles. 'Hello, my love,' he said to Craig in a funny cockney accent. 'How are you, my darling? Are you all right? Hello there, my boy.' His gushing manner hit a wrong note with me.

'Come on then, Craig.' He held out his hand. 'This way.' Craig stumbled into the examination room and I followed and helped him up onto the bed. On the wall there was a picture of a Red Indian. 'Who's that?' I asked.

'It's one of my guides,' the surgeon said.

The stink of liniment was even stronger in here. The surgeon didn't ask Craig to undress. Instead he held his hands over Craig's legs and stomach, first touching them, then letting his hands hover over his legs. I hadn't told him what was the matter with Craig, but I was sure he thought, because of the wheelchair and his problems walking, that the trouble lay in Craig's legs.

The surgeon frowned. 'Oh this little boy is very ill.' He looked at me and smiled. 'But in ten days he'll be better. Bring him back next week.'

Ten days? Blimey, I thought, what did he think he had? Flu?

'You don't know who my little boy is, do you?' I asked him. He frowned at me and I knew he didn't. 'Craig has a tumour on the brain—so why you're doing his legs I don't know,' I said. 'Your Indian guide has let you down this time.'

He looked offended. 'I know what I'm doing,' he said.

As we drove home, Craig lay on the back seat of the car, looking absolutely exhausted. 'I don't like that man,' he said. 'Please don't take me back there.'

That decided it. We never went again. It had been an interesting experiment and I was grateful to Tony for paying for it, but I really didn't believe psychic surgery had anything to offer Craig.

Thankfully I didn't have much time to sit worrying about Craig's health—we were madly counting cards again now, trying to get as many as we could opened before the Guinness deadline of May 16.

Then one day I had a phone call from Keith Wendon, who had taken over Brian Sadler's job in the Marsden Appeals Office. 'Marion, have you heard of the Children's Wish Foundation?' he asked. I had. We'd had boxes of cards from America with slips inside saying, *From the Children's Wish Foundation*. But I hadn't a clue what it was.

'Well,' he said, 'they've got four million cards for you. They want to know when you'd like them.'

'Keith,' I said. 'We can't possibly take them, do us a favour. If we took four million on top of all this lot we're counting now we'd sink. Why don't you ask them to recycle them? Help the kids in their *own* country who've got cancer?'

Keith said he would see to it and I didn't give it any more thought. Card nights had taken over my life again now as the deadline got closer. At last, on May 16, Charlie let Guinness know that we had a new record—16,250,292 cards. The following day we had a phone call to say Guinness had accepted it.

We were still celebrating when we had a phone call from the Mayor's office telling us that two officials from the Children's Wish Foundation were coming over from America at the end of May to meet us. Apparently we had to sign over the American cards and parcels to them before they would be allowed to recycle them. The Mayor of Sutton threw a tea party to celebrate the occasion and it was there that we met Linda and Arthur Stein for the first time.

Linda was an elegant woman in her early forties who reminded me of Jackie Kennedy. Her husband Arthur was a real Southern gentleman, a thoughtful, kindly man. Linda's daughter Susan had died of leukaemia at the age of twelve. Apparently Susan had set her heart on getting her driving licence before she died and it was that which had given Linda the idea for the Children's Wish Foundation. The fund's purpose was to grant the last wishes of dying children.

Linda told me how, last year, people had started asking her if she'd heard of this little English boy and his wish to get over a million cards. She'd been fascinated because most of the children she helped wanted to travel or meet famous people: in contrast, Craig's wish didn't involve a lot of money. The Children's Wish Foundation made its own appeal for him, setting up card-collecting points all over America. Linda had sent me a letter explaining all this but, of course, her letter was at the bottom of a sack somewhere.

'Did you enjoy Disney?' she asked Craig.

'Well yes,' he answered, 'only I wanted to go to Universal Studios, but it wasn't open.'

'Oh really?' Linda looked thoughtful. 'And tell me, Craig, is there any special American you'd like to meet?'

'Yeh, Hulk Hogan and Jake the Snake,' Craig said instantly. 'The wrestlers.' Craig was really into American wrestling.

'Maybe we can do something about that,' Linda smiled. 'Craig, how would you like to go back to America?'

Craig's grin stretched from ear to ear. 'Oh *yeh!*' he said.

Craig would have to improve before he could take up Linda's offer. He'd lost more weight since we'd got back and he hardly ever got out of his wheelchair. But I still remembered Mr Hayward's words to me more than a year ago, 'Every kid needs a dream.'

One Sunday at the end of May, I was helping Craig out of his morning bath when he suddenly gasped, 'Mum,' and passed out in my arms. I carried him to his bed and laid him down and lay with him, afraid to leave him even to phone. After a few minutes he came round, but he looked vacant and he was very tired. I rang the Marsden and spoke to a male nurse.

'Well, you have to expect this sort of thing I'm afraid,' he said. 'The tumour's on the move.'

I felt myself go cold. Next day I took Craig to see Diana Tait, who sent him down for a scan. 'What did the nurse mean by, "It's on the move"?' I asked. She frowned. 'It is possible it's started to grow again,' she said. 'But we won't know till we see the scan.'

I tried not to over-react. Dr Tait had only said 'possible', and the nurse hadn't even seen Craig, so how on earth could he tell?

Craig didn't have another turn. Instead, over the next few weeks, he seemed to rally. On June 24 we had a party to celebrate Kylie's christening and Craig's eleventh birthday. He stayed awake almost to the end and I let myself start to feel optimistic again.

We'd sent letters to newspapers all over the world telling them that the appeal was over, but hundreds of thousands of cards were still arriving every week, and we had to keep on opening them. Apart from anything else, some of them contained cheques for the Marsden. I'd finally decided to recycle the cards. The schools for the handicapped had enough to last for years and didn't want any more. At least this way the cards were raising money to treat cancer.

That summer we organised barbecues, karaoke evenings, trips to the seaside and barn dances for the card people. I realised that the cards had taken over our lives. But we'd made such wonderful friends and felt really blessed to have so many people caring for our son. If the clock was put back I knew I'd do it all again.

Yorkshire Television took us to see *The Darling Buds of May* being filmed. David Jason met us as we arrived. 'What are you going to be when you grow up then, Craig?' he asked.

'I want to be like you—an actor and a comedian,' Craig told him. Later on as we were having lunch in the actors' canteen David Jason came and sat next to us. Craig was playing with his food as usual.

'Come on,' David said. 'You told me you wanted to be like me when you grow up.'

Craig nodded. 'I do.'

David put on his Delboy voice.

'Well, you've got to bloody eat then, you plonker, Craig. Cos if you don't eat you can't be funny.' Craig looked at him with great big eyes and wolfed down his whole plate of cottage pie.

'Good boy. Lubbly Jubbly.' David rubbed his hands together. Craig loved him.

The outings carried on. Craig was getting more attention than a pop star and I felt anxious sometimes that he might become spoiled. But Craig's feet stayed firmly on the ground.

I did worry about his appearance though. Sometimes his head seemed to stick out at the back. But no one else commented on it so maybe it was my imagination. Anyway he was still going up to the Marsden for scans and no one ever called me in afterwards, which gave me confidence. He did still get tired very quickly but I was sure this was due to his weight loss. He really had no appetite, it was almost as if he'd lost his sense of taste. By August his weight had gone down to four and a half stone and he looked very frail indeed.

At the beginning of September, Sharon had another baby. This time it was a boy and she and Steve named him Craig. That month too we finally had our week at the seaside in the Malcolm Sargent Home at Jaywick Sands—the holiday Craig had been too ill to take a year before. The weather was lovely and he got a bit of a tan. He came home looking really well.

On September 17, Craig was upstairs when the telephone rang. 'Marion? How are you?' It was Diana Tait's voice. 'I've just come back from holiday.' There was a little pause. 'I'm afraid the radiographer tells me that the results of Craig's latest scans aren't very good. I'd like you and Ernie to come in and see me on Thursday afternoon.' There was another pause. 'Nina will be with me.'

My heart stood still. Nina was the liaison sister—one of her jobs was to arrange the Macmillan nurses when your child was dying. Calling in the liaison sister meant the beginning of the end. 'No way! I don't need her!' I shouted. 'You'd better not have her there.'

'All right, Marion,' Diana Tait said quietly. 'As you wish. I'll see you at two o'clock on Thursday.'

I put the phone down and I started to shake. I couldn't think straight. Part of me was angry but another part was shocked and numb. Ernie came into the kitchen and when I told him he went completely white. We fell on each other and sobbed. 'Thursday!' I gasped. 'How will we last till Thursday?'

There were three nights before our appointment and I don't think we slept a wink during one of them. I stayed in the house. For the first time I couldn't face seeing people—I knew I'd break down.

I'd thought he was getting better. But I'd just been kidding myself. All this time that horrible thing had been lurking there ready to start growing again. That *monster* with teeth and hair and nails. I hated it. I wanted to tear it out of his head with my bare hands.

Thursday came at last and Ernie and I drove up to the Marsden, leaving Craig with Carol. I felt like an old lady as we walked down the hospital corridor. I could hardly put one foot in front of the other. Ernie shepherded me in front of him and somehow we got to Diana Tait's office. She kissed me and then Ernie as she always did, then she put a scan up on the screen. 'As you can see, the tumour has got a lot larger,' she said. 'It's growing very fast.'

There was a big black mass in the middle of his brain. I stared at it as if hypnotised, not wanting to believe my eyes. 'Isn't there an operation you can do?'

Diana Tait shook her head sadly. 'I'm afraid there's very little we can do,' she said. I looked at Ernie. He appeared to be in shock.

'When will he die?' I couldn't believe I was asking it.

'I can't predict that. I don't know. As you're aware, this tumour is very unusual.'

'How will he die then?' I demanded. I had to know. 'Will he just die in his sleep? Will he be in pain?'

'We'll give him morphine for the pain when the time comes,' she said gently. I felt Ernie's shudder through my jacket.

I stood beside her looking at the scan, Ernie on the other side of me. And suddenly I got this feeling. This tremendous surge of energy. It was as though it was coming up through my feet. One minute I'd been on the verge of collapse, the next I felt incredibly strong and calm.

I knew what I had to do. I had to take Craig back. He was mine. Why should I let the hospital decide if he was going to live or die? If they wouldn't fight for him then I would.

I glared at her. 'No way,' I said. 'He is not going to die.' I jabbed my finger at her. 'You're not having him.' I pointed up to the sky. '*He's* not having him. *I'm* having him.'

Diana Tait touched my arm. 'Marion, I didn't want this to happen. I'm very fond of Craig. Of you all. I am so very sorry.'

That night before I went to bed I took out my diary and under Thursday, September 20, 1990, I wrote: *The very worst day of our life. Please, God in heaven, let the doctor be wrong. All that I have I give to you, O Lord. Please don't take my son. I love him so very, very much. Please answer, Father. Thank you, Marion.*

The next morning it was raining again. Every time we had bad news it seemed to rain. I'd been crying all night and I looked a wreck. Craig came down at about ten o'clock and lay down on the settee. He mustn't see how upset I am, I thought. There were half a dozen sacks in the kitchen and I decided to open some cards. Most of the sacks were from the Post Office but there was one big plastic bag full of letters from private delivery firms. I reached in and pulled out a Federal Express envelope. Inside was a letter on official-looking notepaper headed: University of Virginia Health Sciences Center, Department of Neurosurgery, dated August 7—six weeks earlier.

By the time I finished reading that letter, I was shaking like a leaf. God had answered my prayers.

Seven

Dear Mrs Shergold,

I am writing on behalf of my friend John Kluge. Mr Kluge lives here in Charlottesville. He is the wealthiest man in the United States. More importantly, he is one of the most concerned individuals living today.

Mr Kluge called me this morning because he had been asked to send your son Craig a postcard, and he wanted to be sure that everything medically possible was being done for Craig. In fact, he offered to fly him here if there was any hope that anything could be done. Obviously, not knowing the particulars of Craig's case, I could not advise him.

We attempted to telephone you this morning, but found your phone to be unlisted.

I would appreciate it if you would telephone me collect so we can determine if Mr Kluge can be of any assistance to you.

Very truly yours,

Neal F. Kassell, MD
Professor and Vice Chairman of the Department of Neurosurgery, University of Virginia School of Medicine.

'Oh my God! Oh! Oh! Oh!' I screamed. I was in a complete panic. Luckily Craig was sound asleep on the settee. My sister Kate couldn't have chosen a better moment to knock on the door. 'Kate! Look at this letter!' I waved it at her. 'What shall I do?'

Kate took me in hand. 'You've got to ring him now,' she said firmly. She made me a cup of coffee and gave me a cigarette and sat me down, then she dialled the number. I took the receiver from her and took deep breaths.

The phone was answered straight away. 'Neal Kassell speaking.' For a moment I was lost for words. I'd expected to have to go through secretaries first.

'This is Marion Shergold,' I stammered. 'I'm ringing from England.'

'Oh, hello, Mrs Shergold. You got my letter then?'

'I'm ever so sorry,' I said. 'But I've only just opened it. We've got six hundred sacks of mail coming in every week . . .'

He gave a little chuckle. 'I understand, don't worry. How is Craig?'

'You're not going to believe this,' I said, 'but they told me yesterday to take him home and let him die. I thought I was seeing things when I read your letter. It was like a message from heaven.'

'We'd really like to help Craig if we can but I don't want you to build up too many hopes at this stage,' Dr Kassell said. 'The reason Mr Kluge thought we might be able to do something is that we have a treatment for brain tumours here in Charlottesville, called the gamma knife. It's a new instrument that fires high-energy radiation beams directly into the brain. It might offer a possible treatment for Craig but that's all it is—a possibility. OK?'

'OK,' I agreed.

'Now,' the professor's voice turned businesslike, 'before we can make any decisions about bringing him over I must have all his medical notes and scans. I'd like you to Federal Express them straight to us. We'll pay. Phone me when you know what's happening.' He chuckled again. 'And call collect next time.'

'Oh thank you! Thank you!' I gabbled. I put the phone down and threw my arms round Kate. Leaving her in charge of Craig I drove like the clappers up to the Royal Marsden Hospital and galloped up the stairs to Dr Tait's office.

She wasn't there. I was told she was away and that Craig's notes could not be released without her permission. I couldn't believe it. I pleaded. I stormed. Then I pleaded again. But the answer was no, so I phoned Dr Kassell and explained we would have to wait a week until Diana Tait got back. It was the longest week of my life.

While we were waiting I went to see Richard Hayward. 'Dr Kassell is a fine doctor,' he said. 'He's a world-renowned surgeon.' But he wasn't too enthusiastic about the gamma knife. He looked thoughtful then said, 'I have to warn you that it would be extremely risky to operate on Craig a second time, but if you would like me to try . . .'

I thanked him but I said no. Eighteen months before, instinct had told me Mr Hayward would save Craig's life. Now the same instinct told me it was Dr Kassell who had to do the next operation.

Diana Tait returned to work on October 1. 'I will send the notes on, Marion,' she agreed. 'But please don't build too many hopes up on it. Craig is very, very ill you know.' But how could I stop hoping?

At last, on October 16, Dr Kassell's secretary Kim phoned to say they'd received the scans from the Marsden and details of Craig's treatment so far. 'We'll be in touch with you again very shortly to talk about when Craig should come over,' Kim promised.

Two days later Linda Stein from the Children's Wish Foundation phoned. It was uncanny. I hadn't spoken to her since the summer. 'Hi, honey. How is Craig?'

'Not so good.' I told her Diana Tait's news.

'Oh, Marion, I'm so sorry. The reason I rang was to tell you we'd arranged Craig's trip to come to Universal Studios. We thought he could come to Atlanta first to see all the cards we have for him here. Then we would fly him to Florida. Do you think he's well enough?'

In all the upset of the past few weeks I'd nearly forgotten about Craig's 'wish'. I explained to Linda about Dr Kassell's letter and how we might be flying to Virginia for treatment with the gamma knife.

'Wow, that's fantastic,' she exclaimed. 'Look, if he's coming to America anyway why don't we give him his wish at the same time?'

I wasn't sure. Craig really deserved that wish, but who knew what might happen? Maybe if we took time to go to Universal Studios, Craig would die before they could use the gamma knife.

'Linda, would you ask the doctors if we can do the wish?' I asked. 'I'll do whatever they say.'

'Of course I will, Marion honey,' Linda said. 'Leave it to me.'

Four days later she rang back. 'Get your things together. I've spoken to Dr Kassell. He's seen the scans and he says it's OK to give Craig his wish before he goes into hospital—he doesn't think three weeks will make any difference. In fact, he thinks it'll do Craig good!'

Linda had arranged flights for the following day, so Ernie and I flew around throwing things into bags. Craig was excited, but he only knew about the 'wish' part of the trip. That evening I said casually, 'Craig, while we're in America we might see a doctor.'

'Oh, Mum,' he groaned. 'Not another operation.'

'No, just to look at you, because the doctors are very clever in America,' I said.

The flight from Gatwick took ten hours and I barely took my eyes off Craig for the entire time. The stewardess obviously realised how sick he was and she lifted the arm-rest and made up a little bed for him and he slept for most of the flight. We arrived in Atlanta in the mid-afternoon where Linda and Arthur gave us a warm welcome. We were driven straight to our hotel, and my jaw dropped as we pushed Craig's wheelchair into the Hyatt. We'd never stayed anywhere so luxurious in our lives: the foyer was filled with tropical plants and full-size trees. Our room was on the executive floor and we had Craig's ultimate luxury, a telly in the bathroom. He lay in the bath for an hour after Linda and Arthur had gone, watching cartoons.

That night as I sat in our huge pink bed and looked around

everything felt like a dream. This morning we'd woken up on a council housing estate in South London. Now we were going to bed in a palace on the other side of the world. I snuggled up to Ernie. 'Let's enjoy these three weeks,' I whispered. 'We won't even talk about the operation. Let's just live for the moment.'

And that's what we did. The Children's Wish Foundation made it easy for us: every day was filled so that there was no time to sit and brood. We spent the first week in Atlanta with Linda and Arthur. They had hired a stretch limo and we all travelled in it to a gym where we met the famous American wrestlers Sting and Lex Lugher, the first part of Craig's wish. After Craig had felt the wrestlers' muscles for photographers, the limo took us on to a warehouse to see some of his cards. The warehouse was bursting at the seams: cards were all over the walls, in sacks on the floor, spread over tables ready for counting. Craig went round meeting the American card openers, shaking hands.

After a wonderful Halloween party it was time to say goodbye to Linda and Arthur and move on to Florida to visit Universal Studios and Disneyworld—Linda had added Disneyworld to the itinerary when she learned that Craig had been too ill to enjoy it the last time. The dreamlike feeling continued. We were met at the airport by the Sheriff of Orange County, Walter J. Gallagher. I was presented with flowers. Then four police motorcycles with flashing lights and sirens escorted us from the airport, stopping traffic for us at every junction. 'Oh, I love this,' Craig said, his eyes popping. 'I feel like a king.'

This time round we enjoyed Disneyworld much more. Amazingly Craig seemed brighter, and the two weeks in Florida passed in a flash. Ward and Sandy Grimer of the Children's Wish Foundation looked after our every need and every day they came up with something different for Craig to do—a trip to a basketball game, another ride in a stretch limo, a visit to Wet and Wild. Ward and Sandy had scheduled everything carefully so he could sleep his three hours every afternoon, and as a result he hardly flagged at all.

And then all too quickly the three weeks had passed and it was time to say goodbye. It was a painful parting. For three weeks we had felt a part of a big happy family. Everyone cried as we left, and Ernie and I were both in floods of tears. Partly it was the pain of leaving our new friends, but partly too it was because the dream was over and we had to come back to reality. I don't think I've ever felt so frightened of the future as I did that day as we left Orlando.

AT CHARLOTTESVILLE AIRPORT a pretty, dark-haired girl was waiting to meet us.

'Hi, I'm Mona. I'm one of Dr Kassell's assistants,' she smiled. 'I've

271

a car outside to take you to your hotel.' The drive to the hotel was wonderful. I felt as though I'd stepped back in time into an English colony. The countryside was so pretty with all the red and gold leaves falling. Even our hotel, the Boar's Head, was like a traditional English country hotel that had been picked up and dropped into the Virginia countryside. After settling us in Mona left. 'Get some sleep,' she advised. 'Dr Kassell wants to see Craig at six forty tomorrow morning.' I thought I'd misheard at first. Obviously American working hours were different to ours.

When Mona returned the next morning it was only just starting to get light, but we were ready and waiting. Mona drove for about ten minutes and then we rounded a corner and saw a huge collection of modern white buildings—the University of Virginia Medical Center. Behind it the blue mountains rose into the morning mist.

Mona led us through an impressive entrance and along a corridor to Dr Kassell's office where she knocked on the door. It was opened straight away by a handsome silver-haired man. He held out his hand. 'Mr and Mrs Shergold?'

Neal Kassell looked really warm and human, with friendly brown eyes behind his tortoiseshell glasses. 'And this must be Craig,' he smiled. 'How are you, Craig? How was Disneyworld?'

Within seconds of meeting him I knew that this was a man I could trust with my son's life.

When we were all sitting down Dr Kassell explained about the tests they would do to find out more about Craig's tumour. 'We have the scans from London but they're nearly three months old now so we need to do more,' he said. 'Then, I want to find out if the tumour is feeding off a blood vessel. To do that, we'll have to carry out an X-ray called an arteriogram.'

Dr Kassell explained that if the tumour *was* feeding off a blood vessel they could cut off its blood supply and reduce its size before they used the gamma knife, so it was really important to find out.

'Anyway,' he smiled at Craig, 'that's later. First I want you to have some tests. Are you ready to go?'

It was a long day. We trailed from clinic to clinic doing one test after another. It wasn't until seven o'clock in the evening, when Craig actually fell asleep in the middle of an eye examination, that the doctors decided to call a halt. Another two days of tests followed. We got to know many of the people who worked in the hospital. Everyone was so anxious to make us feel at home.

Craig was admitted to hospital for his arteriogram on Monday, November 19. A nurse took us to the children's ward, where Craig had his own room. His bed had a control panel with so many knobs and switches that it was like the flight deck on Concorde. There was even a telly hanging from the ceiling which moved by remote control so Craig was able to watch it while lying on his back.

Although this was to be only an arteriogram Dr Kassell had warned us it carried a risk. The next morning another doctor brought us the consent form to sign, and spelt out the dangers bluntly. He told us, 'This could affect Craig's sight. It might cause a haemorrhage, or even a stroke. I have to explain all the possibilities so that you know exactly what it is you are giving your consent to.'

I looked at Craig. 'Well?' I asked.

He shrugged. 'If it's got to be done it's got to be done.'

After Craig went into theatre at eleven we waited in the coffee bar, willing ourselves to stay calm. There was a balcony nearby and I wandered out for a cigarette. Sitting out there, puffing on a roll-up, was a real old hillbilly with only one tooth in his head. We started talking and I told him about Craig, and then he said, 'You know what you have to do, don't you?' I looked at him, puzzled. 'You have to pray to the mountains,' he said, pointing to the blue peaks on the horizon. 'I've got cancer myself and I pray to the mountains every night.' He gave me a gummy smile. 'And I'm going to be OK . . .'

The nurses had told us the procedure would take about an hour, and at half past twelve we went back to the recovery room. We arrived just in time to see Craig emerge from theatre. 'He's been really brave,' the doctor told us. 'He'll have to lie flat for a while but he'll be out in a couple of days.'

The following day Craig was already up and about by the afternoon. The day after we took him back to the hotel. It was Thanksgiving Day. Thanksgiving seemed to be a time for family reunions and every time someone had mentioned it I'd felt more and more homesick. We'd been away nearly five weeks and I was missing Dad and Kate and Steve and Sharon and my grandchildren so much. We had no idea when we'd see them again, and I felt very low as we watched the preparations in the hotel for Thanksgiving dinner.

And then the phone rang. It was Dr Kassell's secretary Kim. 'Hi, Marion. Dr Kassell has booked a table in the hotel restaurant for you tonight for a Thanksgiving meal. Dress up. Enjoy yourself. You're going to love it!'

We hadn't eaten in the hotel restaurant before. We'd been eating in McDonald's because although Mr Kluge was paying our hotel bill we didn't want to take liberties with his generosity. But that night we had the works. Roast turkey with fresh vegetables and pumpkin pie. Even Craig tucked in and tried everything. People kept coming up to wish him luck and I realised that I didn't feel homesick any more. It was as

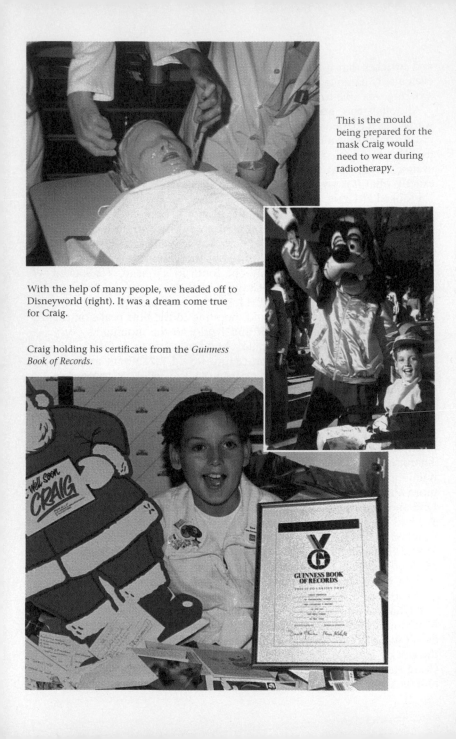

This is the mould being prepared for the mask Craig would need to wear during radiotherapy.

With the help of many people, we headed off to Disneyworld (right). It was a dream come true for Craig.

Craig holding his certificate from the *Guinness Book of Records*.

Craig desperately wanted to visit the set of *The Darling Buds of May* (left) and meet one of his favourite actors, David Jason (kneeling in the centre).

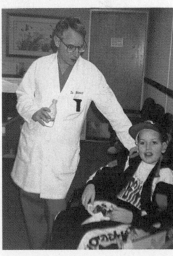

A wish granted. Craig gets to meet two of his idols: wrestlers, Sting and Lex Lugher.

Craig in just one of the American warehouses that are still stacked with cards.

Dr Neal F Kassell, MD, with Craig, in Charlottesville (below).

though we really belonged here in this wonderful country. 'When we get back to England we're going to celebrate Thanksgiving Day every year for the rest of our lives,' I promised.

The following day I woke up with one of my witchy feelings. I knew that Dr Kassell was going to send us home. By the afternoon the feeling had grown so strong I had to share it. 'Dr Kassell won't be using the gamma knife on Craig,' I said to Ernie.

He gave me a funny look. 'How do you know that?'

I said, 'I just know. He'll be sending us home. He'll say he can't do any more. Believe me, we'll be home for Christmas.'

The next morning we went in for our appointment with Dr Kassell with our hearts in our mouths. Kim said he was waiting for us in his office, and we left Craig and went in. Neal Kassell looked very serious. He waited till we'd both sat down, then he said, 'I'm so sorry but things are worse than I thought. The tumour is not feeding off a blood vessel, which means we can't reduce it in size before surgery, and at the moment the tumour is far too large for the gamma knife.'

'Isn't there anything at all you can do?' I asked.

Dr Kassell hesitated. 'There is one possibility,' he said. 'We could carry out another surgical operation to reduce the tumour to a size where we *could* use the gamma knife. We could try to remove about a third or possibly a half of the tumour that way. But the operation would carry a lot of risks. The tumour is in a very bad place.'

'What sort of risks?' Ernie asked. His voice sounded strangled.

Dr Kassell faced us. 'Listen, there is no way I can make this easy. Craig could die on the operating table, or very soon afterwards. Even if he doesn't die, the operation could make him blind or deaf or leave him in a coma.'

I swallowed hard. 'What will this operation mean?' I asked. 'If it's a success will he have a fuller life—will he get back to how he was?'

'No.' Dr Kassell shook his head. 'It would be wrong for me to hold out that hope for you. The most I think it could give him would be another six to nine months of life—but I really don't know.'

Poor Ernie had turned bright red and was gulping. I felt numb. Dr Kassell looked at the floor.

'Have you got children, Dr Kassell?' I asked suddenly.

He nodded. 'Yes, I have three daughters.'

'Would you operate on one of them?'

He looked taken aback. 'Marion, I don't know. Only you and Craig can decide if it's a risk you want to take. Go home for Christmas. Speak to your family and the English doctors, and think hard about what I'm saying.' Then he added quietly, 'If you decide to go ahead then I'm willing to operate in the new year.'

We walked out to the secretary's desk, where Craig was waiting. 'Craig,' I said, 'we're going home for Christmas.'

His face lit up. 'Cor, Mum, that's great.'

Ernie tried to smile but he looked very down. I knew he'd read the same message into the doctor's words as I had. Dr Kassell didn't expect Craig would even live until Christmas.

We arrived back in England on Friday, December 1, and were given a wonderful welcome by all our friends. I felt so relieved to be home. It was great to see my family again, especially little Kylie and Craig.

A few days later I knelt by the side of my bed and prayed, 'Please God, help me. Help me, tell me what to do next.' I climbed into bed and the last thing I remember seeing before I drifted off to sleep was my mum's face smiling at me. It was as clear as if she was standing at the end of the bed. When I woke up the next morning I knew what I had to do. The moment had come to tell Craig the truth.

That afternoon while Craig was sitting in his chair in the front room I sat on the floor at his feet. Taking hold of his hands I said, 'Craig, do you want to go back to America?'

'Yeh!' he said.

'Craig, I've got to talk to you about it.' I took a deep breath. 'You do know you've got to have a very serious operation and if this operation goes wrong, you could die?'

I'd not felt the need to say this to him before the first operation, but then he'd been only nine. Now I was talking to an eleven-year-old. I knew I had a duty to spell it out to him, to involve him in the decision.

He gave a little chuckle. 'I won't die, Mum. Don't *worry*! I won't die. I like that old Dr Kassell. He's going to get me well.'

I squeezed his hands. They felt icy cold. They'd been like that ever since his first operation. 'If you were to have this operation, Craig, you'd most likely have all that terrible pain you had in GOSH all over again. Do you really want to have to go through that?'

'Mum,' he said, 'no pain, no gain.' He gave me an impatient grin. 'I want to go—all right?'

And that was that. I felt the tension that had been tearing me apart lift away. The decision had been made.

I nearly rang Dr Kassell straight away but something stopped me. Not yet, I told myself. Not yet. I was so aware that this operation might mean the end of everything. I wanted to make the very most of the time we had left. To give him every possible second of life that we could steal. I set out to give Craig his best Christmas ever. I had plenty of help in my mission. Soon after we got back, the Rolling Stone Bill Wyman invited Craig for lunch in his restaurant, Sticky

Fingers. He'd held a Halloween Party in aid of Craig's Marsden Fund and wanted to present Craig with the cheque.

Bill Wyman turned out to be a very normal, exceptionally generous man who was only concerned with our comfort. I hadn't realised Bill came from Eltham, just a few miles from Carshalton. *And* he grew up on a council estate just like ours.

'Are you going to eat with me?' he asked Craig.

'Oh, Mum, do I have to?' Craig pulled a face. I couldn't tempt him with food at all now.

'Bill, he might have a little pick,' I said. But Craig was too tired—he kept looking for somewhere to rest his head. Bill promptly took off his lovely woollen scarf and folded it up. 'Here you are, mate,' he said to Craig, 'here's a present for you. Put your head on that. But no dribbling on it, mind, cos my mum brought me that.' Craig had started dribbling out of one side of his mouth and was starting to get embarrassed about it, but Bill saying that made him laugh and he put his head down on the scarf and dozed.

After the meal a photocall had been arranged for the handover of the Marsden cheque. Craig still looked only half-awake but as soon as he saw the gang of pressmen outside his smile sprang into place. 'How can he turn it on like that?' Bill looked amazed. 'He's more professional than some stars!' The photographers snapped away for about five minutes.

Craig really enjoyed himself that day. He liked Bill because he was so down to earth and treated him like a normal kid. Before we left, Bill presented him with a leather bomber jacket with *Sticky Fingers* written on the back—he had asked the Marsden for Craig's measurements to make sure it would fit, which really touched me.

Craig's coordination was deteriorating every day and he was getting worse in other ways. I cringed now whenever I put him in the bath—he was just a little bag of bones. Six months ago he'd been able to walk around without his wheelchair for ten minutes at a time, but now he could hardly walk more than a step or two on his own.

It was Christmas that really brought it home to us. Last Christmas, when we'd just got back from France, he'd been so bright. His hair had been growing. He'd been eating. Now, a year on, everything looked bleak. It rained solidly all day and Craig was really ill.

He managed to open most of his presents but then he just sat, looking far away. I'd cooked a turkey with all the trimmings but Craig didn't want any and Ernie and I couldn't face food either. When we went to bed that night I think both Ernie and I secretly feared we had just spent our last Christmas with Craig.

By the end of January he was spending more and more time in bed and his speech had slowed right down—he was slurring his words badly and often he didn't finish his sentences. Incredibly he was still able to perk up for TV appearances and interviews.

In February a photographer, Anthony Grant, asked Craig to be on the cover of a book called *Take Two*, which aimed to raise money for the Marsden. It would be a collection of photos of famous people posing as their heroes. 'Does Craig have a hero?' Anthony asked. 'Some character in a film he'd like to dress up as?' That was easy. Craig's favourite film was still *Rocky*. When we went up to Anthony's studio I helped Craig get changed into some stars-and-stripes boxing gloves, boots and shorts, and he got into a fighting pose. I worried he wouldn't be steady enough on his feet but he managed it. The result is one of our most treasured photographs.

BY THE MIDDLE OF FEBRUARY Craig couldn't walk at all without support, and his dribbling had got worse.

Then, on Monday, February 25, he woke up complaining that he couldn't feel anything on the left side of his face and I knew then we couldn't put it off any longer. I had to ring Dr Kassell before Craig got too ill to travel. As soon as he came on the line I blurted out, 'Dr Kassell, I think the time has come. We're ready to come back.'

'How is he, Marion?' Dr Kassell's voice was concerned. When I told him about the dribbling and the sudden numbness in his face he said, 'Marion, that's a very bad sign. We'd better get you out here as quickly as possible. Kim will let you know the arrangements as soon as she's made them. Give Craig my love.'

'I will,' I promised. On impulse I said, 'Craig has great faith in you, Dr Kassell. He's certain you're going to get him well.'

'You have to remember what I told you, Marion,' he said quietly. 'I'm not promising you anything.'

'I know,' I said. 'I know.'

I put the phone down and ran upstairs to Craig's bedroom. 'We're going to America!'

His face lit up. 'Great!'

I gazed down at him, propped up high on his five pillows. His face was all swollen and distorted, his eyes dark and bruised. I wanted to kiss him and hug him tightly to me, but I knew his poor frail body couldn't stand it. I felt tears starting down my face.

Craig was watching me. 'Mum, come here,' he said, and he held his arms out to me. I put my head on his chest and he cuddled me as though it was me who was the child and not him. 'Stop worrying,' he said. 'Doc Kassell is going to get me well. I won't die. I love you and Dad and Steve and Grandad too much. All right?'

His words calmed me. I dried my eyes and sat up, feeling ashamed of myself. He was so brave. And I was the one who should be comforting him. 'Go down now,' he ordered. 'Let me sleep!'

The airline tickets were delivered on Tuesday. We were to travel on Wednesday via New York and Washington. Kim rang again to say Mr Kluge would not only be paying Craig's hospital fees but would also foot the bill for our air fares and hotel bills.

In the few hours we had to get ready we ran around in a frenzy. Ernie rang up work to tell them he was taking indefinite leave. 'I hope your job's still waiting for you when you come back,' I said nervously. 'Sod the job,' he said. 'Craig comes first.'

On Tuesday night with our bags packed and ready we held a last emotional card night. Craig was on top form, making everybody laugh. It was a real party atmosphere—with everyone trying to hide their fears and be jolly for Craig's sake. If you searched the world over you wouldn't find a better crowd of people.

Just before nine o'clock on Wednesday morning, Ernie and I took Craig by the hand and went out through the rain to the car. As we piled inside everyone crowded in the doorway and broke into a chorus of 'Good Luck, Good Health, God Bless You'.

The flight left Heathrow at eleven thirty. This time the whole family had turned up to say goodbye. 'Don't worry. I'll be back,' Craig kept saying as Grandad dabbed his eyes with his handkerchief. 'I'll be back . . .'

The flight to Charlottesville took nineteen hours. Craig slept for most of the journey, playing cards with Ernie whenever he woke. I watched the two of them out of the corner of my eye—anyone would have thought they hadn't a care in the world. Would Ernie be playing cards with Craig the next time we crossed the Atlantic?

Eight

It wasn't until very early on Thursday morning that we arrived, by a tiny ten-seater plane, at Charlottesville's little airport. There was a light covering of snow on the ground as we walked out to the car park where a taxi was waiting to take us to the Boar's Head. The night porter greeted us like old friends and took us inside to the lounge where Linda and Arthur Stein were waiting up for us. They had travelled from Atlanta to provide moral support and as they stretched out their arms in welcome I felt we had come home.

Craig was very tired and looked really ill after the long journey. Our hotel room was filled with flowers, but he didn't even notice them. He was asleep before his head hit the pillow.

But the following morning he woke at nine, fresh as a daisy. At ten thirty we lifted him into Linda's and Arthur's hire car and took him to the hospital. Dr Kassell and Kim were waiting for us outside his office and Dr Kassell greeted us all warmly. 'I'm just going to talk to Mum and Dad a minute,' he said to Craig. 'You'll be all right with Kim, won't you?'

'Yeh,' shrugged Craig. 'Great.'

Dr Kassell showed us into his office. I handed him a big brown envelope containing Craig's latest scans and he put them up on the screen and examined them. When he turned back to face us his face was grave. 'I'm afraid things don't look good,' he said. 'If you give us the go-ahead then we'll go for it. But I have to say, I really don't rate his chances very highly.'

Ernie looked shaken. 'What do you think his chances are then, Doctor?' he asked.

Dr Kassell hesitated. 'I estimate the chance of him not coming through this, one way or another, is about twenty per cent.'

I got the feeling that Dr Kassell really didn't want to do this operation. 'Dr Kassell, I've explained everything to Craig,' I told him. 'He knows the danger and he wants to do it. He has so much faith in you. And we have too. I know—'

Dr Kassell broke in. 'Fine. Fine.' Then he gave a little sigh. 'Marion, I only wish I had the same faith as you.'

The next three hours were taken up with scans and assessments. In the afternoon Dr Kassell called us into his office again. 'I'm going to admit Craig tonight,' he said. 'The operation is scheduled for tomorrow.' He outlined what the operation involved. Dr Kassell would lead the operating team, helped by Dr Jane and two assistants. The plan was to try to reduce the size of the tumour by up to fifty per cent. Two years ago Mr Hayward had opened Craig's skull down the back. Dr Kassell planned to take out a disc of bone from the top of his skull. It was riskier but it would make the tumour more accessible.

Dr Kassell shook Ernie's hand, then he turned to me. 'Let's hope everything turns out for the best,' he said. 'I'll see you tomorrow.'

We took Craig up to the children's ward and settled him in his bed. He was very cheerful, and was cracking jokes with Linda and Arthur. At eight, visitors were supposed to leave. I planned to stay in Craig's room—there was a convertible chair which pulled down into a single bed. But when Craig realised my intention he grabbed my arm. 'Mum, I do love you but please can Dad sleep with me tonight?'

I was hurt. 'Why?'

'I know you. You'll be touching me all night, asking me if I'm all right. Linda and Arthur will look after you.' He appealed to them. 'You will, won't you?'

'Of course, honey,' Linda smiled.

It was so hard to leave him. But Craig knew me better than I knew myself. And he needed all the sleep he could get.

I spent a terrible night. At ten to six the phone on my bedside table jolted me awake. It was Ernie.

'He's going down to theatre at seven thirty, Mal.'

'Give me ten minutes,' I said. 'I'll be there.'

'HI, MUM,' CRAIG SAID as we walked into his room. 'I'm having my op this morning.' He was so happy and chirpy. 'I'm not scared, Mum, honest,' he said. 'I *am* going to beat this cancer.'

Linda and Arthur had brought him a big, fluffy grey elephant and he cuddled it and said he was going to call it Arthur. Then at seven thirty on the dot two smiling nurses came into the room to take him down to theatre. We walked on either side of his trolley as they wheeled him down the corridor.

Craig looked at one of the nurses. 'What's your name?' he asked.

'Nurse Butter,' she replied.

Craig laughed. 'Can I put you on my toast?' and she laughed back. Then he started to sing and I bent down to listen. It was our song, 'I Just Called to Say I Love You'.

'I've seen kids more nervous than this just going in to have their appendix out,' Nurse Butter whispered to me. Craig heard her and grinned. Then he saw me watching him and his face changed. 'I'll be all right, Mum, don't worry.'

'Come on then, Craig—in we go,' Nurse Butter said, and he started to sing again. He was still singing when she pushed his trolley through the swing-doors into the operating theatre. I had an irresistible urge to run through the doors and bring him back.

One of the nurses must have guessed what I was thinking because she grabbed my arm. 'Honey, your kid has guts. He'll be fine, don't worry. He wouldn't want his mum upset.'

'We'll be waiting in the West Visitors' Lounge,' I told her. 'Please call us if he needs us.'

The hours that followed were the longest of my life—even longer than the hours we'd spent waiting at Great Ormond Street. This time his chances of dying or worse had been spelt out by Dr Kassell, twenty per cent. One in five. 'You'd have a better chance playing Russian roulette,' Ernie told me.

After a bit he got up and started to pace up and down the room. Linda and Arthur watched him, looking concerned. Linda's own daughter Susan had been almost the same age as Craig when she died. How could she bear to go through this?

From time to time I prayed silently. I knew we weren't hoping for a cure. The only hope this operation offered was a little more time. By midday my mood had hit rock bottom. Ernie had stopped pacing up and down but he looked ill with worry. He cuddled me to him. 'Try and have a nap,' he said. But I didn't want to try. It was as though my body had shut down. I felt a million years old.

No one had told us how long the operation might take. We'd been in the visitors' lounge for about six hours when suddenly I felt a piercing, sharp pain in my head. An amazing sense of peace came over me. Ernie had his head buried in his hands. Linda was still sitting quietly on the next bench. Arthur was starting to look edgy and nervous. 'Arthur,' I said, 'how about coming outside for a fag?'

'Sure, honey. Are you all right?' He followed me out to the balcony. 'You're very chirpy suddenly,' he said, as he lit my cigarette.

'Arthur,' I said, 'I want to tell you something. And I want you to look at your watch so you'll remember the time when you heard it.' He gave a puzzled frown, but he looked at his watch.

'Listen, Arthur. Craig's all right, I know he's all right.' I had heard Craig's voice telling me clear as a bell, 'Mum, they are sewing me up. I'm fine.' Arthur gave me a funny look.

We smoked a couple of cigarettes, then went back in. Just over an hour later the lounge door swung open and Dr Kassell appeared. He was wearing a white coat over his green theatre suit and was smiling.

'We have some terrific news for you.' He walked over to where I was sitting and smiled down at me. 'OK. As best we can tell we really didn't hurt him. And we got at least ninety per cent of the tumour out and maybe a lot more.'

Ninety per cent! They'd only been going to remove fifty per cent. Ninety per cent was even more than they'd taken out in England! I jumped up wanting to throw my arms round this wonderful man, but my legs had turned to jelly. I collapsed back onto my seat and Linda came and put her arm round me. Ernie ran his hand through my hair, his eyes shining.

'So far, so good,' Dr Kassell continued. 'Now, that doesn't mean that he's not going to have a complication of an infection or a blood clot but we got an amazing amount of the tumour out. I'm very pleased with him.'

'When can we see him?' I asked.

'You can go to him now,' Dr Kassell smiled. He turned to go.

Suddenly I remembered something. 'Oh, Dr Kassell. What time did you finish the operation?'

He thought for a moment. 'We started to sew him up at around one forty,' he said.

I looked at Arthur. 'What time did I tell you to look at your watch?'

Arthur looked shaken. 'It was one forty-two,' he said.

I looked up to heaven. Thank you, God, I said silently.

CRAIG HAD BEEN TAKEN to the intensive-care unit on the sixth floor. He was lying quietly on his back, surrounded by machines and drips. His head was wrapped in a white helmet of bandages. His eyes were closed. I whispered to the nurse, 'Is he all right?'

'He's fine,' she smiled. 'But why are you whispering?'

'He doesn't like my voice because of the pain in his head.'

She smiled. 'Honey, we've taken the pain away. Come, talk to him.'

I went up to the head of his bed, Ernie close behind me. 'Craig?' I said softly. 'It's Mummy. Please open your eyes.'

I touched his cheek gently and his eyes flickered open. 'The cancer's gone, Craig. It's all gone. Dr Kassell has taken the tumour away. You're going to be well now.'

Craig took a deep breath and let it all out at once in a big sigh. 'Thank God,' he said.

Ernie and I took it in turns to speak to him. Then I started to sing—the only song I could possibly sing at that moment. He smiled.

'Does it hurt, Craig?'

'No,' he whispered.

I picked up his hand and squeezed it tight. And as I did so I felt something I hadn't felt for two whole years, not since that first operation. I was so happy I was shaking.

'What's the matter?' Ernie asked.

I smiled at him, and tears ran down my cheeks.

'His hands are warm,' I said. 'Feel them . . . His hands are *warm*!'

It was like a signal from heaven that our long nightmare was over.

VISITORS WERE ONLY ALLOWED to stay for ten minutes at a time and we were asked to come back in an hour. We wandered downstairs still brimming with excitement. I wanted to tell the world!

Television crews were waiting outside the intensive-care unit and they fired questions as we came out. I just remember saying, 'My Craig's well! Thank God,' over and over again. I must have looked like a Cheshire cat—my jaw was hurting from smiling so much. As we wandered through the hospital, people kept cheering and clapping. Everyone seemed to know about this little boy from England.

We walked into the cafeteria area to get a coffee. On our last visit I'd made friends with the staff here, sharing cigarettes and swapping stories about waiting on tables. Now as I turned the corner there was a shout. 'Here's the English lady! How is he, ma'am?'

'He's fine!' I yelled back. 'It's a miracle! I want to shout it from the top of the hospital!'

'You do that, ma'am,' the big black guy who worked in the burger bar grinned. A moment later the assistants from the deli, patisserie and salad bar were swarming round us. It was like a carnival!

Suddenly at a corner table I recognised the old hillbilly who had told me to pray to the mountains back in November. He held his arms out to me. 'Honey, your prayers have been answered.' He told me his last check-up had shown he was clear of cancer too. When I heard that I kissed him—one tooth and all!

At four thirty we were allowed back into the intensive-care unit. Natalie, Craig's day nurse, was sitting beside his bed. 'He won't be left on his own for a second while he's in here,' she promised. I picked up his hand—it was still warm. He opened his eyes as he felt my touch and his face looked so peaceful—the tense look that had been there for so many months had completely disappeared. Ernie and I sat quietly beside his bed taking it in turns to hold his hand. A tube on his pillow was draining blood from somewhere under his bandage. Behind us the monitors bleeped and flashed. The intensive-care unit had every modern appliance imaginable. Electric stockings on his legs to keep the blood circulating. Heat lamps which shone on his body to keep him warm. Compared with the English hospitals I had known it was like jumping into the twenty-first century.

After ten minutes Nurse Natalie touched me gently on the shoulder. 'Honey? I'll look after him now. He must rest. You can see him again in the morning.' The expression on her face told me she knew exactly how I was feeling. 'We'll call you if we're worried but he's fine. Go celebrate! Your son has been born again!'

The ITN reporter Stuart Maister was waiting outside the intensive-care unit. He told us about the press conference Dr Kassell had given. 'He said a lot of nice things about Craig, and about you and Ernie too,' Stuart said. 'He said you were a strong family and the fact that you and Ernie loved him so much really helped. "Love is a great healer," he said. He mentioned the cards. He said he felt sure that all the people who were out there rooting for Craig had helped him to pull through.'

I smiled. 'I could have told you that. Did he say anything about the operation?'

'Yes. He said that the tumour was made of a hard material like mother of pearl so they couldn't just cut it out—he'd had to scrape away at it for hours with a tiny instrument chipping little bits off.'

'Did he mention using the gamma knife?'

Stuart nodded. 'He said they may not have to use it. It depends whether the ten per cent that's left is benign or malignant. They have to analyse the tumour in the laboratory to find out—but he sounded pretty hopeful to me.'

I gaped at him and Stuart chuckled. Then he looked at his watch. 'Look, we've got to put the story together now. Why don't you all go out for a meal? We'll buy the champagne.'

'WOW—A NEW WOMAN!' Ernie kidded me when I came out of the hotel bathroom an hour later. But it wasn't just the change of clothes and the fresh make-up that had perked me up. It was hearing Stuart say that magic word 'benign'. When Craig had woken up after the operation I'd told him, 'The cancer has gone.' It had just been a hunch—another witchy feeling. Now the feeling was getting stronger and stronger. It was affecting Ernie too. He looked ten years younger.

Linda and Arthur took us to a Mexican restaurant and insisted I had a pina colada cocktail to celebrate. The news of Craig's operation had been on TV and as soon as we sat down people started to come up to the table to congratulate us. I was overwhelmed. It was a very happy foursome who drove back to the hotel that night, and for the first time in months both Ernie and I slept like babies.

The next morning we arrived back at the hospital to learn that Craig had developed a huge blood clot on the brain which would have to be drained immediately. Dr Kassell was reassuring. He said that complications like this were fairly regular after major brain surgery. Once he'd told us that I didn't get in too much of a panic. God was not going to give us a miracle yesterday and take it back today.

At midday Dr Kassell came back out of the theatre. 'OK. We got it,' he smiled. 'Go and see him. I'm sure he'll be fine now.'

Craig was asleep when he came back to the intensive-care unit and he slept for most of the afternoon. We were allowed to sit by his bed for an hour at a time on condition I didn't say a word!

Stuart was putting together an item to be broadcast in England on Sunday and asked us to give another interview in the West Visitors' Lounge. I put some more make-up on and put my hair up. I knew everybody at home would be watching and they'd be reassured if they saw me with all my warpaint on. Even Ernie overcame his shyness and agreed to be interviewed for the very first time. 'We feel better,' he told Stuart simply. 'We feel we've made it . . . I think we'll start getting a few days' sleep now. I feel happy!' And he hugged me.

All day, telegrams, flowers, videos and toys flooded in to the hospital for Craig. Tom Doran, the hospital's public relations officer, told me that because of the fame of Craig's get-well card appeal, every TV channel and newspaper in America had carried the story.

Towards evening Craig woke up as alert and bright as a button, and his condition went on improving. He'd stopped dribbling, and his speech, though slow, was much clearer. On Sunday morning he greeted us with a wide smile that said, 'It's great to be alive.' I went down the corridor to ring Kate. Our whole family were in her house hoping I'd call. 'My phone's been a real hot line,' Kate said. 'Everyone wants to know how he is.'

I arrived back in the intensive-care unit at the same time as Dr Kassell. 'Hello, Champ, how are you?' he asked Craig and was met with a great big beam. Dr Kassell sent Craig down for an MR scan and the result, an hour later, was reassuring. 'There's been no more bleeding, so I don't foresee any more problems,' he told us..

By Monday morning Craig wasn't even drowsy. He spent the morning playing hangman with Ernie and chattering nonstop. And that afternoon Dr Kassell came in to see us again. 'Craig, Marion, Ernie. We have some good news. We have the pathology report back from the laboratory and it confirms what we suspected when we saw it. The tumour is benign.'

I didn't trust my ears. 'Are you absolutely sure?'

He nodded.

'Craig, did you hear that?' I asked.

Craig's eyes were sparkling.

'How?' I asked. 'How could it change?'

He shrugged. 'I really don't know, Marion. It's something of a mystery. It's possible there were two tumours, one cancerous, the other not. Like twins. But that's speculation. Whatever the reason, there's a very good chance that the remaining ten per cent will lie dormant and not return.' He smiled. 'The tumour has done some damage—it's squeezed the brain stem until it's like a ribbon—and we're going to have to run tests to find out how much of the damage is reversible. But the signs are good. I'm optimistic that Craig will lead a very happy, long, successful life.'

It was what we had all been praying to hear. Ernie put his arms round me. 'You mean he's cured?' He still couldn't believe his ears.

Dr Kassell nodded. 'It's certainly possible. I'd even say it's likely.'

Craig beamed. 'Doc Kassell, you're the best doctor in the world.' Then he took a deep breath and speaking very slowly and carefully, he added, 'You're supercalifragilisticexpialidocious.' There was a stunned silence. Craig grinned up at us, really pleased with himself.

Dr Kassell seemed lost for words, and a moment later he hurried out. Then Kathy, one of the nurses, came in looking puzzled. 'Did something happen in here just now?' she asked.

'Craig said a tongue twister,' I smiled. 'Why?'

She laughed. 'Well, Dr Kassell just came shooting out of Craig's room and gave a little skip and clicked his heels together in the air—you know, like those Cossack dancers do?' She shook her head. 'I've never seen him like this before. Never.'

Craig recovered from his operation faster than I could have dreamed. On the Wednesday after the operation he was transferred from the intensive-care unit back to the children's ward. That same afternoon he walked unsupported for the first time for three months.

Only eight days after the operation Dr Kassell announced that we could take Craig back to the hotel. 'Hospitals are for sick people,' he said. 'He could pick up an infection here. He's safer outside.'

THERE WAS GOING TO BE a lot of work to do to help Craig's recovery along. We learned about it over the next few weeks as he attended the Rehabilitation Center. Sue, his physiotherapist, explained that parts of Craig's brain had been damaged, and other parts would have to learn to take over from them. His muscle control, especially down the left side of his body, had been badly affected, and he had very little feeling in his fingers. To improve his sense of touch Joan, his occupational therapist, hid money in a sort of play-dough material and made Craig feel through the dough till he found it.

Something else which had been damaged by the tumour was Craig's appetite centre. We were warned that learning to eat the correct amount would be difficult and his weight would probably yo-yo up and down while we tried to get it right.

The most obvious damage had been to Craig's speech centre. The improvement in his speech had been so dramatic after the operation that I'd expected it would soon get back to normal. But after a week I realised his speech was still slow. He sounded a bit like someone who'd had a stroke. But I wasn't seriously worried. Nothing could dampen my joy at having him back.

Three weeks after the operation we met Craig's guardian angel Mr Kluge for the first time. All the media had been screaming to meet him too. It was all they needed to make the fairy story complete. But Dr Kassell said Mr Kluge didn't want our meeting to turn into a circus so it was to be kept very hush-hush with only one local TV company and newspaper being invited.

I was terrified. I told Dr Kassell and he smiled. 'Have you ever thought he might be nervous of meeting you too?'

Arthur and Linda drove us in to the hospital. Now the big moment was upon us my stomach was turning over. How do you show your gratitude to the man who paid to save your son's life?

The TV camera and reporters were already there and we sat down and waited. Then we sprang to our feet as a grey-haired man walked through the door. I guessed he was in his seventies and he had a warm, open smiling face which reminded me a bit of Bob Hope.

Dr Kassell followed Mr Kluge into the room and introduced him to us. Mr Kluge held his hands out to Craig, and Craig took them and said simply, 'Thank you very much. I can't say a big enough thank you. I'd kiss you all over if I could.'

'Craig, I don't think anyone has ever said anything so nice to me before.' Mr Kluge leaned over and kissed him.

I took Mr Kluge's hand. 'Mr Kluge, thank you. How can we possibly thank you enough?' I asked.

'You don't have to say thank you, my dear,' he said softly. 'This has to be the best thing that I have done in my life. I thank God I was in the position to be able to do it.'

I gulped. I just couldn't speak. Neither could Ernie. I could see him fighting to stop himself cracking up. And then, suddenly, I saw a tear roll down Mr Kluge's cheek too. Craig looked at the three of us and started to laugh. 'Oh, here they go,' he said.

Mr Kluge smiled. 'Please sit down,' he said. 'Craig, won't you come and sit next to me?' Mr Kluge had a skilled way of putting people at their ease and we were soon chatting and laughing as though we'd known each other for years. We found out that although Mr Kluge supported several charities he had never given money to an individual before. He told us he had made it a rule because he got so many begging letters and it would mean making impossible choices. One of the reporters asked why he had broken his rule for Craig.

'I saw his picture and a story about his appeal in a newspaper and I was going to send him a card,' he said. 'But then it was as if God touched me on the shoulder and told me I had to do something more. All my life I've followed my intuition, so I telephoned Dr Kassell and asked him to contact the Shergold family.'

As a thank-you present for Mr Kluge, dear Arthur had made a metal plaque with a mounted photograph of Craig in his Rocky pose.

While Craig held the plaque up for the cameras Mr Kluge leaned towards me and said quietly, 'I'm very sorry I didn't see you before today, Marion. I wanted to meet you earlier, but if the outcome had been different I could never have faced you. Professor Kassell has kept me informed about Craig's progress ever since his first examination back in November.'

'So you really were watching over us like a guardian angel,' I said. 'It's how I'd always thought of you.'

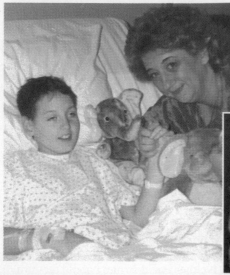

Time was running out, and Craig had to return to Charlottesville before he became too ill to travel.

Craig made a remarkable recovery after his operation. Here he is (below), tired but happy.

After the operation, Craig finally meets his guardian angel, Mr John Kluge (left).

We could have danced all night . . .

Former Rolling Stone, Bill Wyman (right), holding my favourite photograph of Craig. To me it is a moving tribute to a child who has suffered and survived.

'Thank you.' Mr Kluge smiled. 'You know, when I spoke to Professor Kassell after he'd first seen Craig, he told me he didn't want to operate. I begged him to think again. In the end he said it was something you said that changed his mind: you'd asked what he'd do if one of his daughters had a tumour like Craig's, and he decided he would give his own child a chance whatever the risks.' He looked across at Craig, still joking with the camera crew. 'You know, Marion, you have a very special human being there.'

IN THE WHOLE TWO YEARS he'd been ill I had never seen Craig cry. But at Heathrow Airport on Friday, April 19, his self-control broke down. As he flung his arms round Steve, his chin wobbled and tears of happiness poured down his face. 'Hello, Ugly. I'm home,' he said.

Poor Steve was too overcome to speak. Grandad, Carol, Kylie, Kate and Sharon all jostled to kiss him, their faces wet with tears.

As we pushed our luggage trolley up the walkway, flashbulbs started to pop and everyone began applauding. The whole world seemed to be waiting for us, all clapping and cheering as we walked towards them. Craig had been so determined to walk off the plane today and, with a bit of help from Ernie, he made it. As he reached the end of the barrier at last and wobbled into Steve's arms there was a loud chorus of 'For He's a Jolly Good Fellow!'

Talk about a hero's welcome! We arrived home to find the whole house covered with Union Jacks, Stars and Stripes, balloons and bunting. Over a hundred people were waiting in the street to welcome us and someone had set up speakers so that the first thing we heard was Stevie Wonder singing 'I Just Called to Say I Love You'. It was the crowning moment to a magic day.

IT'S NOW MORE THAN two years since that wonderful day, and Craig's recovery has continued. The latest scan shows that the remains of the tumour have shrunk further. It really does seem that God has answered our prayers and the prayers of millions around the world.

Craig's speech has improved dramatically. There's no slurring and it's only slightly slower than normal. But his left leg and the whole of his left side have taken a long time to get their strength back. He still has to use his wheelchair for travelling and shopping, and his walking still looks odd because his left knee won't obey him properly. But slowly, with hard work, his control over his body is improving.

We have had to accept that other things won't improve. Craig's appetite centre has gone for good and he's having to learn to live with that. His pituitary gland, too, has been permanently damaged which means he has to have regular injections of growth hormone to compensate. But those are minor problems. He has a future now.

In September 1992, three and a half years after he last sat in a classroom, Craig went back to school. Chartfield is a special state school for children who have missed lessons through illness or other problems. Craig loves it and is doing well. He loves English, music and maths but his favourite lesson is drama. He still wants to be an actor, and he had a part in his first school play last Christmas.

The press turned out in force for Craig's first day back at school. I thought the media attention would die down but they are still as interested in him as ever, and hardly a week goes by without him being invited to appear on television or radio. Everywhere he goes, people want to kiss him, to touch him. It's as if they hope some of our blessings will rub off on them.

The avalanche of cards continues. We stopped counting cards individually in 1990 but the Post Office still keeps a tally of the number of sacks and by Charlie's estimate we have now received well over one hundred million cards. Even now, in early 1993, Craig is still receiving fifteen thousand a day, and the group of wonderful friends we call the card people are still meeting regularly to open them.

All Craig's fame hasn't brought us riches—we still live in our two-up, two-down house on the St Helier housing estate in Carshalton. In December, Ernie was made redundant from his job at the Electricity Board, so life isn't a bed of roses. But Ernie and I are the richest parents in the world, because we have our son. And every day we count our blessings.

Craig is a teenager now. I try not to fuss over him. I know I must begin to let him take chances and risks like any normal boy. All the same it's hard. I'm sure it will be years before my heart stays calm when he says, 'Mum, I've got a headache.'

Only God knows what the future holds. We continue to live one day at a time. But we're full of hope. For me the most wonderful thing about what happened to Craig is that it shows how many good people there still are in the world. When the news is full of wars and people doing terrible things to each other, it's easy to think there isn't any goodness or generosity left. Craig has proved differently.

Sometimes when I'm putting him to bed in the evening I say to him, 'Can you imagine an island, Craig, with all the people who sent you a card and all the people who've been good to you living on it? What a wonderful place that would be.' Craig always smiles. Thank you, world, for giving my son back to me . . .

MARION SHERGOLD

Three years after the operation in America that saved Craig's life, Marion Shergold is able to view her son's illness in a positive light: 'I honestly think God gave us a miracle. Even now I can't believe it when I remember how bad he was. Not many people can say they had the whole world praying for them, as Craig did. It was definitely all that love that helped save him.'

Craig has certainly made a remarkable recovery. He has almost caught up with the years of schoolwork he missed and he hardly ever needs his wheelchair these days. Equally impressive is the way that the fourteen-year-old has reacted to all the media attention. His mother explains: 'They were dreading having him back at school because they thought he'd be a spoiled brat, that he'd show off about having been on telly. But he never does. He's just great. I'll give you an example of what's lovely about him: last year, Bill Wyman'—of the Rolling Stones—'invited us to a barbecue. He said Eric Clapton would be there, and a car would pick us up. But when I told Craig, he said, "Oh, no. I can't go. We've already said we'll be at Auntie Kate's on Sunday." Now, there aren't many kids who'd do that, are there? I'm so proud of him.'

Marion Shergold continues to devote much of her time to dealing with the TV crews and journalists from around the world who want an update on Craig's story. Her Thursday evenings are still spent opening sacks of get-well cards (five sacks a day on average) that are sent to Craig. 'To be honest, we do wish they'd stop sending them, but I don't want to sound as if I'm complaining. The card-opening nights have become something of a social club, and we do have fun.'

'You know,' Marion Shergold says of Craig's benefactor, Mr Kluge, 'he once said to me, "You think your son is famous now, but he's going on to greater things." And I've always felt that too. Craig is a very special little boy. There aren't many people who have experienced the kind of love we've been touched by. I really can't tell you how lucky we are. We've been blessed.'

Final Argument

Clifford Irving

illustrated by Dan Gonzalez

Ted Jaffe is a lucky man. A partner in a prestigious Florida law firm, he has just about everything he's ever wanted—the swimming pool, the house by the water, good schools for his son and daughter.

There's only one problem. Twelve years ago, Ted Jaffe made a mistake: he sent an innocent man to death row. Suddenly, Ted Jaffe's comfortable life turns upside-down. And he knows he must risk it all—his career, his marriage, even his belief in the law—to put things right again.

A man's life depends upon it.

A time came when my wife and my law partners were convinced I was going crazy, and the best I could reply was, 'I hope not.' That was a year ago. I was forty-eight years old, I had worked hard, I had almost everything I wanted, and once the economy recovered I would achieve the rest. Or so I believed.

In the late afternoon of a golden winter day, I gazed out of my office window at the warm waters of Sarasota Bay and, beyond it, the Gulf of Mexico. The bay spread itself before me—enormous, billowing blue. With the light waning, I turned on a brass lamp. I was reaching for a copy of *Florida Rules of Court Service* when the intercom buzzed with the call that would change my life.

'Ted'—the nasal voice belonged to my secretary, Ruby—'a guy named Elroy Lee is on the line, collect. From the jail. He's in there on a possession charge. Says he met you up in Jacksonville years ago, but from the way he talks, it doesn't sound likely. Shall I pass him along to one of the associates?'

I looked again at the bay, where a few homebound sailboats had spinnakers set before a light breeze. My vantage point was a fifth-floor office at the downtown firm of Royal, Kelly, Wellmet, Jaffe & Miller. (I was Jaffe.) The floor of the office was soft Spanish cork, the walls oatmeal-coloured hessian. The teak desk was shaped like a boomerang. Twelve years earlier, when I joined the firm, after ten years as a state prosecutor in northern Florida, I'd designed all this. It was the office of my dreams.

I was senior litigator at Royal, Kelly—one of the best and priciest firms on the west coast of Florida. But two years before, the firm had invested heavily in one of our clients' luxury condominiums on Longboat Key, and in the gloomy depths of what we still called the recession, the rentals dried up like old leather. At last week's partners' meeting to split up the pie for fiscal 1990-1, Harvey Royal announced that after the basic salary of two hundred thousand dollars, there would be no pool money to split.

'We're hurting,' Harvey said, 'and we need clients.'

So when my secretary buzzed through to me that an unknown man named Elroy Lee was on the line from Sarasota County Jail, I said, 'I'll take the call. Put him through, Ruby.'

A hard-edged southern voice came on the line. 'Mr Ted Jaffe?'

'Yes, Mr Lee, and what can I do for you?'

'For starters, you can get me out of jail.'

'Seems like a reasonable request. What's the charge?'

'Possession of cocaine in my vee-hicle. I got one or two prior convictions.'

'And what made you call *me,* Mr Lee?'

'I'm from Duval County, right? I remember you from up there when you were top dog with the state. I had this bad luck down here, so I'm looking through the Yellow Pages for a lawyer, and there's your name. Recollected it right off the bat.'

I looked at my watch. 'I'll be over to see you between nine and ten o'clock tomorrow morning.'

'You can't make it now?'

'No, I really can't. Sorry.'

'What's so danged important you can't help a man out who's got real serious asthma, and he's scared to death of what might happen in a cell with a buncha bad people?'

'Nothing, except my wife and I are invited to a lobster barbecue in exactly one hour. What've you got to offer me that's better?'

The truth made him chuckle. 'Your danged lobster's more important than a man's welfare? What kind of a lawyer are you?'

'A realistic one. And one who loves lobster. You'll get through the night, Mr Lee. You've had practice.'

But then I glanced up. Above the bookshelf was a framed cartoon that showed a shark about to chew up a grouper, which in turn was about to swallow a minnow, which in turn was about to gobble up a worm. The shark was saying, 'There's plenty of justice.' The grouper was saying, 'There's some justice.' The minnow was complaining, 'There's no justice,' and the worm was crying, 'Help!'

I had a flare-up of compassion for the downtrodden of the species.

So to the worm who called himself Elroy Lee, I said, 'Tell you what I'll do. You keep your mouth shut for another twenty minutes, and I'll drop by and see if I can get you off the hook.'

Elroy Lee chuckled again. 'I hear you, Counsellor.'

I MET HIM in one of the lawyers' visiting rooms at the Sarasota County Jail. He was a lean white man in his early forties, with thinning sand-coloured hair and cold green eyes. A gap between his two front teeth made him look like a squirrel, and he had a rodent's alert expression and quick, furtive movements. The charge against him was possession with intent to deliver, a second-degree felony.

'Tell me what happened to you,' I said.

A few days ago, he explained, he was riding along on Route 41 in his Olds Cutlass, and at a stoplight two cops waved him over to the kerb. They searched the Cutlass, found cocaine in the trunk.

'How much cocaine?'

'Twenty-eight plastic Baggies. Each Baggie's got a gram.'

'You're lucky. One more gram and it would've been trafficking. As it is, it's still possession with intent to deliver.'

From my client's studied silence at the receipt of this information, I deduced that he was a veteran and knew all that I had told him. You couldn't call it luck that he was carrying one gram less than was required to merit the graver accusation of trafficking.

'Elroy, I'll want to know where that car's been for the last seventy-two hours. And I'll need to know if any reliable witnesses can confirm what you tell me. My fee is seven thousand, five hundred dollars, and my firm's policy is simple. You pay it in full up-front.'

He looked unhappy. 'I haven't got that kind of money.'

Elroy dug an asthma inhaler from his pocket and puffed on it twice. I was meant to feel sympathy, I realised. Criminals just never could figure out why lawyers didn't trust them.

'Then it's back to the Yellow Pages, Elroy.'

I stood and walked across the room to the barred window.

From behind my back, Elroy asked slyly, 'Can't we work something out like before?'

I turned to him; now it was my turn to frown. Before what?

'Like up in Jacksonville,' he said. 'I told you I had a couple of priors—under my real name, which happens to be Jerry Lee Elroy, not Elroy Lee. You know me now?'

'No, I don't.' But I *did* know him. I just couldn't place him. 'All right,' I conceded, 'the name's familiar. Refresh my memory.'

'Ten years ago, in Duval County. You were on the other side of the law then, Counsellor.'

'Not quite,' I said. I had been chief assistant state attorney in Jacksonville and Duval County, but a lawyer, no matter what side he was on, was always an officer of the court, bound by the canons of ethics and his conscience.

Then it struck me; I remembered the gap between Elroy's teeth. It was twelve years ago, not ten. 'The Morgan trial?'

'Right!' He looked immensely pleased. 'I snitched on this guy, Morgan.' He gave a shy, toothy smile. 'You got it now?'

I still hadn't the slightest idea what he was getting at. 'What?'

Elroy sighed and rolled his ditchwater-green eyes as if he were dealing with a backward child. 'I was just thinking . . . I help out this here sheriff the same way I helped you out back then, and then these guys could drop the charges on the cocaine.'

I walked back across the stuffy little room and sat down once more at the table. I tapped with my pen on my yellow legal pad.

'What are you talking about, Elroy? What did you do in Jacksonville back in nineteen seventy-nine? Run it by me nice and slow.'

Elroy concentrated for a minute. 'Nigger killed a rich Jew. You remember that?'

Under the table, where he couldn't see, I balled my fists. 'I remember very well,' I said coldly. 'A black man named Darryl Morgan shot a white man named Solomon Zide.'

'Out at the beach, right?'

'Yes,' I said. 'At the Zide estate. After a big party.'

'That's it. It so happens I was in the same cell with Morgan. Big guy, dumb. Cop took me up on the roof of the jail. He asks if this Morgan talks to me, and I say, "That's not likely." Cop wants to know, "You ever hear him say, Yeah I did it?" I go, "He could have." "Well, he *did* do it," the cop says, "'cause he told *me* he did it, so he might just as well have told someone else, right?" And I say, "What's in it for me?" Cop tells me he can cut a deal for me, get me time served and probation. So I go, "OK, I heard him say he done it."'

I remembered how the issue arose in Judge Eglin's court twelve years ago. Gary Oliver, Morgan's lawyer—the names had not been in my mind for a decade, but they rose up now like rocks at low tide—had made a pretrial motion to suppress the testimony of Jerry Lee Elroy. The judge had ruled that the witness would be allowed to testify.

Now, twelve years later in Sarasota, I was finding out that this worm who had been my witness in a capital murder case—my last case before I went into private practice, and moved down here to the good life on the Gulf of Mexico—had perjured himself at a police officer's request. He had lied to me, to the judge and to the jury. He'd lied about a man who was facing the death penalty. I hadn't known he was lying, but that didn't change the fact. And it didn't make me feel less disgusted with myself—or less apprehensive.

'What was the charge against you in Jacksonville, Elroy?'

'Aggravated battery. Beat up on a woman.'

I made up my mind. Something had to be done, and I had to keep this man under my control no matter what the cost. 'I'll find a bondsman for you,' I said. 'I'll get you out of here.'

Elroy seemed surprised. 'What about the fee?' he asked slyly.

'We'll work that out. I need to think about this for a while.'

When I left the jail, the sun was a squashed blood-red ball quivering on the horizon. A chill wind had sprung up to ripple the bay. I hurried to my car, but there was no way to avoid that wind. As it struck me I had the feeling that it blew out of the past.

In December, over twelve years earlier, Solomon Zide and his wife sponsored a benefit concert at the Zide estate at Jacksonville Beach. It was a black-tie affair. Buffet dinner was two hundred and fifty dollars a plate.

I received one of the engraved invitations in the morning mail at my office on the fifth floor of the Duval County Courthouse. The envelope was addressed in blue ink, in a flowing feminine hand, to Edward M. Jaffe, Esq., Chief Assistant State Attorney.

I was a public servant—a prosecutor—not a lawyer who could afford to spend two hundred and fifty dollars for dinner. But the invitation included a handwritten note from Connie Zide: *Please come with Mrs Jaffe. You will be our honored guests.*

When I arrived home that evening, I showed the note to my wife. I told her that I'd called Connie Zide's secretary and accepted.

'Why did you do that?' Toba said. 'You could have called me first. Why did you assume I'd want to go?'

We were in the kitchen. Toba, slim and black-haired, her long neck gracefully curved like that of a Modigliani model, stood at the butcher-block table, chopping onions to go with calf's liver. She was wearing a hand-printed batik sundress. In the living room, Cathy and Alan bickered over the volume level of the television.

'Since when did you have anything against a party?' I asked.

Toba glanced up, the sting of the onions blurring her vision.

'Ted, are you attracted to Connie Zide?'

Radar. Women are born with it. I forced what I hoped would come out as a smile of amused, warm-hearted indulgence.

'Connie's an attractive woman,' I replied with extreme care. 'But no, I'm not attracted to her.'

At the time, I was thirty-six years old. Connie Zide was forty-seven. I wasn't lying to my wife; I wasn't attracted to Connie any more than I would be to a scorpion that had stung me. But I was prevaricating—Connie and I, until recently, had had an affair.

Toba seemed to bow to my denial. 'Ted, you hate these big fancy parties,' she said.

'I usually do. But they're going to play a Mozart horn concerto. That's hard for me to resist. Besides, this is business.'

She raised an eyebrow. 'Business? What's that mean?'

'Come with me to the party,' I said. 'I have a surprise for you.'

ON THE FATEFUL NIGHT, I strolled about the Zide estate with my wife. I could hear the rumble of the ocean surf, and palm fronds clicked in the darkness. Toba's black hair shone in the spotlights that illuminated the pool area. I'm a lucky man, I thought, and life is good. And with a little more luck and some patience, soon it will be even better.

Our hosts lived in a fourteen-thousand-square-foot pink palace fronting the Atlantic. The two-storey entrance foyer was dominated by a curving marble staircase, which soared from the middle of formal rooms crammed with Louis XIV furniture. The Zides had two clay tennis courts and two Jacuzzis, one outdoors and one in the master bedroom suite. The entire jungle-bound estate was edged by massed flowerbeds under crape myrtles and palm trees.

'Have you ever been here?' Toba asked me.

'No,' I lied. We were approaching the buffet tables. 'Let's eat.'

Connie Zide, surrounded by a group of men, passed by and thanked Toba and me for coming. That night she was wearing a necklace of pearls and emeralds and a diamond ring with a large centre pearl. Until just two months ago, this woman had held me in thrall, with the fear that I had lost my mind. But now I was free.

Toba squeezed my arm. 'Are you having fun?'

'Because I'm with you.' I meant it.

'So what's the secret, Ted? Why are we here?'

'Some of Solly Zide's pals in Sarasota want me in their law firm.'

'Sarasota? Tell me more!'

In our view, Sarasota—halfway down the opposite coast of Florida, on the Gulf of Mexico—was where people migrated in order to live the good life. No serious crime, no pollution, no hassle.

I slipped an arm round Toba's waist. 'Did you think you'd always be a prosecutor's wife?' When the puzzled look didn't fade from her eyes, I said, 'I guess I'm tired of putting people in jail—even scum.'

'You want to keep them *out* of jail?'

Once I had, yes. In the early sixties I'd been a history major at Florida State. I led marches for civil rights. One night in my final year of law school in Gainesville, my friend Kenny Buckram, another Jacksonville boy, threw out a question: 'What's your deepest ambition?'

Those were wonderful years. Questions had simple answers. 'To argue a case successfully before the Supreme Court,' I said. 'And to save an innocent man's life. If possible, at the same time.'

Most of our group of friends wound up in civil law, where the money was. A few, like Kenny, joined the public defender's office. And I, for the sake of courtroom experience, joined a clinic programme offered by the state attorney's office. I took four misdemeanour cases to trial before six-person juries in Gainesville, winning all four. I loved winning.

Shortly afterwards, Beldon Ruth, chief assistant state attorney in the Fourth Circuit, invited me up to Jacksonville for lunch. Beldon was in his late thirties at the time. Immaculately dressed in a navy blazer, with a yellow polka-dot tie, he was 'not fat', as he explained when I knew him better, 'just a little short for my weight'. A black man in power—unusual enough in the late seventies, even rarer then, in the sixties.

Beldon Ruth and I ate conch fritters and catfish at The Jury Room, a private club across the street from the courthouse. I explained that I had always pictured myself as a defence attorney.

'You want to help people who are guilty?'

'Why was I under the impression,' I fired back, 'that under American law they're considered innocent until proved otherwise?'

'You can consider them whatever you like,' he said, slathering hot jalapeño sauce on his catfish, 'but if we indict them, you can bet they're guilty. A prosecutor doesn't go to trial unless he has the facts—but a defence attorney goes in there because he has to eat. And before he eats, he has to cosy up to the slimy bugs who rape our sisters and sell smack to our kids. A prosecutor gets to put those people where they can't do any more harm. And that dog'll hunt.'

We were southerners and spoke the same language. This was not a visiting lecturer in jurisprudence, but a man in the trenches. Suddenly I wanted to be there with him, under fire. I shook Beldon Ruth's hard hand and I took the job he offered me. When I passed the bar exam, I married Toba and we moved into an apartment forty minutes from the courthouse in downtown Jacksonville.

Five years later, the governor asked Beldon to be state attorney for

Duval County and the Fourth District: that was Jacksonville. Beldon considered me his brightest young prosecutor—when I went to trial I had a 98 per cent conviction rate—and appointed me to take his place as chief assistant. And that's who I was on the night my wife and I strolled the moonlit lawn at the Zides' party and I told her I had a better offer from a Sarasota firm.

'This firm,' I said, 'represents a string of Solly Zide's luxury condos over on the Gulf. They need an experienced trial lawyer. The firm's offered me eighty-five grand a year.'

Toba's eyes widened; that was more than double my current salary. 'You think it would be good for the kids?'

Alan was seven, a dreamy boy who had trouble paying attention in class. Cathy was ten, a straight-A student. Toba plucked a glass of champagne from a silver tray. She answered her own question. 'Well, maybe. Heaven knows there's no decent, safe high school here in Jacksonville. You know just what I mean—violence and drugs.'

'It would definitely be safer in Sarasota.'

We heard the musicians warming up beneath the peppermint-striped tent: first the French horn, then the moan of the bassoon.

'Ted, what do *you* want to do?'

I hadn't lost all my youthful idealism; I still wanted to be involved, to be proud of what I did. But, beyond that, I wanted a little sailboat, and a car for my wife that didn't break down every other season. I wanted my kids to go to a decent college without my having to pinch pennies. When I told all that to Toba, she smiled.

'It's no crime, darling. You say it as if you're ashamed of it. That's what everyone wants.'

'I used to think I wasn't like everyone else,' I admitted.

'I love you, Ted,' she said.

I fingered her thick black hair. 'So let's think about it, although not for too long. They need an answer by Christmas.' Out of the corner of my eye I saw Connie Zide dancing on the grass to the beat of a steel drum. I dropped my hand to my wife's hip.

Oh, Toba, if only you knew.

If she knew, if she ever found out, would she be able to handle it? Please God, let me never know the answer to that question.

TOBA AND I excused ourselves from the party a little after ten.

Much of what happened I learned later. I was trained at asking questions. I snoop. I have a good memory when it suits me.

JSO, the Jacksonville Sheriff's Office, determined that the last guests left the Zide estate by eleven twenty. The caterers and other staff finished cleaning up around one o'clock in the morning.

Some days later, on December 10, 1978, Connie Zide made the following tape-recorded statement to Detectives Floyd J. Nickerson and Carmen M. Tanagra of the homicide division of JSO:

> We went to bed as soon as the caterers left. But I couldn't sleep, and Solomon is—was—a real night owl. So around one thirty I got up to make him a cup of tea. And he followed me downstairs. We wound up playing backgammon in the yellow drawing room. Then Neil, our son, came home from a party and sat down with us. It was probably 2am, perhaps a little later. Right after that we heard a sound from the patio, as if an urn had tipped over and crashed. Our electronic security is state-of-the-art. There's an armed night watchman at the gate—Terence is not young any more, but he's a former Orlando police officer—and Paco, the Doberman, poor thing, was supposed to be down at the beach cabanas. So none of us was particularly alarmed by this crash. My husband just said, 'I'll go look.' He got up from the table, and I followed him, sort of trailed behind at a distance. Then I heard shots. Three, four, five in a row, I couldn't tell—I still don't remember. I went nuts, ran outside. Solomon was lying there, on the terrace, with blood all around him. Two men were standing on the grass. One had a gun—a young black man, looking very frightened. I recognised him as one of our employees, although at the time I couldn't put a name to the face. And then the other man, who was closer to me, raised his hand and slashed me with something. I imagine it was a knife.

Solomon Zide had been shot twice in the chest with a .38-calibre revolver. A third bullet had been found lodged in the Swedish oak panelling on the far side of the room. Connie Zide had been slashed in the face. Neither weapon was ever found. Minutes later young Neil Zide, unhurt but close to hysteria, called the Jacksonville Beach police and then a man named Victor Gambrel, the head of security for Zide Industries. When Gambrel and the law and the paramedics arrived, Neil was able to describe the murderer. 'Young, black, wearing sneakers, jeans, and I seem to remember a dark T-shirt. There were two of them. I didn't get a decent look at the other one, who cut my mother. They obviously didn't expect anyone to be awake at that hour. My father surprised them, and they panicked. No, I don't know how they got onto the property.'

By the time the JSO homicide team arrived on the scene, the entire estate was locked in the hard yellow glare of its own floodlights. Detective Tanagra found the dead Doberman—poisoned by a piece of meat. She also found imprints of two pairs of sneakers in the wet sand near the beach cabanas. One of the men wore size fourteen or fifteen shoes.

'Let's cruise around,' Floyd Nickerson said to her. 'Pair of bayou rats, where can they go? Feet like that, you can't hide.'

The detectives drove off in their unmarked Plymouth and left the tech squad to do its work. Over the mossy bayous and highways hovered a jungle darkness. They stopped at bars with pick-up trucks out in front, talked to bartenders and waitresses. Black men drinking beer and rye whiskey peered at them with stoic dread. Nickerson, in his late thirties, was burly, moustached, his pockmarked white skin shiny with sweat; he was made instantly as a cop. Carmen Tanagra was thin, flat-chested, good-looking, often taken for a junkie.

The detectives passed car dealerships and pizza joints, empty lots overgrown with weeds, intermittent Lil' Champ food stores. At nearly 5am the air was cool but still humid.

Nickerson had a nose for finding people. 'Turn in there.' He pointed across the highway to a Lil' Champ.

Tanagra slowed the Plymouth.

A blue, salt-pitted 1968 Ford pick-up, which had been smacked in the rear, stood isolated in one of the parking slots. Two young men came out of the Lil' Champ, carrying a six-pack of beer and several bags of potato crisps. One of them, William Smith, was lean and tall. He wore a grey sweatshirt and sported an Afro. The other youth, Darryl Morgan, wore faded jeans and a black Nike T-shirt. He was huge, probably six foot six, could have been a college basketball player except he moved awkwardly. Nickerson glanced down at Morgan's sneakers. Feet like boats.

By the time the detectives stepped forth to be seen, William Smith had climbed behind the wheel of the pick-up and slammed the door behind him. Darryl Morgan moved more slowly.

'*Poh*-lice! Hold it right there!' Nickerson flipped his gold shield. The light shone on it. 'Let's see some ID, boys.'

No one moved. Then Smith turned the ignition key, starting the engine, so that the pick-up rattled violently.

Nickerson tugged at the gun in his waistband.

Tanagra yelled at Smith, 'Hold it! Hold it right there!'

Morgan backed his huge frame against the building.

Nickerson dropped to one knee and fired what he would later describe in the official police report as 'two warning shots when the suspect Smith attempted to escape'. One of the shots passed through the driver's door and into William Smith's left thigh. Smith yelped in pain and fell forward. His left foot lifted off the clutch and the

pick-up hurtled backwards in a screeching curve, smashing into a pair
of concrete posts. It tilted and fell on its side, bounced and settled.
The engine died. A shower of glass fell.

'Go take a look, Carmen,' Nickerson told his partner.

After a couple of minutes Carmen Tanagra walked back from the
wreck. 'Boy seems to have a bullet in his leg and a sliver of windshield
in his throat. He's looking poorly.'

'You gonna stand around talking? Or call an ambulance?'

'No rush for that, Nick.'

'What are you saying?'

'Graveyard dead, that's what I'm saying.'

Nickerson's eyes rolled in his head. He wheeled on Darryl Morgan
and said angrily, 'You and your dead pal been out to the beach
tonight, right? Looking to score a few TV sets. Got caught in the act
and lost your cool, and you shot a man. Big fella, don't pop my cork
by telling me it ain't so! Let's just hear about it. And then I'll tell you
how you got the right to remain silent, and all that other crap.'

TEN DAYS AFTER the murder of Solly Zide, I accepted the job with
the Sarasota law firm. I gave three months' notice to the state
attorney's office in Jacksonville and celebrated by buying a case of
chateau-bottled Bordeaux.

But I was basically a sober fellow and still had work to do. One of
the places to do it was the lawyers' lounge on the fourth floor of the
Duval County Courthouse. One morning I sat on the sofa there with
a young assistant public defender, plea-bargaining a drug case. The
telephone by the coffee urn rang, and one of the defence attorneys
snatched it. 'Your lord and master,' he said, waving the receiver at me.

A moment later, the gruff voice of Beldon Ruth said in my ear, 'Get
your butt upstairs, Ted, if you're not too busy.'

I took the stairs two at a time to the fifth floor and soon sat on the
window ledge of the state attorney's office, the only space available to
sit down. Beldon's legal files were piled on the sofa and chairs. They
were also spread on the floor in front of his desk.

'What a mess,' I said. 'How will you survive when I'm gone?'

'I'll do just fine. It's you I'm worried about.' Beldon rocked back in
his creaky swivel chair. 'I know Sarasota. What's Toba going to do
while you pace the wall-to-wall carpet of your office, wondering
whether to trade your Honda for a Porsche or a Mercedes?'

'Real estate. She may be the one winds up driving the Porsche.'

Beldon sighed theatrically, then picked up a bulky brown accordion
folder from his desk. 'The Zide case,' he said.

I had assigned it to Dale Settels, an eager young prosecutor.

'A slam dunk for the state,' I told Beldon.

'It's for sure a slam dunk for the newspapers and the TV,' he grumbled. 'Two black perps, and one gets shot trying to escape.'

'Or so the detective says,' I pointed out.

'So we're left with one live black defendant in a big murder trial, and he's come up with a black lawyer. Guy named Gary Oliver. You see where I'm heading? Constance Zide knows you, likes you, seems to trust you, and she's asked me if you'll prosecute.'

My affair with Connie Zide was defunct—Beldon didn't know about it; no one did—but it was still something for me to consider. Beyond that was a more worrisome factor. In Florida, first-degree murder now carried with it the possibility of electrocution. The governor had already earned the nickname of Barbecue Bob.

This case, for many reasons, was not for me.

'Tell me about Gary Oliver,' I said.

'Used to be a good private investigator. Then he got uppity and went to law school, like some other people we know. But he's got a problem. Guy's favourite drink is the next one.'

Not that it mattered, Beldon explained. Forty-eight hours after his rights had been read to him, Morgan confessed the murder to Sergeant Floyd Nickerson. A few nights later he repeated the confession in front of a cellmate. And Connie Zide identified him positively. Neil Zide confirmed the ID at a police line-up.

'This Morgan kid's six foot six,' Beldon said. 'A giant. Hard to mistake him for anyone else.'

'So the jury will convict.'

'You can bet on it. But not on part two.'

In Florida a murder trial was divided into two parts. First the jury heard evidence, then voted as to guilt or innocence. If the verdict was guilty, in part two the same jury voted on a recommendation for sentencing. The final decision was up to the judge.

'I've never done a death penalty case,' I said. 'And this doesn't strike me as the time to start.'

'It won't come to that, Ted. Take the case. Handle the media people. Cut a deal up-front with Oliver.'

I looked up. 'If I cut a deal, you'll approve it?'

'Hey, you think I want a twenty-year-old black boy's blood? We got a white cop who got trigger-happy, and some unhappy black folks out there all over the county and the state. I don't want a riot. I don't even want a trial. I want it smooth, Ted. That's your specialty. Do it as a personal favour to your old uncle Beldon.'

He had me where he wanted me, and I nodded. 'For you,' I said.

'Bless your little cotton socks,' he said, handing me the case file.

WHEN THE CLOCK in my office chimed the morning hour of seven, I settled behind my state-issue metal desk and read the rap sheet on Darryl Morgan, who prior to the murder had been an assistant handyman on the Zide estate. He was the third of five children born to Marguerite Little, a cleaning woman in Jacksonville Beach. His biological father was unknown. Marguerite's common-law husband, A.J. Morgan, was a grounds keeper at the Palmetto Country Club. The family lived in a four-room wooden shack on the edge of a rat-infested palm grove, half a dozen miles from the beach.

Since his fourteenth birthday, Darryl Morgan hadn't known two straight years of freedom. Banished to reform school for hoisting a tape deck from a car, he had done time on a penal farm for jackrolling drunks and in Clay County Jail for grabbing money from a cash register. Finally he had been sentenced to a branch of Florida State Prison for burgling an auto-parts warehouse. He was eighteen then. He did nineteen months on that seven-year bit, then was released.

Gary Oliver, his knight in the lists, arrived at my office at 8am.

I poured coffee into two chipped mugs. Then my portly visitor got right to the point. 'Mr Jaffe, do you believe in the death penalty?' This was not a challenge; he was probing.

'I believe in upholding my oath as a state attorney, and that requires me to apply the appropriate law. However'—I eased up—'I have some leeway. If you convince your client to plead out to first-degree murder, the state will accept a life sentence.'

'With a mandatory twenty-five years?'

'That's the law. You know that.'

Oliver's large moist eyes narrowed. 'I'll put it to him,' he said.

The following week, on a warm February morning, he returned to my office. Settling into a chair, he wiped his forehead with a damp handkerchief. 'This Morgan boy's crazy as an outhouse rat,' he said. 'Wants to take it to a jury. Claims he's innocent.'

'I'm sure he does. But you've seen the evidence. You know a jury will find him guilty, Mr Oliver. There are two eyewitnesses and two separate confessions. He's got a criminal record that includes violence. I'm giving him a good deal. I'm giving him air to breathe.'

Oliver sighed. 'He says black folks will see he didn't do it.'

'No,' I said sharply. 'Black or white won't matter. When a juror sees what Morgan and Smith did to Mrs Zide's face, they'll get mean. Your responsibility, sir, in a case like this, where the evidence is strong, is to keep your client alive.'

Oliver said, 'I don't think this client has both oars in the water.'

I shifted position, swivelling to look out at the St Johns River.

Turning back, I said, 'Tell him this. If he goes to trial and he's found guilty, I'll do my best to put him in a coffin.'

Oliver looked glum. 'You think that boy's quiet and repentant?' he said. 'He's got a mouth on hinges. He'd argue with a signpost.'

He wasn't bargaining; he was turning me down. No smooth road. That was how I was trapped into going to trial in a capital murder case—my last case as a prosecutor in Jacksonville.

In Sarasota in early 1991, at the time when Jerry Lee Elroy called me from the jail, I was working on four cases. All seemed headed for trial unless the parties could agree to settle out of court.

In one, a developer was suing a contractor for major construction errors. In another, a professional football player had assaulted a local hooker. In the third case, after a local savings and loan company had been taken over by the government, its former chief executive officer was being sued for fifty million dollars. The last case involved alleged price-fixing by Manatee County milk distributors.

I had lunch at the Colony Beach and Tennis Club with Harvey Royal, senior partner of our firm, and our client, the developer who was suing the contractor. A few yards from the Gulf, we discussed trial strategy and a list of witnesses to subpoena. The food was gourmet, the air unpolluted. I lived five minutes away. This was definitely the good life, recession or not.

When the client left, Harvey and I spent another half-hour over coffee, discussing the savings and loan case.

Harvey called for the bill. 'Any new business coming in?'

'Two-bit stuff.'

'We can't afford two-bit stuff these days, Ted.'

'Keeps me off the streets,' I said.

Harvey offered a watery smile.

I drove back to the office, thinking about Jerry Lee Elroy.

A state's witness had lied. Common enough. We lawyers lived in a jungle of lies. But this was different. Elroy, my witness, had lied because he'd made a deal with a cop—Floyd Nickerson.

Darryl Morgan had confessed to Nickerson, who had shored up his position by suborning false testimony from a jailhouse snitch. If that had come to light during the proceedings, Nickerson would have been booted out of the sheriff's office and Elroy would have been charged with a felony. There would have been a retrial.

Dumb, because the case was good enough already. In fact, airtight.

So why had Nickerson done that? I had no satisfactory answer.

For the last dozen years I had banished from my conscious mind the murder of Solomon Zide and the memory of Darryl Morgan. My unconscious mind was a different story. I had had nightmares. Those nightmares were of a man's head bursting into flames.

At three o'clock I appeared once again at the Sarasota County Jail. With Jerry Lee Elroy, I stood before a judge. Elroy handed me a certified cheque drawn on a Miami bank, and I passed it along to the bondsman. By 4pm, my new client was a free man. While I waited by the wire cage, he collected his red nylon jacket, gold wedding ring, money, baseball cap and Miami Dolphins key ring.

In my office, seated in a green leather chair and looking out at the bay through the tinted plate glass, Elroy was subdued.

I leaned forward across the expanse of polished desk and said, 'What you told me before about what happened up in Jacksonville—I can chew it, Elroy, but I can't swallow it. You follow me?'

'Hey, it was a long time ago,' Elroy said.

'The first thing I want to know is, back then, did you think I *knew*?'

Elroy just shrugged. 'I only knew what the cop and the other lawyer told me. I'm talking about that state chick who was out to get mc on the battery charge.'

'She and Floyd Nickerson made the proposition to you?'

'Who? Oh, yeah, the cop. I told you, he asked me to do him this favour. Then later the state chick says, "OK, we're waiving the bail bond. We'll cut you loose." All I had to do was show up in court, repeat what I told this detective. If not, my butt would've wound up in a sling.'

'You ever talk to Morgan about the shooting?'

Elroy smiled shrewdly. 'Yeah. He talked to me. Four guys in a cell, hard not to talk to the next guy. Morgan goes, "I's in here for a bad reason, 'cause I don't kill no one and they says I do. I's in deep trouble." And I go, "Hey, man, tell me about it." So he did.'

'What exactly did he tell you?'

'Like how he and his pal tried to rob this fancy house, and someone comes out, so they run away. I go, "Hey, dude, you're up for first-degree murder. You gotta say they shoot you, you shoot back. Self-defence, see?" He goes, "I never had no gun." ' Elroy stopped, smiled thinly, then said, 'Counsellor, I ain't learning nothing, doing all the talking. When are we gonna discuss *my* case?'

There was no way out of it. That was my job. And it was a way to get where I had to go. 'Tell me everything that happened,' I said.

He had run a stoplight, he said, at Route 41 and Beach Avenue. When the traffic cops flashed him over, he'd cut through a bank parking lot and tried to lose them on back roads. But he took a wrong turn into a cul-de-sac, and they nailed him.

'They're going to want to know who you got the cocaine from,' I said. 'If you decide to keep your mouth shut, you're looking at ten to fifteen years.'

'You mean if I get convicted.'

'Pay attention, Elroy. If you get convicted, the judge will stick it to you on three separate counts. That could add up to half your life. I'm talking about ten to fifteen if you make a deal.'

'That's what you call a *deal*? Where are we, Red China?'

'It's the best you can get unless you snitch.'

'What do I get if I snitch?'

'Five years, maybe. You might even walk away if you convince them your cooperation is sincere.'

'I can be plenty sincere. But these people they want to know about, these are heavyweight dudes. These people are from Miami. You snitch on them, they inch you. You know what that is?'

'Yes.' I leaned back in the chair and said calmly, 'They cut off your fingers. Inch by inch. With a machete. Right?'

Elroy nodded solemnly. 'It ain't just a bedtime story, amigo.'

'You ever hear of the witness protection programme?'

'I saw a movie about it on TV.'

'Think about it. I'll talk to the state attorney's office and see what they've got on you. Meanwhile, don't leave town.'

RUBY, MY SECRETARY, was printing out the day's letters on the printer, getting ready to hit the singles bars on the quay. I came out of my office at ten past five. 'Just a few things, Ruby, if you don't mind. And if you haven't got a hot date.'

Ruby was a divorced woman in her late thirties who answered ads in the local magazines. But still she blushed. 'What is it, Ted?'

'Book me on a late afternoon flight to Jacksonville tomorrow. Then get in touch with JSO. See if there's a homicide detective named Floyd Nickerson still on the roster. If they give you a hard time, call Kenny Buckram at the public defender's office. Then call the state attorney's office. There was an aggravated battery case back in seventy-nine. The accused was Jerry Lee Elroy. I need to know the assistant state attorney who prosecuted and dropped the case.'

Ruby looked up from her pad. 'Will you need a hotel room?'

'Yes. And call the state prison in Raiford. There was a man named Darryl Morgan committed to death row in April nineteen seventy-nine.' I took a deep breath. 'I need to know what happened to him.'

At six o'clock Ruby bounced in, clutching her steno pad.

'You're booked on USAir 456 at three forty-five. You're in the Marina Hotel. The prosecutor in the Elroy case was named Muriel M. Suarez. She's still there. Floyd J. Nickerson left the Jacksonville Sheriff's Office in nineteen eighty-one. They couldn't tell me where he is now. I put in a call to Mr Buckram at the public defender's office, but he was in Tallahassee for the day. I left a message for him to call you at home tonight up to eleven o'clock. Was that OK?'

'Fine,' I said, my heartbeat accelerating. The worst for last.

She read from her notes: ' "Darryl Arthur Morgan entered Florida State Prison, twenty-four April nineteen seventy-nine. Appeal to the Florida Supreme Court in June nineteen eighty-one—denied. Public defender handling it all. Appeal to the Eleventh Circuit in Tampa, denied in nineteen eighty-five. Atlanta, Federal Court of Appeals, application denied." We're up to nineteen eighty-eight. "Application for review by the US Supreme Court—denied. The governor signed the death warrant on October second, nineteen ninety. Scheduled for execution April eleventh of this year, nineteen ninety-one. One more appeal for postconviction relief to the trial court in Jacksonville. Decision pending." '

I said quietly, 'You're telling me that Morgan is still alive.'

Ruby said, 'He better be, because if they find out a dead man's making all these appeals, they're going to be seriously displeased.'

I first met Connie Zide almost a year before the night of the concert and the murder of her husband. Driving home from work one afternoon, I decided to stop at the Regency Plaza Mall to buy a tie. I nosed the Honda towards an empty slot in the mall parking lot, and at that moment a tall, tawny-haired woman emerged from Dillard's. She wore a tailored grey suit. She was not young. That woman, I thought, can't be as beautiful and as elegant as I believe she is—there's no one like that in Jacksonville.

A young fellow in blue jeans and a white T-shirt stepped from behind a Datsun. Gold chains jangled round his neck. With peppy strides he closed the distance between himself and the elegant woman. I hit the brake. I wanted to yell, Watch out! But I was too far away.

Alejandro Ortega, born in Cuba nineteen years earlier, expert broad-daylight jewellery thief, got rapidly to where he was headed and slipped his hand through the big gold necklace dangling from her white throat. He yanked hard. As he expected, the connecting link snapped. Connie Zide gave a tremulous cry.

Alejandro clutched the necklace in his hand and wheeled, ready to sprint to his souped-up Trans Am. But as he started to bolt, Connie Zide took one quick step, and with her red-tipped fingers she tore one of the gold necklaces from his neck.

Later she said, 'Why did I do that? Because I felt violated, Ted. People think they can do anything they want with a woman who's on her own. You're just a target for these little creeps.'

'You weren't frightened that he'd retaliate?'

'I had a pistol in my handbag. And a licence to carry it.'

'You'd have used it?'

'If I had to . . . who knows?'

Alejandro got four or five quick running steps away from his mark before he realised that something had been wrenched from him. He whirled in the air and moved back towards her. He extended his hand in mute, eloquent demand. At that point he became aware of a presence growing larger by the second.

I'd decided that if this unknown beautiful woman could do what she'd done, then I could lend a hand. I weighed one hundred and sixty-seven pounds and hit that fellow broadside, on the run, with a bent shoulder. He wound up on his knees, visibly amazed, huffing. I twisted his right arm high up behind his back.

I looked up at the woman in the grey suit and said, 'Would you mind, ma'am, going back into Dillard's? Ask someone to call nine one one. Don't take too long.'

And to Alejandro I said, 'Fight back and I'll snap your arm like a twig. I'm a karate black belt. *Cinturón negro, comprendes?*'

There wasn't a word of truth in any of that.

Connie Zide said, 'My hero.' It didn't sound at all sarcastic.

AFTER THE COPS arrived and wrote down Mrs Solomon Zide's name, address and telephone number and bundled Ortega off to jail, Connie slumped against her car and said, 'What a thing to happen! I need a drink. Can you indulge me just a bit more?'

We went to the first bar we could find—a quietly lit pizza place called Ruffino's Kitchen. She ordered a Scotch. We talked, but there was a roaring in my ears and half the time I wasn't able to listen with the required concentration. Connie Zide's blue-green eyes, set in the perfect oval of her face, were large and clear, her lips ruddy and full. Her body was richly sculpted, with a slender neck and long legs. All of this was topped by an affluence of silky light brown hair. She was deep into her forties but looked ten years younger.

'Well, Mr Jaffe, what happens next?'

A question wild with meaning. I held her gaze as steadily as I dared.

It wasn't possible, I decided, that she was reacting to me the way I was reacting to her. Such things didn't happen—not to me.

'You have to go down to the courthouse first thing tomorrow morning,' I said. 'File a complaint. Make a statement. Otherwise they can't hold this guy. He'll be at another mall in a few days.'

She thought it over. 'Who do I make the statement to?'

'The assistant state attorney who gets the case.'

'Won't that be you?'

'It'll be someone who works for me. I'm chief assistant.' I shrugged, meaning, That's a big deal in my world, not yours.

'Would you be able to handle this personally?'

'Why?'

'Do I have to tell you?' She looked at me calmly.

I felt guilty already, and nothing had happened.

'I'm a witness,' I said. 'I'll have to bow out at a certain time. But until such time comes, yes, of course I'll handle it.'

'Are you married?' she asked.

My heart pounded; her bluntness frightened and captured me.

'Happily married. With two kids.'

'And one more dumb question. Are you Jewish?'

'Yes.'

'I knew it. Something in your voice. Old World warmth. My goodness, you're blushing.'

She didn't have a southern accent, and I asked where she was from. Scranton, Pennsylvania, she told me. She had done a little modelling after high school, she said, then gone out to LA to become an actress. But there were too many actresses. Then she got married and was brought by her husband to Jacksonville.

I had never met Solomon Zide, although you could not live in Jacksonville without knowing Zide Industries. Not just the conglomerate, that statewide octopus, but Solly's local projects. ZiDevco, the real-estate development subsidiary, was changing Duval County, buying up mud flats and bay bottom and converting them to golf courses, yacht harbours and home sites.

'May I call you Edward?'

'Ted will do it.'

'I know you're a prosecutor and happily married, but what else?'

'What do you want to know?'

An intense, clear light seemed to pour through her eyes. She said calmly, 'If I said "everything", would I be rushing things?'

I felt a sensation in my spine and fingertips. I didn't answer her question, just moved my hand towards hers; she clasped it, squeezing it hard. Her fingers were thin and cool. Her eyes were knowing.

316

Nothing more happened that evening. I backed off. I said good night to her and gave her my business card.

The next afternoon, at the courthouse, she wore a beige suit, the austerity of which only heightened her sensuality. I took her statement and had it filed.

When Connie had called, she'd said, 'After we get through our business, will you buy me another drink?'

'If you come here at four thirty, Mrs Zide, I'm sure I can manage that.' I was in conference then with two assistant state attorneys.

We went to the Marriott. At a table under a palm tree on the terrace, we chatted for an hour, and then I smiled in what I hoped was a gracious manner and said, 'I'm afraid I have to go.' I realised that I had made a mistake. She was as lovely and dazzling as before, but she seemed nervous. I felt like a fool.

Out in the hotel parking lot, she led me to her pearl-grey Mercedes convertible. When she brushed up against me, I grew a little giddy. I stared at her face in the shadowy light, wanting to say goodbye with at least a trace of style. She sprang the locks of the car with a crashing sound like a great brass gong. With firm and lunatic intent, I strode round to the passenger's door, slid inside, and got all mixed up by the aroma of foreign leather and perfume. 'Connie . . .'

'Ted . . .'

'Look, I know this is crazy . . .'

'No, it's not crazy at all.'

She reached out for me, and I kissed her.

THE AFFAIR LASTED seven months, until two months before Solly was murdered. I'm not in love with Connie, I concluded. That would be the end of everything. But, like the beautiful lady in the poem by Keats, *la belle dame sans merci* had me in thrall.

She was on the board of two Jewish charities, and she asked me to join. I agreed, with reservations. At the charity luncheon I met Solly Zide. In his mid-fifties, he was a medium-sized man with hard little brown eyes. Connie said of him, 'He gets his major thrill from making money.' She had married him not so much for money as for the security that attended it.

'Solly had two daughters by a former marriage. Nasty, spoiled girls. When he met me, he wanted a son and heir. I gave him one.'

Neil was twenty-two when I met Connie. He had graduated from Duke and was living at home, working on the big ZiDevco landfill project with his father. I asked how they got along.

'Like the proverbial cat and dog. Neil's a spiritual person. He can paint, he's got a natural talent in music. He could become a

317

world-class photographer if he wanted. He's the light of my life.'

I really didn't care. I wanted nothing to do with Connie's life outside of us. I was in thrall. I was not wholly happy, and yet I felt wholly alive. I expected some thunderbolt to strike me from heaven, or some terrible revelation that would put my marriage and career in peril. None of that happened, then.

DURING LUNCH BREAK on the first day of Darryl Morgan's trial in April of the following year, I strolled along the south bank of the St Johns River with Connie Zide. I still remember how the grey surface of the water barely moved in the April heat. To the east of Jacksonville, over the Atlantic, lightning flared.

'Ted darling, I need to ask you a favour.'

I let the endearment pass without comment. The hangover of love, if indeed that's what it had been.

Until that past December and the night of the murder, Connie had been a beautiful woman. Now a scar puckered her left cheek, and dark pouches sagged under bloodshot eyes. She had gained weight. But I felt close to her; I had allegiance to memory.

'Ask, Connie.'

'I know there are no guarantees in life, Ted, much less in a murder trial. But I need to know what will happen.'

Her husband had been murdered before her eyes. I thought I knew what she was thinking. What if, by some bizarre mischance, Darryl Morgan walked out of the courtroom a free man? The justice system was not perfect, lawyers and judges less so. I had told her enough to have planted that idea in her mind.

We stopped by the river. Looking into her ruined face, I said, 'The jury will find Morgan guilty.'

'That's not what I meant. Ted, do you ever pity a murderer?'

'Oh, Connie, my love.' That endearment was out before I knew it. I took her arm. 'So many of these kids are dealt bad cards. I pity him, yes, because something had to happen to make him that way.'

'Will you argue for the death penalty?'

I hesitated again. 'Do you want Morgan to die?'

'No,' she said, revealing her purpose and surprising me.

'And neither do I. But you have to understand. After we get a guilty verdict, I'll argue for death. I have to do that.' I touched her arm. 'But perhaps not with sufficient vigour as to win.'

A MARAUDING SPRING SHOWER slanted down. Sunlight glimmered through a pillar of rain that cannoned against the windows of the courthouse. Inside, Gary Oliver had to raise his voice to be heard.

318

'The defence calls Darryl Morgan!'

It was not required. In my experience, guilty men seldom took the stand in their own defence. A good prosecutor would carve them into bite-size pieces. Morgan was a self-confessed murderer. Was Oliver so incompetent as to permit cross-examination?

The defendant slouched to the witness box in just a few strides. He wore a long-sleeved blue denim shirt, khaki trousers, jail-issue black shoes. A youth of twenty, Morgan dwarfed everyone in sight, including the beefy deputy sheriffs on hand to guard him. His hard jaw jutted forth under a powerful face. The oval whites of his eyes were rimmed with pink. The dark irises had tigerish flecks, glinting with suspicion as they stared out at the threatening world. In the air-conditioned courtroom, he sweated.

Oliver led Morgan through self-serving testimony for over an hour. Near the end, he said, 'You're not denying that you tried to rob Mr Zide's house?'

Morgan had a resonant baritone voice. 'I done that,' he said.

'But you didn't shoot and kill Mr Zide?'

'No, sir.'

'Tell this jury the truth, and may lightning strike you dead this minute if you lie! Did either you or William Smith slash Mrs Constance Zide in the face?'

Morgan said, 'No, sir.'

'Darryl, did you throw away a .38-calibre pistol that night?'

'No, sir, I didn't throw no .38 away, 'cause I don't have no .38. William was carrying a .32 that night. He threw *that* away in the ocean before they arrest us.'

'Pass the witness!' Oliver cried, casting a smile towards the jury box, as if his client's denials were triumphant.

I stood up to cross-examine.

'Mr Morgan, you don't deny breaking into the Zide estate with William Smith at two o'clock in the morning, do you?'

'I say I done that.'

'You don't deny giving poisoned meat to Paco, the Doberman, on the beach side of the house, do you?'

'I done that too. But I didn't know it was poison. I thought he just go to sleep. William, he lie to me.'

'But you deny that William Smith ever slashed Mrs Zide in the face with a knife?'

'William never do that.'

'And on the morning of December sixth of last year'—looking directly into the violent yellow eyes, I raised my voice a notch—'you didn't shoot Solomon Zide twice in the chest?'

'I never do that.'

'And on December ninth, nineteen seventy-eight, in Duval County Jail, you didn't confess that murder to Detective Nickerson?'

'Never do that, either.'

'And on or about January third of this year, nineteen seventy-nine, in that same Duval County Jail, you didn't say in front of one of your cellmates, Jerry Lee Elroy'—I glanced at my notes—' "I'm in deep trouble because I was robbing this house and shot some Jew"?'

'Never said that. Ain't so.'

This young giant had gall; I had to give him credit.

'Your contention is that Constance Zide—who testified under oath that you were standing over the dead body of her husband with a pistol in your hand—is lying or mistaken?'

'Don't know why she say what she say. She know it ain't so.'

'And Neil Zide, the victim's son, is also mistaken?'

'Didn't do it,' Morgan said.

'Officer Nickerson and Jerry Lee Elroy are also mistaken?'

'They ain't mistaken,' Morgan said. His voice rose. 'They lying.'

'Mr Morgan, would you lie in order to save your life?'

I waited for an objection, but Gary Oliver chewed the end of a stubby yellow pencil.

'Can't rightly say,' Morgan growled.

I announced that I had no further questions.

'No redirect,' Gary Oliver said. 'And the defence rests.'

But Morgan continued. 'I don't kill no one! You wrong about that, mister.'

'That's enough!' Judge Eglin began to cough. 'Step down.'

After a brief recess, Gary Oliver rose from his chair and launched into his final argument.

'Look at him, folks. Just a simple black boy from the ghetto! He might smoke some dope on Saturday night, he might steal, but it's not in him to murder! Mrs Zide says, "It was Darryl Morgan did it." Her son, Neil, says the same. But it's real dark that awful night, and this defendant, as you can see, is a dark-complexioned boy. So how can they know for sure it's him? I believe this boy when he says he didn't do it. I don't believe his cellmate, that man Jerry Lee Elroy, at all. A professional snitch is what he is.'

When he finished, I stood and after a pause said, 'If I am ever seated in that chair there, facing the possibility of death by electrocution, I guarantee you one thing: I will lie until my teeth fall out.'

A few jurors smiled. Most nodded, for they would lie too.

'Physical evidence has placed the defendant on the Zide estate at the hour of the crime. And he's admitted to being there. Mrs Zide has identified him. Neil Zide also identified the defendant. That is sufficient to warrant a guilty verdict. And yet, beyond that, two men, one of them a veteran police detective, have stated unequivocally that the defendant confessed to the murder. That is conclusive *far* beyond reasonable doubt. But still Mr Morgan says, "I didn't do it." '

I paused to let the next words gather some weight.

'Well, he has to say that, doesn't he?'

I sighed as if saddened by my prosecutorial duty, but that was not all acting. 'The evidence is simply overwhelming. I beg you to do your duty. Find Darryl Morgan guilty.'

It took the jury less than twenty minutes to return. The foreman delivered the expected verdict.

Judge Bill Eglin said, 'Thank you, ladies and gentlemen. Y'all have found the defendant guilty of first-degree felony murder. Tomorrow morning, evidence and argument will be presented by both sides that will help you to recommend one of two punishments for the defendant. You'll recommend either death by electrocution or life imprisonment without the possibility of parole for twenty-five years. In our law here in Florida, there is no alternative. Court is adjourned until nine o'clock tomorrow morning.' He rapped his oak gavel.

Our house on Longboat Key was brick and marble and glass, with an atrium foyer and tropical landscaping. A twenty-eight-foot sloop was tied up at the private boat dock, from where we had views of both Sarasota Bay and the Gulf of Mexico. We had moved here in August 1990 from a wooden A-frame on Siesta Key. We had traded up, no doubt of it, to a home befitting a partner in a prestigious law firm. But that was not why we had moved.

One morning on Siesta Key, I had been squeezing orange juice and trying to read the paper when the telephone rang. Our son, Alan, was an eighteen-year-old high-school senior, and the early-morning caller was his guidance counsellor, Mr Variano. He asked Toba and me to come and see him. We dutifully and apprehensively appeared at the high school that same afternoon.

'Alan is a good-natured boy,' Variano said. 'Sensitive, friendly—'

Toba blushed as if she herself had been complimented. 'We thought you'd brought us here to tell us he was in some sort of trouble.'

'—when he's not stoned,' Variano continued.

Twice, he said, Alan had been caught smoking marijuana on school grounds. He often fell asleep in class. He cut classes regularly.

'Didn't you know this?' Variano asked.

'Not really,' I managed.

Variano looked at his notes. 'We have reason to believe that Alan and his friends—the Becker twins, the Woolford boy—have been selling to the other kids. Are you aware of that, Mr Jaffe?'

'Definitely not the selling.' My stomach tightened.

'Are you talking about hard drugs'—Toba's voice was chilly—'or just marijuana?'

'Marijuana, Mrs Jaffe, although I'll bet my pay cheque these kids have dabbled in other stuff. Everything's available.'

ALAN CRIED WHEN I talked to him that evening. He admitted that the boys smoked in the janitor's storeroom.

'What about crack?'

'No way. That's bad karma, Dad.'

'Do you want to quit?'

'Yes. I know it's ruining my life.'

I was pleased. These admissions had to be therapeutic. 'If you know that, Alan, and you want to quit, you can. And you will.'

In spring the school advised us that Alan would not be graduated with his class. He had failed required courses in American history and science. That was when we decided to move to Longboat Key. Take the kid away from his dope-smoking pals, get him in a new environment for the make-up semester.

'And I want to put him in a drug programme,' I said to Toba. 'I've done some investigating. There's a good one downtown.'

After we moved to Longboat Key, Alan began a twice-a-week evening programme. I drove there with him on that winter day after I met Jerry Lee Elroy at Sarasota County Jail.

That night, on the drive back home to Longboat Key, I said to Alan, 'How are you doing, son?'

'Fine, Dad. We sit in a big group and talk. I'm clean.'

'Do you want to leave the programme?'

'I know what a terrible thing drugs are now. I could use the time for studying. I'm having a real tough time with physics.'

We were home. Alan hit the button that opened the electronic security gate, and it whirred open.

'Let me think about it,' I said. 'I'll talk to your mother.'

Stars glittered above Sarasota Bay. Standing in the driveway, I reached out to give Alan a hug.

Toba was upstairs, watching television. I went to the den, where I read for a while in a new Le Carré novel. A clock was ticking softly in the kitchen. There was a rhythm to any life, I thought, a routine that both sustained and deadened. Countless moments became strung together in the guise of a whole. I was forty-eight years old. It would be over all too quickly, and if I had the courage at the end, I would ask myself, What was it all about? What did you do that really mattered? And what would I answer?

I thought of my seventy-two-year-old mother then, for I knew what she would answer. I visited her whenever I could in her condo in West Palm Beach, where she had moved after Dad's death. To all my musings and soul-searchings, she once said, 'Teddy, most of what happens isn't planned. Who knows what's going to be? So do your best. Be kind, enjoy, try not to worry.'

I tried.

When I went up to bed at half past eleven, Toba didn't even stir. In the silent darkness I thought of Jerry Lee Elroy, and then of Darryl Morgan, the man I had sent to death row. And I didn't even have to dream that recurrent horror. Now I saw it and heard it while I was still awake: the black head in the leather cap, the crash of the switch, the dimming of the lights—the burst of blue fire.

TWELVE YEARS BEFORE, the second part of the Morgan trial in Jacksonville had gone quickly. But in memory it would always have the quality of drawn-out nightmare.

I rose from the counsel table. It was my duty to seek the end of the convicted murderer's life. But Connie had said she didn't want him to die. And neither did I. 'The state of Florida,' I said calmly, 'rests its plea for the death penalty on the previous evidence.'

With a perceptible scowl on his lips, Judge Bill Eglin looked down. I had confused him.

Gary Oliver strode towards the jury again, a hearty man, arms spread as if to embrace the world. He called Marguerite Little as his first witness. With her wild iron-grey hair and Mother Hubbard dress, Morgan's mother had the look of a woman let out of a mental institution for the day. 'He always been a good boy.' That was the sum of her testimony.

A.J. Morgan, the stepfather, in a black suit, took the stand. 'I always told him he was gonna go too far. He never listen to me.'

'Sir!' Oliver shot forward, cutting him off. 'Tell us this: in your home, was your stepson violent?'

'I don't permit that.'

'Outside your home, that you know of?'

'That's what he here for, right?'

Oliver sank back towards the defence table, defeated by this friendly witness.

The time came for final argument in part two.

Rising, Gary Oliver faced the jury. 'This is a young boy,' he begged. 'He shot this man without meaning to.'

From his seat at the defence table, Darryl Morgan rumbled, 'I didn't shoot *no one!*'

The eyes of all the jurors swung towards him. The judge tapped his ball-point pen on the oak bench from which he dispensed justice.

Oliver stared at his client, then turned back to the jury. 'Twenty years old! Be merciful! The boy will be forty-five years old when he comes up for parole, if you let him. He'll be a new man then. Give that new man a chance!'

After Oliver sat, wiping his forehead with his handkerchief, Judge Eglin waved his hand at me. The state, saddled with the burden of proof, was granted the right of the last word.

I stood and said, 'Ladies and gentlemen, the defendant was surprised in the act of burglary by Solomon Zide, and indeed, thinking he was threatened, may have reacted quickly and irrationally. But he carried a loaded weapon he was prepared to use. The brutality of this crime is an aggravating circumstance that may outweigh any mitigating circumstances such as the defendant's youth. Therefore the state moves for the application of the death penalty.'

I HAD A SEAFOOD LUNCH with Toba at The Jury Room, with Connie and Neil Zide at a table on the far side of the restaurant. We went back to the courtroom, and at a few minutes past 4pm the jury filed in and took their seats on the padded wooden chairs. The foreman rose; he was a retired electrical engineer with yellowing hair. He read from a slip of paper in his hand.

' "The jury advises and recommends to the court that it impose a sentence of life imprisonment upon Darryl Morgan without possibility of parole for twenty-five years." '

I met Connie Zide's eyes; she was nodding her head in what I knew was relief. Toba nodded at me too, and smiled. I looked across the table at Darryl Morgan. There was pure hatred in his gaze.

Judge Bill Eglin tapped his pen again. 'I want to remind you'—his voice instantly stilled the light murmur that had swept through the courtroom—'that I have the right to uphold or override the jury's recommendation.' He leaned forward, a pockmarked man in his late forties, and turned towards the jurors. 'I suspect y'all have cast your verdict on the basis of the defendant's youth. But I'm moved by Mr Jaffe's final argument. Now I ask you, is the convicted man penitent? Does he say those simple words we all want to hear: "I'm sorry"? You heard his outbursts! *He does not!*'

The judge was grimly quiet for a few moments.

'I find this a reprehensible crime. And I'm going to override the jury's recommendation. Darryl Morgan, I sentence you to death. I order that you be taken to the Florida State Prison and there be kept in close confinement until the date set for your execution. That on such day you be put to death by electrical current passed through your body. And may God have mercy on your soul.'

I couldn't believe what I had heard. Connie Zide, her face gone white, looked at me. There was nothing I could say, nothing I could do. Twelve years would pass before I would see her again.

I stared dully at the defendant, whose lips twisted in fury.

My college friend Kenny Buckram was a short, thick-chested man with the curly hair and friendly appearance of a teddy bear. Kenny, at forty-seven, was now the elected public defender for the Fourth Circuit of Florida. After Ruby had told me that Darryl Morgan was still alive and on death row, I telephoned Kenny myself at his Jacksonville office.

'You can't stay in a hotel,' Kenny said. 'That's crazy, Ted. I haven't seen you in years! I've got a house out by the beach, with plenty of room. I'm between wives.'

I flew to Jacksonville on Wednesday. At half past six that evening, carrying cold bottles of beer, Kenny and I walked onto Jacksonville Beach. Seagulls screeched in the cool evening air. I finally got round to telling Kenny what I had learned from Jerry Lee Elroy.

'But you were a prosecutor,' Kenny said. 'You're not telling me you didn't know there were people out there who'd sell their souls to get out of jail? Nickerson's supposed to have got a confession out of Morgan? OK, assume that's true. So he thinks, I'll hammer in an extra nail to make sure. No big deal to convince a rat like Elroy to lie. And it paid off, didn't it?'

'Why is it,' I asked gloomily, 'that I never smelt it?'

'Because,' Kenny said, 'you were really into denial, Ted. All Nickerson did was what half the guys in his shoes do all the time. And you should have known. Talk about snitches, listen to this. We investigated a complaint a few years ago—you remember Bongiorno, our local crime boss? This homicide detective was accused of planting a story in order to get Bongiorno on a murder-one rap. Bongiorno had political connections in Tallahassee, and he put a lot of heat out. The snitch changed his mind. They needed a fall guy—come to think of it, it was a fall gal—so they suspended the detective from JSO, and eventually she quit.'

'Kenny, never mind that. I need to find out what happened. Who lied, and why. Do you know where Nickerson is?'

'Long gone, and the sheriff's office isn't that buddy-buddy with me, these days. You'll have to go through Beldon. You still friends?'

'Sure we're friends. Why shouldn't we be?'

Kenny threw an arm round me affectionately. 'You're making too much of this. A snitch perjured himself. So what else is new?'

'But if Nickerson got Jerry Lee Elroy to lie, maybe Nickerson lied, too. Did that ever occur to you? It does to me.'

'But how are you gonna find out? Hunt him down and ask him? And even if he said, Yeah, I made it up—what would you do?'

I had no ready answer for that.

'Your office handled all the Morgan appeals, right?' I asked.

'Up to five years ago. Then the Florida legislature created a job called CCR—the Capital Collateral Representative. It's a political office in Tallahassee, and they take these cases at the review stage.'

'Can I see your files?'

He nodded.

After dinner I walked alone on the beach to listen to the Atlantic crash against the shore. Tiny shining white animals washed up on the sand with each succeeding wave. Things Kenny had said nibbled at my mind. Why do I need to get involved in this now?

I looked down the beach and realised that if I followed its wide path far enough to the south, I would reach Connie Zide's house. I knew she still lived there. Over the years bits and pieces of information came my way. Solly's estate had been divided into five portions: one part each to the two daughters; one part to Connie, one to Neil; and one divided among a clutch of southern universities.

Neil had stayed in the development business, surprising most people by parlaying the inherited millions into many more.

I walked back towards the cheerful lights of Kenny's house. See what you can find out tomorrow, I decided. A day is what you promised yourself. You have responsibilities elsewhere—to your family, your firm, to other clients. A day, then go home.

AT HOME THAT NIGHT, as I learned later, Toba was watching TV in the master bedroom. She had bathed and put on a bathrobe and slippers. She'd had a hard day at her real-estate office and was feeling just a tad sorry for herself. Nobody was buying houses, and even if they were of a mind to do so, they made ridiculously low offers. Sellers were saying, 'We'll wait until this bad period is over.'

Earlier, Toba had cooked lamb chops and French fries. Alan set the table with red linen napkins, took out his old Zippo and, with a flourish, lit a candle. Toba opened a bottle of cabernet sauvignon.

'Mom, the Becker kids are going sailing over the weekend down at Captiva Island. They've got an uncle who has a fifty-six-footer that sleeps seven or eight. They invited me. Can I go?'

'Of course you can. You're nineteen years old—you can do things like that without asking me.'

'We'll probably check out the nightlife on Captiva, which I'm sure is non-existent. But I don't like to be without any money, hang around like a parasite. I hate to ask, but—'

'Don't worry,' Toba said.

'You're great, Mom.'

'Just don't get too sunburned.'

After dinner she heard Alan on the phone in the den, leaving a message for someone to call him back. That was when Toba said good night and went upstairs to bathe. Now, in the bedroom, wrapped in her terry-cloth robe, she lay on the bed, supported by a special backrest with arms, while she watched *M*A*S*H*. I miss Cathy, Toba thought. It's hard when a daughter leaves home. In Ithaca, at Cornell, Cathy would be awake, studying. The question was, Wait until eleven, when the rates went down, or call now?

Toba picked up the phone.

Alan's voice filled her ear. 'Man, good and wasted! I'll get the money tomorrow for sure. It was hard tonight. She drives me crazy.'

Toba's cheeks heated up. She couldn't put down the phone.

A young male voice on the other end of the line said, 'One fantastic blast. Freakin' *wasted* is what we'll get.'

Far across the room, in the mirror above her dressing table, Toba could see the moronic look on her face. Her mouth had fallen open.

Alan said, 'Bobby's holding the stuff.'

'Gotta hang up, dude.'

Toba carefully replaced the receiver.

THE NEXT DAY, in one of the public defender's dusty storage rooms on the third floor of the courthouse, I thumbed through what was left of the *Florida* v. *Morgan* file. A memo told me that on August 22, 1986, most of the original documents had been shipped over to CCR in Tallahassee. At the time, the assistant public defender on the case had been someone named Brian Hoad.

I asked for him, and a legal intern looked up from a volume of Shepard's *Federal Citations*. 'Try courtroom four.'

I entered courtroom 4, on the second floor, and took a seat. It wasn't hard to pick out Brian Hoad, a pale man wearing glasses and sitting next to the defendant, a skinny black man. The prosecutor was a trim Hispanic woman in her thirties, wearing a dark blue suit.

At the recess I introduced myself and asked Hoad if we might talk in the snack bar. I paid for coffee and we sat down in two red plastic chairs. 'Is that a strong case you've got up there?' I asked.

'About as strong as this coffee,' Hoad said glumly.

'Then how come you're in trial?'

'This is a hard-nosed prosecutor. She wouldn't deal.'

'I wanted to talk to you about an old case. You handled the appeal. Darryl Morgan—first-degree murder. Back in seventy-nine.'

Hoad nodded a few times. 'Visible case. Shot Solomon Zide.'

'I was the trial prosecutor.'

'You?' Hoad laughed.

I frowned and said, 'I'm a defence attorney now, down in Sarasota. What's so funny?'

'Well, it's not really funny. It's just surprising. You're kind of a legend around here. You mind if I tell you something?'

'I hope I'm not going to mind.'

'I had that Morgan appeal in my case load for a long time. I've read that trial transcript three or four times. You did fine in the first stage. But in the punishment part, you just gave up.'

'I didn't want the Morgan kid to die.'

'Well, that didn't help me at all. My chief point on appeal was incompetent defence counsel in the sentencing phase. One of the judges up in Tallahassee commented, off the record, "Mr Hoad, just between us, it may have been the other way round." '

I sighed. 'You had the appeal from the beginning?'

He nodded. 'But I didn't get over to Tallahassee until eighty-one. Hopeless. Then we got turned down in the Eleventh Circuit. Didn't have anything to take to the feds in Atlanta, but I went anyway. That's the name of the game. Keep your man alive.'

I told him about Elroy's 1979 deal in exchange for perjury.

'And the cop, Nickerson—he set that up?'

'If Elroy's telling the truth.'

Hoad seemed excited. 'Will your client testify to that?'

'There'd have to be something in it for him.'

He looked at his watch. 'I have to get back to court.'

Going up in the elevator, I said, 'Why did you get so involved with this case?'

'Have you ever been to Raiford, Mr Jaffe?'

'No.'

'An execution is not something you quickly forget. You know, they're having one the day after tomorrow. A local boy—Sweeting. Remember him? Killed a pair of co-eds at Jacksonville eight years ago. Well, he dies on Saturday. You should go and watch Eric Sweeting pay for his sins. Then you'll understand why I get involved.'

The elevator stopped at the second floor. The woman prosecutor was waiting for us. She said to Hoad, 'Can I talk to you?'

They talked; then Hoad returned, the prosecutor preceding him, heels clicking, moving briskly on strong legs into the courtroom. She carried her head high and didn't smile. She was good-looking.

'Making any progress?' I asked.

'Suarez is backing off,' Hoad said. 'Looks like she'll cut a deal.'

'That's Muriel Suarez?' She was the assistant state attorney who had prosecuted Jerry Lee Elroy and let him go.

'Right.'

'I'll hang out for a while,' I said. 'Maybe we can have lunch together.'

BY NOON THE ROBBERY case in courtroom 4 was history. The prosecutor, Muriel Suarez, and the public defender, Brian Hoad, shook hands, and both went off to lunch with me.

In Worman's Deli, near the federal courthouse, at a table at the back, Suarez, Hoad and I had corned-beef sandwiches. When we were finished, Hoad stood and said, 'Folks, I've got a woman over in the jail pleaded guilty to possession. I have to get over there.'

'I've got the bill,' I said. 'I'll call you about the Morgan file.'

When he had gone, Muriel Suarez said, 'That name rings a bell.'

I brought her up to date.

'I remember the case. Floyd Nickerson told me Elroy was a creep, but a reliable creep. Gap in his teeth, right? I remember him.' Her eyes moved away and she reached for her mug of beer.

'Carmen Tanagra was the other detective on the Zide case. She have anything to do with Elroy?' I asked.

'She was Nickerson's partner. I knew her. But it was Nickerson who came to me and proposed the deal.'

'Tanagra still around?'

Muriel shook her head. 'Got more or less kicked out. She wasn't a smart cop. I mean, she was a good woman, but they corrupted her.'

Something clicked in my memory. 'Was she by any chance involved in the Bongiorno episode? The cop who got the snitch to lie?'

'Right. They nailed her to the wall. She didn't like it, so she quit,' Muriel said, an edge in her voice. Then she smiled and looked at me with more cheerful eyes. They were dark and Latin; they actually flashed. 'So, Mr Civil Lawyer, what are you going to do about this?'

'Morgan's still alive. Barely. They're executing him in April.'

'You think you could get him a new trial?'

'I could try for a stay of execution.'

'You care if he lives or dies?'

'Yes, I do,' I said, with a vigour that surprised me. And so I repeated it. 'I care. And I'm going to do something about it.'

'You losing any sleep? That's my standard. You hit the pillow and pass out, you're OK.'

'Do you always hit the pillow and pass out?'

'Not lately,' Muriel said. 'One of my first cases as a felony prosecutor was Eric Sweeting. They're burning him Saturday down at Raiford. And I'm going to be there when they pull the switch.'

'Why do you want to do *that*?'

'Because when I did the case eight years ago, the morning before I asked the jury to bring in a verdict of death, I looked in the mirror and said, "Muriel, this is not a statistic you read in a book. This is a human being, and you're arguing in favour of his being killed. If you haven't got the guts to witness that execution, you shouldn't argue in favour of it." So I promised myself, if it ever happened, I'd go.'

'It's brave of you to go down there,' I said.

'I know,' Muriel said.

THAT EVENING, on the porch of his house in the black neighbourhood where he'd always lived, Beldon Ruth brought out a pitcher of iced tea and settled down in a rocking chair to talk to me. 'I still believe we're on the side of the angels,' he was saying. 'And you defence guys, you do your job, but you don't really help people. The PD's office has got the right idea. Churn 'em out, cut a deal. Hired lawyers waste time trying to show clients they're earning their fee.'

'You're a disgusting old cynic.'

'I'm a disgusting old realist.'

'Why did you ever become a lawyer?' I asked him.

'Fascination of aberrant behaviour,' Beldon said, and let that hang in the air while he poured the tea. Laurette, his wife, was inside the house, preparing dinner.

I hadn't come back to Jacksonville to be lectured, not even by Beldon. I was on his porch because I had new information that I was obliged to turn over to the state attorney, and I had done so.

I said to Beldon, 'What are you going to do about it?'

'Not a thing,' he replied, 'other than to add it to my long list of incidents that tend to prove that the human race at best is capable of anything under the sun, and at worst is generally no good.'

It wasn't exactly a complete vision. I ground my teeth, but didn't comment. 'Where's Floyd Nickerson these days?'

'I somehow thought you'd ask that. He left the sheriff's office nine years ago and went over to Gainesville. Chief of security in a big country-club development. Place called Orange Meadow.'

'Who's the developer he works for? Do you know that?'

After just the barest hesitation, Beldon said, 'ZiDevco.'

I made up my mind the next day, a couple of hours before I was due at the airport. I called Muriel Suarez at her office.

'You want to *see* it?' she asked.

'I want to be there. Then I'll decide if I want to actually see it.'

She called the superintendent at Raiford and requested that I be put on the list. Then she rang me back. 'Done. They allow twelve witnesses other than the media goons.'

We arranged to meet at her place on Washington Street. I called home and Alan answered on the first ring. 'Bobby?'

'No, it's me. How're you doing, kid?'

'Fine, Dad. I was just reading by the pool.'

I liked hearing that. There was hope. 'I've been thinking about our talk the other night. If you're ready to leave that drug programme now, it's fine with me. Where's Mom?'

'Taking a nap upstairs.'

'I was supposed to come home today from Jacksonville, but I have to postpone. Tell her I'll be back tomorrow.'

Alan said he'd write a note; he was leaving in another hour for a weekend of sailing at Captiva. I called Royal, Kelly and spoke to Ruby, who recited a list of death threats from my partners, who needed me on other cases.

'I didn't hear any of that,' I said.

That night, at his house by the beach, Kenny Buckram told me he had a date in St Augustine. 'I probably won't be back until morning,' he said. 'So you are the lord of the manor. You have plans?'

'A late date. Four in the morning.'

'YOUR CAR OR MINE?' Muriel asked.

At four o'clock in the morning, we stood in the cool darkness in front of her house on Washington Street. 'I'm driving a rental. Let's give the wear and tear to Mr Hertz.'

Through silent streets we headed out of town on Interstate 10.

'Twenty miles,' Muriel said, 'and then you bear south on 121.'

We drove through the darkness, past mobile homes and darkened

Baptist churches. Scrub palm grew thick in the sand hills, and the night air brought the smell of woodsmoke.

I followed the signs and turned west on the Raiford road. Some scruffy palm trees rose against a lemony dawn sky. Concertina wire stretched between electrified fences and machine-gun towers.

At the base of a gun tower in front of the prison, a telephone sat in a niche. Muriel spoke into it, and a voice on a speaker told us to proceed to the first gate. We walked through a series of gates into an indoor reception area with peach-coloured walls. The linoleum floors smelt of fresh wax. The air was chilly and musty. Identities were checked. We passed through a metal detector.

Our escort was a clean-shaven, thin-lipped young Florida State Prison administrative assistant who introduced himself as Fred Olsen. He wore a pale grey suit, a pale grey tie and shiny black shoes.

'I'll be taking you through the procedure,' he said quietly.

He led us down a long waxed hall, through a door into a cafeteria with light green walls. The other witnesses were there: reporters, officials, the lawyer who had handled Sweeting's appeals, the father of one of Sweeting's victims and an uncle of the other one. Sweeting's mother sat with the appeal attorney.

'Coffee?' Olsen asked. 'There's no charge.'

When Olsen left, I asked Muriel if she knew the appeal attorney.

'Sure.'

'What kind of a job did he do?'

'Thorough. But he didn't stand a chance.'

'Do they ever?'

'Sometimes. Weird things happen.'

Olsen came back with the coffee. 'Would you like me to tell you the rest of the procedure?' he asked. 'It's what we recommend. It spares you any surprises.'

I heard myself say, 'All right.'

Muriel nodded. There were dark smudges under her eyes.

Olsen reached into the pocket of his jacket and consulted an index card. 'For the last five days, Mr Sweeting has been under surveillance by an officer who sits outside the cell and records in writing every fifteen minutes what the condemned is doing. Four days ago, Mr Sweeting was asked to inventory his property and indicate its disposition, and to specify his funeral arrangements. He requested standard burial and was measured for a suit of clothing. Yesterday, twenty-four hours before execution, our chef took Mr Sweeting's order for his last meal. Would you like to know what he ordered?'

Muriel grunted softly, a word or two that I couldn't understand.

Olsen looked at another card. 'Mr Sweeting ordered a sirloin-steak dinner, a pint of chocolate ice cream with hot fudge, a Coca-Cola and a large-size buttered popcorn—all of which we were able to provide. This meal was served at four thirty this morning, following the condemned's final visit with a clergyman of his choice. Any questions?'

Muriel and I shook our heads in the negative.

Olsen said, 'The rest has to do with the execution procedure, which you'll witness shortly. Witnesses will be escorted at five forty-five to the witness room of the execution chamber in Q wing. At six o'clock, an FSP administrative assistant, namely myself, three designated electricians, two correctional officers, a physician and a physician's assistant will be assembled in the death chamber.

'Meanwhile, the condemned will have his head and right calf shaved to better conduct the electrical charge. Conducting gel will be applied to his scalp and shaved leg. The prison superintendent, Mr Tate, will read the death warrant one final time to the condemned. The condemned will be strapped into the chair. He will be permitted to make a last brief statement. A conducting sponge and cap will be placed on his head. I might mention,' Olsen added, 'that last night I and my colleague, Clive Crocker, noticed that the sponge to be used this morning was, to say the least, dirty. So we went out and purchased a brand-new, clean sponge. I don't think they *ever* had changed that other sponge, if you can believe such a thing.'

Under the table I dug my fingers into the muscles of my legs.

'Mr Wright, the assistant superintendent of this facility, will then engage the circuit breaker. The chief electrician will activate the panel, Mr Tate will signal the executioner to throw the switch, and the automatic cycle will begin. Once it's run its course, the physician will pronounce the condemned as dead.'

'Who's the executioner?' Muriel asked quietly.

'An anonymous local private citizen dressed in a black hood and robe,' Olsen said. 'He'll be paid one hundred and fifty dollars.'

'How many volts?' I asked.

'Two thousand, four hundred.'

'And it takes . . . how long?'

'Oh, instantaneous. Perhaps a few seconds. You may see some movement, but I assure you, consciousness ends instantly.'

Fred Olsen excused himself to go to the bathroom.

I stared into Muriel's eyes. The pupils were dilated. She said, 'I don't know if I can go through with this.'

'Then let's skip it.'

'No. I've got to do it. I took a vow. Will you come with me?' She gripped my wrist. 'Please help me.'

'All right,' I said.

INSIDE Q WING, we were led to rows of white wooden chairs. The chairs faced a glass wall. On the other side of the glass, about fifteen feet away, was a high-backed, solid oak chair with black straps.

The condemned shuffled into the death chamber. He was manacled at his ankles, and his wrists were cuffed to a waist chain.

Sweeting, twenty-seven, looked like a freckled boy dressed for an adult party. He wore a red and blue striped tie that hung well below his waist, a white button-down dress shirt that was too big for him, baggy dark blue suit trousers, black socks. He was about five foot four, thin and sinewy. His mother waved to him.

Fred Olsen was in the death chamber, as were a doctor in a white coat, the doctor's assistant, the superintendent, his assistant, three electricians, two bulky correctional officers, and a small man dressed in a black gown and a hood with a slit for vision.

For some time I had been hearing a regular rhythmic sound, like a feebly ticking drumbeat. Now it grew louder. I looked to my left, two seats away, where Olsen's colleague, Clive Crocker, was seated.

Crocker leaned over to whisper. 'The men on death row know our schedule. They tap on the bars with plastic spoons. I think we can assume it's a form of saying goodbye.'

The correctional officers unchained Sweeting. One of them said, 'Sit down here, please.'

The men helped Sweeting up into the chair, then cinched the various leather straps round his waist, legs and arms.

We heard Olsen ask, 'Would you like to say a few words?'

'Yes, please,' Sweeting said, and turned towards the visitors. 'Goodbye, all. Goodbye, Mama.'

'Goodbye, son,' Mrs Sweeting called.

'Merciful God,' Muriel murmured.

I took her hand, gripped it as if we were husband and wife.

'I'm sorry for what happened,' Sweeting said. 'But I guess y'all know that. So . . . I'm ready to begin my journey.'

Muriel groaned. I clasped her other hand as well.

The superintendent read the death warrant a final time. One of the officers placed a black hood over Sweeting's face. The other officer tilted Sweeting's head back and fastened a chin strap round his small jaw. The new sponge was wedged inside the top of the hood. Electrodes led from the hood to the control box, set in the wall. The first man fastened a second set of electrodes to Sweeting's calf.

He signalled to the hooded executioner. Thumbs up. The executioner pushed the button in the control box.

The automatic cycle began. Lights dimmed. Sweeting's body jerked and he moaned softly, as if in sleep.

334

Blue and yellow flames shot from Sweeting's head, firing radiantly upwards and outwards like the corona of the sun during a total eclipse. Sweeting screamed. Mrs Sweeting started to blubber.

In the witness room with us, Clive Crocker jumped to his feet. Sweeting kept screaming. The flames continued to leap upwards.

The executioner released the switch.

'We seem to have a problem,' Crocker said quietly to the rest of us in the witness room. 'But I'm sure it will be remedied.'

The electricians busily readjusted the straps and the electrodes. In a minute or so they signalled thumbs up a second time. Nodding, the executioner pushed the switch a second time.

The flames jumped forth from Sweeting's shaved skull and out on all sides through the black hood. Sweeting's screams became the baying of a hurt dog. His little body twisted against the straps.

Through it all, the other men on death row beat with their spoons against the bars. Mrs Sweeting buried her head in her arms and whimpered prayers. The electricians shouted something again, and again the executioner removed his finger from the button.

Sweeting shrieked, 'My eyes are on fire! I can't breathe!'

On the third try, fourteen minutes after the first jolt of electricity had surged into his body, Sweeting was pronounced legally dead.

Olsen entered the witness room, wiping sweat from his neck. 'The sentence of the state of Florida has been carried out. Please exit from the rear and proceed to the van.'

In the hallway, Muriel clung to my arm, shuddering.

The dirty sponge that had stood the test of so many executions was a natural sponge. The one that Crocker and Olsen had bought was made of nylon, and when two thousand, four hundred volts rocketed through it, it had caught fire. Blue fire. My nightmare.

I couldn't stand the thought that in some way I was responsible for Darryl Morgan's being sent to this place, where he would suffer, if not the same corrupt fate as Eric Sweeting, then a similar one. Whatever it took, I swore, I was going to save Darryl Morgan's life.

STILL WEARING HER NIGHTGOWN under a terry-cloth bathrobe, Toba curled against silk pillows on one of the sofas in the living room. Slanting afternoon sunlight beat against the picture window facing west. A half-full bottle of Chablis stood on the coffee table.

'I'm going to brew coffee,' I said. 'While I do that, you drink this glass of water. Then I'll cook some scrambled eggs and make some wholewheat toast.'

Toba sat up straighter and put down her glass. 'Ted, you haven't asked me *why* I'm drunk.'

I patted her shoulder. 'I will, after I've fed you. I love you, and I'm trying to be kind to you, not ask a lot of questions.'

She began to weep.

After eating, we sat by the edge of the pool in the early evening light. Toba was drinking her third mug of decaf.

'I just can't get it through my head,' I said. 'You heard this telephone conversation on Wednesday evening. You didn't say anything to him then, you didn't tell me, and on Friday afternoon you just let the kid go. What's the matter with you, Toba?'

'I couldn't handle it. If you had heard them—'

'I know how young men speak.'

'He said, "I couldn't squeeze the money out of her tonight because she drives me crazy!" It just wasn't *him* speaking.'

'It was him. That's the first thing we have to accept.'

She sighed tremulously. 'So what now?'

'Maybe another drug programme. Therapy, psychiatry—I don't know yet. I need some straight answers.'

Evening descended; the land that we could see across Sarasota Bay looked like a picture blotted with ink.

'You think they might have been boasting?' Toba asked. 'You know, being macho, not really telling the truth . . .'

'Toba!'

She hung her head. In the twilight, I clasped her hand. The second time in one day I had held a woman's hand to give comfort.

ON MONDAY MORNING, after Royal, Kelly's weekly partners' meeting, I appeared at the Criminal Justice Building at eleven for a meeting with Buddy Capra, the hard-nosed assistant state attorney handling the case against Elroy. Capra informed me that the sheriff's department had checked Elroy's fingerprints with the computer. He had four prior convictions under various names.

'Buddy,' I said, 'this case may be a bonanza for you guys—if you can cut a deal.'

He and I talked for nearly an hour with Charlie Waldorf, his boss, and then I met Elroy in a little bar on Main Street. I ordered oysters.

'Did you find any witnesses to back up your story?' I asked.

'A couple, yeah.'

'Who are they?'

'Well, one's in Miami. He's in a little trouble. He can't—'

'Forget him. Who's the other?'

'My sister. She lives in Orlando.'

'Was she here in Sarasota those three days before the cops picked you up with that cocaine in your trunk?'

336

'If she says she was, who's to say she wasn't?'

'You're out of your mind, Elroy. Forget it.'

The oysters arrived. I let Elroy ramble for a while, offering theories of how the cocaine got in the trunk of the car. Then I said, 'Let me lay this out for you as simply as I can. You have no reliable witnesses. If you go to trial, a fingerprint expert will swear that your prints were on those plastic Baggies. And when that happens, you are headed to Raiford for a twenty-year bit.'

'OK, OK. You made your point.' Elroy began to pick nervously at his thumb. 'So what's the deal you can get me?'

'I spoke to Charlie Waldorf, the state attorney here. He got on the horn to Robert Diaz, the state attorney in Miami. They know you over there, know who you work for. Guys named Ramos and Palomino, right? I'll give you the bacon without the sizzle, Elroy. Give them Ramos and Palomino, you walk away laughing.'

'I can't do that,' Elroy said quietly. 'They'll inch me.'

'I told you, there's a witness protection programme.'

Elroy mulled that over for a minute. 'Where would I go?'

'Far away. California, Oregon, maybe North Dakota.'

Elroy nodded gloomily. 'I don't wanna go somewhere and freeze. California sounds OK, but forget North Dakota.'

'There's another part of the deal,' I said. 'The business twelve years ago, with that guy Morgan. You'll have to retract that testimony.'

'Are you kidding? Go up there and face a perjury rap? No way.'

'The statute's run out on your testimony. They can't prosecute.'

Elroy considered this. 'When?' he asked.

'Soon. First you provide an affidavit. Then you testify. Then you give them Ramos and Palomino. Then you go to California.'

'Let me think about it.'

'Elroy, you have no choice. It's part of the deal.'

It wasn't, of course. Neither Waldorf nor his counterpart in Miami would have stood still for that. I was lying to one client in order to save the life of another one—maybe. No matter how much I tried to justify it, I knew I had no right as a lawyer to do it.

And I didn't care.

I KNEW A BIT about things such as laserless holograms, DNA replication, Picasso's blue period, Van Allen belts, even gout. But I did not know how to talk to my own son.

On Sunday night, when Alan returned home from Captiva, I had faced him with what his mother had overheard.

'I don't yet know how to handle this,' I said. 'So let's both ponder it awhile. Then you come and talk to me. Cards on the table.'

When I reached home at seven o'clock the next day, sweaty and ready for a swim, Toba was waiting by the side of the pool.

'Alan talked to me,' she said. 'He thinks you don't respect him. You're disappointed in him.'

'He's right,' I said.

'He's depressed. His father's a high-powered lawyer. His mother, in his view, is a successful real-estate agent. His sister's a whiz kid off at an Ivy League college. And he's a failure. Drugs are the only solace in his life, he says. Marijuana is his best friend.'

I raised my eyes to heaven.

'And worst of all,' Toba said, 'I think he's suicidal.'

I felt my shoulders sag, my heart seize up with despair.

'He says he climbs into his car, drives across the causeway, and he gets this urge to shut his eyes. But then he says to himself, "Dad'll be furious, and it'll ruin Mom's life." '

'Did you tell him that was the understatement of the year?'

'No. I just cried.'

That's what I wanted to do. This was my son's life. I would have given anything for none of this to be true.

'Ted, what are we going to do?'

But I had no answer. I was heartsick. Unless I could intervene, my son, like Darryl Morgan, was on the road to death.

In late February I flew to Jacksonville, rented a car at the airport, and drove straight out to Raiford again, and to death row.

At the main building of the prison, I was expected. My ID was checked, I passed through the metal detector and I was led into the cool office of the assistant superintendent. A placard on the desk read RAYMOND G. WRIGHT.

There were two telephones on the desk: a red instrument to communicate with the outside world, a black one to communicate within the prison. Wright wore a white button-down shirt and a striped tie. A creased brown suit jacket hung on a wooden clothes tree in the corner of the room. I remembered seeing Wright for a minute or two in the death chamber when they had electrocuted Sweeting.

'We don't get many prosecutors visiting here,' Wright said.

'You may have misunderstood. I'm not a prosecutor now,' I said, handing him my card. 'The man I want to visit is Darryl Morgan.'

'You're Wizard's attorney?'

'Who is Wizard?'

'That's what the guards call Mr Morgan.'

'No, I'm not his attorney yet. But I will be. I've just come from Tallahassee, from CCR—they're handling his current appeal.'

Wright said, 'But you're not on Mr Morgan's visiting list.'

'I prosecuted Morgan,' I said.

Understandably, this seemed to baffle the assistant superintendent. But he reached for the black telephone.

THE ATTORNEYS' INTERVIEW rooms were in the main building. There were two folding metal chairs and a metal table. Through a glass wall a correctional officer could observe, but couldn't hear.

In another room, Darryl Morgan was strip-searched. His waist chain and handcuffs were removed. I stood up when he entered. I avoided his eyes, conscious only of a physically large, dark presence.

Darryl Morgan was thirty-two years old now. If I hadn't known that, I would have guessed him to be forty. There was grey in the kinky black hair above the temples. The eyes no longer smouldered with anger. They were wintry with resignation. They were old.

I realised that he didn't recognise me. 'You know who I am?'

'They tell me you're a lawyer. You looks familiar.'

'I was at your trial,' I said. 'I was the prosecutor.'

Morgan slowly nodded his huge head up and down.

'Ted Jaffe is my name. Do you remember me?'

Morgan nodded again. The eyes barely changed. After a minute he said, 'Why're you here?'

'To try to help you.' That was all I could think of.

'You help me best by getting the hell out of here.'

I had expected that and believed I could deal with it. 'I understand how you feel, Mr Morgan.'

'You do?'

Abruptly, I felt drained. All that was left was my sense of foolishness. I was an intrusion here, my presence a terrible tampering with what remained of a condemned man's life.

'Darryl,' I begged, 'please listen to me. I have some new information. I know that your cellmate back in Duval County Jail, Jerry Lee Elroy, lied about hearing you confess. If this comes to light, it could win a new appeal for you—maybe even a new trial.'

Morgan, through all this, kept shaking his head. 'You're crazy, man. You put me here.'

'Yes, I did. I was part of that process.'

'Something's wrong,' Morgan muttered.

'I need to ask you a lot of questions.'

'Get out of here.'

'You have nothing to lose.'

'You always got something to lose,' he said. 'Some kind of flimflam here. I told you, I ain't interested.'

'Darryl, I don't work for them any more.'

'You still think I kill that man.'

He was right, but I couldn't tell him that. 'What I think doesn't matter,' I said carefully.

'Better you split,' Morgan said. 'I kill you, what I got to lose?'

'You just said you always have something to lose.'

'Maybe you right and I wrong. Forty-four days, they gone kill me. What do I care if they kill me for doing you, too? Who deserve it more than you and that snitch and that cop?'

There was a light in his eyes now.

'Take it easy,' I said. I had to dominate him. Every lawyer has to dominate his client. In this case, it was a little more necessary than usual. Morgan was a big, powerful man. I held my ground.

'I tell you how it is,' Morgan said. 'They take my cards and my magic stuff away from me, and my cards and my magic was all I got. They hurting me over there, waiting on Big Wooden Mama. The real mean thing what they done in here is keep me waiting. Twelve years gone by. Every day go round, it come in my mind, "When all this be over with?" Feeding me to Mama, they ending my hurt. I get rid of you, dude who put me here, maybe they do me faster.'

I watched him rise from his chair and glide towards me. I didn't have the power to move an inch. I just waited for him.

THE ROOM SLOWLY resolved into focus; it had a sharp smell of disinfectant. 'Rest here for a while,' a voice said.

I didn't argue. My fingers trembled when I held my hands out. I had been taken from the visiting cubicle to the prison hospital. The doctor, a pale young man, said nothing had been broken. My larynx was bruised, that was all. There would be some discomfort for a day or two; I'd be better off talking only when necessary.

I asked the doctor, 'What happened back there?'

'An inmate tried to strangle you. The guards subdued him.'

After I had signed the necessary release papers, I left the prison.

In Jacksonville, I checked into the Marina Hotel, showered, then called Ruby at the office. 'What's new, sweetness?'

'Jerry Lee Elroy wants to know what he's supposed to do.'

'If he calls again, remind him not to leave town. And be cool.'

'I have difficulty hearing you, Ted. Do you have laryngitis?'

'Something like that. Who else called?'

'Waldorf. Says, "Do we have a deal? Miami needs to know."'

'If he calls again, tell him, yes, be cool, I believe we do.'

'Your partners are in varying states of apoplexy.'

'Same message. Be cool. I'll be back on Monday.'

'Are you in the Caribbean with a girlfriend?'

'Goodbye, Ruby.'

I called home. 'How is Alan?'

Toba's voice, like the weather at the end of summer, had a chilly edge. 'He's all right. Today he's at the beach.'

'I'll try to be back by the weekend.'

'Were you out carousing last night?'

'Yes, at the law library. I have a sore throat. I love you.'

She didn't say it back to me, as she usually did.

I put in a call to Brian Hoad at the public defender's office. He had gone but had left me a message: an address I needed.

I LEFT THE MARINA HOTEL at seven fifteen the next morning. A lot of concrete had been poured in Jacksonville since I was a boy; gone were the old savannahs, the wild marsh along the river. Now I drove from strip mall to strip mall, to intersection after intersection. I crossed the Main Street Bridge, and fifteen minutes later stood in front of Carmen Tanagra's front door on Alabama Avenue. The small wooden house was set back from the sidewalk. A plaque by the side of the door gave the following information:

CARMEN TANAGRA

CRYSTAL BALANCING NUTRITIONAL THERAPY

IRIDOLOGY HERBALISM KINESIOLOGY

I rang the bell.

Carmen Tanagra came to the door. I recognised her from her days as a detective: she looked older, but she also looked healthier.

'Ms Tanagra, may I come in? I'm not here to talk about the Bongiorno case.'

In the living room five minutes later, I drank chicory coffee and ate a croissant. I decided I'd better move things along. 'You don't have any connections still with the sheriff's department?'

Carmen Tanagra shook her head firmly. 'And I don't want any. They dump the good cops and keep the bad.'

'You don't miss it at all?'

'What's to miss? Carrying a gun? I have a better life now. Look, Mr Jaffe, what is it that you want?'

'Do you remember the Solomon Zide murder?'

Carmen Tanagra gazed at me waspishly for a few seconds. From her throat blared a harsh sound that might have been a laugh.

'The black kid in the truck at the Lil' Champ,' she said. 'The one who got killed. William Smith was his name.'

'Didn't Floyd Nickerson shoot him when he was escaping?'

In response, Carmen Tanagra made that harsh sound again. 'That's what our report said.'

So there was that, too. I was getting in even deeper. I told her what I had learned from Jerry Lee Elroy.

Tanagra said, 'Uh-huh.'

'You're not surprised,' I said. 'So Nickerson must have told you himself that it was not true.'

'I don't recall what he told me.'

'Morgan is still on death row. They're supposed to pull the switch in April. But there was one witness at his trial who lied.'

Tanagra said, 'And you want to know if there was a second one.'

My heartbeat quickened and I put a clamp on my tongue.

'If I told you there was,' she said, 'what would you want of me?'

I leaned forward in my chair. 'I'd want you to make a statement under oath. Back it up at an appeal hearing.'

'Mr Jaffe, let me tell you a story. A while ago, JSO made a big bust, including some guys in two Mercedes. Amazingly, the two Mercedes wind up in the garages of two high-ranking police officers. But one day a file clerk down at the courthouse snitched on them. The cops had to give back the Mercedes. Were they prosecuted? No, sir. You hear of any resignation? No, sir. The file clerk, though, *he* has to resign. Now he's a cook in a short-order joint downtown. You see what I'm saying? If I snitch on Floyd Nickerson, it won't matter how long ago he was a cop.'

'They busted *you* in the Bongiorno case,' I said, 'and you were a cop.'

'To be in the brotherhood, you have to be a man. That time in the Gambrel murder, the snitch I had was for real. But Bongiorno had real good friends in Tallahassee. Money and political clout is what it came down to. The snitch changed his story and I got dumped. And if I do what you'd like me to do . . .' She drew a finger across her throat. 'I don't have a licence to practise. I could wind up taking orders for grits and eggs.'

'William Smith is dead. There's another man on death row waiting to be executed. Don't you think one dead is enough?'

'I can't help you,' she said, putting down her coffee cup.

'I could subpoena you,' I said. 'You'd have to tell the truth.'

Carmen Tanagra got up from her chair and walked across the room. She banged open the front door. 'Don't bother coming back,' she said.

The rest of the morning I spent in the library at the public defender's office. In the early afternoon I went to the courthouse to visit a judge I knew. I asked him a favour he had the power to grant, and at three o'clock I climbed into the rental car and headed west again on I-10. Twenty-five minutes later I took the now-familiar turnoff south onto State 121. I recognised landmarks: the Country Variety Store, the sagging white clapboard Raiford Road Church. Tuning the radio to a country-music station, I snapped my fingers to the beat.

Back in Sarasota were my wife and son and law firm: problems closer to the bone. This was as good a way as any to keep all that in remission. And to recapture whatever it was I had lost in the last decades. I remembered how once I had wanted to be of service, how my deepest ambition had been to argue a case before the Supreme Court and save an innocent man's life. In the quest for comfort and security, somehow that had faded. Do we do the right thing, I wondered, by giving up our youthful fantasies?

But I might not have to now, for I'd found what I wanted in those old dusty files at the courthouse. Darryl Morgan was six foot six. Now I knew that Neil Zide, on that bloody December night at the beach a dozen years earlier, had not described him as tall.

AT HIS DESK, Assistant Superintendent Raymond G. Wright made a humming sound. 'Mr Jaffe, after yesterday's unfortunate incident of violence, I have a right to deny your request to visit Darryl Morgan.'

'If you deny my right to visit,' I replied, 'I'll have a court order from Judge Krawitz in Jacksonville on your desk by ten o'clock tomorrow morning.'

Wright's hands rested on the desk, motionless, like empty gloves. He said, 'In the light of what happened, we'll have to cuff and chain and shackle your client. You can talk to him on the row. In his cell.'

I looked into Wright's pale eyes. 'All right,' I said.

Wright smiled smugly. 'What we need, then, is for Wizard to agree to the visit. If he doesn't, all this is beside the point. Not even a judge can force an inmate to talk to a lawyer.'

'You're absolutely right,' I said. 'Tell him that I think he may be innocent. And I intend to save his life.'

THERE IS A GREAT DEAL about Darryl Morgan that I learned, then and later, but I'm going to tell it now.

Darryl's first beef was larceny, after he had boosted a tape deck from a Chrysler New Yorker and been caught trying to pawn it. Looking down from the bench, the judge said, 'I want to help you, son. And I think the kind of help you need is jail therapy, because it'll make you think about the consequences of your acts. Let's try six months to a year at ACI.'

Apalachia Correctional Institute was in Liberty County, west of Tallahassee. Darryl was fifteen when he entered ACI. He was housed in dorm 5, a ramshackle white wooden building. His neighbours were seventeen-year-old boys named Hubert and William. William's last name was Smith, and he was destined to die outside the Lil' Champ food store some four years later in Jacksonville.

At ACI, Darryl learned a new language. Your house was your bed, your slice of territory. The hole was solitary confinement. A shank was a knife made from the guts of an iron cot. A one-year sentence was a bullet, five a nickel, ten a dime, twenty-five a quarter.

After seven months Darryl returned to Jacksonville. For a while he had a job at a car wash. He found a girlfriend named Pauline. When Pauline got pregnant, he needed money to pay for an abortion. A friend said, 'Be cool. We go down to the beach tonight. Find us some dudes with cash in their jeans.'

Using planks of wood to threaten, they jackrolled drunks for two weeks, and on the third weekend were caught by an undercover cop. The juvenile-court judge sentenced Darryl to a year at the Arthur C. Dozier School for Boys.

The boys lived in bunks with armed guards outside. When it grew dark, there was nothing to do except talk and play cards. Darryl made friends with two boys named Hog and Isaac.

Isaac had two decks of playing cards under his pillow. He said to Darryl, 'You got big hands. I teach you to shuffle the cards good, do some tricks. We do some neat things.' At lunch breaks he showed Darryl how to shuffle so the cards didn't change places, how to make a one-hand cut, how to deal off the bottom of the deck.

Back on the street after eight months, Darryl discovered that Pauline had gone to Miami. He decided to go down there and claim her and his possible child. But he had no money. He was seventeen. He could work as a dishwasher, janitor, porter, maybe a mechanic or a carpenter if he learned how. Pump gas.

Don't know how to do this, don't know how to do that, he thought. What I know? Know how to jackroll drunks, bust windows.

So he snatched fifty dollars from a Burger King cash register, but was picked up by the cops that evening in Jacksonville—he was too recognisable. He did four months in Clay County Jail.

A few months later he was caught with goods from an auto-parts warehouse burglary. He was eighteen, an adult, and he drew seven years. The joint was called Branville. Isaac was at Branville, and so was Darryl's old friend from ACI, William Smith. Isaac was in the same cell block, happy with his decks of cards. He ran a little poker game, won a few cartons of cigarettes a week. Stupid, Darryl thought. Got to be something better. But what? Eighteen, and this all I know.

On parole after nineteen months in residence at Branville, he returned home to Jacksonville to bunk down on the wooden boards of the back porch of his mother's clapboard house. He worked for a while pumping gas in a Mobil station.

Then one day he went to A.J., his so-called stepfather, at the golf club where he worked as a grounds keeper. He asked for help.

To Darryl's surprise, a few days later A.J. told him that a friend named James was head gardener at a fancy beach estate. James did the hiring of all grounds-keeping staff. They needed a handyman.

That was August 1978. The following April, twenty minutes after sentencing by Judge Bill Eglin, shackled at the ankles and cuffed to a waist chain, Darryl found himself headed for Raiford and death row.

A SEMICIRCLE OF THICK black iron protruded from the wall next to the toilet. The shackles and chains wrapped round Darryl's ankles and waist were looped through the ring bolt. The handcuffs were shackled to the steel waist chain. Darryl sat on the concrete floor of his cell, back braced against the wall, long legs splayed out like a pair of scissors ready to close. He didn't smile.

Two guards seated themselves on the catwalk in opposite directions, each one on a metal chair about fifteen feet away.

I sat at the foot of Darryl's bed. In my lap I had a tape recorder and a yellow legal pad. I said to Darryl, 'I can help you.'

'Why you come back?' he asked, his eyes unblinking.

'I made a choice. Coming back is part of it. Tell me, why do they call you Wizard?'

'If I had a deck of cards, turkey, I'd show you.'

'What can you do?'

For the first time, Darryl chuckled. 'Sweet deception,' he said, 'is the name of the game. I can do things with cards, make you think I's a real magician. You don't gonna believe what I can do.'

'Why did they take away all your magic stuff?'

'This is Q block. They take all you got. What you want from me?'

'I want you to tell me what happened the night you went to rob the Zides' house at Jacksonville Beach.'

'You not gonna believe it. You never did believe it.'

'Try me.'

HE DIDN'T LIKE THE JOB at the Zides' because the chief gardener, James, a sinewy, bald old man, got on his case all the time. Cutting the grass too short, boy. Too long, boy. He was given the job of hunting all over the estate to clean up after the dogs.

The lady had one dog already, Paco, the eight-year-old Doberman guard dog, and now she'd just bought a pair of three-month-old puppies and turned them loose on the lawns.

Darryl rapped now and then with Terence, the chief security guard, and Terence told him that James never taught anything to his assistants. He was sixty-three years old and fearful he would be put out to pasture in favour of someone who knew more than he did.

'That sure won't be me,' Darryl said.

Paco, the Doberman, had to be taken for a two-mile run every afternoon. That became one of Darryl's chores. He and Paco bounded up the beach until Darryl's feet were swollen and his lungs felt on fire. But he liked it when they stopped to rest.

I could be a sailor on the ocean, he thought. Except no one never taught me to swim. Or work on boats. Build boats. Do something with these hands. He spread his fingers. Where am I gonna learn to do that? Go down to Lauderdale where they got boatyards. Find Pauline. I could be a daddy for all I know. And I be a good one.

He told his friend William what was on his mind. William was working from eight to five as a porter at the Greyhound terminal. 'Hey, I go to Lauderdale with you,' William said.

'With what, man? You got no money.'

'Neither have you. We do a little nightwork, man.'

Darryl scuffed his shoes on the pavement where they stood outside a Kentucky Fried Chicken. 'The cops know me too good.'

'Coupla scores down by the beach, we on our way.'

'I don't want to hurt no one, man.'

'This place where you picking up after dogs . . . they wealthy?'

'Wealthy? Man, they *rich*.'

'You know how to get in?'

Darryl mulled that over. He wanted to leave Jacksonville. 'I look around,' Darryl said. 'I figure it out.'

HE FIGURED IT OUT. But he didn't want to hurt Paco, he told William. Paco was trained not to take food from anyone he didn't know, but he knew Darryl. William promised to get pills that would put Paco to sleep for six hours. He'd wake up good as new.

Rich folks were having a fancy party in a few days, Darryl said, and pretty sure they'd do some drinking. They'd sleep good.

So at six o'clock on the day of the concert, William was waiting for

Darryl outside the gates of the Zide estate in his rattly blue Ford pick-up. They drove south through the scrub forest.

'Where we headed?' Darryl asked.

'Got eight hours to kill, man.'

They went to a bar for a while, then drove west to a mall with a triple movie theatre and saw two movies. It was still only midnight. William bought two six-packs of beer, and they pulled the truck into a parking lot at the beach and sat in the dark, popping the cans.

Close to 2am, William said, 'Hey, man, we gotta go. We late.'

They reached the area of the Zide estate, passed by the black gates. They parked half a mile away, in a clump of saw grass off the road. The moon had already set, but the night was thick with stars. Darryl stuffed a pair of wire cutters into his belt and a flashlight into the back pocket of his Levi's. William carried a Colt Python and a plastic supermarket bag with some beef liver in it. They shouldered their way through the brush to the dunes and then onto the beach.

After fifteen minutes of slogging through soft sand, they reached the edge of the Zide estate. A disturbed seagull gave a raucous cry.

William said, 'What kinda TVs you say they got there?'

'Got a big-screen console and three more nineteen-inch babies.'

'Man, how we gonna carry them back to my pick-up?'

Darryl laughed wickedly and said, 'Won't be easy.'

A fog rolled off the ocean as they reached the beach gates, and out of the gloom they could hear Paco growling.

Darryl approached the gate. 'Hey, Paco, it's me. Be cool, boy.'

Moments later the dog lay in the sand near a clump of saw grass.

William cut through the barbed wire with the clippers. They made their way up through more dunes and then along a boardwalk. Off to the right were the swimming pool and tennis courts.

Lights burned on all three floors of the house. With William following, Darryl moved across the soft, springy lawn, along a line of hibiscus, onto the terrace. They cut across the ultraviolet beam of a security lamp. It blazed swirling yellow light across their path. They heard voices, and both youths crouched against a marble column.

The voices rose in pitch. Downstairs in the house, people were arguing. A man's voice snarled in rage. A light snapped on upstairs. Then the Lhasa apso puppies sprinted down the terrace towards Darryl, yipping and baying like baby wolves from hell.

Wearing a billowing white bathrobe, Connie Zide stepped suddenly out of the house through French doors. She was about thirty feet away from Darryl. She stopped and stared at him.

Instantly he jumped from his crouch, bellowed like an elephant, and ran. William followed, crouching low and weaving. Darryl pounded across the grass towards the beach gate, tripping another light beam. He heard a crash behind him, as of pottery smashing, but when he flung his head round to look, he saw only William's long-jawed face bobbing up and down in stride.

I RAISED A PALM, meaning, Stop right there. Darryl nodded, adjusted himself against the cool wall of the cell.

'I have a few questions,' I said.

This story of Darryl's hadn't come out at trial. If Darryl had told this tale then, I would have ripped it apart. Because who were you going to believe—the wife and son of the murdered man, or the hulking youth who had admitted being there on the terrace and confessed the murder to a homicide detective?

The two guards appeared at the door to the cell. 'Sir?'

I turned.

'It's time for this prisoner to exercise.'

I asked if it was possible for him to do it after I'd gone.

'No, sir. It's supervised and we have a schedule.'

I turned to Darryl. 'Can you skip your exercise today?'

'We get up on that roof twice a week, man,' Darryl said. 'Which you think I rather do—rap with you or breathe fresh air and stretch my bones? You don't believe me, nohow.'

We had just finished our weekly partners' meeting, and Harvey Royal, our distinguished-looking senior partner, asked to see me alone. He slid an antacid pill into his mouth, leaned back in the leather chair and said, 'Ted, just what the heck are you doing up in Jacksonville?'

'I explained it last week, Harvey. Darryl Morgan's run out his string of appeals. He's due to be executed in four weeks.'

Harvey knew, of course, that the case hinged on the testimony of the firm's new client, Jerry Lee Elroy. But what I didn't dare tell him was that I'd lied to Elroy and pretended that his recantation was part of the deal to get out of the drug charge. Harvey peered at me over his reading glasses. 'I am not unsympathetic to what you're feeling,' he said. 'But at the meeting today we discussed several cases in which you're involved. Barry Wellmet and Marian Miller have filled in while you were up north, trying to play Good Samaritan. I have to ask you, Ted—are you ready to pull your load with this law firm?'

'I've got to put out the biggest fire,' I said. 'And I don't need to apologise for that. I'm flying up north again in a few days. I'm going to take over the defence of Darryl Morgan.'

'Let me be cruel, Ted. From everything I've learned, you stand no chance of winning. You'll just be drawing out this man Morgan's agony. Can you justify that?'

Darryl Morgan had said, 'When all this be over with? Feeding me to Mama, they ending my hurt.'

'I'm trying to convince the system that it made a mistake.'

'Ted, we need your billing here, not in Jacksonville.'

'Then we have a conflict.'

'How do you propose to resolve it?'

'By doing what I have to do,' I said.

AND I KEPT WORKING. I drove up to Bradenton for a meeting on the milk-price-fixing case. I met with local ZiDevco executives to discuss a witness list for the real-estate lawsuit, and began to prepare a report on what they might say under both direct and cross-examination at trial. I edited Barry Wellmet's brief in the savings and loan case. Work—the word sounded so clean, so meaty. So righteous.

I hurried downtown one afternoon to meet Elroy at Buddy Capra's office in the Criminal Justice Building. While Charlie Waldorf sat on the couch filing his fingernails, Capra laid out the state's deal. It hinged on Elroy testifying against his suppliers, Ramos and Palomino. Elroy asked where this would take place.

'The grand jury is sitting now in Miami. They'd like to indict this spring. Your presence is requested,' Capra said, making a graceful gesture with his hand. 'After you testify, we'll drop the possession charge. You'll walk away under the witness protection programme. California has held a lottery, and you've been won by the city of San Diego. They're thrilled that you're coming.'

We rode down in the elevator, which piped a Vivaldi flute concerto to its passengers. Elroy and I walked west on Main Street in the afternoon heat. 'You couldn't have made a better deal,' I said. 'And there's the other part of it, which I hope you didn't forget.'

'What was that exactly, Counsellor?'

'Jacksonville. Testifying about the Morgan case. You recall?'

Elroy scratched his chin. 'Those guys didn't mention that.'

'Because they didn't need to. But you have to do it. We start with a sworn affidavit. Now. Up at my office.'

THAT EVENING AFTER DINNER, I asked Alan into the den. I sat in an easy chair; Alan sprawled on one of the sofas. Adjusting my horn-rimmed glasses, I felt old.

I leaned across from the easy chair and placed a hand on his shoulder. 'Alan, you talked to your mother about suicide, and it frightens me. I'm sure it's hard to elaborate, but can you tell me what depresses you? I need to know.'

'I just feel useless. You said it—I'm a failure.'

I'd never called him a failure, and the worst I might have said on other occasions was, 'I think you're screwing up your life.' But I didn't contradict. This wasn't court.

'I'd like you to go into therapy. Do you have anything against it?'

'No,' Alan said.

There was more, and I had to get through it. 'You can stay in the drug programme or not,' I said to Alan. 'That's up to you. But if I find out that you're doing any drugs at all, you can get down on your knees and beg and weep—I'll still kick you right out of here.'

A few days later, Toba hunted down a recommended therapist in the high-school system who took patients on a private basis for sixty-five dollars an hour. Her name was Dorothy Buford.

We went one evening to see her. Dorothy Buford was in her early thirties. 'I don't really want to talk to you two,' she said. 'I'd rather not have preconceived ideas. Have your son call me.'

'We'd like to tell you what the problem is,' I said.

'What you'll tell me, Mr Jaffe, will be what *your* problem is. Have your son call me. He'll tell me what *his* problem is.'

In the car on the way home, I laughed. 'You know, she's absolutely right. I like her.'

'I don't,' Toba said. 'I thought that was smart-aleck.'

Sitting on the edge of the bed, undoing her blouse, Toba said, 'Ted, I wish you weren't going on Monday.'

'I'll try to be back for the weekend.'

'Have you got a girlfriend up there in Jacksonville?'

'For heaven's sake, no.'

'If you do,' Toba said, 'I'll break your knees with a sledgehammer while you're asleep in bed. How long are you going to keep this up? This running off to Jacksonville?'

'As long as I need to, Toba.'

'Our son told us he was suicidal. What if *he* dies,' she said, 'while you're off trying to save some murderer's lousy life?'

I didn't know how to answer that. There was no answer.

Sheets of rain swept down on Longboat Key. Boats bobbing at anchor in the bay blinked friendly signal lights into our bedroom.

A few minutes after turning out her light, Toba began to snore lightly. Soon I drifted towards sleep.

'That time in the Gambrel murder, the snitch I had was for real.'

I sat up in the semidarkness. Thunder growled from far away in the night, like a vicious dog. I was awake, focused on a name, hearing it in the reedy voice of Carmen Tanagra.

I remembered that name from twelve years ago. And the man himself: Victor Gambrel. A former Jacksonville cop, and at that time chief of security for Zide Industries. Nickerson's police report had quoted Gambrel as stating that following Neil Zide's telephone call, he'd arrived at the estate a scant few minutes before the homicide team. Gambrel had seen nothing. I had interviewed him, but decided not to use him as a witness.

A few years ago, according to the casual recounting by Kenny Buckram and Carmen Tanagra, Gambrel had been murdered. But why? And by whom? Organised crime, they thought. What else had Tanagra said? I hunted in the debris of memory and found it: 'Bongiorno had real good friends in Tallahassee. Money and political clout is what it came down to.'

Even a blind dog finds a bone once in a while. I had a new vision, one that staggered me. I slipped out of bed and padded swiftly down the stairs to the living room. The sky crackled with lightning. From my briefcase I fished out a legal pad and a ball-point pen.

When I slept again, I dreamed of a woman who resembled Connie Zide. She held a knife to the throat of Darryl Morgan.

CONNIE ZIDE ONCE SAID to me, 'Solly can't stand me. He thinks I'm deceitful, self-centred, vain—I hear it all the time. If he can't control someone close to him, he has to destroy them. A couple of weeks ago, when we were arguing about Neil, he hit me.'

We were having a drink that evening at Ruffino's, which was halfway between the courthouse and home. My fists clenched in anger—how *dare* he hit her?—and I knew I had to be careful. Her life with Solly and Neil wasn't my business.

'You remember when I didn't see you for a whole week? It was because I had a bruise here.' Connie touched her cheek.

'Neil saw it next morning,' she went on. 'I told him the truth, and he went straight to the office. Apparently, he called Solly a few names that even Solly had never heard.'

'They work together, don't they?'

'Neil's a glorified gofer, on starvation wages. Why do you think he lives at home?'

That made no sense to me. 'Why don't you stake Neil to a place of his own?' I asked.

'He won't take anything from me. He thinks I should leave Solly, and if I did, he says, I'd need every penny I've saved. I signed a

352

prenuptial agreement. I can live well, but only if I'm in residence.'

I had met Neil at one of the charity luncheons. The young man had a cold, appraising look in his eyes. He was soft round the jawline, nervous and arrogant. At one point in our conversation he said, 'Well, what good luck to meet you. If I ever get caught speeding, I'll give you a ring.' Neil was wearing Gucci shoes and a black silk sports jacket, draped over his shoulders like a bullfighter's cape. When he left, he drove off in a Lamborghini.

During the seven months of what I came to think of as my period of primal madness, I took care not to fall in love with Connie Zide. I knew it could lead to the destruction of my marriage, my family, maybe even my career. And I didn't want that.

A while later that summer, Connie and I were sailing a borrowed cutter offshore in the Atlantic when she turned to me in the cockpit and said, 'Neil knows about us.'

She saw the expression of dismay on my face.

'It's all right. He approves.'

I looked at her darkly. 'How did he find out?'

'We have no secrets.'

'Connie, you told him?'

I could imagine all kinds of scenarios. Solly, in a rage, confronting me in the state attorney's office. Or at home in front of Toba.

I brought the cutter through the wind, hauling in the sheets and turning the bow into the Atlantic chop. Connie rose in one motion and moved midships to deal with the jib. She glistened from head to toe in the afternoon sun. The job done, she came aft, stalking towards me across the deck. She said, 'Ted, tomorrow will be six months since that Cuban kid mugged me in the parking lot.'

'I know.'

'Ted, I love you.'

Those three words had not been used between us before.

'I told Neil that I loved you,' she said. 'If I could, I would tell the world. I would leave Solly to be with you.'

'Connie, even if—' But I bit that off short. We had never gone in this direction before. It was a collision course.

I set myself to be honest. 'Connie, I don't want you to leave Solly for me. I will not leave Toba and my children. Maybe you and I have come to the end of our good luck. Maybe it's time to quit.'

'How cruel you are,' she said softly. 'If you were honest, you'd give in to your wanting me.'

'I don't want to hurt you,' I said. I was miserable. I hated what was happening. But I knew what I felt and what I had to do.

She let out a wail that made me shudder. 'Is it because I'm older

353

than you? There isn't anything I won't do for you! I swear I'll make you happy!'

This wasn't the woman who'd called me honey when we first met. I looked out at the ocean. Beyond here are dragons, I thought. I now believed that I had journeyed to the edge of the map.

CONNIE TELEPHONED one day and told me that Solly had gone to Hong Kong on business. 'Please come over.'

'That would be unwise,' I said.

'Ted, for heaven's sake, haven't we gone beyond that?'

I didn't *want* to go beyond that. But I suddenly sensed that if I didn't agree, I would be postponing the inevitable.

At five thirty, when I had cleared my desk at the office, I drove south and then east until I arrived at the iron gates of the Zide estate. I had been there only once before. The grey-uniformed security guards were just changing shifts. The older of the two men—his brass nameplate said TERENCE O'ROURKE—looked up from his clipboard. 'May I please see some ID, sir?'

From my pigskin wallet I extracted my driver's licence.

Terence scanned the licence. 'Thank you, Mr Jaffe.'

The electronic gate rolled open.

I parked near the front door, with its etched-glass panes and flanking stone lions. Connie was waiting for me by a hedge of scarlet hibiscus. She wore white. With the two Lhasa apso puppies following, she led me under some awnings to the swimming pool. 'Let's jump in and make love,' she said.

I indicated a large black workman half hidden by a grove of banana trees. He headed towards the lawn, pushing a wheelbarrow.

'Ted, you worry so much.'

'Yes, lately I do.'

There was something portentous in my tone, and it quieted her. We began to stroll round the pool. Hollow-hearted, stomach fluttering, I told Connie it was over. I was no longer at ease in the affair. I feared for my marriage. My voice seemed to come from an inner distance.

Connie looked a little pale under the buffeting.

'You've always told me your wife has your best interests at heart.'

'I'm sure she does.'

'Then if there was someone else in your life, why would your wife want to hang onto you? Isn't that demeaning to your wife?'

The repetitions of the words 'your wife' were like darts inserted to pierce the skin.

'Connie, *this* is demeaning. Let's cut it out.'

Shadows slanted across the pool from the banana grove and the royal palms. In her broad garden hat and white sundress, Connie looked like a haughty and angry princess. I must have looked like a tired man in a wrinkled business suit who'd been sitting in crowded courtrooms since eight o'clock that morning.

'I have to go,' I said.

'Your wife is expecting you?'

'Goodbye, Connie.'

A week later, one morning when I was in court, Solly Zide called and left a message with my secretary. I returned the call later that afternoon. I imagined only the worst.

Zide said, 'I was going to ask you to lunch to discuss this, but now I'm tied up for the rest of this week and the next. Anyway, it's not me you need to talk to.' He told me about the opening at Royal, Kelly in Sarasota. 'If I were in your shoes,' he said flatly, 'I would take the opportunity. Nothing better will ever happen to you.'

Was that a threat? Did he mean leave Jacksonville, or else? I wondered but never asked. Would never have the chance to ask, either. The next time I saw Solly Zide was two months later, at the black-tie concert. The host, in his white dinner jacket, was surrounded by guests. We spoke a few words as we passed each other by the pool. Seven hours later, he was dead.

Beldon Ruth shuffled across his office to dump some wilting red roses into a wastebasket. Then he turned on me and said, 'You can't defend someone you once prosecuted. You *know* that! Cops told you everything they knew. Prosecution witnesses talked freely to you. You can't switch sides!'

'Elroy didn't tell me then that he was lying. He told me twelve years later. Beldon, it was not a fair trial. I think Floyd Nickerson perjured himself, too.'

'Since when does "think" count in a court of law?'

'I may have a witness.'

'Who?'

'I can't tell you.'

'Oh? Now we're being cute? Is this all a bluff?'

'Let me ask you a question,' I said. 'Why are you scared of this thing being retried?'

'Wait a minute!' Beldon yelped. 'Who's talking about a *re*trial? Justice might—just *might*—require a hearing, if only to save this dude from the electric chair and put him away for life. But if it ever comes to a whole new trial, you are emphatically not the right man to do it.'

'Will you let me handle a motion and an appeal hearing?'

'What will you do if I say no?'

I locked eyes with him. 'I'll fight you all the way.'

Beldon was silent for a few moments, thinking things over. 'OK,' he said. 'I'll make a deal with you. You handle your motion for Morgan. The state attorney's office won't object. If you win—meaning if Judge Horace Fleming grants a new trial for Morgan—you step down. Let another lawyer do it. Is that a deal?'

One step at a time. I shook the offered hand.

But at the door, Beldon put his other hand on my arm.

'You're not telling me everything,' he said.

'About what?' He couldn't mean my con job on Elroy; he had no way of even guessing at that.

'This case. Something else is happening here. Why else would you be so anxious to do it?'

I didn't answer. I was smiling woodenly and trying to get out, but he still touched my arm. There was a message in the touch.

'I know something, too,' he said. He let the words hang there.

Wary, I said, 'About the case?'

He said, 'It's just something that makes me feel you shouldn't be involved, not even at this level. So what I'm saying is, be judicious.'

He knew about Connie. It had to be that.

'Think about it,' he said. 'Don't get yourself hurt.' He lifted his fingers from my arm. It was as if a weight had been withdrawn.

That evening I took Muriel Suarez to dinner at my favourite seafood joint at the beach. Muriel dropped into a red plastic booth and said, 'I'm bushed, so would you do the ordering? I eat everything that swims except jellyfish.'

After drinks came, I ordered fresh conch and mesquite-grilled snapper. 'What else do you do besides try cases?' I asked. 'Is there a man in your life?'

'No,' Muriel said, 'there's no man in my life. Who has time?'

She raised her glass to me. 'And what's happening with you these days, Mr Hotshot Civil Lawyer from Sarasota?'

I had told her about the deal with Beldon, so I talked about my family. I had left home at a bad time. I should be there for Alan.

'Your son has to solve his problems by himself,' Muriel said. 'I have a kid brother, David, who's an addict. My father, before he died, persuaded David to go into a drug programme. He stayed there seventeen months. It was in New York State, up in the Catskill Mountains. He told us it was like a prison. He called me once—he said, "Muriel, I'll die if I stay here." He'd been there about five months then. I said, "No, you won't." That was a night, believe me, I didn't sleep. But when he got out a year later, he was cured.'

'He wasn't an addict any more?'

'You're always an addict. No, David's attitude was, "I spent seventeen months in that miserable hole, and if I go back to drugs now, then it was a total waste of time." He's a stubborn kid.'

'What does he do now?'

'He's a cab dispatcher in West Palm Beach. They don't turn you into lawyers and doctors. They just teach you to survive.'

THE ZIDE BUILDING WAS out in the suburbs, behind the Regency Plaza Mall. Neil Zide ran the empire now. He let specialists handle the various arms of the Zide Industries octopus-like conglomerate. But ZiDevco was his. Neil, who had been rich, had become very rich. He had let his hair grow down to his shoulders in unruly brown waves, went to work in Levi's and Italian silk shirts. He looked like a young Hollywood producer. He was thirty-four years old now.

Sitting behind his glass desk, he glanced at his watch to make sure I realised his time was valuable. 'You're here in your capacity as an attorney, I take it. How can I help you?'

'I'm representing Darryl Morgan,' I said, 'to see if I can win a new trial for him.'

The flesh round Neil Zide's jawline seemed to go slack. He studied me carefully, waiting. He was a bright man despite his foppishness. He knew when to shut up.

So I fired from the hip. 'There are a few questions I'd like to ask you about Floyd Nickerson and Victor Gambrel.'

Neil exhaled quietly, then inhaled deeply. 'Go ahead.'

'Nickerson investigated your father's death.'

'I remember that.'

'And until some five or six years ago, Victor Gambrel was head of security for Zide Industries, the Jacksonville office. Right?'

'That's correct.'

'Nickerson took a confession from Darryl Morgan, and Nickerson also dug up a cellmate who heard Darryl Morgan confess.'

'I remember that, too,' Neil said. 'You still haven't told me how I can help you.'

'I'd like to find out what happened to Nickerson. If you know.'

'I'm not sure.' Neil scratched his nose and blinked a few times.

'Well, I didn't mean I didn't know where he was,' I said easily. 'He's chief of security over at Orange Meadow Estates in Gainesville. What I meant was, I wondered how he got there. It's a ZiDevco project.'

'That's correct.'

357

'Do you recall how Nickerson got that job?'

'I'd have to ask someone to check the personnel records,' Neil said, starting to blink again. 'Would you like me to do that?'

'You don't recall giving him the job?'

'Ted'—smiling now, trying to appear friendly, worldly—'that's a long time ago. How could I remember that?'

'Then I *would* like to see those personnel records. If you could arrange to have a copy sent down to me, care of Kenny Buckram at the public defender's office here in Jacksonville?'

'I'll try.' Neil scratched a note on a desk pad. 'If they still exist. We may not keep records like that for as long as nine years.'

I was silent for a moment. 'And Gambrel. What do you remember about Victor Gambrel?'

'Victor . . . well, I remember him, of course. He came to an unfortunate end.'

'Shot and killed in his car at the Regency Square Mall in nineteen eighty-five. I heard, and this is between you and me, that the Bongiorno people were behind it. But I'm not sure why Gambrel would be a target for organised crime. Doesn't make sense. Does it to you? I didn't know Gambrel. You did, though. You knew him well.'

'I wouldn't say that.'

'The night that Darryl Morgan broke into your house and shot your father, you called the police and then you called Gambrel. That's what you told the court, isn't it?'

Neil cleared his throat. 'Ted, the truth is, I don't remember what I said on the witness stand. That was an exceedingly traumatic time for me. I called Victor that ghastly night because he was chief of security and it seemed appropriate to do so.'

'What's your theory as to why he was murdered?'

'What I heard was . . . gambling debts. Large sums. To the wrong people. May I ask you a question now?'

'Fire away, Neil.'

'Why are you getting involved again, and on the other side?'

'Everyone asks me that,' I said, shaking my head sorrowfully. 'My wife, my law partners, the state attorney. I suppose it's because I don't think Morgan received a fair trial and therefore doesn't deserve to die. I've learned something specific along those lines. Nothing earthshaking, but it's significant.'

'Which is?'

I sighed and said, 'It's confidential. Sorry.'

Neil looked at me steadily. 'Is that all?'

'Yes, that's all—and thanks, Neil. My best regards to Connie.'

We shook hands. Then, at the door, I turned and said, 'Oh, by the way, there's just one more thing I wanted to ask you. May I?'

'OK,' Neil said.

'I asked you how Floyd Nickerson got that job over at Orange Meadow, and you said you didn't know. Isn't that right?'

'Yes, that's right.'

'And when I asked you for the personnel records, you said you didn't know if your office kept those kinds of records for as long as nine years. How did you know it was nine years ago?'

Neil stared at me calmly. But he was upset. 'I was guessing.'

'And hit it right on the button,' I said. 'I'll be in touch.'

That afternoon I went to see a judge again and secured a court order. Then I bought two decks of playing cards and put them in my briefcase. The next day I drove down to Raiford. After I'd presented the court order to Raymond Wright, I was escorted to death row. Today Darryl wore a Mickey Mouse T-shirt and blue jeans.

'I'm going to file a petition for a retrial,' I told him. 'There may be a hearing. Will you cooperate with me?'

'You say *may* be this hearing. You don't say going to be.'

'That's right. No promises.'

'You promise, I don't believe you nohow. What you want me to do for you?'

'I want you first of all to agree that I represent you. That I'm your lawyer, your attorney, your counsellor.'

'Lot of weird things happen in my life,' Darryl said. 'This got to be near the top of the list.'

I gave him the two decks of playing cards.

I TRIED TO COMMUNICATE with Toba now and then. How goes it? How's Alan? They were fine, she told me with unremitting hostility. At the offices of Royal, Kelly, I felt the same coolness. I was working on my cases, but not putting in a lot of billing time.

I was not a man who dreamed much. But at night now the dreams were thick with fear. I felt I was always on the edge of the dream where a human head flamed heavenwards. And the head that threatened to burn was not Darryl Morgan's or even Eric Sweeting's. Some part of me feared that the head was my son's.

I submitted my motion to Judge Fleming on March 29. Morgan's execution at Raiford was scheduled for Thursday, April 11.

On Monday, April 8, at noon, Fleming called me into chambers at the Duval County Courthouse. The judge slouched in his chair, silver hair brushed back, glasses perched on the edge of his red, veined nose. He spoke slowly, and he looked as if he should have been in a rocking chair on a country porch, sipping a mint julep. On his desk, surrounded by other piles of papers, were my petitions for a stay of execution and relief in *Florida* v. *Morgan*.

'This is all you got to say?' Judge Fleming asked. He ran a gnarled arthritic finger along the spread-out pile of papers.

'Yes,' I said, agonising, wondering what I had left out.

'You were the prosecutor in this case, Mr Jaffe?'

'Yes, Judge.'

'I talked to Mr Ruth about this. Now, I have an opinion about Mr Ruth that I don't mind communicating to anybody. If Mr Ruth says a squirrel can pull a freight train, you can hitch up that rodent and clear the tracks. You understand what I'm saying?'

'Yes, Judge, and I agree. You can trust Mr Ruth.'

'You want some coffee?'

'That would be welcome.'

'Over there in the corner. Bring some for me, too.'

While I was pouring the coffee, Judge Fleming said, 'I'm going to say yes to your petition. Grant you a ninety-day stay. Least I can do if they're getting ready to fry a man. You bring your witness in here, and Mr Morgan, and anyone else, on June twenty-fourth, nine o'clock in the morning. Suit you?'

'Yes, Judge,' I said, my heart pounding with joy.

On the Saturday before the court hearing, I flew to Miami to pick up Jerry Lee Elroy and haul him back to Jacksonville. It was evening, and below, as the little plane gained altitude, were the blue dots of lighted pools and the yellow chains of headlights on arrow-straight highways. Forty minutes later, from the black void of the Everglades, Miami sprang like an immense treasure chest of neon jewels.

I took a taxi to the address I had in Hialeah. Behind the reception desk of the Man O' War Motel hung old black and white photographs of famous thoroughbreds. A man looked up from a lounge chair near the cigarette machine—a man in his thirties, with a moustache and a Hawaiian flowered shirt under a seersucker jacket. He might as well have had COP branded on his forehead.

Elroy had given me his room number, so I dumped my single piece of luggage in my room and walked upstairs. When I knocked and called out his name, Elroy flung open the door to his room. He wore new decor: baggy mod trousers, a white golf shirt. Above the blare of the TV he cried, 'Hey, Counsellor, how about we eat?'

'Do they let you come and go as you please?'

'They watch, they follow. They're getting paid. What do they care? There's this place down the block, not too bad.'

Even in the night air I felt the pavement heating the soles of my shoes. Horse racing took place nearby, and Lacy's, the restaurant Elroy had chosen, catered to retirees and racegoers. It offered bargain dinners and I ordered meat loaf. I glanced round at the senior citizens in plaid shirts. One couple studied the racing form as if it were a treasure map.

Elroy said, 'The track, that's action, man. That's what I love.'

I looked at Elroy and didn't smile.

The waitress passed by. Elroy called out, 'Hey, sweetie pie, we have a little more gravy here?' He turned back to me, grinning. 'We got an unforeseen problem, Counsellor.'

'How do you mean?'

'Guys downtown at the state attorney's office, they don't want me to leave Miami. Palomino, Ramos, they're out on bail.'

I put down my knife and fork. 'I spoke to you in the middle of the week. You said no problem.'

'There's this guy Baxter, see? I told him I thought Jacksonville was part of the deal. He says no, there's no deal I testify in Jax.'

I had never told Charlie Waldorf in Sarasota or Robert Diaz, the Miami state attorney, that I needed Elroy as a witness.

'See, they got these plain-clothes guys watching me. You saw one of them at the motel. Another one's here right now—I just spotted him.' Elroy's eyes flicked to the left. I looked, and saw the man sitting by himself five tables away: about forty, prematurely grey, with a crew cut, wearing a pale blue silk sports jacket.

'It ain't gonna work, Counsellor,' Elroy said.

'It has to work,' I said flatly. 'That hearing is Monday morning. You don't show up, they'll execute this man.'

'Hey, sorry. They said I don't have to. Maybe you misled me.'

That was what I had feared.

'If you had a girlfriend waiting up in Jacksonville,' I said, 'you wouldn't care what Baxter or Diaz or anyone told you.'

'Yeah, but that's different, ain't it?'

I gathered up all the cold, hard anger that usually stayed trapped beneath the surface of my life as a lawyer. 'Elroy, if you don't go up with me tomorrow, Palomino gets your address delivered by Federal Express to his home on Key Biscayne. I'll remind him, when he comes to visit you, to bring his machete. And his ruler.'

Elroy laughed nervously.

'Keep laughing, pal.' I glared at him.

'Hey, hey, hey . . .' Elroy's eyes darted left, right, then up. 'Just take it easy, Counsellor. Calm down. So I do it, what's in it for me?'

'I'd pay all your expenses.'

'Big deal.' He thought for a few moments. 'Jax, they race in the summer at the Kennel Club, right?'

'Greyhounds?'

'The crazy doggies, yeah.'

I had taken a thousand dollars from Elroy as a down payment on his legal fee. 'When we get up there,' I said, 'I'll give you back the thousand. That way there's no fee on the drug case.'

Elroy grinned. 'How're we gonna get rid of these guys at the motel?'

I considered that problem for a few minutes while I asked for the bill. When I focused on him again, Elroy was still grinning.

'Got any ideas?' I said.

'Leave it to me. Just tell me where you want to meet.'

WAITING FOR ELROY the following afternoon in the jabbering chaos of Miami International Airport, I sweated. At ten minutes to four I began to pace, put on my glasses and checked the departure board again. Our flight left for Jacksonville at four thirty. There was another at six—if Elroy showed up at all. I cursed and scowled.

At three minutes past four I felt a tap on my shoulder. When I turned, Elroy stood there in his baggy trousers, white golf shirt and baseball cap. He was still grinning.

'Worried, huh?'

Behind Elroy, from the revolving door, emerged the grey-haired cop who had been sitting near us at dinner the night before. Or at least someone who resembled him. This one wore a brown cardigan and carried a small airline bag. 'Don't turn around,' I said.

The grey-haired man merged into a group that included a team of laughing athletes wearing purple-striped shorts. He vanished.

'So what is it?' Elroy asked.

'I thought I saw one of your shadows.'

'No way.' Elroy searched for a while, then shook his head.

'Let's go through security,' I said, still sweating.

The plane was full. I walked twice through the aisle to the toilet aft to see if anyone looked at all familiar. Elroy was drinking his second double Dewar's on the rocks when we began the descent into Jacksonville International.

'Where we staying, Counsellor? Ponte Vedra? Plantation Club?'

From the Avis counter I called the Omni downtown. With its upper-middle-class solidity, it seemed safer than a suburban motel.

In the car, Elroy cleared his throat. 'We were talking about what you might call a rebate? That thousand? You got it handy?'

'Not tonight.'

'How about a down payment? I'm down to my last chip.'

'I can give you a hundred. What do you need it for?'

'Hey, I told you—the doggies.'

'Let's get up to the hotel room,' I said, 'and then we'll see.'

Elroy sulked. I took two rooms, hoping that he would settle down on his bed in front of his own TV. But it was useless. Within a minute Elroy knocked on my door. 'Counsellor! You comfortable? Everything cool? I been thinking . . . just give me whatever cash you can. You do your thing; I'll do mine. That OK?'

I thumbed through my wallet. I had two hundred and fifty in cash.

'The last race is over by eleven. I'll be back by midnight.'

He could go anywhere. I'd have to wait up for him, biting my nails. 'I'll go with you,' I said. 'Want to eat first?'

'Get a hot dog out there,' Elroy said. 'Come on, let's move.'

I had been to the dog track once, with my parents and sister when I was a boy. But on the drive out, I let Elroy explain everything. I let him pay the fifty cents' admission and lead me to the seats in the glassed-in, air-conditioned mezzanine.

'You got something on your mind, Counsellor?'

'The hearing tomorrow.'

'Yeah, but it's not a trial, is it? Nothing serious like that.'

'It's serious, all right. That's why you're going to tell your story under oath. We're trying to save Darryl Morgan's life.'

Held by the track handlers, the dogs paraded round the track in front of us. The palm trees swayed in the night breeze. Elroy kept checking the odds as they changed on the monitor. His pale eyes were never still. Finally he jumped up from his seat. 'I'm putting twenty bucks on the number two dog. How much you in for, Counsellor?'

I handed him a five-dollar bill and he marched off buoyantly towards the betting desk. A few minutes later the lights dimmed and the mechanical rabbit was released. The dogs flew wildly round the oval. I stood to stretch, and glimpsed through a gap in the crowd the hard, attentive face of a grey-haired, crew-cut man in a brown cardigan. He was twenty feet away and watching me. He was the man who had been in the restaurant the previous night, and at Miami Airport earlier that evening. He wasn't a cop, I realised.

But why is he watching *me*, not Elroy? Because, a quiet voice whispered, someone else is with Elroy now.

I stood unmoving, my heart jackhammering against my ribs. The grey-haired man blocked the aisle.

Other aisles also led to the betting desk and the payoff windows. I moved towards one of them. I felt as if I were underwater, breast

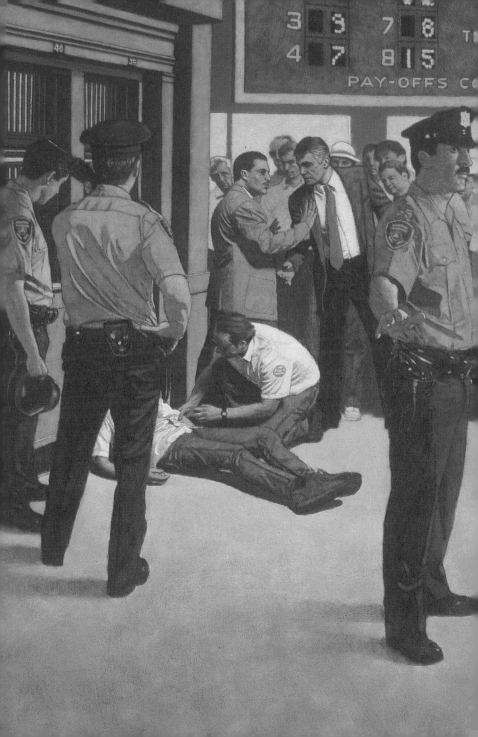

stroking against a stiff current. By the time I reached the betting desk,
a crowd had gathered and the police were holding people at bay. Jerry
Lee Elroy sat upright on the carpet against one of the cashier's cages.
His eyes were sightless. Blood leaked from his side, staining his white
golf shirt. He had been stabbed with a thin blade slid between the ribs.
A thick black object choked his mouth. It took me a minute or two to
figure out what it was. Someone had thrust a sea urchin into his
mouth so that its spines bit deep into the offending tongue.

IN THE CORRIDOR leading from the courtroom to his chambers,
Judge Fleming swayed a few feet to his left in order to write some
notes, resting his paper on the surface of a filing cabinet. The lawyers
for the state, the court clerk and the court reporter shifted with him,
like tick parasites following a water buffalo. A few feet away, Darryl
Morgan's bulk took up most of the space on a heavy wooden bench;
he was manacled to the armrest. Two grey-uniformed deputy sheriffs
with holstered .45s sat on metal folding chairs by the water cooler at
the end of the corridor.

Judge Fleming surveyed this scene. 'Dance floor's getting crowded,'
he said to me and the representatives of the state. 'Care to join me in
chambers?'

Once in there, I slumped in a chair. I had managed about two hours
of restless sleep. The other lawyers found chairs. The slender,
bespectacled assistant state attorney from Beldon's staff was named
John Whatley, and next to him sat Muriel Suarez.

She smiled cordially. I went over and asked her what she was doing
there. 'You and I have discussed this case,' I said. 'I can't remember
what I've told you, but whatever it was, it was in confidence.'

'Beldon seems to think that's irrelevant.'

'He assigned you?'

'What do you think, I volunteered?'

I understood. Tit for tat. I had been privy to the state's thinking
twelve years ago. Muriel Suarez had been privy to my thinking just
days ago. How could I complain? Beldon, you sly dog.

Judge Fleming unknotted his tie, turned to me and said, 'I think we
can save a bunch of time by discussing this informally right here in
chambers. Mr Elroy, your witness, is not present in this court. From
what I gather, he doesn't have the pulse of a pitchfork.'

'Yes, he's shaken hands with eternity,' I said. I heard my voice as
from a distance, enunciating carefully. 'Last night, at about ten
o'clock. Stabbed to death at the Jacksonville Kennel Club.'

'As ye sow.' The judge turned to Whatley and Muriel Suarez.
'What sayeth the state of Florida, besides "amen"?'

Whatley said, 'Your Honour, the entire thrust of the petitioner's position is the proposed testimony of Mr Elroy as to alleged perjury. Nothing else in the appellant's petition is new. Much as the state regrets Mr Elroy's passing, our contention is that the deceased witness's affidavit is not sufficient to establish perjury. The state has no way of cross-examining an affidavit.'

Judge Fleming nodded.

'Your Honour—' I began.

'No, no, no,' the judge said. 'I don't want to hear argument. I know the issues. There's a man on death row. Man wants to live. State wants to kill him. Man's lawyer wants to string things out. Judge wants to get on with the business of his court. Can't make everybody happy. You got any live witnesses, Mr Jaffe?'

'Not today, Judge. But I hope to find some.'

The judge thought for a while.

'I'm going to allow this affidavit, but I'm going to find that this recantation would not have affected the outcome of the trial. What I'm saying is, Mr Jaffe, you lose. I'm going to deny your petition.'

'Judge—'

'Mr Jaffe'—the judge leaned forward in his chair, his pale eyes watering—'nice to meet you again.'

I left Fleming's chambers and walked out into the corridor to tell Darryl Morgan that the state still wanted him to die.

THE SOLES OF MY FEET began to itch. During one Monday morning partners' meeting, I had to take off my shoes and socks in order to rip away with my fingernails at the soles.

My partners stared at me. I didn't blame them. This was the time that both they and Toba believed I was going crazy.

I had taken my chief witness to the dog track and allowed him to be murdered by a Miami drug lord. As a result, Darryl Morgan had received another death warrant from the governor of Florida. Unless some other court granted a stay, he would be electrocuted in the death chamber at Raiford on August 2, 1991, at seven o'clock in the morning.

Desperate, I filed papers with the state Supreme Court in Tallahassee. I had no hope that the court would grant a retrial, but they might grant a stay pending their decision. Indeed, a week later, the court ordered a stay for sixty days. I was invited to appear before them on August 27 for oral argument.

'Go for it, Ted!' I yelled, encouraging myself. I was in the office. Ruby looked in at me. I shrugged and instructed her to cancel all my appointments for the next day.

I flew up to Jacksonville, hired another car and, in the August heat, drove down to Raiford to tell Darryl that the Florida Supreme Court was willing to consider sparing his life.

Darryl refused to see me.

In Sarasota, I was called one morning to Charlie Waldorf's office at the Criminal Justice Building. Buddy Capra ushered me into an office layered with cloudlike wreaths of smoke.

From behind his desk, without any preliminaries, Waldorf said, 'Robert Diaz in Miami is talking to me about indicting you for tampering with a witness.'

I dropped into an armchair. 'Elroy wasn't absent from an official proceeding. And I didn't induce him to withhold testimony. All I did was ask him to testify in another case. And he agreed.'

Capra said, 'You took him out of Miami, where he was under the protection of the state authority.'

'Took him? Not likely. He went willingly.'

'But secretly. He gave the slip to two deputy sheriffs, didn't he?'

'If he did, and I wouldn't know, that was his idea. Lo and behold, he showed up.'

Charlie Waldorf leaned across his desk, like an attack dog ready to spring. 'It boils down to this, Jaffe. Did Elroy tell you that, pursuant to your request, he'd asked permission to leave Miami and that permission was refused? And after being told that, did you knowingly aid and abet him to leave? Care to answer?'

Before I tear your throat apart, he wanted to add.

I said, 'Only two people know the answers to those questions, Charles. One of them ain't talking, and the other one can't. I didn't obstruct justice, I tried to *do* justice. And if Diaz wanted to keep Elroy in Miami, he was tampering with justice.'

Waldorf said, 'You got some nerve.'

A week later I flew again to Jacksonville, where I took Gary Oliver to dinner at a seafood restaurant on the river.

He was older and greyer now, more sure of himself and with more of a sparkle in his eye. Twelve years ago I hadn't thought he was much of a lawyer. Since then, however, I'd come to realise that, in his own way, Gary had done his best for Darryl Morgan.

At the end of the shrimp cocktail I said, 'Gary, we're on the same side now. I came up here because I need your help.'

Oliver nodded warily.

'Back in seventy-nine, you believed Morgan was guilty. Why'd you put him on the witness stand?'

'I told him, "Darryl, don't get up there." He insisted.'

'But when he was on the stand, he never really told his version of what he and William Smith did that night.'

'That's right. I knew it'd hurt him. I just let him say, "No, I didn't kill no one." I figured that's all he really wanted to do.'

'Gary, I want to run a few facts and theories by you, if you don't mind. Just consider that you're singing for your supper.'

'If I can help that kid, I'll do it.'

I told him about everything that had troubled me since I had become involved in *Florida* v. *Morgan* the second time round—about Elroy, about my hunch that Nickerson had also lied, and about Nickerson's job at a ZiDevco country club. About Neil Zide's slip-up over when Nickerson got the job. And finally, about the violent death of Victor Gambrel, security chief for Zide Industries.

'So what's your theory?' Oliver asked.

'Let's assume for the sake of argument that Darryl is telling the truth. He was there at the Zides'—he admits that. But he didn't pull the trigger on the gun that never turned up.'

Oliver looked at me carefully. 'Well, Zide didn't turn that gun on himself, that's for sure. And Mrs Zide didn't cut her own face that badly. *Someone* did it.'

'Someone who looks like Darryl?'

'Not many fit that bill.'

'Someone who *doesn't* look like Darryl?'

'Only other people around were Mrs Zide and her son.'

'Yes,' I said.

'Could be. Unlikely, but could be.' He mulled that over for a while, as I had done on other occasions. 'Husband might have cut her. And then she shot him.'

'Suppose Darryl and William Smith arrive in the midst of an argument, and get scared by someone, and run off. Darryl says he saw Connie Zide outside on the terrace in a bathrobe. So she might well have seen *him*. Then the family argument resumes, and Zide cuts his wife. She shoots him. Kills him. Maybe she didn't mean to do it, but there he is, dead on the patio floor. So she says, "Hey, I'll blame it on Darryl Morgan. He was *here*." '

Oliver shook his head slowly, but I could tell the thought intrigued him. 'You think that's what happened?'

'Not really.' The truth is, I couldn't imagine the woman I had made love to deliberately pointing the finger of guilt at a young man she knew to be innocent. But she hadn't wanted Darryl to die; I remembered that. Maybe because she knew that he was innocent.

Oliver stroked his jowls and said, 'How does Floyd Nickerson getting that job tie in with the rest of it?'

'It's pretty blatant, but it could have been a payoff.'

'And Gambrel's murder?'

'Maybe that doesn't tie in at all.' Finishing my coffee, I called for the bill. 'You were an investigator before you took up lawyering, and Beldon told me you were pretty good at it. Why don't you sniff around? The deal is, if I win the appeal over in Tallahassee, and there's a retrial, I'll ask you to sit second chair with me. For whatever's your standard fee.'

'How much money are you making out of this?' he asked.

'Diddly.'

'Well, I'll take a fair half of your diddly.'

I gave him a copy of my notes.

IN THE FLORIDA Supreme Court, a lawyer is allotted half an hour to persuade the state's seven justices that a human being shouldn't be strapped into the electric chair and burned to death.

The judges looked at me with great interest. I thought, Yes, there's hope. I can do it. They will *see*.

To my left on the podium was a row of small lights. During my given half-hour, the lights would change from green to white, to warn me when my time was nearly up. When the lights flashed red, that was the end. You had to finish your sentence and step down.

I opened oral argument by pointing out that throughout the trial twelve years ago Judge Bill Eglin had called Darryl Morgan by his first name, had even called him 'boy', and in doing so had demeaned the defendant and poisoned the minds of the jury. Defence counsel at the time had not objected.

One of the younger judges raised her hand and said, 'Mr Jaffe, if you're arguing ineffective assistance of counsel, we've been down that road before in *Morgan*. Has anything changed?'

Looking into the judge's ice-blue eyes, I said, 'There's the new factor of perjured testimony by a state witness back in nineteen seventy-nine. You have copies of his affidavit in front of you, Your Honours. I alluded to it in my opening statement.'

The chief judge adjusted his bifocals and glanced at the papers in front of him. 'Counsellor, I have a problem here. I'm looking at the trial record, where the state prosecutor is listed as Edward M. Jaffe. Now I'm looking at your supporting affidavit—the appeal attorney is Edward M. Jaffe. Were you the prosecutor at the original trial?'

'Yes, I was.'

'Added to that, Mr Jaffe, is the fact that the witness you now claim was perjuring himself at the trial was *your* witness!'

'Yes, that's a fact.' I explained the circumstances of my meeting

Jerry Lee Elroy in Sarasota, and Elroy's admission to me. While I was doing that, the light bulbs turned from green to white.

I made my final plea. The judges retired.

In ten minutes they were back in their seats on the bench.

The chief judge said, 'We don't intend to draw this matter out and leave the appellant in suspense. This court stresses that it will not tolerate proceedings whose only purpose is to vex, harass or delay. We believe it is unseemly for a prosecutor to wear one hat at one trial and don another hat for an appeal. It is our view that Mr Morgan's trial was not perfect—few are—but neither was it fundamentally unfair. No relief is warranted.'

The judge tapped his gavel on the table.

My deepest ambition, to argue before the Supreme Court and save an innocent man's life, had danced before me and slipped away.

I HAD FAILED to save Darryl Morgan's life, and that plunged me into a pit of gloom that threatened to have no bottom. But life goes on. There were other things I had to deal with.

Toba was having a hard time, too. 'The country's depressed,' she said, 'and so am I.' Her real-estate office telephone rarely rang.

Cathy had a summer job as a cocktail waitress at a seafood restaurant on the quay. Alan was working at a garage on St Armands Key. He went camping one weekend down on the Caloosahatchee River with some friends. When he got back, he told Toba that they'd never been able to set up the tent properly and, when a heavy rain began to fall, he and another kid found a station wagon with the back door open. They went to sleep in it and were arrested for trespassing.

'Like criminals? That's absurd!' Toba cried.

He would handle it himself, Alan said.

Toba told me about it that evening. 'If he pleads guilty, what sort of fine will they give him in Fort Myers?'

'Couple of hundred bucks, maybe. Don't worry—the court will let him do community service.'

To make it easier for Alan to pay the fine, Toba decided to pay his bill with Dorothy Buford. She called to make the arrangements.

The therapist said, 'Alan's not been my patient for three weeks.'

'Oh? May I ask why you let him go?'

'*He* left. It was his decision that he didn't need more therapy.'

Toba sat on this knowledge for a full week. One evening in September, when I came home from the office, she told me what she had learned about Alan.

I left him a note: *Kiddo, I'll be waking you before I go to the office. I want to talk to you about your leaving therapy.*

When I came downstairs at six thirty, Alan was already pouring milk onto his granola. He said sadly, 'Well, I screwed up again.'

'That's a way of putting it.' I put a kettle of water on to boil.

'This is what happened,' Alan said. He wasn't getting anywhere with Dorothy Buford, and so for the last three weeks he'd spent the money that I'd contributed towards the therapy fee on marijuana.

'And the story I told you about what happened down on the Caloosahatchee, that's bull. We were in a car parked by the river. The cops rousted us about one o'clock in the morning because they were suspicious. They got us on possession. Two ounces.'

And one more thing, he said. He'd told us he'd passed the courses in physics and American history, but that wasn't true.

'Dad, I was thinking of going to San Francisco. My friend Bobby Woolford is out there now. He's got his own apartment and a job, and I can stay with him. Don't worry, he's off drugs.'

That evening I gathered my family together in the living room and told them that I had a proposition to make to Alan. I wanted their input as well as his.

I turned to him and said, 'I want to thank you for your honesty. I understand now why you're depressed, and even why you've contemplated suicide, because anyone who keeps making the same mistake over and over again has to know he's on a treadmill.'

Alan lowered his head.

'I made some calls today,' I said. 'I spoke to the head of a programme in upstate New York, and he said he'd make an opening for you. He wants you to come to Manhattan within a week for an interview, and I have to go with you.'

'Dad, I told you I wanted to go to San Francisco.'

'Yes, you did, and so I also spoke to the assistant state attorney down in Fort Myers. They could hit you with thirty days' jail therapy now. If you go to San Francisco before all that's settled, it makes you a fugitive. But if you go into the New York drug programme, the state of Florida will drop the charge.'

We argued for more than an hour. Toba said little and Cathy said nothing. Finally, I called a halt. 'Alan, I need to know by the end of the week. And the last time we talked, I made something clear to you—I'm not backing down on it. You can't stay in this house any longer. Go into the programme or get out of here.'

On Thursday morning, unshaven, Alan was waiting for me again at the breakfast table. 'All right,' he said quietly.

When you've won, when the other party's agreed to your terms, don't gloat or encourage more debate. Walk away. I made the necessary telephone calls. On Friday we flew to New York.

We stayed in a hotel facing Central Park. Office buildings soared into the sky and homeless men sprawled in their shadows.

'You like New York, Dad?'

'Yes, but I doubt that I could explain why.'

In the morning a warm September rain fell. Our cab driver spoke nearly incomprehensible English. Nevertheless, he got us to our destination on West 104th Street.

The drug programme, occupying a ravaged brownstone east of Broadway, consisted of a reception room, a few offices, and basement dormitories. It was early in the day but already hot. Alan and I waited on a wooden bench. Alan had brought a small suitcase which he clutched between his knees.

Our appointment was with Germaine Price, a frail, sharp-jawed woman in her late thirties, who led Alan into a small windowless office and asked me to wait outside.

Ten minutes later, Alan came out and said, 'Dad, can I talk to you privately?'

We went into a bare room that contained an old school desk. Alan said, in a strangled voice, 'This programme is for crackheads—real ghetto kids. The place they send you to is a hundred and twenty miles north of here, in the mountains. You have to stay sixty days without even making a telephone call. No visits for ninety days. You can't leave the grounds. It's like a prison. I don't need that.'

'What do you need, Alan?'

'I think I could take care of that misdemeanour business in Fort Myers. Go to court, explain things to the judge. Then I'd go to San Francisco, get a job. Get rid of my drug problem.'

'Baloney, Alan. I want to talk to Ms Price. Stay here, all right?'

I went into her windowless office and sat down with Germaine Price. 'Does this kid need your programme, or is it overkill?'

'Mr Jaffe, if he doesn't do this, or something like it, he'll die.'

I felt a terrible chill. 'I have to assume you're exaggerating.'

'No. Before his time, that's really what I'm saying. From AIDS, general deterioration, poverty, overdosing, stuff that happens in prison. They can be bright and they're usually good-natured, like your son seems to be. They lie a lot. They break your heart.'

I returned to the room where I'd left Alan. He was sitting on the desk, tapping his fingers on the scarred wood. His eyes were damp.

I said, 'I don't have the answer for you, son. I have my own choice to make, and I've made it. If you don't go into this programme, I wash my hands of you.' I felt my heart cracking.

Alan's face twitched and he shambled from the room.

Germaine Price came back to me half an hour later to tell me that he had signed up. It wasn't a triumph; it was just a beginning.

He came up the stairs from the basement with two black youths. One of them was tall and looked like a young Darryl Morgan.

'Who are they?' I asked Alan after they went into an office.

'Two guys in the family. They've been residents for a while— they're called expediters. Bucky and Jack. They're down here on a pass. We'll go up to Oakwood together in the van.'

He had the jargon already.

I took Alan with me to the front door and out on the step, while the rain drummed on concrete. I looked into Alan's face and saw that he was close to tears. But he was brave; he was going. I hugged him and whispered, 'Good luck, my boy.'

Withdrawing from the embrace, I twisted my mouth into a smile and walked off into the rain towards Broadway.

I went straight from Broadway and 104th Street to La Guardia Airport. Now it was Darryl Morgan's time, and there wasn't much left of it. But I had a plan. I didn't fly back to Sarasota. I flew to Orlando and changed planes for Gainesville.

He saw me first in daylight. I was sitting behind the wheel of a rented car and staring at him as he came out of a supermarket wheeling a cart full of groceries. He wore the usual floppy pastel-coloured cotton slacks and oversized white golf shirt that middle-aged Florida men wear in order to hide their paunches.

There was a melodic *tweet-tweet-tweet* as Floyd Nickerson hit the beeper that disarmed the alarm on his Buick. He looked up and his eyes locked with mine from a distance of about twenty yards. He probably thought little of it, although I stared pointedly for five seconds and didn't drop my gaze. He looked away.

He had noticed me; that was what mattered.

HIS HOUSE WAS diagonally across the street from the fifth hole of the Orange Meadow golf course. I had to have patience. Even more, I had to have luck.

At seven thirty the next morning I parked by the fairway, across from the two-storey pink house. At a few minutes past eight, the electronic garage door rolled up and a big blonde woman backed out behind the wheel of her Jeep Cherokee. Nickerson took a few steps from the interior of the garage to wave as she drove off.

He saw me again. I started the engine and cruised out along the eucalyptus-lined roads of Orange Meadow Estates. I followed the woman's car north on 441 to a modern glass-fronted real-estate office on University Boulevard in Gainesville. I didn't stop there; I just slowed down, had a good look, then kept driving.

Wherever Nickerson went now, he'd be looking for me. He might even see me if I wasn't there.

That evening I left my motel room and drove to a steakhouse on the edge of town, where I ate a filet mignon. After dinner I drove south on 441 to Orange Meadow Estates.

A Volvo appeared, curving through the streets behind me at a varying distance. I'd thought so when I left the motel, but I wasn't sure until now. The Volvo speeded up, passed me, then swerved to cut me off. I touched the brakes.

Nickerson was out from behind the wheel quickly, and so was another man who stayed by the Volvo. In a few strides, Nickerson was wrenching at the door handle of my maroon Toyota.

'Come out of there, Jaffe. What do you want?'

He wore khakis, his usual golf shirt and, because the night was cool, a poplin jacket. There wasn't much light there, so I couldn't see his expression. But he kept clenching and unclenching his fists. He wanted to harm me. I believe he was frightened.

'Let's talk, Nick.'

'There's nothing to talk about.'

'How about the good old days? Before you were on the take.'

He murmured a swearword. I heard his rapid breathing. No, he didn't want to harm me. He wanted to kill me.

'I have an affidavit,' I said, 'from Jerry Elroy. Remember him?'

'No,' he said, and that was probably the truth.

'Darryl Morgan's cellmate in Duval County Jail twelve years ago. He was the guy you set up to lie on the witness stand that he heard Morgan confess to killing Solly Zide.'

He took a step backwards.

'He'll testify to that, Nick. And you'll go to prison.'

He didn't know that Elroy had been stabbed to death at the dog track. He turned towards the Volvo and said, 'Patrick, this gentleman and I are going for a walk. Keep an eye on his car, OK?'

Patrick's voice came out of the darkness. 'Yes, sir.'

He grasped my arm and guided me past an oak tree, up a slope, onto the fairway. In the gloom I could see two broad bunkers and a pond. A humid night breeze blew from the pond. An owl hooted. When we got to the edge of the first trap, Nickerson halted and placed his hands on his hips, probably to keep them from strangling me.

'I remember Elroy,' he said. 'But your story, that's all bull.'

'You lied in court too, Nick. You testified that Morgan confessed to you. *That* was bull.'

He snickered, but he didn't say any more.

'Carmen Tanagra will testify to that,' I said.

'All lies.'

From behind the clouds a thin crescent of moon appeared.

'Nick, I'm trying to give you a break. You've got a new life, a new girlfriend. You want it all to go up in smoke? Your accounts at the Barnett Bank can be subpoenaed. You flew to the Bahamas in March of nineteen eighty for a little holiday. The cash that Neil Zide gave you went with you, and later it paid off your mortgage in Jacksonville. You want to tell me it wasn't a payoff from Neil Zide?'

Gary Oliver had been doing some good sleuthing.

Nickerson was silent for a few moments. Then he said, 'The big black kid shot and killed Solly Zide, and that's a fact.'

'No, it isn't, Nick.'

'If he didn't kill him,' Nickerson asked, 'who did?'

'I know *you* didn't do it.'

'Good,' he said, chuckling.

'All you did was destroy evidence. Keep witnesses from testifying. I don't think they'll give you more than ten years in Raiford.'

He stopped laughing.

'Of course, if you killed Gambrel, and they can prove it, then you'll swap places with Morgan. Where'd you put the payoff money, Nick? Bank of Nova Scotia in Nassau? A nice little offshore annuity?'

I'm not even sure what he did. I heard him grunt, I smelt his sour breath and felt a combination of pain and nausea all at the same time. He was big and quick. I think he did a karate step to the side and struck me in the groin with the toe of his shoe.

Dirt filled my mouth. I still smelt his meaty breath because he was leaning over me and pressing his fingers into my temples. He was so enraged he could hardly speak. His voice seemed to rasp at me from a watery distance. I couldn't understand most of what he said.

'. . . to lose, so mess with me, I'll *kill* you. Screw with my bank accounts, anything happens to me, you're *dead*.'

He raised his hand then and brought the edge of it down on the bridge of my nose. I heard the crack and immediately tasted blood.

I think he called for help because Patrick came up out of the darkness over the fairway. They dragged me down the hill to my car and I felt myself shoved into the passenger seat. Patrick drove me out of Orange Meadow Estates and, perhaps five minutes later, pulled over behind a gas station on the highway. He never said a word: neither did I. Patrick got out of the car and I never saw him again.

I checked myself into the emergency unit at County General Hospital. They asked me to undress because my shirt was wet with blood. A nurse pointed to the wire taped to my chest. 'What's that?' she asked, frowning.

'A wire,' I said.

'You a narc?'

'No. A lawyer.'

I didn't listen to the tape until I was back at the motel. And the next time I played it, forty-eight hours later, was for Judge Horace Fleming, in his chambers at the courthouse.

Muriel Suarez was present for the state attorney's office. She didn't argue much as to the legitimacy of the conversation—I'll give her that. But she did frown and say, 'There is a certain sense of entrapment here, Your Honour. I suggest that Mr Jaffe goaded him and very nearly put words in his mouth. It seems clear that Mr Nickerson was enraged beyond reason.'

'He sure sounds mad enough to kick the cat,' said the judge.

Judge Fleming looked me over. It was obvious that under my bandages I looked like a man who'd lost an argument with a truck. He nodded and then said, 'I'm going to think on this matter. I'll get back to you both in a day or so.'

Three afternoons later Fleming called us into his chambers.

'You're a persistent fella,' he said to me.

'Yes, Judge.'

'What is it you want?' he asked. 'In your own simple words.'

I cleared my throat. 'I want my client to have his day in court.'

'You want a hearing? With witnesses?'

'At least that, Your Honour.'

He raised a shaggy white eyebrow and turned to Muriel Suarez. 'And, ma'am, what is it *you* want?'

'Your Honour, what I *don't* want is for the state to have to go to the considerable expense of a full-scale hearing when there's already been an eight-day jury trial where Darryl Morgan was convicted of first-degree murder. There is no new evidence.'

'Well, there's this tape,' Judge Fleming said.

'That's not evidence,' Muriel shot back.

'It's a lot of shouting, that's what it is,' Judge Fleming said, nodding. 'But if you listen real good, you get to thinking.'

There wasn't much Muriel could do except shrug.

The judge turned back to me. 'If I give you a day in court, which witnesses would you put on?'

I decided to roll the dice double or nothing. 'Judge,' I said, 'if you grant my motion, you'll of course want to hear from the moving party, which is Morgan. We will have one or two other witnesses. But I believe you'll benefit by hearing the state witnesses, too.'

Muriel jumped forward. 'Judge, watch out. He's just about asking for a new trial!'

'Hang on there, both of you,' Fleming said. 'Mr Jaffe, if you're telling me you want to hear the state's principal witnesses, you've got more nerve than a toothache.'

'I'm saying *you* should hear them, Your Honour, if only for the sake of enlightenment. It would certainly be quicker and simpler than reading that three-thousand-page trial transcript.'

The judge stroked his jaw and looked straight into my eyes. 'You sure have got billy goat in your blood. You wouldn't mind doing a little cross-examination of those folks, would you?'

'Sir, I wouldn't mind a little cross.'

'Judge'—Suarez was angry and didn't hide it—'he *will* retry the case if you allow him to cross our principal witnesses!'

He smiled mischievously. 'Well, Ms Suarez, I'll ask you again: what do you want? Not what you don't want, but what you *do* want.'

Muriel rose to the occasion. 'I want justice, Your Honour, leavened with common sense.'

'Good for you,' Judge Fleming said. 'So do I, most of the time. But most of all, I want to be enlightened. Think of it this way.' He jerked a thumb in my direction. 'By the time it's over, we'll have this fella off our backs. That would make life a lot easier, wouldn't it?'

'Your Honour—'

'Just a little hearing,' Judge Fleming said, 'for the purposes of judicial enlightenment. So make it Monday, January sixth. I'll grant another stay. That gives you both plenty of time between now and then to think things over. Or maybe even cut a deal.'

I FELT TRIUMPHANT, even vindicated, when Judge Fleming granted a hearing in *Florida* v. *Morgan*. To win, I would have to make some sacrifices. How large they would be, how they would reshape my formerly ordered life, I could only speculate. I had to say to heck with it and lower my head to plunge forward through the thickets of deceit and the swamp of denial that my life had become. For now I knew that Darryl Morgan was innocent. What I didn't know was how to prove it and escape with my marriage and my career intact.

Fall moved slowly towards winter. I was nervous; I knew the upcoming hearing was the last chance to save Darryl Morgan's life.

Toba and I were finally allowed to call Alan up at Oakwood in New York. He explained that the telephone was in a hallway and there was a strict five-minute limit.

'What are you doing with your time?'

'There are a lot of family meetings. And I read a lot.'

'Do you run? Can you work out?'

'There's no place to run. And there's nothing to work out *with*.'

'But you're not depressed?'

'I'm doing it one day at a time,' Alan said gravely.

Prison inmates said that.

I FLEW TO JACKSONVILLE in late December. The Friday before the hearing was scheduled to begin, when I was sitting by the pool at the Marina Hotel eating a late breakfast, Gary Oliver called.

'I've got some people here in my office,' he said. 'I want to bring them over now.'

'Who are they? I hate surprises.'

'You might like this one,' he said, chortling.

I was going over the Nickerson tape before I drove down to Raiford that morning to see Darryl. I told Gary I was by the pool. 'If you don't see me, look underwater at the deep end.'

Half an hour later, he showed up at the poolside with an attractive but fidgety black woman who appeared to be about thirty years of age. She was wearing brand-new blue jeans and a pink sweater. With her was a boy. He was tall, lean, a bit surly in manner, maybe sixteen years old. He wore an old sweatshirt with a picture of Magic Johnson. He looked like a young Darryl. He looked *a lot* like a young Darryl.

'This is Pauline Powers,' Gary said, and she reached out to shake my hand. 'And this is Tahaun. He's Darryl's son.'

We drove down to Raiford together in Gary's Cadillac. By the time we turned off the interstate, I knew that Tahaun rooted for the Lakers, Dolphins and Braves, and wanted to be a basketball star but was worried because he was only six foot two. He was a high-school sophomore down in Boca Raton.

Pauline was only fifteen when Tahaun was born, and a few years later she married. Then her husband, Powers, an auto mechanic, was killed by a hit-and-run driver. Recently she saw on TV that Darryl was getting a new hearing for a murder he'd committed thirteen years ago. She hadn't known about the murder. She'd lost all touch with Darryl since he was a resident at Dozier.

'My husband, he was short. Tahaun wanted to know how come *he* get to be so tall. He asked about his natural daddy all the time.'

'You want to meet him?' I asked Tahaun.

'Yeah.'

'We'll try.'

At Raiford, I asked Assistant Superintendent Wright if Pauline and

Tahaun could join me in the visit. Darryl and I had been meeting the last couple of times in the attorneys' visiting room, the same room where he'd once tried to strangle me.

When I explained to Wright who I had with me, he thought it over for a few moments. 'How old is the boy?'

'Eighteen.'

He peered out into the anteroom, where Pauline and Tahaun sat stiffly on two plastic chairs.

'He doesn't look eighteen. Are you sure?'

'Yes.'

'You've got a lot of nerve, Jaffe. Anyone ever tell you that?'

'I've been told,' I admitted.

'They can see him if you're with them.'

So Darryl met his son and the now-grown-up Pauline. He was shy with her, and she with him. They were strangers, of course.

When I introduced him to Tahaun, Darryl blew out his breath in amazement. 'Oh, Lord,' he muttered, 'I *knew* it.' They shook hands, then drew back and measured each other for a while. They looked more like brothers than father and son.

'You play any ball in here?' Tahaun asked.

'Heck, no.'

'What do you do?'

Darryl thought for a while. There was a great deal, I realised, that he could have said. He could have told this boy stories that would raise the hair on the back of his sixteen-year-old neck.

'I'll show you what I do,' he said. Leaning forward a bit, in one smooth motion he slipped out a deck of worn playing cards from his back pocket, one of the decks I'd given him.

He entertained Pauline and his son and me for half an hour. His bony brown fingers seemed swifter than rips of lightning. Pauline squealed with pleasure. Tahaun just stared.

Darryl looked at Tahaun and gravely intoned, 'You're my son, so we got an affinity. I can read your mind, just like your mama can. I'm going to prove it to you.' Then, without touching the deck, Darryl ordered Tahaun to bury a chosen card and fan out the pack. He kept talking. 'I want you to concentrate! Think of that card. Think *hard*, boy!' And he guided Pauline's finger until it quivered over what turned out to be the king of hearts.

'That's it,' Darryl cried, seemingly flabbergasted.

'That *is* it,' Tahaun said, and he *was* flabbergasted. 'Do it again,' he told his father.

'Can't. I got to rest. The strain on my old brain is too much.'

A few minutes later the boy and his mother left, and Darryl and I went to work on what we wanted to happen in court.

When I was gathering up my papers and about to go, he said, 'What you think of my boy?'

'Good kid. Determined. What do *you* think?'

'Don't know what to think.' He seemed mystified, as Tahaun had been at the sleight of hand. 'Seem like a nice boy. I tell you something. I knowed he was out there, knowed I'd run into him one day. Once I got locked up and they got fixing to kill me, seemed like I'd never see him. But I did, man, I *did*.' He thought for a long time, brows knitted together, and then put his hard hand on my shoulder. That was the hand that had nearly strangled me last February.

'They come see me again?' he asked.

'I'll try to arrange it.'

IN THE YELLOW GLARE of the overhead bank of lights, Judge Horace Fleming's bald skull shone like a nearly full moon. His huge courtroom had a twenty-foot-high ceiling. The pale walls weren't particularly clean. The judge's oak bench swept in a magisterial arc halfway across the room. This was the same courtroom where Darryl Morgan's trial had taken place and where Judge Bill Eglin had overridden the jury and pronounced his sentence.

Here now—half-glasses perched on the end of his bulbous nose—Horace Fleming reigned. There was no jury. This wasn't a trial, merely a hearing to determine whether or not there should be any change in Darryl Morgan's status. The judge, after hearing the evidence, could dismiss or grant my motion for a new trial; he could commute the death sentence to life; and in extraordinary circumstances he could even send Darryl home.

It was an open court, and the press had learned what was going on. Zide was a name to be reckoned with in Florida, and the murder was remembered. On Monday morning the courtroom was full.

Muriel Suarez and John Whatley, the assistant state attorney, carried the banner for the state of Florida. As soon as Fleming rapped his gavel, young Whatley sprang to his feet. 'If it please the court, the state of Florida moves to disqualify Edward Jaffe as counsel for the defence in the matter of *Florida* versus *Morgan*.'

'Why?' Fleming demanded.

Whatley gave all the reasons, and it was clear to me he'd been coached by Beldon. He was personable and deeply confident.

Fleming peered over his tortoiseshell glasses. 'I don't mind people thinking I'm senile and stupid,' he said. 'But if any of you lawyers think we've come this far just to turn tail and go fishing, you're in the wrong courtroom. Florida, call your first witness.'

Whatley started to open his mouth again, but Muriel Suarez yanked him by the sleeve of his jacket and stood up at the counsel table. She wore a black wool nipped-at-the-waist Italian-looking creation and filigreed gold glasses. Other than lipstick, she had used no make-up today, so that she looked like a scholarly courtesan. Even Fleming couldn't keep his eyes off her.

'Permission to approach the bench, Your Honour,' Muriel said.

'Come right up,' the judge said. He couldn't refuse.

Up there, we could only whisper. I leaned across the oak bench, with Gary Oliver at my side. Muriel leaned from another angle, backed up by an eager John Whatley. The judge bent forward with an audible creak, turning up his hearing aid. This was all off the record.

'Your Honour,' Muriel said softly, 'the state is now willing to join the defence in a motion to commute the sentence of Darryl Morgan from death by electrocution to life imprisonment.'

'Well!' said the judge, surprised. 'What say you, Mr Jaffe?'

I was surprised, too. I was more than surprised. I cleared my throat and told him that I'd have to consult with my client.

'How long will that take?' the judge asked, a little puzzled by what he took to be my coolness.

'I don't know, Your Honour. Maybe half an hour. Maybe longer.'

'Mr Jaffe, this isn't what I'd call a complicated decision. We'll recess until ten o'clock tomorrow. That should give your client plenty of time for making up his mind whether he wants to live or die.'

IN THE COUNTY JAIL'S air-conditioned room given over to visits by lawyers, Darryl kept clenching and unclenching his fists, and now and then he beat with them against his massive thighs.

'You can live,' I said. 'That's what it comes down to.'

He looked at me. 'How much time I got to do that way?'

'Another twelve years before you're eligible for parole. There's no guarantee you'll get parole. But you'll *live*.'

'I ain't afraid of death,' he said.

'I know that. Listen, Darryl, if you take this deal, you get off the row. You work at a job, you walk around the yard, you have visitors.'

'How it turn out if we keep going?'

'I don't know,' I admitted.

'You want me to take the deal, right?'

'If I tell you to turn it down, and we lose this appeal, and they electrocute you, I can't live with that, Darryl.'

He put his hand on my shoulder again. 'You got to think about what *I* can live with, Mr Lawyer. What you can live with don't matter, 'cause you out there, a free man. Hear what I'm saying?'

I just nodded.

He began to pace the little room. Then he said, 'Tahaun, he came back again with Pauline yesterday. You know that?'

'I heard.' Gary Oliver had told me about it.

'I talk to that kid alone for a time,' Darryl said. 'I ask Pauline to step outside. She a real good woman. She do it for me. You know, he's a nice boy. But he got problems.'

'I have a son too. They all have problems.'

'Black boy got different ones. We talk for a while, then I say, "How *are* you, dude?" And he turn away; he don't want me to see him cry. Then I remembers what it's like to be sixteen, and big, and black. I figure out he's angry. And he got to get past the anger so's he can see who he is and who he wants to be. I tell him that.'

'I hope he paid attention,' I said. 'It was good advice.'

Darryl nodded, but he wasn't really concerned with my reaction; he was listening to himself. 'You got to fight, I tells him.'

He was silent. Then he said, 'I take the deal, where I got to go now? What kind of life? Listen to me, man, 'cause I don't believe you hear what I'm saying.' His dark eyes glowed furiously.

'Where that boy gonna go?' he demanded. 'He a lot smarter than me, but still he do some drugs. I asked him and he told me.'

Darryl leaned forward to me. 'I didn't kill that man. You know that. You get me outa here, you get me free, I can take care of that boy. I can do it. I get a job, I stay with Pauline, if she have me.'

'You're telling me,' I said slowly, 'that you don't want to take the deal the state's offered you.'

'And you're hearing me,' he said.

I felt my heartbeat quicken. 'You're throwing the dice for your life.'

'No. *You* throwing the dice. I just putting up the stakes.'

Darryl smiled at the thought, showing white teeth and frightened eyes. He was taking responsibility for his life, just as he had done thirteen years before with Gary Oliver. I had respect for this man.

'We have a chance,' I said.

'Then go to the whip, dude,' Darryl said.

On Tuesday morning Judge Fleming showed me an emotion midway between vexation and anger. 'Counsellor, it's my duty to remind you that your first responsibility is to keep your client alive.'

'My client knows what's going on, Your Honour. We'll gratefully accept the state's joining our motion to commute the death penalty, but we want a new trial on the guilt-or-innocence issue.'

The judge beckoned and I leaned forward across the bench. He whispered, 'Mr Jaffe, if your client's guilty, you'd do better trying to put socks on a rooster than looking for a new trial in *my* court.'

I whispered back, 'He's not guilty.'

The judge then called shrilly, 'Mr Morgan, kindly step up here.'

Darryl got to his feet and lumbered to the bench.

Fleming wagged a finger at the court reporter, meaning, Stop transcribing. The judge then leaned forward, his white whiskers almost touching Darryl's nose. I could barely hear him.

'Your lawyer,' Fleming said softly, 'claims you're turning down the state's offer of a life sentence. You aware of that?'

'Yes, sir.'

'You agree with your lawyer?'

'Yes, sir. I agrees.'

'You think I'm a pussycat? You think I care if you live or die?'

'No, sir,' Darryl said. 'I don't think you do.'

'You can sit down,' the judge said.

He raised his head then and said, 'Let's get on with this hearing.'

The state called ex-JSO Sergeant Carmen Tanagra, under subpoena, as its first witness. Tanagra was sworn in by the court clerk. John Whatley rose from the counsel table to question her.

In clipped, unemotional prose, the former homicide sergeant set the scene for us: the luxurious beach estate, the tropical night, the hard glare of the floodlights. She and Sergeant Nickerson pulled up in the driveway. The three Jacksonville Beach patrolmen who had first reached the house took them straight to the body on the terrace. The crime scene, as far as she knew, had been preserved. After making sure that Mrs Zide's bleeding had been staunched, she talked to Neil Zide and then walked about the grounds and discovered the dead Doberman near the beach cabanas. In the wet sand closer to the ocean, she found the imprint of the sneakers of two running men.

When she got back to the house, red lights were flashing. An ambulance had arrived and paramedics were bundling Mrs Zide into it. Her partner, Sergeant Nickerson, was questioning Neil Zide. Armed with Neil Zide's description of the two young black men, she and Nickerson set out together into the dark night to see if they could find the perpetrators. Tersely she described the encounter at the Lil' Champ, the death of William Smith, the arrest of Darryl Morgan.

'Pass the witness,' Whatley said.

I rose slightly in my chair. My tone was casual. 'Ms Tanagra,' I asked, 'when you and Sergeant Nickerson arrived at the Zide estate in your car, how did you get in?'

'Through a gate down at the road,' she said.

'The gate was open?'

'I don't really remember. Maybe open, maybe shut. There was a security guard there. Maybe he opened it.'

'Did you wonder, considering that several shots had been fired, why the guard was there at the gate and not up at the house?'

Carmen Tanagra thought. 'I seem to recall that someone had given him an order to stay there because the police were coming.'

'Did he say who gave him that order?'

'If he did, I don't remember.'

'How far was it from the gate to the house?'

'Hard to say.'

'If you don't mind, I'll try to refresh your memory.' I signalled to Gary Oliver, who stepped into the hallway leading to the judge's chambers and returned with an easel and a large sheet of white cardboard. On it was drawn a plan of the Zide estate.

'Your Honour,' Muriel said, 'I don't see the relevance.'

'The purpose of this line of questioning,' I said, 'is clarity. And enlightenment.'

That was the magic word. The judge said, 'Overruled.' He turned to me. 'Just hurry it along, Mr Jaffe.'

I pointed out to Carmen Tanagra that according to the drawing it was a quarter of a mile from the front gate to the Zide house.

'That seems about right,' she said.

'Ms Tanagra, if a shot had been fired in the house while you were passing through that gate, would you have heard it?'

'Of course,' Carmen said.

'When you reached the house, what other vehicles were parked on the driveway in front of the house?'

'Two black-and-whites from Jacksonville Beach. And one civilian car, belonging to a man named Victor Gambrel.'

Gambrel was in the living room, taking care of Mrs Zide, she explained, when she and Nickerson entered the house. He had been there for only a couple of minutes, he told them, after a telephone call he received from Neil Zide.

'Were you able in any way to corroborate that Mr Gambrel had been in the house "only a couple of minutes"?'

'I believe the security guard corroborated it.'

'Oh? The one down by the gate? When did you talk to him?'

'Sergeant Nickerson questioned him the next day.'

'And did either of you question Mr Gambrel?'

'Sergeant Nickerson did, later. He and Gambrel knew each other.'

Gary Oliver was scribbling notes across the lines of his legal pad.

Muriel Suarez's eyes were on Gary as he wrote; she was frowning.

'Did you ask Mrs Zide and Mr Neil Zide if they'd touched anything in that area? And if they'd moved the body at all?'

'Yes, I did ask. They said no.'

I was fishing. The hook was wiggling a little in the murky depths, and I wasn't sure what was on it. But I felt that slight pressure.

Slowly I said, 'Ms Tanagra, why did you go off to find the dog?'

'Because someone had said, "I wonder if the dog's all right. Why isn't he barking?" Something like that. And I went out there to find out. The son said that, I think. Said the dog was down by the beach.'

'Did you go down to the beach alone?'

'No, I took one of the Jacksonville Beach cops with me. Nick said, "Don't go alone, Carmen. You never know who's out there." '

I took a chance. 'When you and the third Beach cop got back from the cabanas, were the two other Beach cops still in the living room with the Zides and Gambrel and Nickerson?'

'I don't think so,' Carmen Tanagra said. 'I think the ambulance was coming up the drive and those two guys were out there to flag it down. Yes, I'm positive of that.'

'Positive . . . after thirteen years?'

'Yes,' she said, but I could see by the fresh lines etched into her forehead that she was troubled by some memory.

'I have no more questions,' I said, 'for now.'

John Whatley said, 'The state of Florida calls Constance Zide.'

Heads turned and necks craned. A uniformed bailiff escorted Connie into the courtroom, down the aisle and to the witness stand. As the door hissed shut you could hear the clicking of cameras. Connie's black leather purse was raised in front of her face.

When she passed in front of me on her way to the stand, I understood why she was covering her face. I hadn't seen Connie since the day Darryl Morgan had been given his death sentence. She was sixty years old now. Her hair was the same colour, dyed now to mask the grey. But her hair was almost the only recognisable feature.

Connie's cheeks were doughy and a roll of flesh moved down from the chin to the thick throat. The scar was gone; cosmetic surgery had taken care of that. She wore a black suit, as if still in mourning. She walked as if it took effort to move her hips down the aisle, and she seemed grateful finally to sit down in the witness box.

Oh, Connie . . . my old dear Connie, what happened to you?

John Whatley treated her gently.

He took her back thirteen years to the night of December 5, and in a slightly hoarse but warm voice, which had hardly changed over time, she told the story of that night. She had heard shots, she recalled, and rushed outside to the terrace, where her husband lay dead. Two black men had been standing there, one with a pistol in his hand. Someone slashed her in the face. That's all she remembered.

Whatley moved a deferential step backwards, like a courtier withdrawing before a queen. 'No further questions. Thank you, Mrs Zide.' He turned to me and said curtly, 'Pass the witness.'

'I have no questions,' I said.

Connie's eyes shone at me with a gratitude beyond deserving.

I added, 'But I would like to have Mrs Zide stay on call.'

Connie stayed in the courtroom to listen to her son testify. Neil's hair was still long and unruly, but he had shaved for this occasion, and wore a black three-piece suit and cranberry-coloured tie. His testimony echoed what his mother had said. No surprises.

When Whatley said, 'Pass the witness,' I rose from my seat.

'Mr Zide, you and I have known each other socially for about fourteen years, isn't that correct?'

'Yes, it is.' He was already wary.

'So you won't mind if I call you Neil?'

'No, of course not . . . Ted.'

'Neil, you heard Ms Carmen Tanagra today, didn't you?'

'Yes, I was here,' Neil said.

I consulted Gary Oliver's notes. 'Sergeant Tanagra remembered that the reason she went down to the beach was because someone had said, "I wonder if the dog's all right. Why isn't he barking?" And she thought that someone was you. Do you remember that, Neil?'

He laughed good-naturedly. 'Ted, we're talking thirteen years ago. I like to think I've got a good memory, but that's pushing it.'

'You didn't tell Sergeant Tanagra where the dog was?'

'Look, I'm saying I *may* have. Or I may *not* have. I don't want to guess or speculate. I'm under oath, Ted.'

'So you are.' I picked up a folder from the table and handed it to Neil. 'Would you open that, please, and tell us its contents?'

Neil opened the folder carefully and flipped through the pages inside. Then he looked up at me calmly. He shrugged. 'They seem to be copies of a statement I made to the police thirteen years ago. And my testimony at the subsequent trial.'

'Your memory was fresh then, wasn't it?'

'Yes, of course.'

I took the folder from his hand and read aloud to the judge: ' "They were young, black, wearing sneakers, jeans, and I seem to remember a dark T-shirt. There were two of them. I didn't get a decent look at the other one, who cut my mother. They obviously didn't expect anyone to be awake at that hour." '

I looked up at the bench. 'That's from the JSO offence report, Your Honour. Mr Zide signed each page in the margin. And now I'll read from the trial transcript:

'Q. [*by Mr Jaffe*]—Did you see them clearly?
'A. [*by Mr Zide*]—Oh, yes.
'Q.—They weren't in shadow?
'A.—No, I could see them quite well. One was a very tall young black man. The other one I don't remember as well. The spotlights on the lawn had finally been triggered, I assume by these two men, so there was a lot of light out there.
'Q.—About how far away from you were the two men?
'A.—Oh ... fifteen or twenty feet perhaps. Hard to say exactly.
'Q.—And for how long did the two men remain there on the terrace before they ran away?
'A.—It's hard to say. A few seconds. But it was long enough for me to see their faces.
'Q.—Is either of those two men in the courtroom here?
'A.—One of them.
'Q.—Would you point to him and identify him?
'A.—The man who shot my father is sitting at the table there. [*The witness pointed to Mr Morgan.*]'

I laid the papers on the table. 'That's accurate, isn't it, Neil?'
'Yes. I believe you read it accurately.'
'Neil, Mr Morgan's in the courtroom today, too, isn't he?'
Neil scowled. He felt I was treating him like a child and he didn't like it. 'Yes, he's here,' he said.
'Mr Morgan, would you please stand up?'
Darryl rose slowly to his full six foot six inches.
'Neil, what's the first thing you notice about Mr Morgan?'
'Objection as to relevance,' Whatley interrupted.
'That will become clear,' I said.
'Overruled,' Judge Fleming said. 'You can answer, Mr Zide.'
'Well,' Neil said, 'he's black and he's tall.'
'Normally tall?'
'What do you mean?'
'Well, there's tall and there's very tall, wouldn't you say?'
'Yes, I see what you mean. Very tall, I suppose.'
'That's how you described him under oath at the trial.'
'Yes, exactly.'
'Thirteen years ago, on the night your father was shot and killed,

when Sergeant Nickerson asked you for a description of Mr Morgan, how did you describe Mr Morgan?'

'That same way. Black. Tall. Young, I think.'

Now came the litany. He had to be led and hypnotised.

'Neil, I read the police offence report aloud, didn't I?'

'Yes.'

'That night you described Mr Morgan as black, isn't that so?'

'Yes.'

'And you did say he and Mr Smith were young, didn't you?'

'Yes.'

'And you described what he and Mr Smith were wearing?'

'Yes.'

'And did you also describe Mr Morgan as tall?'

Neil was silent.

'Did you mention his height or size *at all*?'

Neil sighed.

'Isn't it a fact, Neil, that less than an hour after your father's murder, you didn't describe Darryl Morgan—the man who allegedly shot your father—as tall?'

Neil looked to the judge for help, but none was forthcoming.

'And yet,' I said, 'three months later, in the courtroom at the trial, you described him to me as *very* tall—isn't that so?'

'Because by then I remembered.'

I waited, but Neil said nothing more. So I started to turn away, then stopped, scratched my head.

'There's just one more little thing,' I said. 'I nearly forgot it.' I shuffled through the papers in the folder I still held and came up with one page more of Neil's thirteen-year-old testimony. 'What you swore to thirteen years ago,' I said, 'is that you heard a noise, and your father got up and went out to the terrace. Your mother followed him. And you heard three shots.'

'Yes.'

'Not two shots, or four shots, or five shots?'

'No, three . . . as best I recall.'

'How long did it take, Neil, between the time you heard the shots and the time you reached the terrace?'

'Probably ten seconds.'

'You reached there just in time to see a black man, who we later learned was William Smith, make some movement with his hand towards your mother's face?'

'Yes.'

'No more shots were fired?'

'No.'

'No more questions,' I said.

Whatley ended his presentation by reminding the court that the state had no burden of proof and therefore no more witnesses.

Now it was my turn.

It was also time for the lunch break, and I welcomed it. I needed to talk to Gary Oliver. I made my way to the back of the courtroom and started carving a path between the reporters and the TV cameras.

Then suddenly, startlingly, there stood my wife. She wore what I called her travelling outfit: a pair of floppy khaki trousers, a camel-hair blazer and leather boots. I shoved through the mob to Toba's side and she fell into my arms.

It was Alan, of course. He had called at seven that morning. He said, 'Mom, I can't stand it here any more. I'm going tomorrow. I just thought I owed it to you and Dad to let you know.'

'And what are *you* doing?' I asked Toba.

'I have a plane ticket that gets me into Newark at six o'clock. I'll rent a car and find this Oakwood joint. If he still insists on going, at least I can make sure he doesn't go on the road like a pauper.'

'The road to where?'

'San Francisco, he said. He was going to hitchhike.' She hunched her shoulders. 'Can you imagine? In the middle of January?'

I shook my head in despair. 'It's a mistake for Alan to quit.'

She straightened up. 'Well, Ted, you've done all you can. You can't leave in the middle of a trial. So I'll go up and deal with it.'

Wrong. If I was battling to save Darryl, didn't I owe the same allegiance and effort to my son? Judge Fleming had given me until 5pm tomorrow to finish the hearing. It didn't seem that I could go up to Oakwood with Toba and get back in time. But I had to.

'Let's go find Gary Oliver.'

TOBA AND I flew to Newark, grabbed a Hertz car, and by six thirty had struggled through the maze of highways onto Route 17 into New York State. The night was dark and the temperature well below freezing. The highway rose gradually into the Catskills. The cold wind ripped past the car. Toba was at the wheel.

We had telephoned from the airport. When we bumped down the icy dirt road outside Oakwood and spotted the ramshackle buildings of the therapeutic community, a flashlight beam shone out of the darkness. Toba slowed to a crawl. I opened a window.

'Dad? Mom?' It was Alan, bundled in a thick winter parka.

Inside the main building, Alan looked grave, a little confused. He seemed leaner but healthy-looking, and certainly looked older. He embraced us. Behind him, Germaine Price, still frail and pale, bustled in from another room. 'I'm sure you want to talk to Alan alone,' she said. 'So I'll join you in a minute.'

Alan led us upstairs into an office with a sagging sofa, a desk and a single easy chair. 'Well, this is what's happening,' he said, easing himself onto the surface of the desk. 'This was the wrong programme for me, but I needed help and I got it. Sticking it out here was the hardest thing I ever had to do. The thing is, it's time to go.'

And we couldn't stop him either, he said. He had fifty dollars he'd saved from his last job. He wanted to borrow a few hundred more from us. But if we wouldn't lend it to him, he was going anyway. He'd hitchhike out west, work along the way, survive.

'What will you do when you get to San Francisco?' I asked.

'Study and work.'

'What will you study?'

'Art, or maybe journalism.'

Germaine Price slid into the room. 'What has he told you?'

Toba repeated most of what Alan had said and finished with, 'I'm impressed. I trust him. I think we have to trust him.'

Germaine dropped into the one empty chair and gave a thin laugh. 'Why? He's a lying junkie.'

Alan smiled nervously. Toba's lips quivered; her cheeks brightened, as if she'd been struck. 'That was unnecessary,' she said.

'A little rough,' Germaine said, 'but no less true.' She lit a cigarette, then took a deep drag. 'Mrs Jaffe, he wanted you to come up here. You understand that, don't you? If Alan wanted to, he could have taken off yesterday, the day before, any time.'

Toba leaned back against the sofa. 'You think it's money.'

'I know it's money.' Germaine sucked at her cigarette. 'Didn't you bring it?'

Toba reddened.

'Without money,' Germaine said, 'he won't go. He can't go. He'd freeze to death in a ditch. He uses you. He's clever at it.'

Alan sprang up and said to Germaine, 'Will you please keep out of this?' He faced his mother. 'Now, just yes or no, like Dad would say. Will you lend me the damn money, or not?'

I felt myself flush. 'Watch your language,' I cautioned.

Alan glared at me; I'd never seen that much anger on his face.

'I'd like to talk to you,' I said. 'Alone, if no one minds.'

Toba and Germaine went out of the door.

'Is it true you called Mom just to get money from her?'

'Probably,' he said, a bitter smile twisting his jaw to one side. 'So what? I sure didn't ask her to come up here. I asked to borrow money. Big deal! Isn't money the big thing in everyone's life? What's so terrible about asking for it?'

Alan had never lost his temper with us. He always tried to con us with amiable sweetness and apologies and promises, usually with some success. But that sweetness seemed to have fled.

'Alan, I'd like to explain something to you—'

'I don't want to hear it,' he said sharply, raising his open palm.

I ground my teeth. It had been a long day.

'A few minutes ago,' Alan resumed with fervour, 'Mom said she had faith in me—you remember? And Germaine said that was dumb, because I was a lying junkie. Well, I saw the look on your face and I knew right away you agreed. So I want to ask you, why don't you have any faith? Because you always think I'm going to mess up, unless I do it by the rules? Your rules?'

I hadn't thought of that; he might have been right.

He kept going. 'Who cares if you're right? Give *me* a chance to be right! Or wrong! You can't run my life any more, that's the bottom line. I'm getting out of here, Dad. Tomorrow.'

Yesterday, when the state had offered him life instead of certain death, Darryl had made a choice. He had turned down the offer and chosen to throw the dice, risking everything. That was a human being's final privilege.

My son's, too. He was declining this sanctuary, which he hated, in favour of risk. And he had no advocate to argue for him. He had to do it all alone. I began to respect him. 'Good luck,' I said.

'I will!'

He was hearing words other than the ones I spoke. But that was all right. We all do that.

I yawned and said, 'Let's go. I'm bushed. I'm hungry, too. Would you like to go into town and have a hamburger and coffee with us?'

He took a few deep breaths and studied my face, looking for hidden motive, but there was none. I was just tired.

'Sure,' he said.

'Is there a place that's open?'

'A diner on 17 outside the town of Oakwood.'

We drove through Oakwood and ate at the diner. Alan ordered eggs with a double ration of bacon, which he hadn't tasted in three months. After we ate, I realised he didn't light up a cigarette.

'No,' he said. 'I quit.'

'Why?' Toba asked.

'To prove something to myself, I guess, and because I always wanted to. It's a disgusting habit.'

Alan went to the men's room.

'What happened?' Toba asked. 'He seems so calm.'

'I'll tell you on the drive back. Meanwhile, I'm going outside. Give him a few hundred dollars. He'll take it from you, but not from me.'

'But—'

'Let him throw the dice and do it his way, Toba, whatever that is.'

I TRIED TO SLEEP on the drive to Newark Airport, but at one o'clock in the morning it began to drizzle, and then sleet fell. My forehead pressed against the car window; it was like cosying up to the shady side of an iceberg. Toba skidded on a curve and asked me to drive.

By 4am, when we returned the car to Hertz, my nose was dripping, my eyes felt ragged and I had trouble keeping them open.

'I'll come to court with you,' Toba said. 'I'd better be there if you fall asleep at the counsel table.'

My heart seemed to slow another beat or two. 'That's good of you, darling, but—'

'Oh, knock it off, Ted. I'm coming.'

There was nothing I could do. She would be there, and she would hear my witnesses.

TOBA AND I reached the courthouse just before eleven in the morning.

Floyd Nickerson was to have been my first witness. He was under a subpoena that Gary Oliver had hand-delivered one evening a week before to Orange Meadow.

The previous day, after lunch, Gary had gone to Judge Fleming and explained that I'd been called out of town on urgent family business, but that I'd be back the following morning.

In a midnight call from Oakwood, I had prepped Gary on how to examine Nickerson. 'Draw it out until I get there. Whatever you do, save the other witnesses for me.' But as soon as I pushed open the courtroom door on Wednesday morning, I realised that Floyd Nickerson was not on the witness stand.

Darryl Morgan, in a khaki jumpsuit provided by the jail, filled a wooden chair at the counsel table. Gary Oliver, seated next to him, was questioning a medical examiner named Duckworth.

Toba and I passed by Connie and Neil Zide. With a gracious smile, Toba squeezed herself into a seat on the wooden pew across the aisle from them. I continued to the counsel table.

Gary looked up and spotted me. Without hesitation, he said, 'No further questions, Your Honour, and we request a brief recess.'

Judge Fleming banged his gavel in agreement.

I sat down, nodding to Darryl. Clutching Gary's arm, I said softly, 'Where the devil is Nickerson?'

Gary told me. At three that morning, Nickerson had killed himself.

'I don't believe it,' I whispered.

'Believe, Ted. Ate his gun. In his garage.'

Jerry Lee Elroy, now Floyd Nickerson. I could understand how you might think twice about becoming a witness for Ted Jaffe.

'Go get Terence,' I said. I stood up, brushed past Whatley, grabbed Muriel Suarez by the arm and made a dash for chambers.

JUDGE FLEMING PEERED at me. 'You lost another one?'

'Yes, sir.'

'You got any other witnesses worth my listening to?'

'Yes, sir.'

'They in court or close enough to hear you yell?'

'Yes, sir.'

'And by the way,' the judge said, adjusting his glasses and letting his eyes roam over me, 'what the heck happened to you?'

'I had a long night, Your Honour.'

'Worth it?'

'Too early to tell.'

'Usually is,' the judge said. 'Well, we're here, and we've got a few hours left of precious court time. Seems a shame to send all these snoopy TV folks home early. How long will you take?'

'Not too long,' I said.

Back in the courtroom, I dropped down in a wooden chair next to Darryl and said, 'The defence calls Michael Stanzi.'

Mike Stanzi, the JSO ballistics expert, was still working at the same job. I had his report and trial testimony in front of me. He was a man of forty-five, with curly grey hair and a big moustache.

'Mr Stanzi, tell us briefly what you observed on December sixth, nineteen seventy-eight, when you reached the Zide estate.'

No secret about that. Stanzi had observed a corpse with two bullet holes. The rounds were from a .38 revolver. A third shot from the same weapon had struck the wall on the far side of the living room from the terrace and embedded itself in the oak panelling.

'You found no other spent rounds?'

'No, I didn't.'

'And you never found the gun?'

'Never.'

'Then it's possible that more than three shots were fired from that .38-calibre pistol, isn't it?'

'We didn't find any evidence of that.'

'Did you look outside the house?'

'No, because the pistol had been fired by someone facing the house from the direction of the terrace.'

'But how did you know that?'

'I was told by a fellow officer.'

'Which fellow officer told you that?'

'I believe it was Sergeant Nickerson, when we arrived.'

'The bullet in the woodwork didn't tell you anything about any bullets that might have been fired from inside the room in the direction of the lawn, did it?'

'There weren't any other bullets out there,' Stanzi said smugly.

'How do you know that?'

'Because there were only three shots fired, and those rounds were all accounted for.'

'And how did you know *that*?'

'Sergeant Nickerson informed me.'

Nickerson! Nickerson was the key, and Nickerson was dead.

'Did anyone conduct a paraffin test of the hands and face of Darryl Morgan? And of William Smith down at the morgue?'

'Yes. I did.'

'With what results?'

'Negative. But that didn't mean that neither of them fired a gun. It's only proof if there *is* paraffin. People can wear gloves.'

'Did you do a paraffin test of any of the people in the house?'

Stanzi looked puzzled. 'No, sir. Why should we? The people in the house were the victims.'

I said, 'Pass the witness.'

Muriel didn't know in what direction I was heading, but she saw that thus far I hadn't done any damage to the state's old case.

'No questions,' she said.

When we broke for lunch, I looked towards the rear of the courtroom. Connie and Neil were still there. She was dressed in a grey suit today, as she had been when I first met her.

At lunch with Toba, I ate a grilled cheese sandwich and drank nearly a quart of coffee. Then we went back to the courtroom. The bailiff called for order as I moved forward to the counsel table. The throng settled into the wooden pews and became quiet.

'The defence,' I said, 'calls Terence O'Rourke.'

We had located him in a small rest home only a hundred yards from the ocean, south of St Augustine. It was pricey there, but that wasn't a surprise. Terence had been given a handsome pension.

He was lucky to be alive.

The courtroom door swung open to admit Terence, Gary and a bailiff. Terence was a round-bellied man with sparse white hair, protuberant eyes and horn-rimmed spectacles, and he wore a sports jacket and tie. He had been a cop in Orlando, and had a lilting Irish brogue. I had him identify himself as a former security guard at the Zide estate and provide some background. Then I said, 'Sir, were you a witness in nineteen seventy-nine, in *Florida* versus *Morgan?*'

'No, sir, I was not.'

'Were you ever interviewed by any police officers?'

He related to the court that Sergeant Floyd Nickerson had talked to him on two or three occasions and had finally thanked him and said that he wouldn't be needed as a witness.

'Mr O'Rourke,' I said, 'did you follow the Morgan trial in the newspapers and on television?'

'No. I was on vacation around that time. I have a daughter in Colorado and a son near Los Angeles. I went out to visit them.'

'Do you recall anything unusual about that vacation?'

'Well, the way it came about was a little unusual, you could say. I had a week due me in summer, but Mrs Zide came to me one night in February—poor lady still had her face all bandaged up—and she said she'd prefer I take my holiday earlier, in the spring, for reasons that I don't at this moment recall. And because it might be an inconvenience, she said, I could take longer than was due. She indicated she was pleased with my work too, so she gave me three weeks off with pay, she did. The Zides were fine people to work for.'

'And so you missed the Morgan trial?'

'I was away for all of it, yes. That's what I'm telling you.'

'Mr O'Rourke, cast your mind back and tell us what happened on that night of December fifth, nineteen seventy-eight.'

He was on duty, he said, down at the main gate. There was a party. A good many cars moving in and out.

'You were alone at the gate?'

'Yes, I was alone.'

'You stayed awake?'

'Not all the time. I must have been dozing at one point.'

'What woke you?'

'A shot.'

'When you say "a shot", do you mean, literally, a single shot, or many shots?'

'A single shot is what I meant.'

'And what did you do in response?'

Terence O'Rourke sighed a bit mournfully, a bit bravely. 'Nothing. I waited . . . a minute or two.'

'And after that minute or two, did you hear anything else?'

'I heard more shots.'

'How many more?'

'Three or four, I believe. If I had to choose, I'd say three.'

'The three shots were together or spaced out?'

'Close together. One after the other. Like *bang bang bang.*'

'When you heard the three shots, what did you do?'

'I took my pistol out of my holster and I went up to the house.'

'You walked up there?'

'With a flashlight in my hand, I did indeed. When I reached the house, Mr Neil came out and said to me, "Terence, a terrible thing has happened. We've sent for the police. Go back to the gate and wait for them." And I did that.'

'And did the police come, as Neil Zide had said they would?'

'Yes, indeed they came.'

'How much later?'

'Thirty-five minutes later. We kept a log. I wrote down the times.'

'I see. And did anyone else come before the police got there?'

'One person. Mr Neil called down to the gate and said a man would be arriving shortly and I should let him in and not talk to him.'

'Do you remember the name of that man?'

'Gambrel, it was.'

'And the man named Gambrel arrived approximately when?'

'About twenty minutes before the police.'

'You're sure of these time intervals because you wrote all this down in your log?'

'I did indeed.'

'What happened to that log?'

He sighed. 'I gave it to Sergeant Floyd Nickerson.'

'Did Sergeant Nickerson ever give it back to you?'

'He did not.'

'Did you ever tell Sergeant Nickerson that you'd heard a single shot, and then three evenly spaced shots a minute or two later?'

'I told him that, sir. Indeed I did.'

'Were you aware that at the trial, back in April nineteen seventy-nine, Mrs Zide and Mr Neil Zide testified that there had been only three shots fired by the accused, all fired at the same time?'

'No, sir. I've told you, I was in Colorado and then California.'

'How soon after the death of Mr Zide was your employment terminated?'

'About five years later.'

'Can you tell us the circumstances?'

'Mrs Zide came to me and told me she wished to reward me for faithful service. She said the time had come for me to retire.'

'Did she give you severance pay?'

'Yes.'

'Tell the court how much.'

Terence hesitated. 'Two hundred and fifty thousand dollars.'

I was silent a few moments to let that sink in for the judge's benefit. Then I asked Terence if he thought that was a lot of money.

Predictably, he did.

'Has Mrs Zide paid you any more money?'

'She has not, but I receive a cheque from one of Mr Neil's companies, every month, for four thousand dollars.'

'Health insurance and major medical?'

'I have that from them, too.'

'Did you ever expect such handsome retirement benefits?'

'No, but I've told you, they are good people.'

'Pass the witness,' I said.

This time it was Muriel who jumped up to do the cross. She beat at Terence, she insulted him, she questioned his sobriety, his mental capacity and even his loyalty to his former employers, tried to twist his words and degrade his story in any way she could—as any lawyer would have done in her shoes.

Terence wouldn't budge. Finally, she said, 'I have no more questions.' I thanked Terence and the court told him he could leave.

Judge Fleming looked down from his lofty bench. 'Is that all?' he asked me. 'You look like death on a cracker. Are you ready to go home and get some sleep?'

'No, Judge. I'm just fine, and I have one more witness. And possibly a second one.'

'Can we get them done this afternoon before we close up shop?'

'Yes, sir,' I said, somewhat recklessly. 'They're both here in the courtroom. The defence calls Constance Zide.'

Connie Zide sat in the witness box. Her eyes were quiet and dull; she almost seemed drugged. I began.

'Do you recall, Mrs Zide, how you and I met?'

Connie smiled gently, and briefly related to the court the story of her mugging in the mall parking lot.

'I asked you a question that day, Mrs Zide, and I imagine you've forgotten it. But I'll ask it again, if you don't mind. When you ripped the gold chain off the young man who had attacked you outside Dillard's, weren't you frightened that he'd retaliate?'

Muriel looked puzzled, and so did Judge Fleming.

'No,' Connie said, 'not really. I was just acting on impulse.'

'Were you armed?'

A little nerve in Connie's cheek twitched. She said, 'Armed?'

Muriel jumped up swiftly to object. 'Where's this going, Your Honour? Can we have a proffer on that?'

A proffer was an offer made before the court in the presence of opposing counsel stating what you planned to do.

The judge looked at me, shrugged and nodded his approval.

'Of course, Your Honour,' I said. 'Mrs Zide told me on that occasion that she carried a pistol in her handbag.'

Muriel exploded. 'Your Honour, out of line! *He's* not testifying!'

'You asked for a proffer,' the judge said. 'And he gave you one.' Judge Fleming focused again on Connie. 'I'll allow the question,' he said. 'You may answer, madam.'

'Yes,' she replied. 'I was armed.'

I was over the first hurdle. She could have said no.

'Armed with what, Mrs Zide?'

'A pistol.'

'What kind of pistol was it?'

She hesitated. 'I really don't remember.'

'Are you sure you don't remember, Mrs Zide?'

'Objection!' Muriel said angrily. 'Asked and answered.'

'True,' the judge responded. 'Go forward, Mr Jaffe.'

'Withdraw the question,' I said. 'Did you have a licence for that pistol, Mrs Zide?'

Connie had little choice. In a trembling voice she said, 'I don't remember.' She had good instincts; it was the safest place to hide.

I turned to the judge. 'Your Honour, perhaps I can refresh her memory,' I said. I reached into a folder on the counsel table and took out a cream-coloured document. 'I would like to place this in evidence and then have my witness examine it.'

Connie blanched. She blew out her breath and said quietly, 'Wait. I remember. It was registered. It was a Smith and Wesson .38.'

'May it please the court,' I said, 'that this document in my hand be marked defendant's "A" for identification?'

I walked to the bench and handed the cream-coloured piece of paper up to Judge Fleming. He stared at it in puzzlement.

'Mr Jaffe, this is your sworn affidavit that Mrs Zide told you she carried a pistol in her handbag. It's not a registration permit.'

'I never said it was, Your Honour.'

'Damn you!' Connie cried at me before Muriel could intervene.

'That was sheer trickery,' Muriel said. 'It's cheap, Your Honour!'

'Flashy, maybe. Not what I'd call cheap.' He turned back to me and wagged a crooked finger. 'No more stunts, Counsel. Once is enough. Just ask proper questions.'

'Yes, sir,' I said, and I began again.

'Mrs Zide, you've been in this courtroom during previous testimony, haven't you?'

'Yes. You've seen me here.'

'You heard certain contradictions between what Terence O'Rourke swore to and what you and your son said here in this courtroom under oath, didn't you?'

'I'm not sure what you mean.'

'Do you recall Mr O'Rourke saying that on the night of your husband's murder there was a single shot and then, a minute or two later, three more shots?'

'Yes, I believe he did say that.'

I glanced down at my notes. 'And didn't you say yesterday in this court, "The shots came one after the other"?'

She had been bluffed and hurt once; she wouldn't allow it to happen twice. That was where her calmness came from. 'I don't recall saying that yesterday, Mr Jaffe.'

'I'll put it another way. Was Mr O'Rourke telling the truth when he said there was a single shot, and then three more shots?'

'I don't know.' She sighed. 'It was so long ago.'

I handed her the piece of paper in my hand. 'Would you identify this, please, Mrs Zide?'

She stared at it. 'It seems to be part of a trial transcript.'

'And the date, as notarised by the court clerk?'

'It says April eighteenth, nineteen seventy-nine.'

'And who is asking the questions?'

'I believe you were,' Connie said softly.

'And who is testifying?'

'I was.'

'Mrs Zide, if you please, read the part marked in yellow ink.'
She read:

'Q.—You heard the shots?
'A.—Yes, there were three, or maybe even four. Shots, I
      mean. They came one after the other. I ran outside.'

A trickle of sweat appeared at Connie's temple.

'Mrs Zide,' I said, 'did you, back then, identify this man sitting beside me as the murderer of your husband?'

'Yes.'

'How did you do that?'

'I don't recall.'

'You don't recall?'

'I mean, I did it because the police arrested him . . . and showed me photographs . . . and I knew him. He had worked for us. I was told that he had a criminal record.'

'Who told you that he had a criminal record?'

'I don't recall.'

'Did your son tell you that?'

'I don't recall!' Her voice rose shrilly. 'Don't you believe me?'

Muriel sprang to her feet. 'Your Honour, may we have a break so that the witness can compose herself?'

'We don't need a break,' the judge said. 'Keep going.'

Connie moaned softly.

'Mrs Zide,' I resumed, 'let's get back to what Terence O'Rourke said about the single shot and then, a minute or two later, three evenly spaced shots to follow. That's what he said, isn't it?'

'I think so.'

'And, by the way, do you at all dispute Mr O'Rourke's figures about the money you gave him when he left your employ?'

'Not at all. He was a faithful servant.'

'Did you ever consider having Terence O'Rourke killed?'

'I beg your pardon?'

'Would you like the court reporter to read back the question?'

'No, I heard the question,' Connie said, her lip quivering. 'I was just a little shocked. Killing Terence? *No.* Definitely *no*.'

'You never discussed that possibility with your son?'

'No!'

'Did you discuss the idea of having Victor Gambrel killed?'

'No!'

'Did Neil elect to do that on his own?'

'Objection!' Muriel, her face inflamed, jumped to her feet. 'There's no predicate for this insinuation. This is bizarre!'

'Objection sustained,' Judge Fleming said. He wagged a finger of admonishment at me.

'Mrs Zide, let's go back to the night of December fifth, nineteen seventy-eight,' I said. 'The night of the murder.'

She nodded; she seemed almost relieved. 'Do you want me to tell you again what happened, Ted?' she asked.

Oh, poor Connie. It was as if we were having a conversation on her living-room sofa, as if we were still what we once had been.

'No,' I said, smiling sadly. 'I want you to answer my questions, Mrs Zide, if you don't mind.'

Connie clasped her hands like a child and nodded obediently.

'Mrs Zide,' I said, 'on the night of the murder, what *first* alerted you to the presence of intruders on your grounds?'

Blotches of colour appeared on her pale cheeks. 'An urn crashed on the patio,' she said. 'We heard the noise. Solomon got up—'

'Mrs Zide, stop.' I wanted to be casual at this stage, but I had to control her. 'Just answer my questions. Don't volunteer information. Do you understand?'

'Yes, I thought . . .' She wanted to be friendly, to defuse me.

'Didn't you have a security system with spotlights which would snap on if anyone broke the path of their ultraviolet beams?'

'I'm not sure, but yes, that's what was supposed to happen.'

'It didn't happen? None of the lights went on to alert you?'

'I don't think so.'

'Do you recall, Mrs Zide, when your son took the stand here on Tuesday, that I read aloud some of his testimony from the trial thirteen years ago?'

'Yes, I believe so.'

'Do you recall that he said, "The spotlights on the lawn had finally been triggered, I assume by these two men"?'

'I'm not sure. I think so.'

'Isn't it a fact, Mrs Zide, that you *did* see the lights go on outside—while your husband was still alive—and that you then went outside on the terrace in your bathrobe?'

'Objection! Asked and answered.'

'Sustained.'

I pointed my finger at Connie like a pistol. 'And that's also about the time, isn't it, that you heard the Lhasa apso puppies barking?'

'Objection!' Muriel was still on her feet. 'There's no predicate for any barking Lhasa apso puppies.'

A murmur of laughter flowed through the courtroom.

'Objection sustained.'

'Isn't it a fact, Mrs Zide, that you came outside in your bathrobe and saw Darryl Morgan on the lawn or on the terrace?'

Connie waited for Muriel's objection, but none came.

'No, it's not a fact,' Connie said. 'I saw two men. I didn't know then that one of them was Darryl Morgan.'

I moved two steps closer to the witness stand. She could see the look in my eyes. There was none of the mercy she was looking for.

'Mrs Zide,' I asked, 'what happened to the Smith and Wesson .38 you carried in your handbag fourteen years ago?'

'The what?' She seemed confused. 'You keep changing the subject, Ted.'

'Your pistol, Mrs Zide. You told us about it earlier.'

'I don't know.'

'Do you still own it?'

'No.'

'You threw it away?'

'No, I didn't.'

'Neil threw it away?'

'Neil did what?'

'I'm asking *you,* Mrs Zide. Did Neil throw it away?'

'I don't know.'

'It just vanished? Disappeared?'

'I think so.'

'Soon after the death of your husband?'

'I think so. I mean, no. I don't remember.'

'Didn't it vanish the night your husband died? Didn't Neil throw it in the ocean, or the Intracoastal Waterway?'

'I don't know.'

'Did you shoot your husband, Mrs Zide?'

'No, I didn't. I swear that to you.'

'But on the night of December fifth, in the early morning, *someone* fired your pistol, your Smith and Wesson, isn't that so?'

She didn't answer. Her lips twisted into a skeletal grimace. Her blue-green eyes had sunk deep into their sockets.

'Your husband was in a rage that night, wasn't he, Mrs Zide?'

She nodded her head slowly. 'He was angry at me, yes.'

'After the party?'

'Yes, after the party.' There was a half-smile on her bloodless lips and a cunning look in her eyes that slowly resolved itself into an expression of superiority.

'There in the living room, after the party, Solly was in a rage?'

'Yes.'

'And he screamed at you and frightened you?'

'Yes.'

'And then Neil came home?'

Her eyes grew stony, darker. 'Yes.'

'Isn't it a fact, Mrs Zide, that before any shots were fired from your pistol, you heard the puppies barking, and you went outside and surprised two black men on the lawn, and they ran away?'

'Objection. Asked and answered,' I heard Muriel say, but without the vigour of a short time ago.

'Withdrawn,' I said. 'And when you came back into the living room, the argument with Solly grew worse?'

'I don't remember.'

402

I had it now. 'And *you* took your pistol out of your handbag, Mrs Zide, and you fired a shot into the woodwork, as a warning?'

'No.' But that look of cunning fled her face.

'And then Solly broke a bottle and cut you, didn't he?'

'No.' The cunning look returned.

'And you shot him, didn't you?'

'No.'

'You shot at him three times. One shot missed and went outside. The other two struck him and killed him.'

'No,' she said, and the cunning look didn't fade. Because, I realised now, that *wasn't* what had happened. My mind swerved from one possibility to another.

'And then,' I said, 'Neil took over, didn't he?'

'Took over?' Connie looked frightened, paler than before.

'Neil made a telephone call to Victor Gambrel, didn't he?'

'No, not then.'

'Then who did call Victor Gambrel?'

'Neil did, of course,' she said, confused. 'I'm sorry.'

'And Victor Gambrel arrived before the police did?'

'Yes, I think so. Does that matter?'

'Victor Gambrel helped Neil move your husband's body so that it looked as if he'd been shot by someone *outside*, isn't that so?'

'No, that didn't happen.'

'Victor Gambrel helped you and Neil work out the story you needed to tell the police, didn't he?'

'No. There was no story we needed to tell.'

'When you saw Darryl Morgan outside the house that night, you didn't recognise him as a man in your employ, isn't that so?'

'That's true. Yes, that's so.'

'You didn't know who they were—*you* hadn't seen them clearly, and Neil hadn't seen them *at all*. Isn't that correct?'

'I don't know,' she said, as if by rote.

'And that's why no one described Darryl Morgan as tall, or big, until *after* he was arrested, isn't that correct, Mrs Zide?'

'I don't know.'

'And then, that night, after you'd cooked up your story, Neil called the Jacksonville Beach police and Gambrel called his friend Floyd Nickerson at JSO homicide. Isn't that what happened?'

'I don't know.'

'And the reason Nickerson sent Carmen Tanagra down to the cabanas to see what happened to the dog was so that he'd have the time to listen to an offer from Gambrel on behalf of Neil.'

'I don't know.'

'And to your surprise, after Nickerson and Tanagra picked up Morgan and Smith at the Lil' Champ food store, you found out that Darryl Morgan worked for you as a handyman, isn't that so?'

'I don't know.'

'You had no idea he and Smith would be caught, did you?'

'No.'

'You didn't want Darryl Morgan to be blamed for the murder of your husband, did you?'

'No.'

'Because he hadn't murdered him, isn't that the reason?'

'No, that's not why.'

'But by then it was too late to back out, wasn't it?'

'I don't understand.'

'And so it was a choice between Darryl Morgan—an uneducated, violent black criminal who wasn't fit to do more than clean up after your dogs—taking a fall on a first-degree murder charge or you taking a fall on a manslaughter charge that might easily turn into murder . . . and that was hardly a choice, was it?'

'It's not true,' Connie said.

'But you didn't want Morgan to die, did you?'

'I didn't want that at all, Ted.'

'You wanted me to go easy on him in the trial, didn't you?'

'Yes.' She brightened suddenly. 'Yes, darling.'

I felt a terrible chill, and my heart fluttered like a torn wing, but I had to go on. 'The argument with Solly, before he died—that final argument—that was about Neil, wasn't it?'

'No, Ted.'

'And then Neil came in at two o'clock, didn't he, Mrs Zide?'

'He came in, yes.'

'Solly was violent, wasn't he, Mrs Zide?'

'Please, my sweet, don't call me that. You know my name.'

I remembered Beldon's hard warnings to me last spring in his office: 'Something makes me feel you shouldn't be involved.' He had tried to stop me from moving too far into the past, where dragons lived.

But for Darryl's sake I had to go back. And then go on.

'Solly threatened you, Connie, didn't he?'

'Yes.'

'Somehow, in this argument, you enraged him to the point where you feared he'd do you bodily harm, isn't that true?'

'He hit me, Ted.'

'In the face?'

'Yes. In the face. He cut my cheek.'

I realised now that she was telling the truth. She had turned a

404

corner and was racing down a track and couldn't halt herself.

You try not to ask a question where you don't know the answer, but we were beyond that now.

'What was the argument about, Connie?'

'You. He knew,' she said. 'And he hated you.'

Oh, Lord. I couldn't back out of it—but I could step aside.

'He slashed you with a knife, Connie, didn't he?'

She wouldn't let me. *She* was in control now. 'I couldn't stand him any more,' she said. 'I wouldn't let him touch me. I told him I loved you. You never believed that, did you?'

I wanted to shut my eyes. I wanted to run away. I felt Darryl, at my side, staring up at me. I could see the wide wondering look of Judge Fleming. I felt Toba's presence in the courtroom.

But I went forward, because there was no choice.

'What did he do to you, Connie?'

'I told you, Ted. He hit me with his hand.'

'You grabbed your pistol out of your handbag and fired a shot over his head, didn't you, Connie?'

'Yes.'

'And then?'

'He hit me again. He knocked me down.'

'So you shot him and killed him, to protect yourself?'

'No, my darling, no.'

I became aware of a commotion towards the rear of the courtroom. Neil Zide was in the aisle, and he had wrenched free of the bailiff, a man forty pounds heavier. Neil hurtled down the aisle into the well of the courtroom. The blood had fled from his cheeks as if he had been struck. His hair flowed behind him like a lion's mane.

'You swine!' he yelled at me.

Connie was crying his name, trying to stop him. The judge was shouting, 'Bailiff!' Connie rose from her seat in the witness box and reeled forward towards us as Neil's body slammed against mine and we tumbled back together against the counsel table.

THE TUMULT SUBSIDED. The bailiffs held Neil, while the judge rapped his gavel to quiet the courtroom. Connie's eyes looked stony and unfocused. I turned to her as her hands searched the air like the claws of a wounded animal. I pointed at Neil. 'He took the pistol from you, didn't he?'

'Yes,' she murmured.

'And he shot your husband.'

'He didn't mean to.'

'Neil was enraged because Solly hit you, isn't that true, Connie?'

'Yes. He's my son. He loves me. He despised Solly.'

'Connie'—I approached her—'who cut your face?'

'I did,' she said. 'It was cut when Solly slapped me. I had to explain that. They told me to do it. I knew it would heal.'

'Who is "they", Connie? Do you mean Neil and Gambrel?'

She just nodded, and that was good enough, or terrible enough.

'What did you use?'

'A piece of glass. It was just my cheek.'

How brave. How desperate. How insane. To keep her son from a manslaughter charge that might have turned into murder, she would scar herself and send another man to his death.

We stayed in Jacksonville for a week after the hearing. Toba was in a form of shock. The revelations in Judge Fleming's courtroom, which the media took such pleasure in relating for the next several days, were like poison for her to absorb.

I wanted to say to Toba, 'Darling, it's been fourteen years. That's a lifetime ago.' But, wisely, I didn't. For one thing, the word darling was definitely out of favour for a while. For another, infidelity of that sort doesn't have a statute of limitations.

Toba forgave me in time, because not to do so would have crippled our lives. She thought things over and decided she loved our marriage as it was: whole. It gave her security and freedom and love, and it had a history; what better combination is there? She was silent and tearful for that week in Jacksonville and scowled at me for the next month in Sarasota, but then one Sunday I persuaded her to go out with me in the boat. On the bay, I said, 'Who's your best friend? Tell the truth.'

'You are.'

'So let's drop anchor and do what friends do.'

She laughed at that, and the worst was over.

For us, but not for me. Day after day, when I was alone, I relived that moment in the courtroom when I had asked Connie the subject of the argument.

You.

That argument had led to Solly's death and Darryl's thirteen years on death row. Each time that realisation flashed clear to me, my heart beat violently, my stomach throbbed with pain.

There's a price to pay for every act. In this case, the wrong man paid. And now Connie and Neil would pay their small share. They were not arrested right there in court, but once the court reporter had delivered the transcript of the hearing to the state attorney's office, Muriel Suarez filed charges and the wheels of public justice began to clunk slowly forward. The charges that could stick were only second-degree murder and perjury. Neil hired lawyers from both Tallahassee and Washington, and the feeling round the Duval County Courthouse was that he would eventually cut a deal for fifteen years' pen time, of which he'd serve two or three, and Connie would walk out of the door with a suspended sentence.

So that left Darryl.

In court that memorable day, I made a motion for his immediate release. Leaning down into the clamour, Horace Fleming said, 'Mr Jaffe, get the transcript of this last bit from my court reporter and make a formal motion in writing. You look a little on the ragged edge—it shouldn't take you more than all night. The Morgan man's got to sleep somewhere, so let him go back to the jail and bunk down one more time. It won't kill him, and we know some things that would've—ain't that right?'

He turned to Muriel Suarez. 'You want to oppose that motion, State, go right ahead. I can tell you, it'll be a hard crop to grow.'

'The state will not oppose, Your Honour,' Muriel said.

I sat down with Darryl for a while in the judge's chambers and explained what his options were. He was still in handcuffs.

'You can probably sue the state and win,' I said, 'but you'll grow a beard to your knees before it's over. On the other hand, you file suit against Neil Zide and Connie Zide, and my blind old dog, if I had one, could win that case.'

Darryl laughed deep in his belly. 'You a lawyer to the end, ain't you? You gonna do that suit for me?'

'No, my friend. But Gary Oliver will. He'll make you rich.'

He mulled that over. 'Then I send that boy to school. If they's enough money.'

The next morning, in Judge Fleming's court, Gary filed the motion for release. At noon, Darryl was formally released from the Florida state prison system. Gary, Tahaun and I were waiting for him outside, in the mercy of the warm winter sunlight. His son approached Darryl with an outstretched hand. After thirteen years in a cage on death row, Darryl could fit his worldly possessions into a battered cardboard carton, which he carried under his arm. His clothes, his two decks of worn playing cards and his toothbrush were inside it. He sniffed the air as though it were honey.

My eyes misted, but I said, 'You want to go somewhere for a beer?'

'Hey,' Darryl rumbled at me in The Jury Room, where he slowly sipped a Heineken, 'you remember that day you come see me at

Raiford? Day I put these round your neck?' Setting the bottle down, he raised those huge hands. 'Remember what I try to do?'

'Yes, I remember.'

'Lucky for me you was such a tough little guy.'

That was as close as he ever came to thanking me.

TOBA AND I FLEW HOME to Sarasota.

A storm howled in from the Gulf that evening. During the night the rain overflowed ditches and gushed down the fairways of Longboat Key. The leaves of banana trees bowed under the lash of water. At dawn the rain stopped; the planet still spun, therefore the sun appeared to rise.

With carnal intent, I stroked the back of my slumbering wife. Later, I scratched the stubble on my jaw. Should I let my beard grow? It might come out even greyer than my hair, but so what? Yes, I will. I will, therefore I can.

I called Kenny Buckram's office and asked him if he thought the public defender's office in Sarasota would have a place for me.

'Are you serious?'

Within a month I was offered a job in the special defence division of the public defender's office. I would be based in Sarasota County but would travel all over the state. The salary was not quite a third of what Royal, Kelly guaranteed me.

'What do you think?' I asked Toba.

'I think it would be crazy,' she said. 'Cathy's talking about graduate school. Alan's out there in art school, and he may want to go on to college. We just can't afford it.'

'And I can't afford not to take the job,' I said. 'I want it. It will make me feel I'm a useful human being instead of a parasite.'

She had seen that look in my eye before. But she didn't back off or sulk. She hugged me and said, 'Do it, Ted. We'll work things out.'

I took the job. Toba and I went to services at our local temple that Friday evening, and a line from the prayer book struck me and stayed with me: 'There will we serve with awe as in the days of old.'

CLIFFORD IRVING

Author of sixteen books, Clifford Irving is 'bookish' only by trade. A native New Yorker, Irving dotes on travel, enjoys sports and, by his own account, likes to take a risk now and then. To him even the writing of novels is an exotic activity—an 'adventure of the mind', he calls it.

An interviewer recently caught up with the six-foot-four, burly and bearded writer in Aspen, Colorado. Irving had retreated to a friend's house, knee in a brace, nursing sprained ligaments from a misadventure on the slopes. 'The snow's been great, but no skiing for a while,' he said with a sigh, adding, 'at least I get a lot more work done.'

Now in his early sixties, Irving likes to recall some of the real-life adventures that moulded his career: striking out for Europe as a callow (his word) graduate from Cornell University in the 1950s; a stint as a Middle East correspondent for NBC-TV.

Then there was the time when he answered a newspaper ad for experienced sailors to take a three-masted schooner from Mexico to Spain. Not really experienced, Irving reckoned that he could learn along the way. The problem was that all six of the other men who signed on reckoned the same thing. Was it fun? 'Fun?' he quipped. 'It was harrowing.' They got lost, were hit by the tail end of a hurricane and they ran out of fresh water. 'Everything that can go wrong at sea did,' he said. 'It's like most adventures—it's more fun in the telling than in the doing.'

But whether telling or doing, this author clearly relishes both—and always with a pinch of humour. His accident on the slopes made no difference. 'I treat life as an adventure,' he said with a chuckle. 'I took up skiing eight years ago. And that's certainly been an adventure.'

GɾOWTH

Max Marlow

illustrated by Gino D'Achille

At thirty-eight years old, Georgina Playle of Playle plc is a highly successful London architect and proud to be working in the firm founded by her father. Her latest impressive project has just been completed—the immense headquarters of the Global Banking Corporation—but suddenly disaster strikes and everything Georgina stands for and believes in, including her father's firm, is under threat. She soon realises, however, that her desperate fight will involve something a great deal more important than her career and her family's reputation—the safety of today's cities.

1

The taxi pulled into the kerb, and one of the morning-suited men waiting on the pavement immediately hurried forward to open the door. Georgina Playle stepped out and slowly drew breath. At twelve thirty on a June morning, even in the City of London, the sun was shining from a cloudless sky; the day was pleasantly warm rather than hot. She looked left and right, at the waiting policemen, and the crowd behind them, to either side. It was a small crowd, composed in the main of those clerks who for the past two years had watched the immense headquarters of the Global Banking Corporation rising out of the pile of rubble from which it had originated. Now it dominated even the Bank of England, the Old Lady of Threadneedle Street.

'Looks like the architect copied the Senate House, in Rome,' someone muttered uncharitably.

Georgina smiled, and allowed herself to look up, and up. The building was certainly fronted by the high Corinthian pillars of a bygone age. These supported the first roof, some forty feet above the pavement. Beneath them was a broad flight of four steps which led up to the main banking hall, and at the top of these steps waited Sir Trumpton Dauntsey, with his fellow directors, all smiles as they greeted their guest of honour.

'Welcome to Global Banking, Miss Playle.' Sir Trumpton gave a brief bow. 'The finest building in London.'

Round and florid, he carefully disguised the accent of his origins. His effusive bow irritated her, but as the architect he had chosen to employ, Georgina could only smile her agreement, and nod her thanks for the compliment. Inside, the hall was conventional enough at first sight. Marble counters and glass partitions would shelter the tellers once the bank was open for business, and behind them the various computers waited in rows. It needed a second glance to appreciate the subtle use of windows angled to catch every possible ray of sunlight at any hour, the quiet colours which contained the light yet absorbed none of it, and the hidden artificial lighting which could supplement the natural at the flick of a switch.

'This place is a palace,' muttered Geoffrey Teigne, the intended chief manager of the headquarters branch.

'Thank you,' Georgina murmured in reply, and allowed herself to be escorted towards the elevator.

POLITELY GEORGINA sipped champagne and felt like a mother who had given birth after a four-year pregnancy, only to have the infant immediately handed over for adoption. Admittedly it was always like this at the completion of a contract, a matter of conflicting emotions: pride and relief on the one hand while feeling drained and exhausted on the other.

'I want you to meet all the directors,' Teigne said. 'Come over to the window. We are all admiring the view.' He put a hand under her elbow and propelled her across the room to where the huge picture window looked out at St Paul's. 'Here she is,' he announced proudly.

'Miss Playle! This is fabulous!'

'Congratulations!'

'May I pre-empt the speeches and raise a glass to you and your firm?' Teigne asked. Everyone clinked glasses and sipped.

Georgina Playle remained near the window and let the crowd revolve round her, gradually relaxing. She placed her empty glass on a salver and took another, catching sight of her reflection in a length of mirror set into the window embrasure to reflect light. She paused for a second to check, turning her head slightly, but not a single dark hair had strayed from the severely swept French pleat, not a crease showed on her Saint-Laurent suit. It was black with red braiding and buttons on the wide-shouldered jacket, the short skirt revealing her shapely knees and long calves. Black and gilt designer earrings swayed against the high ruched neck of her red blouse, which perfectly complemented the handsome, slightly severe face above.

'Looking for grey hairs?'

Georgina swung round at the sound of Patrick Turner's voice. 'None yet, thank goodness,' she grinned, flashing the wide smile that dispelled all severity from her expression.

'I should think not, at your age!'

'I've got a friend of thirty-two who is almost white, and I'm thirty-eight!'

'Big deal! Wait till you get to my age, my girl!'

Patrick was a dear. He had been with Playle plc since starting work with her father, George Playle, back in the early sixties, and his pale blond hair was now liberally streaked with white. Although her father had been the founder and senior partner of the firm, life could have been very much more difficult for her when she first pinned up her nameplate on the office door—Georgina A. Playle, ARIBA. As well as her extreme youth, she had the enormous disadvantage of being a woman. Patrick had been kind and encouraging, and it was to him, rather than to her father, that she had turned for advice, and for comfort when things went wrong. Her father had too short a fuse and Patrick was so patient.

'I would like to pursue the subject of grey hair further,' Patrick said behind a serious mask, 'but Sir Trumpton is bearing down . . .'

Georgina composed her features and turned to smile into the beetroot face.

'Luncheon is served, Miss Playle. May I escort you to the executive dining room?' He offered his bent elbow and waved his free arm to encompass the surroundings. 'What do you think, when you look at this, knowing it all came out of your brain?'

'Amazed that it has all actually happened,' Georgina replied truthfully. 'But . . .' she grinned, 'right now I feel on top of the world!'

SECURITY GUARD Jim Onslow leaned on the counter of his little office on the ground floor of the Ashmore Tower block behind Regent Street, picked up his telephone and punched a couple of numbers. 'Mr Hardisty here for Mr Browning. Righto!' He replaced the receiver. 'Take number three lift, sir. Sixteenth floor.' Mr Hardisty marched off without a word, and Jim gazed after him, reflectively. Everyone was in a hurry nowadays, he thought. He didn't see the point.

The door to the basement opened and Charlie Trent emerged, wiping his lips on a handkerchief. 'That's better. How's it going?'

Jim shrugged, picked up his Thermos and sandwiches and headed for the door. The guards ate their lunch in the basement.

'Smells like last week's cabbage down there,' Charlie remarked. 'Damp, that's what it is.'

Jim scratched his head. He couldn't accept that. He was proud of the building he minded. Ashmore Tower had been designed by the world-famous architect George Playle. There was absolutely no chance of any damp getting into one of his creations, even after fifteen years. Yet as he went down the stairs, Jim had to admit that Charlie had a point. There was a definite musty smell filling the basement. Last week's cabbage? More like overcooked mushrooms! Jim placed his lunch on the table, put the kettle on, and wandered through the various cellars trying to locate the smell.

The basement of Ashmore Tower was actually part of the foundations, and the ceiling, which served as the ground floor of the building itself, was a solid slab of reinforced concrete. Several inches thick, and maintained by massive pillars, it had for fifteen years effortlessly supported the twenty floors above. But today, immediately above his head, paint was flaking off a large part of the ceiling, forced away by a bulge which had appeared in the concrete.

It would have to be reported after his lunch. He returned to the main room, ate his sandwiches and read his newspaper, while he reflected that in this modern age all work was shoddy.

'What d'you think?' Charlie asked, when he went back upstairs.

'Damp, all right. Hard to believe.' Jim leaned on the counter and punched out the number of the maintenance firm. 'Mr Timmins? Jim Onslow here, Ashmore Tower. You're not going to believe this, Mr Timmins, but there's damp getting into the basement.'

'Damp? At Ashmore? Tell me another.'

'Funny thing is,' Jim said, 'it's not in an exterior wall. It's in the ceiling right in the middle of the boiler room.'

'Hm. Could be a leak. Look, my men are all out at the moment. I'll have someone round first thing Monday morning.'

'If it's a burst pipe, it could be in a mess by then,' Jim objected.

'Can't be more than a minor leak. If it was a burst you'd see water. Listen, Jim, it's Friday, right? When the building empties this afternoon, turn off all your heating, and close all the valves. That way any leakage will be contained.'

During the next couple of hours there was a steady stream of callers needing to be directed, and parcels being sent down for collection. Ashmore Tower was an office block which rented space to every variety of business, from publishers' agents to insurance companies. It was past four before Jim had time to think about the basement again, and then he was thinking of his cup of tea. He went downstairs. Now the smell was even stronger. Overcooked mushrooms gone bad, he thought. He put the kettle on, and strolled through to the boiler room.

The bulge had grown enormously during the past three hours. If ever he had seen a ceiling about to come down, this was it. He ran back upstairs. 'Seen a ghost?' Charlie enquired.

416

'We have a problem.' Jim punched out the maintenance number again. 'Let me speak to Mr Timmins. This is an emergency.'

Charlie had never seen his friend so agitated.

'Jim Onslow, Ashmore Tower, Mr Timmins. That bulge in the ceiling is growing by the minute and I don't think it is damp. It's not like anything I've ever seen before. Someone'd better come, pronto, and bring steel girder supports. There's a hell of a lot of concrete above there waiting to come down.' He knew he sounded a bit panicky, but anything to make Timmins hurry. 'And there's a funny smell, too. Mouldy. Like overcooked mushrooms.'

Timmins changed his mind about what he was going to say. Ashmore Tower Limited was a good customer. 'I'll stop by myself,' he promised. 'Fifteen minutes.' He hung up.

'What's it all about, then?' Charlie wanted to know.

'Have a look.'

Charlie went downstairs, and was back up again in a minute, his face ashen. 'Hell, it's coming down.'

'D'you think we should get everyone out?'

Charlie pulled his nose. It was a quarter past four on Friday afternoon, and most of the people upstairs would be packing up for the weekend. 'They'll all be gone anyway in half an hour,' he said.

'And suppose someone puts a foot through that floor and sues for a million?'

'Better than a false alarm. And your friend Timmins will be along any minute.'

Jim grunted, but he saw the point. Neither really felt like a cuppa any more. They watched the swing doors open with some concern; it was a pretty girl. 'Hello. I've an appointment with Mark Lewis, Mather and Associates.'

'Your name?' Jim asked.

'Liz Brettell.'

Jim punched the appropriate numbers, made the right noises. 'You're to go right up, miss. Use the third lift, and get out on floor fourteen. Mr Lewis will be waiting for you.'

'Thanks ever so.' She hurried off towards the lifts.

A minute later there came a rumble from below. 'It's come down,' Jim snapped.

Charlie walked out of the office into the centre of the foyer. 'Hello.' He stooped. 'Could be a crack.'

Jim chewed his lip in indecision; the lifts were humming, and now he watched the first come to a halt and discharge a group of young men and women, shouting goodbyes to Charlie and himself.

'You just stay there,' he told Charlie, 'and make sure nobody steps on that piece of floor. I'll go and see what the damage is.' He ran down the steps; at least he'd have something to show when Timmins got here.

He stood in the doorway to the boiler room and gazed at a pile of rubble; it was as if the reinforced concrete had been hit by a shell. It really was a miracle that the floor above was still standing. The smell was stronger than ever.

He turned to go back up, and stared in horror at the wall beside the stairs. An immense crack had appeared in the smoothly painted concrete. He listened to an immense groaning. An earthquake, he thought. Has to be an earthquake. In Central London?

The wall came crashing down.

2

Sinking back onto the pale tan cushions of Patrick's Mercedes, Georgina closed her eyes. 'I thought that idiot Trumpton Dauntsey was never going to shut up,' she sighed.

'You were nervous,' Patrick accused.

'Weren't you?'

'What, about a building designed by Playle plc? But seriously, Gina, you have worked bloody hard. You deserve a rest.'

'I intend to have one, this weekend.'

'Mike coming home?'

'No, he's with his father.'

'Ah.' Patrick was not going to pursue that matter. 'So it's you, and Philip and the moonlight.'

Georgina opened one eye. 'I have a growing feeling that you don't care for Philip.'

'My dear Gina, you're a big girl now.'

'But I still can't pick men, right?'

THE CAR WAS ALREADY in Hammersmith, and a few moments later they were at the Playle Building. 'I'll say goodbye now, I'm leaving again in five minutes. See you Monday,' Georgina said to Patrick, as she hurried along to her office. 'Get me a cab, will you, Anne,' she instructed as her door closed.

'Right away. How'd it go?' Anne Bladen was her secretary, a slender young woman whose languorous demeanour disguised her considerable energy.

'I suppose, very well. Pretty boring. Let's tidy up these loose ends and go home.'

Half an hour later a taxi was depositing her at Waterloo Station.

Finding herself in the midst of the rush hour, she clutched her season ticket and forced her way towards the platform she wanted, and checked, as did everyone else, at a distant rumbling sound.

'That's all we need,' someone commented. 'A thunderstorm!'

THE OLD PEUGEOT Estate was waiting in Haslemere Station car park. She eyed the Mercedes sports parked alongside and sighed. She kept meaning to get rid of this cumbersome old relic from the days when it was filled with Michael and his friends, dogs and picnic gear every weekend. The traffic lights in Hindhead changed twice before she reached them in the line of cars, to turn left down the hill and right to Headley Down.

The house was just beyond the village, at the end of what was little more than a track until reaching the automatic gates. She had stayed in the flat in Hammersmith during the week, so that a pile of accumulated mail had been stacked on the hall table by Mrs Dobbs. Oddly the evening had remained calm and clear, despite that rumble of thunder. She went to pour a Bacardi and Coke.

The sun was still warm on the patio outside the conservatory. Blackbirds and sparrows were busy supplying a late supper to their noisy broods before retiring into the shrubbery.

She tried to enjoy the tranquillity but loneliness kept invading her thoughts. If only Michael was at home instead of spending this weekend with his father . . . but that would probably lead to endless arguments. To say the boy was going through a difficult stage would be the understatement of the year. And unfortunately her ex-husband, Tom, wasn't helping. He seemed to encourage the sixteen-year-old in the belief that now he was virtually adult he should be allowed to enjoy a succession of wild, alcoholic parties.

Her marriage had been a disaster. Mother had seemed so old-fashioned when she had insisted that Tom Carden was not a suitable prospective husband, but she had been right. What Georgina had taken for snobbery had proved to be clever perception. Far from the exciting person she had naively imagined him to be, Tom was a cadging layabout who needed the Playle money to finance his chosen lifestyle.

Two years after they parted came an acrimonious divorce. Fortunately the house had been part of the family trust so Tom hadn't been able to get his hands on it. That had been three years ago, the worst period of her life, both her parents dying within months of each other, her mother from cancer, her father from a massive heart attack . . . all while the lawyers were wrangling. Thank goodness for Patrick, and Thelma his wife: they had been wonderful.

She shivered. It was getting chilly outside, so she went indoors.

It was time to go through her mail and check if there was anything on the Ansaphone. She carried the post through into her study, and flicked the switch of the Ansaphone. She stood absolutely still as she listened to the several almost incoherent messages, one from Patrick and two from Thelma, saying something about 'the Ashmore Tower disaster'.

She grabbed the phone and dialled Patrick's home number. Thelma answered. 'Oh Gina, thank goodness, where have you *been*? We've been trying to contact you for hours.'

'Sitting in the garden. What's all this about Ashmore Tower?'

'Good Lord, do you mean you still don't know? It's all on TV. The whole building has collapsed . . .'

She continued talking but Georgina was no longer listening. Ashmore Tower! Designed and constructed under her father's supervision . . . collapsed! 'Rubbish, Thelma, it couldn't just fall down,' she interrupted. 'It must be the IRA.'

'I think Patrick wants you there, Gina.' Thelma sounded very anxious. 'Something about the layout of the building to help the rescue services . . .'

'Oh Lord! As bad as that?' She felt her knees go weak. 'OK, tell him I'm on my way.'

She pressed the TV remote control and gazed in horror at the picture of the collapsed building on her screen.

Ashmore Tower seemed to have imploded, but even so, the immense amount of concrete and glass coming down had spread across the street. The camera was panning to show a bus cocked at a crazy angle against the wall of the opposite building, kept there by a massive chunk of reinforced concrete. Two cars had been squashed, and several more were scattered around the street, obviously badly damaged by falling masonry. 'The explosion occurred at half past four,' the commentator was saying.

The noise she had heard, just as she was boarding the train, and had supposed to be thunder!

'No organisation has as yet claimed responsibility, but the event appears to mark a whole new dimension in the category of terror bombing. The death toll is expected to mount as police and firemen hunt through the rubble of this modern London landmark.'

Georgina switched off. She felt physically sick. Fifteen years ago, when Ashmore Tower had been opened, she hadn't even been a member of the firm. Yet a Playle building was a Playle building, and as the only Playle now in the firm, she had to be there.

420

3

The rescue services' command centre was in a camper-type vehicle parked a little way down the street from the collapsed building. Patrick Turner leaned over a table piled with architectural specifications, trying to sort out the ones most useful at the moment, hedged in by senior police and fire-brigade officers who all seemed to be speaking at once on their walkie-talkies.

If only Gina were here, he thought. She had planned the latest redecorations at the owners' insistence. She'd know exactly what she was looking at. He turned his head and there she was, standing just outside the roped-off area. She looked shocked and angry as she argued with the two policemen who attempted to bar her way.

'Gina!' He hurried forward, closely followed by the police superintendent, and the constables apologetically raised the tape for her to duck underneath. 'This is Superintendent Michelsen,' Patrick said. 'Georgina Playle, Superintendent.'

'Miss Playle.' The policeman looked tired. 'Did you design the building?'

'No. It was designed by my father. There was talk of a bomb . . .'

'The collapse of the building certainly suggested a bomb, Miss Playle. But we have been able to find no evidence of such a device.'

'Is it possible to have a look down there?'

Michelsen hesitated. 'I'm afraid it is not a very pleasant place right this minute. We aren't sure all the bodies have been recovered.'

'I understand that. But I cannot possibly help you if I don't see where the building came down,' Georgina pointed out.

Michelsen nodded. 'Mr Turner thought you might be able to identify from the decor which part of the collapsed structure came from which floor. That way we can establish who might have been in which office at the time of the collapse. Bring a hard hat for the lady, will you, Sergeant?'

A yellow hat was brought and Georgina put it on.

'Over here,' the superintendent said.

She followed him between battered cars, her tough site boots crunching on broken glass, Patrick at her elbow. Then they came to the broad front steps, scarred and pitted where huge chunks of concrete had crashed onto them.

Beyond was what would have been the foyer, save that it was now a pit out of which two of the steel lift shafts pointed skywards. On the far side of the building, an exterior wall still stood, some ten storeys high she estimated. From it hung sections of floor, on one of which remained a filing cabinet, clinging dizzily to the edge.

'Were there many casualties?' Georgina asked in a low voice.

'Eight bodies had been recovered at the last count, Miss Playle. I'm afraid there may well be more. Seventy-three people have been taken to hospital. You could say we've been lucky. I understand something like two hundred people worked in this building, but many had already left for the weekend when it came down.'

'Yes,' Georgina muttered. 'That was lucky.'

Michelsen picked his way through the rubble, and reached the head of a flight of stairs. 'This leads down to the basement, or it did.' He began a careful descent, and Georgina and Patrick followed, nostrils dilating at the various odours.

'You wanted me, Superintendent?' A man had appeared behind them. He wore a hard hat, was tall and thin and had a moustache. His suit was crumpled and dusty, and he looked exhausted.

'Oh, yes, Mr Timmins. I think you know Miss Playle and Mr Turner, the architects. Would you tell them what you told me?'

'G'devening, madam, sir. Well, it's just that we received a telephone call from one of the security guards, Jim Onslow. Jim said they had a bit of a problem, something about a possible water leak. I agreed to send someone over first thing Monday, hoping Jim could trace it and cobble it up for the weekend. But then Onslow called back just after four this afternoon to say that the problem was more severe than he had first thought, and he needed instant help. He said something about a ceiling bulging. He thought it might be on the point of coming down. I promised to come right over. By the time I got here, the whole building had come down.'

'We found Onslow here,' Michelsen said, indicating the first landing on the basement steps. This had been cleared of rubble, and there was a dark stain on the pitted floor.

Georgina stared at the stain. All that was left of a man. 'What's that funny smell?' she asked.

'Overcooked mushrooms,' Michelsen agreed. 'It was stronger when we first arrived. I suppose maybe something survived on a stove for a while even after the crash.'

'There was no kitchen in the basement.'

'Funny thing,' Timmins said. 'Onslow mentioned something about a mouldy smell when we spoke . . .'

A whistle blew above them, and there was a flurry of shouts. 'She's alive. Easy now.' Georgina ran back up the steps and watched the men in the pit which had once been the foyer. A dog was barking excitedly, and the men were cautiously moving pieces of concrete. 'Easy now,' the fireman in charge said again.

It was several minutes before ambulancemen came up the steps carrying a stretcher. The ripple of excitement seeped back out to the waiting crowd. 'They've found someone!'

Georgina swallowed as a young woman was brought out. She looked virtually unharmed from the waist down, but the white shirt above was dark with blood, and her face was a crimson mask. She was moaning and writhing. 'She needs a shot,' the fireman said.

'Get her over here,' one of the stretcher-bearers said.

'Crikey, here's her handbag,' said one of the men in the pit.

The bag was passed up, while the girl was carefully laid on the stretcher. A medic swabbed at the flesh exposed beneath the ripped sleeve of her blouse, needle in hand. The fireman had opened the bag. 'Elizabeth Brettell,' he said. 'Make a note of that, Harry.'

Georgina moved closer, willing Elizabeth Brettell to fight. The writhing had stopped. 'Is she all right?' Georgina asked the medic.

He grimaced and put away his needle. 'I reckon she's had it.'

GEORGINA REMAINED sitting on the steps, head in hands, while the stretcher was being loaded into the ambulance. 'That makes nine,' Michelsen remarked with an air of finality.

Georgina forced herself to stand. Better get on with the job before anyone else died. 'Are those the decorators' plans you've got there?' she asked Patrick.

'Yes.' His expression was grim.

She balanced on a pile of concrete, facing each compass point in turn, examining chunks of wall and sections of flooring. 'This came from the first floor; the offices of Huyton Associates. There were usually two male and one female seniors in the carpeted area behind, and five clerks and secretaries in the front general office.' She pointed, while a fire officer nodded to two of the dog handlers. She clambered higher onto another vantage point.

'For heaven's sake be careful, Gina,' Patrick called up to her.

Gina ignored him as she turned over the plans. There was a blast from one of the dog handlers' whistles, and more men converged on another hole in the masonry. Two hours later she allowed herself to be led back to the control vehicle. Patrick had removed his helmet, revealing deep lines etched in concrete dust around his eyes. 'I don't think there is anything more we can do for you, is there?'

'Well . . .' The superintendent hesitated. 'There are questions which have to be answered. If it was a bomb it will all be relatively straightforward. Trouble is, some of the characteristics are wrong . . .'

'It could've been faulty construction. Is that what you mean?' Patrick enquired.

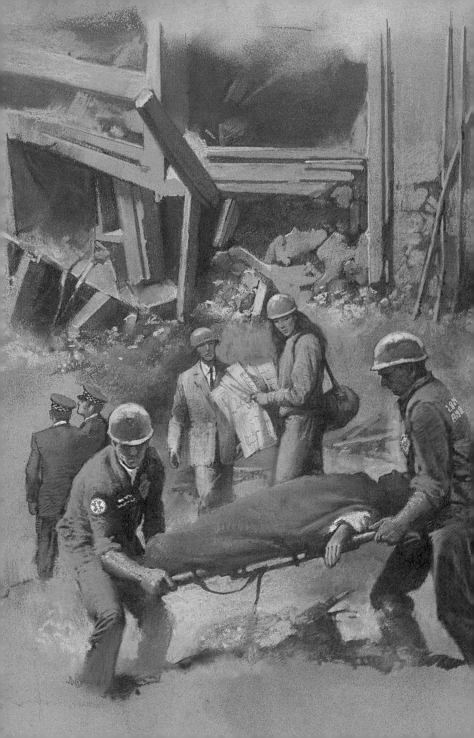

'We have to take every possibility into account,' Michelsen pointed out. 'There will have to be an inquest, of course. But hopefully we will have come up with some solid evidence of an explosion before then. Or whatever . . .' There was an uncomfortable pause. 'Well, I shan't detain you any longer. You must be extremely tired. Good evening to you, Miss Playle, Mr Turner. Thank you for your help.'

'Just what did he mean by those last remarks?' Georgina asked as they stepped out into the now darkening evening.

'I imagine there will be claims and counterclaims flying around in various directions, and some of them may be aimed at us.' Patrick's voice was weary and despondent.

Georgina shivered, and hugged herself. She watched a man with a microphone coming towards her, accompanied by his cameraman. 'Miss Playle, the police have told us that the destruction of the building was not caused by a bomb. Can you tell us then what did cause the collapse?'

'No,' Georgina said.

The camera was now very close. 'Could it have been concrete cancer, Miss Playle?'

Patrick thrust the microphone aside. 'Of course it was not concrete cancer,' he snapped. 'Now, if you'll excuse us . . .' He grabbed Georgina's arm and pushed her towards the barriers. 'My car's just down that road,' he muttered.

Georgina slumped into the passenger seat. 'Patrick?' she asked. 'There's no chance it *could* be concrete cancer, is there?'

'Absolutely not. Concrete cancer is caused by either carelessness or false economy. Do you seriously suppose your own father would have been guilty of something like that? Anyway, concrete cancer reveals itself as cracks in exterior walls long before it becomes dangerous. There is no evidence of that at Ashmore Tower.'

'Patrick . . . I have to *know*. Let's go to the office.'

'I was going to take you home for a drink.' He swung the wheel almost savagely and headed for Hammersmith.

GRIFFITHS, THE NIGHT watchman, peered at his two principal bosses as they got out of the car. There was a TV in his little office, and he knew why they were there at such an hour. 'Evening, Miss Playle. Evening, Mr Turner. I hope they'll catch the beggars what did it.'

'Yes,' Georgina said, and stepped into the lift.

They reached the fifth floor, where the records were kept, and entered the multi-banked filing room. Georgina went straight to the 'A' section.

She was trying to isolate her feelings, because that was essential if she was going to retain her sanity. The sight of the girl, Elizabeth Brettell, hung over her consciousness. Her pain must have been dreadful, endured for hours, between the moment when the floor had given way beneath her feet and the moment she had been found by a dog. That moment too late. Georgina shivered.

'Here we are.' She went over to the table and opened the file. Five minutes later she sat back, triumphant. 'There. Read all about it,' she invited.

Ashmore Tower.

Cement Mixture Requirement: tricalcium silicate; dicalcium silicate; tricalcium aluminate; tetracalcium aluminoferrite; *Proportions*: lime sixty-five per cent; silica twenty-five per cent; alumina five per cent; iron oxide three per cent; sulphur trioxide one and a half per cent; alkalis half a per cent. *Additional Requirements*: sulphonated hydrocarbon; oleic acid.

'Happy?' Patrick leaned over her shoulder. 'There you have a standard Portland mixture, supported by sulphonated hydrocarbon and oleic acid to prevent any risk of damp. Right. Next page.'

Georgina placed the completed page neatly upside-down on the pile to her left, revealing further details underneath.

Concrete Requirements: one part cement to three parts of fine aggregate to six parts of coarse aggregate; cold-worked high carbon steel bars. *Testing Requirement*: pressure of six thousand pounds per square inch. *Curing Requirement*: concrete must be kept damp for three days after placement.

'Pick a hole in that,' Patrick recommended. 'Turn over.' Georgina obeyed. Patrick remained at her shoulder to point out the various items which he regarded as important. 'You'll see the floors were flat slab, jacked into place. Which makes the idea of damp getting into them from nonexistent piping the more absurd.' He rested his hand on her shoulder. 'Gina, we are not responsible for what happened.'

'There was something wrong with that building, Patrick. Buildings do not stand for fifteen years and then suddenly collapse.'

'Well, we're not going to find anything here,' Patrick said. 'I think you should come and spend the night with us.'

Georgina hesitated. It was past ten, and she was exhausted. On the other hand . . . The phone buzzed.

Patrick picked it up. 'Turner.'

'Pardon me for interrupting, Mr Turner,' Griffiths said. 'But there's a gentleman here. Says he wants to speak to Miss Playle.'

426

Patrick looked at Georgina. 'Do you want to speak to anyone tonight? My bet is he's from the media.'

'No, I don't want to speak to anyone,' Georgina decided.

'Tell the gentleman Miss Playle is busy, Harry,' Patrick said. 'Tell him he can make an appointment for next week.'

'He says it's personal, Mr Turner. Says his name is . . .' Griffiths hesitated, obviously reading a card. 'Mr Philip Rossmore.'

'Oh, damn,' Georgina remarked. Patrick raised his eyebrows. 'My dinner date,' she explained. 'He must have realised I'd be here. Tell him I'll be right down.'

4

Beethoven's Seventh filled the house. Georgina opened her eyes, breathed deeply and smiled up at Philip. 'Thanks for putting it on. Brilliant idea. Balm for the soul after the horrors of yesterday.'

Philip had a towel wrapped round his lower half. His hair was uncharacteristically tousled, and his eyes remained puffy from sleep.

'This Ashmore Tower thing can't possibly be your fault, or your responsibility,' he said firmly. 'All buildings eventually fall down.'

'Not after fifteen years. A well-designed and constructed building should stand for just about always, barring man's interference.'

Gina dressed quickly and was heading for the kitchen when the front doorbell chimed. That would be her neighbours, Tim and Sally Buckenham, coming to offer moral support.

She flung open the door and reeled back from a battery of flashing cameras. 'What the . . .?' She tried to push the door into its frame, but a burly character in a scruffy blazer stood in the way, thrusting a microphone in her face.

'Miss Playle . . . Mrs Carden . . .' They were all shouting for her attention at once.

She kept her cool. 'I have absolutely nothing to say, except to request you to leave.'

'You must have some theory about what happened . . .'

'The police say there is no evidence of an explosion . . .'

'Need any help?' It was Philip's voice from the stairs. All she needed was a shot of her half-naked lover standing beside her on the front page of the Sunday tabloids.

'No,' she called over her shoulder.

'Who was that?' asked the burly invader, still pressing against the door. Georgina didn't answer, just released the door sufficiently to throw him off-balance then shoved again, hard. The door slammed into place and she shot the security bolts. Her heart was thumping furiously as she leaned, panting, against the wood.

Philip was standing in the hall. 'How the devil did that crew get here without us hearing them?'

'Easy. They parked on the road and sneaked through the shrubbery.'

The phone was ringing in competition with the doorbell. 'Are you going to answer it?' Philip asked.

'The Ansaphone is on. I'll wait to hear who it is.'

It was Sally Buckenham's voice. '. . . we tried to come round but turned back when we saw your visitors.'

Georgina had gone into the study. She picked up the receiver. 'Sally, dear. Good to hear a sane voice.'

'Anything we can do?'

'Yes. Help get us out of here. If we sneak out of the back and down to the gate through the bottom fence, can we come round into your garage and beg a lift into Haslemere?'

'No problem.'

'Thanks. See you in about half an hour, then.'

Philip looked fed up at the wreck of his weekend plans, but tried to be helpful. 'Shall I drive you up to town? I can stay on in the flat and keep you company.'

'That's sweet of you, but there's no way you can get your car out of my garage without revealing all. However, if you really fancy a trip to Hammersmith you can come up on the train with me. I would appreciate the company,' she added sincerely.

THE ESCAPE WENT according to plan. The Buckenhams insisted on collecting Philip's car and returning it to his house, later in the day, and inviting Georgina to their house for lunch on Sunday.

Georgina kissed them both goodbye and she and Philip hurried into the ladies and gents to wait out of sight until their train was announced on the Tannoy. Philip was not amused, when they finally got together in a first-class compartment. 'How long do you think this will be going on?' he asked.

'You know the media. Give it twenty-four hours.'

'But wait a minute, what about tonight? You're coming with me to the Round Table Ladies' Night.'

She'd completely forgotten about it. 'Oh, Philip, I am truly sorry. I'm afraid I don't even know what day I'm in. Do you mind if I duck this one? What with all the work I must do in the office today, I'd be the ultimate wet blanket.'

'Well, we'll see.' He wouldn't press the matter now, but he'd talk

428

her round later. Across the compartment he watched her eyes flicking vacantly over the passing scenery, a deep frown between her brows.

They picked up a taxi outside Waterloo, and went straight to the Playle Building. 'You can help me, if you like, Philip,' Georgina told him as they rode up in the lift.

'What I know about architecture wouldn't cover a postage stamp.'

'You don't have to know anything about architecture.' She unlocked the door of the records room, and switched on the light. The Ashmore Tower file lay on the table where she and Patrick had left it. She unlocked the filing cabinet. 'What I am going to do is take out the files of every building we designed during the period between sixteen and fourteen years ago, and we are going to go through them and find out if the Ashmore specifications for materials and construction differ from the rest.'

Gloomily Philip sat at the desk. 'Do you know what I had planned to do this weekend?'

'Listen,' she said. 'After we've finished here we'll buy some food, take it to the flat, and not budge until tomorrow morning. I'll make all my phone calls from there.'

The last bit didn't sound too enthralling but Philip elected to ignore it and at twelve thirty they bought some cold food at the local delicatessen and walked to Georgina's flat, which was in nearby Loveridge Square. Philip went into the kitchenette, which was built into a corner of the sitting room, and dumped the groceries on the kitchen counter. 'Do you realise this is the first time I have ever been here?' he remarked.

'Do you know you are the first man I have *ever* brought here?'

'Then I'm flattered. Where do you keep the hard stuff?'

'In that corner dresser, under the glasses. I'll have a Bloody Mary.'

Philip made one for himself as well. He pressed her glass into her hand. 'Drink this. Real spicy. Doctor's orders.'

Georgina drank, then opened her briefcase and spread the pile of notes she had made on the desk.

Philip eyed the papers. 'We're not doing any more work now, are we? I would have supposed someone like Georgina Playle would have made a couple of phone calls, and the place would have been packed with eager secretaries, pencils at the ready.'

'This is something I have to do for myself.'

'I thought we'd come here to relax.'

'Are you hungry?' Perhaps if she changed to a more popular topic he'd cheer up.

'What are you offering?'

'Tomato soup. Cold meat and salad. Fresh fruit and Camembert.'

'In that case the answer is yes.' He drained his glass. 'Where do you keep the cutlery?'

While the soup was heating she listened to the Ansaphone. Patrick had tried to get her at home to say the police had definitely ruled out any possibility of an explosion. Big deal, she thought. And they weren't prepared to look for any other cause, apart from jerrybuilding.

Georgina clipped a cassette into the player, adjusting the volume on Elgar's Cello Concerto. 'I'm dishing up the soup now. Ready?'

Philip looked aggrieved, despite the playing of Jacqueline du Pré. Georgina tried to lighten the conversation as they ate, but without success. 'You don't look very happy,' she commented at last.

Philip attempted a smile, and shrugged. 'What's there to be happy about? The weekend has not been an outstanding success, so far.' He sat back, put his paper napkin on his plate and looked her in the eye. 'But all is not lost. If we can retire, now, for a nap, and make it back home in time to get ready for the Round Table dinner tonight, it could take a beautiful upswing. Right?'

Georgina stood up and started piling the dishes onto the kitchen counter. 'If you mean we can enjoy a happy siesta hour together, before I make my calls then all right. But, as I told you before, I am not going back to Headley Down tonight. Or anywhere else.'

'Well then, there's no point in me hanging around, is there?'

'Certainly not if you're going to sulk for the rest of the day.' Which remark put paid to any chance of reconciliation. Georgina watched him stride out of the flat. She wasn't sure whether to be sad or relieved that he'd gone.

'PHILIP NOT WITH YOU?' Sally asked next morning. To Georgina's surprise, she was waiting at Haslemere Station.

'No. He had a function on last night. Something up?'

'I thought it might be a good idea to leave your car here and let me drive you home.' They walked out to Sally's car and a rapturous reception from a pair of black poodles.

'Are we still being besieged by newsmen?' Georgina asked.

'Yes, there are still a couple sitting in a blue van. Look . . .' she produced a plastic bag, 'I've brought a wig of mine for you to put on.'

They both burst out laughing as Georgina adjusted the fake hair in the mirror of the passenger sun visor. The ruse worked. Sally drove quite slowly along the lane, chatting casually with her passenger, and the men sitting in the blue van ignored them completely.

The Buckenhams had a heated pool in which Georgina joined them, in a borrowed swimsuit, before a happy barbecue lunch. Talk gravitated to the disaster from time to time, but once the Pimms took effect the three friends relaxed onto lighter topics. By the time Georgina returned to her own house, the van had disappeared.

'THERE IS A LIST of phone messages,' Anne Bladen said first thing on Monday morning.

Georgina sat behind her desk and tapped her teeth with her pen. 'How many?'

'A dozen or so. Where would you like to start?' Anne asked.

'Put them on the desk,' Georgina said. 'I have something more important for you to do, Anne. You have a boyfriend in Fleet Street, haven't you?'

'I wouldn't exactly describe him as a boyfriend.'

'But he'd do you a favour?'

'If I offered one back.'

Her boss laughed. 'It would be in the line of duty. I want you to spend the day going through all the newspaper files you can get hold of, and see if you can find any reports of apparently sound constructions which have suddenly failed.'

Anne frowned. 'How far back?'

'Well, recently, I suppose. But go back a few years as well.'

Anne picked up her handbag. 'You may never see me again.' She went to the door, and paused there. 'Denys Wright has been on the blower repeatedly, about Riverview. He wants to know how the arrangements are coming along.'

'Oh, yes? And *I* want to know . . .'

'When he's going to make the next interim payment. Just thought I'd mention it. Ta-ta.'

ANNE BLADEN HAD thoughtfully placed the Riverview file on Georgina's desk.

Riverview had turned out to be a number one pain in the butt. The project was a block of luxury flats overlooking the river, on the south side, not far east of the Festival Hall. Playle plc had secured the contract, and Georgina had drawn up the designs. The foundations had been laid . . . and the consortium had gone bankrupt!

Georgina had not been too sorry at the time: three years ago, when it had happened, she had been in the middle of her divorce. But then two years ago a consortium headed by the whiz-kid businessman Denys Wright had taken over and the green light had been flashed. The building had been completed, but for minor details, three months ago. Since then Playle had been trying to obtain the penultimate payment—a matter of seven figures—out of the consortium. Wright, always promising that the matter was in hand, was pressing for a gala opening of the building and had suggested that Georgina should organise it.

She managed to get on with some work on a couple of existing projects, and was in the drafting room when Anne telephoned in just after eleven.

'Listen! My reporter friend has come up trumps. When I told him what I was looking for, he took me straight to a news item reported last summer. Several underground stations in Moscow have had to be closed because of concrete failures. Seems that when they took this collapsing concrete apart, they found it was riddled with some kind of mould, or fungus, which developed inside the aggregate, causing it to bulge and then collapse.'

Georgina stared at the telephone. Mould, she thought. Fungus. Overcooked mushrooms! And bulging ceilings!

'Are you there?' Anne asked.

'Yes. Yes, I'm here. You'd better come on back. And congrats.' Georgina replaced the phone, continued to gaze at the wall for several seconds, then went along the corridor to Patrick's office.

'I was just coming along to see you,' he told Georgina. 'This has just arrived, by messenger. It's addressed to me, as senior partner, but it concerns you. It's virtually a subpoena. You are required to give evidence at the inquest next Monday.'

'Hell. That gives me one week.'

Patrick raised an eyebrow. 'For what?'

She told him about the Moscow mould. 'I must get as much information out of the Russians as possible, and also get some concrete from that basement ceiling at Ashmore Tower analysed.' She headed for the door.

'Just a minute!' Patrick was leaning back in his chair, the nails of his right hand clicking on his desk. 'I don't see how there can be any connection between the Moscow underground and Ashmore Tower.'

She shrugged. 'Surely it can't do any harm to follow it up?'

'Personally I think you will be wasting time. Do it if you must,' he told her. 'But I suggest you keep it to yourself. At this stage of the game the media would have a field-day if they got wind of this idea. There's also the question of whose fault it is the mould got into the concrete. We don't want anyone even to sniff at an admission of liability on our part.'

PATRICK'S WASN'T the only opposition Georgina ran into. When she sent one of the clerks down to Ashmore Tower to collect some concrete, he was turned away by the policeman on duty. Apparently to obtain anything from the Ashmore Tower site required a court order. Georgina sent Anne off for the necessary form, but she returned empty-handed. The whole affair was sub judice.

By now it was midafternoon on a particularly frustrating day. Georgina was unable to make any progress in obtaining information from Moscow through the Russian Embassy. Finally she got through to a charming under-secretary who, on hearing her problem, commiserated about the disaster but informed her that the newspaper reports concerning concrete failures in the Moscow underground were much exaggerated. However, if Ms Playle really felt they might be connected, they would be grateful for a sample of concrete from Ashmore Tower!

'They'll be lucky!' she exclaimed to Anne, who had just come in with the news of the refused court order.

Georgina looked at her watch. 'Damn, nearly five already. The day that got away.'

'Did you return any of those calls?' Anne asked.

'I haven't even looked at them.'

'Well . . . one was from your ex.'

'Cheer me up.'

'And one from Martin Garrard.'

'You really are trying to make my day.' Martin Garrard was a brash, self-opinionated fellow architect who worked for Harvey & Associates, Playle plc's rivals for a lucrative project at Dudlington Marina.

'Gina . . . you mustn't let this thing get to you.'

'It's not getting to me,' Georgina lied. 'I just want to stay on here a while to look at some more specifications.' Anne went home, and Georgina brooded over the papers on her desk. But she wasn't seeing them. She was seeing some kind of mould, swelling inside a slab of reinforced concrete. How had it got there? If it *had* got there.

The telephone rang. 'Miss Playle?'

'No calls, Jean.'

'It's transatlantic . . .'

Georgina raised her eyebrows. 'Then I'll take it.' Out of curiosity.

'Miss Playle?' The voice contained both a brogue and a slightly nasal twang. 'Hi. I'm Billie Malandine. Freelance journalist.'

'I'm afraid I'm not talking to any journalists right now.'

'Don't hang up, please.'

Georgina waited. The woman had an appealing voice.

'I read in this morning's paper a report on the collapse of a building in London. Your name was mentioned as the architect.'

'I told you, Miss Malandine, I am not prepared to discuss that.'

'Sure, sure. But I just thought you might be interested to know that there was a building collapse, just like yours, in Chicago a fortnight ago,' Billie Malandine said. 'An apartment block. Upwards of twenty people killed. And a whole lot seriously injured.'

'You said this happened a fortnight ago?' Georgina asked.

'Eleven days, to be exact.'

'What caused the collapse?'

'That's the big question. It's why I'm calling you. Nobody knows for sure. There's gonna be an inquiry, and there's talk of lawsuits in every direction. And I'm telling you, it's about big money.'

'Well, thank you very much for the information, Miss Malandine.'

'Say, don't you have any to give me? I thought maybe we could work together on this.'

'Work? In what way?'

'Well, you tell me what you have, and I'll tell you what I have.'

Georgina held the phone away from her ear and stared at it. She didn't have anything, save the nebulous fungus, and she wasn't keen on telling anyone about that. 'I don't have much at the moment. I am working on it, naturally, but I really don't feel like passing on any preliminary findings by phone to someone I don't know.'

'Absolutely. I'll be with you tomorrow morning. I'll call you back in an hour and confirm the flight I'm on.' The phone went dead, leaving Georgina feeling as if she had just been hit by a truck.

It took several minutes before the fact that the girl intended calling back sank into her dazed brain. 'Damn!' She flicked her intercom through to the switchboard. 'Jean, thank heaven I caught you. Look, will you leave an outside line through to my office? I'm expecting another call from the States.'

'Yes, Miss Playle. But I hope you don't get pestered by reporters. They've been wanting to speak to you all day.'

Georgina smiled to herself. 'Thank you, Jean, for fending them off for me. I'll just have to hope they've given up and gone home. Good night.'

It seemed that the reporters had indeed called it a day. But not everyone had. The phone jangled. 'Hello,' Georgina said.

'I'd like to speak to Miss Playle, please.'

Her first reaction was relief as she recognised her ex-husband's fruity voice, quickly followed by exasperation. 'Really, Tom, what a time to ring.'

'Oh, you are there, Georgina. I've been trying to get you all day.'

'Well, I have been rather busy.'

'This Ashmore Tower thing, eh? Always told you that father of yours couldn't design anything worthwhile. Haw haw haw.'

'Oh, get lost.'

'Hold on. You and I have to get together. It's about Mike. He has a big problem.'

This was an old ploy. 'Tom, if Michael has a problem he will tell me about it himself. And I am not, repeat not, having a meeting with you. I am simply too busy.' She banged the phone down.

Once again the phone tinkled. What a fool she'd been to request an open line. 'Yes?' Her voice carried a sigh of boredom.

'Georgina!'

'Oh, shoot,' she muttered.

'What's that?'

Georgina couldn't help laughing; it was the comment she made every time she saw or heard Martin Garrard. 'I'm sorry, Martin. Don't tell me: you've been trying to get hold of me all day.'

'Well, I can imagine you've been busy. Listen . . . lunch on Wednesday suit you?'

'Lunch? Wednesday? Martin, look, I'm up to my ears . . .'

'You still have to eat, from time to time. And I think we have one or two things we could usefully discuss about Dudlington Marina. As it's a very big project, there could be room for possible cooperation rather than competition.'

The swine, she thought. He knew that Playle, being the bigger and more reputable firm, was likely to get that contract. Or would have been likely to get that contract, up to four thirty on Friday afternoon. Now . . .? Well, just what did he have in mind? She'd better find out. 'All right, lunch on Wednesday.'

'Super! Shall we say twelve forty-five, at L'Escargot?'

'Fine. I'll see you.'

She replaced the phone, idly scratching her chin. Well, she had waited long enough for the call from the States. She pushed her chair back, picked up her bag and coat . . . and the phone tinkled again.

'Hello?'

'Oh, Gina. Sir Trumpton here. I rang earlier and your secretary said you'd call back.' He didn't seem pleased.

'I do apologise. I've been extremely busy.'

'I can imagine. Hm. Gina . . . well, I wonder if you'd lunch with me some time? Some time soon?'

'I'd be delighted,' she lied. 'But I'm going to be tied up all this week. I have to prepare for the Ashmore Tower inquest.'

'Ah! Yes. Actually it's Ashmore Tower I wanted to discuss.'

'Yes?' Lumps of lead were forming in her stomach.

'Well . . . I want you to know that I, personally, have the highest possible confidence in you and your work, Gina.'

'Thank you.'

'However, there can be no question that this business has upset a lot of people. Have you discovered what caused the tragedy?'

'Not as yet. We're working on it.'

'Quite. The fact is, it has been put to me by various members of my board that until the cause is established as having been beyond your control, well . . . the final payment on the Global Building should be withheld. As I say,' he hurried on, 'I have no doubt at all that Playle will be exonerated of any blame, but I must represent the views of my fellow directors.' His voice was heavy with insincerity.

'I am sure you will do as you think best,' Georgina said coldly. 'I suggest you call me again after the findings of the inquest have been published. Now I really must go. Good night.' She replaced the phone, and left the office before it could ring again.

5

The small, dainty blonde who was sitting in reception bounced to her feet when the lift doors opened next morning to admit Georgina to the executive floor of the Playle Building. Extending a tiny hand, she said, 'You have to be Miss Playle. I'm Billie Malandine.'

Georgina did not need telling. Wearing an immaculate navy-blue suit, white blouse and a big artificial flower pinned to her lapel, the girl could only be American. 'Yes. How do you do?' The hand was lost in her own, but the grip was firm and businesslike. Looking down at the visitor who, despite her high-heeled navy courts, did not reach up to her shoulder, Georgina immediately found herself liking her. 'Let's go straight to my office,' she said, leading the way.

Billie launched into a detailed report on the collapse of the Mossburn Grove Building in Chicago. 'High-rise luxury apartment block.' She flipped a page of her notebook. 'The building was well maintained, and thoroughly surveyed every three years.'

'And there were no problems reported?'

'One couple complained the lid of the garbage chute was too hard to shift on level thirteen . . . oh, and three separate residents had reported a stink in the laundry.'

'The laundry? They shared one?'

'Sure. In the basement. Several washers and dryers, for the use of residents. Someone had an idea maybe a rat had dragged hunks of bread behind the machines and they had gone mouldy.'

Georgina jumped. Mouldy! Exactly what Jim Onslow had said to Timmins! Which tied in with the report from Moscow. Fortunately

Billie didn't notice her agitation. Georgina didn't want to talk about Moscow at this stage. Instead she repeated the Ashmore Tower story, in no more detail than had been reported in the press.

'Did you actually design the place yourself?'

'My father, George Playle, did.'

'You never married?'

'I reverted to my maiden name when I divorced.'

'Ditto. But please call me Billie.'

'Billie. And my friends call me Gina. Now, perhaps we should get down to specifics. Have you any details on the construction of Mossburn Grove?'

Billie opened her bag again and produced a floppy disk. 'Have you got a computer in here?'

'My secretary has one in her office. I'll ask her to get a print-out.'

Anne came in to collect the disk and whisked it away, leaving a print-out of Georgina's findings on the desk. These were unfolded and Georgina invited the American girl to pull her chair round beside her so they could examine the sheets together. 'Hmmm.' Billie sat back after some minutes. 'You know, Mossburn Grove was built real good, just like your Ashmore Tower, and both buildings came down in incredibly similar fashion.'

The time had come to tell Billie about the Moscow underground. The American girl listened to the story without moving a muscle, and when Georgina finished the two sat staring at each other. 'Jeez!' the blonde hissed under her breath. 'And no one else knows about it?'

'Only my secretary and the senior partner, and he thinks I'm crazy.'

'But if there is a connection . . . What are we gonna do? No way we can sit back and watch if there's something happening to all concrete of a particular age . . .' She gave a little shiver.

'But the Moscow underground is a lot older than Ashmore Tower.'

'You are saying it can be any concrete of any age? That sure don't make me feel any happier.'

'If there is some kind of concrete rot going about, which can't be detected except by smell, and then only just before the building gives way, any building could collapse at any moment.'

'That's scary. So . . . what's the drill, skipper?'

Georgina found herself liking this effervescent little creature, whose appearance totally belied her character. In Georgina's experience, fluffy blue-eyed blondes in high heels and heavy make-up usually had nothing between the ears but sawdust. But this girl, who could be barely out of her twenties, applied immense energy to her work. 'Where are you staying?' she asked.

'Haven't a notion. I just came right over.'

'Ah. Well, would you care to stay at my place while you're here?'

'Gina! That would be great. But I don't want to impose.'

'You wouldn't be imposing. I have a spare bedroom.' Besides, Georgina thought, she didn't fancy the idea of Miss Malandine wandering all over London, interviewing people, airing her views . . .

'Thanks, Gina. Now, may I use your phone?'

'Feel free.'

Billie dialled a long number. 'Hi, Mac. It's Billie Malandine, used to be with the *Chicago Chronicle*. Gimme Ed's desk.' Pause. 'Oh, come on! What's he doing?' Another pause during which she turned her wrist to see the time. 'OK, gimme his home number.' She scribbled on a pad, then dialled again. 'Hi, Ed, it's me, Billie . . . London, England . . . well, Ed, I know that, but you're a bright morning person . . .'

Georgina grinned. A few minutes later Billie put the receiver back triumphantly. 'There! I've got an agency tracking press coverage of all constructional failures, worldwide, in the past five years.'

Georgina shook her head slowly. 'Has it occurred to you that there are high-rises and dams and flyovers collapsing almost daily in some part of the world? And for no other reason than appalling construction?'

'OK, OK, I hear you. So what? We'll sieve it.'

Georgina shrugged and stood up. 'Let's go to my flat for lunch.'

THEY WERE EATING LUNCH when the phone rang. 'Ah! I hoped you'd be at home,' Philip purred. 'I was wondering if we are ever to meet again.'

'Are you sure you want to?' Georgina asked.

'Frankly, I don't have too much choice at the moment. You're the only woman in my current orbit who interests me.'

Georgina chuckled. 'You are the ultimate male chauvinist pig! I should hang up on you, right now. But why don't you come and have supper here, tonight?'

'Seriously? A beautiful, candlelit supper *à deux*?'

'Er . . . no. *A trois*. I have a girlfriend staying with me.'

'Oh hell! What's she like?'

'She's overweight, with long black hair and pebble glasses. But she's very nice.'

Billie had picked up the drift of the conversation and had both hands over her mouth to suppress her giggles. Philip was silent for a moment, then said, 'You're deliberately trying to put me off, aren't you? Well, I'll call your bluff. I'll be there at eight. Till then.' The phone went dead.

'Is he coming, after that terrific build-up?' Billie asked.

Georgina nodded, grinning. 'Now. Let's be serious. You must be jet-lagged. Why don't you take a siesta this afternoon?'

'You have to be kidding! I'll be along with you.'

Georgina noted the determined jut of her guest's chin and gave up.

THE AGENCY had been busy, and already a clipful of data was on Georgina's desk. 'I knew this was going to be the job to end all jobs,' she groaned.

'Is Anne able to help?' Billie asked.

'That's why I'm here,' Anne said.

'OK. So we each take a sheet, examine it and list separate categories. One list will be anything that was definitely speculative or substandard. On our second list we put any collapse the cause of which remains unresolved.'

They divided the fax sheets, Anne returning to her office, Billie and Georgina at opposite sides of the desk. Most of the reported incidents came from the Mediterranean or other tropical locations, and the majority could be dismissed immediately as speculative building.

The telephone rang. Georgina flicked the intercom. 'Yes?'

'Oh, Miss Playle,' Jean said from the switchboard. 'It's Mr Wright. He seems to be in a bad mood.'

Georgina sighed. 'Very well. I'll accept the call.' She listened to the click. 'Good afternoon, Denys.'

'Georgina, you have been avoiding me. Have you arranged the grand opening of the Riverview Building yet?'

'We're working on it. Though I'm sure you appreciate that it has taken second place in the current emergency. It's scheduled exactly four weeks tomorrow.'

'Hm. Yes, that's acceptable. If the building is still standing, eh?'

'I'm afraid that doesn't come across to me as a joke, Denys. However, I'll ignore it. By the way, I assume you received our account rendered?'

'I did.'

'Then may we anticipate your cheque before the end of the week?'

'I've put that on ice, Georgina. I want guarantees.'

'You have the guarantee of our name and that of the builder, plus the usual indemnity clauses.'

'I don't think those are quite sufficient, in the circumstances, Georgina. And neither do my associates. We need something more.'

Georgina began to get annoyed. 'I cannot give you more than that, Denys. I shall therefore follow your example and put all preparations for the gala opening of Riverview on ice. There is no way you can take possession of a building if you have broken a contract.'

'Look here! I'll sue.'

'Denys, on your instructions, we designed and oversaw the construction of Riverview. It is now complete, and if you wish possession you must fulfil your part of the contract.' Georgina hung up.

Billie was gazing at her, open-mouthed. 'Sounds like you might have a problem,' she observed.

'Excuse me a moment.' Georgina headed for Patrick's office to put him in the picture.

His face was longer than usual when she had finished. 'He will probably sue,' he commented. 'And we're not in a good position.' He gestured at the papers on his desk. 'Those are two cancellations of projects. The time isn't right, they say. What they mean is, the name isn't right. Playle plc is a dirty word right now.'

'But that's ridiculous. There's been a failure just like ours, Mossburn Grove in the States, and . . .'

'I read your memo. I don't think one coincidental failure is going to be enough for us. No, I'm afraid we are just going to have to sit this one out and pray that the coroner isn't too bolshie. And in the meantime,' he pointed with his pen, 'I think we should preserve a cool, calm, collected, and above all polite exterior to all clients, potential or actual. And that includes toads like Denys Wright.'

Georgina went to the door. 'And suppose there is another failure while we're pussyfooting about? It could happen, Patrick.'

'It could,' he agreed, and began looking at his papers.

Georgina went back to her office, and found Billie and Anne in a state of high excitement. 'Got one,' Billie said. 'In Italy.'

THE DOOR PHONE buzzed at eight sharp. 'It's me,' Philip's voice announced, and Georgina pressed the release button.

He saw the three place settings on the table as soon as he entered, and raised an eyebrow. 'You still keeping up this game?'

'It's no game, Philip dear. Come in, Billie. I want to introduce my good friend Philip Rossmore.'

Philip swung round and did a double take. Billie had changed into a soft crinkle-cotton dress in shades of turquoise. Her arms were bare except for a few dozen bracelets and bangles, and huge earrings which swung vigorously against the background of soft blonde shoulder-length hair. Smiling, she held out a tiny hand, and said, 'I am so happy to meet you, after all Georgina has told me about you. I'm Billie Malandine.'

Philip stood stock-still, mesmerised, holding the little hand very tenderly, as if afraid it might break.

440

Georgina watched his reaction with amusement before asking, 'Martini, Philip?'

'Please.' He released Billie's hand but couldn't take his eyes off her as she sank into an armchair and crossed her legs.

Georgina left them talking together while she dished up the meal, but interrupted to ask Philip to pour the wine. 'Not for me, thanks,' Billie said. 'Excuse me one moment. I just have to powder my nose.'

She left the room, and Philip whispered, 'Where on earth did you find her?'

'She's an American journalist. Working with me on this Ashmore Tower thing.'

'Hm! She may be here awhile, then.'

'Could be.' It occurred to her that she might no longer be the only woman who currently 'interested' him. Feeling neither upset nor jealous, she invited him to dinner at Headley Down the following weekend. She knew now that she could never have a meaningful relationship with Philip Rossmore.

'What a super guy,' Billie commented at breakfast.

'I promise you, the feeling is entirely mutual.' Georgina grinned. 'And you can take that any way you like. Now listen, what I want you to do is to promise that not a word of what we are working on goes anywhere beyond you, me and Anne.' Billie scratched her nose. 'I know your reporting instincts are crying out for you to deliver a scoop,' Georgina said. 'But honestly, it would cause more trouble than it's worth, until we have some proof.'

Billie sighed and nodded. 'You think that guy in Italy is gonna call back?'

'I hope so.'

However, when the time came to find her way to L'Escargot, Signor Carvello had not yet called. At least, Georgina thought, she could get Ashmore Tower and concrete off her mind for the next hour ... she hoped. Martin Garrard was waiting near the door for her, looking almost tidy for once.

'Gina!' He squeezed her hand in a huge, hairy paw. 'I am so glad you could make it. You must be snowed under with work and worry. Don't you find it difficult to think of anything but the Ashmore disaster, at the moment?'

She smiled in amazement. The last thing she expected from Martin was sympathetic understanding. 'Very. In fact I am hoping we can forget the subject of concrete for a while,' she replied as he led her to their table.

The restaurant was small and intimate. They sat opposite each other and a shaft of sunlight escaping from behind a cloud caught the posy of flowers on their table.

'So, what's on your mind?' she asked eventually.

'You mean apart from the pleasure of seeing you?'

She raised her eyebrows. 'You didn't say that with conviction.'

'Well, I suppose it's not something I normally say.'

'Quite. So let's stop playing games. What would you normally say?'

He sliced his steak, thoughtfully. 'Heard from the Dudlington people recently?'

'No. Have you?'

'Not officially, no. The various tenders are still being considered. However, I do have a little bird in the office there. Seems your bid was some ten per cent below ours.'

Waves of relief began to drift through Georgina's mind. She could afford to be generous. 'Well, I suppose that's because we're a bigger firm, with more experience.'

'Quite. According to my dickybird, however, you are not going to get the contract.'

Georgina swallowed a lump of steak, unchewed. 'Every customer has the right to make up his own mind,' she pointed out, having regained her breath.

'Absolutely. And I won't deny we would be delighted to get that contract. But not by default, as it were. So, I have given the matter some thought, and discussed it with my partners, and, well, what about if we both withdraw our tenders, and submit a joint one?'

'I see,' Georgina said. 'Our expertise, and your name.' The remark sounded bitter and she regretted making it the moment it was out.

Martin ignored it. 'I meant joint, in every way.'

'I apologise. But don't you think you're jumping on a very unpleasant bandwagon?'

'I'm trying to find a solution to both our problems, Georgina. If it were Harvey and Playle, well, at least we'd be showing the world we have confidence in each other.'

Georgina studied him. He had grown on her during the first part of the meal, and she was finding him a pleasant and charming man. But was he trustworthy? Just how much did he know about what was going on, anyway? she wondered. Was there a mole in her own office, telling him about the two other clients who had cancelled projects? Yet the idea of a merger, even if very temporary, was attractive. Nobody wanted the name Playle plc outside their construction right

442

at this moment, and the Dudlington Marina project was a big one.

'Well?' Martin asked.

'Could you accept the idea that Ashmore Tower didn't collapse because of faulty design or construction?'

'I would say it is very unlikely, and in the absence of any proof to the contrary, yes, I accept that.'

'Thank you for those few kind words.' She sat back with a sigh of relief. 'If there was no design fault, it follows that there must have been some outside factor at work. As you can imagine, we have been giving the matter considerable thought. Well . . .' She toyed with her napkin, and then told him about the Moscow underground, Chicago and their latest discovery in Milan. 'We haven't had any confirmation from Italy yet, but it seems to fall into the pattern.'

'But this is absolute dynamite,' he said. 'Are you going to put this before the inquest?'

'No.'

'Why not? It would clear your reputation at a stroke. In any event it should be released to the media. If there is some kind of fungus which attacks cement, every concrete structure in the world is at risk.'

'Unfortunately, I have absolutely no proof. All I really have is the entirely coincidental fact that there was an unpleasant mouldy smell just before each building collapsed.'

'But, my dear girl, if the fungus is there, it's there. Surely all you have to do is break up a piece of concrete from Ashmore Tower, preferably from the basement, and find your proof.'

'But they won't let me do it. Ashmore Tower is sub judice.'

He drank his wine, wiped his lips on his napkin and grinned at her. 'Well, the answer to that is very simple, if you're game. Why don't we just go along there tonight and pinch some?'

Georgina's eyebrows shot up. She stared at him for several moments while he sat watching her reaction. 'That would be stealing, Martin. It belongs to the owners of the building.'

'Well, I suppose we could go and see them . . . but then we'd get involved in all kinds of arguments. No, better just do it ourselves.'

'Ourselves? I don't see why you should want to involve yourself in something criminal for the sake of Playle.'

'Don't you think it's my business as well? If there is some kind of destructive fungus emerging, it is the business of every architect and construction engineer in the world. Listen, I'll collect you tonight. We can't move until eleven at the very earliest, so how about you invite me to supper first? We must wear black, and soft-soled shoes.'

She found herself entering into the spirit of the adventure as they made plans. 'By the way, you don't know where I live in London.'

'So tell me. Or is it a deadly secret?' She gazed at him for several seconds before divulging that precious address and telephone number. 'Right.' He entered them in his notebook.

BY THE TIME Georgina regained the office, Billie and Anne were both in a state of high excitement because Signor Carvello had called.

'It's good and bad news, I'm afraid,' Anne said.

'There is no evidence of explosives, and the specifications indicate that the building was constructed to the highest standards,' Billie said. 'Everyone is as mystified by what happened as they have been here, or in the States.'

'The bad news is that Signor Carvello has no evidence of any unusual smell immediately before the collapse,' Anne said.

'Which doesn't prove there wasn't one,' Billie argued. 'All the people who smelt it might have been killed.'

'Equally, it doesn't give us anything to work with,' Georgina said. 'We haven't learned anything about the fungus yet, or even if it really exists. But,' she smiled mysteriously, 'we may know more in a day or two. Close the door and I'll tell you how . . .'

'WELL, HELLO,' Billie said, as she opened the front door of Georgina's flat later that evening. 'You must be Martin Garrard.'

'And you must be Billie Malandine, if I'm at the right place.'

'Oh, you're at the right place,' Billie said. 'Gina's just preparing supper.'

They sized each other up. Martin was wearing a black rollneck and a dark track suit. 'You even look like a burglar,' Georgina commented from the kitchen doorway.

The doorbell rang, and Martin turned, somewhat sharply.

'That'll be Anne. My secretary. She and Billie are coming, too.'

Anne came in, also dressed in black, and Georgina served pizzas and Chianti. 'I like your flat,' Martin remarked. 'I must come here more often.'

'Tell us what the form is,' Georgina said, ignoring his comment.

'What we want is a block of concrete from the ground floor, because that's where the initial cave-in took place, as I understand it.'

'The ground floor is no more. It's all down in what was the basement.'

'So we go down into what was the basement.'

'Of course we don't know it was caused by a fungus at all,' Georgina said. 'If we're to have any chance of proving it was, we'll need several small pieces of concrete, rather than one large bit. We must try to collect them as far apart as possible.'

'That's good thinking,' Martin agreed.

'I've unearthed several holdalls and put them in the hallway. They should be strong enough to carry several pieces each.'

'Good girl. Any of you got a car handy?'

'My Mini is in the square,' Anne said.

'Right. Better if we go in two cars, just in case we run into a problem. I will drive up Wigmore Street, park a few streets away from the perimeter fencing and approach it on foot with my partner. Anne can come down the Bond Street end, and will follow the same pattern in reverse.'

'Damn! I've forgotten about the torches,' Georgina cursed herself.

'No torches,' Martin said. 'To show a light would be too risky.' He finished his wine. 'I think we must face up to the possibility of being spotted. In any event, they will probably have policemen on duty day and night. The vital thing is that at least one of us gets away with some samples large enough to be worth analysing. Once we are clear, we take the stuff to this address. It's a chemical laboratory.' He gave Georgina a slip of paper. 'It only remains to decide who goes with whom.'

'Me with you!' Billie announced. 'Gina and Anne are used to working together, and they know London.'

Martin looked at Georgina, and she shrugged. 'Makes sense.'

He looked as if he would have liked to argue, then changed his mind. 'Right. Synchronise watches. Three minutes to eleven.'

'Check,' Anne said, getting into the spirit of things.

'Now.' He hauled his vast frame out of the armchair. 'Let's go!'

They drove into the West End, where the theatre crowds were still in evidence. Anne handled her car expertly, and parked in a quiet side street, two streets from the collapsed building.

When Georgina and Anne reached the corner, they paused to consider their next move. The road remained closed by a simple red No Entry sign. The entire street was dark and apparently empty, although there were probably watchmen and a policeman or two lurking somewhere close. Work had already begun on the houses opposite which had been damaged by flying masonry, while the street itself, though cleared of the wrecked cars, was a minefield of deep ditches and lengths of piping waiting to be laid.

To their left, where Ashmore Tower had once dominated the entire block, there was a gaping hole in the skyline, only the

445

lift shafts still standing. Beneath them were tilting chunks of wall and piles of rubble.

They crept along the side of the street, hugging the shadows and feeling with their toes before putting weight on each step. There was no sign of Martin and Billie. They had covered half the distance to the front steps when they heard a scraping sound and saw the gleam of a torch. Instantly they both dived behind a silent generator and crouched, waiting. There were two men, just beyond the steps, talking. Georgina could not hear what they were saying, but one of them was wearing a policeman's helmet. Then they moved off, towards the far end of the street.

Georgina realised that Anne was holding her arm, very tightly. 'I'm not sure I'm enjoying this,' the girl admitted.

'It may get more exciting later.' Georgina stood up as the men faded into the distance. They reached the steps, mounted cautiously—but not cautiously enough. Anne tripped over a pile of rubble and landed on her hands and knees.

'Damn!'

'That you?' Martin asked.

'Oh Lord, I nearly jumped out of my skin. Where are you?'

'Here.' He and Billie had crawled into the basement.

Georgina led Anne down to them, stumbling over broken concrete, and cursing as a piece of iron reinforcing ripped the leg of her trousers.

'Here we go,' Martin said, holding up a fair-sized lump. 'These are ideal.' They picked up several pieces of concrete in varying sizes and thrust them into the holdalls. Then they crawled and scrambled to the back of the building, where Martin selected some more chunks. 'OK, girls, let's split.'

They returned to the steps and Martin started walking up, Billie behind him, and checked as a voice said, 'Stop there!' and a beam of light shone down.

Georgina and Anne, still in the deeper shadows at the foot of the steps, huddled against each other. Billie, whom the policeman had not seen, merely dropped on her face. 'Ah, officer,' Martin said, continuing up towards him. 'I'm just collecting concrete.'

The policeman peered into his face. 'I'm sorry, sir, but you can't do that. It's against the law.'

'Is it?' Martin sounded dumbfounded.

'This building is the subject of a judicial inquiry, sir.' The policeman unhitched his walkie-talkie. 'You'd better wait a minute, sir. The inspector might want a word with you at the station.'

'Is that really necessary? I had no idea I was stealing. Look, my car is parked just round the corner. Come along with me and I'll give you my card, then you'll know where to get in touch with me.'

'Well . . .' The policeman was uncertain, but Martin was already past him heading onto the street. He followed.

'Let's get out of here,' Billie gasped.

They gave Martin and his escort time to reach the end of the street, then hurried the other way.

COLIN WORTHINGTON was a young man who wore steel-rimmed glasses and a little moustache. He peered at each of the women in turn. 'Where's Martin?' he asked at last.

'Taken into custody,' Anne said.

'Well, we don't actually know that, but he was last seen with a bobby on his heels,' Georgina corrected, confident that Martin was capable of talking himself out of his problem.

'But we have these samples,' Billie said eagerly.

'Bring them in.' Worthington showed them into his laboratory.

It was the most untidy room Georgina had ever seen, with jars and bottles scattered round the two microscopes on a bench which occupied the centre of the floor. Overstuffed shelves lined the walls and a battered roll-top desk was almost hidden under a single huge mound of papers. 'Where shall we put them?' she asked.

'Oh, anywhere you like.' He waved an arm over the chaos.

Georgina put the bags under the bench and placed pieces of concrete from each bag beside the microscopes. 'It's rather urgent that we have some sort of analysis by the weekend,' she said sweetly.

Colin nodded. 'Martin said you were in a hurry. I'll get my assistants working on them first thing tomorrow.' He looked at his watch. 'This morning.'

'And you do realise this is absolutely confidential,' she added.

'Certainly.' He grinned. 'Most of my work is confidential. Well, I'll be in touch.' He ushered them to the door.

'Not so much as a cup of coffee,' Billie groused as they squeezed themselves into the Mini. 'What now?'

'If Anne would be kind enough to drop us home, I suggest we call it a night.'

'GOOD MORNING, Miss Playle,' Anne said formally next morning as Georgina entered the office. They had chatted excitedly about the evening's adventure until two o'clock, drinking coffee laced with brandy, and they were both now fairly bleary-eyed.

'Good morning, Miss Bladen.' Georgina went through to her office and sat down. Anne followed. 'You look terrible,' Georgina commented in a flat voice. 'Have you phoned Martin Garrard?'

'He called you,' Anne replied. 'Would you like to borrow some make-up?'

'Is it that bad? I thought I had done my face.' She got up and staggered to a wall mirror. 'What did he say?'

'Only that he had talked his way out of trouble, and that he'd be in touch whenever he had the analyst's report on the concrete.'

Georgina was tempted to lift the phone anyway, for no better reason than . . . hearing that lovely deep growl? She straightened her back. She would have to be mad to consider getting involved with a business rival. 'We'll wait for him to call back.'

'Right. Now . . . Mr Turner wants to see you.'

Georgina drew a long breath, got up and went to Patrick's office. 'You look like something the cat dragged in,' he remarked.

'Billie and I sat up chatting rather late last night.'

'Billie? Oh, your little American friend.' Patrick drummed his nails on the edge of his desk as Georgina sat down. 'I have decided not to attend the inquest,' he said. 'Mustn't appear to take it all too seriously.'

'What?'

'Of course we know it is serious, Georgina. Of course we are deeply concerned at the deaths and the injuries. But it is not our responsibility. We have the proof, and you will take it with you, that that building was designed and constructed to the highest possible specifications. It is up to someone else to discover why it fell down. Any mention of theories about a fungus would inevitably be interpreted as an attempt to off-load blame.'

Georgina opened her mouth, and then closed it again. She stood up. 'I'm sure you're right, Patrick. Now I must get on.'

There was so much to be done . . . and she hadn't even mentioned Martin Garrard's proposed joint tender to Patrick. Worrying about Dudlington Marina seemed so irrelevant compared with the feeling that there was something silent, unseen, but utterly malignant stalking through this city, and every other city in the world.

When Georgina got back to the flat that evening, Billie was preparing to go out. 'Thought I'd take in a show,' she explained. 'Care to come along?'

'Sorry, I'm for an early bed.' She collapsed into a chair.

'Got anything from Worthington yet?'

Georgina shook her head. 'Billie, there's something we have to chat about. This weekend.'

'I guess you go home to your cottage in the country, eh?' Billie gazed at her and waited.

'I'm sorry,' Georgina said. 'I would love to invite you, but I can't. It's the weekend my son comes home. He's having problems and I know we're going to have to do a lot of talking. But you're welcome to stay on in the flat here, see something of London.'

'I might just do that.' But for once her lips were pinched tight. She was obviously disappointed.

'You can come down next weekend,' Georgina suggested, hoping to appease. 'And in the meantime . . .'

'I don't talk to anyone about funny smells or cracking concrete. I got the message, Gina. See you.'

Billie was definitely miffed. Well, she'd have to sort that out for herself. Georgina had a shower, pulled on a dressing gown, mixed herself a drink and watched the news. She had just stuck a TV dinner in the oven when the doorbell rang. She picked up the entryphone.

'Hi. Martin. May I come up?' For a moment Georgina was tempted to say no. In her present mood maintaining a cool business reserve could be quite a strain. 'I've a preliminary report from Colin,' he added, sensing her indecision.

'Oh! Well, then, you had better come up.' She dashed into the bedroom, pulled on track-suit trousers and a top, and was back in time to open the door to him. 'I'm afraid you caught me about to relax with a fast-food dinner. I hadn't expected a result so quickly.'

He came in, peering around suspiciously. 'Where's Billie?'

'Out.'

'That's a relief. I find her so exhausting.'

Georgina laughed. 'I have to agree. There is something very sweet and appealing about her, but she can be infuriating. Drink?'

'Maybe later. Let's talk about this.' He removed a long manila envelope from his inside pocket, and took out several sheets of paper.

She took the sheets somewhat gingerly. 'You seem excited.'

'I'm not sure that is the word. Scared would be more appropriate. Colin *has* found traces of an unknown Mycota inside those blocks we gave him to analyse.'

'Mycota?'

'Fungi. It's a generic term.'

Georgina sat down. 'I'm afraid I don't know much about fungi.'

He sat beside her. 'Well, basically, Mycota are plantlike organisms, but they have no organised structure, like stems or roots . . . and they don't have chlorophyll.'

'So they don't need light to grow, like mushrooms, right?'

'Well, when most people think of fungi they think of mushrooms and toadstools. But mushrooms are only a small subdivision of all the Mycota in the world. Now, the thing about Mycota is that some of them don't need to crossbreed to reproduce. The thallus simply fragments, and begins to grow all over again.'

'Sounds horrendous.'

'It is. Just imagine, one tiny thallus, perhaps not even big enough to be seen with the naked eye, in, say, a matchbox, for example. Then it fragments, and you have ten thalluses. They grow, and fragment, and you have a hundred. They grow, and fragment, until eventually the matchbox just splits apart.'

'And that's what happened at Ashmore Tower?'

'It would appear so.'

'You say Colin doesn't know what this Mycota is.'

'He's working on it. He's pretty sure that it belongs to the Class Zygomycetes. It's a strictly terrestrial fungus, doesn't have anything to do with water, reproduces asexually by conidia. That's the splitting technique I mentioned. He hopes to narrow it down further in the next week or so.'

'I'm afraid I don't see we are any further ahead,' Georgina remarked. 'To claim that Ashmore Tower was destroyed by a fungus can't absolve us of responsibility, unless we can prove that we weren't responsible for the fungus being there. That's what Colin really has to work on. And there's no use alarming the whole world unless we can tell people how to cope with it, and which buildings are at risk.'

'You don't think you're taking on rather a lot of responsibility? Keeping it quiet, I mean.'

'What else am I to do? Go on the box and tell everyone to move out of their houses because they may collapse at any minute?'

'Well . . . Do I smell burning?' Martin asked suddenly.

'Oh damn!' Georgina wailed. 'My supper!' She dashed to open the oven which was belching black smoke. 'Blast!'

'Now what will you have for supper?' he asked.

She saw the invitation coming and knew she must stop it. 'Beans. A tin of beans. I haven't the energy or the will to get anything else.' She saw he was about to say something, so quickly added, 'I'm definitely too shattered to go out for anything.' Martin closed his mouth again, looking a bit disappointed. 'You can share my beans if you like.' The offer was made before she could stop herself.

'Love to. I'm quite professional with a tin-opener. Where will I find it?'

'In the drawer next to the hob.' She heard him fiddling with the CD player and smiled as a Beethoven sonata filled the room. The disc was only half through when he called her to the table. 'Wow! Haven't you been busy!' she exclaimed, eyeing the mound of food on her plate which included eggs, frankfurters and fried tomatoes.

'Hope you don't mind me raiding the cupboard to add a few things to the beans.' He uncorked a half-empty bottle of red wine. 'Found this, too. Thought it looked in need of tidying up.'

From the other side of the dining table, Martin studied his companion. Strange girl. Good-looking, certainly, but far too tall, obviously very strong-minded and determined . . . well, she would have to be to achieve all she had. And yet there was a very attractive feminine streak. He had been married once, years ago. It had lasted three long months of bickering, sulks and repeated walkouts and reconciliations. Since then, he had withdrawn to peaceful bachelorhood. It bothered him that he found Gina's company so relaxing and enjoyable.

They talked about wine and France, about skiing holidays and gardens and visiting Australia—anything but architecture. They listened to another CD with coffee and she was amazed when, having helped clear up and load the dishwasher, Martin announced it was eleven thirty and he was going home to bed. 'Thank you for cooking supper, and for keeping my mind off the current problem,' she said, standing at the open door with him.

'Thanks for inviting me to stay.' He held her hand. 'A really nice, quiet evening which we both needed.' Then he was gone. He hadn't attempted to kiss her good night . . . which was probably just as well.

'HOW WAS your evening?' Billie asked at breakfast.

'Quiet. As I intended it to be. How was your show?'

Billie shrugged. 'I guess I don't quite understand your British sense of humour. Did you hear from Martin?'

Georgina carefully stirred her coffee. One copy of Worthington's report was in her handbag, the other in the desk in the corner. 'Not yet. What are your plans for today?'

'Hoped I might get to do some of your London stores. But I guess it's more important I hang around here, in case he calls.'

Georgina raised her eyebrows. 'Well . . . I'll be back for lunch.'

'DENYS WRIGHT CALLED,' Anne told Georgina when she reached the office. 'He really is agitated about the Riverview opening.'

'Has his cheque arrived?'

'It wasn't in this morning's mail.'

'Then the Riverview opening stays on ice.'

'Um,' Anne commented. 'Martin Garrard been in touch?'

'Early days,' Georgina said. She disliked holding out on the faithful Anne even more than on Billie, but she didn't want either of them to know about the analyst's report until she had decided on her course of action. 'Don't put any calls through for a while. I'm going to talk to Patrick.'

'I LUNCHED with Martin Garrard on Wednesday,' Georgina began. Tentatively, she outlined the Dudlington proposal.

'Hm,' he commented. 'Goddamned vultures.'

'Might make sense, though, in our present circumstances.'

'Oh yes, it would make sense . . . if we could be sure we can trust the beggar. We've had two more cancelled contracts. And Bascom tells me there are more lawsuits being prepared, awaiting the coroner's verdict.' Bascom was the company's solicitor.

'The coroner's inquest may put us in the clear.'

'It could also put us firmly in Queer Street.'

'Well, I've a notion we may be able to influence the verdict. Read this.' Georgina handed him the top copy of Colin Worthington's report, and studied his expression as he perused it.

He raised his head. 'How many people know of this?'

'Well, the analyst of course, Worthington. And Martin Garrard.'

'What did you say?' Patrick shouted. 'Garrard?'

'No need to get excited. You may as well know the whole story.' Georgina told him the rest of their lunchtime conversation, and the events of that night.

'Let me get this straight,' Patrick said when she had finished. 'You have committed a criminal offence, and in the company of one of our rivals. Gina, sometimes I despair . . .'

'I was thinking of Dad's good name—and that of the firm,' she snapped.

'Is his name going to be helped by your going to jail?'

'Don't talk nonsense! No one is going to jail, Patrick, for pinching a lump of concrete. The point is that any building could be at risk, if that fungus has somehow invaded the concrete. What I have come to discuss with you is what we do with this information.'

Patrick tapped the sheet of paper. 'If this is true, we have the reason why . . . but not the how or the when.' He pushed the report across his desk in her direction. 'I suggest you get that how and when, just as rapidly as possible. Until we have that information, if we make this report public we'll be branded scaremongers.'

'My own view exactly. So I tell Worthington to drop everything else and concentrate on our concrete.'

452

'WHEN ARE YOU OFF?' Billie asked after Georgina had prepared their lunch.

'I usually try to get to Waterloo before four. Otherwise it can be sheer hell, especially on a Friday.'

'So you won't be going back to the office?'

'Oh, I will, for an hour. Something might turn up.'

'From Martin, you mean?'

Georgina frowned. In fact, she was hoping to speak to Worthington, who had been in his laboratory all morning. 'Why, yes,' she said. 'Hopefully.'

'What do you think Martin will be able to add to what he gave you last night? You gave me the run-around,' Billie complained.

'What makes you think that?'

Billie got up, went to the little antique walnut desk and picked up the copy of Worthington's report.

'You took that from my desk drawer,' Georgina accused.

'Sure. I admit it. I sussed you'd ratted on me this morning, when you said Martin hadn't been in touch. When I went out last evening the dishwasher was empty. This morning there were two dinner plates in there. And I ate out.' She was obviously pleased with herself.

'And you decided that gave you the right to ransack my desk.'

'Sure,' Billie said, coolly. 'I had supposed we were partners. But you've been holding out on me since the start.'

Georgina's hurt transformed into anger. 'You have abused my friendship and my hospitality . . .'

'I'm not in your class,' Billie retorted. 'OK, you want to play this game your way? Then I have the right to play it mine, too. I want you to release me from my promise to keep this thing under wraps.'

'I am trying to do what's best,' Georgina said, as evenly as she could. 'For everyone. The moment Worthington comes up with some idea on how the fungus got there, how it can be found before the concrete crumbles, and how its growth can be checked, then I am prepared to go public. Until then, no. And your promise stands.' She got up, thoroughly disgruntled. 'I'll be back about three.'

Billie's bottom lip stuck out, her diminutive frame quivering with tension. But she remained silent, for once.

'WORTHINGTON CALLED,' Anne told Georgina when she returned to the office.

'Then get him back for me. Mr Worthington,' Georgina said as he came on the line. 'Look, my company is prepared to make it worth your while to concentrate all of your staff on this Mycota. What we have to know is where the fungus originated, how it got into the concrete, and how it can be checked and then destroyed. Do you think you can find those answers?'

'Of course I can, Miss Playle, given enough time.'

'Time is what we don't have, Mr Worthington. I am authorising you to charge whatever you feel is justifiable, if you can come up with an answer by ten o'clock on Monday.'

'I'll do what I can.'

'All right. I'll call you at nine on Monday. Good luck.'

9

The flat was as spick-and-span as Georgina had ever known it. And empty. The latchkey she had given Billie lay on the desk. 'Billie?' she called, as she wandered through to the spare bedroom.

She opened the door. Billie's bed was made, and everything was in place. Billie had definitely done a runner.

Georgina hated herself, but she couldn't resist rushing into her own bedroom to check things out. Nothing was missing from the flat.

Except for the copy of Colin Worthington's report.

GEORGINA DIDN'T GET to Waterloo until half past five, and then it was a standing affair for nearly the entire journey home. By the time a seat did become available, she was so close to Haslemere it didn't seem to matter. Her life had suddenly taken such a peculiar turn. One week ago, on this same train, she had been reflecting that with the opening of the Global Bank building she had just about reached the peak of her profession. Now her firm was in danger of being kicked off the map. Her brain was revolving in circles as she left the train and went in search of her car in the station car park.

Traffic had thinned, giving her a chance to reorientate her mind to her son, Michael. She longed to see the tousled hair, long leggy body and challenging blue-green eyes ... her eyes. Let's hope his latest problems have been resolved, she muttered to herself as she swung round the drive to face the garage doors. The savage throb of amplified drums met her before she reached the front door. Michael was home.

She had just had time to put down her cases when his strong young arms wrapped round her waist and lifted her bodily from the floor to swing her round and round. 'Michael! Stop, I'm dizzy,' she yelled at him over the music. But she was grinning, and he knew she loved the way he always greeted her, now he was large enough to handle her height and weight.

She picked up her cases and headed for the stairs. 'And I gather from your father you have plenty to say!'

He took the cases from her. 'Did he tell you anything?'

'No. I'd rather hear it from you, whatever it is.'

He sat on the ottoman in the bay window of her bedroom, while she disappeared into the dressing room to change into a T-shirt and shorts. When she was ready she padded barefoot across the carpet to stand beside him, surprised at his silence. 'Must be a big problem, darling.' She put an affectionate hand on his shoulder.

He sighed. 'It is. Mum, I've fallen in love.'

She was glad he couldn't see her smothering a relieved smile. Poor Michael! So he was being troubled by the first pangs of puppy love. She gave his shoulder a squeeze. 'It happens to us all, eventually.'

He stood up, and she noticed he wasn't smiling. 'Can we go and sit in the garden with a drink or something?'

They sat on patio chairs watching shadows lengthening across the lawn. 'Linda's a super girl,' Michael began. 'I'm sure you'll both get on well together. I'd have brought her down this weekend, only she thought it might be better if I broke the news to you first.'

'News?' Georgina was beginning to get bad vibes.

'Yes. We want to get married and I hoped it would be OK for us to come and live here for a while . . . until we get our finances sorted out.' He spoke very fast, spilling the words as though to get rid of them as quickly as possible.

'Hey, hold on! Don't you think you're jumping the gun a bit? You are still only sixteen.' Oh dear! And he looked so serious.

'Yes. Well, I'm afraid we have already jumped the gun . . . she thinks she's pregnant.'

For some ungodly reason Georgina had a desire to throw back her head and roar with laughter. It was a purely hysterical reaction, of course, but there seemed little else to do in the circumstances.

'Well?' Michael was staring at her, waiting anxiously.

She swallowed. 'A bit careless, weren't you?'

'You mean you're not going to read me the riot act?'

'Bit late for that. But . . . oh, Mike, what about your education?'

'We accept that we'll both have to leave school, of course. I'll get a job while she has the baby.'

'You mean she *wants* to have the baby?'

'Of course, so do I. No matter what happens we are not going to have an abortion.'

Georgina's brain was going round and round. Another thought struck her. 'Your father knows all of this?'

'I told him last weekend.'

No wonder he had been so agitated, Georgina thought. 'What did he say?'

'That we'd have to put our heads together. He said he'd call you.'

'Yes,' Georgina said grimly. 'Michael . . . are you positive that marriage is the answer? I mean, well . . . what age is she?'

'Fifteen. But she'll be sixteen in three weeks' time.'

'Oh, no! You could be had up for statutory rape!'

'So who's going to accuse me? Not Linda. Honestly, Mum, I know you'll think we're crazy, but we know this is the real thing. We really are in love.'

Georgina looked at him, as though seeing him as an adult for the first time. 'So who is Linda? Where did you meet her?'

'She's at White Grange, the girl's boarding school near Shipcombe College. Pupils from the top two forms at each school are allowed to get together for dances and special events each term.'

Well, at least if she was at a respectable school one might presume she had a fairly respectable background. 'Who is she?'

'Oh, that's no problem. You know her parents.'

'Do I?'

'In fact,' Michael went on, 'it was when we discovered that you and her father were doing business together that we first got friendly.'

'Business?' Georgina asked, with a sinking heart.

'Yes. Some huge project down by the Thames, Linda said. He's Denys Wright, the property developer.'

10

'I'll have to ring your father now, I suppose, to arrange a time to discuss this business.' Georgina dragged her fingers through her hair, trying to let the tension out of her scalp. She picked up the remote phone and pressed the numbers. 'Tom, it's Georgina. We will have to get together to discuss this. Can you come down this weekend?'

There was silence while Tom spouted a river of sarcastic comments, at the end of which he surprised her by agreeing. 'OK, Sunday morning,' she sighed again. 'And yes, we will give you lunch.'

SATURDAY PROVED to be a very pleasant day, Michael plugged into a Sony Walkman while he played computer games in his room; Georgina pottering among the delphiniums and lupins. She tried to convince herself that if Michael set his heart on marrying Linda, and the Wrights agreed, then she had to accept the situation and hope it worked out. Their finances would be the main problem.

On one thing she was absolutely agreed with her son, now that she had had the time to think about it—there should be no abortion. They would never forgive themselves if they agreed to an abortion, nor would they forgive anyone who talked them into it.

Sunday, however, started badly, and never improved. They woke to clouds which lowered by the hour until a steady curtain of rain blotted out the day. Georgina settled at her desk sorting out household bills and replying to invitations.

Tom arrived at eleven thirty. He was a big, immaculately groomed man, crinkly hair firmly lacquered into place, expensive casual clothes belying his invariable poverty. He refused the offer of coffee and helped himself to a large martini.

'So have you convinced our young idiot that an abortion is the only way out?' he demanded, in front of Michael.

'Hey, Dad! What's got into you? This is a sudden change of tune.'

'Don't take that tone with me! You got yourself into this. Now we've got to make the best we can of a bad job.' He stood with his back to the empty fireplace in the sitting room, carefully trimmed beard jutting aggressively at his audience.

'I had thought we were all agreed that there was no need for an abortion,' Georgina said quietly.

'I can't imagine where you got that idea . . .'

'From me.' Michael jumped up. 'Last weekend you seemed perfectly happy with the idea of Linda and me getting married.'

'Anything for a peaceful existence. But you surely don't imagine I was serious?' Tom had placed his glass on the mantelpiece while he performed a cigar-lighting operation, sucking steadily until the end glowed an even red. 'What do the girl's parents say about it?'

'They don't know yet,' Michael mumbled from the window.

'What! Well, isn't it about time they did? Come on. Get them on the phone now, Mike. Either you call them or I'll do it for you.'

'Tom! Stop it!' Georgina snapped. 'Michael and Linda decided to tell us first, hoping for a positive reaction, before telling her parents.'

'So what does Michael do now? Leave school and become a street cleaner?'

'Michael will leave school, yes,' Georgina said. 'They can live here for the time being.'

'I have never heard such nonsense in my life,' Tom declared. 'And who is going to finance all of this? Don't look at me. I don't have the money to throw around on people who can't manage their lives.'

Georgina could feel Michael starting to bristle, and squeezed his hand. 'Michael's finances are my responsibility, Tom, as they have always been. I don't recall you ever providing for either of us.'

'Never miss an opportunity to turn him into a mother's boy, do you?' Tom sneered.

Georgina kept her temper with an effort. 'There is absolutely no point in having hysterics about this. It's happened, and we must all cooperate. But if this is the way you are going to carry on, then there was little point in your coming down here to discuss the matter.'

'What is there to discuss? Until the girl's parents know what's going on we can't decide anything.' Tom spread himself over an armchair, poking his beard at her.

As an exercise in family discussion the meeting was a total failure. She served a lunch of steak and salad, steering the conversation onto general topics and sweeping Tom out of the house after coffee before he had time to protest.

'But he's right, isn't he?' Michael said, as the car tyres crunched on the drive.

Georgina sighed. 'I suppose so. You say Linda's getting the result of the second test tomorrow?'

'Yes.'

'As soon as you hear from her you contact me, and I'll set up a meeting with Mr and Mrs Wright. OK?'

'You're still hoping that it'll be negative, aren't you?'

She grinned. 'Either way, I'm on your side, right? Now, I've asked an old friend to dinner tonight. His name is Philip Rossmore and you must be nice to him.'

Michael's turn to grin. 'Butter won't melt in my mouth.'

IT WAS A CONSIDERABLE bind having to cook seriously twice in one day, Georgina reflected. As they had had steak for lunch she opted for pork chops Provençal, and had everything ready to be turned on twenty minutes before dinner when she heard the growl of a motor.

'You get it, Michael,' she called, and then cocked an ear as she heard a female voice. Not believing the evidence of her senses, she ran into the living room . . . and gazed at Philip and Billie Malandine.

'Hi,' Billie said. 'Sorry to burst in on you like this.'

Georgina looked at Philip. 'It's a long story,' he said. 'I know you weren't expecting Billie. Let me take us all out to dinner.'

'There are five chops,' Georgina told him. 'One of you men will have to settle for one, that's all. If it's a long story, I suggest you tell me over a drink. Come on in.'

Philip looked at Billie. 'Swell place you have here,' Billie commented. 'And isn't Mike something?'

Georgina sighed. 'Make some drinks will you, please, Martin?' She sat down. 'Thanks for leaving without even saying goodbye, Billie.'

'Gee, I felt awful about that.' Billie sat down as well. 'But I reckoned you and I were not on the same wavelength.'

'And you were probably right. Which makes this visit all the more surprising. I suppose when I told you that I wasn't about to give you permission to hold a press conference you went to Philip. Am I right?'

'I guess you are. Well . . . I thought he might be able to talk you round,' she hastily added.

'And are you staying at a hotel?' Georgina asked.

Philip coughed. 'You know I have that small guest apartment downstairs in my house? I told Billie she could use that for the rest of her stay in England.'

Georgina's eyebrows shot up. 'I see.'

'Now don't go getting any wrong ideas,' Billie said, flushing.

Michael returned from the sideboard with a tray of drinks. 'I'm afraid I don't really know what is going on.'

'Come and sit beside me, Mike.' Billie patted the other cushion on the sofa. 'It's straightforward, really. Your mom and I have information which I believe should be released to the media as soon as possible, and which she wants to keep private. I gave her my word to let her make the decision. All I'm asking now is that she gives me the green light.'

'The information should be released now, Gina. In fact, I'd say release is long overdue,' Philip adjudicated.

His interference did not help. 'As far as I am concerned, nothing has changed,' Georgina snapped.

'Don't you watch TV?' Billie enquired.

Georgina frowned at her, aware of a slow tightening of her stomach muscles. She had not had the set on today, certainly. She had been trying to put non-family problems out of her mind.

'Is that today's paper?' Billie got up to look at the neatly folded newspaper on the coffee table.

'Here we are,' she announced. 'Concealed on page four. The Atterbury factory in Yorkshire. Nothing of the remotest importance to anyone—save us, and the poor gink who owned the factory. You wanna read it?'

Georgina took the paper and read the article. 'It says here only one wall and part of the roof collapsed,' she said.

'So he was lucky. But see what the night watchman said? A rotten smell, for some time before the collapse.'

Georgina chewed her lip. 'I don't suppose you designed that building?' Philip asked.

'No, I didn't. It's not a Playle construction.'

'That's not important!' Billie sat down again, beside a totally bemused Michael. 'You have to see, Gina, that this has gotten too big to hold down. No one has observed the connection between all of these failures, except ourselves, because no one else is in possession of all the facts. Now it's essential we make those facts public.'

'I'm sorry, Billie, but that's not the way I see it. By tomorrow we may have discovered some way of dealing with the Mycota. The analyst is working on it through the weekend. But in the meantime, I still think it would be wrong to panic the public.'

'Oh, come on!' Philip interjected. 'That excuse won't wear. People should at least be warned to look out for the smell, so that if necessary they can take evasive action.'

'Philip, that's naive.' Georgina drained her sherry glass. 'The entire population would sniff imaginary smells . . . or claim they had, simply to get off work. The country would grind to a standstill in twenty-four hours. It would be criminal to alarm everybody until we have some idea of how to handle it.'

'What you're saying is, until you have some proof that the fungus couldn't have gotten into the concrete through some shoddy building methods on the part of your firm,' Billie snapped.

'Shoddy!' Georgina shouted angrily. 'Listen, no one knows what causes that fungus . . . why don't you try being honest with yourself, for a change? All you want is to be able to print a scoop, get into the big time. Well, that's not on, until we find out the truth. So my answer is no, not until we hear again from Colin Worthington.'

Philip looked more apprehensive than ever, and Michael more bewildered. 'So, shall we have dinner?' Georgina asked, standing up.

Billie also stood up. 'Thank you, no.' She looked at Philip.

He also struggled to his feet. 'I . . . ah . . . Perhaps we had better be getting along.' Billie was already at the door. Philip continued to look uncomfortable, hesitating in the doorway. Then he gave an embarrassed smile and followed her out into the evening.

'Would you like to tell me what that was all about?' Michael said.

'Over dinner. Would you like three pork chops, or four?'

11

On Monday morning Anne greeted her with, 'Mr Turner would like a word, in his office.'

Georgina nodded. 'Get me Colin Worthington first.'

For the moment it was necessary to put family affairs out of her mind. 'Good morning, Miss Playle,' Worthington said.

'Have you anything for me?'

'I'm afraid nothing I'd care to put into writing, as yet. This Mycota has some very unusual properties, and until we can recheck our findings, anything I might say has to be pure speculation.'

'Speculate.'

'Only in confidence. Would it be possible for you to come down here, say around ten this morning?'

'Mr Worthington,' Georgina said patiently. 'At ten this morning I shall be attending the inquest on the Ashmore Tower deaths. That is why I was hoping to have some information about the Mycota.'

'Well, I'm sorry, Miss Playle. We'll keep at it. Drop in whenever you can, and I'll show you what we have so far.'

'Yes,' Georgina said. 'Thank you.'

She replaced the phone, and gazed at Anne. 'No joy?'

'Not a thing. I'd better go along and bring Patrick up to date.'

JAMES BASCOM was also in the senior partner's office. Though a clever lawyer, he always struck Georgina as being more concerned with politics, both in and out of the firm, than with legalities. Long and thin and of indeterminate age, he walked with a stoop, his long straight hair dangling over his spectacles.

'You've read the papers?' Patrick asked.

Georgina nodded. 'Best thing that could have happened. Especially as no one was hurt.'

'A long shot but it just might be useful,' Bascom shrugged.

'Playle didn't design the Atterbury factory,' Patrick said, backing Georgina. 'But what we have to worry about is the risk to Playle. People like to have scapegoats. And we are the number one target. My information is that there are letters on the desk of just about every solicitor in London from nearly every tenant in Ashmore Tower, all wanting to file claims re liability. Up to Friday,' he tapped the papers in front of him with the tip of his pencil, 'that liability pointed squarely at us. This Yorkshire failure could possibly put a new complexion on things.' He sat back with a pained expression. 'At least that is the message we can try to get across, starting with the inquest. I'm not saying it'll put us in the clear, but it should help.'

'Surely the inquest will be concerned solely with the deaths of those nine people,' Georgina argued.

'Agreed. But a verdict of why they died has got to be recorded: accident, human error, criminal negligence . . . I just want you to bear in mind what I've said, when you take the stand.'

'And the fungus?'

'The more I think about that, the more I become convinced it's too hot to handle, until we know a lot more about it. The instinctive reaction of everyone who hears about the fungus theory will be that there was something wrong with the initial cement mix for which we are attempting to invent an excuse.'

Including yourself, she thought angrily. 'Well . . .' She looked at her watch. 'I suppose we'd better be getting along.'

'OUR PURPOSE TODAY is to determine the cause of death of the people who lost their lives in the Ashmore Tower disaster,' said the coroner, Dr Henry Milling, when the jury had been empanelled. 'Their names are as follows . . .' He read the list, and then looked over the crowded room. Georgina, seated beside Bascom four rows from the front, had already spotted Billie, on the far side of the room.

She had also seen Sir Raymond Bentley, the distinguished barrister who was acting on behalf of the tenants' association and they had met on several occasions. She smiled briefly in his direction but Sir Raymond gave a perfunctory nod in return. Sir Trumpton Dauntsey was sitting with Geoffrey Teigne, Global's chief general manager, and their greetings had also been cool. At the end of the aisle opposite her, Martin Garrard gave an almost imperceptible wink of encouragement. She needed it.

'I would remind everyone that this is not a court of law,' Dr Milling went on, 'endeavouring to apportion guilt. We are concerned with the cause of death, only. However, in view of the nature of the disaster, and the number of solicitors present, I will permit questions from interested parties, where they are relevant. Dr Pitman?'

The doctor took the witness chair, and confirmed that he had been the senior registrar at the hospital to which the dead and the injured had been taken on the night in question.

'The deaths, and injuries, were all consistent with falling, in some cases from a considerable height, and with being struck by collapsing masonry. Two of the victims died of asphyxiation, but their injuries were such as to indicate they would have died in any event.'

Georgina swallowed and glanced at Bascom. He remained expressionless, but over his shoulder she got another wink from Martin.

'Thank you, Doctor.' Dr Milling glanced at the pad on the table before him. 'Mr John Anstruther.'

Anstruther, a middle-aged man, walked on crutches and had adhesive plaster on his forehead. His had been a quite miraculous escape. Apparently he worked in a suite of top-floor offices and had been alone when the floor had given way beneath his feet. The streetside wall had fallen outwards, carrying him and the floor with it. It had struck the wall of the building on the far side of the street before subsiding and that had absorbed some of the force. But he had broken one leg and two ribs, as well as receiving cuts and bruises.

'It is courageous of you to come here today, considering the extent of your injuries,' the coroner remarked.

'I'm lucky to be alive.' Anstruther laid aside the crutches and lowered himself gingerly onto a chair.

'Before the collapse, did you have any intimation that anything might be wrong?' the coroner asked.

'No, sir.'

'There was no tremble, no noise?'

'One minute I was sitting at my desk talking to a client on the telephone, and then there was a series of strange sounds, like a cross between rifle and mortar fire . . . and the next minute I seemed to be flying through space. The building just collapsed.'

'Thank you, Mr Anstruther.'

There were another fifteen witnesses who had been working in the building at the time of the collapse and had had lucky escapes. Their evidence was similar to Anstruther's: a complete absence of any warning, either noise or movement, until the very last moment. Mr Timmins was next. He confirmed that he had received a telephone call from security guard Onslow at four fifteen that afternoon.

'Mr Onslow had called previously,' the coroner commented, looking at his notes.

'Yes, sir. He reported damp in the basement ceiling. We assumed it was a leak, and promised it would be seen to first thing Monday.'

'But then he called back.'

'Yes, sir. He called back at four fifteen, as I said, and reported a serious bulge in the basement ceiling. He thought it might be going to come down. I said I'd be right along to look at it, but by the time I got there the building had collapsed.'

'Did Mr Onslow indicate that he felt the building was in danger?'

'No, sir. He was worried about that ceiling only. He was pretty agitated, mind you. But on account of the ceiling.'

'Did he make any other observation at all, which might be relevant to this inquest?'

'Well, sir . . .' Timmins looked embarrassed. 'He did say something about an unpleasant smell.'

'A smell. Have you any reason to believe that this smell was in any way relevant to the failure of the building?'

'No, sir. Probably to do with the drains.'

'Thank you, Mr Timmins.' The coroner looked over the room. Bascom raised a questioning eyebrow at Georgina, but she shook her head. There was nothing to be gained by asking Timmins anything.

Superintendent Michelsen then took the chair and reported on the events of the night after the collapse. 'My first reaction was obviously that it must have been a bomb planted in the basement,' he told the court. 'But no trace of any explosive was found.'

'Then what, in your opinion, Superintendent, caused the failure?'

Michelsen cleared his throat. 'The failure was caused, almost certainly, by a complete collapse of the ground floor of the building. Ashmore Tower was of what is known as slab construction, in which each of the floors is an integral part of the overall strength of the structure. Had one of the upper floors collapsed, the damage, while extensive, would not have been catastrophic. The total collapse of the lowest of these floors produced an excessive strain on the remainder, and the walls they in part supported.'

'Have you any idea why that floor, that so vital floor, should have suddenly collapsed?'

'You'd have to ask the architect that, sir,' Superintendent Michelsen said, carefully.

'WOULD THE REPRESENTATIVE of Playle plc please take the chair?' asked the coroner.

Georgina took a long breath and stood up. As she moved forward, there was a low hum of interest round the room.

'Please be seated, Miss . . .' The coroner was looking at his list. 'Miss *Playle?*'

'Yes,' Georgina said. 'I am a partner in Playle plc. My father founded the firm.'

'And your company designed Ashmore Tower, and oversaw the construction? Have you visited the site since the collapse?'

'I visited the site within four hours of the failure.'

'You have listened to the evidence presented before this court. Here we have a building which stands for fifteen years, and suddenly collapses. You must have a theory about why it happened?'

'I have several theories,' Georgina said, picking her words as carefully as had Superintendent Michelsen. 'But they are, at the moment, only theories.'

'You have theories which you will not divulge?'

'I do not think vague theories could possibly assist this court, sir. I am sure that what you wish for are facts, and I have none.'

'Beyond your certainty that there was nothing faulty with either the design or the construction of the building.' Dr Milling sighed. 'Very good, Miss Playle. You may step down.'

Georgina gave a sigh herself, of relief that it had been completed so painlessly, and stood up. She checked at an interruption from the floor. 'With respect, Dr Milling.'

464

'Yes, Sir Raymond?'

'I represent the Ashmore Tower Tenants' Association. I wonder if I might be allowed to ask Miss Playle one or two questions?'

'Certainly. Would you remain in the chair, Miss Playle?'

Georgina sat down, feeling as if she had been kicked in the stomach. Sir Raymond Bentley cleared his throat noisily. 'Miss Playle, I am sure you have the necessary documentation to prove that Ashmore Tower was designed and constructed, in every way, to the highest possible standard. Yet the building fell down. This is a most disturbing event. The implications are vast. It is also a unique event. Unique to a building designed by Playle plc. I would have said you owed it to yourself, quite apart from the public, to explore, here and now, every possibility.'

Georgina took a deep breath. 'I should like to point out,' she said, 'that what happened to Ashmore Tower is *not* unique. There was a concrete failure in Yorkshire on Friday night, and the failure of an apartment block in Chicago three weeks ago.'

'Are you suggesting these failures are linked?'

'Yes,' Georgina snapped.

There was a huge burst of noise in the court, and the coroner banged his gavel. 'I will have quiet,' he said. 'Or I will have the room cleared. Now, Miss Playle, I am going to have to ask you to be more specific in your replies.'

He paused to allow her to prepare herself for whatever Sir Raymond Bentley might ask next. 'Sir Raymond?' Obviously Milling was quite willing to give the famous barrister his head.

'Miss Playle,' Sir Raymond continued. 'You feel that the Ashmore Tower failure is somehow linked with other similar events. I must ask you to tell us in what way.'

'I believe there is an agent at work which is destroying certain cements,' Georgina muttered. She had backed herself into a corner.

Once again there was an uproar, punctuated by the banging of the gavel. 'An agent?' Bentley said when the room was reasonably quiet. 'What kind of agent?'

Georgina sighed. 'A type of fungus. Traces have been found inside specimens of concrete taken from Ashmore Tower.'

Once again it was several minutes before the coroner could take up the questioning. 'Do I understand that you have had blocks of concrete from Ashmore Tower analysed?' he asked.

'Yes.'

'I have no information as to this here.' Dr Milling riffled through his papers.

'It has been done privately.'

'Privately.' They stared at each other. 'Very well. What is the result of this analysis?'

'It has not yet been completed.'

'Miss Playle, should you withhold evidence from this hearing you may well find yourself in contempt.'

'The analysis has not yet been completed,' Georgina insisted. 'The moment it is, I will see that you have a copy of the findings.'

'Miss Playle,' said Sir Raymond, who had remained on his feet, 'I put it to you that you adopted this very curious course of action because you were afraid it might be discovered that there was something substandard about the concrete used in the construction of Ashmore Tower.'

'I wanted to find out what had caused the failure.'

'And now you are not prepared to release your findings.'

'As yet there are no findings. I have said I will release the report as soon as it is finalised.' She was keeping her temper with an effort.

'I'm afraid you will have no choice. The report will be made subject to a court order. However, let us take your point that there may have been something in the concrete which has caused the concrete to rot. Is it possible that this, ah, fungus was present from the first? In the original cement mix?'

'It is possible. But highly improbable.'

'What you are saying is, it is highly improbable that the fungus managed to get into the concrete ... but it is there.'

There was a ripple of laughter round the room, and Georgina began to feel like a wet rag. 'I am trying to explain that I am not prepared to speculate until the result of the analysis is known. What I am also saying is that it is certain Ashmore Tower was not an isolated incident.'

'There have been one or two others which may, or may not, have arisen from the same cause. I understand that, Miss Playle, although I cannot see that these other incidents have any bearing upon what we are investigating here today.'

'I am saying that there may be hundreds, thousands of concrete structures at risk,' Georgina almost shouted, at last losing her cool. 'There is some agency at work of which we know nothing! But it is highly destructive ...' Her words were lost in the upsurge of noise from behind her, and several people hurried from the room.

Georgina and Sir Raymond continued to glare at each other. Then the coroner nodded. 'Thank you, Miss Playle.'

Georgina got up, uncertainly, and made her way back to her chair.

The coroner consulted his notes. 'I propose to call no other witnesses.' He looked at the jury. 'You have heard the evidence. A

466

building collapsed, and nine people were killed. You have the option of offering any of four verdicts. The first is that these people were wilfully killed with malice aforethought; that is, your verdict will be murder, charged against a person or persons, either unknown or named. Such a verdict in this case would be patently absurd.

'The second is manslaughter, by which you would indicate that the victims died through negligence or carelessness on the part of a person, or persons, entrusted with their safety.

'The third verdict open to you is that the victims died by accident, or misadventure, which means that the deaths were caused by chance, even if they were caused by someone going about his or her lawful business. The fourth option open to you is to record an open verdict, which in effect means that you would like to see a further investigation of the facts of the case by a properly constituted authority. Now, do you wish to retire to consider your verdict?'

'No, sir,' said the foreman.

'Then will you return your verdict now?'

'We wish to return an open verdict, with a recommendation that the facts of the collapse of Ashmore Tower be further investigated by the proper authorities.'

The coroner nodded. 'Then I must concur with your decision,' he said, and looked over the assembly. 'The verdict of this inquest is, as you have heard, an open one. The proceedings will therefore be forwarded to both the Department of Trade and Industry and the Department of the Environment for further study. Thank you, ladies and gentlemen, for your time.'

Anne wore a long face. 'I gather things didn't go very well.'

'The coroner had virtually made up his mind Playle were responsible.' Georgina grinned. 'And I didn't make things too much better by losing my temper.'

'Mr Turner would like a word.'

'I thought he might.' She went along to Patrick's office. 'Just don't bother to say it.' She threw herself into the chair before his desk. 'I'm sorry. Bentley got under my skin.'

'So I gather. Did you know it's already been reported on Sky news? Gina . . . don't take it too hard. It's my fault. I should've gone.'

She glared at him. 'Meaning you'd have handled it better than me.'

'Of course I don't mean . . .' His head jerked round as there came a tap on the door. 'Yes?'

His secretary looked in. 'There's a letter for you, Mr Turner. Special delivery.' She placed the envelope on the desk.

Patrick looked at Georgina, then somewhat gingerly he slit the envelope, took out the sheet of stiff paper inside, glanced at it, and threw it across the desk. 'Number one.'

Georgina picked it up. Solicitors representing Mr John Anstruther had issued a writ charging Playle plc with having caused injury and loss of business, through incompetent building techniques.

'That's absurd,' she said. 'Can he make it stick, Patrick?'

'Not before the outcome of the inquiry. He's just putting himself at the head of the queue for punitive damages when we go bankrupt.'

'The bastard! Well—' She got up, and nearly sat down again as the door burst open.

Anne Bladen stood there, pink-cheeked. 'I'm sorry, Mr Turner, Miss Playle, but there's been another failure! The cooling tower for an electric power station in the Midlands. It's just come down.'

'Was anyone hurt?' Georgina asked.

'They don't know yet. But no one normally worked inside the tower and there were only a few maintenance staff around.'

'Like Atterbury,' Georgina said. She sat back, the lines on her forehead relaxing a little. 'This has to put us in the clear, coming on top of the Atterbury business. But, Patrick, what are we going to do? You must see that this is bigger than just Playle, now.'

'Why not get hold of your friend Worthington again?' Patrick suggested. 'He has to come up with some answers, fast.'

GEORGINA RETURNED to her office and began dialling Worthington. 'Look, all hell is about to break loose,' she told him when he answered. 'Haven't you got anything yet?'

'We've got some leads, Miss Playle. This is a most unusual Mycota, in its growth requirements.'

'Well, for goodness' sake let me have all the information you have so far.'

Her brain was spinning as she replaced the phone. It was impossible to follow exactly what Worthington had said. She turned to other matters. What was Billie doing? What was everyone doing, with what she had made public knowledge at the inquest? The collapse of the cooling-station tower must be concentrating a few minds.

Georgina hadn't managed to swallow one mouthful of the sand-wich Anne had brought in for her when Michael came on the line.

'Linda called,' he said, his voice filled with suppressed excitement. 'It's positive. Are you there, Mum?'

'Yes, I'm here. Well, that's splendid news, isn't it?'

'She feels she should tell her parents, right away. Have you spoken to Mr Wright yet?'

'Well, no, I haven't. I've only just got back from the inquest.'

'Oh! How'd it go?'

'Like a lead balloon in a large bowl of sulphuric acid.'

'Well, I suppose you can't win 'em all, Mum. When are you going to make a date to see Mr Wright?' Georgina resisted the urge to throw the phone out of the window. 'I think,' Michael went on, 'that it might be better if you did it before he hears from Linda.'

'Yes,' Georgina said. 'You're probably right. Oh Lord . . . I've just registered the fact that I'm going to be a granny!'

'GET ME DENYS WRIGHT,' she told Anne.

Georgina waited, fingers drumming lightly on the desk. 'Denys!' she said brightly. 'Long time no speak.'

'Yes,' he agreed, his voice cold. 'Have you got a date for the Riverview opening yet?'

'That's only one of the things we have to talk about,' she told him. 'I thought it might be a good idea to have lunch together.'

There was a prolonged pause before he said, 'Fi . . . ne. When and where?' His voice was heavy with suspicion.

'Wednesday? The White Tower? And Denys, why don't you bring Caroline—that is your wife's name, isn't it? I'd be delighted if she could join us.'

'Whatever for? Isn't this to be a business lunch?'

'I thought it was about time we all got to know each other a bit better. And do you know, Caroline and I have never met?' She realised she was sweating. 'Wednesday at a quarter to one,' she added hastily. 'Bye.' She put the phone down. Anne had come in and was standing in front of the desk, papers in hand, her expression one large question mark. Georgina smiled sweetly.

'There have been these calls from the media,' Anne said. 'The BBC would like you to have a five-minute slot on their evening news and Sky would like to come round and interview you here. There have also been several newspapers . . .'

'Tell them all that I am not available for comment at this time.'

'Do you think that's wise? Doesn't that give them the right to put any construction they wish on what you said at the inquest?'

'They can't libel me. Anyway, I'm not seeing anyone today. Now, do you think you could get me Tom Carden and then book a table for four at the White Tower, for Wednesday, one o'clock.' It was the nearest she had ever come to seeing her immaculately groomed secretary scratch her head.

ONCE AGAIN IT WAS time to attempt some work divorced from the thought of collapsing concrete. Difficult, because so much of her work eventually wound up *as* concrete.

She was home by five to six, and put on the news, hoping to see a film of the most recent collapse, and instead stared at a video of herself as she left the inquest that morning.

'Georgina Playle,' said the newsreader, 'top woman architect, who today suggested that a large proportion of all the concrete structures in this country could be at risk due to attack by a concrete rot. Miss Playle is not available for comment, but with me in the studio I have American journalist Billie Malandine, who has been investigating this startling phenomenon. Good evening, Miss Malandine.'

'Good evening.' Billie smiled at the camera.

'Now, Miss Malandine, as I understand it, you were the person who first brought the idea of this fungus to the attention of Playle.'

'Well, I wouldn't exactly put it like that,' Billie said. 'We've had several unexplained building failures in the States . . .'

Several? Georgina wanted to shout. But the newsreader beat her to it. 'Several, Miss Malandine?'

'That's right. I've been investigating one in Chicago, but since then there have been four more . . . All of these, as I say, are unexplained collapses of apparently well-designed and constructed buildings. Now you've had at least three over here.'

'All as a result of this mysterious fungus?'

'It seems likely.'

'Briefly, Miss Malandine, would you tell us what kind of structures are specifically at risk from this rot?'

Once again Billie smiled at the camera. 'I would say every concrete structure in the world could be at risk, right this minute.'

Georgina switched off the set. Her heart pounded furiously. It was impossible to sit still. She paced from the front door to the window and back again. Then the door phone beeped.

She stopped pacing, and frowned. Now what? Reporters? She grabbed a tea towel from the kitchen counter and held it over her mouth before lifting the phone. 'Yeah?' she growled.

'Er . . . is Miss Playle there, please?'

'Martin! Thank goodness. I thought it might be reporters.' She pressed the door release. 'Come on up.'

A glance in the mirror revealed a terrible mess, half her hair having escaped the pins in her French pleat. Not that it would matter. Martin always looked dishevelled himself: he'd never notice. She opened the door and found him waiting outside, filling the door frame, holding a bunch of roses and looking absolutely immaculate.

'Crumbs!' The exclamation was out before she could stop herself. He shoved the flowers at her. 'I thought I'd tidy up a bit in the hope of persuading you to come out for a meal.'

She sniffed the roses—only realising then that there were twelve of them, deep red. 'Martin! They are magnificent!'

He closed the door behind him and followed her into the kitchen where she rummaged at the back of a cupboard for a suitable vase.

'Well,' he asked. 'Will you? There's a little place I'm very fond of down by the river.'

'Sounds lovely! Yes, I'd love to. But, as you see, I will have to change.'

'There's no hurry. The table is booked for eight thirty.'

'Really! You knew I'd come!'

'No! But I was prepared to work on it.'

She laughed as she passed him in the cramped doorway, carrying the filled vase into the sitting room, and a warm comfortable feeling spread through to her toes.

IT WAS AN OLD PUB overlooking a footpath along the river. There were three separate dining rooms, all tiny, two upstairs and one in a conservatory with lovely views up and down the river, where Martin had reserved their table.

'This is marvellous. How did you find it?' Georgina asked.

'I can't remember. I've been coming here for years.' He handed her a menu. 'The food is not exotic. Pretty plain, in fact. But I confess I come for the ambience rather than the cuisine.'

'Suits me. My digestion has gone for a Burton over the past week. Let's see. I'll have the roast duck. And melon with port to start.'

Martin looked up at the waiter who had appeared at his shoulder. 'Make that for two, please. And a bottle of your excellent Pauillac.'

The duck was good and the wine was smooth as velvet. After dark, moths and flies were attracted in by the table lamps, but the evening was too perfect to close the windows. Georgina and Martin dawdled over soft, ripe Brie, finishing their wine, talking irrelevancies, anything but Mycota . . . or the other thoughts that were surfacing in their minds.

'Coffee?' he suggested at last.

'Shall we have it at the flat?'

'I'd love that, if you don't mind.'

He managed to wedge his battered VW into a very small slot on the far side of the gardens. It was nearly midnight, and the flat was cosy and welcoming. Georgina made coffee and they drank it in companionable silence.

'I can't think why you haven't married again,' Martin said at last. 'Your son must be getting quite big now.'

'A lot bigger than I am.'

'You don't look old enough!'

'Oh, funny! I'm about to become a grandmother.' Damn it, it was out!

'Good grief! I had no idea he was married.'

Her mouth quivered and she started to giggle. 'He isn't! But he insists he is going to marry the girl, despite the fact he is only sixteen.'

'Oh Lord! So Mycota is not the only problem on your mind at the moment. My poor Gina!' Quite without intending to, he put his arms round her. It seemed the most natural thing in the world to slide her arms round him in response, and nestle her forehead against his neck. When she looked up they stared at each other for only a moment, before his mouth came down over hers.

13

The sun didn't reach into Georgina's bedroom at the flat, but from the bed she could see it shining through the maple leaves in the square. She was smiling. It was the first time she had woken to happy thoughts since the Ashmore disaster. Martin Garrard! Of course she shouldn't be smiling at all, the situation was ridiculous. He was the opposition, one of Playle's competitors. She rolled over onto her tummy, remembering the warmth of his huge frame as they had stood in front of the fireplace in the sitting room, kissing. When they paused the first time to draw breath, his fingers had combed up through her hair, grasping it in his hand as he pressed his mouth against hers once more. Then they had collapsed into separate chairs, both obviously shocked. They knew, without the need of words, that they both wanted more ... She had shaken her head. 'No, Martin. No. Let's give ourselves more time.' She watched him breathing deeply, nodding agreement. He stayed only a few minutes longer.

It was difficult not to be amused by Martin's reticence. How different he was from the suave Philips of this world who were so practised in the art of the 'come-on'. Womanising was their sport, hobby and pastime. Yes, Martin was definitely different.

THERE WERE SEVERAL reporters and a TV cameraman waiting outside the Playle Building when she arrived.

'Miss Playle, would you care to make a statement?'

'Miss Playle, is it true buildings are at risk because of their smell?'

'Miss Playle . . .' They surrounded her, barking their questions, barring her way into the building, tugging at her clothing. Fortunately the doorman, Ken Lovat, noticed what was going on and came out to her rescue, pushing her inside and locking the door.

'Whew!' Georgina gasped. 'Thanks a million, Ken.'

When she got to her office, Anne was fluttering, rather like a trapped bird. There was a large man, wearing a lounge suit but with policeman written all over him, rising from the sofa.

'This gentleman wishes to speak to you, Miss Playle,' Anne explained.

'You'd better come in,' she said, and led him into her office. 'Do you have a problem?'

He looked embarrassed. 'Sergeant Lucas, Miss Playle. I have to present you with a summons. You admitted at the inquest that you removed several pieces of concrete from the Ashmore Tower site and that means you broke the law. There's a magistrate's court sitting tomorrow morning, at Bow Street.' He laid a paper on her desk. 'You will have to answer that summons.'

She wanted to laugh hysterically, but managed to keep a straight face. 'Yes, I'll be there.'

When he had left, Anne appeared in the doorway. 'Are we all for the high jump?'

'Only me. You'd better get hold of Mr Bascom. And . . .' She gazed at the telephone as it buzzed.

Anne took the call, raised her eyebrows and passed over the receiver. 'Department of the Environment for you.'

Georgina took the phone. 'Georgina Playle.'

'Miss Playle. Jonathan Lloyd here.'

'Yes?' she said cautiously.

'The minister would like a word.'

'Ah!' The penny dropped. Jonathan Lloyd was the Parliamentary Private Secretary to the Minister of the Environment. 'Certainly. Would you like to put him through?'

'He would prefer it if you could come here to see him. Just as soon as possible. Shall we say . . . this afternoon at three?'

'Er . . . Yes. Certainly.'

Georgina replaced the phone and raised her eyebrows at Anne. 'High society,' she commented. 'After you've got Bascom, Anne, call Worthington and tell him I'm on my way.'

'Right,' Anne said. 'Have you seen today's papers?'

'No. And I'm not going to look at them. I suppose there's a photo of Miss Malandine on every front page.'

'Not exactly,' Anne said. 'Although she's prominently featured in the *Daily Echo*. It's just that there have been some more failures. Down in Cornwall, a luxury hotel was evacuated because of the smell and sudden bulges in the walls. Just in time, because half of it fell down. It's like you said: every concrete structure in the world is at risk.' She went to the door. 'Wait till a big bridge collapses.'

So! Maybe Billie had been right to go public with the findings. If she hadn't, dozens of people might have been killed in that hotel.

Bascom came on the line and listened to what she had to say. 'You have to play it very, very straight, Georgina,' he told her. 'Don't worry about the court appearance. We'll plead guilty, and there'll be a fine. But you can't withhold any information you may have from the minister, or you'll wind up in deep trouble.'

'Message received and understood,' Georgina said.

Anne dashed into the room. 'Colin Worthington is expecting you,' she said. 'He sounds quite excited.'

'Then call me a taxi.' Pray God he has something worthwhile, she thought as she crossed Vauxhall Bridge.

GEORGINA HAD FORGOTTEN how much like a junk room Colin Worthington's laboratory was. But at least it was a busy place, with half a dozen young men and women using microscopes, little saws and hammers, tapping away, frequently pausing to inspect their samples before resuming, muttering to each other.

Worthington himself escorted her to his desk, and sat her on a chair which he swept clear of papers to make room for her. 'My secretary seemed to think you had something for me.'

'Progress, Miss Playle. Progress. I'm sorry we're a day late, but these things don't work by numbers. I read the report of the inquest. Sounds quite exciting.'

'I was cornered, I'm afraid. Finished up putting my foot in it,' Georgina said. 'Now I'm relying on you to get me back out.'

'Right! Well, as you will probably have gathered, there are thousands of different forms of Mycota, which cover everything from slime moulds up to toadstools. All Mycota conform to certain patterns, need certain requirements, the two most important being temperature and moisture. Nearly all Mycota only grow in temperatures between twenty and thirty degrees centigrade. However, this Mycota—I am calling it *Mycota concretus*, by the way—is unique, in that it does not have any of the above qualities.'

'Eh?'

'Instead of requiring temperatures of between twenty and thirty degrees centigrade, it only grows when the temperature is between seventeen and twenty degrees. This is appreciably cooler.' Georgina frowned as various ideas began roaming through her mind. 'Additionally, and this is even more important, it abhors moisture. Moisture drives it into total hibernation.'

'And it eats lime.'

'It would appear to be able to obtain sustenance from the lime in its very early stages,' Worthington said cautiously. 'But of course no organism could possibly sustain itself on lime. No, no, another unique feature of this Mycota is that it is homo-cannibalistic.'

'You mean it eats itself?'

'After subdivision of the thallus, yes.'

'It sounds a thoroughly unpleasant piece of work. But I'm not sure where this gets us.'

'It gives us the outlines of the life story, Miss Playle. We have the Mycota. Right? For the time being, you may take it that it is inside the cement, drawing sustenance from its surroundings. It lies dormant for as long as the temperature is outside that very narrow band I mentioned, and as long as there is any moisture in its vicinity. However, the moment its environment is absolutely dry, and the temperature of its environment reaches the required levels, it starts to grow. When a certain stage of growth is reached, however, it subdivides its thallus into as many as ten new growths. But of these ten new Mycota, only a portion survive because they consume the remainder.'

'Wait a minute,' Georgina objected. 'If we have five Mycota subdividing into ten, and the first five eat the second five, then how can there be any growth?'

'You're quite a mathematician, Miss Playle. But you misunderstood me. *Each* thallus can subdivide up to ten times.'

'You mean five thallus can suddenly become fifty?'

'Exactly! And they don't just split into two down the middle. Only about a third breaks off in total. We have a situation, therefore, where if the conditions are right for any lengthy period of time, five Mycota can project themselves into fifty, eat perhaps twenty of the subsidiary growths while again reaching maturity, then the remaining thirty subdivide into perhaps three hundred . . . well, you can take it from there.'

'What a scenario,' Georgina muttered.

'This explains why there has been no evidence of this Mycota in tropical countries,' Worthington continued. 'Because of the excessive damp, you see. It explains why no bridges have as yet been affected, because of the proximity to water.'

'But that surely eliminates England altogether. No place can have a wetter climate than ours.'

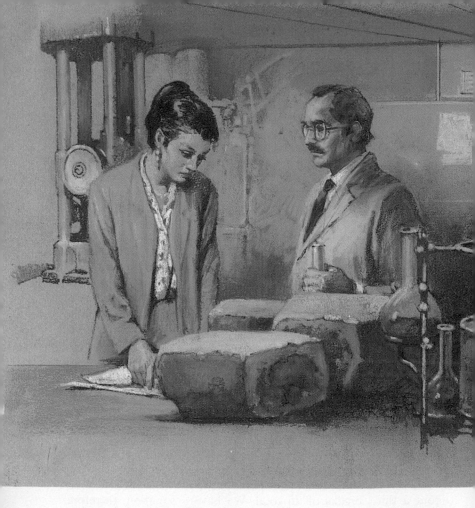

'Now,' he went on, refusing to be interrupted, 'there have undoubtedly been cases of building failures in more temperate zones, caused by this Mycota, in the past. But of course, the cause has not been suspected. You see, normally it would take many years for the Mycota to grow to a size large enough to crack a concrete structure. And growth only takes place in a favourable environment.'

'And this sudden spate of failures . . .'

'. . . in this country, is because the last couple of summers have been abnormally dry. Given that, all that has been needed is the right temperature, and it has grown like weeds, as I indicated earlier.'

'And you think some of this stuff may have been dormant in the affected concrete for years.'

476

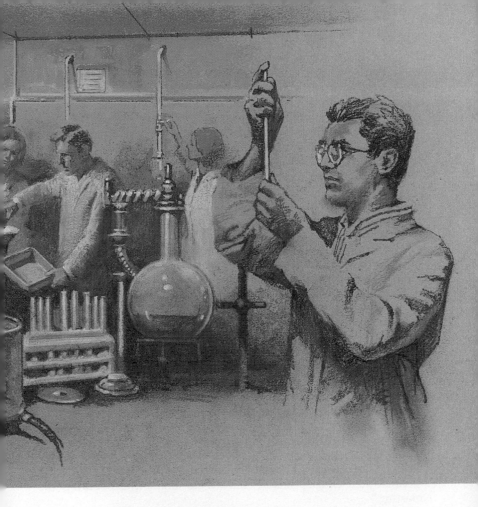

'It could be hundreds of years.'

'But Ashmore Tower was only fifteen years old.'

'The last fifteen years have been a period of increasing dryness in the United Kingdom. But there is another, more important factor involved: central heating! This would account for this sudden upsurge in its appearance. How many houses in the UK were centrally heated at the end of the Second World War? How many are *not* centrally heated now? I think you'll find the difference is enormous! Central heating means an elimination of damp, as well as the maintenance of a constant temperature. Now, there is most certainly a period each day in each house where the temperature passes through the vital band. There again, the Mycota would be activated.'

'That is absolutely horrifying.' Georgina thought of her own central heating, which came on for a couple of hours every morning and every evening when she wasn't there, just to keep out damp . . . and was set for eighteen degrees centigrade! Four hours a day in which the Mycota could be growing away. If it was present.

'All right,' she said. 'Supposing you're right about all of this, you are confirming my worst fears. There may be thousands of structures in this country, and more in others, which are just waiting to come down with an almighty bump. How do we find out which buildings are at risk?'

'Well, fortunately, there is the smell element. This is a strong-smelling fungus, as you are aware. When it reaches a dangerous stage, the smell certainly provides a warning.'

'Mr Worthington,' Georgina said with restraint, 'when the smell provides a warning, it is usually a matter of a few hours before a disaster. We need something a little better than that.'

'I accept that is a problem. But it is not yet one to which we have found a solution. I'm sure we will, given time,' he added brightly.

'Time,' Georgina muttered. 'All right, let me ask you the big one, then, Mr Worthington. How does the Mycota get into the concrete in the first place?'

'I'm afraid I can't answer that one yet, Miss Playle,' Worthington said. 'It looks likely that it is present, probably in a minuscule state, in one of the ingredients of cement. I would go for lime, but I can't be certain until we have conducted many more tests.'

'But how does it get into the lime?'

'Very simply. Lime, or more correctly, quicklime, is produced by roasting limestone, or chalk, under controlled conditions. If the limestone or chalk used already contained the fungus . . .'

'Could the fungus survive such high temperatures during the roasting?'

'It's survived all the temperatures we've inflicted on it since we've had it. It won't develop in any sense, of course. But it doesn't die.'

'Forgive me for being just a little self-centred, but is there any way in which any architect, building or cement merchant could tell that the fungus was in the chalk before he roasted it?'

'Only if he specifically looked for it, and then it would be a slow and expensive business.'

'Right! Now would you put all of that in writing for me?'

'Surely. I'll let you have it in a day or two.'

'I'd like it now.'

'Oh! Ah . . . it'll take half an hour.'

'I'll wait.'

478

14

It was too early to go to the Ministry of the Environment, so Georgina went to a quiet little pub she had known in her student days, bought a ploughman's lunch and sat in a corner with a pile of newspapers. They seemed to be treating the Mycota as something of a joke so far, except for the *Echo* of course which, having purchased Billie's story, featured it prominently and seriously.

At three o'clock she arrived at the ministry, gave her name to the security guard, and was sent up in the lift to the third floor.

A smiling secretary greeted her. 'The minister will see you in a few minutes, Miss Playle. If you'd care to wait in here . . .' She opened the door to a comfortably furnished room.

THE DOOR OPENED, and a somewhat harassed young man appeared. He shook hands with her. 'I'm Jonathan Lloyd, PPS to the minister. Sorry to have kept you waiting, Miss Playle. Will you come this way?'

Lloyd opened a door and she was shown into a spacious office. Behind the huge desk the minister stood waiting. Georgina had met Charles Campbell before, at a reception, but she did not expect he would remember her. She was gratified when he came round his desk to take her hand. 'Georgina Playle! When did we meet, now, April of last year?'

'March actually, Minister.'

'Of course it was.' Charles Campbell was six foot tall, had the shoulders of a rugby player and the hips of a ballet dancer, and his strong aquiline features suggested great powers of decision. 'Sit down, sit down,' he told her.

Georgina chose the sofa facing an antique marble fireplace. The minister sat in one of the leather armchairs. 'This business,' he remarked. 'Upsetting. And you are suggesting that these failures are being caused by some kind of a fungus. Am I right?'

'Yes, that is so. In fact I commissioned an analysis immediately after the Ashmore tragedy, and I have here copies of the two reports.' Georgina held them out. 'You will of course have to decide whether or not this latest information should remain confidential,' she added.

'It can't remain confidential for very long,' Campbell said. 'A question has been put down in the House, and will have to be answered on Friday. Also, we are receiving reports of some agitation arising out of Miss Malandine's articles and television appearances. What I propose to do is this. I have already instructed government analysts to obtain samples of concrete from the collapsed sites in this country, and to subject them all to rigorous examination. In the meantime, this office will immediately issue a statement recommending that in the event of anyone detecting an obnoxious smell in any concrete structure, the building should be vacated until local building inspectors have cleared it of possible contamination by fungus.'

'Thank goodness for that,' Georgina said.

'Of course we hope that all of our findings will entirely exonerate your company, or any other, from the charge of poor design or construction. I'm sure that will please you, Miss Playle.'

'That will please me very much.'

'Now you told me that your man is experimenting on possible ways of dealing with this . . . Mycota. Keep him at it, please. I'm sure I need not add that the moment he finds anything, I expect to be told.'

Georgina nodded. 'Of course.'

'Good.' Campbell stood up. 'Well, it's been very pleasant meeting you again. I only wish the subject had been more agreeable.'

'NO RED ROSES tonight, I'm afraid,' Martin said when she opened the door. 'I thought this might be more practical.' He headed straight into the kitchen and dumped some plastic carriers on the counter. Having invited himself round for a drink after work to hear the story of Georgina's meeting with the minister, he obviously had plans to extend his visit.

'What on earth have you got there? It must be enough to feed the five thousand.' Georgina eyed the bags with misgivings. The day had been exhausting—and nerve-racking. Now, apparently, she was going to have to cook Martin a meal, instead of settling in an armchair with a sandwich.

Martin read her expression correctly. 'Forget it! I'm in charge of supper and I don't allow women in the kitchen when I'm busy.'

'Oh heck! Was I that transparent?'

'Yes! However, before you sit down you can do two things. First, allow me to greet you with affection, now my hands are free. Second, pour drinks. Then you can kick your shoes off and put your feet up.' He grabbed her arms and pulled her into a smothering hug.

Her tiredness drifted away. Leaning against him she felt the tension behind her eyes ease. She looked up, laughter lines around her mouth. 'I am glad you came.'

He kissed her forehead, then pushed her away. 'Drinks,' he said. 'Before I lose interest in this meal.'

They talked across the kitchen counter as he worked, Georgina recounting all the details of her meeting with Campbell. By the time she had finished, Martin was able to leave the kitchen and join her for a top-up of his gin and tonic.

She leaned forward and fidgeted with her glass. 'I keep expecting Worthington to come up with an answer to all this. There must be one. If we could only find some way of determining whether or not a building contained the fungus, without having to wait for the smell, we could take all the steam out of the situation.'

'What about lasers? A laser beam can penetrate almost anything. Suppose we could bore an infinitesimal hole in the wall of a building, and draw off a specimen of anything that is movable . . .'

'That sounds incredible! Could it be done?'

'I'm sure it could be done. We'd have to get the experts on it, of course . . . I think I know some people in that business.'

'Oh, Martin . . . if only it would work . . .'

'I'll fix it first thing tomorrow morning.' He paused. His eyes narrowed as he studied her face. 'Go on. What's niggling you?'

'Oh, it's a personal matter. I think I mentioned my son, Michael, to you, last time you were here. He has a problem which needs sorting out. I've got to tell the girl's parents over lunch tomorrow.'

'They still don't know? Any idea how they'll take it?'

'Yes, I can guess how they'll take it. Very, very badly.'

Martin stood up. 'Come on. Let's eat. You can tell me over the meal.' He held her chair, shook out her napkin and put it across her lap, then took plates from the counter and set them in each place.

Georgina tasted the first mouthful of chicken Kiev and said, 'Brilliant. And it all looks so appetising.'

'Well, you don't have to sound so surprised! Remember I have lived a bachelor existence for years and I'm very fond of my stomach.'

'Yes,' she giggled. 'I had noticed.'

'Now. Tell me more about Michael's problem. Who are these formidable prospective in-laws?'

'Mr and Mrs Denys Wright.'

'Good grief!'

'You know them?'

'I know him. A bigheaded, loudmouthed beggar. How do you come to know him? Business?'

'He owes me a couple of million pounds. And he's stalling on payment. Says he's waiting to see if the building falls down.'

'The real reason is his cash-flow situation.'

'Really! How do you know?' Georgina sat wide-eyed, her fork poised halfway to her mouth.

'We've had the same problem. We virtually had to take him to court to get the last payment out of him for Skyways.'

Georgina frowned at him. She knew that the Skyways apartment block was Harvey & Associates' biggest and most prestigious project. 'I never knew Wright was involved in that.'

'One of his consortiums. When the money was slow in coming, we made some investigations. Apparently Denys still owes four million on a Scottish Components factory deal. He'd sold his shares in the Grand International chain to do it, but their audit is under review by the Inland Revenue and the money hasn't been released. Denys had been trying to pull a fast one.' Martin paused to clear away the plates and put a bowlful of fresh raspberries on the table. 'Did you know he has been in dispute with Carling Brothers, too?'

'Carling Brothers? The commercial ducting engineers?'

'Denys has held up payment to them, claiming professional negligence.'

Georgina frowned. 'He's got his fingers in an awful lot of pies!'

'Yes. And his fingers are getting badly burnt. He rode a high when the economy was booming, and he has been wrestling with his blunders ever since. So don't let him give you any stick tomorrow. You call his bluff.'

'Oh, Martin, that's brilliant. Looks like I might just enjoy tomorrow's lunch after all.'

How could I ever have doubted his intentions? Georgina asked herself as they cleared the table together. Martin talked about Michael, asked questions, and made suggestions which were all practical and sensible. When they sat side by side on the sofa with their coffees, listening to the Brahms Violin Concerto, it seemed the most natural thing in the world for her to lean her head against his shoulder.

'You are a great comfort,' Georgina murmured. 'You're the first man I've known, apart from my father, who I haven't had to mother. Maybe it's because you're one of the few men I know who are bigger than I am.'

'You're the first woman I've known, including my mother, who hasn't tried to nag me to death. In fact,' he sat up so that he could turn and face her, frowning, 'I'm afraid I've done something I'd vowed never to do again.'

'What?' She frowned back.

'I've fallen in love with you.'

GEORGINA WORE a coral linen suit with matching high-heeled shoes, which meant Denys would have to look up to her. A white silk rose was pinned to her shoulder. She had chosen large gold and ivory earstuds and a matching bracelet, and her perfume was Dior Poison.

482

It seemed appropriate. Certainly it had its effect in the magistrate's court, where everyone smiled at her and she was fined twenty-five pounds in very rapid order.

'That wasn't too bad, was it?' Bascom asked, as they settled into their taxi.

'As a matter of fact, no,' Georgina agreed.

'So, back to the office?'

'No, drop me at the White Tower. My day hasn't even begun yet.'

15

'Miss Playle, how nice to see you.' The lady maître d'hôtel at the White Tower was welcoming as ever. She led Georgina to a table beside a Victorian-style French window.

The Wrights arrived within five minutes. 'Hope we're not late,' the shapely blonde said anxiously.

'Not at all.' Georgina stood up. 'You must be Caroline.' She held out her hand. 'I'm Georgina. Won't you sit here beside me?'

'Sorry. Forgot you two hadn't met,' Denys growled.

By the time they had ordered drinks and studied the menu, Tom had arrived and Georgina made the introductions.

Caroline's eyebrows rose faintly. Denys frowned and said, 'Really?' making no attempt to hide his surprise. The atmosphere was stiff and Georgina feared it was going to be a difficult meal.

Denys was the first to speak when the waiter left with their order. 'Seeing you've got your lad's father in tow, I imagine we're here to discuss the mess the boy's got our Linda into.'

'Now look here . . .' Tom began, flushing.

'Denys! We agreed before coming here today that we would not pretend that Linda didn't know full well what she was doing.' Caroline was smiling as she replaced her glass of Perrier on the table.

'Well, I gather Linda must have told you all about it.' Georgina glanced from one to the other. 'So how do you feel about the youngsters getting married?'

'Is there any question?' Caroline asked.

'Of course there is!' Denys scowled. 'She doesn't have to have it.'

'Quite,' Tom agreed.

'Tom!' Georgina said hastily. 'We have already agreed that if the kids want to keep the child and marry, then they should do so. Don't you agree, Caroline?'

'Of course. Linda has made it quite clear that this is what they both want. All we can do is decide how best to help them.'

'With money, I suppose. Well, they're not getting a ha'penny from me.' Denys drained his whisky. 'I'm not paying for their mistakes.'

'We all do make mistakes, don't we, Denys?' Georgina said quietly.

'Suggesting what? If you mean I was wrong to employ Playle to design Riverview . . .'

'I'm afraid that excuse for not paying your account with us will no longer work, Denys. The mistakes I was referring to,' she continued quietly, 'were made by those people who have expanded too fast, left themselves with severe cash-flow problems and now find themselves unable to meet their debts.'

Tom and Caroline were swivelling their heads from side to side, as if they were at Wimbledon. Through gritted teeth Denys demanded, 'What the hell are you talking about?'

'Carling Brothers, Scottish Components . . . Playle plc.'

Denys closed his eyes. 'Where did you get all that? Are you threatening me or something?'

'Good gracious, no. I was only going to suggest that as we all want the best for Michael and Linda, we should think of ourselves as family, from here on. So we must give family first consideration in all matters. It would be so sad for the kids to start married life with you heavily indebted to me. Don't you agree?'

The other three were sitting listening with their mouths open. So she continued. 'I have a block of flats in Hammersmith. Michael and Linda can have one, rent-free, until they are in a position to pay something. It will be very small, but it's near Playle plc and Michael plans to work for the family firm while studying for exams.'

'That sounds very reasonable,' Caroline said.

'We can do better than a poky flat in Hammersmith,' Denys declared. 'They can have a decent apartment at Riverview. As a wedding present from me.'

Georgina found that her mouth was open. She had caught a glimpse of how this man wheeled and dealed himself to millionaire status, even if the millions were in debit rather than credit.

Caroline was smiling. 'Have we any idea when the wedding is to be? Linda would like it to be a proper one.'

'Of course it'll be a proper one,' Denys asserted. 'With all the trimmings. We'll have the reception at Riverview, too. I'm assuming it'll be open?' He cocked an eyebrow at Georgina.

She had no intention of being steamrollered. 'Well, that's up to you, isn't it?'

He grinned. 'Bloody women! All right. You'll have your money. Providing you can give me your guarantee that Riverview is free of this fungus of yours.'

Back to square one. She could only pray Martin had contacted his laser experts.

'Right,' she said. 'You're on. Bring your money this afternoon, and I'll supply your proof.'

'HOW'D IT GO?' Anne wanted to know, when Georgina got back to the office.

'About eight hundred per cent better than I had hoped,' Georgina told her. 'Denys Wright is actually coming here this afternoon, with cheque. He will pay up when we guarantee the safety of Riverview.'

'Which we can't do.'

'Yes, we can,' Georgina told her. 'Get me Martin Garrard.'

Martin was on the line in five minutes, and Georgina outlined the situation to him. 'So,' she concluded, 'the big question is, have you made any progress with your lasers?'

'As a matter of fact, I have ... Hell, you're not thinking of Riverview?'

'This afternoon. In front of Denys's eyes, if that's how he wants it.'

'Well ... OK. I'm not guaranteeing anything, mind.'

'I have total confidence in you,' she told him.

THE ROLLS PARKED, and they got out. 'Afternoon, Miss Playle,' said the watchman. 'You reckon she's going to stand?'

Denys glanced at Georgina to see how she took the quip, but Georgina merely smiled. 'It'd better, Bill. I'm thinking of moving in.'

The Riverview project rose higher than its neighbours. Georgina had not attempted to imitate a period in its design, but had styled it to blend into its background, yet maintaining a character of its own.

Bill unlocked the huge lobby doors, and they stepped into a vast, high-ceilinged area and the smell of recent paint and plaster. 'No rotting vegetables, at any rate,' Denys said. 'So where's your proof?'

'On its way,' she said.

A few minutes later Martin appeared.

'Is that Garrard?' Denys asked. 'The fellow from Harvey and Associates?'

'That's right. Like me, he's trying to get to the bottom of this concrete fungus.'

Martin was accompanied by three men in overalls, and a laser gun.

'Let me get this straight,' Denys said. 'You are intending to take concrete samples from this building?'

'Explain it, Mr Linton,' Martin said.

'It's this laser, sir,' Linton said. 'With it we can bore a hole several feet deep into the concrete, and draw off a sample.'

'You are proposing to bore a hole several feet deep in my building?'

'Thinner than a pencil lead,' Martin said reassuringly. 'It won't affect the strength of the building in the slightest, and will immediately be filled in again.'

Denys snorted. 'And then what we draw out can be analysed, don't you see?' Georgina asked. 'If there's no trace of fungus present, then the building is absolutely safe, because there's no chance of fungus getting in once the cement has hardened.'

Denys scratched his head as the engineers got to work taking a sample. Finally, as he watched the liquid concrete being pumped into the pinhole, to fill it, he asked, 'How soon before we know what's what?'

'A couple of days. Maybe less.'

'And then you'll have your guarantee,' Georgina told him.

'And you'll have your cheque,' Denys grunted as they trooped to the next floor for another sample.

'GEORGINA? CAROLINE. You're not the easiest of people to locate!'

'Sorry about that. I'm afraid life is rather hectic at the moment.' Georgina was holding the receiver against her ear with a hunched shoulder, leaving her hands free to pass three current files to Anne across the desk and to scrawl a note of instructions.

'I thought maybe we should get started on details re the wedding,' Caroline was saying.

'Agreed. Have you had a chance to speak again to Linda? What does she think of the ideas we had over lunch?'

'Fortunately she seems keen to go along with Denys's desire for a splash. I suppose every young girl dreams of being a beautiful bride once in their lives.'

The two women got down to details. The wedding was set for a fortnight on Saturday, which meant a rush to get the invitations out and make the arrangements. They had made a good deal of progress when Georgina looked at her watch and said, 'Hell! I've someone arriving at my flat in twenty minutes and I won't be there to let them in. I really must fly, but I'll call you later to hear how you're getting on. How about Sunday morning?'

'Great. I'll be at home.'

'Even better, why don't the three of you come over to our place in Headley Down for lunch?'

'That would be marvellous, if it won't be too much bother.'

MARTIN WAS STANDING on the steps looking baffled when she arrived at the flat. 'Sorry, darling,' she said, and pecked him on the cheek before pushing the key into the lock.

When the flat door slammed after them he took her into his arms and kissed her. He realised her brain was still doing overtime, so the embrace was brief. 'Marks and Sparks supper tonight, I'm afraid,' she said, pulling away. 'There are two or three different ones in the fridge. You decide what you want while I take a shower. I can't do a thing till I've cooled off.'

'OK. I'll get things under way in the kitchen.'

Martin had always admired Georgina from a distance. In business she never attempted to use her sexuality, remaining unselfconsciously an architect, pure and simple, using only her artistic perception to compete with her male peers. Yet she was utterly, magnificently feminine, from the sweep of her dark hair and deep green eyes to the full, rounded breasts and long, long, elegant calves.

He listened to the sound of the shower water through the half-open door and hurriedly dried his hands. Wagner seemed a good choice of music, and as the prelude to act one of *Lohengrin* filled the flat he went and stood in the bathroom doorway.

'If you want a shower, too, I'll fetch you another towel,' Georgina mumbled through the folds of cloth as she rubbed her hair.

'Thanks. I will.'

Georgina sat at her dressing table, directing the heat of the hairdryer through the long dark tangles, but it was still very damp when Martin came in from the bathroom. He stood behind her, waiting, till she switched off the dryer, stood up and turned into his arms.

'Isn't it marvellous reaching that stage in life when you no longer have to pretend that it all happens accidentally?' she murmured between kisses. They both knew they'd waited long enough.

16

'Well?' Anne greeted Georgina the following morning. 'You look like the cat who swallowed the canary! What's the good news?'

'Life must go on,' Georgina said sententiously. 'Now, first thing, will you get onto the Ministry of the Environment and set up another meeting with Charles Campbell. It's for Martin Garrard and myself, and we would like it to be as soon as possible. It is very urgent.'

'Right,' Anne said. 'Any joy with Denys Wright?'

'Soon, I hope.'

'It's just that the caterers are getting a bit agitated. They want to know if we are going to have that gala opening or not.'

'Twenty-four hours,' Georgina said. 'Arrange that meeting.'

'THE MINISTER isn't available until three this afternoon,' Anne told her. 'And then it has to be a very brief meeting, as he's due in the House at four.'

'Anyone would think this wasn't important. OK, get me Sir Trumpton Dauntsey.'

Georgina sat at her desk, fingers drumming, until Anne came back. 'He's in a meeting.'

'You mean he doesn't want to talk to me. You tell him or his secretary that he'd better. It's me or our lawyers.'

Dauntsey was on the line a moment later. 'Now look here, Georgina,' he said, 'you can't threaten us. Playle is the party in the hot seat. Not Global Banking.'

'And if I can prove to you that the Global Building is fungus-free?'

'How?'

'It'll mean boring a few test holes in the building. They'll be filled again the moment we have our samples, and no one will ever know they even existed.'

'Well, I don't know . . .'

'If you don't, we are going to take you to court, when we will claim that we offered this guarantee and you refused it.'

'Well, really, Gina . . . when would this take place?'

'Tomorrow morning.'

'And this will prove that the building is safe?'

'Absolutely.'

'Well . . . oh, all right.'

'Thank you, Sir Trumpton.'

She hung up, and Anne came in. 'That was telling him. What happens if the building is contaminated?'

'The next person who suggests that to me gets the sack,' Georgina told her. 'Now will you get me Martin Garrard, please.' Martin came on the line, and she put him in the picture, both about Campbell and the bank.

'I'll get onto Linton right away. Why don't we lunch together, and go along to the meeting afterwards? I know a little trattoria just round the corner from the ministry.'

SHE WAS THERE FIRST, but Martin had booked a table and she was given a drink by the beaming waiter. Martin was obviously a well-established client. He arrived five minutes later, looking decidedly hot and bothered. 'Sorry,' he said, 'I got held up.'

'Not to worry. We'd better order.'

He nodded, called for some house wine and leaned on the table. 'I love you,' he said, solemnly.

She raised her eyebrows. 'I won't say the feeling isn't mutual. But what brought this on?'

'I had a telephone call this morning from Bob Jacobs.'

'Jacobs?' she said. The name was familiar.

'He's handling the negotiations for the Dudlington Marina job.' Martin drank some wine and got entangled in his spaghetti, which had arrived with amazing speed. 'We've got the contract.'

'Oh, that's tremendous. But why . . .'

'I mean Harvey and Associates.'

'Oh! Ah! Yes.'

'There's a letter in the mail for you, to Playle plc I mean, but he wanted me to know in advance. He and I have been friends for a long time. I put the merger idea to him, and . . . he said to forget it.' Martin paused, but when Georgina didn't speak, he went on. 'I told him that was a lot of nonsense, that you had only designed one of the failures, that it was utterly unreasonable to pillory you just because you were, so to speak, first in the field. He listened, then said he was sorry, but that was the way it was. His backers didn't want to touch anything to do with Playle.'

Another pause, and again no comment from Georgina. 'They'd apparently got wind of people like Global withholding payments,' Martin said miserably. 'We talked back and forth, and then he suddenly said, Look, do you want the contract or not? Well, there didn't seem much to say after that.' He looked at her, unhappily.

'Of course you had to say yes, Martin. It was very gallant of you to attempt to cut us in at all.'

He drank some more wine. 'You know what I hope? I hope some of those samples I took along to Colin come up positive, for one of our buildings. Then I can plonk that report on Jacobs' desk and say, well, now, do you want us, Playle, or both together?'

Georgina squeezed his fingers. 'You are being so kind.' Their eyes met and held, full of love and gentle reassurance. She released his fingers and picked up her fork. There was no point in brooding over her disappointment. 'I think we'd better eat up, or we'll be late for the minister.'

CHARLES CAMPBELL was waiting for them. 'Has your man come up with anything?' he asked, the moment Martin had been introduced.

'Not yet,' Georgina said. 'But we have an idea.'

Campbell sat down and gestured them to seats. 'Ten minutes.'

'You're due in the House, I know,' Georgina agreed. She outlined the laser plan as succinctly as she could.

Campbell stroked his chin. 'You are recommending we bore these holes in every concrete structure in Great Britain? Have you any idea of the cost?'

'With respect, Minister, have you any idea of the cost if you just left those buildings to fall down?' Martin enquired.

'It can't be any greater. Aren't you implying that wherever the fungus is found the building should be pulled down anyway?'

Martin looked at Georgina, then back at Campbell. 'No, not necessarily. We hope that an antidote might be found in time to treat them. But, in the meantime, the buildings should be vacated.'

'It is the possible cost in lives we are thinking about, Minister,' Georgina said quietly.

'Harrumph,' Campbell commented. 'Well, I shall put your idea before the Cabinet tomorrow morn . . .' He looked up as the door opened and Jonathan Lloyd virtually fell into the room.

'I do apologise, Minister. But . . .' His face was white.

'There's been another failure?'

'Sir . . . the Palace of Westminster . . . They're evacuating now, sir.'

'Good Lord! I must get down there.'

'Mind if we come too?' Georgina asked.

'Perhaps you had better.'

THE MINISTER'S CAR was already waiting, and within minutes they were in Whitehall, where they were halted by police barriers some distance from Parliament Square. The square was filled with people, most of them irate MPs and peers who had been forced to evacuate the buildings.

Campbell got out and proceeded on foot, followed by Lloyd, Georgina and Martin. It was not immediately obvious that anything was the matter with the Palace of Westminster. Above their heads Big Ben rose majestically against a clear blue sky, and immediately in front of them Westminster Abbey looked as solid as ever.

Campbell was accosted by a man in a dark suit. 'Ah, Charles! What a shambles, eh?'

'What exactly happened?' Campbell demanded.

'Damned if I know. A message was passed to the Speaker, who ordered the chamber to be evacuated, and everywhere else as well.'

'We need to get inside.'

'The building has been closed pending the arrival of experts.'

'My dear fellow, I have two experts with me.'

The MP looked at Georgina and Martin for the first time.

'Well . . . you'll have to see if they'll let you in.'

'Come on,' Campbell said. He led the way across the street to the gate to New Palace Yard, where there was another cordon of policemen. Close by, the Prime Minister and several other Cabinet members all looked extremely hot and bothered.

'Campbell!' the Prime Minister said. 'What are we going to do? This damned fungus of yours seems to be in the House.'

'May we have a look at it, sir?' Georgina asked.

The Prime Minister gazed at her, eyebrows arched.

'Georgina Playle, Prime Minister. And this is Martin Garrard. Miss Playle and Mr Garrard are architects who are working with me on solving this business,' Campbell explained.

'We really need to look,' Georgina said.

'Then you better had, I suppose.'

Campbell was already hurrying towards the inner police cordon. 'Where exactly is the problem?'

'I believe in one of the downstairs dining rooms, sir,' the superintendent told him.

'Right.' They hurried across the courtyard and up the steps into the lobby. Campbell hurried towards the stairs leading down to the private dining rooms. They were only halfway down when he stopped, and sniffed. 'What a pong!'

'That's it,' Georgina snapped, and pushed past him to gain the downstairs lobby, following her nose. Some distance down the corridor the smell made her halt, feeling like choking, and she gazed in horror at the huge bulge in the wall.

'Good heavens!' Martin stood at her shoulder. 'You know this is the first time I've actually seen it at work?'

'Is it going to come down?' Campbell asked.

'Any moment now, I'd say.' Martin grasped Georgina's arm. 'We'd better get out of here.'

He pulled her through the doorway and into the corridor, pushing her in front of him. 'Run like blazes!' Georgina obeyed instinctively, reached the stairs, and turned round at the rumbling crash. Martin and Lloyd were immediately behind her. Behind them was nothing but dust. 'Up the stairs!' he shouted.

'Campbell!' she shouted in return, and started back.

Martin caught her round the waist, thrust her at the stairs again. 'We'll get him!' Lloyd had already disappeared back into the gloom; the lights had gone out.

Georgina stumbled to the stairs, fell to her hands and knees, her nostrils filled at once with dust and the stench of rotting vegetables. But her mind was filled with the apprehension of catastrophe. She went up a few steps, on her hands and knees, and looked back again, in time to see Martin emerge from the dust-mist, carrying the minister. Lloyd stumbled behind him. The cracking, tearing sound was spreading. They fell up the stairs, dropping Campbell's limp form and retrieving him, and sprawled into the lobby. Pieces of wood and plaster fell on Martin's and Georgina's shoulders as they regained their feet and ran for the door.

A policeman in the courtyard was staring up at the northeastern tower of the palace. It had disappeared in a cloud of dust and rubble, as it collapsed across Bridge Street, its debris pitting Big Ben itself as it scattered into the entrance to Whitehall. People ran in every direction, but several unlucky ones lay on the roadway where they had been struck by flying masonry.

Policemen rushed forward to pull Georgina away from the danger and to help Martin, who was carrying Campbell, Lloyd at his shoulder. Martin's knees buckled as he reached the grass and laid the minister down as carefully as he could, while from behind them there was yet another series of rumbling crashes and another tower came tumbling down.

The minister lay dreadfully still, eyes wide and head turned at an odd angle towards the police superintendent kneeling beside him.

'Is he going to be all right?' Georgina gasped.

'No, ma'am,' the superintendent said. 'Mr Campbell is dead!'

17

The day was hot. The water in Georgina's shower had been hot and the mug of tea clasped between both her hands as she sat wrapped in an old dressing gown was boiling. But Georgina could not stop shivering.

The Houses of Parliament. Gone! Destroyed . . . by this monstrous Mycota. Westminster, the symbolic centre of Western civilisation and culture, just wiped out. Was this then the end of all the cement cities of the world, the concrete jungles filled with teeming humanity? Were they witnessing not merely the collapse of a few buildings, but also the commencement of the disintegration of world civilisation?

Georgina shuddered again and sipped the tea. 'I really must pull myself together,' she said out loud and switched on the TV.

Great Britain was to be tested for the fungus. The spokesman was a little bit vague about how long this would take, reiterating phrases such as 'this has maximum priority'. The collapse of part of the Palace of Westminster had concentrated minds wonderfully.

Martin came for supper and again spent the night. 'We seem to be making a habit of this,' Georgina commented, but she wasn't objecting. She needed the comfort of his arms.

NEXT MORNING Georgina decided to get into the office early. She hadn't been back yesterday afternoon—she had simply felt too shocked. When Patrick arrived she hurried along the corridor to tell him of her adventure.

He listened, grim-faced, but when she was finished he managed an attempt at humour. 'At least no one can say we designed the Houses of Parliament. When do we get a report on those tests your friend is making?'

'Hopefully today on Riverview, Monday for Global. I'm seeing Denys Wright over the weekend, so I mean to arrive at work on Monday morning with his cheque for one point two million.'

'We'll pray it doesn't bounce,' Patrick commented.

VERY LITTLE WORK was done that day, as everyone was watching a pocket television brought in by one of the junior staff. A wave of panic was gathering among people who lived or worked in high-rises, many of whom insisted on evacuating immediately or refused to work. Some of the people who had moved out began to camp in the parks or in adjacent squares.

Georgina spent the day waiting for the phone to ring. The only calls she was prepared to accept were from either Martin or Colin Worthington. She tried to concentrate on work, and tried to compose what she was going to say to Michael's headmaster, the next morning. But as the minutes ticked slowly by, a deepening depression settled over her. The firm which her father had painstakingly built up from nothing was slipping down the drain, along with her own career. They were left with almost no projects and a host of dissatisfied customers.

When the phone did finally ring, just before five, she nearly jumped out of her skin. 'Hi.' A subdued Martin.

'Give.' The lumps of lead were back in her stomach.

'Colin has completed his analysis of the first dozen samples we submitted. Ten are clear, but two have the fungus.'

'Well, that's a better average than I'd hoped for. From your tone I gather there's a down side.'

'I'm afraid so. One of the infected samples comes from a block of flats in the Midlands. The other is from Riverview.'

GEORGINA SAT motionless at her desk breathing irregular gasps. Martin had remained on the phone for several minutes after breaking the news, but she had no idea what was said. Riverview! Oh, no! Denys would have to repay all the purchasers of the flats, to date, which could possibly put him out of business. He would never pay

Playle now and even if the Global test was clear, one could lay heavy odds that most of their clients would use the excuse to follow suit. It was tempting to delay passing on the news to Patrick, but he would have to know in the next few hours, and better from herself than anyone else. Leaden legs carried her along the corridor to his office, and she slumped into a chair.

'It's Riverview. The analysts have found Mycota.'

Patrick's eyes closed. For several seconds he remained silent, then muttered, 'Well, that's curtains, isn't it?'

Georgina swallowed. 'Does it have to be? Just because it was a Playle building that first hit the headlines doesn't mean that we have to carry the can from here on. That would be grossly unfair.'

Patrick raised his eyes to study her expression and gave a thin smile. 'My dear Gina, I am so very sad that this has happened. You are still so young . . . young enough to believe that life should be fair to us all, that honest endeavour will always be rewarded.' He brushed back the thick, wavy light-coloured hair that had fallen across his forehead, stood up and walked round the desk to put a hand on her shoulder. 'Why don't you come over to our place this evening for a drink?' He obviously pictured her alone at home with her worries.

She reached up to place an affectionate hand over his. 'Dear Patrick, you are so kind. I would dearly love to come over, but I have to collect Michael from school. Tomorrow I have to break the news to his headmaster that he is leaving school to get married.'

'What! Michael? Married? That's crazy, Gina. He's far too . . .'

'Yes, Patrick, he is far too young. But his girlfriend is pregnant and they want to get married.' Patrick staggered back to his big leather chair, sat heavily and stared at her, speechless. Georgina nodded slowly. 'Yes. I know, don't tell me.'

'Do her parents know? What do they say?'

'They've agreed to the marriage, but right this minute I reckon they are wishing the father could have been anyone but my son.'

'You know them? Who are they?'

'They are Mr and Mrs Denys Wright.' Patrick sat with his mouth open, and watched as Georgina started to laugh, more than slightly hysterically. 'Can you believe it? They are coming to lunch on Sunday to meet their future son-in-law. And while they are at lunch I have to break the news to Denys that the building we designed for him could fall down at any minute.' She threw back her head and laughed helplessly, tears running down her cheeks.

Patrick continued to stare at her, amazed, but Georgina's laughter became infectious, and much against his will he found himself unable to smother the laughter that welled up in response.

'Thank goodness for the blessed relief of laughter. I believe in situations like this the only alternative is suicide,' he remarked.

'You're probably right, but think of all the fun one would miss.' Gina threw her sodden tissue into the wastepaper basket. 'Now, if you'll excuse me, Patrick dear, I have to leave.'

THE INEVITABLE DEPRESSION followed Georgina's laughter as she drove across the Surrey countryside to Michael's school. It was a school with a fine tradition and Georgina's heart lurched with sadness that her son would not be able to complete his education there.

Michael was waiting at the top of the front steps. He waved as she drew up, then ran down and slid into the seat beside her. 'You're late,' he growled.

'Yes.' She hadn't the energy to list her excuses.

As the car turned out of the gates Michael asked, 'Do you want me to come with you tomorrow to see old Willie?' He was hoping for a negative answer.

He got one. 'No. I don't see the point in you being there, other than to act as punchbag. I imagine he's going to be furious.'

'You betcha! Mind,' he added, 'I wouldn't mind being a fly on the wall. Aren't you a bit scared yourself?'

'Me? No! I shall make it perfectly plain that I consider the entire predicament to be his fault. Lack of supervision *in loco parentis.*'

And indeed at her meeting with the headmaster the following morning she let him have it, straight from the shoulder, working on the theory that attack is the best means of defence.

Mr Willis was accustomed to handling awkward and complaining parents, and to administering justice to the various miscreants in his charge. But the beautiful, smiling and forthright woman who had come to explain that her son wished to leave school to get married and commence employment was outside the realm of his experience.

GEORGINA COULD SEE she'd won the day, but she knew she couldn't hope for such an easy ride through the Sunday luncheon party.

The Wrights arrived ten minutes early, before Georgina had put the finishing touches to her face and hair. But at least the house was reasonably tidy and the preparations for lunch were completed. Michael had led them straight through the sitting room and out onto the patio when she ran down the stairs pressing the last butterfly onto the modest gold earstuds she'd chosen.

'Caroline! Denys! Welcome! How nice to see you!'

'Gina! It's lovely to be here.' Caroline leaned forward for the customary brush of cheeks. 'I do hope we are not too early.'

'Not a bit. And Linda.' She grasped the girl's hand. For some inexplicable reason, Georgina had pictured Linda as a smallish girl with pert features and a challenging expression . . . in fact, the exact opposite of the tall, charming young woman whose hand she still clasped. Her light brown hair was drawn back in a ponytail and her smiling blue eyes and freckled nose were devoid of make-up. Georgina liked her immediately.

The feeling was obviously reciprocated. 'Mike has told me so much about you, Mrs Carden. I'm only sorry that all this has happened right now when you must have so much on your mind. What a terrible tragedy this Mycota is proving.'

'Yes,' Caroline agreed. 'Almost makes one want to camp out in the open for fear of waking up under the weight of a ceiling.'

Before Denys could add his thoughts to the subject, Michael suggested drinks. 'Mum has made a jug of Pimms. Would you like some, Mrs Wright, or shall I get you something else?'

'I adore Pimms, thank you, Michael, but I loathe being called Mrs Wright by friends and family. What do you reckon, Gina, shall we stick to Christian names?'

'Definitely,' Georgina smiled. 'Now, Denys! What are you drinking?'

'Nothing, so far. But Pimms would suit me fine.' Georgina wondered how such a coarse man could have such a charming wife and daughter. But then she discovered another side of his character as he led her off round the garden, questioning her about various plants and trees.

If only we could maintain these pleasantly mundane topics all day, Georgina thought. She still hadn't decided when to break the news about Riverview. Now, or wait till after lunch? She glanced at her watch. She had stuffed pork fillets roasting in the oven. If she launched into the story now they'd be ruined before she escaped Denys's wrath. Better to wait. Linda joined them. 'Aren't your azaleas marvellous,' she remarked. 'Ours were finished ages ago.'

'They don't get much sun on this side of the garden so they always start later than most,' Georgina explained. 'Tell me about yourself. What are your hobbies?'

'Trust a woman to ask about hobbies rather than work,' Denys said, but there was a smile on his face.

'I love swimming and tennis, and I play, or should I say played, in the school lacrosse team,' Linda added.

Michael remained sitting with Caroline. Georgina could see they were laughing and chatting quite happily . . . it was all going so well.

They sat outside under the shade of a huge royal-blue parasol and began the meal with thin slices of smoked salmon and brown bread. Michael poured Frascati for the three parents and Cokes for himself and Linda, and conversation was light and jovial. There were quips about weddings and Denys told the story of his and Caroline's ceremony.

The loganberries were so ripe they needed little sugar and as no one wanted cheese, Michael helped his mother to clear, leaving the guests to talk among themselves. 'Why don't you take Linda for a walk or something,' Georgina hissed at Michael as she filled the coffee machine, 'while I break the news about Riverview?'

'Happily. I'd rather not be within earshot!'

He and Linda refused coffee and escaped hand in hand round the side of the house. Georgina poured and handed cups to the other two, trying to frame the necessary words in her mind. However, fate took a hand. Or rather Caroline did. 'I've been over the flat the kids are to have in Riverview,' she said, 'discussing carpets and curtains. It's a lovely place, I think they're awfully lucky.'

'Yes. Well, I'm afraid there is a hitch.'

'What's that?' Denys woke out of a reverie and a cloud of cigar smoke. 'What hitch?'

'I'm afraid I have some devastating news, Denys.' Georgina took a deep breath. 'The analysts have found Mycota in Riverview.'

Caroline gasped. 'Oh, no!'

'When did you hear? Why didn't you tell me before?' Denys demanded.

'On Friday after . . .'

'Friday!' he yelled. 'Friday! And here's Sunday before you deign to relay the news! Damn it, woman, I should have been told—'

'No you should not!' Caroline said severely. 'Georgina was absolutely right to wait until we'd finished our lovely lunch with the kids.'

'You realise what this means, don't you?' Denys persisted. 'I'm going to have to refund payment received so far on those flats. And as for Playle p-l-c . . .' the name was spat out with fury.

'You don't have to tell me.' Georgina sat shaking her head.

'But Linda and Michael!' The thought suddenly struck Caroline. 'What about their flat? Where will they live now?'

'I promised them a flat for a wedding present,' Denys declared, 'and they'll have one. The Skyways building. The penthouse is still vacant there. We'll have the reception up there, and the guests will see what the kids are getting.' He stared hard at Georgina. 'Skyways was designed by Harvey and Associates. I had a letter from them on Friday informing me that it, and, incidentally, *all* of their buildings, are Mycota-free.'

18

The day was grey. As grey as Georgina's thoughts. Dark yellow clouds hung over London, close and threatening. Even with the windows open there was no movement of air, the curtains hanging limp and lifeless in the heat of early evening. Georgina was sitting at her little antique desk in the living room with the intention of making a list of wedding guests but she hadn't got very far. It was impossible to concentrate on weddings and presents when more buildings were failing daily, when one's business was collapsing around one's ears and every structure one entered was suspect. In fact life itself, as she knew it, seemed to be on the point of collapse. Half the buildings in London were empty. Staff were refusing to risk sitting all day surrounded by concrete which could be disintegrating. Those businesses in the City which were still operating, and had not yet been tested and pronounced Mycota-free, were paying people to walk through their premises sniffing, checking, all day long. They had someone sniffing at Playle, because even their test results had not yet been analysed, so heavy was the workload on every available analytical chemist.

Georgina added Martin Garrard's name to the list and smiled. At that moment the door buzzer sounded. She got up, stuck her head out of the window and saw Martin below, standing at the top of the steps. 'Hello! Just coming!' she called, and ran across the room to press the door release.

Martin put down his briefcase before taking her in his arms. They didn't kiss, just stood pressed together, giving and receiving comfort. 'Was the day very awful?' he asked.

'As Mondays go, it has to have been more horrendous than the worst nightmare. What about you?'

'Could have been a lot worse. For some unfathomable reason we still haven't had one building failure. Yet!'

'You don't have to worry: you were born under a lucky star. When I broke the news about Riverview to Denys he decided to transfer the reception to the penthouse suite he has in your Skyways building. What's more, he's giving it to the kids as a wedding present.'

'Oh!' Martin's expression was suddenly very serious. 'Hell, darling. I'm so sorry. This is all such damnably bad luck for you.'

She blew him a kiss. 'But are you really sure Harvey and Associates still want to know Playle plc?'

'They don't have a choice.'

'Why?'

'Well, once Playle and Garrard have amalgamated . . .'

'Have what?' she exclaimed.

'I mean, once you and I are united . . .' He paused, staring at her. Georgina stared back. Slowly a smile spread across her face, the first that day. 'Martin Garrard! You wouldn't by any chance be . . .'

'Yes.' He smiled back. 'I am. Proposing marriage, that is.' Her green eyes continued to hold his, unblinking. Her lips formed an O, but no sound came. 'Well?' Martin began to look anxious. 'Don't you think it would be a good idea?'

She reached up and put her arms round his neck. 'Of course I do, silly. I feel quite crazy, choosing a time like this to fall hopelessly in love, and with a business rival. However, it's happened, and I've no intention of letting anything come between us.'

Martin couldn't reply because she was kissing him, very fiercely. So he kissed her back, and assumed that her answer was yes.

SUDDENLY LIFE TOOK on an entirely different aspect. The prospect of settling down with Martin, if and when this ghastly Mycota problem was resolved, was a great incentive to hold the business together, talk positively to as many people as possible from ministerial and council level to clients and other business associates. She was determined to make people understand how the fungus worked, as well as all that was being done towards finding an antidote. It was wonderful how much more confident she felt, knowing Martin not only backed her opinions but loved her, wanted her as much as she wanted him.

Caroline Wright was a tower of strength. Unlike her husband she was intent on maintaining a happy relationship with her daughter's prospective mother-in-law, and although a fortnight was all too brief a period in which to make all the arrangements she still found time to call Georgina to offer help with matters which were traditionally the responsibility of the groom's family. Denys, of course, wanted to combine the reception with a publicity stunt to advertise the building, plugging the angle that Skyways had been declared free of fungus.

Within her own business, the news that Playle had had another high-rise condemned caused the cancellation of all their remaining contracts. Even at places like Global, which had been given the all clear by Colin Worthington, Sir Trumpton Dauntsey and his fellow directors were being slow with their penultimate payment.

'While bankruptcy stares us in the face,' Patrick said, peering at the latest figures presented by the accountants, 'these indicate that we can keep going for another month, before liquidating assets.'

'I suppose we could always approach Global Banking for a loan to tide us over until things improve,' Georgina suggested.

'I'm glad you can smile about it. In fact I'm surprised you can smile at all, with that son of yours going ahead with his shotgun wedding, on top of everything else. I can't make out why you allow it, and it's certainly nothing to look happy about.'

'I'm in no mood to cry, Patrick. I'm getting married myself, soon.'

His head jerked up, eyebrows raised in alarm. 'You! You didn't tell me you were contemplating . . .'

'I couldn't have told you before,' Georgina explained. 'He has only just proposed. And anyway, it's taking a little time to sink in.'

'Good Lord! Not to that bounder Rossmore?'

'No.' Georgina shook her head vigorously. 'Not to Philip. I'm going to marry Martin Garrard.' This time Patrick was speechless. 'You know we've been talking about this merger . . . Well, things sort of developed from there, I suppose.'

'You mean, if we go under, you're going to be shifting your desk down to Harvey and Associates?'

'We are not going to go under, Patrick. I am determined on that. I'm just trying to explain why I'm prepared to look on the bright side right now.'

'Well, try looking on the bright side of Riverview. We have a building which nobody wants, and which is liable to fall down at any moment. Plus the fact that the contractors are screaming for the money, which we don't have. I'd like to hear your thoughts on that.'

'Well . . . I suppose it'll have to be pulled down before it falls down and causes a lot of damage.'

'And who foots the bill?'

'It's insured . . .'

'Against fire, theft, robbery, storm and flood. Not against something that was built into it.'

'If we refuse to pull Riverview down, and it collapses, they could be liable for the whole ten million. It's unlikely to cost more than half a million to demolish. I should think the insurers would happily pick up a settlement in the neighbourhood of, say, two million.'

'What a complicated mess. Anyway, before we approach the insurers, I think you want to get some kind of statement out of Worthington to the effect that the Mycota is a natural disaster, and can be classed under one or other of the insured headings.'

'Um. I'll have a go.'

GEORGINA WANTED to see Worthington again. She hadn't spoken to him for a couple of days, although she had received another list, only last night, of buildings which had been found to contain Mycota.

She hurried round to the laboratory, to find even more than the

500

usual chaos. Worthington had been forced to hire extra staff, but had not been able to expand his premises, so that a dozen young men and women were now crowded into the little laboratory.

He seemed pleased to see her. 'We're making progress, Georgina. I was about to get in touch with you when your secretary called.'

'Tell me about it.'

'Well, not all of it is good, I'm afraid. The good news is that we've been able to determine that just about all the infected cement was obtained from chalk quarried in one part of the Downs. Now, I want you to take this with caution, because, of course, overseas failures cannot be related to any specific British area. However, we can now say that we are dealing with a specific type of chalk, and I have no doubt at all that this will prove of enormous value.'

'Absolutely,' Georgina agreed. 'It will enable us to decide not to take any more quicklime from areas containing that particular kind of chalk. That saves the future, maybe. What about the present?'

'That's a tricky one. We are running a series of tests, attempting to discover some agent which will destroy the fungus. Having established that it is unaffected by any known fungicide it might appear obvious that we would have to find our answer in water. But of course the difficulties there are just about insuperable.'

'You are not exactly making my day,' Georgina told him.

'The ultimate solution, as I see it,' Worthington went on, 'lies in treatment of the cement before it is ever mixed and set.'

'You've gone back to the future again,' Georgina pointed out. 'Which means you have no hope of saving any presently affected buildings. In that case I want you to give me a report of your findings phrased in such a way as to establish that when all these constructions were taking place *Mycota concretus* was an unknown natural phenomenon and therefore cannot be covered by any exclusion clauses. Demolishing Riverview is going to be a costly business, and frankly, we have a cash-flow problem just now. So we would like the insurers to pay for the demolition, in order to avoid having to fork out the full insured sum should the building collapse.'

'They won't like that.'

'Quite. They'll claim they are not responsible for something which was in the concrete before the building was constructed. We have to fight them on that point, and win. This is where you come in. We have to prove that we could not have known of its existence in advance.'

Worthington took off his steel-rimmed spectacles and polished them. 'I'm not asking you to perjure yourself,' Georgina said.

'No, no. But I have to obtain several samples of soil from the area,

where the original chalk was quarried in order to establish beyond
doubt that the Mycota is present, as you say, as a perfectly natural
but hitherto unknown and undetectable phenomenon.' Worthington
scratched his head. 'We're up to our ears as it is. But I'll put a couple
of people onto it.' He ushered her to the door, and checked, his brow
puckered. 'Georgina, if you really are going to pull Riverview down,
would you mind if we took more samples from it first?'

'Why?'

'Well, this is the bad news I mentioned earlier. You see, that
building is only five years old. That's the foundations. The actual
building is less than two years old. Yet we found evidence of the
fungus, not in the basement, oddly enough, but in the samples taken
much higher up. The point is, there is only one other sample we have
taken which is less than six years old. That was the Skyways building,
from Harvey and Associates, and that of course was clear. The most
recent building, other than Riverview, which was found to contain
the fungus, is nine years old.'

'What are you trying to tell me?'

'Well, simply this: I don't think there is any way that the fungus
could develop from scratch, as it were, to such a dangerous state as
we found in Riverview, in just two years. Therefore we are faced with
the possibility that in some cements the fungus is already fully
developed even when it is being poured. I'd like to take a whole lot
more samples from Riverview to see if we can come to any proper
conclusion about this latest development.'

'All right, Colin, you get onto that. And let me know the moment
you come to a conclusion.'

19

Caroline was thankful the church was so small, otherwise it would
have been more than half empty. Two hundred and eighty invitations
had been sent, but for various reasons—short notice, summer
holidays and most of all the concrete problem—only one hundred
and sixty-seven acceptances had been received.

The other good point about the church was that it was within five
minutes' drive of Skyways. So far everything had gone amazingly
well. She studied the tall stands of floral arrangements either side of
the altar steps and the garlands suspended from each pew end; they
looked lovely. So they should be for the price she had paid!

She glanced at her watch. Denys and Linda were three minutes late.
From across the aisle Georgina caught her eye and smiled before

leaning forward to whisper something to Michael, who kept shifting uncomfortably in the front pew, alongside his extremely youthful-looking best man. She wondered who the huge man could be, sitting with Georgina. Michael's father, Tom Carden, on Georgina's other side, looked distinctly uncomfortable.

The organist stopped, then burst into the Trumpet Voluntary. The congregation stood and all heads turned to watch the bridal procession. Denys had never looked so proud, and Linda was exquisite.

Caroline and her daughter had chosen a dress made entirely of the palest pink and white lace flowers, touched with delicate threads of lavender. The bodice fitted tightly over a white satin lining which spread wide over stiff net petticoats, almost like a crinoline. Linda looked radiant and relaxed as she smiled at the waiting groom who had sprung anxiously to attention. She was followed by two attendants, her best schoolfriend and a three-year-old flower girl, daughter of Caroline's younger sister, who looked gorgeous in her tiny pale turquoise dress.

Georgina smoothed the creases from her biscuit-coloured silk dress. She didn't really like her outfit; the colour was all right, but the shape was very ordinary. However, Michael had said he thought she looked terrific, and Martin had nodded appreciatively when he arrived at the house to escort her. They were the only two people who mattered, although even Tom had grunted a compliment when he had joined them.

Linda's bridesmaid had taken the bridal bouquet, and Denys gave Linda's hand to Michael. Georgina sighed. Michael was looking so tense. Thank goodness Linda could appear so cool and composed. When they all trooped into the vestry to sign the register, Georgina squeezed his arm reassuringly.

COLIN WORTHINGTON was exhausted. He and his team had worked virtually nonstop for thirty-six hours. They had begun by checking and rechecking their Riverview findings. They had even returned to the building and taken more samples. And they had found no trace of fungus at all. Then it had been a matter of rechecking the original concrete taken from the site. The fungus had still been there, and at an advanced enough stage to suggest that the slightest stress might bring the entire building down.

Colin himself, and two others of his team, had been to the Downs, collecting chalk samples from the established Mycota-infected areas. Their results had been positive. Now he had to face this unacceptable situation.

'What's happened is obvious,' he declared, 'however unpalatable it may be. There's been a mix-up, unless any of you believe that this fungus managed to self-destruct within the past fortnight.'

'Wouldn't that be lovely?' Jennie Gibbs said. She was regarding her finger, which she had managed to cut open on a sliver of concrete, and which was oozing blood.

'You want to put something on that,' Patsy Hartwell told her. 'The first-aid box is under that bench over there.' Patsy regarded herself as second-in-command.

'Life just isn't that simple,' Colin pointed out, impatient at the interruption. 'No, those original samples must have come from somewhere else.' His staff exchanged glances.

'There's only tincture of iodine here,' Jennie complained. 'Really! When was this box last used? Iodine went out with the ark.'

'I put that iodine there myself,' Patsy told her. 'It's what my mum used when we cut ourselves as kids. Here, let me put it on.'

'You mean there is another building in London on the verge of coming down, and we don't know which one it is?' Joe Bridewell demanded.

'That's right,' Colin said. 'Which explains everything. Riverview is far too recent a construction to be so severely affected.'

Joe couldn't resist a grin. 'Georgina Playle isn't going to be happy when you tell her that. Isn't she about to have it pulled down?'

'Well, at least we've caught it in time to stop that,' Tom Spencer said. 'She'll just be happy the building is sound.'

'Georgina Playle!' Colin snapped. 'Oh no! What time is it?'

'Just gone three.'

'I'm supposed to be at the wedding of her son. It began at three!'

'Ow!' Jennie cried as Patsy applied a rather liberal dose of the iodine to the cut. 'Ow-ow-ow!'

'Oh, you clot!' Patsy shouted, as Jennie's jerk knocked the bottle from her hand. It struck the floor and smashed; a dark brown stain spread across the floor.

Colin raised his eyes to heaven. 'I haven't even typed up that report she wanted. Anyway, we have to find that building. It'll be one of those brought in at the time of the first tests a fortnight back.'

'There were over a dozen of them,' Joe pointed out. 'And those samples, having been pronounced Mycota-free, have been thrown out.'

'Then we'll just have to take more, and right away.'

'One of them is the Skyways building. Isn't that where Georgina Playle is holding her son's wedding reception? Are we going to show up in the middle of it armed with lasers?'

'I suppose we'll have to leave it until tomorrow,' Colin agreed, and was interrupted by another shout from Patsy, who had dropped to her hands and knees with a cloth to mop up the spilt iodine.

'Just look at this.' The men and Jennie clustered round. Some of the powerful antiseptic liquid had dribbled against a lump of contaminated concrete, in which the fungus had been so advanced it was visible to the naked eye. Tentatively Patsy touched the greenish mould with her finger, and it crumbled into dust.

'Wow!' Joe commented. 'You don't suppose iodine . . .'

Colin snapped his fingers. 'You guys get working on it.'

'What are you going to do?'

Colin grinned. 'Maybe I'll attend the reception after all. This may be the best wedding present Georgina Playle could possibly have.'

EVEN FROM THE PENTHOUSE suite, the view from Skyways couldn't match that of Riverview, but it made up for the fact with spacious, airy rooms. Georgina had given Michael a cheque to buy a few basic pieces of furniture and today, with caterers' trestles filling the sitting room, the sparseness of the furnishings was unnoticeable.

'Lucky kids,' Patrick remarked when Georgina joined him and his wife Thelma after breaking away from the handshaking routine.

'Let's hope it all works out well for them,' Thelma added, looking doubtful.

Etiquette had demanded that Georgina stand with Tom in the reception line, but she had now unloaded him next to a makeshift bar from whence the champagne was being dispensed, and hastily summoned Martin, drawing him into the group. 'You two men know each other, don't you?' she smiled sweetly. 'But, Thelma, I don't think you've met Martin Garrard, have you?'

Martin smothered the elderly woman's tiny hand with his. 'Gina has told me so much about you. You've always been so kind to her.'

Georgina exchanged some words with Tim and Sally Buckenham, then went off to find Caroline to congratulate her on the buffet. She saw her with two of the maids and a waiter over by the kitchen door, but as there was obviously some problem she waited a few moments.

'Anything wrong?' she asked, when Caroline left the group.

Caroline laughed. 'There is always something wrong! Too many people: not enough people. They sample the buffet before we can get to it, then keep half of it in the kitchen because, they claim, it's gone off. Smells rancid. More likely they fancy it for their tea! I think I've sorted it out.' She took Georgina's arm. 'Now let me introduce you to some of our friends.'

Champagne flowed and people flocked round the magnificent three-tiered cake, admiring the craftsmanship of the icing. Everyone Georgina spoke to referred, if only obliquely, to the extreme youth of the happy couple, their good fortune in having understanding parents, this penthouse in which to start married life. And then Georgina heard a high-pitched squeal she recognised and turned to the door in time to see Billie bounce into the room.

'Gina! Good to see you! I just got back from a couple of days in Chicago. Sorry I missed the ceremony!' A massive shocking-pink cartwheel hat was zigzagging towards her. It was pinned precariously over blonde curls, beneath which a microscopic navy-blue dress ended a third of the way down shapely thighs.

Obligingly, Georgina bent to receive a kiss as the enormous brim flopped back to reveal Billie's upturned face. 'Glad you managed to make it at all. Hello, Philip.' This time she held out her hand. Then she looked past him, at Colin Worthington.

NEVER THE MOST tidy of men, Colin managed to appear as if he had stolen his morning suit from a scarecrow. 'Colin!' Georgina presented her cheek for a kiss. 'I thought you weren't going to make it.' She peered at him. 'You look exhausted.'

'I am exhausted. But, Gina, I have the most tremendous news.'

She grabbed his arm and pulled him into the hallway. 'Tell me.'

'Well . . .' He drew a long breath. 'There are two bits of good news, actually. One, we may have found the antidote.'

'Oh, Colin! Seriously?'

'Entirely by accident.' He told her of Jennie's knocking over the bottle of iodine, and what had happened after. 'That Mycota just curled up and died.'

'Oh, if that could only be true. But how would it work?'

'Leave that one with me. Now we know that it will work, the rest is detail. The second bit of good news is . . . how's your heart?'

'Still thumping.'

'Riverview is clear of Mycota. It's our fault. Two samples must've got mixed up. Those new samples we took are clear.'

'Oh, Colin!' She felt quite weak at the knees. 'Wait until Denys hears this. This is the best news I've had in weeks. But . . .' She frowned. 'If Riverview is clear, then where did the infected samples come from?'

'God knows. Don't worry, my people are starting a recheck now. We'll find it quickly enough. Like I said, that Mycota is in such an advanced stage, it has to be the rottenest structure in England.'

'Ye-es,' Georgina said slowly. So many thoughts were tumbling through her mind, but they were interrupted by the loud noise coming from the room behind her. She stepped through the doorway, Colin at her shoulder, as the master of ceremonies called out, 'Ladies and gentlemen! Your attention please!' Conversation subsided. 'If you would care to form a semicircle in front of this table then everyone may be able to see the happy bride and groom cut the wedding cake.'

Waiters threaded through the guests to recharge the champagne glasses. Georgina saw Martin looking for her, and gave him a quick wave. She watched as Michael and Linda were positioned beside the cake, brandishing a large, silver-handled knife.

Georgina sighed. The kids looked so terribly young and vulnerable, but what a handsome pair! Michael stood tall, with Linda smiling encouragement at her husband, obviously adoring him. Four hands together, they pressed the knife through the coating of icing into the dark fruity mixture beneath. Everyone clapped, raised their glasses and shouted good luck.

Caroline hurried in from supervising another catering crisis, and Georgina noticed that a waiter was gesticulating.

Caroline came up to Georgina. 'He says someone in a downstairs flat is complaining that we are causing a blockage in the drains. Can't be anything to worry about, can it?'

'No. The building was given a clean bill of health.' But then a chill ran up her spine. 'Colin,' she muttered. 'Wasn't Skyways one of the first buildings you tested?'

'Yes. We'll test it again as soon as this shindig is finished.'

Georgina's chill grew. Including the serving staff, there were more than two hundred people in the penthouse, twelve storeys above the basement. 'Look,' she said to Caroline. 'Why don't Colin and I pop down and see if we can placate this tenant of yours?'

'No. Please don't worry. I'll go . . .'

'It's important for you to stay here. We won't be more than a couple of minutes.' Dragging Colin by the hand, Georgina followed the waiter through the crush to the lift. They stared at each other as they rode down. 'Please tell me it's not possible,' she said.

He licked his lips. 'I wish I could.'

The lift came to a halt, and they ran across the lobby. The complainant occupied the ground-floor flat, and the moment he opened his front door Georgina's knees turned to jelly. There was no question about the smell: the place positively stank.

'And about time too,' the man snapped. 'Come and look what you people have done to the wall of our kitchen.'

Georgina dashed ahead of him to stand in horror in the kitchen doorway, gazing open-mouthed at the line of cupboard units which had been pushed inches out of alignment by the building wall behind them. 'Colin!' she gasped.

'Good grief!' he muttered. 'This *is* the one.'

20

'We have to get everyone out of here,' Colin gasped.

'Wait!' Georgina's brain was still racing. Her son was up there. Her daughter-in-law and unborn grandchild. Martin. She would not save them by losing her head. Mr Frankom, the tenant, was looking from one to the other, his face ashen as he realised what was happening.

'How long have we got?' Georgina asked Colin. 'Think, now!'

Colin licked his lips. He was obviously thinking, but about how this looming catastrophe was the fault of his staff and himself, and of the confusion in which he invariably worked. 'It is in this wall and has almost certainly spread to the first floor,' he said at last. 'I'll have to check it out. And the basement. There's a chance it might only be a partial collapse.'

'Then how long would we *have*?' Georgina was keeping her voice even with an effort.

'Maybe a couple of hours, providing there's no excessive noise or vibration.'

'A couple of hours is ample time to get everybody out, providing we don't have everyone trying to leave at once. You go to the porter, Colin. He will know who's at home. Everyone in the building must be alerted, and told to leave, quietly and without fuss. Tell them to use the lifts rather than the stairs.'

'Surely the stairs would be safer?'

'Not in this instance. The stairs are on this side of the building, where the fungus is. The lifts are on the other side, where there is nothing, so far as we know. And while you're at it, you'd better call the emergency services.'

'Where's the fire escape?'

'On the outside of this wall. Again, I think we will be better off if we just evacuate everyone by the lifts. The vital thing is to avoid panic. Mr Frankom.' She turned and smiled gently at the terrified man. 'I would like you to collect up whatever valuables you wish to take, and then get out onto the street.'

'You think it's going to come down?'

'Yes, in due course. Now please do as I ask, and please, do not do anything which may start a panic and put everyone else at risk.'

Georgina ushered Colin through the door and headed for the lifts.

'You're going back up there, yourself?'

'I have to try to get everyone out, quietly, remember?' She stepped into the lift. 'Call me the minute you find evidence of Mycota anywhere else in the building.'

508

STEPPING INTO THE LOBBY, she took a deep breath to steady herself, and looked back at the lifts; there were three of them, each capable of holding twelve people. Did she dare use them all at once? Martin was standing in the penthouse doorway. 'Gina? Where on earth have you been? You're missing Mike's speech.'

'Martin . . .' She grabbed his arm, put her mouth to his ear and hissed. 'This building has only a couple of hours left.' He stared at her in horror. 'I'm serious. The samples from here got mixed up with those from Riverview. Skyways is the one with the fungus.' Rapidly she outlined what she and Colin had discovered downstairs. 'We must get everyone out of here. But if there's panic, the vibration may bring the building down even more quickly.'

'OK,' he said. 'You say the lifts are safe?'

'At the moment.'

'Think this lot can stand an announcement?'

'I think they'll have to. Shall I make it?'

He shook his head. 'I designed the place. I have to.'

MARTIN WENT BACK into the penthouse, where everyone was laughing and clapping as Michael finished his speech. Georgina watched Michael as Martin sidled up behind the table and muttered at him. He was so young, so handsome, so confident . . . and so happy with his radiant bride beside him. And so unaware that the world was literally about to crumble beneath his feet.

Martin held his hand up for silence. 'Ladies and gentlemen,' he said in a loud, clear voice. 'I have something very important to say to you. Is everyone here? Could we have the staff in as well, please?'

Denys appeared at Georgina's elbow. 'Who does the bloody man think he is?' he demanded.

'Now please,' Martin said, 'what I have to say may shock you, but as long as everyone keeps his or her head there should not be a problem.' He drew a long breath. 'It has just been discovered that this building, Skyways, is contaminated with *Mycota concretus*, in an advanced stage of development. This means that we cannot guarantee the safety of the building.' He held up his hands as there was a wave of excited comment.

'It has therefore been decided to abandon the premises as quickly as possible,' Martin went on. 'The important thing is that there be no panic, and above all, no excessive noise, which might start a vibration and bring about some failure earlier than would otherwise happen. There are three lifts in the lobby, and each will hold twelve people. The lifts will take approximately seven minutes to descend and return. That means we can clear this floor in forty-two minutes using the lifts alone. Now I am sure we are all agreed that the first thirty-six must be women and children, with one exception. I think the bridal couple should be the first to leave.'

'No way!' Michael said, getting back to his feet. 'Linda goes first, of course. But I'll stay to the last load.'

'No!' Linda protested. 'I'll stay with you.'

'What about the baby?' Caroline asked.

There was a fresh hubbub. 'Please!' Martin called, holding up both hands. 'No noise. It is essential to remain as quiet as possible.

'Right,' Martin said. 'Let's move. Every moment is vital. Mothers with small children, first to the lifts. That includes you, Linda.'

'I'm for the stairs,' muttered one of the staff, laying his tray on a table and hurrying through the emergency door.

'Please don't make a noise,' Georgina begged as several other servers followed him. She had no means of stopping them.

'Of all the damnable fiascoes!' Denys announced loudly, striding towards the lobby. 'I am going to sue Harvey and Associates for every last penny.'

'Denys, please,' Caroline said.

'You know they aren't responsible,' Georgina told him.

'What a story,' Billie remarked, coming up to them with Philip at her shoulder.

'You'd better hurry,' Georgina suggested.

'What, and miss all the reactions up here?'

'Close the doors,' Denys ordered. The three lifts had now arrived and been filled. The children were looking hopelessly bewildered, their mothers white with terror; among them were Caroline's sister and both bridesmaids, as well as a weeping Linda.

The remaining women muttered at each other and glared at Billie, who had whipped out her camera and was flashing in every direction. 'Really!' someone said. 'Fancy taking photos at a time like this! The idea is obscene.'

'That's exactly what sells newspapers, honey,' Billie told her.

'Come on!' Denys grabbed Caroline's arm. 'Linda's on her way. Let's take the stairs.'

'I can only advise you against it,' Georgina said, irritation in her voice. 'Using the stairs could start a collapse.'

'We'll use the fire escape.'

'I think I'd rather wait for the lift to come back,' Caroline said.

Georgina went back into the lounge. She glanced through the glass doors to the roof garden, and saw Tom, standing moodily at the balustrade and looking down at the street. 'Tom!' she cried. 'Whatever are you doing?'

'It's a long way down.'

'Well, I hope you're not contemplating jumping. We'll be evacuating the men next. Come on, take your place in the queue.' She held his arm and pushed him into the lobby, where people were still milling about, gazing at the red lights which were moving upwards again.

'So far so good,' Martin said grimly. 'Come on, now, ladies.'

The children had gone, and several of the women were obviously unhappy at having to leave their husbands. 'You must lead the way, Mrs Wright,' Martin said.

'Please, Caroline,' Georgina begged.

Caroline still hesitated, staring at Denys, whose face had turned beetroot. 'Well, I'm going,' Sally Buckenham announced, having said goodbye to Tim, and stepped into the centre lift. 'All by myself?'

That caused a general forward movement. 'In you get,' Denys said firmly, and pushed Caroline in beside Anne Bladen.

The telephone in the lounge jangled. Georgina picked it up. 'What's happening up there?' Colin's voice was hoarse.

'Second load just leaving,' Georgina told him.

'I don't think you can wait for a third,' Colin said. 'I've located fungus in the wall of the lift shaft.'

'Oh, no! How long?'

'Could be minutes.'

Georgina slammed the phone down. 'We'll have to chance the fire escape for the rest.'

They hurried back into the lobby. 'What's happening?' Denys wanted to know.

'Colin Worthington feels we should change our plan and use the fire escape, that's all,' Georgina said as evenly as she could.

'Well, I'm certainly going to,' Denys declared. He led the way to the emergency door. As he reached it, the building shook. There was a deep, rumbling sound, swelling like approaching thunder, and with a series of whiplike cracks, splits began to appear in the floor.

THE LIFT DOORS closed, and it slipped gently away from the penthouse floor. 'Three and a half minutes,' Sally Buckenham told the anxious women around her. 'Three and a half minutes.'

Three and a half minutes, Anne thought, while her stomach was doing a series of handsprings. 'Two and a half, now,' Sally said, watching the numbers. 'Two. One and a half.'

The light changed from 1 to G. 'That's it, folks.' The doors opened to reveal even more anxious faces in the lobby, then there was an enormous rumbling crash, and the lift seemed to gather pace again and kept on going, down to the basement.

DENYS WRIGHT, standing on the top landing, the wind whipping at his frock coat, checked as the building shuddered. 'What the hell . . .'

'The lift shaft's gone,' Martin snapped.

Denys stared at him. 'The lift shaft? My God, Caro was in one of those lifts!'

'Sally,' Tim Buckenham muttered.

'We must hope they were at the bottom of the shaft when it gave way,' Georgina said, determined to keep everyone calm as long as possible. 'Now, these stairs are our only chance.' She looked over their terrified faces. 'All right, Denys, you lead. Then the women.'

Denys looked down. By now word of what was happening had spread, and there was a large crowd down there. The onlookers were being pushed back to the head of the next street by a cordon of policemen, and, with screaming sirens, more and more police were arriving. There were also several fire engines, and some of the ladders were already snaking upwards, but they could not reach above the seventh floor.

One of the fire officers used a megaphone. 'Can you get down?' he bellowed.

'Yes,' Denys shouted back. 'We're on our way.' He looked round at the crowd of women. 'Follow me, ladies!'

'Come on, Thelma.' Georgina grasped the older woman's arm.

'I can't go without Patrick.'

'Patrick will be right behind you,' Georgina promised.

There were still roughly sixty women left, and most of these unwillingly followed Denys onto the exposed steps. 'God, I hate heights,' someone said.

'Easy now, ladies, easy.' Denys was negotiating the first landing, just above the tenth floor.

Georgina watched the women, save for herself and Billie, disappearing through the emergency doorway. 'Time for you, Billie.'

'Nuts,' Billie said, writing busily in her notebook. 'I'm working.'

'All right, gentlemen,' Georgina said. 'You've been very patient. Patrick, would you lead the way?'

ANNE BLADEN KNEW she'd lost consciousness, but only for a few seconds. Then she was aware principally of weight, making it difficult for her to breathe. It was the soft weight of human bodies, several of them squirming and moving. In the distance there were voices, shouting.

'Please,' she gasped. 'Can you get off me? Please!' She tried to take a breath, and found she couldn't. She could hear noises now, of people scrabbling above her head. If only she could see through the dust and gloom. The person immediately on top of her moved, and Anne blinked into the darkness. She recognised Caroline Wright's voice. 'Oh, God!' Caroline was whispering. 'Oh, God, my back . . .'

Funny, Anne thought, I don't feel any pain. Voices! 'Quickly,' they were saying. 'Get them out. This ceiling is going to come down at any moment.'

Lumps of concrete were heaved aside from outside the doors, and Anne wanted to shout with relief—she could see light. But she didn't have enough air in her lungs. She could see faces, now, anxious and frightened, among them Colin Worthington. They were clambering into the pit that had been the lift shaft, moving the crumbled stone which had cascaded through the mesh roof of the cab, lifting out bodies, coming ever closer. 'Oh, thank God,' Anne whispered. She looked past the faces and the hands reaching for her, at the high ceiling of the downstairs lobby, and the huge bulge which was seeping out of it. She was able to watch it fall.

21

Georgina had moved away from the outer wall. Rounding up the men who had gravitated to the bar for a last drink, she was nearly thrown from her feet by the rumbling crash, which was accompanied by a chorus of shrieks of terror and dismay.

'The fire escape!' Martin snapped, and ran to the parapet to look down. Georgina stood beside him, and felt sick. The outer wall of the block had fallen outwards, from about the sixth floor down to the first, she estimated, carrying with it the fire escape, crashing down into the street below. From the noise she realised several people had been hit by the falling debris. But worse, the resulting stress had pulled the fire escape out of the wall above the seventh floor, where the lower section had snapped off. The upper section now swayed away from the building in the breeze, held only by the very first few stanchions. A couple of the women had already let go and dropped like stones to the ground ninety feet below. The others screamed and shrieked their terror as they clung to the swaying iron.

'Come on,' Martin snapped at the gaping men. 'Get them back up.'

They grasped the arms of the women nearest to them and pulled them to safety, but most of them seemed too afraid to move. 'I'm going to have to go down to them,' Martin said.

'Martin!' Georgina grasped his arm. 'That thing could break loose at any moment.'

'Exactly! We have to get them back up before then, right?'

She bit her lip, but knew he was right. 'For God's sake, be careful!' she begged. Her brain was doing somersaults. There had been two separate crashes, one from each side of the building, yet this floor was still intact. Hooray for Martin's technique and that of his builders. But it wasn't going to stand much longer.

Men crowded the emergency doorway behind Martin. Michael, alarmed for the safety of his father-in-law, and Patrick, worried about Thelma, took steps to follow. Martin made his way down the top flight to the first landing, crawling past the women who had sunk to the iron steps, whimpering with terror. 'Ladies,' he begged, 'please go back up. Look, these chaps are waiting to help you.'

Slowly, reluctantly, they began to move. The men behind him reached for their arms.

Gingerly Martin went down to the first reverse bend, and on again to the next, where the women were even more terrified.

'Help me!' Denys wailed from below. 'For God's sake!'

Martin stepped past the women, reached the landing, and gazed at the broken ladder, dangling into space. And Denys.

When the wall and the fire escape had disintegrated beneath him, Denys had managed to grab hold of the metal railings, which continued to trail downwards towards the street. He was a good nine feet below where Martin was standing on the last remaining landing. He was still clinging on, knuckles white, his face contorted with fear and agony, body hanging over eternity.

'I can't hold on much longer,' he gasped.

'You'll have to,' Martin told him. 'See if you can pull yourself up far enough to lodge your elbows through those bars.' He looked over his shoulder, at Michael. 'We need rope . . .'

'There's none upstairs.'

'There are tablecloths. Get some!' Michael climbed back up the steps, past the last of the women.

'My wife!' Patrick muttered. He sat on the iron steps staring down at the ground and the ambulances, into which the broken bodies of those who had fallen were being loaded.

'Come on, now, Denys,' Martin coaxed. 'Get your elbow through.'

Puffing and gasping, face purple, Denys strained to lift himself. He was a heavy man, badly out of condition. Slowly he got himself up, and thrust an elbow through the bars.

'Good lad,' Martin said. 'Help's on its way.'

MICHAEL RAN BACK up the stairs, into the lounge. He jerked the tablecloths off the top table, sending glass and crockery to the floor.

'What on earth?' Georgina asked.

514

'We're trying to reach Denys,' he gasped.

'Do you need help?'

'Yes. Several strong men.'

She looked left and right. Volunteers were quickly forthcoming. 'How many fell?' she asked Michael.

'God knows! Several.'

'Thelma Turner was there.'

'She's not there now. Patrick's distraught.'

He was away, hurrying through the emergency door, while Georgina bit her lip. Thelma . . . it was hard to believe. She should go to Patrick. But it was equally hard to believe that they were now cut off, more than a hundred feet above the ground, in a building that was about to collapse. Their only remaining hope was the inside staircase, but if that wall had gone . . .

She went back out onto the terrace. Tom had returned there and was sitting down near the balustrade, peering up at the brilliant blue of the afternoon sky, and on his second bottle of champagne.

'Do you realise we could be about to die?' he asked, waving the bottle at her. 'Can you think of a better way to go?'

She stood at the balustrade and looked down. This street also had been cleared of spectators, but the crowds were there, at the heads of all the approach roads, and growing every minute. A great shout went up when they saw her. There were calls for silence and a fire officer raised his megaphone. 'Can you hear me? How many of you are up there?'

She cupped her hands round her mouth. 'More than a hundred. Can you get a ladder to this terrace?'

'Negative. How about the inside stairs? Can you come down some floors?'

'I'll have to check that.'

He didn't have to tell her to hurry.

'HOLD ON, DENYS,' Martin said for the umpteenth time.

'My arms hurt,' Denys groaned.

'Where the devil are those tablecloths?' Martin asked over his shoulder.

'They're here.' Michael paused to glance at Patrick, who had slumped to the steps just behind Martin, his head sagging, then turned his attention to the job in hand.

'All right. Give them to me.' Martin took the tablecloths, joined them together to make a rope with several fisherman's bends, then tied a large bowline knot in one end, to make a loop sufficiently wide for Denys's head and shoulders. 'Where's our support?'

'Right behind me.'

Martin glanced up at several of the younger and larger men. Crouching behind Michael, their combined weights were causing the ladder to sway disturbingly.

'OK. Stand by.' He lowered the looped end of the tablecloth rope until it dangled beside Denys's head. 'Now, Denys, let go with one arm and grab the rope.'

Denys groaned and, with infinite care, eased one arm up and reached for the rope.

'OK,' Martin said. 'Now put your arm through it. You fellows take the strain.'

The men behind him grasped the rope, and the one at the back tied the end round his waist. Denys had got his arm through the loop. 'Now let go with the other arm, and if you can, get it through the loop as well,' Martin told him. 'But in any event, grab it.'

Denys sucked air into his lungs, then with a convulsive effort released the balustrade and grasped the rope. 'Hang on!' Martin shouted. 'All right, heave.'

The men heaved, slipping on the iron steps and desperately trying to stop themselves going towards the edge. 'Heave!' Martin said, grabbing the rope himself. 'All together now, heave!'

Denys's head appeared over the landing.

'Once more!' Martin cried.

Another heave, and Denys groaned with pain as he was dragged over the rough metal at the lip of the broken steps, ripping the flesh of his hands. But at least he was safe. Martin grabbed his jacket and pulled him away from the edge. 'Gotcha!' he said.

Denys was crying. 'For what?' he moaned. 'The whole lot is coming down.'

THE NEXT CRASH shattered several windows in the penthouse. Georgina ran back onto the terrace, where ominous cracks were also appearing. 'What's happening?' she yelled.

'Some more floors have come down,' the fire chief replied. 'We have helicopters on their way.'

'They can't come down on this roof! The whole lot will collapse.'

'We understand. They'll use their rope ladders. But get as many of your people as possible down to the seventh floor. We reckon we can just reach that with our ladders from down here.'

'Gee,' Billie said. 'If we get out of this, I am gonna have the scoop of a lifetime.'

'I need a drink,' Denys muttered, and headed for the bar. Patrick just slumped to the floor, staring vacantly into space. He was

obviously in deep shock and Georgina desperately wanted to comfort him, but there was no time.

'Martin,' she said, leading him aside. 'They reckon they can get ladders up to the seventh floor. Can we reach there by the internal staircase?'

He looked exhausted, his hair whitened with dust. 'Should be possible. Just. It was below there the wall gave way. It'll be dicey.'

She grinned. 'More dicey than staying here?'

'No, you're right. Mind you, morale about tackling those stairs will be pretty poor at the moment.'

'Let's see what we can do.' She beckoned Michael. 'Martin and I are going to investigate a way down. There are helicopters on their way. They can't land, but they can drop their rope ladders.'

Michael looked to right and left, assessing age and relative agility. 'This lot are going to be able to climb rope ladders?'

'Most of them, probably not. But the young and vigorous can. Anyway, if the choppers turn up before we get back, organise it.'

Michael gulped, but nodded. His immaculate morning coat and pearl waistcoat had been abandoned, exposing a now-scruffy shirt and braces. Under the dust Georgina could see his face was white, eyes red-rimmed and wide with horror. Impulsively she paused to throw her arms round him and whisper, 'We'll make it, darling. We'll make it,' and felt comforted by his responding hug.

'CAREFUL,' MARTIN WARNED, as they made their way down the steps. For the first couple of flights there was no sign of any damage, and Georgina had a brief spasm of hope that they might actually be able to get out this way. But then, just as they reached the seventh floor, she saw the steps suddenly end, disappearing into a vast pit. To their left the collapsed wall exposed the staircase to the light. To their right, below them, several floors had lost their interior walls and were sagging. But beside them the wall still stood, and Martin cautiously pushed open the door. He entered the lobby and crossed to the door of the flat opposite.

'Locked,' Martin grunted.

'Can you force it?'

He grinned. 'Sure I can. If you don't reckon I'll bring the building down.' He took a heavy, multibladed penknife from his pocket and got to work. It took him only seconds to force the lock. He pushed it open, went inside and to the windows, looked down and waved at the firemen. The crowd gave a great cheer as they spotted him, and the ladders were already brushing the wall just beneath him. 'All systems go.'

518

GEORGINA RETURNED to the penthouse. 'If you ladies will come down to the seventh floor, we'll get you to safety,' she explained.

'You want us to go down those collapsed stairs?' someone asked, plaintively.

'And then a fire ladder, seven storeys up?' someone else wailed.

'Well, would you rather climb a rope ladder to a helicopter? You have to do something,' Georgina told them, 'or you're going to find yourselves all alone up here. Billie!'

'Right,' Billie announced. 'I'm supervising the ladder brigade. We'd better do it in sections, to avoid too much weight on those steps. Come along now, I need twelve volunteers. You, and you, and you.' She rounded up twelve women, who seemed mesmerised by her calm assumption of authority. 'Follow me,' she commanded. 'You come too, Philip. You can help get them onto the ladders.'

'Choppers!' Michael called. 'Come on! Let's be having you.'

'It's all happening,' Georgina said, buoyantly cheerful.

'I'll have a go,' said a skinny blonde in a microskirt.

Georgina went with a group of them onto the terrace, to watch the first helicopter, coming closer; she could already feel the downdraught. Then its doors opened and the rope ladder came snaking down, to end some twelve feet above their heads. Immediately a crewman descended. 'Who's first?' he shouted.

'Ready?' Georgina asked the girl.

She nodded, biting her lip, and then as an afterthought kicked off her shoes. The helicopter came lower, and the loop came down.

Georgina and Michael fitted the loop over the girl's head and under her arms, then gave the thumbs up as the crewman put his arms round her. The girl gave a little shriek and clutched frantically at her rescuer as she was lifted from the ground and the line was reeled in.

While this was going on the pilot had manoeuvred his machine away from the building to allow a second helicopter into position, when the drill was repeated. Georgina felt almost hysterical with relief. People were actually being saved, and now Martin appeared. 'It's all go down there,' he said.

Georgina ran to the parapet, and watched the ladders being placed against the seventh-floor windows. The first of the women climbed out, assisted by Billie and Philip inside the building.

'Oh, Martin,' she said. 'Are we going to pull it off?'

'If we do it'll be a miracle. The only thing holding this building up now is faith.' She turned, into his arms. 'Listen,' he said. 'You'll go in a helicopter.'

'Of course. When the time is right.'

'Which is when the last of these women has gone.'

It was slow work, but it was happening. All fifteen women who were prepared to risk the helicopters were taken up. Philip returned periodically to take another twelve down to the seventh floor. Several were on their way down the ladders, and several more had already reached the ground.

'It's your turn on the winch,' Martin pointed out.

She shook her head. 'Send some of the boys. Michael, up you go.'

'Now, Mum . . .' he argued.

'That's an order. Linda's down there, waiting for you. I'll be along in a minute.' She clutched his hand. 'You must never forget that from now on your first duty is to your wife and child.'

She kissed him, and went inside. Tom and Denys were at the bar, apparently drowning each other's sorrows. With them were Patrick and Tim Buckenham.

'Mike's away.' She looked at Martin. 'The way things are going we'll have the building empty in half an hour.'

'Hallelujah!' he said, and checked, as from outside there came a gigantic wail.

'A HELICOPTER must have crashed!' Georgina ran for the terrace. But the two machines were still circling, and on each of their winches there was a man being hoisted to safety. The remainder, however, had moved in a rush to the balustrade. Georgina ran into their midst. 'It's cracking,' they gasped.

She went to the balustrade, looked down at the crowd, many of whom were pointing up at the walls of the building. She heard a dreadful groaning sound. Superbly designed and built as it was, Skyways' upper exterior walls were at last finding the strain too great. There were still some fifty people on the terrace.

A helicopter was approaching, its crewman still at the end of the rope ladder to grasp their next passenger. Georgina ran beneath him, hair flying in the downdraught. 'The ladder!' she screamed. 'They'll have to use the ladder! There's no more time for the loop!'

He nodded, gave her a thumbs-up sign, and spoke into the radio that was clipped to his harness. His pilot understood, and the helicopter moved lower yet, until the ladder was within a foot of the terrace floor. The crewman promptly jumped down. 'Come along now,' he called. 'Madam?'

Georgina shook her head, pointed at the waiting men. 'Up you go. Hurry now.'

'Six at a time,' the crewman said. 'It'll be moving. Throw one leg round the reverse side of the rope if there's a problem.'

The first of the men licked his lips and then started his climb. Face rigid with fear at the understanding that only his hands and muscles stood between him and a plunge to his death, he inched his way up. As soon as he was six feet up, the crewman beckoned the next in line. Martin scowled at Georgina. 'You don't intend to leave at all, is that it?' His voice was fierce with anxiety.

'I said, I'd leave when you do.'

'And I have to be last. I designed this heap of scrap.'

BILLIE AND PHILIP were just assisting two women through the windows when they heard the wail and felt the shudder. They saw the crack appearing in the exterior wall. 'We've had it,' Philip snapped.

'You'd best make haste, miss,' said the fireman on the ladder.

Billie glanced over the lounge; there were only a dozen of them left. 'We'll make it,' she said. 'Come along. Quick!'

One of the women began to scream, a high, wailing sound. Billie stepped up to her and gave her a crisp slap across the cheek. 'No hysterics. Get out there.'

She pushed the woman to the window where the ladder was resting, helped her onto the rungs where the fireman waited to grasp her.

'Just us now,' Billie said triumphantly, and went to the window herself. The ladders were all full. Billie kicked off her shoes, clambered through and paused. 'Say, I wonder how they're doing upstairs? Shouldn't someone tell them we're clear down here?'

'I'll do it,' Philip volunteered. He turned away, and the wall gave way, carrying the floor outwards with it.

Billie, still straddling the gap between window and ladder, had one hand on the top rung as the ladder moved away violently, carrying her with it. She gave a shriek and threw her other arm round the rung, dangling from underneath the very top of the ladder. Around her there seemed nothing but swirling dust and a welling volume of screaming noise. Through the dust chunks of masonry were falling, and bodies too; one struck the upper side of the ladder just below her with a jar which nearly threw her off. Swaying to and fro as she was, she managed to lodge her toes on a rung further down. The woman immediately beneath her was not so fortunate, as the falling man had landed immediately on her, and she let go with a despairing shriek to accompany him to the ground.

The ladder was swaying away from the collapsing building, whirling giddily out over the street as the fire engine backed up to avoid the falling debris. Billie realised she was sobbing and shouting incoherently. She tried not to look down, looking back instead at the huge pall of dust which had once been Skyways building. Of Philip there was no sign.

GEORGINA HAD JUST GONE back into the lounge to fetch the last of the men when the second exterior wall collapsed. She had waved Tom and Denys and Tim out of the terrace door when she felt the floor starting to go. As the wall beside her gave way, she hurled herself forward to throw both arms round the doorpost which now stood naked on its mounting. She clung there, gasping, afraid to look round as from behind her she heard the sound of tearing masonry. She was waiting for the final collapse to plunge her into eternity . . . while above her head the helicopter engines whirred helplessly.

So this was it. The end. Thank God Michael and Linda were safe, but how sad that she'd never see their baby. And Martin. She had no idea where he had been when the floor gave way. Darling Martin, I suppose our love story and our joint business venture were never meant to be . . .

Clouds of dust rose around her, leaving her blind for several moments. Then she realised that although the front and interior walls had collapsed, the rear wall was still standing, and for the moment the rear third of the penthouse floor was still attached. The door to the bedroom corridor was the outer edge of the remains of this floor. And to this perilously perched bit of doorpost she was clinging, her legs dangling over the dust-filled abyss. Vaguely, through the pain and weariness, she knew that if she was to survive, she had to drag herself up onto the remains of the floor.

Gritting her teeth she began to attempt to drag herself up. Tears of exhaustion mingled with the sweat pouring out of her hair as she strained, exerting her very last ounce of strength, and at last lodging her elbows over the door jamb. She cautiously swung a leg sideways, terrified the movement would cause the door frame to break away, and felt her heel curl over the sill. A moment later she rolled onto her back, pressed both heels against the doorpost . . . rolled again and grabbed the door opposite a split second before the whole lounge door frame twisted away from its anchorage to fall out of sight.

She had no idea how long she lay there, on the edge of eternity. When full consciousness returned, the dust cloud had thinned, and above her, beyond what had once been a ceiling, she could see the helicopters moving to and fro.

She had to think, to plan what she was going to do next. Every move threatened danger; the floor on which she was lying was giving a series of jerks as it tried to tear itself free of the exterior wall.

Then the drone of an engine came closer, and she saw a helicopter immediately above her, its rope ladder dangling, and at the end of the ladder a crewman. Georgina sat up, one leg still hooked round the doorpost. Adrenalin pumped through her arteries. She was being given a chance at life. Closer and closer came the loop, while beneath her the collapsing floor gave another shudder and groaned like a giant about to expire. She wasn't going to make it. So close, not more than three feet now. But clearly the line was at its full extension, and the pilot could descend no further because of the risk of his rotor blades touching the exterior wall. She had to jump at it, if she dared. She knelt, sucking air into her lungs as a gust of wind caught the helicopter and the noose moved away to her left. But it was coming back. If she could just make herself jump and grab it . . .

She looked up, saw the crewman gesticulating, willing her to take the risk because he knew there were only split seconds left; above him at the open doorway of the helicopter was Martin, shouting at her! Even from this distance she could sense his terror for her . . . and his love. Martin! Georgina took a deep breath, and leaped at the loop, arms extended.

'COME ON, WAKE UP, Georgie love!' Someone's hand was on her shoulder, shaking her. She didn't want to know. Go away and leave me alone, she wanted to say . . . but she couldn't hear any sound.

'Can't she just go on sleeping until she's ready to wake up?' a man's voice asked from a long way away. Georgina withdrew into the blissful darkness.

Hours, or was it minutes, later, she was shaken again, but this time the nurse persisted until her eyelids flickered enough to allow a tiny glimmer of light into her brain. Reluctantly she opened one eye, saw Michael and smiled.

'Well, now, that's more the thing!' The nurse lifted her very gently, arranging pillows to support her back, then retreated, leaving two anxious-looking men to stand either side of the bed, each holding one of her hands. 'What's happening? What time is it?' she murmured.

Martin spoke first. 'It's two thirty, Sunday afternoon, darling.'

'Oh.' She closed her eyes and lay silent, thought processes working very slowly. She felt Michael's fingers squeeze her hand very gently, and she forced her eyes open. 'Tell me. Everything. What happened? Who else survived?' She bit her lip. 'Who didn't?'

Michael hesitated. 'Perhaps you'd better have a bit more rest . . .'

She tried to shift on her pillows; every part of her body ached. 'Come on! Let's have it. Is Linda all right?'

'Linda's fine, but terribly upset about losing her mother,' said Michael.

'Oh no! Poor Caroline.' Yes, of course she'd been in the lift with Anne. 'Anne! What about Anne?'

'She's alive but badly injured. That's all we know at present. Nearly all the others in that lift died. Not so much in the fall as in the collapse of the ceiling on them immediately afterwards.'

'How ghastly! Were there many other deaths?'

'Yes. But Dad came through. He and Denys went down with the floor. They both have broken legs and Dad's broken his arm and four ribs. He's just down the corridor. But he's going to be all right.'

She opened her eyes wide. 'Your father! I'm so glad, darling.' She meant it, although she couldn't help reflecting that being totally anaesthetised with alcohol must have had something to do with his remarkable escape. 'And Thelma Turner?'

'Died. And I'm afraid Patrick is in hospital after suffering a severe stroke. He collapsed after being pulled into the helicopter.'

Martin leaned over the bed to kiss her cheek. 'Sweetheart, don't you think it might be better to have a bit more rest?'

'No, darling. I'll rest after I've got the whole picture. Tell me, what about Colin Worthington?'

'They haven't found his body, yet,' replied Martin.

It was impossible not to think that it was as well he wasn't among the survivors. He would never have recovered from the feeling of guilt at having been responsible for so many deaths. 'And Billie?'

'Not a scratch,' Martin laughed. 'She's having a ball with her scoop and her exclusive photos. She wants to pop in and see you before leaving for Chicago tomorrow.' Georgina rolled her eyeballs towards the ceiling. 'But I'm afraid your pal Philip didn't make it. And Sally Buckenham. She's upstairs here, on life-support. Multiple injuries including a broken spine.'

'Oh God, how awful. Poor Sally. And poor Tim. Is he OK?'

'I believe so.'

'So, what happened to me?'

'No broken bones, but you've torn ligaments in your left shoulder and right arm. And you've had to be stitched up in a few places where you ripped yourself open on jagged bits of metal and wood.' Martin grinned at her. 'What the doctors described as minor injuries.'

She again tried to adjust her position in bed, winced with pain and lay silent for a few minutes before asking, 'Come to think of it, how did you survive?'

'Promise not to laugh?'

'No. But tell me anyway.'

'I must have slipped sideways. I landed on someone's settee, I think, bounced off and found myself across a girder which had been bent right over by the weight of wall adhering higher up. It was curved down to the top of a pile of rubble. I just slid down it.'

'And you weren't injured?' A grin was spreading across her face.

'Indeed I was. Look!' He held up his left hand to show off the plaster on the end of his little finger.

A bubble of happiness exploded in Georgina's throat and the two men joined in. Her two most precious men.

There were tears in their laughter.

THE GOLDEN RETRIEVER puppy, lying on her back, four oversized feet in the air, was sleeping on the grass in the shade of a laburnum. The June afternoon sun was hot, here behind the high, sheltering hedges. Nobody spoke. Even the usually noisy sparrows and starlings were silent. The only sound came from the tall poplars, their leaves rustling in the breeze fifty feet overhead.

Georgina felt her fingers taken into Martin's gentle grasp as he reached across from his sunbed. She gave his hand an affectionate squeeze and a small, contented sigh escaped her lips. She could allow herself the luxury of contentment, at last, but it had been a long, uphill struggle. So much had happened since the horrendous tragedy at Skyways, just a year ago today. Overhung by a black cloud of public despair, the country's top scientists had worked all hours God gave to develop the antidote for the dreaded Mycota. Colin Worthington's theory about iodine had provided the basis for their research, and within a matter of weeks they had presented a formula for mass production of a substance which, injected into infected buildings with laser guns, had proved highly successful—where the fungus had been caught in time.

Of course nothing could overcome the tragic loss of life. Caroline, Thelma and Patrick, who had not survived his stroke. Philip . . . and so many others. And poor Sally Buckenham, now confined to a wheelchair for the rest of her life.

But for some the disaster had been a beginning. Billie was now a world-famous journalist, her status enhanced by her undoubted heroism in marshalling the escape of most of the women, at the risk of her own life.

A soft gurgling sound came from behind her. She sat up and turned, swinging her feet off the bed, in time to see her grand-daughter's tiny fingers grasping at a plastic toy attached to her pram. Linda was walking across the lawn to fetch the baby, watched by her adoring husband. The youngsters had recovered comparatively quickly from their disastrous wedding reception, but nothing could have persuaded them to move into the Riverview flat afterwards. Instead they had agreed to stay with Denys for a while.

The construction industry had come to a complete standstill for many months and was only just beginning to pick up again. Michael was working very hard at Playle & Harvey Associates, and studying most evenings for A levels next year.

And Martin? Georgina twisted the plain gold band on the third finger of her left hand. He had whisked her off to a registry office within a fortnight of the tragedy. It had seemed almost indecent haste, amid all the misery and bereavement around them, but Michael and Linda had agreed with Martin that it made sense to legalise their union.

Georgina looked at her watch and stood up. 'I'm going to put the kettle on. How many for tea?'

Various hands were raised, and she went into the kitchen. She was filling the kettle when her nostrils twitched, at the same time as her knees went weak. The house had been tested and been pronounced safe—but there had been mistakes. 'Oh, my God!' she muttered, and ran to the door. 'Martin! Michael!' she shouted.

They came running in. 'That smell . . . Behind there!'

Martin knelt beneath the sink, tore open the cupboards, peered inside, while Georgina looked at the wall and ceiling, seeking the telltale bulges that meant catastrophe.

Slowly Martin's head and shoulders emerged from the cupboard. 'Is it . . .?'

He held out his hand. From the forefinger and thumb there drooped a dead mouse.

'Oh, Martin!'

He threw the carcass into the bin, and held her against him.

'It's over,' he said. 'Really and truly. Even if we'll all never be quite the same again.'

MAX MARLOW

Back in 1988, when Reader's Digest Condensed Books published a condensation of the novel *Her Name Will Be Faith*, the real identity of its author, who wrote under the *nom de plume* Max Marlow, was a closely guarded literary secret. Now the truth is out. And the fact is that Max Marlow is not one person, but the pseudonym of a husband-and-wife team—Christopher Nicole and Diana Bachmann, both successful novelists in their own right.

They have travelled widely around the world. For five years, the couple made their home on the sizable but sparsely populated island of Eleuthera in the Bahamas. It was ten miles to the closest village and they lived on an isolated headland, doing all their shopping by boat to the nearest island, where there was a supermarket. After leaving the Bahamas, they spent four years in Spain before settling in the Channel Islands, where they live in an old house on the edge of St Peter Port, Guernsey. 'Diana is a Guernsey woman,' says Christopher Nicole. 'She was born and bred here, so in a sense we've come home. We do all our work here. We have an office out the back, well away from the rest of the world.'

They have now collaborated on six Max Marlow novels, all dealing with disasters—either natural or human—in one form or another.

The idea for *Growth* arose from an item spotted in a newspaper a few years ago: a report that several Moscow underground stations had had to be closed because of a deterioration in safety caused by a fungus which attacked the concrete.

Nothing more has ever been heard of this Russian experience, but the author started to wonder what would happen if such a fungus really does exist . . .